Dear Reader,

It's hard to believe that the Signature Select program is one year old—with seventy-two books already published by top Harlequin and Silhouette authors.

What an exciting and varied lineup we have in the year ahead! In the first quarter of the year, the Signature Spotlight program offers three very different reading experiences. Popular author Marie Ferrarella, well-known for her warm family-centered romances, has gone in quite a different direction to write a story that has been "haunting her" for years. Please check out *Sundays Are for Murder* in January. Hop aboard a Caribbean cruise with Joanne Rock in *The Pleasure Trip* for February, and don't miss a trademark romantic suspense from Debra Webb, *Vows of Silence* in March.

Our collections in the first quarter of the year explore a variety of contemporary themes. Our Valentine's collection—*Write It Up!*—homes in on the trend to online dating in three stories by Elizabeth Bevarly, Tracy Kelleher and Mary Leo. February is awards season, and Barbara Bretton, Isabel Sharpe and Emilie Rose join the fun and glamour in *And the Envelope, Please....* And in March, Leslie Kelly, Heather MacAllister and Cindi Myers have penned novellas about women desperate enough to go to *Bootcamp* to learn how *not* to scare men away!

Three original sagas also come your way in the first quarter of this year. Silhouette author Gina Wilkins spins off her popular FAMILY FOUND miniseries in *Wealth Beyond Riches*. Janice Kay Johnson has written a powerful story of a tortured shared past in *Dead Wrong*, which is connected to her PATTON'S DAUGHTERS Superromance miniseries, and Kathleen O'Brien gives a haunting story of mysterious murder in *Quiet as the Grave*.

And don't forget there is original bonus material in every single Signature Select book to give you the inside scoop on the creative process of your favorite authors! We hope you enjoy all our new offerings!

Enjoy!

Marsha Zinberg

Marsha Zinberg
Executive Editor
The Signature Select Program

MINISERIES

Coffee
in the
Morning

ROZ
Denny
FOX

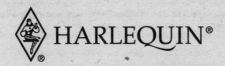

HARLEQUIN®

TORONTO • NEW YORK • LONDON
AMSTERDAM • PARIS • SYDNEY • HAMBURG
STOCKHOLM • ATHENS • TOKYO • MILAN • MADRID
PRAGUE • WARSAW • BUDAPEST • AUCKLAND

ISBN 0-373-83696-1

COFFEE IN THE MORNING

Copyright © 2006 by Harlequin Books S.A.

The publisher acknowledges the copyright holder of the individual works as follows:

ANYTHING YOU CAN DO...
Copyright © 1998 by Rosaline Fox

HAVING IT ALL
Copyright © 1998 by Rosaline Fox

CONTENTS

Dear Reader,

I love the characters you'll find in the two stories contained in this volume. Emily Benton, of *Anything You Can Do...*, is a strong woman who stuck out a bad marriage. And even after her self-indulgent, spoiled husband died, she had to battle affluent inlaws to keep her teenage son and daughter from sliding down the same path. When her friend Sherry Campbell talked her into a summer getaway with her kids, she had no idea that she'd have so many adventures or meet the man of her dreams. That man, Nolan Campbell (Sherry's brother), organized the wagon train reenactment of the Sante Fe Trail as a historical project for a study he hoped to publish to get the dean of the department off his back. It was a summer of laughter and tears, and lessons learned for all who made the long trek.

And at the time, I'm sure Sherry Campbell had no clue that she'd meet a stranger on the trip who would turn up in a sequel, *Having It All*, the second story in this volume. Sherry Campbell has her eye on moving up the staff ladder in her small Missouri college. Garrett Lock, single dad, not only had *his* eye on the job Sherry covets, but on Sherry as well. Sherry, the epitome of an independent woman, has always doubted that love and independence are compatible. Garrett and his lovable eight-year-old son eventually prove that all her theories about love are wrong.

As a writer, I found it satisfying to forge happy relationships for Emily and Camp, and Sherry and Garrett. Next month, look for a brand-new story from Signature, *Hot Chocolate on a Cold Day*, in which I revisit the Campbell and Lock families and do my best to find lasting relationships for their kids, Megan and Mark Benton, and Keith Lock. I hope you'll enjoy spending time with all these folks as much as I have. I'd love to hear from you.

Roz Denny Fox
rdfox@worldnet.att.net
P.O. Box 17480-101, Tucson, AZ 85731

ANYTHING YOU CAN DO...

CHAPTER ONE

*Most historic accounts of western trailblazing are
written by men, about men, to eulogize their feats.*
—Catalyst that provoked the wagon train reenactment.

NOLAN CAMPBELL, professor of history, stared
woefully at a skinny white Christmas tree standing in
one corner of the staff lounge at his Columbia,
Missouri, college. The tree was virtually smothered in
pink ornaments and cellophane bows. Several strings of
hot-pink bulbs flashed intermittently, and every few
seconds his conservative blue tie turned a ghastly shade
of green.

Two colleagues brooded beside him. Camp, as he
was known by his peers, gestured toward the tree with
a glass cup too dainty for his masculine hand. "Fake or
not, Lyle, Christmas trees should be green. What's
wrong with the world today?"

"Plenty," snorted Lyle Roberts. "Especially with the
people in charge of this party. Did you get a load of
those dinky sandwiches at the buffet table? No crust and
less filling. Takes four to make a decent bite."

"Who planned this do?" asked Jeff Scott, economics
prof. "Invaders from another planet?"

"Yeah," Lyle said sarcastically. "Aliens. In other

words, our women's studies department. Hey, that reminds me of a joke I heard. How do Columbia housewives call their kids to dinner?"

Camp and Jeff shrugged.

"They say, 'Come on, kids, get in the car.'" Lyle tittered. "Women don't cook anymore."

Unlike his associates, Camp didn't laugh. "I eat out a lot, too," he said, recalling all the evenings he stopped at a café near his home rather than face a solitary meal. "It's a sign of the times, I guess. Home is no longer the focal point of a family." Camp's gaze traveled to a huddle of women instructors. "Eight-plus hours at a job doesn't allow time for domestic chores."

"Are you kidding?" Roberts exclaimed. "Modern women have erased the word *domestic* from their vocabularies. I've said it before and I'll say it again—my great-grandmother's generation spawned the last real women. In her era they cooked tasty meals on wood stoves. No boxed crap of undetermined origin. She planted a garden and sewed for herself and the kids. And she was happy doing it."

"Get a life, Lyle." Camp's sister, Sherry, department chair for women's studies, left her group to confront the men. "Try stepping into this century. Women pioneer in a *lot* of fields. Politics, medicine, corporate America— to name a few. And Lyle," she added sweetly, "we live longer than Great-grandma did."

Lyle wagged a finger in her face. "If settling the West depended on coddled women like my ex-wife, civilization would be permanently stalled east of the Ohio."

She batted his hand away. "Those so-called historic facts about the West are fantasies dreamed up by men. And if you think women today are all pampered, spend an hour in the Women's Hub listening to the battered ones left penniless by well-heeled exes."

"Really? My ex spends the child support I pay her on cosmetics and manicures."

Camp insinuated himself between the two. "Sherilyn, you missed the crux of our conversation. Lyle's referring to basic evolutionary changes—like, if modern women had to wash without a machine, cook without gas or electricity, they'd have difficulty surviving."

"That's right," Jeff interjected. "Economically speaking, women still expect men to be the hunters, the main breadwinners in the family."

"Oh, pu...leeze! Like you three men could skin a bear and put him in a pot." Sherry thumped her chest. "*I* could live primitively. Thank goodness I don't have to."

Camp lifted a brow. "Toss your electric toothbrush, hot comb and microwave, sis. Then we'll talk."

"Horse feathers. You history types always lament the loss of the *good old days*." Her sarcastic sneer was suddenly replaced by a wide smile. "The other day I received a brochure at the Women's Hub advertising a wagon-train reenactment along the Santa Fe Trail. Led by a woman, incidentally. Her train leaves Boonville, Missouri, in June, if I recall. Sponsor a few women on that trip, brother dear. See how they compare with your precious pioneers."

Lyle hooted. "Don't waste your hard-earned money, Camp. I daresay they wouldn't make it as far as Independence."

"Oh, yeah?" Sherry met him glare for glare.

"It's a silly notion," Camp said impatiently. "Just accept that today's women are softer."

"Camp's spouting sour grapes," a woman behind

them shouted. "Because Greta Erickson refused to spend *her* life shackled to that hundred-year-old house he'll be restoring for the rest of *his* life."

Pain licked ever so fleetingly through Camp's brown eyes.

Sherry dealt the speaker a dark look. She could grumble at Nolan and call him bossy. That didn't mean she'd stand for others picking on him. Greta had hurt him.

Yet it was Lyle who spoke up. "Greta thought Camp's house was fine until she met Mr. Gotbucks, who upped the ante with a fancy new rambler in a gated subdivision. Man isn't important to a relationship anymore. Only the perks he provides."

"Bull, Lyle. One of these days you'll have to eat your words." Sherry thrust out her jaw pugnaciously.

Camp felt the discussion was getting out of hand. "I might consider your experiment, Sherry—if you'd agree to drive one of those wagons." He knew his sister's penchant for luxury and figured that'd end the argument.

"Go for it, girl. Show him." The other women egged Sherry on.

Sherry mulled it over. Spending a summer vacation plodding across the dusty prairie was the last thing she wanted to do. However, she knew a couple of women who were capable of making these men eat their words. Gina Ames, a freelance photographer who last year backpacked across the Sierras. And Emily Benton, Sherry's counterpart at a college nearer St. Louis. Widowed young, Em had returned to the workforce to pay off a philandering husband's debts rather than take one penny from wealthy in-laws determined to drive a wedge between her and her two kids.

Deciding to settle the argument once and for all,

Sherry hooked her arm through her older brother's and steered him toward the stairs. At six foot two and leanly muscled, he cut a dashing figure. Too bad these guys from the history department were all several generations too late. "I'll grab that brochure on the wagon train before I leave on Christmas break. We can discuss my proposal some more at Mom and Dad's. I assume you'll be there for Christmas dinner."

"A forty-year-old man should have someplace more exciting to spend Christmas than with his parents," Camp said glumly.

"You're not forty—you're only thirty-eight." She punched his arm playfully. "If you add years it makes me older. I prefer to think that at thirty-one, I'm in the prime of life."

"Prime, huh? Then why are *you* spending the holiday with Mom and Dad instead of serving plum pudding to some lucky guy?"

She smacked him harder. "Very likely for the same reason you're not fixing stuffed goose for a special lady."

Nolan rubbed his shoulder. "So Lyle was right—you can't cook."

"You really are a Neanderthal moron sometimes, Nolan. Women are quite capable of surviving without a man. I certainly don't need one around."

He frowned as she stomped off. Nolan had forgotten how bulldog-stubborn she could be. Wasn't she ever lonely? He was. Thrusting his hands in his pockets, he clattered down the stairs. "I'd just like to find a woman who enjoys the simple things in life," he muttered as his steps faltered on the bottom landing. Wrenching the door open, he stepped out and breathed in a lungful of noxious city fumes.

"Ugh!" For a minute Camp stared at the cars whizzing past and actually recognized merit in his sister's challenge. Give women a chance to prove they could cope as well as their pioneer ancestors. The real question, though: could *anyone* today, man or woman, give up modern conveniences for an entire summer? "Hmm, the answer to that does have the makings of a great academic paper."

Absently, Camp dug out his car keys. For two years his department chairman had been hounding him to write and publish. A comparison-and-contrast piece on modern versus pioneer women might be the ticket. Although, if such a comparison was to be real and valid, information would have to come directly from the women involved.

Driving home, Camp played with the idea. What if he leased and stocked a few wagons in exchange for the participants' feedback? That'd work. But to remain an impartial observer, he'd have to dissociate himself completely. By following the train on horseback, say, and sleeping in a tent. Except he hadn't ridden a horse in—how long?

Bad idea. Okay, what if he stopped at motels along the route, instead? That way, he could input the women's findings every night on his laptop computer and all but have the paper written by trip's end. Suddenly, what began as an irrational dare sounded pretty darned good.

With a grin, Camp turned off the highway onto the graveled lane leading to his old farmhouse. What better opening for this paper than to point out the author's dependence on a most modern convenience—a computer? Both witty and modest, if he did say so himself.

Sherry would never know what a coup she'd handed him.

BY THE TIME Christmas dinner was over—a dinner during which her brother talked of nothing but what he now referred to as *his summer project,* Sherry regretted having butted into the men's conversation, no matter how irritating. All she'd been trying to do was shake them out of the past. Now here was Nolan reading excerpts from his stupid history books about the he-men who'd tamed the West. The simple fact was, her brother needed some modern woman to boot him into the twenty-first century. Him *and* his pals.

"Suppose the wagon train still does have room?" Sherry asked as they stood together on the porch, preparing to make mad dashes to their separate cars through the falling snow. "How will you choose your guinea pigs?"

Camp chucked her under the chin. "Did you see *Field of Dreams?* The movie where Kevin Costner cleared his cornfield and put in a baseball diamond? I'll lease Conestogas and women will wade out of the corn rows to volunteer."

"Dream on." Sherry jerked away. "You may look a little like Kevin, but even he had to work to entice players to his field."

Camp flipped up his jacket collar. "Let's have it, Ms. Nineties Organizer. How should I attract female adventurers?"

"Advertise in the local newspaper and neighboring college papers. Of course, you'll need an application form that'll weed out kooks. To prove I'm a good sport, I'll help with that. Heck, I'll even mail your applications."

"Hmm. I thought maybe word of mouth around our campus would be easiest."

"Taking all your participants from one pool will skew results, Nolan. Besides, aren't you afraid colleagues will steal your idea? You know how much pressure there is to publish these days. Which reminds me—what about professional liability? Participants should sign a release giving you permission to use their input. And that would be easier if you offered a small stipend. I mean, you *are* asking women to give up vacation plans or work."

"I hadn't thought of liability. What makes you so savvy?"

"I am woman," Sherry said smugly. "So…shall I put together an application?"

"Sure. I guess," he muttered. "Although sending defenseless women on the trip outlined in Maizie Boone's brochure will probably give me nightmares."

"Poor baby." Gritting her teeth, Sherry stepped into the driving snow and left him standing there. She hurried home to call Gina Ames, the wilderness photographer. After twisting Gina's arm and making her promise not to reveal their friendship, Sherry said that her friend should be on the lookout for an application.

Next morning, Sherry decided to visit Emily Benton.

"Sherry, what a delightful surprise," exclaimed the attractive redhead who answered Sherry's knock. "I thought you were my kids. They're at a neighborhood snowball fight. Come in and warm up. I was just making tea." She released the chain and opened the door to one half of a small duplex. Emily hung Sherry's coat on a wrought-iron coat tree, then skirted a shiny new bicycle, two boxed TVs and the components for two or more computers as she led the way to a tiny kitchen.

"Wow!" Whistling through her teeth, Sherry absently handed over a box of homemade cookies she'd brought. "Fencing stolen goods are you, Em?"

Emily frowned. "My in-laws' presents to the kids. It

doesn't matter that our house won't hold all this stuff. It's their latest ploy to convince me to move in with them." Her blue eyes frosted. "As if I'd let them get their hooks in Megan and Mark after the way they overindulged Dave."

Sherry slid into the compact eating nook. "Maybe they feel bad because their son turned out to be such a rat. Guilt does funny things to people."

"A Benton suffer guilt? Hah! It's always someone else's fault. Dave's backers lacked vision. His womanizing was my fault. Don't you know I spent too much time volunteering at church and at the kids' schools?" She poured water over tea bags with a trembling hand. "Sorry for dumping on you, Sherry. The holidays have been a trial. If I didn't owe Toby and Mona so much money, I'd take the kids and move to Alaska or Timbuktu. I told you Dave's folks literally own this town. I had to look long and hard to find a place to rent that didn't belong to them or one of their companies. I desperately need the job at the college here, but…"

"I wish we had an opening in our department. My dean may retire at the end of the school year. New deans almost always hire additional staff."

"What if he doesn't retire?" She gave a small shrug. "I'm checking the ads in the *Chronicle of Higher Education.* So far, nothing."

"At least let me offer you a short-term reprieve." Sherry dropped a brochure on the table and quickly described her brother's project.

Before Sherry had finished talking, Emily was shaking her head. "There's more to this, right? Something you're not saying. Oh, no—I hope you're not planning to set me up with your brother. You're one of the few people who know what a nightmare my marriage was. I'm sure your brother's a nice man, Sherry, but I'm not interested. I don't care if I'm thirty-four and life is passing me by, I'm just not interested. Okay?"

"Boy, have I bungled this. I'm not setting you up, Em. I love Nolan, but I wouldn't wish anyone that chauvinistic on a friend. I'm doing this because...well, you could call it gender rivalry."

"Do I ever understand that. Megan just turned fourteen. She's constantly lording it over Mark, who's only twelve and still pretty much of a kid. To tell you the truth, Sherry, a wagon train in the middle of nowhere sounds like heaven. A whole summer without grandparents, shopping malls and TV." She fingered the brochure. "Will your brother want children in his study? What makes you feel he'd choose me? Oh, I can't go, Sherry, I really need to teach summer school and earn some money." Jumping up, she began to arrange cookies Sherry had brought on a plate. "I heard through the grapevine that Dave's parents want me to default on my loan. It'll give them leverage to petition for custody of the kids. You wouldn't believe how many times they bailed Dave out of bad land deals. On the last scheme, he lost all the front money for building a casino."

Sherry got up to hug Emily. "Those creeps. Hey, I forgot to mention that Nolan's trip comes with a small stipend. You need a break, Em. Fill out this application exactly the way I've penciled it in. Then mail it. Just don't tell Nolan we're friends." With a final bracing hug, Sherry left her to chew on the idea.

CHRISTMAS WAS a dim memory in Camp's mind and spring break loomed on the horizon before he got around to selecting candidates for his trip. Today, in spite of a drizzling rain, he was set to interview prospects. Not that he had many.

He refilled his coffee cup, sharpened several pencils and returned to his desk to frown at the three applications he'd received. Three! After weeks of advertising, only these few women appeared willing to spend their summers trekking the Santa Fe Trail.

He hadn't expected a flood of would-be adventurers, but considering that he was providing a virtually free summer vacation and paying his participants for their time, Camp had imagined he'd have more than three.

He'd already leased four Conestogas through Mrs. Boone's Frontier Adventures outfit. They weren't cheap, so it was fortunate that he'd shamed Sherry into going or he'd be paying for an unused reservation as well an extra wagon. Yesterday, she said she'd talked her roommate, Yvette Miller, into going, too.

Camp smiled. Yvette had grown up next door. He knew for a fact that she traveled with a hundred pounds of luggage—half of it cosmetics. Maybe she'd have even more now that she repped for an exclusive line of women's apparel. At this rate, his paper would write itself.

He sipped coffee and gazed out the window at the gloomy sky. Assuming the applicants were all suitable, that still didn't allow room for last-minute cancellations or unexpected illnesses. The way it stood, Sherry's wagon would have two drivers. Each of the other women would be forced to drive the entire route alone.

"So?" he said out loud. "Sherry claims they're as strong as pioneer women."

Unfortunately, Camp knew another of the applicants. Brittany Powers. A starry-eyed college sophomore better suited to modeling than anything athletic. She'd been in two of his history classes. Camp suspected she had a crush on him. Such things happened on occasion. He was very careful never to give these young women any encouragement, and most of them soon found boyfriends their own age. Brittany hadn't as yet.

But perhaps he was reading too much into Brittany's reasons for going on this trip. Maybe she really *was* interested in American history. Well, the list of questions Sherry had helped him design for the interviews should reveal how committed each of the women was. He'd conduct Brittany's meeting with his office door open. That ought to give her the right message. Before telling the secretary to send her in, Camp donned horn-rimmed glasses that were like window glass. He figured they gave him a nerdy look.

"Hi, Mr. Campbell." Brittany sashayed past the department secretary, tossing a tangle of blond curls over one shoulder. Camp simply pointed at the chair she was to occupy.

"I'm so excited about this trip," she gushed. "Summers are positively boring." Crack went her gum.

Camp shuddered as he sat behind his big oak desk. Lord, he hated gum-chewers who felt five sticks were a minimum. "You don't have a regular summer job you're turning down then?" he asked politely.

She scooted forward and batted heavily mascaraed lashes. "Are you kidding? That's why this is so perfect. Otherwise, I'd just veg out at the house."

"Really?" Nolan picked up her application, along with a sharp pencil whose lead he promptly broke. Grabbing another, he eased back in his chair. "What's your main goal after you graduate, Brittany?"

She looked at him coyly. "To marry somebody rich."

"Ah." Camp relaxed. Everyone knew professors weren't rich. Briskly, he worked through the remaining questions. Brittany's answers weren't as clear as Camp would have liked, but given her age and lack of focus, they were what he'd expect.

It was the way she hung on his every word and followed his slightest move with cosmetically enhanced baby blues that made him nervous. And yet they'd be well chaperoned when he collected the data sheets once a day. That fact let him continue. "It's not a vacation, Brittany. I'll expect you to keep an accurate daily log, which I'll incorporate in my academic paper."

"Kind of like a diary, you mean? Oh, cool. My best friend says my diaries could be published as bestsellers."

Camp's doubts concerning Brittany's motivation tripled. But in the next breath, she made an issue of saying her parents wanted her to do this, so he handed her a release form to sign. Not that she needed parental consent—after all, she was nineteen. It just made him feel better knowing she'd discussed it with her folks.

Assuming his best teacher-to-student smile, Camp ushered her back to the door. "I'll be handing out more detailed information later," he said. "Tomorrow, in class, I'll lend you a book on the history of the Santa Fe Trail. The trip could take ten weeks. It's no picnic. I want you to be prepared."

"Oh, I will be, you'll see." She gazed at him adoringly. "Out there we'll be more like equals—right? I guess everyone will call you 'Nolan'?"

Camp cleared his throat. He was infinitely relieved at the appearance of the department secretary, heralding Gina Ames's arrival.

A suntanned, robust woman with blunt-cut brown hair, Gina steered the conversation to a professional level the moment she sat down. "I'm a freelance photographer. Two national publications have expressed interest in a photo-journey like this."

Had a plum fallen into his lap? "Gina...may I call you that?" Ignoring the thinning of her lips, he said, "Let your work support my scholastic paper, instead. Are you aware that the Santa Fe Trail was the first highway of commerce? A vital link to our past. And it was the last trail saved under the National Historic Trail Preservation Act."

"Spare me the dissertation, Campbell. I was married to a stuffy historian who considered it crass to sell my photographs to tabloids. He and I parted ways."

Removing his glasses, Camp coughed. "Ri-ght. Outside of funding, the extent of my involvement with the trek is to assure simulated nineteenth-century living conditions for modern women traveling a pioneer trail. Our wagon master, or in this case...mistress, is Maizie Boone. Says she's a direct descendant of Daniel. We haven't met, but on the phone she sounds like quite a character. Claims she birthed eight kids at home and is a grandmother of twenty. Most of them work in the business. There may be a book in all this." He drummed his fingers on the desk, envisioning Gina's photos interspersed with pictures from archives.

"Poor woman. It's a wonder she's not dead. I have to

say I'm glad to hear you're not gathering a harem. I found it curious that you only wanted women. Okay, I'll go—provided I have a wagon to myself. I don't like strangers handling my equipment."

Camp was quick to shove a release form across the table for Gina to sign. Odd woman, but he needed her expertise with a camera. Somewhere out there, he thought, a deserving fellow historian was no doubt kicking up his heels. "I'll be in touch," Camp promised, trailing her to the door.

What a diverse group this was shaping up to be. Camp rubbed his hands together. He couldn't wait to meet Emily Benton. The name Benton came from pioneer stock. Last week he'd read an article on a *Jessie* Benton's travels. Daughter of a once-prominent senator, Jessie had married a man known for his explorations along the Oregon Trail. According to Jessie's letters, she loved trail life. She dispatched regular chores easily, and at night, by firelight, she pieced intricate quilts by hand.

Camp had visited the historical society in the hope of finding her journal. As it turned out, they had little trail history from a woman's perspective. He'd never imagined that he might have difficulty finding data to compare or that Sherry was right—history books all seemed to be written by men.

"Hey, Camp," called the department secretary. "There's nobody else waiting."

He glanced at his watch. "Mrs. Benton's scheduled at four."

"Well, she's not here. I'll buzz your intercom when she shows."

Camp returned to his desk. He had papers to grade. But the minute he hauled them out, she'd probably walk in. Then again—he checked the wall clock—she was already fifteen minutes late. If this was indicative of Emily Benton's punctuality, she might not be a good candidate. Maizie Boone had made it clear that she didn't mollycoddle anyone. Camp knew *he* wouldn't want to cross the gruff wagon mistress.

Ten more minutes of fidgeting and he was ready to write Emily off, pioneer name or not. He pulled out a folder of tests and was busily grading when a disheveled redhead in a rumpled blue suit stumbled through his doorway. She promptly dropped a bulging briefcase of the type mature students preferred over backpacks. Papers and books spewed from the doorway clear to Camp's desk.

Mumbling to herself, she scrambled awkwardly on hands and knees to collect the mess.

Startled as he was by the intrusion, Camp jumped up to lend a hand. From the array of textbooks, he judged her to be a student. And not a very good one if the low grades on the papers he scooped up were any indication.

He frowned. She must be from his overcrowded freshman lecture course, An Introduction to American History. Surely he'd remember her otherwise. But he'd left strict instructions at the desk that he wasn't available to students this afternoon. Maybe she'd be more organized next visit.

"Here," he said gruffly, stuffing papers neatly into her satchel. "I can't meet with you today. See Bess at the outer desk. Tell her to make you an appointment tomorrow during my free period. I hope rescheduling isn't terribly inconvenient."

"Well, it is." The smoky voice climbed. "I raced home from work, took my son to baseball practice and waited to make sure it wasn't canceled due to rain. It wasn't, so I drove my daughter across town to a friend's house. Freeway traffic was impossible." She shifted the bulky case. "If I'm keeping you from happy hour, we can make this brief." She scraped two stubborn locks of fiery hair from a pale forehead, revealing angry, wisteria-blue eyes.

From his superior height, Nolan Campbell scowled at her, prepared to deliver a rebuke that would let her know in no uncertain terms how unwise it was to talk back to one's professor. The rebuke stuck in his throat, squeezing the breath from his lungs as he was sucked, spellbound, into those amazing blue eyes. Twice Camp opened and closed his mouth, feeling as if he were going down for the third time. Unable to lay claim to a logical reason for clammy hands and suddenly incoherent speech, he floundered back to his desk and flopped into his chair with all the grace of a beached whale.

Something must be terribly wrong. He had to get rid of this student quick. "Look, I'll give you a few seconds. What is it you need?" he croaked, sneaking two fingers to his wrist to take his pulse. It bounced erratically. Oh, God! Maybe it was his heart. He was at that age. And he didn't eat right. If he didn't die, he'd lay off cheeseburgers.

Camp blinked at the woman who'd followed him to his desk. Sweat popped out on his brow. Did she have sense enough to dial 911 if he fell off his chair? Not according to the scores written in red on the papers he'd picked up.

"What do *I* need?" Eyes narrowed, she thumped her bag and purse to the floor and perched gingerly on the edge of the chair that faced his desk. "Did I land in the right room? Are you Nolan Campbell?"

He nodded, keeping his gaze on the tiny frown lines

that crinkled above her perfect nose rather than risk a second collision with those killer eyes.

"Then *we* have an appointment, Mr. Campbell. At least, I doubt there's more than one Nolan Campbell at this college who plans to take a wagon train over the Santa Fe Trail." Dimpling prettily, she said, "I'm Emily Benton, by the way. And I believe that's my application you're turning into confetti."

Shocked to see his fingers shredding her application, Camp dropped the paper as if it were a hot potato. Things went from bad to worse as his gaze shifted to a spiky heel dangling enticingly from a shapely foot. He snapped his eyes to her face again.

Her smile broadened, and Camp felt as though he'd been kicked in the stomach. This time he had a clearer grasp of his symptoms. It'd been so long since he'd experienced lust that he'd failed to recognize the signs.

Emily Benton was nothing like he'd imagined. In addition to huge, captivating eyes, she had an air of fragility that made her totally unsuitable for his project. Why, the woman didn't have enough meat on her bones to attract a buzzard.

Camp closed his eyes and massaged his temples. "So," he said, dragging one hand over the hollows in his cheeks, "Judging by the address on your application, I assume you're attending our sister college. Instead of trekking across the prairie this summer, Mrs. Benton, I suggest you sign up for bonehead classes to help bring up those abominable grades." His words were cold, Camp knew. But her application stated she was a widow. She probably needed extra schooling to ensure a better job to help raise those kids she'd mentioned. Actually, he was doing her a favor, turning her down.

Not only that, he didn't want to deal with the tension of seeing her every day—something he was loath to admit. Folding his hands, he squared his shoulders and met her eyes. Almost.

"Student? Abominable grades?" Emily clapped a hand to her head a moment. Then it dawned. "Oh, the papers." She kicked the bag at her feet. "I teach in the women's program. Those are my students' papers." She grimaced. "They *are* deplorable, aren't they? But I imagine that the women in our program are lucky to be in class. Some we barely coached through GEDs. A few of our older students finished high school, but thanks to crafty divorce lawyers they're being forced into an alien work environment. Most have no marketable skills, nor have they cracked a textbook in years." Her speech faltered. Why was she telling him this? According to Sherry, the man had some pretty dated ideas about women.

Emily lifted her chin, gathering her dignity. "I hold a Master's in psychology and one in sociology. I didn't realize a degree was required to go on your wagon train."

"I, ah, no, it isn't." Taking in a deep breath, Camp forced himself to study her application. Damn, she looked as if a stiff wind would blow her away.

Emily couldn't say how she knew he was getting ready to turn her down. But the feeling was strong. She'd promised herself that after the humiliation of dealing with Dave—after years of trying to be the perfect wife and putting her career on hold—she'd never beg another man for anything. Lowering her gaze to clasped hands turning white at the knuckles, she murmured, "Please, Mr. Campbell. My children think money grows on trees. I need this trip to teach them some solid values this summer."

Camp's stomach churned. He hated looking down on her bent head. He needed her, too, dammit—to fill his contracted portion of the train. But the last thing he *wanted* was daily contact with this woman. Wait a minute, though. Pioneer women traveled with children. Emily Benton and her kids offered a unique opportunity to contrast a contemporary single mother with her pioneer cousins. For goodness' sake, this was business. Nothing more. Besides, he'd only see her at night when he collected the data sheets.

"Sign here." Brusquely he handed her a release form. "I'll mail you the final packet of information in a week or so."

Emily didn't trust herself to meet his eyes. Her hand shook as she scribbled her name. If it wasn't for the fact that her in-laws were stealing her kids' affections by buying them everything under the sun, she'd tell this SOB exactly what he could do with his trip. And it wasn't pretty.

CHAPTER TWO

"Naturally, men take credit for winning the West. Hollywood says they did."
—Camp overheard a woman tell Sherry this.

AFTER POSTING his spring-semester grades with the registrar's office, Camp loaded his laptop computer in the car, along with his suitcase, and headed for Boonville. He felt curiously lighthearted—sort of like Tom Sawyer or Huck Finn. Probably because it was the first year in ten he'd skipped teaching summer classes. Until he'd begun to pack, he hadn't realized how stagnant his life had become. Or how badly he needed a break.

The thirty-mile drive seemed less. Historically speaking, Franklin, across the Missouri River from Boonville, was the "Cradle of the Santa Fe." But old Franklin was destroyed by a flood in 1826, and Boonville took up the slack. Maizie Boone's wagon train, the one Camp had begun to refer to as *his train,* would leave from the original cobblestone square in Boonville. This was real history, not some Hollywood script.

He reached the town's outskirts, slowed and navigated tree-lined streets, looking for the lot where Maizie had told him to park. He rounded a corner and saw them—a complement of Conestoga wagons framed against the riverbank. He gawked. Seeing the wagons up close, Camp suffered his first stab of apprehension. White canvas billowed above gigantic blue boxes, their running gear painted bright red. They reminded Camp of a fleet of sailboats on wheels. Lordy, he'd booked four of those monsters on a dare. Had knowingly filled them with greenhorns—or whatever they called novice trail drivers. With women yet. Women whose stamina he had reason to doubt. With the exception of Gina Ames.

Camp passed a hand over his sagging jaw. He'd agreed to arrive a week ahead of his researchers in order to stock the wagons and rent the draft horses destined to carry city dwellers many miles from the comforts of home.

The image of one particular city dweller, Emily Benton, loomed starkly before his eyes. Camp pictured her, reins in hand, clad in a flowing, flowery pioneer dress—a matching sunbonnet tossed carelessly back so that her riot of red hair caught flame in the afternoon sun.

He blinked hard to dispel the vision. A sudden cool breeze lifted the hair on the back of his neck, as if ghosts from the original Becknell caravans mocked his imprudence in accepting Emily's application. *Why did you?* they taunted.

"Hey, they all read the brochures." Not a woman had backed out, even though he'd half expected it after his secretary mailed out Maizie's six pages of rules and regs.

Camp stripped off his sport coat and tossed it in the back seat. Rolling his shirt sleeves midway up his arms, he sauntered toward the rustic building that housed Boone's Frontier Adventures.

A young, freckle-faced woman sat at a desk, phone to her ear. Karen Boone, according to her nameplate. One of Maizie's many grandchildren, Camp decided, gazing around the cracker-box office. Two chairs flanked a glass-topped table stacked with brochures like the one Sherry had brandished like a red flag to start this madness. Rather than sit, he studied a laminated, parchment wall map boldly marking the Santa Fe Trail. He'd memorized the route, but the old map reminded him of the risks encountered by the original wagon trains. So did the watercolor paintings depicting the old forts along the trail. Perusing each, Camp felt an odd kinship with the pioneers.

"May I help you?"

He spun at the sound of the girl's voice. He'd been so immersed in his own thoughts, he hadn't heard her hang up the phone. "I'm Nolan Campbell." He ambled up to her desk. "I believe Mrs. Boone is expecting me."

The girl's green eyes twinkled. "I could ask which Mrs. Boone. There are fifty here. More spread all the way to Boone's Lick. I've typed your name a zillion times these last few weeks, so I'd guess you mean Maizie. Want a tip? Don't call her 'Mrs.' If you haven't already figured it out, my grandmother is her own woman."

"I gathered that. But based on your smile, her bark must be worse than her bite."

"True, but I'll deny it if you tell her I said so. The image, you understand? Right now she's two miles out of town at her son Micah's ranch. We board the horses there. Let me draw you a map. She said to send you out to pick the animals that'll pull your wagons."

"Me? You mean it's not just a matter of paying rental fees?"

The girl glanced up from her drawing. "Another tip. Don't let Maizie hear panic in your voice. March right into the pasture and examine each horse. Run a hand over their legs and say 'um' a few times. Then casually ask her expert advice." No spark of humor showed this time when Karen passed Camp the map.

"Uh, thanks. For everything," he said, folding the paper several times as he backed out the door.

On the sidewalk again, Camp took a deep breath. What he knew about draft horses you could inscribe in capital letters on the head of a pin. A very small pin. Oh, during his preteen years he'd ridden his uncle's saddle horses. He'd curried them and seen to their care when his aunt and uncle took vacations, but...

"I suppose...a horse is a horse is a horse," he muttered, hurrying back to his car.

He drove the length of the small picturesque town and beyond, to where lush fields of sorghum replaced rural homes. When the road split around a huge, gnarled oak—the one sketched on his map—he slowed the car and began to search for the Boone mailbox. It wasn't difficult to locate. A green valley off to his left suddenly sprouted gargantuan horses contentedly munching grass. It struck Camp how wrong his earlier assessment had been. A horse *wasn't* just a horse. Each of those bruisers could easily make two saddle horses.

Car virtually at a crawl, he whistled through his teeth. "Some of those suckers have feet the size of dinner plates."

Farther along, he spotted someone inside the fence filling water troughs with a hose. Maizie, he presumed. The wagon mistress was everything he'd imagined and more. Calamity Jane without the cigarillo. Iron-gray hair hung straight to the woman's shoulders from beneath a battered, wide-brimmed hat. A shirt of fringed buck leather topped a split denim skirt. Her scuffed Wellingtons were caked with dirt and run-down at the heels.

As Camp climbed from the car, she glanced up and greeted him with a grin that pleated her sun-weathered cheeks into a profusion of wrinkles. His mind had already begun spinning the human interest portion of his paper.

"You'd be that Campbell fella, I suppose," she rasped. "I'm Maizie." After crushing his fingers in a solid handshake, she spit a stream of tobacco less than an inch to the right of his new black loafers. "Them'er pansy-ass shoes, boy. If you got boots in the car, you better fetch 'em. These Clydes, Percherons and Belgian drafts leave ankle-deep calling cards." She placed one foot on the bottom rung of the fence and scraped a layer of dark muck onto the wood rail as if for emphasis.

The pungent aroma told Camp he'd been wrong about that being dirt caked on her boots. It also crossed his mind that Calamity's cigarillo might be preferable to Maizie's chew. He jerked a thumb toward his car. "I brought boots. Give me a minute to change." Thankfully, he'd packed his oldest jeans. He doubted if new denim would pass her muster. As he poked the legs of his best worsted wool slacks into his boot tops, Camp wished he'd changed clothes before leaving campus.

"Ready," he said, rejoining her. "How many horses are we talking?" As Karen had suggested, he knelt and ran a hand down the iron-hard leg of a horse with gentle eyes.

"Four per team, and two per wagon spare. I'm a stickler for rotating stock. We have vets meeting us in Fort Larned and McNees Crossing. My son Terrill will deliver us feed and fresh water. We won't run our animals into the ground the way pioneers did. This is a reenactment, not the real McCoy. That's why I asked drivers to arrive a day early. So you'll all learn to hitch, unhitch and handle these babies."

Babies? Hippo babies, maybe. Camp stood. "Uh, Maizie...all my drivers are women. I never mentioned it—never presumed that *my* role mattered. I'm a college professor conducting a study comparing modern and pioneer women. My volunteers aren't exactly the types who work out with weights or anything." Again, Emily Benton came to mind. Smooth, unblemished skin and a waist Camp could span with his hands. If her head reached his shoulder, he'd be surprised. Camp suffered a second wave of guilt as he eyed the tons of muscle. "Why don't I leave the choosing to you," he said smoothly, remembering the last part of Karen's advice.

"Uh-huh!" Maizie stroked a callused hand down the back of a massive brown-and-white horse. "We'll go with the Clydesdales for your ladies. At seventeen to eighteen hands, they're a little taller than the Percherons, but more even-tempered. Perches are bred with Arabians, so they're more feisty. Belgians are the biggest. Strongest, too. Most are nineteen to twenty hands. You men can drive them."

"Well, I..." He tugged an ear. "I'm not exactly going with the train."

"Uh-huh. Where *do* you fit in, sonny? You're laying out a passel of dough for somebody who's missing the fun."

Camp summarized his plans and ended by saying, "I'd prefer others on the train didn't know about my study. I don't want them purposely helping the women. Ruins the results, you understand."

"It's been my experience that people on these trips either start out friendly and hate one another before the end, or they begin every man for himself and finish up pulling together. Thing I can't see...is women with any guts a'tall lettin' you study 'em like pet rats, 'n you stayin' out of the maze." She spit another stream past his ear, pinning him with faded, all-knowing eyes.

"Of course they will. My paper isn't about how *I'd* fare in the wilds. Men haven't gone soft. We still do manual labor."

"Uh-huh." Maizie gave the horse a final pat. "How well do you know women, boy?" she asked, leading the way out of the pasture. "Claim to be an expert, do you?"

Camp's laughter held a nervous edge. "Show me a man who claims to be an expert on females and I'll show you a bald-faced liar. Even so, I know some in my group will stick until death to prove that anything pioneer women did, modern women can do better."

"Uh-huh!" Maizie dug a stubby pencil and a wrinkled pad from her skirt pocket and wrote out a rental slip for the horses. "Stop by the office and pay Karen. Meet me at the general store on Market Street tomorrow at ten to buy supplies. I hope you've got the muscle to stock four wagons. It's definitely manual labor—loading bags of flour, coffee, sugar, salt, beans, crackers and sides of home-cured bacon."

Camp took the bill and climbed into his car. Had he made an error taking her into his confidence? The way she said *uh-huh,* a body would think Maizie Boone had a Ph.D. in psychology. He chuckled as he started the car. Her advice, like little Lucy's in the *Peanuts* cartoons, was probably worth the same—about five cents.

WHEN SATURDAY rolled around, the day Maizie had set aside to teach drivers how to hitch and unhitch the teams, Camp expected his research subjects to trickle in one by one. They surprised him, arriving en masse, accompanied by a television crew from Columbia and a woman reporter from the campus newspaper—which didn't please him.

"Whose bright idea was this?" he muttered, sidling up to his sister.

"Yvette's. What's the matter, Nolan, afraid they'll steal your thunder?"

Camp shrugged. "No, but neither do I want them turning this into some kind of farce. Why do you all look like you stepped off the pages of Mule Creek Mercantile's catalog?" The women, all except Sherry's roommate, sported spanking new boots, blue jeans and Stetsons. Yvette was Hollywood all the way, in white jeans and a purple suede halter top trimmed with fringe, feathers and beads. She wore matching purple moccasins. Camp would have bet the farm she'd come dressed like this.

"Ugh! What stinks?" Yvette ran up to them holding her nose. Her pristine moccasins landed in a fresh pile of manure. She slipped, slid, then went down squarely on her rump. "Ick! Yuck," she squealed as Camp hid a smile and stretched out a hand to help her up.

"You're laughing, Nolan Campbell." She smacked his hand away. "Don't touch me." Instead, she accepted help from a member of the press. The instant she was up, Yvette turned on Sherry. "I assumed they'd pull the wagons with something civilized, like tractors." Sniffing the air, she wrinkled her dainty nose. "This is positively gross. I'm not spending ten weeks smelling horse poop." She clapped a palm over the closest camera lens. "Those shots had better end up on the cutting-room floor, my friend. I know the station manager. Grab your stuff out of my car, Sherry. I'm outta here."

Sherry gaped at her roommate's retreating figure.

"Yvette, wait! You promised. Darn it! I paid your half of the rent for the whole summer."

The blonde gingerly picked her way to the car, paying no attention. She peeled off her moccasins and threw them in a nearby trash barrel. Hopping the remaining distance on bare feet, she unlocked the car and tumbled inside.

Sherry took one look at Camp's smirk and ran after her friend. "Oh, for pity's sake, Yvette. I'll pay off your Visa," Sherry wheedled. "Come on, this is exactly what Nolan expects. What happened to striking a blow for modern womanhood?"

"You strike it." Yvette knelt on the front seat, leaned over into the back and started pitching Sherry's bedding and duffel bags out on the ground.

"Fine! Leave. Be a traitor." Sherry grumbled as she snatched her things. "And I want that money back!"

Yvette slammed her door, cranked the engine and peeled out of the lot.

Maizie Boone jabbed an elbow into Camp's side. "Uh-huh! What'd I tell you?"

He scowled. "Shall we proceed with the lesson? My sister's capable of handling a wagon alone. The way I see it, I still have four drivers."

Maizie inclined her head toward his dwindling group. "Maybe you haven't been listening to those kids. They've been bellyaching to leave since they got here. Seein' how frazzled the mom looks, I'll bet you a long neck at Sammy's Bar that she splits next."

Camp had sampled the cheeseburgers and brew at Sammy's last night. Good as they were, he didn't want to meet Maizie there to pay off that type of bet. But now that she'd mentioned it, he heard kids squabbling. He zeroed in on them. Neither resembled Emily. The boy was taller than his mother, and sturdier, his hair auburn, not red. The girl was shorter by a head and as thin as a reed. Rings circled each of her red-tipped fingers. Except for the mop of mahogany hair, she'd pass for a younger version of Yvette. Flounced like her, too. *Brother!*

Emily's jaw was locked in place. She didn't look as if she'd give an inch. "I'll take your bet," Camp told Maizie impulsively. He knew, as Maizie didn't, that Emily's kids were the main reason she'd signed up.

He turned, planning to introduce himself to Emily's offspring. Instead, he nearly mowed down Brittany Powers. Camp's eyes bugged. Brittany's fingernails weren't painted red—they were half silver and half black. At least, on the hand possessively clutching his sleeve.

"Nolan," she whispered breathlessly, a speech pattern he'd noticed her developing over the last weeks of the semester. "I'm positively freaked by horses. You'll take care of mine, won't you?" Her fingers walked up his shirtfront and fiddled with the silver medallion he wore around his neck.

He frowned into eyes outlined in kohl and shaded in luminous silver—colors that matched her nail polish but left her looking oddly like a raccoon. Debating how to handle an effective rebuke in the midst of so many people, he caught Emily's expression of disgust. Surely she hadn't pegged him as a cradle robber.

"I'm not traveling with the train," he snapped at Brittany, firmly setting her away. "Follow Maizie. She'll show you how to harness the teams. According to her, the Clydesdales are big, lovable teddy bears. You'll do fine, Brittany."

"What do you mean, you aren't traveling with the

wagon train?" A chorus of angry voices almost blew Camp off his feet. Suddenly, Sherry, Gina and Emily all converged, hands on hips, eyes flashing.

Warily, he sidestepped a cameraman, and aligned himself with the wagon mistress. She spit a bead of tobacco, two drops of which splashed on his boot.

"Uh-huh," she mused in that way Camp had come to find exceedingly irritating. "These the gals who'll stick until death to prove you wrong?" she murmured.

Smile plastered to his lips, Camp held up a palm. "Listen…ladies…I figured I'd make you nervous breathing down your necks. Maizie gave me a list of your scheduled stops. I plan to pop in at regular intervals and pick up these data sheets."

"If you aren't going," Brittany said, pouting, "then I'm not, either."

Gina gathered the others to caucus. After a brief discussion, she broke free. "That's about the size of it, Campbell," she said. "If you don't go, we all quit."

"Hooray," chorused the Benton kids. "Let's go home, Mom."

Emily advanced on Camp. "I'll have you know I gave up a chance to teach summer school. I need that stipend. What do you plan to do about it?"

"Look." Camp raked a hand through his hair. Mentally he added up how much he'd already forked out. The money was nothing compared with the fact that he'd promised his department chair a publishable paper by the start of fall term. "You all agreed to be part of my study. No one said I had to travel with the train."

"I thought it was understood," Sherry said.

Gina crossed her arms. "Well, we could go and write

any old thing on his data sheets. Skew his study all to hell! He'd be none the wiser."

"Oh, but that wouldn't be right!" Emily exclaimed, eyes bright with concern even after the others silenced her with glares.

As if things weren't already going down the toilet, Camp's colleagues drove in next. Hearing a reporter explain to the newcomers why everyone was milling about, he shook his head and groaned. "Listen to this great front-page caption," the man bragged, "'Local College Prof Fails Test.'"

Sherry snapped her fingers. "Could you maybe add 'Beaten By Women'?"

Camp's knees all but buckled when Lyle Roberts clapped him hard between the shoulder blades. "Camp's just fooling around. I assure you he's one hundred percent committed to this project. *Of course* he's driving a wagon. He wouldn't dream of backing out before every last woman here falls by the trail."

"Lyle!" Camp weighed available options for digging out of this mess.

"Uh-huh," grunted Maizie. "Gonna be the shortest wagon train in history."

"Okay...hold on," Camp shouted. "It's no big deal. Brittany, you go in Sherry's wagon. Gina asked to be on her own. Emily and her kids will take the third Conestoga, and I'll drive number four. Now, if everybody's satisfied, can we get this show on the road? I have bedding to buy before the stores close."

It was hard to tell who was more disgruntled by his capitulation, Emily Benton's children or Camp himself. Megan Benton stamped a dainty foot, declaring her mother couldn't *make* her go. As if to prove it, she flung herself down on a park bench. Mark grabbed his boom box and turned it up to deafening decibels, refusing to turn it down as Emily ordered. He glared when Camp walked over and shut it off. Sullen, the boy flopped next to his sister. "This summer sucks."

Camp was relieved that Lyle and Jeff had trundled off to Sammy's Bar with the last of the nosy reporters. He felt doubly glad they were gone when Maizie gave his team of teddy-bear Clydesdales to strangers—Doris and Vi, two elementary-school teachers from St. Louis who'd joined the trek. Then she delivered to Camp a quartet of nasty-tempered Belgians. One stepped on his foot, possibly crippling him for life. Another continually tried to eat his hair, blowing foul-smelling breath in his face. "Stop it," he hissed.

An hour after all the women had mastered the task of hitching and unhitching, Camp remained in the park, tangled in the harnesses and singletrees that yoked the teams together. The face-saver was that a loudmouthed man from Philadelphia had done no better. Philly, as Camp dubbed the braggart, claimed he'd fished Alaska, shot the rapids of Oregon's Rogue River and single-handedly sailed through the Greek islands. That was where Camp tuned him out and got down to business. He'd be damned if he was going to let a few scrawny women and four fat horses make an ass out of him.

By the time he'd performed to Maizie's liking, Camp was more than ready to slug down the beer the woman owed him. But it was four-thirty. He had less than thirty minutes to make it to the general store to purchase bedding. No way would he sleep on bare planks just to prove he was a manly man.

Let the women jeer. He intended to scare up spare

batteries for his laptop, too. It turned out no store in town carried the type he needed. Giving up, Camp raced into a stationery store at five minutes to five to buy every ruled tablet they had in stock. At this point he was beyond caring that the pads came only in pink and lavender. Although he drew the line at pencils with grape-and strawberry-scented erasers.

By the time he poked his head through Sammy's swinging doors at six-thirty, he found the place jammed with Saturday-night locals. Ah, well, he could do without a drink. Maizie had warned everyone it was "wagons ho" at 5 a.m. She didn't sound as if she'd be inclined to wait for anyone shuffling in late. Besides, the wail from the jukebox only intensified Camp's headache, and the smoke was thick enough to cut with a dull knife. All in all, it'd been a most trying day. He recalled passing a mom-and-pop café somewhere between Sammy's Bar and Maizie's office. A quiet dinner appealed more than a cold beer.

He found the place easily enough. But as he reached for the door, Camp noticed Emily Benton and her kids seated in a front booth. Megan and Mark were clearly still sulking, and Emily looked positively grim. The very last thing he needed to round out his day was to step into the middle of a family feud.

"What the hell," he said with a yawn, "I'll skip dinner in favor of extra z's." Retracing his steps, he again resisted the smell of onions wafting from Sammy's. At the corner, he crossed the street and didn't stop until he'd claimed his room at the motel. Too tired to shower, Camp shucked his clothes and tumbled into bed—the last real one he'd see for weeks. He sighed as the mattress adjusted to his contours. Seconds before sleep took him, he sat up, snapped on the light and set the alarm on his watch, advancing the time to allow for a leisurely shower and a big breakfast.

What seemed like nano-seconds later, the sound of car doors slamming jarred Camp from a pleasant dream. Where he lived—the outskirts of town, almost in the country—nights were so quiet he almost always slept solidly until the alarm went off. Rolling toward the wall, he pulled the pillow over his head. Then someone banged insistently on his door.

"Wrong room," he yelled. Some fool must have stayed too long at Sammy's Bar and as a result, misread the room numbers.

"Campbell? Is that you? Open up!" At Emily Benton's voice he jackknifed to a sitting position, then leaped out of bed. Heart hammering, Camp yanked the door open the length of the chain. It vibrated out of his hand and slammed in his face. Cautiously he opened it again. "What's wrong? Was Maizie right? Are you quitting?" His sleepy eyes failed to register full daylight.

"Me? The others bet that you'd run off during the night. Maizie sent me to check. It's five-thirty. She's fit to be tied."

"*What?* Come in." The chain jingled, then clanked against the door. "Wait," he said in a muffled voice. "I'm not decent." Snatching his watch from the table, Camp shook it, only to discover that it'd stopped shortly after midnight. "Hell and damnation!" He dug in his bag, dragged out a clean pair of jeans and jumped into them. Socks, boots and a pullover shirt followed. Wadding his dirty clothes into the bag, he raced across the room and threw open the door. "My watch stopped. The battery must have died. You're saying everyone's already hitched their wagons?"

"Everyone except you. Maizie's...annoyed. The wagons are probably strung the length of Broadway by now."

Camp's curse was muffled by the growl of his stomach. "I'm starved," he said. "I skipped lunch and dinner yesterday." He rubbed his jaw. "I haven't shaved and my teeth feel scuzzy."

"Well, it's too late now. You'll have to get something out of your stores."

"You're kidding?" His steps slowed. "Beans, rice, flour, coffee—those are Maizie's idea of stores."

Emily failed to cloak a look of pity. "Sounds like good pioneer fare to me. Isn't that the object of this trek? To simulate what happened in 1821?"

Because she'd spoken the truth, Camp shut his mouth and accepted his fate. Except that Emily had been wrong on one count. Maizie hadn't gone ahead. She'd waited to chew him out.

Pinching the bridge of his nose between thumb and finger, Camp endured her verbal flogging. This he could definitely do without.

Amid a rousing send-off by townsfolk and a marching band from Santa Fe Trail High School out of Overbrook, Kansas, Camp's four horses decided to act up.

Maizie's son, Robert, and his boy, Jared, occupants of the final wagon, helped subdue Camp's nervous team. If Robert Boone had looked less like his mother, or had been built less like a linebacker, Camp would have tried bribing him into going after coffee and a couple of Egg McMuffins. Or he would have if Mark Benton hadn't kept leaning around the canvas-covered bows of Emily's wagon, leering at him.

By the time they pulled out, a full hour late, Camp

was ready to strangle the kid. And just where was the boy's mother during all of this? The starchy woman who'd jerked Camp out of bed at an unholy hour, acting as if he was a no-good slacker.

Emily Benton had absolutely no control over those brats. Camp recalled her saying in the interview that she wanted to remove them from the harmful influence of overindulgent grandparents. He'd sympathized and silently applauded her. Now he discovered that she herself was turning a blind eye to the antics of her little darlings.

If he had children… But why even get into that? A family was out of the question when you didn't have a wife. The only woman he'd asked to fill that bill had dumped him. After she'd accepted his ring, Greta decided she didn't want to spend vacations renovating a musty old house or being dragged through museums. He *hadn't* dragged her. Those things were a big part of who he was. But Greta's departure still hurt. Oh, he'd pretended to shrug off the loss as inconsequential—had even set about playing the field—which only left him more confused.

As the wagons stretched out, and the sun spread fingers of pink and gold across an endless blue sky, Camp realized it was a mistake to have this much time on his hands to let his mind wander. Colleagues saw him as a man in control of his destiny. Intelligent, happy and smart to remain single. Sherry's pals saw him as a callous guy on the make. Both groups were off base. When he wasn't busy, he was lonely as hell. The older he got, the more he wanted a close relationship of the sort his parents enjoyed. And children of his own. Nice, well-behaved kids.

He shifted on the hard wooden seat, staring blindly

at the rumps of the plodding horses. No doubt about it, he was going to be pretty darned sick of his own company long before they reached Kansas, let alone Santa Fe, New Mexico.

Emily Benton grabbed her son, who was once again leaning too far off the seat. "Mark, what's so interesting about watching where we've just been? Why don't you crawl in the wagon bed and play a board game with your sister?"

"Are you kidding? Megan wouldn't lower herself. She's probably got her nose in one of those horror stories she sneaked into her duffel. Besides, I'm bugging the old far— I mean dude. The one who shut off my tunes. He knows I'm slagging him and it drives him nuts."

"What old dude? And what's 'slagging'?" Emily asked absently, overlooking his slip of the tongue as she debated trying to roust Megan from her book. Communication of any sort with Megan had been almost nonexistent since Dave died. Emily had great hopes they'd reconnect on this trip. Her daughter was growing up too fast.

Mark jerked a thumb over his shoulder. "Slagging is like to insult somebody. I meant the old dude you guys forced into driving a wagon. The con man."

"Professor Campbell? Mark, don't call him names."

The boy screwed up his face. "I don't care. He reminds me of Dad. All smiles, making himself out to be the big man, while he's conning you into doing the work."

Emily shot her son a sidelong glance. "If you saw all that, why is it so hard for you to see your grandfather's attempts to manipulate?"

"Toby has the bucks to do nice things for us. We're poor."

"Don't call your grandfather by his given name. It's

disrespectful, no matter what he and your grandmother say. And we aren't poor, Mark. We're not rich, but you have food on the table, a roof over your head and clothes on your back."

"Megan says Toby has the Midas touch. He's a king who had rooms full of money. Like Gramps. Why not let him and Mona spend some on us?"

"Oh, honey, it's hard to explain. Gifts sometimes come with strings attached. Like if you accept gifts, the giver considers that you owe him in return. A payback. But his idea of an acceptable payback may not match yours."

Faint lines etched the child's brow. "I don't get it. Toby and Mona have everything. What could they want from us?"

"Nothing, birdbrain." There was a stirring inside the wagon and Megan thrust her head between her mother and brother. "Mom's jealous because they can do more for us. Mona said so."

"Megan, that's not true." Emily did her best to hang on to her temper.

"It is so, or else why did you drag us on this smelly old trip? You didn't want us swimming in their pool or having them take us to the mall for school clothes. You'd rather let us die out here on some moldy trail."

Emily gripped the reins too tightly and the Clydesdales ground to a stop. "Megan, must you be so melodramatic? No one's going to die on this trip." Her lecture was interrupted by harsh snorts. Turning, Emily saw Nolan Campbell's team pull abreast of hers.

"What's the matter with you?" he shouted. "Can't you signal or something? I almost ran you down. Are you totally irresponsible?"

"You might have slowed your horses," she said through

clenched teeth. Mark was more right than he knew. Nolan Campbell seemed just as dictatorial as Dave.

"Sheesh!" Mark rolled his eyes in disgust. "You'd better fan it, Mom. I told you, the old dude's a loose cannon."

Emily gazed at the huge wagon inching toward hers. Snapping her reins, she sped ahead of Camp. "Just stay away from me," she ordered. "From us."

Mark's lips curled in an impudent grin.

Camp coughed and spit out grit thrown from the Bentons' wheels. In a flash of brilliant insight he wondered why on earth he'd wasted time regretting that he didn't have a wife and kids. Especially a wife!

CHAPTER THREE

"Historic reality is a far cry from men's version of it."
—Gina Ames's observation on her first data sheet.

THE SETTING SUN CAST long shadows behind the wagons before Maizie gave the signal to stop for the night some five miles outside the community of Arrow Rock.

Camp had bounced up and down on the hardwood seat so long his butt felt numb. Blistered even. He wanted desperately to leave his perch, yet he was half-afraid to get down in case he couldn't walk. Too humiliating. *You have to do something, dolt.*

What he did was watch the others unhitch their horses and hobble them in the carpet of grass beneath a stand of yellowwood and hickory trees. His best view was of Emily's wagon, since he'd parked beside her. Damn, but she looked positively chipper the way she hopped down and bent to loosen the singletrees. Camp was struck by an urge to ruffle the wisps of hair escaping her hat. Curls that shone like new copper pennies in the peachy afterglow of the sun.

His gaze slipped automatically from Emily's hair to her nicely rounded backside. It was plain to see why pioneer men chose to walk or ride horses and let their wives drive the wagons. The simple fact was, women had more natural padding than men.

Would you look at that! Padding be damned. Emily Benton had a thick bench cushion covering that hard plank seat. How would Sherry justify *that* bit of comfort?

Camp scowled, then moaned as he shifted his position, checking to see if the other women had cheated, too. They had! Of all the nerve… Yet on another level— the one that hurt—Camp wished he'd been as smart.

"Are you all right?" Emily's quiet question jarred him from his stupor.

He straightened quickly, ignoring the hot prickles shooting up his thigh as feeling returned to one leg. "I'm fine. Just wondered why we aren't circling the wagons."

Her low laughter sent hot prickles of another sort along Camp's already tender nerve ends.

"And you call yourself a historian, Campbell. For shame. Pioneers only circled the wagons to ward off attacks by marauding Indians. Which didn't occur nearly as often as Hollywood would like us to believe, I might add."

He bristled. "Wagon circles are well documented in the journals I've read. They guarded against more than Indian and outlaw attacks. Circles discouraged scavenging by coyote, cougar and bear."

Mark and Megan Benton tumbled out of Emily's wagon in time to overhear the last exchange. "Mo…th…er!" Megan wailed. "We'll all be eaten in our sleep."

"Bears. Cool!" Mark discarded his sullen look for one of delight—the first Camp had seen from either of the kids.

"I'll bet there're rattlesnakes, too," the boy announced in a loud, shivery voice, his face shoved close to his sister's.

She shrieked and scrambled back inside the wagon. Camp felt sorry for Emily. She had her hands full with those two.

"Megan, get back out here," Emily called. "It's time to pick up our list of nightly chores from Maizie. It'll be dark before you know it."

"Chores?" Camp looked blank. His stomach felt caved in to his backbone. The apples Maizie dispensed at the noon water stop had barely whetted his appetite. But starved though he was, Camp wanted to record his impressions of the trip before they faded. Every bone-jarring memory.

"Didn't you read the rules you mailed out?" Emily asked. "It's number four. Maizie doles out a list of chores every night. She'll rotate duties so one person doesn't always get the cushiest jobs and vice versa."

"You have the rules memorized?" Camp paused in the painful act of climbing from the high wagon seat. "I barely glanced at the packet. My secretary ran copies and sent them out. Why would I study the rules? I hadn't intended to travel with the train," he said, as if blaming Emily for his change in plans.

"That was evident. Still, you'd better try to borrow a copy, unless you're expecting special privileges."

"Not at all." Camp reacted to her sarcasm.

"Then I suggest you unhitch your team. Everyone else is already headed for Maizie's wagon."

"Bully for them," he snapped, uncaring that he sounded as fractious as Megan had earlier.

Emily pursed her lips. "Let's go, kids." She checked the Clydesdales' hobbles one last time before hurrying off.

Megan Benton didn't budge. Mark sidled up to

Camp. "I've never seen a bear. Are they really out there in the woods?"

Camp considered possible answers, then discarded all but the truth. He'd decided on the policy to which his father subscribed—that all questions asked by kids deserved an honest answer.

"Bears were a problem for the original Santa Fe trailblazers, Mark. We're more apt to run afoul of those rattlers you mentioned. If you gather wood, take care. Roll the piece over with your toe before picking it up. Wood provides homes for a variety of spiders, as well as snakes."

"Hot damn!" Mark exclaimed, then rolled his eyes as his sister let out another shriek and climbed to her knees on the wagon seat.

"Mona said the fact Mom's dragging us on this trip shows how weirded out she is. Toby *begged* me to tell some judge friend of his about this nutty plan. I wish I had. We could've stayed home. And I'm not doing any stupid old chores."

"Who are Mona and Toby?" Camp asked Mark, who—without being asked—helped stake Camp's last horse, a Belgian named Renegade. All day Camp had called him numerous other names under his breath.

Mark waited until they'd finished before answering Camp. "Mona and Toby are my grandparents. Since our dad died, they want us all to live with them. Mom won't. They fight about it all the time. Megan and me hear…'cept I don't think they know."

Camp, who rarely got involved in matters that didn't concern him, was moved to support Emily. "Talk to your mother. I'm sure she has valid reasons."

"She'd lie," Megan said bitterly. "Mona says it's

Mom's fault that Dad drank too much. She didn't try to understand him."

Camp thought he was hearing more about the Bentons' private lives than Emily would want discussed. He cast around for a way to extricate himself. Unfortunately, it came in the form of Brittany Powers. She ran toward him waving two slips of paper.

"Nolan. Nolan," she yelled, apparently forgetting the breathy voice. "I have your chore assignment. We're working together. Isn't that awesome?"

Reluctant to be teamed with Brittany, Camp nevertheless accepted one of the slips. "Well, Mark," he said, frowning after reading it, "don't worry about fending off snakes tonight. We're the wood hunters." He indicated himself and Brittany.

"Snakes?" Brittany shivered, cleaving herself to Camp's side. "I hate creepy crawlies. You're just soo brave."

Embarrassed, Camp tried peeling the young woman off his arm. "I need to grab a pair of gloves. You'd better do the same, Brittany."

"I didn't bring any, Nolan." She drew out his name. "But I'll tag along and keep you company." She wound both arms around his biceps this time.

Damnation, but she had a grip like a boa constrictor. "I'm sure there's something you can do around here. Let Mark help me." Camp snatched at the boy's shirtsleeve with his free hand. "Okay with you, kid?" He hoped Mark hadn't heard how desperate he was to avoid going into the woods with Brittany. But Mark was definitely astute.

"What's it worth to you, man? Five bucks?"

Little blackmailer. Luckily, Emily returned then. Before she gave her kids their assignments, Camp hit her with a smile. "Would you give Brittany Mark's job and let him go with me?" At Emily's arched brow, he explained Brittany's lack of gloves.

Emily saw how Camp took a step and Brittany moved with him, as if they were joined at the hip. Her husband had had younger women swarming over him, too. Dave had loved the attention. "I'm sure you'd rather Mark lent Brittany some gloves, right?"

Mark seemed surprised by his mother's caustic tone.

Camp was plain angry. For crying out loud, she seemed downright eager to toss him to the wolves.

"What'll I have to do if I don't help him haul wood?" Mark bargained with Emily.

"Locate rocks and build a fire ring for each wagon."

The boy jerked a thumb toward Camp. "I'll go with the dude. Her witchy fingernails'll poke holes in my gloves." He pointed at Brittany. "Ain't never seen nails like hers 'cept at Halloween."

"Twit. If I were a witch I'd turn you into a toad." Brittany gave him an evil eye. She clung to Camp's sleeve a moment longer, then reluctantly let him go. "I don't want to break my nails on rocks, either. Maybe I'll go see what Sherry's doing. We'll meet later, won't we, Nolan? I mean...you're collecting our data sheets, aren't you?"

Her affected whisper was back, Camp noticed with a wince. Avoiding her question, he said, "I suspect all the chores will be hard on hands, Brittany. I'd hate to see you tear a nail badly and, uh, risk infection."

Brittany's hands fluttered. "You are so thoughtful, Nolan. Nobody else cares if I rip a nail clear off. Or an arm or a leg, for that matter."

"I'm sure your parents expect me to judge these situations in their place."

"My folks don't give a damn what I do as long as I'm out of their hair. I'm a burden they'd like to be shut of for good, not just this summer."

Taken aback, Camp didn't know how to respond.

"You guys run along," Emily said softly, coming to Camp's rescue after all. "I'll carry the rocks. Megan and Brittany can push them into circles with their feet if they don't want to mess up their nails."

"Hey, thanks." Relieved beyond words, Camp wasted no time grabbing his gloves and striking off ahead of Mark into the copse of trees. He'd certainly misjudged Brittany Powers. Since the day she'd walked into his classroom, he'd figured her for a spoiled kid who had everything. Expensive clothes. Car. Enough spending money to feed a third-world nation. Everything but parental love, it seemed.

"Yo' dude," panted Mark as he caught up to Camp. "That Brittany chick has the hots for you."

Camp peered down his nose at the boy. "Don't be silly. And don't call women 'chicks.' I'm Brittany's college professor. I'm old enough to be her father."

Mark stopped and tipped his head back to gaze at his taller companion. "Uh-huh," he grunted. "Guess she digs old dudes, then."

Camp snatched up a long stick and parted the shrubs. The kid sounded so much like Maizie it was scary. "Look, here are three pieces of dry pine. Take them to one of the wagons while I look for more. And don't call me 'dude.' Understand?"

"It's cool if you don't want to talk about your love life. My mom sends me off to do stuff when I make her uncomfortable, too."

"I don't have a lov—we're not—oh, blast." If he

wasn't half-starved he'd leave the kid on his own and go log today's experiences. He had some beauts. But undoubtedly there'd be time while the women cooked dinner. Which would be speedier if he hurried back with wood for the cook fires. As if on cue his stomach rumbled again. Camp muttered a silent prayer that the people Maizie had assigned to the chore of cooking would allow plenty for ravenous men.

By the time they finished gathering wood, the sun had dropped. A stiff night breeze carried the smell of wood smoke and the mouthwatering aromas of onions and garlic. Saliva pooled in Camp's mouth as Mark darted off. Cheery campfires crackled in front of every wagon. Correction: every wagon but his.

In the flicker cast by Emily's dancing flames, Camp saw that someone had shoved rocks into a circle in front of his wagon. If not for the fact that the air had grown chill and he'd prefer to stay warm while he ate, he wouldn't even bother lighting a fire. The minute he finished eating he intended to collect the data sheets and hibernate.

Plans set, Camp strolled nonchalantly past the Benton wagon.

Emily called out, stopping him. "Maizie said to tell you that your wagon tilts left. She wants you to redistribute your load. Even out the heavier stuff."

"I don't have much that's heavy. But sure, I'll get right on it."

"Oh, another thing. Robert Boone has a big can of oil. We all picked up our ration and oiled our harnesses. You'll need to do yours."

Camp tried to see her face, but she stood in the shadows mixing something in a metal bowl. "Anything else?" He spread his feet, hooking thumbs in his belt.

"No. Just start a fire and cook your meal. Robert and Jared hauled water up from the creek for washing dishes. He said to use water from the wagon barrels for cooking and making coffee."

"Wait! You mean we're not eating potluck?"

She raised a sticky hand and brushed a springy lock of hair back with her forearm. "You mean everyone makes a dish and we eat together? No. The rules clearly state that we're on our own for meals."

"But…" The only food he'd fixed over an open fire had been an occasional hot-dog or toasted marshmallows. And that was about thirty years ago. Now he ate all his weekday meals out. On weekends, he popped prepackaged frozen dinners into the microwave. Now he really wished he'd read those frigging rules. The packet probably included recipes. If he'd only known— the store in Boonville where he'd bought his gear stocked boil-in-a-bag meals for backpackers.

Well, he had to do something fast. The kitchen goddess was looking down her nose again. One thing he knew for sure, he'd die before letting the truth of his culinary ineptitude leak out to his research subjects. "Argh…" Camp cleared his throat. "Believe I'll just mosey up the line and see if Maizie has an extra set of rules."

"Not that I want to keep you…" Emily smiled sweetly. "But if you light a fire now it'll be ready for cooking when you return. See…I've put water on for tea. Once the flames die down, I'll set out my Dutch oven." She pointed to a set of stacked pans. "Your coffee will be drinkable while your meal cooks—if you drink coffee, that is," she stammered.

"I do. Rarely this late, but tonight it sounds good."

"All this fresh air. Sharpens the appetite," she said with a laugh.

When Emily Benton laughed low in her throat like that it sharpened *his* appetite, Camp discovered. But not for food.

He shifted uncomfortably. If there was anything he didn't need, it was to lust after a grieving widow—and definitely not one who couldn't seem to control her kids. Grunting his thanks, he withdrew and built a fire without glancing her way again. Five matches later, it stayed lit.

As long as he was going to visit Maizie, Camp decided to ask if he could change places in the line—so he wouldn't be parked next to *her* tomorrow night. He pawed through his supplies, unearthing a fire grate, a coffeepot and the apparatus Emily called a Dutch oven. The coffeepot didn't have a device to hold filters like the one at home. It was galvanized inside and out. Camp figured you filled it with water and tossed in coffee beans.

Only, how many beans? Maizie's supply list had called for generic canned coffee. He wasn't picky about much, but he was about coffee. The minute he found out he'd be driving a wagon, he'd traded in the can for a sack of gourmet beans.

Settling on a handful, Camp dropped the grate over the fire and sat the pot on it before he took off to see Maizie. Cooking wasn't so hard, he thought smugly.

At each wagon, Camp paused to sniff. The elementary-school teachers had potatoes roasting in foil wrap and were frying a thick slab of ham. Vi, the taller of the two, said the mouthwatering confection cooling on a flat rock was cinnamon apple cobbler.

Refusing to lick his lips, Camp left. Robert's and Jared's plates were piled high with beans and franks.

Camp skirted the couple from Philadelphia. That guy was so obnoxious he probably made his wife whip up baklava and lamb wrapped in grape leaves so he'd have another opportunity to brag about his trip to Greece.

Camp skidded to a halt at Sherry and Brittany's fire. "Who fixed that?" He pointed to something that had the look of strawberry shortcake.

"Me." Sherry blew on her fingers and scraped them lightly across her shirt. "Emily discovered a patch of wild strawberries along that fencerow. I also made tomatoes, peppers and onions over brown rice. Tomorrow, it's Brittany's turn to cook. We decided to trade off."

Camp swatted at a curl of smoke. "When did you learn to cook?" he demanded "As I recall, you got a D in home ec."

"In freshman sewing—because we didn't have a machine at home. At the condo, I do most of the cooking. Yvette's rarely around. Here, take your data sheet. Brittany? Where's yours?"

The girl flashed Camp a wide smile. "I'll bring mine later. I'm redoing my nails." She beckoned to Camp. "I'm painting them ravishing red instead of black. Tell that little creep, Mark."

Ravishing red? Camp edged away, remembering what Mark had said about Brittany having the "hots" for him. "He wouldn't have noticed if you'd worn polish or not."

"No polish? Not wearing any color is like…like going naked. But if that's what you want…" Her rapt gaze traveled slowly up Camp's torso.

Reflexively, he closed the top button on his shirt. No way would he touch that statement. "I'll leave you ladies to eat. I'm off to have a word with Maizie." He couldn't retreat fast enough to their leader's wagon. She had stew bubbling in a black pot, and a coffee mug sat within reach of where she straddled a log, mending a cinch.

"Howdy, there, sonny. Did you get the word about redistributing your load and oiling tack?"

"Emily told me. I came to see if you have a spare set of rules—and to ask if I could move my wagon up in the line...say, between my sister and Doris and Vi."

Maizie took a swig of her coffee, eyes narrowed from the steam. "Spare rules are in my saddlebag. Bad idea for you to move. That little gal ridin' with Sherry ain't here to learn trail history, if you get my drift."

"Dammit!" Camp exploded. "She's my student."

"Uh-huh."

"It takes two to tango, Maizie. And I'm not dancing."

"Glad to hear it, boy. Help yourself to the rules. You might wanna hit the sack early, too. Today I went easy. Tomorrow we'll make fifteen miles or bust."

Camp put a hand to his sore butt. "That far? Are you forgetting this train's made up mostly of women?"

She slapped her thigh and cackled. "Ain't the gals I've seen rubbin' their backsides."

"Joke all you want. The trip is young," Camp reminded her as he walked stiffly to retrieve a set of rules. He thumbed through the pages, disappointed to see there were no recipes attached. "You didn't give the women extra help, did you, Maizie?" he asked suspiciously.

"Extra help, like how?"

"Oh, like while you had me hitching nags, maybe someone held a sideline cooking school?"

"I never play favorites with customers. Rule number seven says each wagon fixes whatever food they eat on the trip. Number nine says the same about laundry. Next town we hit, you might wanna stock up on canned soup, boy. It gets old, but it's easy to open and heat. Had a fella went all the way to Oregon eatin' soup three meals a day. He couldn't cook, either."

"I can cook," Camp lied.

"Uh-huh! See that you memorize those rules. We're keepin' a tight schedule."

There wasn't enough light for Camp to study the list on his way back to the wagon. Most people, he noticed, had eaten and were washing dishes. He hadn't even started his dinner. He might have to forgo writing anything tonight. Especially if tomorrow was going to be an even longer day. Every bone in his body hurt now.

The Bentons were dishing up their food as he passed. Bacon, scrambled eggs and biscuits. Golden, fluffy, steaming biscuits. Camp drooled on the top page of rules.

His dad had always made biscuits on weekends. He should be able to remember the ingredients. Flour. Water. Salt. And baking soda? No, baking powder. Darting another glance toward his neighbor, Camp saw Emily serve bacon from the bottom third of her Dutch oven. Biscuits were in the middle, eggs on top. He could practically hear Mark Benton taunting him for being a copycat. As if he cared.

Digging out a rasher of bacon, Camp popped it into the pan and set it over the hot coals. Estimating, he tossed approximately two cups of flour in a bowl, to which he added a pinch of salt—uh-oh, he'd forgotten oil. How much? Equal parts? Why not?

According to the baking-powder can, it was double-acting. Camp took another guess and shook some in. Wow, the mixture was stiff. He added more water. He had no clue how Emily Benton made her biscuits so symmetrical, but looks didn't count squat with Camp. He plopped spoonfuls of the stiff dough into the Dutch oven's second level—just like Emily had—and turned the bacon before settling the biscuit pan into the grooves. See, cooking wasn't so hard. Oh, but how long should they bake? Twenty minutes? Half an hour? That sounded good. It'd give him time for a cup of coffee before mixing up the powdered eggs.

Yuck! The coffee was barely brown. Camp tasted it. Weak. Very weak. One handful of coffee beans definitely wasn't enough.

Mark and Megan Benton's arguing diverted his attention. Neither wanted to do the dishes. Well, he'd never had to pull KP as a kid, and look at him now. Maybe Emily Benton had the right idea forcing those two on this trip. A body should be able to survive in the wilderness. Especially a man.

Camp sipped his colored water and watched Emily wrap leftover biscuits in foil. She didn't bustle. He liked that she seemed to do everything with an economy of motion. Well, almost everything. She could scramble, too. Take the incident with the papers she'd strewn across his office floor. She'd fluttered like a bird then. A bluebird in that bright-blue suit. Camp grinned. A red-headed bluebird.

Emily glanced up and caught her neighbor scrutinizing her. "You're burning something," she said, pointing to the smoking pan on his grate.

"Oh, shi…" Leaping up, Camp poked at the bacon. "Sorry," he mumbled. "Guess it's time to start the eggs."

She fought a smile as he picked up a small aluminum bowl and held it over the top pan.

"Wait," she yelled. "Did you put oil in the pan?"

Lord, was he supposed to have done that for the other two, as well? Not wanting to appear ignorant, he opened a bottle of oil and poured till it covered the bottom—followed immediately by the egg mixture, which sizzled, bubbled and blackened in no time flat. He snatched it off, then yelped and nursed a burned finger. "What's wrong now?" he snarled as Emily continued to gape at him.

"Nothing." Hooking a loose strand of hair over one ear, she spun and called to Mark, who stood nearby talking with Jared Boone.

Emily was furious that Sherry Campbell's brother had caught her staring like a ninny. Worse, she was doing it again—feeling sorry for a man. It'd been Dave's charming helplessness that had first ensnared her. Emily the nurturer. Vanguard to the vulnerable. A role that became oppressive when her husband's boyish foibles had ballooned into endless affairs and lies. A shudder coursed through her. The sight of Mark loping back fueled her resolve to ignore Nolan Campbell from here on out. She pasted a smile on her face lest Mark see more than she wanted him to see. Though maybe she'd been wrong trying to keep the unpleasant side of her marriage from the kids…

"Mom…Mom! Jared brought fishing gear. He said I could buy a rod and stuff in Council Grove. His dad says we'll be camping on the Neosho River, and that he'll take Jared and me fishing."

"I don't know, Mark," Emily said carefully. "How…how expensive is fishing gear?" After paying bills out of her last check, plus their rent in advance for the summer, she had exactly three hundred dollars in the bank for school clothes and food until she got paid again in September. Not counting the stipend Camp was paying.

Mark's excitement died. He stuffed his hands in his pockets and kicked a rock into the fire. It clanged against the coffeepot and ricocheted off their neighbor's grate. "I didn't wanna go fishing anyhow." Brushing past his mother, he darted between the wagons.

Sighing, Emily massaged her temples. At least Nolan Campbell had disappeared. Her money woes were no one else's business. She freshened her tea and sank onto a log bathed in silvery moonlight. A perfect setting for a mythical hero to gallop through on his white charger. The fantasy, at least, restored her sense of humor.

Megan Benton reached out of the wagon and grabbed her brother as he ran past. "Psst...Mark. Day after tomorrow in Council Grove, call Toby. He'll let you put the fishing stuff on his credit card. Better yet, maybe he'll come get us."

The boy perked up, then slumped again. "Nah, Mom don't want us callin' them."

"Who cares?" Megan jutted her pointed little chin. "Mona and Toby footed the bills while Dad was alive. You tell me why Mom's suddenly so picky."

"How do you know they paid?" he asked, turning to run smack into Camp, who'd stepped to the back of his wagon to throw out his inedible biscuits. The bacon, charred beyond recognition, he'd scraped into the fire.

The boy sucked in a deep breath. "You spying on us?"

"No, but I heard you mention fishing gear." He tossed one of his rock-solid biscuits into the air and caught it. "These'd double as a sinker," he said around a laugh.

Mark dug one out of the pan. "What are they?"

"They're supposed to be biscuits like your mother's." Camp heaved one into the woods. It cracked against a tree. "I'll give you ten dollars for the ones she has left."

"No way!" Megan spoke up. "We're toasting those for breakfast."

"Oh. Tell you what, Mark. I'll lend you my fishing pole in exchange for her recipe. Only…don't mention that I want it."

"Why not?" Suspicion laced Mark's words. "Why not just ask your sister?"

Camp drew a hand over his jaw. "I figure she's gone to bed," he muttered. "It's no biggie. You kids go ahead and turn in. Soon as I wash dishes, I'm headed for bed myself." He fired the remaining lumps of hard dough into the trees, and walked back to the basin where he'd put the other pans to soak. In a final act of despair, he poured out the weak coffee. If he wasn't so tired, he'd double the beans and try again.

From the corner of his eye Camp noticed that Emily sat gazing at the moon. Occasionally she sipped from a cup. If it'd been coffee, he'd have crawled over on hands and knees to beg a cup. But it was tea. He didn't like tea. And besides, neither of them cared to get chummy.

He knew why he didn't want to get chummy with *her.* Obviously she had her reasons, too. That was evident from the way she'd sneaked her data sheet onto the stack the minute his back was turned. The other women had handed him theirs. The only sheet missing was Brittany's. She'd said she'd bring it by, but maybe she'd been too tired.

Speaking of which—Camp yawned as he emptied his dishwater. Leaving the pans to air-dry, he carefully doused the coals. Plunged into darkness, he stood a moment to let his eyes adjust. Gradually he realized that Emily's was the only fire left burning. He considered telling her he was turning in, then decided against it. She must know it'd be pitch-black once she put hers out. Camp hoped she didn't break her fool neck groping her way into her wagon.

He had his shirt unbuttoned and one leg hiked up over the feed trough that hung on the rear of his wagon—when he suddenly froze and thanked providence for Emily's fire. Now he knew why Brittany hadn't brought him her information sheet. She was in his wagon—her blond hair fluffed out over bare shoulders.

Bare. Holy shi…! Camp scrambled out as fast and as quietly as he could. Fear left a dark taste in his mouth. Where the hell was his sister? Did she know what Brittany was doing?

No. Sherry wanted the women to show him up. But she'd never be party to anything so damaging.

Damn. Unless he wanted to ruin Brittany's reputation, he couldn't roust anyone who was sleeping. That left him one option—to throw himself on the mercy of Emily Benton. He tiptoed between the wagons, almost afraid to breathe. Stopping near the front of her wagon, he whispered as loudly as he dared, "Mrs. Benton…Emily."

She jumped up, slopping tea over the rim of her cup. "I thought you'd gone to bed. Why are you prowling around in the dark?"

"Shh." He held a finger to his lips as he cast furtive glances over his shoulder. "I have a problem. I need your help."

He looked so genuinely flustered, Emily found herself agreeing before she'd heard him out. By the time he'd finished his story, anger gripped her chest. "Of all the spineless…weak willed…why didn't you just tell her to leave?"

Her unexpected fury rocked Camp. Before he could gather his wits, she launched a second verbal attack.

"My husband didn't have a backbone, either. He got himself into jams all the time, only with married women." Her voice shook. "He said if I didn't provide him with alibis, he'd divorce me and his folks would see he got custody of the kids." She hauled in a deep breath. "I feel sorry for Brittany, so I'll help—this once. But hereafter, Campbell, stay the hell away from me." She slammed her cup down and hurried past him.

Camp latched on to her arm. "I don't need an alibi." He spun her around. "Believe it or not, I'm concerned about Brittany's reputation. And her self-esteem. No one at home gives a damn." Releasing Emily's arm, he shrugged. "Okay, I admit finding the kid in my wagon threw me a bit. But mainly I thought if *you* talked to her, she'd be less embarrassed."

"Oh." Emily felt like a fool. She was glad of the darkness. What must he think of her after all the things she'd revealed about her marriage?

"Believe me, Emily, I'm open to any suggestion if you have a better one."

She clasped and unclasped her hands. "I'm…sorry I blew up like that."

"Not to worry," he said lightly. "I've had students with crushes before. But never to this extent. I shouldn't have let her come. Hindsight is always 20-20." He sighed.

"I'll talk with her, of course. If it were Megan, that's what I'd want. I, uh, left a couple of flashlights on the log, if you want to take a long walk."

"Thanks, but no. Once you have her out, assuming she's decent, I have a few things to say. I certainly don't want any repeats of tonight."

Emily handed him a flashlight and took one for herself, sizing him up as she slipped past. Twice she glanced back, expecting him to have vanished. He trod silently at her heels. She fought an unexpected rush of warmth pooling in her abdomen. Darn it...she didn't want to have these feelings for *any* man.

The minute they reached the back of his wagon, Camp cupped his hand for Emily's foot and boosted her inside. He listened to the murmur of voices, steeling himself for fireworks that never developed. In a very few minutes Brittany emerged, followed by Emily. The girl wouldn't look at Camp and refused his help down. Once out, she crossed her arms and hunched her shoulders, face sullen. He was relieved to see her wearing jeans and a respectable cardigan.

Forcing her to look up, he said sternly, "Brittany, we need to talk. Emily and I will walk you to your wagon."

"We don't need *her.*"

"You may not, but I do. It isn't my intention to make mockery of your feelings, Brittany. I'm flattered. Any man my age would be. But that's my main point—age. Had I married at the age my peers did, you'd likely be a classmate of my daughter's."

"I don't care."

"Maybe not now, but you would in a few years when I'm gray or bald and you're still young and beautiful," he said with a touch of humor.

"You think I'm beautiful?" Her gaze flew to his, hope blossoming.

Camp floundered. He flashed his light on Emily as a plea for help.

She thought about letting him deal with his own problem. But over all, he deserved an E for effort. Taking pity on him, she slipped an arm around Brittany's shoulders. "Honey," she said as they walked toward Sherry's wagon. "Mr. Campbell's talking ten years from now. He's trying to say that most women reach their full beauty at thirty, while at fifty men start going to pot. *Everything* starts to decline…." Without spelling out details, she boosted Brittany into the wagon. "Hit the pillow, hon. Maizie plans to make fifteen miles tomorrow."

The minute Brittany disappeared, Emily swung toward her own wagon.

Camp fell into step. "You enjoyed saying that about men going to pot, didn't you?"

Her lips tilted up at the corners, but she said nothing.

"For your information, I don't expect my *everything* to decline until I'm ninety."

Throwing her head back, she stopped and laughed out loud.

A husky, pleasant sound that brought Camp's *everything* to attention and made his palms sweat. And made him want to kiss her luscious lips. Fortunately for him, they'd reached her wagon, which brought a return of Camp's sanity.

"If you're ready to turn in, I'll see to your fire," he said stiffly. "It's the least I can do to repay you." Almost formally, he handed back the flashlight she'd lent him.

"No thanks needed," she said, suddenly as brusque as he. "Keep the torch. I have others." Vaulting gracefully into her wagon, she yanked the drawstring, closing Camp out. Emily didn't move or breathe for a minute, knowing he still stood where she'd left him, probably hurt by her abrupt dismissal of his gratitude. But she could ill-afford to crack the door on friendship, to say nothing of the more dangerous currents that Nolan

Campbell stirred within her. Considering her bills, her unhappy kids and the problems with her in-laws, Emily had all the trouble she cared to handle. Hadn't she learned her lesson about men?

CHAPTER FOUR

Men's version of taming the West leads us to believe it was easy—all in a day's work—and even kind of fun. What a crock of lies.
   —Gina Ames. Entry on data sheet following the first
day on the trail.

AN OBNOXIOUS CLANGING penetrated Camp's sleep. His eyes flew open, only to encounter darkness. Then he remembered rule number two. Maizie's version of reveille was an old-fashioned triangle dinner bell.

Stifling a groan, he rolled from his back to his stomach. Lord, every muscle in his body protested. Inch by inch he climbed to his hands and knees. At first he tried rocking back and forth to gain leverage enough to stand. "Those pioneers must have been one big callus by the end of a trip," he gnashed between grunts and moans. He'd thought he was in fair physical condition from all the manual labor he did on his house! Wrong. And if *he* had this kind of trouble, imagine how the women must feel.

Lumbering like a giant sloth, Camp crept to the front of his wagon. There, after two attempts, he managed to heave himself onto the slab seat. Yesterday's aches were minor by comparison.

This was an unholy hour to get up. No respectable rooster even crowed before dawn. "Tell yourself this is fun, Campbell," he chanted, recalling the pointed observation on Gina's data sheet. Uncorking his canteen, he poured cold water over his head. "Jeez," His teeth chattered so hard, he clung to the canvas water bag, wondering how long till he could safely lather up and use a razor blade without danger of draining his life's blood.

"You sure look scummy today. Didn't you bring clean clothes?"

Camp set the canteen aside and scowled down at Mark Benton, who wore saggy pants that ended midcalf and a shirt five sizes too big. "Someone who buys his clothes at the Salvation Army reject store has no room to talk." Seeing his remark hadn't fazed the kid, Camp said, "A lot of pioneers only owned one set of clothes, you know."

"Gross. It probably still stinks in Santa Fe. Me and Mom hauled water from the river about an hour ago so we could wash. So did your sister and the others."

Camp refused to be baited. "What's on the morning agenda? More chores?"

"Nope. Mom says we have half an hour to fix and eat breakfast and fifteen minutes to hitch teams and roll."

Shapes began to materialize around fires that sprang to life along the meadow. A whiff of coffee and something cinnamony drifted in on the cool breeze, sending Camp's stomach into a cramped tailspin. He should have buried his pride last night and begged Emily for the rest of her biscuits. Hunched over the canteen, Camp sincerely doubted the truth of what he'd read about Kit Carson—that he'd survived a week on two slices of beef jerky. "Get lost, kid. I think I hear your mother calling."

Mark shook a mahogany sweep of hair from in front

of coolly assessing eyes. "Mom said to ask if you needed help starting your fire."

"Certainly not!" Camp jumped down from the wagon, and nearly collapsed when he landed hard. "But…" he gritted his teeth. "It's nice of her to ask."

"Her asking don't mean nothing, understand," Mark informed Camp. "She's always helping strays."

Camp declined comment. Whether aware of it or not, Emily Benton was partly responsible for his condition this morning. After they parted last night, he couldn't seem to stop dreaming about her. He hadn't slept two hours straight. At first he'd tried to write, but her name cropped up far more often than the others in his study. He'd tossed the tablet aside in disgust and crawled into his sleeping bag. He'd continued to dwell on the things she'd let slip about her marriage. Half the night he'd mulled over why a woman with two academic degrees had stayed married to the bastard she'd described. Surely no judge would give child custody to a sleaze-bag like that.

Automatically, his eyes sought Emily's dark shape. Sometime before sleep had claimed him, he'd begun to realize she possessed more strength than he'd first given her credit for. So why hadn't she flown the coop with her kids? Money? The way Mark and Megan talked, they didn't have any. "Hmm," he muttered to himself. "With her earning potential?" There had to be more to it. Some piece he'd missed.

"Here." Mark extended several scraps of paper. The raucous tune on his boom box assaulted Camp's ears. Did that kid have an endless supply of batteries?

"Well, take 'em," Mark drawled. "They won't bite. Mom wrote down her biscuit recipe, and one for potato soup. Maybe a couple others. You musta asked her. I sure didn't tell her you wanted 'em."

"Th-thanks. Thank her." Camp all but knocked the boy down grabbing for the papers. The top recipe she'd scribbled on the back of an envelope. How to make campfire coffee. In capital letters, Emily had written: GRIND COFFEE.

Camp struck his forehead with a flat palm. At home he had a small electric grinder. He'd been so rattled at the time he bought supplies, he'd forgotten that he always ground his gourmet coffee beans before he poured them into his expensive, easy-to-use coffeemaker. So, grind them. But how? Tie the beans in a clean handkerchief and smack it hard with the flat of an ax? Okay. That'd work. Quickly he leafed through the remaining sheets. Soup, biscuits, corned beef hash were a few of the recipes he saw. "Tell your mom she's saved my life…again," he said, belatedly recalling the help Emily had given him with Brittany last night. Man, did he need these—even though he hated being called one of Emily's strays. Was that how she saw him? The pitiful professor? His jaw tightened.

"How'd she save your life before? And when?" In the manner of a young tough, the boy removed the old Saint Louis Cardinals baseball cap he wore and reset it on his head backward.

Either Mark was deadpanning or dead serious. In the dim light, Camp couldn't tell which. It didn't much matter; he wasn't about to explain the saga of Brittany. "That's just a figure of speech, Mark. Your mom, ah, loaned me a flashlight." Camp rubbed a hand gingerly over his stubbled jaw, congratulating himself on fast footwork. "It was after you and Megan had gone to bed. I never thought to buy a flashlight."

"Yeah, well she's good at stuff like that. It's what moms are for. I bet you wish you had one."

"I do. She and my dad live in Columbia. In fact, she's keeping an eye on my house and taking care of my dog."

"I meant…I bet you wished you had one on this trip," Mark snickered. "Megan told me how you took your sister's dare. Not smart, dude. They'll whip your butt." The kid disappeared into the shadowy dawn, leaving Camp's sputter hanging on the smoke-laden breeze.

Why let a half-pint kid get his goat? This trip wasn't a contest between him and the women. It never had been. Well, maybe that was how Sherry saw it. Surely Emily didn't. Or was that why she ran hot and cold? Tonight when he collected the data sheets, he'd set the record straight. Right now he'd better scare up something to eat.

Striking a match to the tented kindling, Camp blanked his mind, pulled out a couple of Emily's recipes and went about gathering utensils.

Again it seemed as if he was two steps behind everyone else. Emily and the teachers in the wagon behind her were cleaning up as he sat down to eat. So what? Everything had gone like clockwork today and he intended to enjoy every last morsel. His biscuits and fried potatoes looked perfect. Coffee had never smelled so good—even if he *had* ruined a brand-new monogrammed handkerchief. Part of a set his mother gave him for Christmas. Well, Mom would understand.

Twice, he tried catching Emily's eye to thank her personally for the recipes. She never once glanced his way. He paused, slathering honey on his first biscuit. Strange code Emily Benton lived by. It was all right to do a man favors, but not be his friend.

Oh, well, to each his own. *Her own,* he amended, all but moaning orgasmically after taking the first bite. Camp sneaked another peek in Emily's direction. Couldn't tell where she was. Uh-oh, why was Maizie Boone bearing down on him? He'd seen that look before—the day he showed up late. Camp couldn't imagine what he'd done to displease her today. He wasn't late...yet. Didn't intend to be. So what had put a bee in her bonnet this time?

The closer she came, the more evident it was that she had something serious on her mind. However, Camp didn't care to be flayed on an empty stomach. He deliberately filled his mouth with fried potatoes and eggs, only rising politely as her smelly boots came to a grinding halt four inches from his own cleaner pair.

"Dammit, boy. Renegade took a powder during the night."

Camp plunked his plate down and vaulted the fire, dashing to the edge of the meadow. Sure enough, Goliath, Little Lizzie and Spike all grazed where he'd left them. But not the tobacco-colored Belgian—the one that'd fought him yesterday.

His breakfast turned to rubber sliding down his throat. "How...how far could he roam, do you suppose?"

"Who knows?" Maizie pulled a new packet of chewing tobacco from her pocket and gnawed off a chunk. "Find him," she ordered after she'd softened up the piece and spit a stream into Camp's fire.

"Me? Do I look like the Lone Ranger?"

"If you end up saddle-sore, you'll double-check your hobbles from here on out. It's rul—"

"Rule fifteen," he broke in. "Yes, I know." Camp thought he had rechecked the hobbles. Obviously not well enough.

"Sooner you start, the better. We ain't waitin', mind you. Follow Renegade's tracks from where you staked him out. Once you nab him, hitch your wagon and head out. Pick up our tire tracks and follow us, fast as you can. We'll be burnin' up the miles today."

"What if I don't find him?" Camp had no worry about being able to follow the tracks left by the balloon tires they'd installed on the wagons before leaving Boonville. That was child's play. Horse tracking was another matter. How did you tell one hoof print from another?

"Reckon you'll find him by and by. He's big as a buffalo. Pretty hard to mistake him for a jackrabbit. The land hereabouts is flat as a flitter 'cept for these few trees." A rumble Camp took for laughter shook Maizie's squat frame.

"It's more a worry over some farmer mistaking me for a cattle rustler that concerns me," he said. "So which of these horses do you recommend I ride for the search?"

"I'll saddle my pinto gelding while you put out this fire. Throw the rocks from your fire ring and any extra wood into your wagon. It'll save repeatin' chores tonight. The pinto's name is Mincemeat, by the way. I bought him from a down-and-out cowboy. Guy wanted everyone to think his horse was a mean one. But I guarantee he'll be fine tied behind the wagon. Just see that you tie him tight."

"Yes, ma'am." Resigned to finding his strayed horse, Camp couldn't help but gaze longingly at his first decent meal in two days—now stone-cold. Again he dumped out his potatoes and eggs. He decided to wrap the biscuits and take them along—in case finding Renegade took him longer than Maizie thought.

Telling himself there was no excuse for delay, he set

to work doing exactly what she'd outlined, trying to sort out the various horse tracks.

Gina's wagon pulled out, followed closely by the couple from Philadelphia. One by one the others fell into line. Camp climbed aboard Maizie's saddle horse, then just sat. The string of wagons made quite a sight leaving the meadow. Matched teams stepped in unison as chalky canvas ballooned against a deep-blue sky. Today the sky was the exact shade of Emily Benton's eyes. A subtle blend of lavender and cobalt, like the wisteria trailing over his porch at home.

Rather than moon over eyes that refused to seek him out, Camp knew he should get under way. If he found Renegade soon, he might even catch up with the train before they took their first break.

Even so, he waited until Emily, now the last wagon in line, left the clearing. Her hair sparked in the rising sun, reminding Camp of his vision last Saturday, when he first saw the wagons. But instead of a long, flowing pioneer dress, she wore faded blue overalls over a creamy T-shirt. In place of the imagined sunbonnet, a battered Kansas City Chiefs cap failed to restrain her curls.

Try as he might, Camp couldn't seem to turn away. Not until Emily's wagon became a speck in the distance. "Okay, Mincemeat," he murmured to the restless pinto, "Let's find that truant horse."

Renegade's tracks weren't hard to follow. He left a hoofprint the size of a barn door. But the benighted creature had covered a lot of ground. He'd crossed the river and meandered through a field of wheat. It was nearly noon before Camp ran him to ground, and then only because the lead line had caught on a spindly bush—one of many red-leafed shrubs dotting the knoll.

"Thank you, Lord, for the bushes. Otherwise this miserable piece of dog food would have walked all the way to Colorado."

Camp had to cut away woody branches to free Renegade. The sun beat down unrelentingly, so it was lucky for both of them that Camp had remembered to bring a canteen of water. While the horse drank deeply from the baseball cap, Camp checked to see that the animal hadn't sustained any injury. Renegade was fine. He must have dragged the entire length of rope behind him.

"Why couldn't you have stumbled into this patch sooner?" Camp grumbled as he hacked away the last twig with his dull pocketknife. "Come on, you son of a gun," he muttered as the rope pulled free. "Let's move. At this rate, it'll be dark before we meet up with the others."

The big horse turned and gazed at Camp with unblinking brown eyes. He trudged obediently after his rescuer, even going so far as to nuzzle Camp's neck. "So you missed me, did you, you big lug?" Camp laughed and patted the soft nose.

On the return trek Renegade didn't display any of the spirited nonsense Camp had put up with yesterday. As they retraced the route, only man and his beast, Camp experienced a curious satisfaction at having successfully carried out a task that must have been routine to his pioneer brothers. Maybe the ability to hunt and track was passed down through a man's genes. Hmm, it was certainly something to consider.

He wasted no time hitching his team after arriving back at his lone wagon. Once they stood ready, he unsaddled Mincemeat and double-knotted the reins through a metal ring drilled into his tailgate for that purpose. Camp imagined Sherry would be crowing if he came back empty-handed. Well, she was in for a surprise. He felt pretty smug about his success.

Tracks left by the caravan were distinct. Beyond the copse of trees, the prairie opened into miles of gently undulating hills. Camp unwrapped and ate the last of his morning biscuits. It had taken longer to find his delinquent horse than Maizie's best guess; if he wanted to rejoin the others today, he'd have to crank up the speed. Which turned out to be easier said than done.

Too often his mind wandered to what it must have been like for the early pioneers. No commercial planes overhead like the ones he saw jetting every so often across the cloudless sky. No automobiles whizzing to unknown destinations along U.S. highway 24, which, if he strained, Camp could just hear. The thought occurred to him that, accurate simulation or not, this trip was cheating. It held few, if any, surprises. A reenactment couldn't compare with the excitement—not to mention the dangers—of facing the unknown that pioneers had experienced every day. He'd have to note that in his report.

Camp continued to amble along, drinking in the trill of the songbirds. Much of the earlier soreness had been worked out of his muscles. He was getting used to the roll and pitch of the wagon. Around two o'clock he crossed a small bridge that he recognized from Maizie's brochure. Some distance off the trail sat Neff's Tavern, the Santa Fe Trail's first stage station. All that was left was a stone smokehouse.

There—he spotted it over to the left. Darn, he wished he could spare the time to stop. If the pattern of tire tracks was any indication, the main column had toured the site. Unfortunately the sun had passed its zenith; he needed to push on. As he plodded past the historic spot, Camp swore he'd triple-check every hobble tonight. With a last regretful glance at the place, he hoped Gina Ames had photographed it from all angles.

Somehow bringing up Gina triggered thoughts of Emily again. Camp was at a loss as to why the woman intrigued him. She was unlike any woman who'd ever caught his fancy. Starting with the horny days of youth, he'd tended to pant after statuesque blondes. All clones of Bunny McPherson, the first girl to initiate him into the wonders of sex. Bunny, two years his senior, had been voluptuous and generous. She'd had a sense of humor and zero inhibitions, the type of mentor every fumbling fifteen-year-old boy needed. Bunny knew about things Camp and his pals talked about out behind the barn—like wet dreams and birth control.

Odd, he hadn't thought about Bunny in years. Yet at fifteen, he'd sworn that when he finished college he'd marry her. It wasn't until the week following his six-teenth birthday, after she'd abruptly moved away, that he learned how many of the boys in his high school had the same idea. Most of them quickly found substitutes. Those guys had no discretion—or loyalty. Camp had a more difficult time transferring his allegiance.

That summer, his history club visited the Smith-sonian, and he'd found a new love. Museums. Did that mean there was something wrong with him? Because years later, Greta had bitterly accused him of being married to moldy old museums. Come to think of it, Greta had little in common with Bunny.

Did Emily Benton? Not in looks. Emily was the opposite of tall and voluptuous. Not that there was a thing wrong with her proportions. What she did for a pair of jeans was downright sinful.

She wasn't sleek or blond, either. But the riot of wildfire framing her oval face attracted him. A halo of shades that changed color with each flux of light. He'd dreamed the other night about what it would feel like to bury his fingers deep in those corkscrew curls.

He let his mind meander so long that when next he glanced up, he saw the sun dipping low. Surprisingly, he faced the Blue River ford. Someone—Maizie, he supposed—had tacked a message on a withered tree: His name in block letters, followed by "Water your team." Then it read, "Cross here and turn directly into the sun. Stay between the Blue and the Little Blue till you reach Rice Farm. Go straight five miles to our campsite. Hopefully!" Yep, that was Maizie—she of little faith.

At the base of the tree, in a plastic bowl, someone with more trust in him had left three honey-drenched biscuits and a bag of trail mix. Camp grinned. He'd bet his bottom dollar that was Emily's doing. Maybe she really was a reincarnation of Jessie Benton Fremont, the pioneer lady said to have nursed the sick and settled feuds within her husband's caravans on a regular basis.

Camp owed Emily again. Big-time.

He worried about the river crossing, but he needn't have. His team plunged into the water with little urging.

Problem was, they didn't want to climb out. He lost a good half hour coaxing, cajoling and finally leading them. Fortunately, the Blue wasn't deep at this point, only a few inches above Camp's hips. And he didn't mind, as his skin had begun to feel hot and itchy. So much so that he soaked his shirt and put it back on wet.

At first it felt good. But as the afternoon lengthened, the sun beat down without mercy, drying his clothes stiff. The itch came back—worse. His legs, his arms, his neck grew hot and tingly. The more he scratched, the more he itched. Camp tried concentrating on the serenity of the river that flowed in the direction he was headed. And on the beauty of the evening ambers streaking the sky. Nothing worked. Each passing mile became more unbearable than the last. He watched the sun sink into a flat puddle of molten gold, and even the coolness of evening didn't help.

At one point he stripped off his shirt to check for fleas. There were none, and no welts, but rather a bright red, slightly bumpy rash covering his chest, arms and legs. An allergy? To what? His shirt was old and his jeans had been washed a hundred times.

Stars blanketed the sky and a crescent moon had risen by the time Camp spied a row of campfires in the distance. He was quite positive he'd never been so happy to see anything in his life.

Maizie and Robert ran to meet him. Sherry, too. Camp identified Brittany lurking in the shadows with Megan Benton. Gina lounged against her wagon. Only Emily was missing. Funny, but she was the one he wanted to see.

"Yo, there, weary traveler. You're a sight for sore eyes." Maizie grabbed the lead horses and guided his team in a circle until Camp's wagon lined up with the last one in the row. Vaguely he registered that it was Emily's.

Maizie instructed Robert to unhitch Camp's team. She ambled back just as he climbed down. "I was beginnin' to worry, boy. What took you so long?"

Camp snorted. What a stupid question. *She'd* sent him on that chase. Instead of answering, he pushed up his shirtsleeves, continuing to scratch his arms as he passed her. He intended to handle his own unharnessing.

Maizie grabbed his arm and whistled through her teeth. "Looks like Renegade wasn't all you found today. Got yourself a right smart dose of poison sumac, I'd say. I warned the kids and out-of-staters. Didn't think to caution anybody who'd grown up here." Tobacco juice sailed past Camp's shoulder.

"Stop that," he bellowed. "Tobacco chewing is a dirty, filthy habit. Not to mention bad for your health."

Her eyes popped wide. Emily materialized from the blackness, gliding between them. "Camp, don't take it out on Maizie because you're tired and out of sorts."

"I have plenty of sorts," he said curtly. "I also have this damned rash itching me to death. It's a little late to be telling me I should've had sense enough to keep out of the stuff. There's no poison sumac where I live."

"How like a man to yell at women for his own stupidity. I should've known." Throwing up her hands, Emily stalked away.

Camp felt bad. She wasn't to blame for any of this.

Sherry inspected his blotches with a flashlight. "Leaflets three, let it be. I learned that as a kid in Girl Scouts, Nolan."

"That's poison ivy. And I was slightly more concerned with finding my horse than counting leaves. What in my first-aid kit will cure it?" he asked Maizie.

She tucked her thumbs in her belt. "Nothing I know cures it, boy. Cortisone cream takes away the sting and some of the itch. Water spreads the rash the first couple days, so don't wash."

"Great. I got plenty wet fording the Blue. That's about time I really noticed something was wrong."

"Why did you get wet?" Gina asked. "We never left our wagons."

"Yeah, well, somebody forgot to tell my team that. Damned animals loved the water." Camp thanked Robert nicely for helping him unhitch, but he rechecked every hobble himself. From now on, he'd *know* their tethers were secure.

"Don't touch me," Sherry said, jumping aside as he accidentally brushed her on the way past. "I read you can give that rash to people during the weepy stage."

Camp ignored her. Robert gazed on him with sympathy. However, he and Maizie carefully avoided any contact as they left.

"Well, are you finally ready to concede that we women are better suited to pioneer life than modern man?" Sherry demanded.

"The trip is far from over. The deal, as I recall, was to determine whether or not modern women have what it takes to get from Boonville to Santa Fe." Camp didn't know why he was being surly. He wished everyone would leave him alone.

"Oh, you're so stubborn. You should see yourself. Three days' growth of beard, filthy clothes, and that rash is probably going to close one of your eyes."

Somewhere, he dredged up the will to grin. "Today, me. Tomorrow, maybe you."

"Are you ready to bag it?"

"I'm sticking it out," he said. "How about you? Had enough?"

"Certainly not. It's just…you're the only brother I have. A lot's happened to you the last few days. Megan told Brittany how you ruined last night's meal. Speaking of which—what did you do to her? She said it'd serve you right to starve. I thought she had a mega-crush on you."

"Brittany's a troubled girl, Sherry. Can you take her under your wing? Head her in the right direction?"

"At least she isn't living hand-to-mouth trying to support one or two babies like some of the young women we counsel in the Hub."

"If she keeps on her present course, it may happen. She's obsessed with finding a husband. She could hook up with some total jerk."

"Tell me about it. Most of my students wouldn't be in the predicament they're in if they hadn't fallen for the wrong man. Marriage doesn't mean happily ever after."

"You sound bitter," Camp said as they ambled toward his wagon.

"Informed and wary, not bitter. Then again, maybe you're right. It's not only young women who get mixed up with rotten men."

Camp suddenly realized they were both gazing at Emily's wagon. "Do you know anything about Emily's marriage? Her application said she was widowed," Camp said, careful to keep his tone light and his voice low.

Sherry shot him a narrowed glance. "Why would I know? She's your applicant." Sherry bit her lip. Had he found out about her bringing in Gina and Emily?

"No special reason. She's your counterpart at her college. I know history profs at other institutions. I thought maybe you two had met at a conference or something."

"Look," she said. "I've gotta run. You're beat. Why don't I collect the data sheets tonight?"

"Would you? Hey, thanks. I'll see what I can do about making myself presentable." He scrubbed a hand over his ragged, itchy jaw.

"You'd better not shave, Nolan. The rash may be under your beard."

"That's a switch. What happened to my looking as scruffy as hell?"

"Can't a sister have a change of heart?"

"While you're feeling charitable, would you see if you have anything in your first-aid kit that I can put on this rash? I know mine only has the bare essentials."

"I'll look. If I have something, I'll bring it when I drop off your info sheets."

They parted. Camp's first priority was to get out of his dirty clothes and to wash, even if he spread the rash. He didn't want Mark Benton pointing out how rank he smelled. Or Emily. Not that she'd venture that close to him.

He'd just stripped off his shirt and was headed for the enticing *lap, lap* of the half-moon curve in the Little Blue River when Sherry rushed up carrying everyone's data sheets. Camp retraced his steps and tossed the papers in his wagon.

She tagged after him when he started off again. "I didn't have cortisone cream. Ooh, that rash looks awful. I'll bet you don't sleep much tonight. How long will it last?"

"Darned if I know. I've never had anything burn, sting and itch at the same time. I don't suppose there's a closet herbalist around," he joked.

She wrinkled her nose. "Ask Philly—Harv Shaw. He has an opinion on everything."

"Good thing I'm bringing up the rear. If I had to listen to him pontificate, they'd haul me off for assault and battery."

"Murder's crossed my mind. Maizie has the patience of a saint."

Camp laughed. "A tobacco-chewing saint? That's a picture."

"Come on, she's perfect for this job. And she'll add spice to your paper." Sherry stopped short of the river. "Have you asked permission to include her?"

"No. I will before the trip's over." He dug at his rash. "This is driving me nuts. I don't care what Maizie said, I've gotta wash off some of this trail dust. I doubt I'll sleep anyway. Are you up for a game of poker? I'll ask Robert and Maizie to join us."

"Sorry, I'm going to bed. Three more days of eating dust before we reach the park in Council Grove—and then we get two blessed days of rest. I can't wait to find a beauty shop and treat myself to the works. You'd better try to sleep. Maizie says it'll hit a hundred degrees tomorrow."

"I doubt pioneer women had beauty shops along their route," Camp said dryly.

"Or doctors, either. You may have to ride into Independence to see one."

"No, I won't," he called as she left, taking the only light with her. Most of the campfires were already banked for the night. He intended to build one and cook dinner after bathing. Too bad if he disturbed his neighbors. He still half expected Mark Benton to show up and get in his licks. "Trip must have worn the kid out today," Camp muttered. "Thank you, Lord."

The moon, almost a quarter tonight, cast ripples across the water. Camp pulled his boots off, then his socks, and quickly shed everything else. He wadded the dirty clothes into a ball, taking care to drape his clean cutoffs and a towel over a jutting granite rock. Looking neither right nor left, he dived into the icy stream. God, it felt good.

Seated on a mossy outcrop about ten yards upstream, Emily Benton stifled a gasp that threatened to give away her position. She realized now that she should have called out before Sherry left. But she hadn't wanted to appear to be eavesdropping. Emily had never dreamed he'd strip naked and plunge to his neck in water after what Maizie said about water spreading the rash. *Now what?* Should she reveal herself, or try to skulk away unnoticed? If it wasn't happening to her she'd laugh. She'd read this scene a thousand times in books.

As she wrestled with her conscience, Camp charged out of the water and shook like a shaggy dog. Moonlight spilled over his dark hair and broad shoulders, gilding water droplets that slid down his chest. Emily held her breath. Dressed, the man was one to notice. Unclothed, Professor Campbell was a work of art. His chest was wide, muscular and not too hairy. His hips were narrow, his thighs… Emily's mind stalled there as she felt his eyes discover her. "I, ah, I…" She struggled to speak—to lower her gaze. All she did was stare, thinking it'd been so long since she'd been able to appreciate a naked male body. Too long. Her knees jelled.

Cold though he was from his swim, the minute Camp saw her wide eyes, so dark they looked purple in her moonlit face, heat pooled in his groin. For a moment the itch numbed, as did his thoughts. In truth he was far more embarrassed than she appeared to be. "Sorry for the striptease. But you might have cleared your throat," he said, snatching up the towel.

Suddenly overcome by jitters, she whirled around.

Realizing that she was shaken, too, Camp gave a lick and a promise with the towel and struggled into his cutoffs. "There, I'm decent," he said, slinging the towel around his neck. "I suppose it's too much to hope that you brought me something to relieve this itch."

Although his voice sounded light and relaxed, Emily was slow to turn back. She was afraid a vision of how he looked emerging from the water would be forever emblazoned in her mind. As she gathered her nerve and finally faced him, her tender heart reacted to his angry rash. "Ouch! Camp...a...a homemade concoction of soda and vinegar works on poison oak and ivy. I'll go mix some." Sweeping by him, she snapped off her flashlight.

"Hey, leave the light on. I'm barefoot."

She hesitated, a dark wraith in the moonlight. "Where are your boots? This dry buffalo grass will cut your feet."

"Yes, Mother."

She tensed again. "Apparently *someone* needs to watch out for you. Have you eaten today?"

"Only what the Good Fairy left at the Blue River ford."

"Oh." Emily hadn't meant for him to know she'd left the food.

"I'm not complaining. And I'll sure accept the soda treatment. How is it you know how to mix some old-fashioned remedy?"

Happy to have her mind off the river incident, Emily explained as they walked. "Trail rides in the wilderness with my dad and his horsey pals. I didn't realize how much I missed those outings until this trip."

"Why didn't you continue the tradition in your own family?"

"My husband—" She broke off, pointing to her wagon, and touched a finger to her lips. "I'll see if I can find what I need without waking the kids. Meet you at my fire. I'll mix the paste and bring it. Oh," she called softly after his retreating form. "In the top section of my Dutch oven there's some leftover stew. It may still be warm."

Camp tried to thank her again, but she'd climbed nimbly over the wagon's tailgate. He dumped his bundle of dirty clothes into his wagon. As he ladled himself a bowl of stew, his thoughts remained on Emily. However, the heat from the smoldering coals soon increased his itching. By the time she returned, he'd sought refuge on his own wagon tongue.

Peering around, she finally spotted him. "There you are." She waved a container. "Come into the light and I'll pat this stuff on."

He set the bowl of stew aside. "Aren't you afraid of catching the rash? Everyone else is."

She shook her head. "On one of our outings, my little brother dismounted in a patch of poison oak. I slathered this stuff on him five times a day or more, and I never broke out. This stuff doesn't hurt. My brother said it felt good."

"I wasn't worried about me. I wouldn't wish this miserable stuff on a dog. But if you're not afraid, have at it."

No sooner had she dabbed the first patch than Camp wished he could retract his words. He hadn't counted on the soft glide of her fingers over his bare skin causing an erection.

Emily had started on his back. Too quickly she moved to his legs. Camp thought he'd burst. "I'll do the rest," he said gruffly as she rose from her kneeling position and stretched toward his stomach. Her touch was bad enough, but when she stood, she left a trail of some sweetly provocative perfume. He'd have bet it wasn't possible to grow harder, but he did.

"Don't tell me you're ticklish?" she teased, coming at him with hands covered in white paste.

He opted for the easy out she offered. "Yeah, I am. Here, do my arms. Stay away from my ribs."

"Chicken." Clucking, she drizzled white goo down his arms. "How about your face? Is your face ticklish underneath that beard?"

"As a matter of fact, it is. And you're enjoying torturing me far too much, Mrs. Benton. Give me that." Camp nearly upset his cooling stew as he grabbed at the plastic container.

Emily didn't let go. She landed in his lap—and promptly discovered the very reason he'd been trying to keep her away. Their eyes met, his darkening with need. Hers, surprised at first, then pleased, then wary as she released the bowl and scrambled up.

"Look, I wasn't trying..." She clasped her hands tight to stop their trembling, and started again. "I should know better than to tease a man. I'm not looking for involvement. And I don't do one-night stands. I'll write down the ingredients for the paste. When we reach Council Grove, I suggest you buy a book on outdoor survival."

Denial that he wanted either a relationship *or* a fling hovered on Camp's lips. However, she was gone before he acknowledged that it would have been a lie. Apparently his body knew something his mind refused to admit—since the day Emily Benton blundered into his life, he'd been barreling full-speed toward involvement. Question was—what, if anything, should he do about it?

"Dammit," he hissed into the velvety darkness. "I'm not looking for one-night stands, either."

If Emily heard, she didn't reply.

CHAPTER FIVE

*"Our national folklore romanticizes the adventure—
the male adventure—of conquering the West."*
　　　　—Sherry Campbell's data sheet. With elaborate
　　　　　doodles drawn around this statement.

CAMP SAT OUTSIDE the circle of heat from Emily's fire
and picked out various constellations in the star-littered
sky. He'd long since finished a second bowl of stew.
Now he marked time while his dishwater heated.

After the dishes were washed and the fire out, he
applied another coat of the soda paste to the areas he
could reach. He'd just climbed into his wagon when a
movement near the tailgate of Emily's Conestoga
caught his eye. At first he thought maybe she'd had
second thoughts, but in the bluish beam of the moon,
he saw that it was Megan. Curious. A bathroom run? If
so, where was her flashlight?

He watched her glance furtively around, then haul
something from beneath the coach. A day pack. What
the…? A chill snaked the length of Camp's spine.

The girl shrugged into the pack and set off with
purpose. Before she slipped out of sight, Camp made
the decision to follow her.

He expected her to head for the highway, even though

it was a five-mile hike. But she didn't. She'd disappeared. Camp panicked. His heart jackhammered until Maizie's string of saddle horses began to wicker, and he glimpsed Megan tiptoeing among them.

"Where's the ruckus, boy?" Camp nearly jumped out of his skin as Maizie's raspy whisper struck him. Wheeling, he blankly took in her frazzled gray hair and a ratty old sheepskin coat she had buttoned over a long flannel nightgown.

"Megan Benton," he murmured. "She may be running away. Damn...look there. She's nabbed herself a getaway horse."

Maizie chuckled. "The kid won't go far on Dumpster. Robert's hoping to unload that nag in Santa Fe. What're you waitin' for? I reckon you'll catch her at the river."

The rapidly fading hoofbeats spurred Camp to action. "Wake Emily. Tell her I'll bring Megan back."

The wagon mistress nodded.

Camp dashed off, thankful for the moonlight and the stillness of the night that let him follow the sound. Breathing hard, he added a burst of speed as he heard the horse snort and whinny, then falter. Obligingly, the river bank sloped gently. Not so much danger of the horse breaking a leg.

At last Camp saw Megan urging her mount into the water. He cupped his hands to yell and saw the horse slow. The animal pranced a bit, then abruptly sat down in the middle of the stream. A bright moon provided Camp with a ringside view. Megan lost her grip on the mane. Inch by inch she slid down the broad back, over the rump, and hit the water with a loud splat. She bobbed immediately to the surface, gasping and flailing her arms. The horse arched his neck and trotted blithely back to shore, uncaring that he'd left his rider behind, bobbing like a cork.

Camp had one boot off and was tackling the second when Emily stumbled through the tall grass, followed by Maizie, who puffed like a steam engine.

"What happened?" Emily's face was pasty white.

Shaking his head, Camp splashed into the river after Megan, now drifting downstream.

Maizie finally caught her breath. "Told you," she hollered at Camp around a chortle. "Trait of that horse is to sit every time he lands up to his knees in water. It's why he's named Dumpster. Hope the gal swims." She sobered, peering at Emily.

Still not comprehending, Emily nodded dumbly.

Cold water lapped at Camp's chest as he carried the coughing, sputtering girl to the bank.

Dumpster shook his head and danced out of reach. Maybe it was a trick of the moon, but Camp swore the roan's lips peeled back in a grin. Camp wasn't smiling, though, his eyes glued to Emily's stricken expression.

"Why?" she asked in a shaky voice, stripping Megan of her soggy pack.

The teen glared defiantly. "I was going to town…to call Mona. This trip sucks. It's hot and sticky, and the mosquitoes are as big as helicopters." Huddled in her wet clothes, she burst into tears.

Camp figured Emily would crumble in the face of Megan's crocodile tears. He pictured all three Bentons leaving the train in Council Grove.

"I'm sorry you're unhappy, Megan." Emily's voice held an edge of steel. "I chose this outing, and I make the decisions for you and Mark until you're of age. Your grandparents have no say in the matter. Now dry off and go to bed. Apologies can wait until morning." Emily's stiff gaze skimmed Maizie and Camp briefly before she grasped Megan by the arm and marched her off.

"Un-huh." Maizie sounded satisfied. "Well, don't just stand there, sonny. Rub that horse down and give him an added measure of oats." She waddled off, avoiding the swish of Dumpster's cold, wet tail.

Rub *him* down? As if Camp himself wasn't soaked. Obviously, the whole incident had amused Maizie. All along she'd known the outcome. But as his unplanned dip had washed off all his soda paste, Camp was not amused.

Once he sat in his wagon again, dry and slathered with paste, he felt more benevolent. He supposed it was funny that of all the horses Megan might have swiped, she'd picked that one.

Poor Emily. She fought an uphill battle with those kids.

Wide-awake now, Camp decided to compile the data sheets Sherry had collected. He pulled out Gina's. She'd devoted a half page to the invasion of giant mosquitoes at Neff's Tavern. With uncharacteristic wit, Gina stated that at one point she had to fight them for possession of her camera. Camp shuddered. It was just as well he hadn't stopped. It hurt to imagine mosquito bites on top of sumac poisoning.

Sherry grumbled about Brittany's petulance. In between doodles and snide comments, she wrote that she was sick of the same scenery. Camp expected similar criticisms from Emily. Instead, she described the prairie in terms of rich colors and unending vistas. And she wrote eloquently of the sorrow she'd felt visiting the Neff family cemetery, because they'd had lost so many children in infancy. Camp imagined tears in Emily's lovely blue eyes as she poured out her heart.

He tapped his pencil to his lips. Clearly he was going soft on Emily. And he shouldn't. For the sake of his paper, it was imperative that he remain objective.

An admirable plan, but Camp's dreams that night and the next were far from objective. Still, Emily's sympathetic smile and the memory of her soothing touch kept him plodding through the days; her homemade concoction offered him relief from the terrible itch during long, sleepless nights.

The day before they were due to reach Council Grove, Camp noted how everyone's spirits seemed to lift. He felt it, too. His rash had subsided enough for him to shave at last. This morning, he felt almost human. All in all, Camp thought things were finally looking up.

Mark Benton had quit bugging him and had started hanging out with Jared Boone. Brittany and Megan cloistered themselves each evening, trading books and teen magazines. A much subdued Megan, Camp noted.

His mind still on the youngsters, Camp circled to the rear of his wagon to dispose of the water he'd used for shaving. He startled Mark, who guiltily thrust a stack of shiny metal objects behind his back—so suddenly, that he dropped one.

"What do you have there, Mark?" Camp inquired offhandedly. "Are you and Jared collecting coffee can lids to use as slingshot targets?"

Mark grabbed for the fallen items, and in the process dropped two more. Camp saw they were cut in shapes—like road markers. Rusted stakes protruded from each.

He set his shaving kit and basin aside and went for a closer inspection. Being less encumbered than the boy, Camp bent easily and retrieved two that still lay on the ground. His gaze lit on green Conestogas etched on a white tin background and stenciled letters that said: Santa Fe Trail. They were markers. Shooting the boy a glance, Camp saw that he was poised for flight.

Camp stopped him with a look he reserved for students cheating on a test. "Mark, the historical society spent a lot of time and money placing these markers along the trail route. Removing them is a serious matter."

"I found them," Mark said, but he also licked his lips nervously.

"Found them where? The dirt on some of these stakes is fresh."

Mark dumped the markers he still held at Camp's feet. "Take 'em. I don't even want the stupid old things."

"You need to put them back where they belong, Mark. When did you start this collection?"

The boy's color drained. He backed away. "Yesterday. But what difference does it make? Nobody but us'll see 'em."

"A lot of tourists visit the trail. Besides, it's stealing. This trail is under federal protection. There's a fine attached to taking markers—if not a stiffer penalty."

"Then I'll call Toby from town. He'll pay the dumb old fine. So it won't do you any good to run and squeal to my mom."

"I'm not going to tell her, Mark. You are." Camp's voice remained calm as he stared coolly into Mark's mutinous eyes.

The boy hunched his shoulders and kicked at a rock. "It's Megan's fault. She wanted one for her bedroom."

"Did Megan take some of these?"

"No," Mark admitted with a sniffle. "I can't put 'em back. It's a long way, and I'm just a kid."

"You're old enough to be responsible for your

actions. I want you to go tell your mother and Maizie what you've done. If you do, I'll help you return the markers. But I won't cover for you."

"Sheesh!" Mark scraped at a lank fall of hair. "Okay, but I don't know why you'd help me."

Camp arched a brow. "I recall getting into a few scrapes at your age."

"You? But you're a teacher."

"I wasn't born a teacher." Camp's lips quirked in a smile. Sobering quickly, he said, "We all make mistakes. The trick is to learn by them and try not to repeat any."

"Toby says you shouldn't ever admit to making a mistake."

Camp shied from touching that statement. On the other hand, someone needed to. "It takes a big man to admit to being wrong. And it makes sleeping easier."

"I guess I know what you mean. I didn't sleep so good last night. I was scared my mom would see 'em." He nudged the markers. "I wish I hadn't done it."

"That's the spirit. I'm proud of you, Mark. Your mother will be, too. Say, can you ride a horse?"

"You bet," the boy bragged. "I've ridden lots of times."

Camp smiled in relief and the two went off in search of Emily.

"What?" she exclaimed after Mark had stumbled through his confession. Closing her eyes, she rubbed her temples. "Honey, whatever possessed you? How will we put them back where they belong?"

Mark jerked a thumb toward Camp. "He said he'd help."

Emily acknowledged Camp for the first time. "How?" she asked, frowning. "We've traveled at least five miles."

"If Maizie agrees, I thought Mark and I could saddle two horses and ride back. We can make it in half the time it took the wagons. Less if we push. I'll ask Robert if he'll allow Jared to drive my wagon until we catch up."

"Yes. I suppose it's the only way."

Because she nibbled worriedly on her bottom lip, Camp cleared his throat. "I could go faster alone. It wouldn't teach him as much. But it's your call, Emily."

Considering what Camp had said, Emily glanced up and caught Mark's hopeful smile. "No," she said decisively. "That's the Benton way out. He did the fiddling—now he needs to pay the piper. I'll go with you to talk to Maizie, son, after you thank Camp for doing this."

After a few false starts, Mark managed a passable thank-you.

"If you leave now," Emily asked Camp, "will you be back before dark?"

"Run that question by Maizie. She may know a shortcut. Otherwise, I guess we'll have to take bedrolls and more in the way of food."

An unexpected smile lit her face. "We know you won't run into the Good Fairy who left you food at the Blue River ford."

Camp grinned as she curled a hand over Mark's shoulder and walked him toward Maizie's wagon. His smile faded as soon as Megan parted the canvas and climbed onto the wagon seat, blowing on newly painted fingernails.

"My brother is such a dipstick."

"Why do you say that?" Camp braced a hand on a wagon bow.

The girl smirked. "Because Toby would hire

someone to put the markers back. Why should Mark get saddle sores?"

Camp tucked three fingers of each hand into his back pockets. "Guess you didn't listen to your mom. Comes a time guys and girls need to stand on their own two feet to look at themselves in the mirror." Leaving it at that, Camp walked away. He met Emily and Mark cutting between their two wagons. Emily's eyes were grim, Mark's downcast. Something in his demeanor made the boy appear younger to Camp. Younger and more vulnerable. His heart gave a little crunch. Maizie could deliver a blistering rebuke; he knew that for a fact. Had he done right, making Mark fess up? After all, he didn't have children and he worked mostly with young adults. He'd handled it the way he thought his father might. Maybe there was a better way.

Emily stopped in front of him, her hand resting lightly on Mark's neck. "Maizie read us the riot act." Absently, her fingers smoothed her son's shirt collar. "What he did was wrong. I'm not trying to make light of his transgression. I just wish the couple from Philadelphia hadn't been there at the time. Harv Shaw made it sound like a capital crime. Said kids who'd steal government property would burn flags and…and become traitors." She pulled Mark close as he began to sniff against his sleeve.

Camp felt a surge of anger, soon replaced by an odd feeling of protectiveness toward this mother and child. "Shaw's mouth is bigger than his belt size, which is saying a lot." Kneeling, he forced Mark to meet him eye to eye. "You knew all along it was wrong. Now you're making restitution like a man." Camp gave him a friendly nudge on the arm. "Hey, I see Maizie's bringing our horses. Stuff those markers in a saddlebag and let's be on our way."

Mark edged closer to Camp, his wide eyes on the approaching horses. "Wha...what if a guy hadn't ridden a horse lots of times like he said?"

Camp heard the quaver in his whisper. "You mean," he said, "you've ridden only a few times?"

Shuffling his feet, Mark hitched up his belt but said nothing.

"Uh, Mark," Camp muttered. "How many times—exactly?"

"I sat on a plow horse once," the boy said eagerly. "A farmer Toby knows owned it. But I can ride. I know I can."

Camp straightened fully, his gaze flying to Emily. He did indeed see worry shadowing her deep-blue eyes, and he reached out automatically, wanting to soothe it away. But her eyes went darker. She flinched and ducked to avoid his hand.

"What? Emily...I..." Camp slid his palms against his thighs.

"Sorry." She reddened a bit and looked sheepish. "You startled me." Tugging her son with her, she ran to where Maizie had stopped to shorten the stirrups on the smaller of the two horses. "How gentle is he?" she inquired.

Camp stared after her. She didn't look back. He noticed that Emily rubbed her upper arms as if to ward off goose bumps, even though the sun had bloomed fully and the day was warming. He swallowed a growl. Had there been more to the fear he'd seen in her eyes—more than just the fact that she was "startled"? In addition to sleeping around, had her no-good husband abused her?

Again the pieces didn't fit. She wouldn't have stayed

in an abusive relationship. The more he saw of Emily Benton, the more puzzling she became—as if she were two different women.

Maizie whistled, jolting Camp from his thoughts. He jogged over to the trio.

"I gave Mark Silverbelle. She's a honey. Has a gait like a rocking chair. The boy'll do fine, and you've already got a feel for this bronc."

"Mincemeat and I are old friends." Camp stroked a hand down the pinto's nose. "Aren't we, boy?" Rechecking the cinch for himself, he turned to Maizie. "Is it possible to make the round-trip in one day?"

She nodded. "Pour on the coals going. Easy on the return. Follow the river coming back. You'll cut off a lot of miles. Water the horses often. Mark will beg for stops. Expect he'll be hurting. You're probably broke in by now. But I'll ask Robert to go, if you'd rather."

Camp studied Mark. He saw that both the boy and his mother expected him to jump on Maizie's offer. "Thanks, but no. Mark and I will see this through. Will you have Jared drive my wagon?"

Maizie dug in her pocket and pulled out a chunk of chewing tobacco. Suddenly aware of Camp's grimace, she tucked it away again. "We Boones are Kentucky hill people," she said by way of explanation. "My daddy smoked and my mama chewed. Out here chewin's safer. The least little spark can set off a prairie fire that'll burn a thousand acres of grass almost before an eye can blink. Lost my brother and two cousins to one of them fires." She patted her pocket. "Seein' how you're paying most of the freight, I'll have to say the customer is right. But dang, old habits die hard."

"I appreciate your trying." Camp relieved her of the

pinto's reins and nodded as she drew his attention to a packet of beef jerky and a few apples she'd stowed in his saddlebags. As he boosted Mark into the saddle, Camp said, "At college there're a lot of farm kids who've already started to chew. Last year alone we lost two young men to throat cancer. Death by fire or cancer, it's all a waste. I'd hate to see the kids on this outing go home with the wrong message." He pulled himself into the saddle.

Maizie slapped Mincemeat on the rump and stepped aside. "Be off with you. Anybody ever tell you that you missed your callin', boy? You shoulda been a preacher."

Camp had his hands full keeping a rein on the crow-hopping pinto.

Sherry joined Emily at her campfire as Nolan and Mark melted into the distance. Maizie had already gone about her business.

"Did that doofus brother of mine lose another horse?" Sherry shaded her eyes.

Emily sighed. Reluctantly, she told Sherry the whole story.

"He's being noble? Did someone slip a mickey in Nolan's morning coffee?"

Emily bristled. "You know, Sherry, I don't see him as the man you described. Are you aware that Brittany sneaked into his wagon the other night? He asked me to flush her out, but he could've run or treated her like dirt. Instead, he stuck around and talked with her, careful not to hurt her feelings. And he didn't let Mark wiggle off the hook the way Dave would have, and Toby does."

Sherry cocked a brow. "So, are you saying I misjudged Nolan's attitude about women? That it's all my fault we're out here busting our buns, frying to a crisp?"

"You said yourself it had to do with sibling rivalry. Remember that I've lived with a genuine old-fashioned man who really disrespected women. So far, I haven't seen anything about Cam—Nolan that compares."

"I said gender rivalry. Nolan's a historian, and the stuff they teach distorts women's true role. Brittany is his student. Of course he's going to handle her with kid gloves, even if she is a twit. By the way, she and Megan are palling around. I feel sorry for the kid, but I don't think I'd want a daughter of mine sharing beauty secrets with her."

Emily bent over her campfire and poured them each a cup of Earl Grey. Throwing a glance toward her wagon, she lowered her voice. "I wish you did have a daughter, Sherry. Maybe then we could compare notes. Lord knows, I could use some reassurance. Or advice. I'm not happy about the girls' blossoming friendship. But something I've learned about Megan—she goes out of her way to do the things I object to." Emily gripped the cup with both hands and breathed in the pungent bergamot. "I'm the counselor, yet your brother seems to know how to handle my kids better than I do. So, if you have any tips, Sherry, I'm all ears."

A flush stained Sherry's cheeks. "I'm sorry, Em. The last thing you need is a friend haranguing you and adding to your problems. The fact is, teenage girls are a mass of belligerence and hormones. I was. I imagine you were." She sipped her tea. "Nolan's a few years older than me. There was enough of an age difference that he had zippo patience dealing with me storming through puberty. Hey, why are we always discussing him? It's not as if you're interested in him romantically or anything. I know you've sworn off men."

Sherry's words created a rumble of tension in

Emily's stomach. Or was it hunger? "Look, Doris and Vi are packing to leave. Megan and I haven't eaten yet. Our oatmeal's probably dried in the pan. Mark disrupted our breakfast coming in with that tale of his. I'm not used to him volunteering information. Generally, I have to pry it out, or have it come back to me through some member of the community who isn't under Toby's and Mona's thumb. And that's darned few."

Sherry tossed out the last of her tea and gave her friend an impetuous hug. "If I had the money from my trust, I'd lend you enough to pay your in-laws so you guys could blow that popstand. What about your family, Em? Is there no one you can borrow from?"

"Over a hundred grand? That's a big chunk of change. My family are all blue collar. They have mortgages and credit card debts like everyone else. Just pray I find a good job on the West Coast. If I got offered a higher salary, I don't believe Toby's toady judge could block my leaving. Do you?"

"I wouldn't have thought he could, anyway. I'm afraid I don't have any legal experience, Em. Not outside of referring needy students who come into the Hub to the Legal Aid Society. Do you think you could make an appointment with them at their Columbia office? How far does Toby's influence stretch?"

"Throughout our county. Plus, he's into politics at the local and state levels. Money talks everywhere. Lord knows he always managed to get Dave off without consequence. I'm almost ready to throw caution to the wind and chance it." She managed a humorless smile "I'll be old and gray before I pay Dave's debts. If I don't do something soon, Toby and Mona will choose a man for Megan to marry and pick Mark's college."

"What? They don't believe in college for girls?"

"You know they don't. According to Mona, if I hadn't had two degrees Dave wouldn't have felt inadequate and he wouldn't have strayed."

"Bah, humbug. How can you put up with them, Emily? I'd be in Leavenworth doing ninety-nine years of hard time, I'm afraid."

"Don't think it hasn't crossed my mind. Luckily, I'm also a coward."

"Well, pacifist, maybe. I wouldn't call you cowardly. That's one reason I thought of you for this trip. I can't say what or how, but I predict—I feel it in my bones— one of us will do something heroic that Nolan will have to report in his article. Picture this, Em, we'll have redeemed twentieth-century womankind."

Emily inspected her chapped hands. "Wouldn't it have been easier to write the article yourself, Sherry?"

"There's still the old glass ceiling. I could write it. Or you. It wouldn't carry the same weight as Nolan's article. Have you been to conferences where papers are presented?"

"No. But heavens, Sherry, we outnumber men in academics these days. There must be lots of women professors who go and present papers."

"Sure there are. They're accorded about as much respect as you could stuff in a billy goat's navel. When a woman gets up to read, the men in the audience go for coffee or take bathroom breaks. Or they steal her work. Well, I might be exaggerating a *little,* but…"

"In that case, I understand why this excursion is so important to you. I'll try my best not to screw up, pal. And I'll take more care filling out my daily data sheets. Rest easy, Sherry—I'll do my part."

"Good. We women have to stick together. Which reminds me...we'd better get our fannies in gear. Maizie's ready to hit the trail."

"It's so dusty I'm going to put a little distance between my wagon and the teachers'. It's not as if a straggler can get lost. This country's so flat you can see all the way to Oklahoma."

"Kansas City, at least." Sherry screwed up her face. "You're one hundred percent right about the dust. Did you see that road sign advertising Itchy's Flea Market? I'm itchy from all the cottonwood blowing around. I guess we're spoiled in Columbia, with our rolling hills and pine and maple trees. What do you suppose kept pioneers trekking through this desolate land?"

"The promise of Spanish money. I tell you, money rules the world."

Sherry chuckled. "Not my world. Work rules my world. If my boss retires...a big *if*. No sense counting on a promotion. Anyhow, in four years when I come into my trust, I'll be able to afford a house."

"Or you could marry someone who owns a house."

"Emily, I'm shocked! That's no reason to walk down the aisle."

"I didn't mean you'd marry to gain a house. It goes without saying that you'd love the man who owned the bricks and mortar."

"I've decided to remain a happy bachelorette."

"Sure. The tougher they talk, the harder they fall."

"Yeah, yeah!" Sherry waved at Emily over her shoulder.

Emily smiled long after Sherry had boarded her wagon and pulled into line with the main caravan. Sherry was tall, willowy and possessed the most luscious peaches-and-cream complexion of any woman in Emily's acquaintance. She also had a sharp mind and a wonderful sense of humor. It was easy enough to imagine men falling crazy in love with her. Emily knew Sherry hadn't met anyone who made *her* feel that way. But if ever the right man came along, she'd be a goner.

As for herself, well—she was the more likely of the two to remain single. Except that widowed and single were different. Still, the prospect of living alone once the kids flew the nest sent a trickle of dread down Emily's spine. All those years, all by herself... It wasn't the sex she missed. Long before Dave's death, his philandering had driven her into sleeping in the spare bedroom. Listening to colleagues, Emily knew sex could be pleasant. Even fun. No, she couldn't say she'd missed the sweaty coupling Dave called lovemaking. But she did miss the aftermath. The quiet time after he'd fallen asleep when his body warmth reached out, cocooning her in the darkness.

Winter nights were the hardest to get through alone. It was dark by the time she got home from work, and cold. To save money, she lowered the thermostat during the day.

She felt foolish wrapping herself in flannel sheets and dragging out her tattered, childhood teddy bear. He sat like a lump on the empty pillow, neither breathing nor exuding warmth; all the same his presence comforted.

After Dave's plane had crashed, so much crap came her way from Toby and Mona that Emily took her comfort whenever she could find it. A cup of tea with a friend. Rereading a favorite book. Watching a TV game show with the kids. Her teddy bear...

Emily might have daydreamed the morning away had Jared Boone not called out that she was being too slow.

"If you're in a hurry, go around me, Jared. I don't mind bringing up the rear."

"Gram wouldn't like that. She wants a man covering the rear of the train."

"Gram? Oh, you mean, Maizie. Why on earth…? Never mind. I get the message." Emily stewed, until it dawned on her that Jared's directions had probably come through Robert rather than Maizie. It didn't sound like Maizie's philosophy. "Hold your horses, junior," she told him. "I'll get under way when I'm ready."

The boy, who wasn't much older than Mark, gave a long-suffering sigh. "Yes, ma'am. Only, I'm not 'junior.' The Boones have enough juniors without me."

Ah, she thought, *even the management's a little touchy this many days out.* Emily made mental note to add that to her data sheet. She also vowed to remain pleasant throughout the entire trip, even if it killed her.

As the day wore on, that promise grew harder to keep. Mile after endless mile, they slogged past fields of waving grain and red-crested tassels of milo. Twice their path ran parallel to Highway 56. Truckers hauling baled hay to market honked their horns. The noise made the horses skittish and difficult to handle. The few cars that passed all slowed down; people opened their windows and cheered the trekkers on. A man on a tractor pulled up next to Emily and chatted. He thought the reenactment was great. He'd lived near the trail his whole life, he said, yet had never found time to drive the route. He warned of thunderstorms brewing in the Texas gulf, and in the next breath wished her Godspeed.

It seemed as if God had traveled at a snail's pace for the last five miles. Emily frequently found herself looking back over her shoulder, expecting to see Mark and Camp overtake them at any minute. Funny, how she thought of him as "Camp," although Sherry always called him "Nolan."

The nickname fitted him, in spite of the fact that camping was foreign to the man. However, he was no slouch on a horse. Emily's heart had beaten faster this morning, watching him ride off, so straight and easy in the saddle. His handling of the pinto was at odds with his ability in other areas of trail life. Emily didn't see him as the type to own horses and muck out stalls. But she'd been wrong about a man before. Horribly wrong.

As the sun began its western descent, the lead wagon turned and set a course into the sun, toward tree-covered undulations. Blessed hills. This turning of the whole column brought Megan out of hiding.

"Where's the town? You said we were stopping in Council Grove."

"We'll be there tomorrow. In time for the morning walking tour."

"I'm not taking any old walking tour. Brittany and I plan to shop."

"You girls had better take notes. Never know when you can use them in a school history paper."

"Brittany said they'll have neat antique stores. We're going to look for old hats, funky jewelry and stuff."

"Hats? Megan, we don't have money for someone else's junk." Emily practically yanked her team to a stop. She did slow enough for Megan to hop off.

"I'm going to ride with Sherry and Brittany. All you ever do is rag on me. I don't need your money. Mona gave me her credit card numbers."

"Megan—you come back here! You're not to charge *anything* to Mona, do you hear?" Her words echoed back from a curve they were rounding. Maizie had already pulled in beside a bubbling stream. Emily decided to unhitch her team first and argue later. Megan was *not* going to use Mona's credit cards this time.

With dusk settling in, she had more to worry about than her mother-in-law's far-reaching tentacles. There was still no sign of Mark and Camp.

Emily fretted as she and Sherry gathered wood. "I wonder what's keeping them. They didn't take bedrolls or much food."

"Speaking of food," Sherry murmured. "Megan wants to eat with us, Em. I said okay without thinking. If you'd prefer, I'll send her back to your wagon."

"No. Let her stay. That'll be one less thing for us to fight about." Emily brought Sherry up to date on her latest confrontation with Megan."

"I'll look for an opening to talk with her," Sherry promised. "I can see your mind's on other things. Do you want me to ask Robert to ride out and have a look around?"

Emily shook her head. "That's not what our pioneer sisters would do. They'd suffer in silence. I'll be fine, Sherry. I'm sure I'm worrying needlessly. I've been more of a worrier since Dave died in that crash."

"I understand. Why don't you come eat with us, too?"

"No. I'll be fine. Really." Emily patted Sherry's arm as they dropped their last load of wood and prepared to part.

Sherry gave Emily's hand a squeeze. "I may gripe about Nolan, but he's dependable. Did I mention he's renovating an old farmhouse? Down to the bare wood. Nothing is too tedious. You'd be impressed. I'm telling you this so you'll know he's not a quitter. He's totally reliable and he follows through on things. Trust me, Mark is safe with him."

Emily smiled. "Thanks. I won't tell a soul you paid him a compliment."

Sherry screwed up her face. "On most things, Nolan and I actually see eye to eye. He's not half as bad as his colleagues. Lyle Roberts thinks women are useless."

"Careful, or you'll talk yourself into siding with Nolan. Go on and fix your dinner. I'm sure he and Mark will roll in shortly."

But they didn't. Darkness occluded the skyline. Nothing but the wind moved out of the east—the direction they'd travel. The temperature dropped appreciably. Emily fixed a whole pot of navy bean soup in anticipation of their riding in hungry.

Megan slunk back at nine. She climbed in the wagon without saying a word. Emily was too weary to argue about Mona's credit cards. She paced and stared into the black night, drinking cup after cup of tea. No doubt the caffeine was adding to her unrest, making her feel even more jittery. One by one the other fires were extinguished, until only hers and Maizie's were left.

It was after ten, going on eleven. Emily sensed more than heard approaching hoofbeats. She jumped up and ran to the edge of Camp's wagon, clutching a hand over her heart. "Yes!" A steady clip-clop shook the ground.

Then, so as not to appear unduly anxious, she walked sedately back to her campfire, poured another cup of tea with shaking hands and sat. The instant the plodding horses appeared, she sprang up. Camp led the horse Mark had been riding. Her son was draped limply across the front of Camp's saddle. "What happened?" Emily barely choked back a turbulent cry.

Camp reined in the pinto, awkwardly placing a finger

to his lips. "It's okay, Emily," he whispered. "Poor kid fell asleep. My arm's about to fall off. I doubt he'll wake up. Let me figure out how to slide off, and I'll help you put him to bed."

Emily steadied the horse, grateful for Camp's offer. It was years since she'd been able to manage Mark's dead weight.

A lack of feeling in the arm and leg that'd borne the bulk of the sleeping boy caused Camp to dismount awkwardly.

"Shouldn't we wake him?" Emily murmured. "Won't he be hungry?"

"At five o'clock we met a family picnicking along the river. They shared sandwiches, fruit and cookies and picked our brains about the Santa Fe Trail. Mark enjoyed the food—almost as much as he enjoyed playing Santa Fe Trail guru."

"All the Bentons make wonderful instant experts. I'm sure it's in the genes."

Camp chuckled as he bundled Mark into Emily's wagon. "I see Maizie's still up. I'll go report in and see to the horses. Then I wouldn't object to a plateful of whatever it is that smells so good."

"Soup. I hope it's still edible. What took you so long?"

"You'll want to discuss that with Mark. I'm afraid his life of crime started a few miles earlier than he let on."

"Oh." She fumbled for words. "I'm really sorry."

Camp gazed down on earnest features hauntingly etched in moonlight. Moved, he gently held her shoulders. "Mark's a good kid, Emily. But he's easily led. I may not have a right to say this...but after things he let slip today, I'd say you'd be smart to remove both kids from their grandparents."

Struggling against a lump lodged in her throat, Emily

pulled from his loose grasp. "You'd better take care of the horses. I'll go check on the soup."

Impulsively, Camp caught her arms again. He hated the pinched look that killed the lively sparkle of her eyes. Instinct urged him to kiss away the sadness. Carefully cupping her soft face, he bent and tilted Emily's chin until their lips met. What started out as a desire to comfort flamed on contact. She arched away, frustrating Camp. He wanted more from her than a simple kiss. But the instant she wrenched away, he released her. Confusion clouded his eyes.

Panting, she licked her tingling bottom lip. It'd been years since any man had kissed her with such compassion, let alone with passion. The coil of need clutching her abdomen tempted her to lose herself in body-numbing foreplay. But with Dave, foreplay always led to unsatisfying sex, which caused more problems, solving none. "I'm going to bed," she said brusquely. "Get this straight—I am not a sex-starved widow. My appreciation for what you did for Mark doesn't extend to payback of that sort. The Bentons taught me there's always a price to pay for favors. Help yourself to soup and coffee. And consider my debt to you paid in full."

Camp barely had time to suck in his breath before she vaulted into her wagon bed and jerked the canvas closed. He glared at the flimsy material that he could so easily rip aside. Bone-weary though he was, he was sorely tempted to do just that and set her straight about his intentions. The fire that shot through his veins died as he heard one of the kids stirring and Emily answer in a low, soothing tone.

To top it all, he was as baffled as she by his caveman tactics. One thing Camp did know, he wasn't anything like her husband. Or her father-in-law. Tomorrow he'd have something to say to Mrs. Spitfire Benton. And when he'd finished, dammit, she wouldn't lump him in with the Benton men again.

CHAPTER SIX

A restrictive ideology prevailed in the written history of the American West. That men were courageous, women passive and dependent.

—From Nolan Campbell's notes.

EMILY FOUND IT impossible to relax. Blood rushed to her ears—and everywhere else her body had touched Camp's. She burrowed under the covers, then kicked them off, trying to concentrate on the even breathing of her children. As she'd told him, she wasn't a sex-starved widow...but she was sure acting like one. Every time she closed her eyes, she pictured straight, sable eyebrows and softly curled dark hair. Her fingers itched to feel the texture, the traces of silver that feathered his temples. Exactly right for a professor. Nolan Campbell's hands were well manicured but not smooth against her skin. Were they, and the solid muscles she'd felt in his chest and thighs, a result of the carpentry work Sherry said he did on his home?

It wasn't easy for Emily to admit that she liked the feel of Camp's hard, masculine body. Because she remembered being drawn to Dave's athletic build at first. The abuse of his body with too-rich food and an over-abundance of alcohol began gradually. He'd developed a paunch well before they stopped sharing a bed. Her numerous attempts to alter his eating habits gave him all the more reason to complain about her to his parents. Looking back, Emily realized that was just an insignificant part of the erosion of respect between them.

Nolan Campbell didn't seem like a man of excess or overindulgence. *Or maybe he was.* Emily ran her tongue lightly over her tender lips. He'd certainly delivered a three-alarm kiss. Unless it'd been too long for her to gauge, she'd venture to say he'd been well on his way to turning that kiss into a four-alarm blaze.

Flopping over on her stomach, Emily punched her pillow into a pulp.

"Mom?" Mark's restless voice floated out of the darkness. "Is something wrong?"

"I'm fine, honey," Emily lied. "Are you hungry? You were asleep when Camp brought you home."

"Not hungry," he mumbled, kicking at his covers.

"Do you want your pajamas on?"

"Nah, don't need 'em. Camp said real pioneers slept in their clothes. He knows all about that stuff." Another, longer yawn. "He's rule, Mom."

Into the silence, Megan piped up. "'Rule' means he's boss or cool," she grumbled sleepily. "*Good* in mom talk."

"I see," Emily muttered. "Anyhow, I think I do."

"Sheesh, Mom. It's heavy-metal lingo. You know, *metal rules.* I'd have thought you'd be up on stuff like that at college," Megan said scornfully, rising briefly on her elbow.

"In college when you mean good, you say good," Emily retorted dryly. Which wasn't necessarily true, of course. With all the cultures and countercultures a teacher encountered, communication was often confusing. What she did find interesting in this midnight exchange with her children was that Mark had gone from calling Camp a "loose cannon" to deciding he was "rule." Kids—Mark in particular—didn't switch allegiance easily.

Megan huffed a little and turned over. Her breathing soon evened out again. Mark had gone back to snoring softly. As her own blood finally cooled, Emily decided she might have acted rashly, tarring Camp with the same brush she reserved for Dave and his father.

She sat up and reached for her jeans. Pulling them on, she muffled a yawn. Oddly, the conversation with her kids had brought things into focus. If nothing else, she owed Camp an apology for acting like an outraged virgin.

CAMP WAS IN NO MOOD for idle chitchat. Maizie had other ideas. He tried to cut their conversation short, insisting he didn't need or want help with the horses.

"Bah, two sets of hands are quicker than one. You look bushed. I hafta say you did a good deed today, sonny. I found out Jared knew Mark had swiped those signs. He stayed mum because of some warped code these young 'uns go by."

"How can you fault loyalty? Truth is, I doubt Mark will pull that stunt again. I'm just glad I discovered it then, rather than farther afield."

Maizie gave the horse Mark had ridden a last, brisk rub and a scoop of oats. "Mark's the lucky duck. I'd probably have skinned the kid alive if I'd caught him. His mother needs to tune in before it's too late."

"Give Emily a break. She's doing the best she can."

"Uh-huh." Maizie dug in her pocket for a chew, stopped and gave a wry shake of her head. "So are you reforming her, too?"

"Nothing of the kind," Camp replied too quickly. "In the beginning, I felt like you. I know now that her in-laws spoil the kids rotten. I gather they're some piece of work." He paused. "Look, if you want to know any more about the Bentons, you'll have to talk to Emily."

"Fair enough. You hungry, boy? I could probably rustle up some grub."

"Thanks, but Emily left soup warming. I may as well take her up on the offer. Also, I promised to bank her campfire. She and the kids already went to bed. Mark was exhausted—slept the last few miles." Camp massaged the arm that'd held the boy as he eyed the long row of dark wagons. "Appears everybody made an early night of it. What's our agenda for tomorrow? You said about three hours to Council Grove?"

"Yep. On the road by six sharp. We need to arrive in time for the town's summer celebration. There'll be a parade, tours, all that folderol. Guess folks are anxious to hit town for a spell. All except that Ms Ames of yours." Maizie scowled.

"Gina? I'm sure she'll want to photograph the folderol, as you put it."

"Yeah, well, she's got her tail in a tizzy. Had her mind set on filming a patch of sunflowers. We got here too late. She's in a snit. Asked if we could start later. I tried to explain if I adjusted the schedule for one, everybody would expect favors."

"Gina strikes me as being a professional. The snit will be over by morning."

"'Spect so. Well, sonny, I'm scrammin' these old bones off to bed. You better eat quick and grab some shut-eye yourself."

"I will. After I jot a few notes. I noticed someone

collected my data sheets. Remind me to say thank-you tomorrow."

"Your sister. I like that gal. She's surprisingly cheerful for having to put up with that ditzy miss you stuck her with."

"Ah, yes, Brittany." Camp massaged the back of his neck. "I should feel guilty, but I'm banking on Sherry's levelheadedness rubbing off."

"Humph, if she doesn't tear her hair out first. Only time will tell. Well, good night, boy. Don't want your food gettin' cold for my jawing."

Camp gave the two saddle horses a last pat, then made a beeline for the only beacon left burning—Emily's still-glowing fire.

Entering the empty campsite, he crouched on his heels to stir the soup. The only sounds were the wind rustling through clumps of tallgrass and the occasional whicker of horses. Loneliness struck Camp without warning. He wavered between partaking of this solitary meal or chucking it in and going to bed.

In the midst of his indecision, the hairs at his nape stiffened. Sensing something or someone behind him, Camp straightened and whipped around, slopping hot soup on his jeans. "Who's there?" His heart beat unsteadily. What would he do if it was Brittany? *Send her back to her wagon, that's what!*

Emily, not Brittany, separated herself from the coal-dark outline of the wagon.

She hadn't meant to sneak up on him. However, once she'd glimpsed his broad back crouched over the grate, her heart began to pound again, and her feet took on a life of their own. Thoughts muddled, Emily had entertained the idea of going back to bed, of saving what she had to say till daylight. Now she'd shown herself, leaving her no choice but to follow through.

"It's just me." Her voice cracked.

"Emily?" Camp rose. The spoon continued to drip on his boots. "Did Mark wake up hungry?" Realizing he still held the spoon, he quickly stuck it back in the soup. "He's in luck. I stopped to feed the horses and haven't had time to finish this up."

She gave a shrug, eyes on the bubbling pot as though it contained witches' brew instead of harmless bean soup. "Mark's sleeping like a log. So is Megan. I, uh, I came to apologize."

He followed her gaze. "Apologize for the soup?" He sent her a puzzled smile. "If it's scorched you can hardly blame yourself. We were late. Anyway, I'm not fussy."

Sighing, she clasped her hands solidly in front of her. All the while her restless gaze traveled skyward, then swooped to lock on the ground near Camp's feet. "I'm apologizing for my earlier outburst." The last word sank into a whisper. She tried again. "I don't know you well, but I've seen firsthand that you possess more integrity than Toby. More than Dave ever did. Forgive me, I shouldn't speak badly of the dead."

Her tone pricked his conscience. It was too polite. "Don't give it another thought. I was out of line." He glanced at the dark canopy overhead. "I can't even blame my bad behavior on a full moon," he joked.

But Emily found she couldn't laugh. She'd said her piece; now it was time to leave. "I should—"

Camp judged she was about one second from bolting. "You're cold," he broke in. "Come, sit by the fire. You're an answer to my prayer, you know," he said too quickly. "I hate eating alone." He hooked his foot around one of the canvas stools she'd left grouped around the fire ring and offered it with a smile.

Emily relaxed a little. She didn't rush to take the seat.

"Scout's honor. It's not good for a person to eat alone."

"I don't believe you were ever a Scout," she snorted. "And I've never heard that company aids digestion."

"Sure it does. Mine, anyway," he said, grabbing another stool and dragging it close to the heat. He sat down and he calmly filled a bowl with soup. As he spooned up a mouthful, he presented Emily with a long face.

This time her sigh spelled resignation. "Stop that. You know I'm a sucker for cow eyes. Would you like crackers with your soup?" Stepping into the light, she bent easily and plucked a packet of unopened crackers from a metal canister. Gingerly she perched on the stool he'd prepared.

Camp hid a grin. He'd take victory any way he could achieve it. "I'll never turn down food. Emily, this soup hits the spot. It's thick, the way I like it." He accepted a handful of crackers, but stopped speaking as their fingers brushed. He felt a sensation that reminded him—oddly enough—of the shock he'd once suffered when his electric sander shorted out. It traveled to his elbow and weakened his grip.

He and Emily both lunged for the fumbled crackers. Camp experienced hunger of a different nature. Emily exuded a tantalizing scent of coconut and almond that put his hormones on alert. He jerked away, knowing he smelled of leather, horse and sweat.

Her stomach churning, Emily made a big production of closing the cracker packet and returning it to the covered tin.

Something was definitely happening here. Camp fought an urge to taste the creamy pulse that had begun to throb in Emily's neck. He bit into a cracker, instead. Once he'd devoured it, he went back to methodically eating his soup. In the sudden descent of silence, Camp was terribly afraid he'd begun to sound like a dry camel taking on water. But if he stopped...

Emily's scent filled him. He found it almost impossible to concentrate on satisfying his hunger for food. Making a concerted effort to act at ease, Camp stretched his long legs toward the fire. "Tomorrow we roll into Council Grove," he said inanely. Darn it, he'd never been inane. Normally he was quite articulate.

"Tomorrow. Yes." Emily bent and set the canister down before straightening and crossing her feet primly at the ankles. She didn't know what to do with her hands and finally left them loose in her lap. *What was wrong with her?* Friends generally considered her a witty conversationalist. However, she wasn't quite sure what had happened with that simple touch they'd shared. No. The real problem—she *was* sure.

Frowning, Camp ladled himself a second bowl of soup, although he barely remembered having tasted the first one. He wished she'd quit rubbing one ankle on the other that way. He imagined her naked flesh slowly massaging his calves. Shifting uncomfortably, he muttered in a gravelly voice, "Are the kids looking forward to the tours or to visiting the Last Chance Store?"

"No."

After waiting several heartbeats with nothing more forthcoming, Camp set his bowl aside. In an all-out attempt to sweep the provocative visions from his mind, he viciously rubbed the bridge of his nose. "Hey, help me out here, Emily. If our students gave one-syllable answers, we'd be all over them in a minute."

The absurdity of two adults—professors—floundering for dialogue, worse than shy preteens, propelled a bubble of laughter past the lump in Emily's throat. Leaning toward him, she clasped her hands between her knees. "I deserve to flunk. My only excuse is that I've been out of the singles scene a long time. I'm afraid I saw an accidental touch and a simple kiss as a prelude to hopping into bed. It's my problem, not yours. That's how Dave operated. It's probably not how you act."

Camp's stomach fish-flopped. The glow from the fire picked up a dusting of freckles on Emily's cheeks— a result of these last few days in the sun. What could he say? He felt guilty knowing she'd hit squarely on what lurked in his mind. What it did was make him face facts. In Emily's case, he did operate differently. Everything she'd blurted out was true; this wasn't his normal style. But his reaction to Emily wasn't the way he normally reacted to a woman, either. He sure as heck didn't want to scare her off until they figured out what it was that spiced the air between them every time they got within shouting distance. At the moment she looked about half a step from taking flight. Again. Camp definitely didn't want to screw things up.

He cleared his throat. "At our age, Emily, everyone carries a lot of baggage. Maybe we should just let the past be. Not worry about it?" He already knew she'd had a bastard for a husband—an experience that'd left her wary of men. So what? According to Greta, a man who hung out in museums was a zero in the relationship department, too. So why not keep things superficial? "Do you see any reason we can't be friends?" He carefully steepled his fingers.

"Friends." She turned the word over on her tongue

and in her mind, recalling how his lips had made her feel. Heart knocking, she eyed him skeptically. "Define 'friend.'"

"I'm lousy at crossword puzzles—but I'll give it a stab. Friends lend a helping hand, laugh together, maybe eat together. Hopefully, share a common interest or two."

Emily nodded. That didn't sound too threatening. He didn't flippantly say friends were playmates. "In a way…" She hesitated. "We, uh, do have a common interest. Sherry said you're remodeling an old farmhouse. My hobby is refinishing furniture."

"See, I knew we were kindred spirits. Do you work with any special time period?"

"I'm partial to the country-styled hard maples, but I tend to mix and match so long as it's real wood and not veneer. I guess you could say my taste is eclectic."

Camp felt the tension slide from his limbs. "Have you ever refinished kitchen cabinets? That's where I am. Sherry says I should gut the room. I want to modernize, but there's a brick-walled fireplace I'd like to save. And an old icebox I thought would make good storage until Gret—someone called it an eyesore."

"Not after it's refinished. Does your friend know people would practically kill for a real icebox? I'd love to see your place," she ventured softly. "Maybe I could give you a few tips."

"More than likely you'd turn tail and run. Even my parents refer to the house as Nolan's white elephant. They're convinced I'll have one foot in the grave before it's ready for guests. I've been working on it in my spare time for eight years. Four bedrooms and two bathrooms are complete. I've stripped the living-room and dining-room walls and floors. My bedroom and one I use as an office are the only rooms I've furnished. In the kitchen I have a refrigerator, a microwave, and a table and two chairs my folks were throwing away."

"Think how satisfying it'll be once it's finally done. I loved my house. It didn't need as much work as yours, obviously, but I redecorated every room."

"You say *loved* as if it's in the past."

Her face fell. "I had to sell for financial reasons after Dave died. The kids and I moved into a small duplex. Luckily the people who bought the house wanted a lot of the furniture, too, or else I'd be paying storage every month."

Camp read the look. He wouldn't call it luck at all. He thought giving up her house had been tantamount to driving a stake through Emily's heart. "When we get back to civilization, I'll draw you a map to my place. I've already invited Mark, but if you're moved to do a little consulting on the side, I'd be happy to hire you."

"Oh, I couldn't take money. I wouldn't."

"Well, then by all means drop by and toss out opinions."

"I'd like that. I'd like Mark to do more riding. Do you, by chance, have horses?"

"No, but there's a stream behind my house that's great for fishing. I understand Jared's going to teach Mark how. And I do have a lop-eared mutt who loves kids. A ten-year-old golden lab. He and I walk together every morning. He doesn't understand why I don't have time to take him fishing anymore."

"Mark used to beg for a puppy." Her lips tightened. "I was afraid—well, his father didn't like animals. And now," she lamented, "our place is too small."

Camp had to temper the rush of anger he felt. Only— as she'd said earlier—there was no sense arguing with

a dead man. Nor did Camp want to sound as if he chastised Emily for staying with the jerk. She said he'd
threatened to take away her kids. Not that he fully understood how that could happen. It seemed, on the
surface anyhow, that someone possessing the tools to
work with disadvantaged women could have used those
same tools to break free of her own situation. But there
he went, judging her unfairly again.

"Why are you looking at me like that? I'm not
kidding, Camp. My place is too small for a turtle, let
alone a dog. It wouldn't be fair to the animal."

"Hey, your word is good." He stood, wishing he
didn't have these doubts. But the question kept cropping
up, and their friendship was too new for him to ask. He
faked a yawn. "I'll wash these dishes before the fire dies
and leaves me with cold water. Go on to bed, Emily.
Maizie plans to be on the road by six."

"I'm awake now. You go to bed and let me do the
dishes."

"My mother wouldn't believe I'd argue if someone
offered to wash dishes. See, you've warped my psyche.
Going by the rules in my house, you fed me, so scram,
I'll handle cleanup."

"Could I convince you to repeat this conversation to
Mark sometime? His father and grandfather voiced
definite ideas on what constitutes men's work compared
with women's. Oh, forget it, the kids'll just point out that
Toby and Mona have a cook and a maid." She jumped
up and poured the basin full of water, then set it on the
grate. "I tend to view housework as a team effort. Since
that's my philosophy, we'll share cleanup and both get
to bed faster."

Camp was struck by a picture of the two of them

winding down for the day and walking off to bed hand in hand. A picture so clear that he stopped folding the stools and stood, gazing hungrily at the delicate feminine curves of her back.

As if sensing his scrutiny, she turned from scrubbing the bean pot. "Camp?"

"Fine." He passed a hand over his eyes. "I'm all for teamwork. Let's cut the small talk and dig in."

Because there was no other conversation between them, Emily wondered what in their brief exchange had made Camp act so moody. Just as she'd begun to let down her guard with him, too. Well, she'd had a bellyful of moody men. He needn't worry that she'd press her unwanted company on him again.

"I don't need an escort service to find my way to my wagon," she said. A gentleman through and through, Camp padded at her heels, shining a light on the path between their wagons. She didn't respond to his grumpy "good night."

Emily had no sooner climbed into her wagon and closed the flap than she decided it'd been churlish to pretend not to hear him. He had put in a full day helping Mark. And Camp had said to begin with that he was tired. It was another example of her past intruding. Emily hated that she'd reverted to the passive-aggressive tendencies she'd developed to cope with staying married. Darn, why did she always end up owing Nolan Campbell apologies? She'd set out to clear the air and now she was back at square one. Fumbling with the ties, Emily threw open the canvas she'd just cinched shut. She expected him still to be there. But he wasn't.

Just as she considered going to his wagon, his lantern sprang to life. Backlit against a canopy of white was a clear silhouette of Camp removing his shirt. Emily's mouth went dry. He shed his jeans and then... What in the world was she doing? She wasn't a voyeur, for pity's sake. Sucking in a huge gulp of night air, Emily drew her canvas closed with shaking fingers. She stumbled on hands and knees to her bed and dived under the covers without removing her clothes. For a long time she lay absolutely still, her mind locked in battle with an unforgivably acute imagination.

CAMP ROUSED at the faint sound of Maizie's dinner bell. He groaned. That woman loved to punish late sleepers with the clang of iron against all three sides of that blasted triangle.

He sat up slowly and heard the thump of books hitting the floor. Snapping on a flashlight, he realized he'd fallen asleep in the middle of comparing the women's data sheets with what was listed in his texts. According to the books, men like Crockett and Boone shunned towns, preferring to live off the land. *His* group, however, looked forward to the promised layover in town.

And not one woman mentioned that the firewood they stocked here would have to last or else, like their pioneer sisters, they'd be out collecting cow chips to burn. Sherry wrote that she was dying to find a bookstore and a beauty shop. Gina wanted to develop her film. Brittany filled two pages with the plans she and Megan had made: a visit to the rodeo, junk food and shopping. Only Emily mentioned visiting historical points of interest. She named some that Camp had never heard of.

In a moment of weakness, he imagined viewing history through Emily's eyes. Such beautiful eyes. Forced to deal with a quickening in his blood, Camp thrust thoughts of Emily aside. He gathered the papers and bundled them with the others, then dressed and took a walk in the woods. A dip in the icy stream effectively cooled his ardor. By the time he returned, preparations for the day had begun.

Mark and Megan were stuffing their faces with pancakes. Emily didn't seem to be around. Mark glanced up and greeted Camp with a sticky smile. "Hi. Jared's dad says if me and him collect piles of wood this morning, he'll loan me a fishing pole to use for the rest of the trip."

"Him and I, stupid," Megan growled before Camp could say a word. "Instead of dragging us on this crappy trip, Mom should have stayed home and sent you to summer school."

"No more'n you. I didn't get any Ds on my report card."

Megan's brows drew down. "Mona said my teachers shouldn't have given me so much homework. She said they were insensitive to Daddy's death."

"A year later?" Mark jeered. "'Sides, what was different? Dad was never home anyway."

"There's a lot different. Mona and Toby made sure we lived in a nice house. Wait till you're my age and have to explain to friends why you moved to a dinky duplex."

Camp listened to them argue as he built a fire and waited for his coffee to brew. Life must have been hell for Emily. Still was, he acknowledged as he sliced the last of his potatoes to fry with a can of mushrooms. Her in-laws sounded like people who'd stepped straight out of a Stephen King novel. Camp felt like waltzing into that town and telling them to lay off Emily. The idea took shape before he remembered the way they'd parted last night. He stirred the mixture, lamenting how things had turned out.

Sherry ran up, saving Camp from dwelling on the subject.

"Nolan, I'm worried about Gina. She left at dawn to photograph sunflowers. Said she'd be back in half an hour. We're due to leave soon and she's not back."

Camp washed his first bite down with a swallow of coffee. "Gina's a big girl. She probably decided to skip breakfast in favor of a big lunch in Council Grove."

Sherry's troubled gaze drifted along the foothills, where gusts of wind turned the bluestem tallgrass into ocean waves.

"I can tell you believe something's happened to her. Isn't it possible she just lost track of the time?"

"Not Gina. She runs her life on a schedule. A lot of us just buy daily planners. Gina actually uses hers."

"How can you know her so well? You only met two weeks ago."

Emily passed by carrying an armload of wood and abruptly dropped several sticks. She hadn't meant to eavesdrop, but did hear Sherry's gaffe.

Sherry shifted from foot to foot. Her eyes made contact with Emily's in a silent warning.

"Really, Camp," Emily chided, crossing to stand beside Sherry. "You don't have to be very observant to see that Gina runs her life by the clock."

His gaze skipped to Emily's open smile. Darn, how did she manage to throw him into a tailspin with one smile? "You think Gina should be back by now, too?"

"Yes, I do."

"Okay. Let me stow my gear and I'll ask Robert to help me take a look." Camp assumed his offer would appease both women. Instead, Sherry bounced a suspicious glance between him and Emily.

"You wouldn't take my word, but the minute Emily asks, you turn into the Lone Ranger. What gives with you two?"

Emily's cheeks flushed. Camp sensed where Sherry was headed and tried to ward her off. "It was the buildup of concern, sis. I still doubt there's a problem, but I'm willing to take your collective word."

"Oh. Guess I let Brittany influence me. She swears there's a romance developing between you two." Snatching the plate from Camp's hand, Sherry pushed him toward Robert's wagon, missing the look that passed between him and Emily.

"Why don't we go ourselves?" Emily asked. "Aren't we as capable of finding Gina as the men are?"

"Robert's been over this route," Camp countered. "He knows the area. Worst-case scenario is Gina had a run-in with a rattler, and Robert's the best person to deal with that."

Emily's eyes glittered angrily for a moment until she registered Sherry's interest in their spat, and she said through clenched teeth, "No doubt Robert is the best choice."

Camp came within a hair of responding in kind to her sarcasm. Reconsidering, he tugged the bill of his Kansas City Royals cap over his eyes and went in search of Robert—who was inclined to agree with Camp that Gina had either strayed farther than planned or that she'd lost herself in her work.

Robert dug out a dime. "I'll flip you for who breaks the bad news to Maizie. She's raring to get under way. This isn't going to make her happy."

"Better you take her tongue-lashing than me, old son," Camp said, delivering a friendly slap to the man's back. "Sherry said Gina followed that trail." He pointed to a faint track leading up the hill. "See where it splits? I'll search the east branch. After you tell Maizie, hike along the other side. If neither of us finds Gina by six, let's touch base back at the fork and switch to plan B."

"Which is?" Robert frowned.

"Beats me," Camp said. "I just made up plan A. She supposedly hiked the Sierras alone. I'm counting on her to beat us back."

Robert nodded, and the two went their separate ways. Camp soon discovered that his portion of the trail petered out. He loped to the fork, expecting that he'd engaged in this morning exercise for nothing. He broke into a jog the minute the crossroads—where Robert paced irritably—came into sight.

"Don't tell me," Camp panted, removing his sunglasses to blot away the sweat trickling into his eyes. "No Gina."

"That's right, and this trail dead-ends on the other side of the hill in a cornfield. As far as I can see is farmland. Some fallow, most planted. I'm going back for my binoculars. Hell, the way the wind whistles through the corn stalks, it's impossible to tell if she's out there wandering around."

"You think she might be?"

"It'd be my guess. Philly opened his big mouth last night and blabbed about this being the place where they've reported odd circles in the middle of cornfields. Circles some fool claims were made by spaceships. If she went in to take pictures and got turned around, it could take her two days to find her way out."

"You're kidding?"

"'Fraid not. I can tell you've never farmed corn. Some places it grows so tall you can't see daylight."

"Yes, but can't you just follow a row to the end?"

"Yep, providing you're headed in the right direction. The rows crisscross."

"I see. Well, let's not waste any more time."

MAIZIE ANXIOUSLY awaited their return. "Damn," she said. "If this ain't a pickle."

Harv from Philadelphia shoved his way between Robert and Maizie. "Don't waste our time because of some broad's stupidity. I say we go on to town and send a search party back. Your brochure promised a frontier day's celebration. Why should the rest of us miss the parade?"

Maizie glared at him. "Nobody's stopping you, Mr. Big Mouth. But it's a far piece to Santa Fe. If you have trouble with your wagon, don't count on help from trail mates."

He made an ugly gesture, but he did shut up.

Robert rummaged in his wagon and pulled out binoculars and a rifle. "Gina might have run afoul of a rattlesnake or a rabid coyote."

Emily handed Camp several clean white dishtowels. "If Gina's injured, you may need to cover a wound or make a sling."

Camp accepted them grimly. He pressed Emily's hand in appreciation.

"Can Jared and me go?" asked Mark eagerly. "We wanna help."

Searching his mind for some polite way to say no, Camp was relieved to hear Robert say it first. "You guys stay and help the ladies lay in a good supply of wood. Best thing you can do is have these wagons ready to roll the minute we return."

Near seven-thirty the searchers stumbled across Gina's footprints leading into a cornfield, just as Robert had predicted. Forty-five minutes later, Camp grabbed Robert's arm. "Is it my imagination or are we covering the same ground twice?"

"It's not your imagination. She wandered in circles for a while."

Cupping his hands around his mouth, Camp shouted Gina's name. Both men strained to hear over the moaning wind that sounded almost human at times.

Robert shook his head and turned to plunge deeper into the field.

"Wait!" Camp's sharp command stopped him. "This way. I heard a shout." Camp pointed in the opposite direction from the set of tracks.

"You may be right," Robert said excitedly. "Listen." Faintly, they heard what sounded like "Help," above the constant rustle of the leaves.

The men angled diagonally through some forty rows before picking up Gina's tracks again. This time they shouted in unison. The answer sounded weak but clear. Keeping up a running discourse, Camp stumbled through a wall of corn and fell over the woman they sought.

"Thank God you found me. I feel like a fool," Gina gasped through parched lips. "I'd set up my tripod for a close-up of the sunflowers mixed in with the corn. I stepped back and landed in a blasted prairie-dog hole. It threw me into the tripod, which toppled over on me. I'm afraid I broke my left leg and my right arm."

"The arm is really swollen," Camp concurred. He carefully immobilized her arm with a sling fashioned from the towels Emily had given him. A cursory glance at the odd angle of her leg had Camp fighting a queasy stomach. "Moving you will hurt like hell. If we take you and your equipment, we'll have to immobilize this leg and trade off carrying you."

"Don't think I'm going to louse up your paper, Campbell. I'll need somebody to drive my wagon into Council Grove to a doctor. He'll patch me up."

Camp didn't want to disillusion her, but he didn't think Gina Ames would be continuing with this trip. There went the professional photographs he'd coveted. Oh, well, accidents happened now as they had to the pioneers—the difference being that Gina's pioneer sisters would have tossed her into a wagon and forged on. She might or might not have healed properly. Today, medical equipment and techniques virtually assured her of a full recovery.

Forcing his disappointment aside, Camp made his decision. No part of this reenactment—or his project— was worth taking risks with Gina's health. She'd stay behind in Council Grove.

CHAPTER SEVEN

"Pioneer women were little more than passive participants in their husbands' ventures."
—A statement in one of the standard history texts used by Nolan Campbell.

THE MEN TOOK TURNS carrying Gina and her heavy equipment. Camp developed a new respect for the scrappy woman who worried not about her injuries but for the safety of her camera and lenses. Her arm and leg had to hurt badly, yet she never once complained of her own discomfort.

Maizie, Emily, Sherry, Doris and Vi ran to meet the returning expedition. Sherry gripped Gina's good hand.

Emily fussed and adjusted her sling. "What can we do to help, Gina?"

Mark and Jared sidled closer. Brittany and Megan hung back. The couple from Philadelphia showed no interest whatsoever in the plight of a fellow traveler.

"That ankle and knee look nasty," Maizie said after giving Gina's injuries a cursory once-over. "You step in front of an eighteen-wheeler, gal?"

Through clenched teeth, Gina retold her story.

"Boys." Maizie waved Jared and Mark over. "We need splints, or the ride to town will be murder. See if you kids can round up some magazines for braces. We women will rip up an old sheet for ties."

Mark screwed up his face. "Brittany's got a slug of movie magazines. I ain't gonna be the one to ask her to give 'em up."

Sherry rallied. "I'll talk to Brittany," she said. "You boys hitch Gina's team."

"Sure," replied Jared. "That's easy. C'mon, Mark."

Mark dawdled. "She can't drive a team with that arm," he noted. "Ms Ames, I'll drive for you," he volunteered.

It had been on the tip of Camp's tongue to suggest that Sherry have Brittany drive their wagon, and his sister take over Gina's. Mark's request both surprised and pleased him. Ultimately, however, the decision to let the boy drive or not rested with Emily. Along with the others, Camp anxiously awaited her verdict.

Maizie clapped the youth on the back. "I'm proud of you, Mark. That's a right gentlemanly offer."

Megan hooted. "My brother a gentleman? He's a baby. Who'd trust him to drive a wagon?"

Though it was one of the first smiles Camp had seen Megan crack, he still would have backed Mark on general principles. Except that Maizie beat him to it.

"For your information, missy, at the time of the real wagon trains, a twelve-year-old lad was considered a man."

"Yeah, Megan, so shut your trap." Mark glared at his sister.

"Enough, you two." Emily shook a finger at both. "This is no time for bickering. We need to settle Gina in her wagon before she goes into shock." As Emily spoke, Robert carried Gina toward her wagon. Jared ran to help his dad.

"Gina's white as a ghost," Emily announced at large. "Sherry, do you have any extrastrength analgesic on hand? Does anyone?"

"I do, dear," Doris volunteered. Pointing to her white-haired wagon mate, she said with a twinkle in her eye, "Between us we have a pharmacy of across-the-counter pain medicine. Taking this trip at our age was defying nature. We didn't want to be caught in the middle of nowhere and be a burden with our achy joints."

Emily smiled. "I should be so spry after I retire from teaching. Ask Gina which of your medications she'd prefer, while I help Maizie tear sheets."

"Mom." Mark tugged at her arm. "Is it okay for me to drive Ms Ames's wagon?"

Emily hooked her thumbs through her belt loops. "Ask Camp."

At once Mark plied Camp with reasons he should be allowed to drive.

Camp listened intently, his eyes still on Emily. When Mark wound down, she was the one Camp addressed. "I'm glad you value my opinion."

"You leased the wagons, after all."

"Oh." Camp's smile fractured. "It's fine by me. But the ball's in your court."

Emily tensed, then shrugged. "I have a tendency to try to protect my kids from possible failure. Mark," she said, spinning toward him, her energy building. "I know you've watched me drive the team, but it's a matter of threading the reins properly through your fingers in order to apply even pressure on the driving bit. Please have Maizie or Robert show you the basics."

"You mean I can do it? All right!" Those near enough to hear him grinned.

GINA'S ACCIDENT resulted in a several-hour delay. They all accepted that they'd miss the parade. Robert saddled a horse to ride ahead to set up a doctor's appointment for Gina, and to try to reschedule tours. Jared drove their wagon, a switch that left two young drivers one behind the other. Maizie took it upon herself to exchange Gina's wagon with the Shaw wagon. Of course Harv complained bitterly.

Regardless, Emily was grateful to Maizie. Experience had taught her that mothers weren't always the best overseers of their children in new situations. This way, if Mark needed direction, he'd accept it much more readily from Maizie. Which didn't mean Emily wasn't worrying. Eventually she stopped leaning out to try to see how he was doing. It hurt her neck, and there was absolutely nothing she could do to help him.

Camp watched Emily's head bob out time and again. He knew the agony she felt. It was like that first day on the trail, when they were all new to driving. He'd worried constantly—when he wasn't in pain from the hard plank seat and the jolting ride—knowing he'd gotten everyone into what might be a risky undertaking. It'd given him a devil of a headache, until it occurred to him there wasn't a damn thing he could do except look out for himself.

He laughed now. Then he'd been about as ill-equipped for this job as an ape from the wilds. Both he and Mark Benton had come a long way. Surprisingly, Camp felt a curious paternal pride in what the boy was doing.

Paternal! Camp hauled back on the reins, slowing his team. That revelation was a shock. Or maybe not, considering his protective feelings for Emily. And her family.

In "family," he'd included Megan. Teenage girls were scary. They resided in a mystery world of clothes, makeup and volatile moods. Megan and Brittany provided plenty of fodder for contrast to the young pioneer women Camp had become acquainted with through old diaries.

For instance, Megan and Brittany avoided work like the plague. Given chores, they either dinked around until someone else, usually Emily or Sherry, got fed up and completed the task. Or they grumped and finished their work only after constant nagging. Pioneer girls had toiled from sunup to sundown.

In all fairness he had to say Brittany and Megan were fastidious about their persons. Come hell or high water, their hair got washed daily. Would they, Camp wondered, if faced with the peril of a rattler, neatly dispatch the snake with one of their battery-powered curling irons? Or would they fall apart?

A few weeks ago, his money would have been on the latter. Now, after Mark's surprising turnaround, Camp wasn't so sure. The last few days he'd begun to revise a number of the notions he had held at the start of this trip. *Some* modern women might be wimpier than their pioneer cousins. Not all, by a long shot.

What would Lyle Roberts say about his discovery of the flaws in their teaching texts? He'd probably harp on Gina's dropping out. Camp didn't plan to make an issue of her accident. She had options that weren't available to pioneer travelers, as he'd make very clear in his paper.

AN HOUR AFTER they pulled into Council Grove and set up in a park on the town's outskirts, everyone grouped around Gina with long faces, staring at the splint on her arm and the long white cast on her leg.

"I've hired Mark to drive my wagon and me to Santa Fe," she announced, and named a figure that was more than a generous wage.

Both Emily and Camp sucked in a sharp breath.

Mark, grinning like a fool, dug a wad of bills out of his pocket. "This is the first payment. Enough to buy me a fishing pole of my own. I'll help settle Gina in the hotel room she's rented for tonight, then me and Jared are going fishing with his dad."

Sherry knelt by Gina's side. "If you're doing this to show Nolan that modern women are as tough as his precious pioneers, forget it. Thanks to modern medicine we don't have to suffer the way our predecessors did. Em and I agreed that we'd put our heads together and find someone to drive you home."

Camp nodded to show he approved. "Gina, I don't think you should stay—"

"I've made up my mind." Gina stubbornly waved them away with her good hand. "The doctor said my cast stays on for six weeks. Said I can remove the splint myself in four. We've already arranged transportation home from Santa Fe. There's no reason to disrupt the schedule for me."

The way Emily and Sherry were glaring at him, Camp was half-afraid to say anything lest it be misconstrued. Except that he agreed with them wholeheartedly. "Gina, how do you plan to manage simple things like climbing in and out of the wagon? Not to mention tending to…to, ah, personal matters."

More blunt than Camp, Maizie came right to the point. "How are you gonna get to a bush, gal, let alone squat behind it?"

"Mark and I already had this discussion." She looked

affronted. "Not that my ablutions are anyone's business, but the doctor's providing me with a portable potty. Everything's resolved. Mark will build my cook fires and set up my tripod as needed. For a fee, of course." She met Emily's eyes and winked. "Your son is a sharp financier. I predict he'll make a killing in the stock market someday."

"I don't object to Mark's pitching in," Emily said. "But he shouldn't take Gina's money."

"Sure he should," Maizie asserted. "Gina wants to pay, and Mark wants the job. Teaches the kid solid work ethics. 'Nough said if you ask me." She turned to Mark and her grandson. "You two run along before them fish stop bitin'. Tell Robert I've got a hankering for catfish for breakfast." One by one, she made eye contact with the others in the circle. "Why are y'all standin' around? Go soak up some history. I'll take Gina to her room. Believe I'll sit with her a spell and rest these old bones."

"Only thing I'm going to soak is my body in a bubble bath," Sherry said.

Megan and Brittany didn't have to be told twice to go. They were itching to explore. But before they could cut and run, Emily pulled her daughter aside. "Megan, I'll expect you back at the wagon for supper. Six-thirty, and don't be late."

"Mo...th...er!" the girl huffed indignantly. "Brittany and I planned to grab something at the rodeo. I wish you'd stop treating me like a kid."

"You've been fourteen for all of a month, Megan. I'll concede that you're not a *kid*-kid, but neither are you an adult. I'm willing to negotiate curfew. What time is the rodeo over?"

"Ten," the girl said sullenly. "But there's a dance later. Cripes, I'm going to be with Brittany, and she's nineteen."

"Yes…I know." Emily definitely wasn't reassured. After all, she'd witnessed Brittany's assault on Camp. His back was toward Emily, and he was chatting with the older girl. Emily couldn't gauge his reaction. For all she knew, things might have changed between those two. But no—she was replaying old tapes. Camp had handled Brittany with the utmost discretion. Anyway, Emily had no call to be jealous. Nolan Campbell had made it plain that all he wanted from her was friendship.

As if she wanted more from him. So why was she having such a hard time staying focused on this skirmish with Megan?

"Mom!" Megan's lower lip stuck out an inch. "Is it all right to eat at the rodeo with Brittany or not?"

Sensing Emily's eyes on him, Camp turned. He broke into a smile and started toward her, making her blush.

"L-let me check with Camp," she murmured. "Brittany and I are part of his project, remember. He may have specific tours he wants us to take for his study."

"Oh, brother. I knew this trip was going to be a drag." Megan kicked a loose stone. Brittany stood to one side cracking her gum.

"What's going to be a drag?" Camp strolled up, hands casually tucked into his pockets. "According to Brittany, you two ladies have a full day planned."

Megan slanted her mother an angry glance. "Tell that to my mom. She's treating me like I'm no older than Mark."

"No such thing. I'm not sure it's safe for the girls to walk alone at night that's all."

Head swiveling, Camp studied the tree-lined streets, alive in the aftermath of a parade. Families collected in groups, talking. Girl Scouts sold lemonade. Craft booths littered the wedge-shaped park. "Town seems pretty tame to me."

"Yes, but a rodeo and dance…" Emily wasn't ready to give in.

"Sounds like fun." Camp flashed a smile at the girls. "I heard two couples discussing the bands. The first half of tonight's dance is bluegrass music, followed by a local country band. Wouldn't you like to hear them, Emily? That way we can all walk back to the wagons together. Unless you plan to take a room at the hotel."

"No, I'm not…" Emily wasn't sure if he was asking her to go with him to the dance or just to meet afterward. Either way it solved her immediate problem. "Okay." She caved in because of the girls. "I don't know where the dance is being held, so I have no idea how to choose a place to meet. Do you?" she asked Camp.

"It's somewhere on the rodeo grounds. In a town this size, we're not talking Madison Square Garden. There's bound to be a main gate where we can meet."

The girls didn't look overjoyed, but they nodded. So they could be off and about their business, Camp thought with a grin. "Hey," he called, watching them exchange worried glances as if to say *Now what?* "There's probably a fee for the dance as well as the rodeo. You two have enough money?"

The girls shrugged, but when Emily began digging in her purse, Camp placed a restraining palm on her arm. He pulled out two twenties and passed one to each girl. "Have fun on me. Just know that I may pick your brains later for my paper."

Giggling, they stuffed the bills into their pockets and dashed off.

Emily rifled through her purse until she found a

twenty, and slapped it into Camp's hand. ",I can pay my children's way."

Camp tested the spark of annoyance he saw in Emily's eyes. "Out-of-pocket expenses should all have been listed on the sheet I mailed out. Maizie forgot to include the rodeo and the dance. I didn't intend there to be hidden costs, Emily."

"All right…if that's the only reason." She accepted the money back, zipped her purse and slung it over her shoulder. "I have to scoot if I'm going to make the one o'clock tour of historic sites. See you later." She took off like a deer in flight.

Camp scratched the back of his neck, then jogged to catch up. "Do you mind if I tag along? I don't mean to crowd you, but I planned on going."

"It's a free country." Her steps quickening, she continued toward the old building that housed the visitors' bureau, where Maizie said the tour started.

Thrown off by her cavalier response, Camp broke stride. Even with his longer legs, he didn't catch up easily. When he did, she ignored him. Darn it, he wanted to spend time with her. If he'd upset her over the money, he was genuinely sorry.

"You must be leading the monument tour," Emily said to a man holding a fistful of maps and brochures. "Am I early?"

He peeled off one of each for her, then did the same for Camp. "This explains the sites. It's a self-guided tour," he said, checking his watch. "Guess you're it for this hour." Snapping his cuff down again, he went back into the building.

Emily scanned the street in both directions. "Where are Doris and Vi?"

"We can give them a few minutes if you like. But considering the loose way this tour is run, they may have already gone."

"You're right." She took a deep breath. "I'm glad you decided to go, Camp. It's not as much fun seeing the sights alone."

"For a minute there, I wasn't sure I'd be welcome."

"I know, and I'm sorry. I was annoyed about your giving Megan that money. My in-laws throw cash at my kids as a way of making me look bad. It doesn't help matters that I have to watch every dime. I know you meant well, but..." A sigh shook her frame.

"I'm the one who's sorry, Emily. I should have asked your permission."

He looked so contrite that Emily felt bad for foisting her troubles on him. She definitely didn't want him thinking she'd make a habit of it. "Maybe this tour isn't even worthwhile. If you have things to do, I really can go on my own."

"I don't have any plans—other than picking up a coffee grinder. In fact, I was going to suggest we have lunch first. Then we'll be able to walk off the calories. Across the street is Hays House Restaurant. Maizie told me it was opened in 1847 by Seth Hays, a great-grandson of Daniel Boone. She said it's the oldest eating establishment west of the Mississippi."

Emily gazed at the old stone building. "I wonder if it's expensive?"

Camp opened his mouth to say it'd be his treat, then thought better of it and feigned interest in the brochure. "Might be worth the price to see the antiques. This says the building's been remodeled, but some original pieces still exist. Oh, maybe you don't like museums and such...." He remembered Greta's snide remarks and curbed his own enthusiasm.

"Are you kidding? I love them. And I love historic houses. Look, this says the fireplace has a hand-hewn mantel." She frowned slightly. "Surely they serve appetizers for people who don't want a full meal."

Camp let her work it out in her own mind. Eventually she smiled and stepped off the curb, preparing to cross the street. He took her arm, pleased that she'd decided to join him. But it went against the grain to have a woman he'd invited to lunch pay for her meal. On the other hand, Emily wore her pride very close to the skin and he didn't want to risk offending her again.

While they waited for seating, they wandered around, checking out the antiques. Even after the hostess showed them to a table, Emily spent more time examining the needlepoint fabric on the chairs than she did looking at the menu.

In Camp's opinion, the dinner salad she ended up ordering wasn't enough to keep a bird alive. As it turned out, his meal would feed three people. As they ate, they discussed a range of subjects. Everything from the tintypes on the walls to their job goals and aspirations. A little at a time, Camp cajoled Emily into tasting most of what was on his plate.

"It's none of my business," he said as the waiter cleared away the remains of his baked apple dessert, "but why haven't you moved if your in-laws make life so miserable? With your education and experience, I'd think you could get a job in almost any college or university."

She rearranged the salt and pepper shakers. "You mean, why don't I quit whining about Mona and Toby and take the advice I give students?"

"In a word, yes." Camp stirred a dollop of cream into his coffee.

Emily practically squeezed the life out of her tea bag. She took a sip, wondering how much to say. "To an outsider, I guess it seems an easy decision. I wish it was."

Camp watched her over the rim of his cup, troubled by her bleak expression. "I've gathered from what you and the kids have said that your lifestyle changed, went downhill, after your husband's death. The more I see of you, Emily, the clearer it is how you feel about their money."

She set her cup in the saucer, but still held it tight with both hands. "No matter how hard I try, the skeletons in my closet have a way of popping up."

"We all have them," he said dryly.

"Compared with you, I have enough to fill several walk-in closets."

Camp tried to imagine Emily-of-the-sunny-smile with some terrible blight on her record. Nothing came.

Surreptitiously, she studied his blank features. "Ha! I thought as much. Your life has been a bowl of cherries." Emily grimaced as she polished off her tea. "Don't ever get married, Campbell. When I took vows for better or worse, my life landed in the pits."

He signaled for the check. "The marriage wasn't a total failure. You have Mark and Megan."

"Which brings us to your original question. Why don't I take them and relocate?"

Camp slipped money into the folder. Emily passed him her portion. He let it lie there for a time, but in the end heaved a sigh and added it to the tip.

"My in-laws are the biggest wheels where we live," she said as they rose. "In retrospect it seems foolish, but

I never had reason to question where Dave's money came from. He called himself a developer and boasted about finding backers for casinos and posh resorts. I hadn't a clue how many times his parents bailed him out of get-rich-quick schemes. Often, it turns out, and after he died they tallied up the bill. The sum is staggering. It's like a sword hanging over my head. If I moved but missed a payment for any reason, they'd use it to force me back. I'm in a catch-22 situation unless I locate a job with a sizable salary increase."

"Did you cosign notes any of the times your husband borrowed money from his parents?"

"No. But they showed me a pile of canceled checks. They even paid the mortgage on our house."

"If you didn't sign anything, how can they collect from you?"

"I told you the Bentons virtually own the town. They have subsidiaries owning subsidiaries. Three-fourths of the businesses are in debt to them in some way. Believe me," she said bitterly, "I lie awake nights trying to figure out how to take the kids and disappear. But what lesson is that for the children? Even if I ran, there's still a matter of references. And I owe the college credit union on my car. There'd be no hiding."

"What if you consolidated your loans at your new site and paid everyone in your old town off?"

She rose, slinging her purse over her shoulder. "Banks don't exactly rush to lend money to a single mother, to say nothing of someone new in town. They're all good ideas, Camp, but I've examined this mess from every angle. Frankly, I don't see any way out."

He trailed her to the front door, then reached around her to hold it open. "I'd be surprised if Mona and Toby are on the up-and-up. People who'd treat family the way they treat you are bound to be all-round jerks. You want to make them sweat? Sic the IRS on them. Those boys don't owe allegiance to anyone."

Emily laughed. "Remind me never to get on your bad side. You play hardball."

"I really don't. Their hold over you and the town smells fishy. People with that kind of money and power usually cut corners someplace, or they pull a few shady deals."

"Toby was an only child of wealthy parents. He inherited big, plus he has a knack for making money. Mona's major problem is that she spoiled her only son to distraction and refuses to believe he could do anything wrong. Therefore it stands to reason she'd blame me for his excesses."

"I guess you loved him, huh?"

"Everyone loved Dave. He radiated charm. He could have had any woman he wanted. And did, if even half of what I heard later in our marriage was true. The thing I ask myself regularly is why he chose to marry. And why me? The girl he dated before me is a fashion model, and many of the ones who came after could have stepped off the covers of *Cosmo*."

"Don't put yourself down, Emily." Camp took her hand as they strolled down the street. "I suspect old Dave knew exactly what he had in a wife. Pretty, talented, loyal. A great mother to his kids. From the way you've described him, he fits the mold of a man who needed order in his chaotic life. Men like that have to present a picture of normalcy to the world. And they want a son to carry on his name."

"Are you sure your degree isn't in psychology?" Emily raised her eyebrows.

"History, and you know it. But all disciplines intertwine. History teaches that there are Daves in every culture and in every generation. And an equal number of Emilys who become ensnared. History definitely repeats itself. Don't ask me why."

"How did you know that was going to be my next question?"

"You're pretty easy to read, Em. Your face is an open book."

"Great! Gullible as a sheep, that's me." She tried to untangle their fingers, but he wouldn't let go.

Without making it an issue, Camp kept hold of her hand as they wandered from site to site. He dropped it once to peer in the smoked windows of the Last Chance Store, which according to a sign on the door had recently closed for good.

"I'd say chances ran out for the Last Chance," he quipped.

"It's a shame," Emily said. "According to the brochure it was the last trading post where pioneers could buy supplies until they reached Santa Fe. Look, they've built a supermarket on the corner. That's progress, I guess."

"At least the sign says the historical society has taken over the building."

She nodded. "Well, I guess there's only one more point on the tour."

"Lead on." Camp took her hand again, content to let her guide.

"It's a statue of the pioneer mother in Madonna Park." Crossing the street, they headed for a slab of carved gray marble set in a small triangle of grass. A young boy clung to the calico skirt of the woman in the statue. She cradled a babe in her arms.

Camp and Emily gazed without speaking at the careworn features on the lined face framed by a sunbonnet. Beneath her long dress the woman wore an unflattering pair of lace-up drover's boots that looked too large for her feet, and too masculine. Sadly, there was little softness about the so-called Madonna of the Trail.

"She looks old before her time," Emily whispered. "You can practically see the miles etched in her eyes."

"But determination in the set of her jaw, too." Camp said, backing away to take a picture with a small, disposable camera he pulled from his shirt pocket. He quickly snapped a second shot that included Emily. Her slender, jeans-clad figure beside the statue contrasted *then* and *now* more effectively than any words he might write in his paper.

Emily stuck out her tongue, stuck her thumbs in her ears and wiggled her fingers at him. "I hate having my picture taken. I hope it breaks your camera."

"I hope not. It would be a shame to miss recording something so poignant, don't you think? Even at that, my shots won't compare with Gina's."

"I'm going to stop and see her now. I'll tell her not to worry—that you're taking up the artistic slack—shall I?"

"Somehow I'm not sure hearing there's a camera in my hands will improve her morale."

Emily laughed. "You may be right. Gina is a do-it-myself person. Odd that she trusts Mark to help out."

"I get the distinct impression that, in her estimation, the world would do well without men. Perhaps she sees Mark as young enough to be trainable."

"What's the magic age beyond which a male becomes untrainable?" Emily asked in all seriousness.

Camp contemplated her through his eyelashes.

"Does anyone in education believe a person is ever too old to learn? Isn't learning and change exclusive of gender bias, Emily?" He gathered her hand in his again.

"That's idealistic, Camp. Not everyone *wants* to change."

"I'll agree that desire and ability depend on the individual. I assume you have a specific person in mind."

She glanced up sharply. "No. Well, yes...maybe. I know Dave was smart enough to make informed choices. He never did. I'd like to think Mark will. I wondered how long I'll have any influence."

She sounded so discouraged, Camp dropped her hand and slid an arm around her shoulders. "It doesn't sound as if Dave received any positive direction as a kid. I'd say your odds with Mark are significantly higher."

Emily reached up and threaded her fingers through Camp's. "Thanks for the vote of confidence. You're a nice man. I can't imagine why some woman didn't snap you up years ago."

"I, ah, came close to marrying once." It was on the tip of Camp's tongue to tell her about Greta, except he found the whole experience hard to talk about. He was spared by Mark and Jared, who ran up, each dangling a string of fish.

Mark had changed from his sag clothes. Both boys wore overalls without shirts, and straw hats that left them looking like Huck Finn.

Emily broke from Camp to walk a slow circle around her son. "Wow. Do I know you? What a difference. I'm impressed. Also with the fish. Now I don't have to worry about what to fix for dinner."

"Maizie said they're for breakfast," Jared explained. "My dad's gonna take Mark and me out for hamburgers tonight, Ms. Benton. Is that okay?"

Emily seemed taken aback. "I, well, that's fine. I'll fix something for myself."

Camp frowned. "I thought we'd eat in town, Emily, and then go on to the dance."

"'We'?" She stopped and raised a brow. "Oh. I assumed we were only going to meet afterward, to walk the girls home."

Camp tried unsuccessfully to hide the disappointment sweeping through him. The last thing he wanted to do was press her into a date if she was reluctant. But she seemed as unsure as he was, so he decided to try again. "I thought I'd asked you to go with me, Emily. If you don't like to dance we can just listen to the music."

"I like to dance. It's been a long time," she said, ducking her head to keep him from seeing her flushed cheeks.

"That's good." He battled a sudden urge to touch her face. To lift her chin so he could read those huge compelling eyes. "I want to dance with you, Em." He winced. "Unless you don't want to dance with me?"

"Of course I do," she retorted, then lowered her voice. "I shouldn't even have to tell you that. But if you want your ego stroked, you're barking up the wrong tree." She nervously clasped and unclasped her hands.

Camp caught both in one of his and let his gaze run slowly from the tip of her toes to the crown of her head. "Looks like the right tree to me," he murmured huskily.

Her breath escaped like a puff of steam. "I'm going by to check on Gina to tell her what we saw. Perhaps we should just meet at the dance."

He felt her withdrawing. "This is a date, Emily. Get used to the idea. I'll meet you in front of Gina's hotel two hours from now. That'll give us time for a leisurely dinner. I hope you aren't the type to stand a guy up." He winked at Jared and ruffled Mark's hair. "Don't wait up for your mom, sport. I intend to have the last dance."

As Camp strolled off, Mark grinned slyly at his mother.

Clearly flustered, Emily swallowed three retorts. Finally she gave up and shooed the boys on their way.

CHAPTER EIGHT

*"I think cowboys tamed the West. I don't believe what
Sherry said, that a cowboy's horse and six-gun were
more important than girls."*
        —From Brittany's data sheet, filled with praise for
cowboys

THE DANCE WAS in full swing by the time Camp and
Emily joined the line waiting to enter. At her insistence,
dinner had been casual—Coney Island-style hot dogs at
a Lions Club booth. They laughed with strangers over the
antics everyone went through to keep mustard, catsup
and sauerkraut from dripping onto their clothes. Emily
called a halt at one. She dabbed mustard off Camp's chin
after he ate his second right down to the paper.

He loved seeing the funny faces she made at his
pathetic attempts to clean the sticky condiments off his
mouth while they waited to get into the dance. The
playful banter contributed in part to the subtle difference
Camp detected in their relationship tonight. Was it
because he insisted they call their evening a date, or
because Emily had changed into a dress made of some
soft, pale-yellow material? Not frilly, yet it underlined
her womanliness, or so it seemed to Camp.

As soon as he paid the nominal entry fee and they

stepped inside the converted barn that'd been lit with lanterns and dressed up with hay bales and checkered tablecloths, he noticed a return of Emily's cool reserve.

A large area of the plank floor was packed with people doing circle dances to lively bluegrass tunes. Camp felt the beat of the music through the soles of his boots as he and Emily jostled around the perimeter of the dance floor.

"I don't see the girls." Emily paused frequently to rise on tiptoes and peer through a maze of cowboy hats.

Camp guided her with a warm hand flattened at the small of her back. "We've barely made it a fourth of the way around the building, Emily. At the hot-dog stand I heard someone say the younger crowd often gravitates to the loft, where they have pool tables and free soft drinks."

"Pool? Megan doesn't know the first thing about pool!"

"While we're this close to the stairs, we may as well have a look."

"I suppose," she said grudgingly. "But I'm sure it's a waste of time."

They'd no sooner cleared the top step than Camp heard Emily's sharp exhalation. Following the direction of her gaze, he saw Megan, pool cue in hand, give a saucy toss of her head and bend over the table. Judging by the roar of approval that went up from bystanders, Camp guessed that little Megan, who supposedly didn't know the first thing about pool, was creaming her partner. Craning his neck, Camp saw the girl's difficult, kitty-corner shot spin into an end pocket. Megan, too, looked different tonight. An old-fashioned crocheted hat crushed her auburn curls. A ribbed cotton crop top showed off her narrow waist.

Brittany spotted Camp and Emily. She leaned in front

of a tall cowboy, saying something to the cocky winner. As Megan turned slowly, remoteness replaced the animated smile that'd brightened her face a moment ago.

Breaking away from her pals, she stalked up to her mother. "I thought we agreed to meet at the end of the dance. You can't resist spying on me, can you?"

"Nothing of the sort," Emily denied. "I wanted to let you know we were here. Who are these people you're with? Why aren't you dancing?"

Megan cast a quick glance over her shoulder at a slim-hipped young man in cowboy garb, who'd finished racking the balls. "Come on, Meg," he called. "I hope you don't plan to run off with my ten bucks without giving me a chance to win it back."

"Megan, you're betting?" Emily gasped. "I forbid it. We don't have money for you to throw around foolishly. Whatever possessed you? What do you even know about this...this game?"

Megan blew a large turquoise bubble, let it pop and hauled the gum threads back into her mouth with her tongue. "Dad taught me years ago on Mona and Toby's table. I'm good," she boasted. "How do you think I get spending money? I'd be laughed out of my old crowd on the skimpy allowance you dole out."

Camp saw the color leave Emily's face. He felt her slender body begin to shake. Pulling her into the curve of his side, he panned the group huddled around the table. None looked like high rollers. If she just stepped back a minute, Emily would see they were all clear-eyed, clean-cut youngsters.

Megan's rudeness was another issue, and not one to be dealt with now. Not one that was really his problem....

"Take it easy on these guys, ace," Camp teased Megan

as he smoothed a hand up Emily's rigid back. "Your mom and I would hate to see you sucker some poor cowboy out of his rodeo entry fee. Isn't that right, Emily?"

Megan sniffed disdainfully. "I could."

Willing Emily to loosen up, Camp continued to massage her stiff neck. Lazily scoping out the players a second time, Camp let his eyes meet Brittany's. He couldn't tell if her smoldering anger was aimed at Emily or at him. At both of them for being together, he surmised. Too bad; she needed to get past that crush.

"Your mom and I are going down to see if we can convince the band to play some old-fogy music," Camp informed Megan casually. "We'll meet you and Brittany at the close of the dance. Oh, and Megan…if you want the guy in the black shirt to ask you to dance, don't take all his money."

The girl frowned for a moment, then tossed her head and laughed. "My dad had a big ego, too. He hated losing. 'Course, I usually let him win." The laughter died suddenly. Eyes overbright, she blinked them clear and swung gaily back to the table.

Camp sensed Emily gearing up to explode. He didn't know who she was maddest at, Megan or him, but he figured the fallout would enlarge the chasm between mother and daughter. He all but bullied Emily down the stairs.

"How dare you," she said in a furious whisper after he hauled her into a relatively vacant corner below the stairs. "That's my child up there betting. *Gambling.*" Cupping her elbows, Emily began to pace. "Now I find out her…her father taught her. Oh, God! And you…*you condoned it.* You and Dave. I suppose if she'd lost, you would've given her money the way

Mona and Toby do." Hugging her waist, she seemed almost ill.

"No." Camp tried to take her in his arms, but she shook him off. "This isn't Atlantic City, Emily. It's Council Grove, Kansas. These are penny-ante games to while away an evening. The stakes aren't high enough to send anyone to the poorhouse."

"You find it funny? I've seen Dave drop a thousand dollars in a few games of pool. He always thought the next game he'd win it back."

"It sounded to me like Megan saw through her dad. Couldn't you give her the benefit of the doubt? If they don't come down to dance in half an hour or so, I'll go put a stop to it and we'll leave. Megan's underage and Brittany's in my care for the duration of the trip."

Emily looked moderately relieved, but Camp still wasn't able to persuade her to dance. Her gaze strayed time and again to the stairway. Only after she saw the group of laughing young people trip lightly down the stairs did color return to her face.

Later, though, Megan and Brittany slipped outside with two boyish-looking cowboys. Emily fretted that they'd gone out to sneak drinks.

"It's possible," Camp said calmly. "Do you know for certain that Megan drinks?"

Near tears, Emily shook her head. "But then, I didn't know Dave taught her to play pool, either. He always had a glass of gin in his hand," Emily said as if that was a telling factor.

"They may just have gone out for air. Or maybe the guys smoke. Dance with me, Emily. If this was anyone's kid but yours, you'd advise her parents to loosen the reins, wouldn't you?"

She rubbed her temples. "I guess. Yes, I would. But until this past, awful year, I never believed I'd be sitting on the other side of the table."

Camp gathered her in his arms and waltzed her out on the floor. The bluegrass band had been replaced by a country group. For their first number, they played a love ballad. Though his back was to the door, Camp knew the minute Megan returned. Emily went pliant against his chest. Not that he minded. Her breasts were soft, and his chin nestled comfortably atop her silky hair. Her warm breath tickled his throat. They danced the next four numbers straight, occasionally passing one or other of the girls. Megan avoided eye contact. Brittany dealt them frost.

It took three rounds of slow dances before Emily felt the tension leave her body and began to enjoy herself. She tried to look at Megan as others must see her. As a pretty, popular girl. Megan danced with an easy grace that reminded Emily of herself before she'd married Dave. A jolting thought. And sad. They'd been happy once. The disintegration of their marriage came on gradually, starting with her first pregnancy. When morning sickness, expanding middle and swollen feet left her drained, Dave simply went places and partied without her. That Megan was born in winter only served to keep Emily and the baby more housebound. At the time she couldn't know that Dave was on a roller-coaster ride downhill.

"A dollar for your thoughts," Camp ventured, tilting her chin so he could smile into her suddenly distant eyes.

She gave a start. "A dollar? Talk about inflation."

"Well, you'd drifted so far away, a penny hardly seemed enough to entice you back. They've announced the last dance. Shall we brave it or do you want to sit it out?"

"The last dance? Already?"

Chuckling, Camp molded her close. "We've been dancing for an hour. I'm running out of steam, while you're like a kid gathering speed."

His remark coaxed a smile. "Tomorrow I'll pay for all my youthful ambitions. You'll be fresh as a daisy and I'll probably look like a hag. I'd just realized when you asked about my thoughts that I haven't danced like this since before Megan was born. More like before she was conceived," Emily laughed.

The thought of her making love with that bastard, even if he had been her husband, spoiled what remained of Camp's good mood. "Emily, are you telling me that a man who loved to party, drink and shoot high-stakes pool never took you out?"

Emily drew away the length of their arms. "I'm not lying. And I'm not angling for your sympathy. There—" she pointed stiffly "—I see the girls heading out the door. Let's go."

Camp twirled her back and folded her into an embrace. "You deserved better treatment, Em. The last thing I want to do is hurt you," he murmured in her ear. "I'm sorry. It galls me to imagine the way that selfish jerk must have hurt you."

The smell of Camp's aftershave and the feel of her cheek pressed to his taut muscles awakened a shiver of need in Emily that she hadn't experienced in a long time. "I think what bothered me most were the cruel remarks Toby and Mona made within my hearing— about things like our not sharing a bedroom after Mark was born. I couldn't bring myself to tell her that Dave had brought his best friend's wife into our bed while I was in the hospital. I found her makeup and a nightgown. I would've divorced him then if he hadn't told me Mona and Toby would see that he got custody of both kids. I had every reason to believe him. And I'd have walked over hot coals to keep that from happening."

Camp stopped dancing. He cradled Emily's face between his hands, and without breaking eye contact, he bent slowly and kissed her softly. At least, it started out soft. As her warmth seeped into his pores, his hands slid down her neck, over her shoulders and fanned across her back, which deepened the kiss. He held her so tightly he felt her lashes brush his cheek as her eyes drifted shut. Spinning out of control, Camp knew he wanted more than simple kisses from Emily Benton. He wasn't sure what made him finally lift his mouth from hers to take in air. It might have been a change in the beat of the music, or a subtle shift in the dancers. But when Camp looked up, he and Emily were standing alone under a blue spotlight. As he peered dazedly through a break in the crowd, his eyes connected with those of a shocked Megan Benton. Her lips were pressed so tight a white ring bled into a face red with anger. Near her stood a stunned Brittany.

His hands grew sticky with sweat where they'd slid to Emily's narrow waist. The instant he cleared his throat, her eyes popped open and she blinked several times, out of touch with her surroundings.

"What's the matter? Are you embarrassed?" she asked quickly.

"Not me. The girls."

She leaned out, still in the curve of his arms. One look at the unforgiving faces, and Emily groaned.

Camp's hold on her rib cage tightened. "We did nothing to be ashamed of, Emily. We're both single and certainly past the age of consent."

"You're right," she said firmly.

However, Camp noticed she wasted no time disengaging their limbs before she self-consciously straightened her blouse. Her cheeks were crimson.

"Their cowboys must have called it a night," he said crisply. "I don't feel we have to explain ourselves, do you, Emily?"

"No."

As it turned out, that was the last word any of them spoke on the long walk back to the wagons. The girls said nothing. It was a silence brimming with accusations and loathing and it spoke for them as they set a punishing pace.

Emily, head held high, marched three steps behind them and two ahead of Camp.

A charley horse in Camp's right calf irritated the hell out of him and kept him from catching up.

Thunder rumbled in the distance. Every now and then a flash of lightning cut through the black sky. There were no stars out, and the moon, which had been bright earlier, had gone into hiding. Camp tasted dampness in the air with each indrawn breath. Before now he'd given little thought to the summer storms that frequently rolled across the plains. In the eerie quiet, broken only by their rapid footfalls, he recalled an incident from a pioneer journal. A man's hat had blown off in a high wind. His horses had spooked, causing the entire wagon train to stampede. One wagon turned over, leaving a young mother and child dead.

Camp rubbed at the ache in his hip. It must be the mood he was in. Thunder didn't mean the storm would pass through the area.

With effort, Camp managed to close the gap between himself and Emily. "Robert probably double-checked the stock, but I think I'll have a look around. Maizie planned to visit friends in town. She may or may not be back yet."

Emily nodded. "Sherry and Gina are both staying in town. Mark's in charge of Gina's wagon. Brittany should take care of Sherry's—if it enters her mind. Since Megan's sleeping there tonight, I'll make sure everything's tied down."

"You'll be alone in your wagon?"

"I didn't say that to give you ideas," she hissed. "A kiss is not an invitation to share my bed."

"I never thought it was," he said gruffly. "The prospect of a storm is making everyone edgy. I was merely going to say that if you're as wide-awake as I am, maybe we could fix a pot of coffee and sit outside for a while."

"Herb tea would be nice. I need to unwind." She glanced at the sky. "We may get rained out. I wonder if the wagons leak."

"The original ones were waterproofed. I assume these are. Maizie has run the Oregon Trail with the same wagons. I'm sure it rained on those trips."

"She doesn't strike me as a woman who'd be deterred by little things like flood and famine."

"Flood? Did you have to say that? I figured our biggest worry would be lightning."

They laughed together, and both girls turned around to glare.

"All that over a kiss?" muttered Camp. "I thought kids who had three holes in each ear were unshockable."

"Megan's never seen me kiss any man before. I imagine it did come as a shock."

"Never? Really?" Camp caught her elbow and turned her toward him.

Emily hoped it was dark enough to hide the heat she felt spreading from her neck into her cheeks. "I explained that Dave and I were little more than strangers living under the same roof. Since his death, what with juggling a job, kids and the squabbles with my in-laws, I haven't had the energy to date."

Camp picked up her hand and kissed the palm. "I figured I'd have to fight my way through a crowd of men at your door."

They felt the first splat of rain on their connected hands before Emily broke free. "I know how many miles there are between your house and mine, Camp. Don't tease."

He shook off raindrops that seemed to fall faster, cursing his leg that had cramped up again. "I'm not teasing, Emily," he whispered, huffing to keep in step. "From the first minute I laid eyes on you, I felt…interest. I know you didn't then, but you have to agree it's there between us now. The last thing I want to do is rush you or scare you. So say the word and I'll back off."

They were nearing the copse of trees where the wagons waited. Emily hunched against the increasingly fierce rain. "Everything would be simpler if you *were* the chauvinist Sherry described," she said with a sigh. "To use kind of a dated term…."

She sounded so earnest Camp hated to laugh. It was just that he'd never thought of himself that way. He gave women colleagues as much credence as the men in his department. It wounded him to think Sherry would say such things to someone she'd only met at the start of this trip. So they didn't see eye to eye on everything. Camp had thought most of their bickering had been in jest. Sherry had to know he'd move heaven and earth to keep her safe—to keep every woman on this trip safe.

"I see I caught you off guard, Camp. I'm sorry. Sherry said something about sibling rivalry. Or maybe it was gender rivalry."

"Listen, Emily. If there's any rivalry, it's all on her part. I'm proud of Sherry's accomplishments. And I thought she was proud of mine. Obviously we're coming at this reenactment from different angles."

"Don't tell her I said anything. I'd hate to be the cause of some new feud."

"There isn't an old feud. Believe it or not, this trek was Sherry's brainstorm. She and I definitely need to talk. Enough said. Do you still feel like sharing a cup of coffee with me? Er…I mean, my coffee, your tea. While I'm checking the horses, you'll have time to change into jeans and grab your slicker."

"All right." Emily saw that Megan and Brittany had already climbed into Sherry's wagon and had lit a lantern. "After I have a word with the girls, I'll build a fire and put on a pot of water. I know Sherry has instant coffee. I'll borrow some while I'm there."

"Emily, I will build the fire and put the water on," he declared. "I don't want you to assume I brought it up so you'd fix my coffee."

"Have it your way. You won't catch me stepping on a man's toes when he's trying to prove a point."

Camp heaved a sigh as she scurried off. Obviously he *hadn't* gotten his point across. She still believed Sherry, or she'd never have made that parting comment. As he followed the gentle sway of her hips, Camp realized he wanted Emily to think well of him. Better than well, he admitted unabashedly.

He wandered among the restless horses, absently checking hobbles. A jagged bolt of lightning forked across the sky, illuminating the grassy slope where the animals grazed. Sweat broke out on Camp's upper lip. Damn, the storm was breaking fast. He wondered if the horses would be all right out here in the open. He stuck around for a few minutes, but when there were no new bursts of lightning he circled the herd one last time before heading back to the wagons. The smell of coffee wafted out on the wind, teasing his nostrils.

Feeling guilty for loitering after making such a big deal of building the fire and fixing the coffee himself, Camp veered off to wash his hands in the stream. It surprised him to see water lapping to the top of the bank. Earlier, when he'd collected water to shave, the current had flowed gently with barely a ripple. Now, unless he was way off base, the creek had risen considerably. In Maizie's absence, he needed to alert Robert.

Emily smiled as Camp charged out of the trees. "I was about to go looking for you. I wondered if a wild animal had carried you off." Fat raindrops hissed and spit as they hit her fire.

"The stream's climbed the bank by about six inches. I'm going to tell Robert."

"I'm surprised you didn't pass him on the trail. He and Maizie went to check. Maizie heard about the storm while she was visiting friends. She said if the rain doesn't let up by morning we'll have to cut short our stay in Council Grove. According to Robert she took plenty of flack about that."

"Tough. I'm sure we know who complained. Philly. Did Maizie say what problems we might face?"

"Not specifically. I gather she was concerned about the lowlands near Diamond Springs. Robert said it's pretty hard crossing the Arkansas River in a storm."

Camp squatted on his heels and accepted the cup Emily handed him. "I thought that's the reason they equipped our wagons with balloon tires instead of the standard wagon wheels. So we wouldn't bog down in wet weather."

"I don't know. They'll be back this way," she said, pouring water over her tea bag. "You can ask them then."

"Um." Camp blew on the liquid to cool it. He hoped they wouldn't come back too soon. If Maizie said to leave, they'd leave. But the rain wasn't too bad yet, and Camp wanted this time alone with Emily.

"You look uncomfortable. Here, I got out four lawn chairs, Camp. I couldn't find Sherry's instant coffee, so I brewed a pot. And I invited Maizie and Robert to stop by for a cup of tea or coffee."

"Um," Camp mumbled again.

He'd no sooner accepted a chair and sat than he saw Brittany jump from Sherry's wagon and head their way. "Our idea seems to be turning into a full-scale party," Camp muttered. "What do you suppose *she* wants?"

Emily crossed her legs. Mild curiosity appeared on her face as Brittany waltzed up and helped herself to a chair, wedging it between Emily and Camp.

"I smelled coffee over Megan's nail-polish remover. I always have a cup before I go to bed. It seemed stupid to build a fire just for me. I didn't figure you'd mind my horning in." She produced a cup from her jacket pocket and filled it to the brim.

Camp looked irritated, Emily merely amused.

"The rodeo was awesome," Brittany exclaimed, facing Camp. She deliberately presented her back to Emily as she regaled Camp with details of each event, barely pausing to take a breath and an occasional sip of her coffee.

Feeling ignored, Emily got up once and paced to the trail head and back, checking for Robert and Maizie.

Camp leaped up at the same time to stoke the fire. "Can't you send her to bed?" he implored Emily out of one side of his mouth.

"Me?" Emily darted a glance over her shoulder at Brittany's carefully composed face. The girl was the picture of innocence.

"Yes, you. After all, she's here at Megan's request. No doubt to act as chaperone."

"Yeah." Emily looked over at the wagon where Megan was reportedly doing her nails. She saw a dark head jerk out of sight. "I suspect that's exactly what's going on."

"Shall we try and outwait them?" he whispered.

"Hey, you two," Brittany grumbled. "No fair keeping secrets. Here, Camp, I brought you my data sheet." She pulled some crumpled papers out of her pocket. "And Sherry's. Oh, and she said to give you Gina's."

Emily bit her lip. "Darn, I didn't fill mine out. I'll go do that now."

Camp reached for her arm to tug her back, but it was too late. She'd set her cup on a log and sprinted for her wagon dashing between raindrops. Reluctantly, he gave the fire a last jab before returning to sit beside Brittany.

She refilled her cup, casually scooting her chair closer. "What kind of papers will I have to write for your fall class? I figured I'd get a head start. With your help," she added.

Camp choked, spewing his mouthful of coffee all over his jeans. In the classes Brittany had taken from him, she'd never once handed a paper in on time.

"I'm turning over a new leaf," she said sweetly, as if reading his mind.

"That's good." He plastered on his best professor's smile. "We'll be doing a unit on forts. There are several on this trip. I can't give you special tutoring, though, Brittany. It wouldn't be fair to other students in the class. The stuff you just told me about the rodeo might make a good English composition. You should go back to the wagon and jot everything down. Otherwise, you run the risk of forgetting."

"Yeah, right," she drawled. "You want me out of the way so you and Mrs. Benton can make out."

Camp was about to tell her in no uncertain terms that what he did and with whom was *his* business and nobody else's, but he'd no more than opened his mouth when Maizie and Robert clomped into the firelight bringing the smell of wet forest.

"Welcome to Grand Central Station," Camp muttered, his eyes tracing Emily's return from her wagon.

Oblivious, Emily passed him her data sheet. Her attention shifted to the mother and son who scraped layers of mud from the soles of their boots. "I scribbled my first impression of things we saw on the tour," she said absently. "I'll add more tomorrow if you need it."

"We'll be pulling out at first light," Maizie rasped. "The Neosho is rising and spilling into our creek. I'm gonna wake everybody now and give them the news. Robert's riding into town to tell those at the hotel. Take your coffee with you, son."

"What about Gina?" Emily asked. "Shouldn't she rest another day?"

"I wish she'd stay put, but as Robert said, we still have to drive her wagon to Santa Fe. All eight wagons are booked for the return trip. Mark can pick her up on our way through town in the morning. We won't drag her back here tonight."

"Mark isn't an experienced driver. Do you expect a lot of problems due to the weather?" Emily automatically moved closer to Camp.

He slid an arm around her waist. With his free hand, he filled cups for Maizie and Robert. Robert thanked him, waved backward as he slogged off through the puddles.

Maizie took a bracing sip before answering Emily. "I always expect problems with the weather. Sometimes I'm pleasantly surprised. Sometimes not. We're a whole lot better equipped than the pioneers. If we can't ford the Arkansas, well, at least we won't be fighting cutthroats and thieves. Thanks for the coffee, Campbell. Fill a Thermos or two. It's gonna be a long night."

Camp jerked the pot and slopped the coffee. "What do you mean, long night?"

"Hear that thunder gettin' louder?"

He acknowledged by dipping his chin.

"Well, till Robert makes it back, I'll need your help keeping those horses in line. Can you sing, boy? Cowboys sang ballads to quiet their stock during thunderstorms. I sound like a damn cat that's got his tail caught in a door."

"You're kidding, I hope," Camp flared. But even as the words fell from his lips, he saw that she wasn't.

"Wish I was. We'll be in a helluva fix if those horses stampede. How was I to know Philly wouldn't be worth a tinker's damn or that I'd have our group all split up when it decided to storm?"

Emily hovered on the balls of her feet. "I'll help ride herd, Maizie."

"You will? I appreciate that. With two of us riding in

opposite directions around the horses, that'll leave one to keep the coffee hot and the fire stoked. We'll trade off, one every half hour, until Robert returns."

Camp grasped Emily's wrist and swung her around. "You'll do no such thing. The middle of a potential stampede is no place for a woman."

The light of battle sparked in Emily's eyes. "What does that make Maizie?"

He gulped. "I…I'm sorry, Maizie. But you're an old hand at this."

"And you're Clint Eastwood?" Emily smirked, dander clearly rising.

"Emily, be reasonable."

"I am being reasonable. You're the one spewing testosterone. And for your information, I can even sing on key."

Maizie tipped her face to the rain and laughed. "Entertaining as this is, I gotta break it up. That last bolt of lightning hit yonder in those trees. Emily, you and I will take the first shift." Maizie grinned at Camp. "Give you time to cool down, sonny."

Taking Maizie at her word, Emily folded the extra chairs and tipped them up next to the wagon so the seats would stay dry.

Brittany dragged her chair closer to the fire. "Who cares if Emily wants to pretend she's Annie Oakley? I'll keep you company, Camp."

Maizie lifted Brittany out of her chair, one hand tucked firmly in the girl's armpit. "If you're gonna stay up, you can help ride herd. Four makes trading off easier."

At first Brittany acted as if she thought Maizie was joking. As soon as it became clear that she wasn't, Brittany pulled loose and flounced off.

Frustrated by Emily's stubbornness and the sudden

crash of thunder that shook the ground, Camp pushed his face into Maizie's. "There's nothing I can do to stop Emily. I won't, however, sit by the fire while you ladies risk your necks."

A gleam flashed in the older woman's eyes. "Then quit flappin' your gums and saddle up. The closer the riders, the less chance those big brutes'll bolt."

By morning, Camp was so cold, weary and saddle-sore that he hardly knew which end was up. It didn't help that the park floated in three inches of water where the stream had overflowed its banks.

Sometime during the long night, the heavy rain had put out Emily's fire. Between the thunder and the lightning, they'd had their hands too full keeping the teams clustered to even worry about the absence of coffee.

Emily tried to assist Harv, who was attempting to start a fire.

"Forget it," snapped Maizie. "We'll grab coffee in town."

Mark and Jared complained about having to forgo the catfish breakfast. By the time they hitched the horses, drove to town and picked up Gina, not even their slickers warded off the rain that washed down in torrents.

At noon the wagons were mired up to their hubcaps, and there wasn't a tree in sight to give travelers or horses any relief from the steady downpour. For lunch, Camp ate a cold hot dog, plain. He figured the bun would be soggy before it hit his mouth.

Tempers were so short that Maizie called a halt to the day's travel before they reached the Arkansas River. "We won't be able to cross anyway," she said in explanation.

"How do you expect us to start a campfire in this crap?" shouted Philly.

"I'll show you," Emily told him. "We all have tarps. Let's string a couple of them between two wagons."

Camp stood in awe of her spunk. Despite his tiredness, he did as she asked.

Everyone admired Emily's resourcefulness in using dry wood from her wagon to build a fire in the largest of her cast-iron pots. She soon had coffee perked and passed around. Then she proceeded to mix a huge batch of scrapple, which she cooked and served to everyone.

"I'm impressed, gal," Maizie said between bites of the leftover cornmeal mush seasoned with ham and onions. "I told Robert to hand out beef jerky. But it's nicer having something hot to warm the innards."

Others heaped praise on the cook. Yet no one except Camp offered to help her wash up after they'd cleaned their plates.

"Don't you have sense enough to go in out of the rain?" Emily yanked the stack of plates out of his hand and dumped them into a pan of hot water.

He smoothed a hand down her rain-wet cheek. "Not if it's the only opportunity I have to spend time alone with you."

Emily's stomach did a jig. A pocket of heat warmed her from the inside out as he bent down to join their cool lips. She didn't even notice that water dripped down their noses from the bills of their caps.

Neither was aware that the dishpan began to fill with rainwater. They strove to bond tighter as the kiss wore on. Megan's petulant voice finally drove them apart.

"Mother," she whined from the wagon, "Are you planning to stay out in the rain all night?"

Breathing hard, Emily clutched her slicker with one hand. She didn't know how or when it'd fallen open. Her eyes searched Camp's and found them dark and dangerous.

"It's pouring," she whispered. "What are we doing?"

"All that steam isn't coming from the dishpan, Emily. I'm not ready to go inside and leave you. Tell Megan to buzz off."

"I would, but if we stay out in this we'll catch pneumonia."

He could see that she felt as reluctant as he did to call a halt. It was enough for Camp. At least, for now. "Your mother'll be in once we finish the dishes," he called to Megan. "Unless you're volunteering to come out here and take my place."

As Camp expected, his challenge was met with silence. He managed to steal several more kisses from Emily before an awful deluge forced them to say good-night.

For the second night in a row, he didn't sleep. But this time the taste and scent of Emily Benton filled his head. He was getting in deep. Maybe too deep for someone who'd landed on the bad side of Emily's first-born pride and joy.

CHAPTER NINE

"It's been said that women had little to do at river crossings except knit. The men did all the dirty work."
—Something Sherry read in a non-fiction book she bought in town.

FOR FIVE DAYS the column wound slowly through waterlogged farmlands. Wagons got mired up to their hubcaps in muddy sinkholes. Regardless of age or gender, everyone scrambled through the muck to help unstick wagons. The single most important goal was to keep moving.

Brittany and Megan moaned, groaned and griped so vocally, they alienated people who might have been inclined to agree that the trip was no longer fun.

Camp, especially, felt like throttling the less-than-dynamic duo. It was as if in addition to complaining from dawn to dark, the two had appointed themselves watchdogs over him and Emily. The girls found ways to foil his carefully engineered plans to spend time alone with Emily, sabotaging his schemes almost before he set them in motion.

Emily merely chuckled. "I'm enjoying this immensely, Camp. Normally Megan does her best to ignore the fact that I exist."

Camp rolled an empty water barrel to the lip of Gina's wagon. "I'm glad you find their Hardy Boys surveillance techniques amusing."

"Nancy Drew," she said, breaching his wrath to help lift the barrel down.

"What?"

"A girl sleuth—not boys."

"Before this trip, I never realized it was so easy to step on toes in the battle of the sexes. Let go of that barrel. Even one end is too heavy for you." He bent and rolled it toward Terrill Boone's water wagon. Maizie's middle son hadn't had an easy time delivering fresh water to their stopover on the outskirts of Fort Larned. He'd also brought a vet this visit. Bad weather had taken its toll on the horses. The vet retired several of the big animals due to strained ligaments. Camp figured if he hauled many more of these oak barrels full of water, he'd have to be retired, too.

"Who keeps the battle of the sexes alive?" Emily asked. "Not women."

"An interesting observation. One I'd gladly explore more fully if we ever managed any time alone. We need to talk, Emily."

"About what? The fact that you're going to kill yourself with these barrels? Why don't you fix some sort of skid?" she suggested matter-of-factly. "I saw an old snow sled at an antique store in town this morning when some of us went to do laundry. Wouldn't its runners slip through the mud as well?"

"Might." Camp turned the idea over in his head. What he found even more appealing was the fact that he'd require Emily's help locating the store. "After I fill this barrel, maybe you could show me where you saw the sled."

"Sure." Her smile broke slowly. "I swear I can hear the wheels turn in your head, Campbell."

"Shh. Not so loud. The wind around here has ears."

"Ah…you plan to ditch our spies?"

"You've got it," he said. "Let's meet at the bridge that crosses the Pawnee fork."

She squinted at the sky, face hopeful. "The rain has finally let up. I wish we could visit the wagon ruts that are supposed to be near here."

"Your wish is my command. Sherry rented a car to take Gina, Doris and Vi to the fort. No reason we can't rent one, too. Terrill's laying over tonight. I'll fill barrels later. Let me wash off some of this sludge in case we want to eat in town."

"I look so scroungy no self-respecting café would let me in the door."

"No, you don't." He eased the barrel onto the filling rack, his gaze cruising slowly over her face and down her body. "You look grr-eat."

"Stop, you're making me self-conscious."

Smiling, he placed gloved hands on her shoulders. Intent on kissing her, he jumped a foot when Megan Benton leaped out from behind the truck.

"Mom," Megan cried, virtually yanking Emily right out from under Camp's nose. "I changed my mind about seeing the fort. Can we go now?"

Emily swept the hair from her eyes—while her feet remained firmly rooted. "This morning you stomped around and refused to talk about visiting the fort with Sherry. Now I have other plans, Megan."

"What plans?" The girl threw a mean look at Camp, who tried valiantly, behind Emily's back, to signal her silence. Without success, apparently.

"This morning," Emily said, "I discovered a sled in an antique store that I think will allow the men to haul water more easily. I was just about to show it to Camp."

"Well, no problemo, then." Megan snapped her fingers. "Brittany and I will go with you. We'll leave him at the store and go on to the fort. All right, Brit?"

At the sound of her name, the second girl appeared from behind the truck.

Camp busily filled the barrel. He felt Emily's beseeching eyes on his back, but he wasn't up to dealing with another of Megan's manipulative displays. "You ladies go on. Take in the sights. Robert and I can manhandle the rest of these."

Sorrow washed over Emily. Spending the afternoon with Camp had sounded exciting. Megan's sudden interest in the fort didn't fool Emily. Although—she sighed—the sole reason for making this trip had been to build a better rapport with her kids. "I'll go run a comb through my hair and grab my billfold," she said resignedly. "If you change your mind about the sled…" She turned to Camp. "The store is on Eighth."

He nodded, not trusting himself to speak. A longing glance in her direction revealed her looking back wistfully. Their eyes clung for several seconds. Breaking the contact, he encountered the smug coconspirators. It was all Camp could do not to vent his anger on them. Except that fighting with Megan wasn't the way to win Emily over. Camp forced himself to say generously, "Have a good time, kids."

"Absolutely!" Megan's tone hadn't dipped so much as an octave.

THEIR SECOND MORNING at Fort Larned brought clear blue skies and the return of a bloodred sun, giving the weary travelers a new lease on life. Dodge City was their next stop. Maizie promised a break that would extend over the Fourth of July weekend.

All day they trudged through fog curling damply off the saturated ground. Camp spent his time plotting to finagle time alone with Emily in Dodge. The very name, Dodge City, carried a certain romantic mystique for Old West aficionados. Camp thought surely Dodge—the so-called Cowboy Capital—would offer enough diversions to capture the interest of two impressionable girls. To say nothing of a huge fireworks display attached to the Fourth of July celebration.

If all of that failed, he could spirit Emily off to the old fort. The girls had complained at length about their boring visit to Fort Larned. Megan announced that if you'd seen one fort, you'd seen them all.

Camp was beginning to feel desperate.

The column of wagons was met on the outskirts of town by the mayor and hordes of curiosity seekers. For the first time Maizie did circle the wagons. She passed the word to unhitch and hobble the horses in the center, saying the mayor planned to present her with the key to Dodge City.

"This is perfect," Camp whispered to Emily. "After the hoopla, we'll slip away. No one will notice we're missing." *Please,* his eyes begged.

"You're sure?" Emily didn't sound convinced.

Camp didn't dream his own sister would scuttle his plans.

"Ladies," Sherry called, sidestepping city dignitaries as she rounded up Emily, Gina and the elementary-school teachers. "What do you say to renting a car again? There's a metal sculpture at the local college campus—*The Plainswoman.* From there we can visit the Kansas Teachers' Hall of Fame and then go on to the old fort."

Emily's despairing eyes sought Camp.

With a sinking feeling, he realized it'd be impossible to object to Sherry's agenda. Pioneer women *were* the focus of his study, after all. But he proved to be quick-witted. "Hey, sis, do you mind if I tag along?" He hoped he sounded casual.

Brittany barged in and jerked a thumb toward Sherry. "She invited Megan and me to go first. Unless you sit on someone's lap there won't be room."

Sherry Campbell stuck a finger in her ear and shook it as if something was wrong with her hearing. "Excuse me, Brittany. Five minutes ago you said in no uncertain terms that you and Megan wouldn't be caught dead traipsing around with a group of 'brainbuckets.'"

"We, uh, we talked about it, and agreed it'd be good research for school." She kept her eyes on Sherry, refusing to meet Camp's hard stare.

"I have an idea," he said, crossing his arms. "I'll rent a van. That way we can accommodate everyone. We'll get one with a lift for Gina's wheelchair."

Gina beamed. "Great idea. We had problems at Fort Larned. I told the boys I wasn't going today, and they've been moping around ever since."

Camp was careful to cover his glee at outsmarting girls who thought they couldn't be outsmarted. "Then it's settled. I'll meet you in front of the Santa Fe Railroad depot in half an hour." Whistling, he strode off before Brittany and Megan found a way to scuttle his plans to spend the day with Emily.

They all fitted nicely in the twelve-passenger minibus. Camp knew the girls were bent out of shape about the fact that he'd maneuvered things so Emily sat up front beside him. The others were so busy loading Gina's cameras that no one noticed Megan's and Brittany's pouts. Camp did, but he was through playing into their hands.

"Hey, ru-le," Mark bellowed as later Camp drove into the parking lot at the Teachers' Hall of Fame. "There's a gunfighters' wax museum next door. Can me and Jared go there while you visit the college and the fort? Look, we're right across from Boot Hill Museum. Okay if we bum around town and meet you for the fireworks?"

Since his plea was directed at Emily, Camp continued to search for a parking place. When he'd found a spot, Emily still hadn't answered her son. Both boys sat on the edge of their seats, waiting. Camp suspected she was worried about allowing kids that young to run loose in the crowded streets.

"Maybe Brittany and Megan would prefer to check out the gunfighters, too, and maybe poke around those old board-front stores at the museum village," Camp said lightly. "The mayor said there'll be gunfight reenactments and other entertainment all day." He worked to keep from sounding as if he had an ulterior motive.

Unwittingly Sherry aided his cause this time.

"You want them to ogle Miss Kitty and her cancan dancers? How educational can that be? Honestly, Nolan, it's just another amusement park."

Camp spread his hands. "You're right. They'll get more out of a visit to the fort than watching actors sensationalize legends that may or may not be true."

"To say nothing of missing a trip to the old wagon swales," Doris added.

"So what?" Mark whined. "Do me and Jared have to traipse out to dumb old ruts 'cause Brittany and Megan hafta act grown up?"

"If only this wasn't a holiday weekend," muttered Emily. "There're so many people in town…."

"If I didn't have this bum leg," Gina said flatly, "I'd go with the boys. I'd rather ride in a real stagecoach and learn to do the cancan," she said, surprising everyone. "The mayor's wife told me Miss Kitty's girls give free dance lessons."

Megan and Brittany exchanged pensive looks. "Free lessons?" Brittany ventured weakly. "What do you think, Megan?"

Camp sensed the girls wavering. Acting deliberately uninterested, he thrust open the driver's door. "Stay here and argue if you like. I'm going to see what's so great about Kansas teachers."

If nothing else, that tipped the scales for the girls. Immediately they clamored to go with Jared and Mark. "We're doing this so you won't worry, Mom," Megan told Emily.

Oh, sure, Camp thought. But he didn't let his reaction show.

"Yeah, Mrs. B.," Brittany chimed in. "It was a tough decision. Say, why don't you come with us? Then tomorrow we'll all go to the fort—like we did at Fort Larned."

"Brittany!" Megan shook her head.

Camp held his breath as he helped Vi climb down. He willed Emily to refuse the girls' suggestion.

"Uh, thanks for asking, Brittany. But you two hated

Fort Larned. And there are other forts along the trail. Go on, have a good time today. But I want everyone to meet inside Boot Hill Village at five. Do…do any of you need money?"

Camp knew better than to offer any this time. Heart soaring, he happily kept a low profile.

With the youngsters gone, the adults paired up to wander through the teaching museum. Sherry pushed Gina's wheelchair. Vi and Doris fell into step. That left Camp and Emily bringing up the rear. Any guilt he suffered for wishing the kids out of the way was lost in the joy of simply being in Emily's company. Even though they spoke little, they shared an occasional touch or a quick smile. By the time the group finished the tour, Camp and Emily had fallen into an easy camaraderie.

"I'm hungry," Gina announced after they'd left the sculpture and headed for the fort. "Hey, look there! A salad bar with a wheelchair ramp."

Sherry craned her neck to see. "Sounds good."

Vi clapped her hands. "It's next door to the steak house a friend suggested."

Emily screwed up her face. "I'm not very hungry. There's a frozen-yogurt place across the street with tables outside. Maybe I'll just enjoy the sun."

"That'd suit me." Camp rubbed his flat stomach. "Someone set a time to meet back here."

Emily jerked her gaze away from Camp's midsection.

Sherry checked her watch. "Steak will take longest to fix and eat. Will an hour and a half give everyone time enough? We passed an interesting clothes store down the block. Gina and I'll check it out after we eat. Do you want to go, too, Emily?"

Camp resigned himself to losing her. He hadn't met

a woman yet who'd pass up an opportunity to shop. She surprised him.

"There's nothing I need, and I don't want to be tempted. Maybe I'll talk Camp into visiting the Carnegie Center for the Arts."

"Fine with me," Camp put in. "Although I find it hard to believe Carnegie funded a center for the arts in a lawless cow town."

"The lawless era ended twenty years before Carnegie issued the grant," Doris chided.

Camp grinned. "I stand corrected."

Sherry rolled her eyes. "Some historian. We'll have to preview the paper he's writing. Emily, make sure you set him straight."

Camp dropped an arm around Emily's shoulders. "It's a tough job, but you picked the right lady. This one has a backbone of steel."

Laughing, Emily jabbed him in the ribs. When it failed to dislodge his arm, she gave up. "We'll see you all later. If we don't get moving, our free time will be gone." As they loped across the street, both missed the curious look Sherry aimed their way.

Instead of sitting in the sun with cups of yogurt, Camp and Emily got waffle cones and wandered the tree-shaded boulevards, stopping to read historical markers. Down the street a long drumroll sounded. Very soon a brass section struck up a patriotic tune. The music faded as they crossed to look at the Carnegie Center, and grew louder again once they'd cut across a cobblestone street to peek into the Ford County Courthouse, where so many outlaws had met their fate.

"Can't you almost feel the ghosts of all those old gunfighters?" Emily asked in hushed tones.

Camp swallowed the last of his sugar cone and grasped Emily's hand. "Kind of a shivery feeling? Like a breeze cooling your body, only there's no wind?"

She nodded, automatically seeking his warmth.

He smoothed a hand up and down her arm. "That's what I experienced the time my high-school history club visited Meramec Caverns outside of Sullivan, Missouri. Our adviser said the caverns had been a hideout for Jesse James. The first cave I looked at, I saw huddles of frightened slaves. They seemed so…real. It shook me. I didn't mention it until after the tour. Our guide admitted Union troops stored powder kilns there during the Civil War, and that the caves were part of the Underground Railroad. Jesse James really visited there only once, briefly." He paused. "Needless to say, for the rest of that trip, everyone avoided me."

"Oh, Camp. It must have frightened you."

"Yes. But my folks had a plausible explanation. Of course, they come from an intuitive Scots ancestry. Dad said strong souls from past eras reach out to the future so we can build on what they learned. It made sense to me."

"Ye-s," she said slowly, thoughtfully.

"You're not put off?"

"No. Should I be? I don't understand, though—with all that Scots blood, why weren't you cursed with red hair and freckles, Nolan Campbell?" Reaching up, she ruffled his dark hair.

He exhaled explosively, all but hearing Greta's snide comments. "Here I thought you were getting ready to say I had a screw loose. What's wrong with freckles, I'd like to know? *Yours* are nice."

"Ha! Kids didn't call you carrot top and measles face."

Camp studied her upturned face so long and hard, and with such hunger, it had Emily sucking in her breath.

The moment was lost as the band they'd heard earlier now rounded the corner. A brace of coronets, trumpets and slide trombones made the sidewalk vibrate. The musicians led a full-fledged parade flanked by a gaggle of followers.

Camp found himself irritated at a clown who darted up and made Emily laugh out loud by finding coins behind her ear. Or maybe it was the garish stalk of fake flowers that the guy pulled from his sleeve to give the "pretty lady."

With a delighted smile, she stood on tiptoe and kissed the clown's cheek, heedless of the white greasepaint. Jealous, he wanted to buy her a million real bouquets; even more than that, he wanted to be clever enough to drive her cares away. She should laugh more often.

Still smiling, Emily tapped her watch and shouted over the din that it was time to meet the others. In fact, they had to run.

Partway down the block, Emily dropped her paper flowers and tripped on them.

Camp caught her before she fell. He scooped up the colorful bouquet and held it away from her, demanding a kiss for its return as he jogged backward.

She danced around him, trying to grab her flowers. Convinced he wouldn't give them back until she complied with his zany request, she threw her arms around his neck and kissed him full on the mouth.

For a minute Camp's hand went limp and he nearly lost the flowers. In the nick of time, he clutched the stalk, awkwardly flattening it against the small of Emily's back as he claimed the kiss he'd craved all day.

Hard to say how long they would have remained locked in their embrace if a passing teen hadn't shrilled a wolf whistle.

Groaning, Camp released her slowly. And happened to glance over her shoulder into the dismayed faces of their companions, who'd gathered at the van.

Sherry appeared the most confused. "What was that about?"

More for Emily's sake than his own, Camp wagged the bouquet under the ladies' noses and explained that the amorous clown had led to his teasing kiss.

Emily snatched the flowers from his hand so quickly, Camp wasn't sure she appreciated his efforts on her behalf. But it was for her sake that he kept quiet about their relationship—if relationship it was. For one thing, he didn't want his sister giving her a hard time. And judging by the speed with which Sherry lay claim to the front seat, Camp knew he'd handled the explanation correctly.

"Where to now?" he asked briskly, as if Emily and Sherry hadn't clammed up.

"To the fort, Romeo," Gina sang out, making matters worse. "From there we'll visit the swales. It'll still be light enough for taking pictures."

The old fort sat between U.S. highway 154 and the Arkansas River. Its buildings, made from limestone, had been quarried north of the city. This time, as they piled out of the bus in the parking lot, Sherry hooked arms with Emily. "Come across the street with me to the cemetery. I heard Bat Masterson is buried there. You can help me find his headstone. Nolan, I trust you'll stick with Gina. The cemetery ground is too soggy for her wheelchair. She'd better stay on the walkways inside the fort."

Camp agreed. What else could he do? Still, he deeply resented the roadblocks his sister placed between him and Emily. He understood Megan's attitude, and even Brittany's, who had fancied herself in lust with him. But what was Sherry's problem? Racking his brain, he drew a blank.

However, once he resigned himself to not making waves, he got on well with Gina. She knew a lot about the history of Dodge City. Camp, Gina, Vi and Doris had nearly completed a circuit of the outbuildings by the time Emily and Sherry reappeared.

"All that trouble for nothing." Sherry sighed. "The cashier in the gift shop said it wasn't Bat Masterson buried here, but his brother who was once the marshal in Dodge."

"Why are you so interested? It's not as if we're related," Camp said jokingly.

"No. But as a kid you got all pumped up over moldy museums. I found gunslingers intriguing. Be still, my heart," she said with a laugh.

Camp snorted. "I guarantee if you ever met one of those tough hombres from the Old West, you'd run so fast smoke would roll from your boots."

"In your dreams, brother. I held my own in neighborhood brawls. I guess you've forgotten that I smacked Roy Keller in the teeth my senior year and walked home from the Sadie Hawkins dance."

"I remember. All because the poor joker ran out of gas."

"Well, he tried to take some squirrelly way home. His story sounded flaky to me. So I took off. It wasn't my fault he had to push his car for miles."

The women tittered over Sherry's escapade all the way to the van. Camp barely managed to herd everyone aboard. Their jovial mood lasted until they disembarked at the wheel ruts carved by the wagon trains that had passed through Fort Dodge.

There were no buildings to block the wind. They stepped into hip-deep prairie grass that undulated across the flat land like breakers on an incoming tide. Deep swales, six abreast, disappeared from the naked eye to a point where the purple horizon met a floating sea of grass. In the silence, Camp thought he heard babies crying. Or was it the tears of pioneer women torn from their families?

The minute his eyes met Emily's and he saw the sheen of tears, he knew she felt the connection, too. He put out a hand, and she slid hers into his larger palm. They stood like that, joined to each other and to the past by a thin thread of emotional understanding, until Gina cleared her throat and Sherry coughed, interrupting the moment. Camp struggled to reconnect with the here and now.

Powerful feelings lingered. No one spoke on the last leg of their journey. It was as if each person sat wrapped in his or her own cocoon. Camp dropped the women off at the entrance to Boot Hill Museum while he turned in the rental. He was sure Emily would stay in the van. But no, she let Sherry entice her out.

Dusk fought for possession of an orange sky as Camp hurried back on foot. He entered the museum village as electric lights winked in the stores lining the main street. Camp soon found the others. They'd stopped to listen to a variety of barkers hawking their wares.

Mark and Jared dashed up, apologizing for being late. Megan and Brittany arrived just as Emily was ready to send out a search party.

"Sorry," they breathed as one. "We had to see the end of the gunfight. Those guys die so cool," Megan explained.

"There you go." Camp nudged Sherry. "A chance to get yourself a gunslinger."

"I've got dibs on the one in the black hat," said Brittany. "In fact, we want his autograph. If you let us go back, we'll stake out a place to watch the fireworks in front of the Long Branch Saloon."

Mark tugged Camp's sleeve. "Have you guys seen the neat old steam engine parked at the north end of Main?"

Camp shook his head.

"It's the train that replaced the Conestogas on the Santa Fe Trail. Me and Jared climbed all over it. Mom, you oughta come look, too."

"Gina? Are you interested in seeing the train?" Emily turned.

"I'd rather the girls parked me outside the saloon. I'm running out of steam."

"The saloon serves sarsaparilla," Megan announced. "I'll get you one if you'd like." Everyone gaped at the girl who never volunteered to help with anything.

Sherry placed her hands on the handles of Gina's chair. "A drink would hit the spot. You kids take off. Maybe Gina and I will find out if the Long Branch serves something stronger than sarsaparilla. How about you, Emily?"

"I'll go with the boys. I'm hungry, and I smell corn dogs. Save me a place to watch the fireworks, all right?"

"Sure," Sherry agreed. "Are you ready for a cold beer, Nolan?"

"No," he said without hesitation. "Mark wants to show me the train." He walked off before Sherry could come up with another excuse to separate him and Emily.

The train engine truly was an old iron horse. The boys importantly demonstrated all they'd learned for the adults.

Emily and Camp were properly appreciative. They admired everything, then were ready to move on.

"Can we stay awhile?" Mark begged.

More easily convinced this time, Emily nevertheless extracted a promise to meet outside the Long Branch before the fireworks started.

She and Camp picked their way through the crush of people. "There's the vendor with the corn dogs." Camp took Emily's hand and pulled her along. "Or there's hot pocket sandwiches if you want something that'll stick to your ribs."

"Look." She slowed. "A booth selling baked potatoes. If I buy a potato and you get a hot pocket, we can trade bites."

Camp would have bought sushi, which he hated, to please her if she'd asked. He couldn't take his eyes off her as she stood in one line and he in the other. Afterward, totally immersed in each other, they wandered along the board walkway.

Camp stole kisses every chance he got. Or maybe they weren't stolen. After the first one, Emily rose to her toes, clasped his shirtfront and did a little kissing herself. During one such silly exchange they parted to find Sherry, Gina, Brittany and Megan bearing down on them.

"Oh, no," Camp groaned. "Not *again*."

"Where have you been?" demanded Megan. "Mark and Jared came back ten minutes ago. We lost our good spot for watching the fireworks 'cause we had to hunt for you."

Camp deposited the remains of their meals into the trash. "I can't speak for Emily, but I haven't lost my way since I was a kid."

"How fitting," Sherry murmured. "You're both acting like adolescents."

Gina wheeled to the front. "Love scrambles the sanest brains."

"Love?" The word erupted in chorus from three sets of pursed lips.

The only thing Camp noticed, however, was how quickly Emily denied any involvement. Out popped that reserved coolly private second side of her again.

Just then the crackle of rockets overhead kicked off the fireworks display. Funny, he hadn't exactly labeled what he felt for Emily. Camp did know she made him feel young again. And happy. And a little reckless—which made him wonder what, if anything, she felt for him. Suffocating smoke from the Roman candles falling around them—not to mention the presence of their companions—precluded his asking anything so intimate.

On the brisk walk back to the wagons after the finale, he and Emily were kept apart, constantly surrounded by others. He couldn't say with certainty whether this was by action or design.

Determined to have a word with her, he whispered a hurried invitation to meet outside his wagon for tea after everyone had gone to bed.

She nodded, seeming as anxious as he.

Restless, Camp set about brewing her favorite tea. He'd even drunk some of the nasty stuff by the time she showed up.

"Whew!" Short of breath, she accepted the steaming cup he handed her. "I haven't sneaked out of bed to meet a boy since eighth grade."

Camp was taken aback to think she ever had. Realizing he didn't know her at all, he decided it was time to bring whatever it was between them into some kind of perspective. "I'm not a boy, Emily. We're adults, you and I."

Sensing a subtle shift in his tone, she set her cup aside without a word. He did the same in time to catch her as she walked straight into his arms.

"It doesn't sit well with me to sneak around." Camp leaned back and framed her face with both hands.

Heart speeding, Emily murmured agreement as she stretched up to capture his lips.

She sighed when Camp slipped open a button on her blouse and rubbed a knuckle over the aching swell of her breasts.

Needing desperately to feel his flesh, too, Emily tore a button off his shirt, in her haste. She had barely reached her goal of touching his skin when a series of small pops culminating in a loud explosion shattered their treasured interlude.

"What the—" Camp released her abruptly as a horse screamed in fright and lanterns winked on in nearly every wagon.

"Firecrackers," Emily gasped hoarsely as another series of loud pops sent two of the mighty Belgians plunging against their flimsy ropes.

"Damn those boys." Camp fumbled at his shirt. "I'll wring their necks."

"If I don't beat you to it." Emily tidied her blouse as she ran toward the tent Jared and Mark had erected near Gina's wagon. Seconds later she backed from the enclosure shaking her head. "They're both still sleeping like the dead."

"Then who?" Camp frowned.

The who really didn't matter. Robert Boone hollered for Camp to help corral two horses that'd managed to break loose. The chore ended up taking Robert, Terrill, Camp, Emily and Sherry all night.

Near dawn, the crisis was controlled. The gritty-eyed men and women dragged back into the wagons, only to have Maizie greet them with a troubling announcement.

"I've called a meeting," she said sternly. "It's time we talked straight about responsibility to one another. And we need to take a hard look at our route."

CHAPTER TEN

The wagon master's word was law on the trail. He ruled with an iron fist. His way or they parted ways.
> —From one of Camp's reference books.
> (All his sources assumed that, without exception, wagon-train bosses were men.)

MAIZIE SAT ATOP her wagon seat and gathered everyone around. "Serious mischief afoot last night. We're lucky a horse didn't break a leg."

"We know who done the deed," shouted Philly. "Them brats. Make their parents pay. Teach 'em the consequences of having the little buggers."

Camp was supremely glad to hear that Philly and his wife hadn't spawned any more of their kind.

Mark, his face pale in the cloudy light, stepped closer to his mother. "Me 'n' Jared didn't set off any firecrackers," he insisted, even though his voice quavered.

Jared concurred in a stronger voice.

Emily brushed at the cowlick that set Mark's hair awry. "He's telling the truth. Camp and I were up having…tea," she said, stumbling over the partial lie. "The boys slept through the whole thing."

"Ha!" yelled Philly. "I'll bet they were playing possum."

"My son doesn't lie." Robert Boone loomed over the other man, his hamlike fists knotted. "It could have been kids from town."

Maizie stuck a thumb and little finger between her teeth, emitting a deafening whistle. "Those who did it know." Her gaze drifted to where Brittany and Megan huddled against Sherry's wagon, faces pinched.

Camp saw the girls turn several shades grayer. He wondered why he hadn't thought of them sooner. Setting off fireworks at that strategic time was obviously another attempt to drive Emily and him apart.

All heads turned to follow Maizie's faintly accusing stare. It wasn't hard to tell from the girls' guilty expressions who the culprits were.

"In my day girls played piano and crocheted things for church bazaars. We didn't run the streets causing trouble," lectured Philly's wife. "Those two should be punished."

"Make them groom the horses for a week, and scrub a few pots and pans," shouted her husband. "It'd kill 'em to get their hands dirty."

Camp listened to the undercurrent of remarks, expecting Maizie to call a halt. When she didn't, he did. "Setting firecrackers isn't a capital offense, folks. I'm sure they're sorry." Although from their mutinous expressions, Camp wasn't sure at all.

"Nolan's right." Sherry insinuated herself between Harv Shaw and the girls. "We've risen above making outcasts wear scarlet letters. It's over. Let's get on with business. Maizie, you said you wanted to discuss our route. Is there some problem?"

"Before we do that," Emily said, holding up a hand. "If my daughter set off those cherry bombs, she *will* suffer the consequences."

Maizie crushed the rumble of voices. "Then that's that." She jumped down and unfolded a large map, which she pinned to the wagon canvas. "The long-term weather forecast is for a series of storms rolling up across Texas from the gulf. They may peter out. They may not. It's raining buckets in the Oklahoma panhandle right now—heading our way. Rain here means snow over Raton Pass. Do we take the longer northern route, or the shorter Cimarron cutoff?"

"The Cimarron route has more creek and river crossings," Robert said. "If they're swollen that'll slow us down. We could spend days waiting for the rivers to drop."

Maizie broke off a piece of tobacco and started to put it in her mouth. Then, catching Camp's eye, she tossed it into the fire, unwrapping two sticks of gum, instead. "In bad weather neither route's a clambake. Personally, I'd rather dry a wagon out than lose it over the edge of a thousand-foot precipice because the tires slipped on ice."

"Speaking as someone responsible for women, kids and four wagons," Camp said, his voice quiet but firm, "I vote for the cutoff. We know we can make it through ankle-deep mud."

Sherry strutted into the circle. "You think we women are afraid of a little snow, Nolan? If the pioneers scaled the pass, so will we."

Camp refused to be provoked. "From accounts I've read, both routes were used equally by the pioneers. Wagon trains suffered loss from outlaw and Indian attacks on the cutoff. But more people died in treacherous snowstorms on the mountain trail."

"Will taking the cutoff be cheating?" Emily calmly injected a note of reason. "I'm talking about your article now." She took a deep breath. "What bearing will changing routes have on your work?"

Brittany shoved her way through the huddle. "Don't listen to her. She's looking for more time to make out with him." She jerked a thumb at Camp. "Ask him what those two were really doing when those firecrackers went off."

"Why can't we just go home?" Megan delivered dirty looks at Camp and Emily.

Mark Benton's eyes popped. "You mean Mom and Camp—hey, ru-le." The boy gazed adoringly up at Camp. "All right!"

Sherry gaped as if Emily had suddenly turned into a two-headed snake.

Emily's cheeks reddened. Neither she nor Camp confirmed or denied anything.

Maizie snapped her fingers to gain attention. "Pioneers faced floods and cyclones along the Cimarron. If you're dying for adventure, there'll be plenty. Either way, this train is going on to Santa Fe."

"And we don't have all day to decide." Robert stroked his unshaven jaw. "Guess I'll stand with Camp on this one."

Doris and Vi quickly sided with the two men.

"We were promised a trip over Raton Pass, and by the devil, I want what I paid for," Philly insisted.

Terrill Boone, who had rounded up the lame horses to drive home, announced that he was leaving. "Why not review the weather at Caches? That's where the trail splits," he said for the benefit of those who didn't know.

"I need a consensus now," Maizie said stubbornly. "I don't want to wait until we hit bad weather, then have to make snap decisions. Take a look at the sky off to the south. We're in for a squall." As if to prove her point, a black cloud obliterated the horizon and began to spit rain. "Well, what'll it be?" she pressed.

Gina hobbled forward on her crutches. "I'd hate for anyone to have to haul my bag of bones up nearly eight thousand feet over Raton Pass."

Philly's wife urged him to reconsider voting for the shorter route.

"You're all a bunch of wimps," he snarled. "I'm calling the Better Business Bureau the minute me and the missus get home. None of our friends'll fork out dough for this rip-off trip," he said, climbing into his wagon.

"News to me that he has friends," Emily muttered.

Camp cornered Maizie. "If we decide on the cutoff, will that allow us some extra time here? Some of us need sleep. And I'd planned on hitting the laundromat this morning. This is my last pair of jeans." He pointed to the mud-caked denims he wore.

"Depends on what the rain does to the river. I'll give you as much time as I can. Long as you agree to take your clothes wet and leave without question if I say so." She let her gaze touch each individual. "That means no aimless wandering around town. I don't want to chase in ten directions if the Arkansas starts to rise."

"I missed doing laundry in Fort Larned," Sherry said. "But I'm beat, too."

"Throw your clothes in with mine. I'll do them," Camp offered.

"Not on your life, big bro. You'd love a tidbit like that for your paper."

"Must every issue be confrontational, Sherilyn? What sense is there in both of us sitting around a laundromat?" Seconds slipped by and she didn't answer. "In that case—" he grinned "—how much'll you charge to do my washing?"

"You don't have enough money. Not even if you throw in your trust fund from Gramps. I believe in total equality between the sexes. When I get married—I'll do my laundry and my husband will do his. Put that in your old report."

"All I can say is get it in writing, Sherry, *before* the ceremony," Gina shouted.

Camp reached into his wagon and hauled out two duffel bags of dirty clothes. "You forget how well I know you, sis. I have never in my life dry-cleaned my jeans, while you—"

"I do that so they'll stay new longer. So there."

"Enough." Maizie held up her hand. "Quit bickering, you two. Time's wasting."

Camp backed off. Later, at the laundromat, he filled a third of the washing machines and sat by himself, while Sherry and Gina talked quietly in a corner. Between cycles, he daydreamed about Emily. Why were so many people conspiring against them? Megan probably felt threatened. With one in three marriages splitting up, kids discussed the trauma of bad experiences with their peers. And around the college, he'd heard all manner of stories dealing with wicked stepmothers and equally wicked stepfathers.

Sherry's attitude puzzled him. They'd had a stable home, where affection was openly shown. Their parents were still deeply in love. He'd entered graduate school the year Sherry started high school. Camp recalled a flock of boys hanging out at the house on weekends. These days, of course, they moved in different circles at work. To his knowledge there hadn't been anyone serious in Sherry's life during the last few years—although he tried not to listen to scuttlebutt on who dated whom. The rumor mill in that place could be vicious, he'd had a taste of it after Greta threw him over.

"We're leaving," Sherry trilled near his ear, causing Camp's eyelids to fly open. "I fed your dryers with my leftover dimes. It'll cost you a king's ransom to dry eight pairs of jeans. Don't fall asleep and let them lock you in here. On the door it says they close at noon on Sundays."

He stifled a yawn. "If I don't put in an appearance in the next hour—or as long as it takes to use another roll of dimes—will you send the dog with the brandy?"

"I'll send Maizie. Brr," Sherry said as she maneuvered Gina's wheelchair out the door. "That rain's flat-out comin' down."

Forty minutes later, Camp's clothes were dried, folded and stuffed back into the two duffel bags. He was soaked again by the time he'd gone two blocks—as were his canvas bags and most of their contents. Compared with the previous day, the streets of Dodge were near deserted.

Not so the wagon circle. It was a beehive. "What's up?" Camp cornered Jared, who led two of the spirited new Percherons toward the wagons.

"Maizie's got it in her head to ford the river ASAP. Some old geezer she talked to said the level's risen six inches in two hours."

"Well, there goes my nap," Camp grumbled.

"You're right about that. Don't even talk to my dad. Gram woke him up and he's growling like a bear who got rousted out of hibernation." A horse snorted and danced around Jared, tangling the lead line.

"The Perches are going to be hard to control," Camp

noted. "Why don't you split them up? Maybe the Clydesdales will calm them down."

Jared untangled the ropes. "I was going to give 'em as they are to ol' Philadelphia." A twinkle shone in the youth's normally placid eyes.

Camp looked away, over Jared's head. "Can't fault your reasoning. But who has to make sure everyone crosses the river safely?"

"Hadn't thought of that. S'pose I'd better give one to you and the other to Dad then."

As he nodded absently, Camp's gaze lit on Emily. Coatless, hatless, she flew across the field toward him. His lungs cinched so tight it hurt to breathe. Darn, he wished Jared would take those horses and go. The kind of welcome he had in mind could use a little privacy.

Emily skidded to a stop in front of him. It wasn't joy Camp saw in her eyes, but dark waves of worry.

"Camp, I'm so glad you're back! Maizie says we have to leave, but I can't find Megan anywhere."

Camp dropped his duffels and swept a glance over the wagons, as if expecting Megan to materialize out of thin air. He took a mental count of the saddle horses and felt better noting they were all there.

"You've checked everywhere?"

"Yes." She clasped her hands nervously. "I thought maybe you saw her walking into town. According to Brittany, Megan said she wasn't going one step farther."

"That's hotheadedness talking. Who does she know in Dodge? Nobody, right?"

Emily shrugged, looking miserable.

"You're soaked to the skin," Camp said softly. "Find a jacket. I'll toss my bags in the wagon and meet you back at Maizie's. We'll have her call a meeting. People may know more than they've let on."

"You mean Brittany?"

"Or someone who might not have realized that she was doing anything out of the ordinary."

"Oh, Lord, I hope so. It's such a helpless, awful feeling."

Minutes later, a sour-faced Maizie clanged the bell, calling everyone together.

"That river's rising higher by the second. If anyone's seen that girl today, spit out when and where. If we don't cross the Arkansas within the hour, we don't cross. So if you're covering for her out of loyalty—don't." The wagon mistress pinned Brittany, then Mark and Jared, with a steely look.

"I told you what I know," exclaimed Brittany. "She said she wasn't pushing wagons through the mud ever again."

Mark, eyes big in his face, simply shook his head.

Philly hitched his belt over a protruding belly. "The brat probably stowed away on Terrill's wagon. Everybody knew he was heading home."

Emily ran up just then. "Megan didn't take any clothes that I could tell. But she rooted through my purse and has my phone card. And she has Mona's credit card number."

"Credit card info, but no clothes. Hmm. Maybe she figures on taking a bus or train," Camp said, sliding a thumb over the itchy stubble on his jaw. "Maizie, you and Robert start the wagons rolling. Emily and I'll swing by the depots. If we don't turn something up, I'll let Jared handle my wagon and I'll ride after Terrill."

"Camp, you're dead on your feet," Emily protested. "She's my daughter. If anyone rides after her it should be me."

Camp shook his head. "We'll talk about that if the need arises."

Maizie added more gum to the wad already in her mouth. "I don't like splitting a tour group. 'Specially not with a flooding river between. I hope you find the sassy little miss. And when you do, I'm gonna give her what for."

Emily's sigh could be heard over the clattering rain. She and Camp gratefully donned slickers that Sherry produced.

"Don't be too hard on her when you find her," Sherry murmured. "According to Brittany, Megan was smarting from Philly's drubbing. I gather the firecracker incident scared the girls as much as it did the horses."

"Pray we find her, Sherry. I know Megan talks big and she tries to act tough. But she's lived in a small town her whole life." Emily's voice cracked.

Camp touched Emily's arm, indicating they needed to go. He heard the splash of the lead team being forced into the swollen stream as they set off down the trail.

Outside the bus depot, near a bank of phones, the two of them sighted their quarry at the same time. Megan's auburn hair clung wetly to her neck. She was hunched under a dripping overhang, looking cold and slightly dazed.

Camp couldn't be sure from this distance if that was rain or tears tracking down her cheeks and dripping off her chin. In case it was tears, he put out a hand to caution Emily. "Let's hear her side of this before we pounce."

Emily indicated that she understood, but her steps quickened. "Megan, honey..."

The girl covered her face with her hands and began to sob—sad, gulping sobs. She didn't, however, object when her mother gathered her close.

Camp, never comfortable with women's tears, stood back feeling powerless. He didn't know how much time had elapsed before he made sense of Megan's words through her hiccups.

"I—I thought Mona would c-come for me," she cried into Emily's shoulder. "But she has an appointment in St. Louis tomorrow at the spa. She—she said I should find my own way home. Toby's busy, too. Tomorrow's his poker night. He said he'd wire me money. That's their answer to everything."

Emily could have told Megan that—had tried to in a hundred ways or more. Maybe she'd been wrong not to strip the kids' blinders off after Dave's crash. She hated hearing her daughter's heartbreak.

Camp didn't want to interrupt, but the rain was falling harder. "Emily, I know you two have a lot to discuss. Can it wait? If we don't leave now, I'm afraid the river'll be too high to ford."

Megan scrubbed at her eyes. "What's he doing here? Mark thinks he's so great, but I want him to leave us…leave…*you* alone." She wailed the last.

A couple walking down the street turned to look, and hesitated as if considering whether or not to intervene.

Camp broke from his frown to give them what he hoped was a reassuring smile. As they seemed inclined to linger, he whipped off his yellow raincoat, threw it over Megan's shoulders and hustled both women back to the park.

Maizie alone paced the clearing. One wagon remained on this side of the Arkansas. It was Camp's.

"You three are a sight for sore eyes," Maizie rasped. "We got no time for palavering. The river's running fast and she's running high. Robert had his hands full crossing Emily's wagon. River carried him downstream to where the bank was almost too slick for the horses to climb out."

"Well, what are we waiting for?" asked Camp. He boosted Emily and Megan into the back of his wagon and motioned for Maizie to join him on the seat.

Camp fought to keep the horses lined up with the tire tracks emerging on the far side. His jaw and his muscles ached by the time he pulled to a stop next to his sister.

Sherry let out a whoop on seeing Megan huddled between them.

If Camp thought Maizie would let them rest once they cleared the difficult crossing, he'd called it wrong.

"Snap to it," she said, gritting her teeth as she jumped down into the mud. "I want to see everybody driving his or her own wagon. This ain't the only river that'll be over its banks today. I know some of you haven't slept in twenty-four hours. I can't promise it won't be twenty-four more. I never claimed to be able to control the weather. What you see is what you get. Let's roll 'em."

Camp wanted a word with Emily. But that wasn't to be. She handed his slicker back with the barest whisper of thanks and climbed aboard her own wagon. He noticed Megan slunk into her mom's wagon bed, looking neither right or left.

Next thing Camp knew, Emily had pulled in front of Sherry.

As if the day hadn't started out rotten enough, the clouds sat down even lower and rain lashed them with all the fury of hell. Midafternoon, instead of allowing a break, Maizie handed out small bags of dried fruit. There'd be no hot meal, not today.

Rain poured without letup. If they made two miles today, it'd surprise Camp. The flat prairie offered no shelter, and the day turned into one round after another of stuck wagons. He'd never dreamed that a reenactment could be this realistic.

When Maizie finally consented to calling a halt that evening, not even Emily could coax a fire to start. Everyone fell into bed, too tired to even gnaw at the beef jerky Robert Boone said they needed to eat for energy.

Camp slept like the dead.

Morning produced a break in the rain, but no slack in the schedule. Maizie whipped them in gear after insisting they eat bread and jam for breakfast.

Noonish, a pale sun came out. Hordes of mosquitoes descended on the spot Maizie referred to as Middle Crossings. There, drivers toiled to ford an engorged Cimarron River.

Under the wet cottonwoods on the opposite bank, the humidity rose even higher. And tempers rose right along with it—as the first wagons to cross had to wait for the others.

Megan Benton, who'd spent the morning riding with Sherry and Brittany, cried over ugly red lumps that itched and marred her pretty face. Camp and Robert took the brunt of the girl's griping as they strained to dislodge Sherry's wagon from a sinkhole in the center of a swift-running river. "I want to go home," she cried.

Brittany and Megan clung to each other. "I hate you, Nolan Campbell," Brittany sniffled. "If the pioneers did this voluntarily, they were nuts."

Camp and Robert ignored her comments and put shoulders to the wheels. The minute they got the wagon ashore, Megan ran to Emily. Camp suspected it was because the girl didn't want anyone to see how the bites had left her face splotched and swollen. At the moment, he had more to worry about than mosquitoes. Several wagons had shipped water during the crossing. Maizie consented to an early stop in order to dry things out. It wasn't just clothing that'd gotten wet. Doris and Vi lost all their oatmeal. Sherry's flour was ruined, as was Gina's sugar.

Philly had insisted on fording the swollen river without help. He nearly capsized his wagon and wasn't half so belligerent when he caught up to the others.

The heat remained unbearable. Steam rose from everything.

Maizie gathered the disgruntled group for a pep talk, pointing ahead to a desolate, barren plateau. "It's gonna be hotter than a pig fry tonight. I recommend tearin' off some cottonwood branches here. They'll dry fast. You can throw your sleeping bags on top of 'em and sleep under your wagons tonight. Wet canvas blocks the wind—not that there'll be any. Inside, the wagons'll be virtual bake ovens."

"What about critters and creepy crawlies?" Brittany inquired in a small voice. "Jared said he saw coyote tracks along the river."

Emily put a hand on Brittany's shoulder. "Animals like coyotes, badgers and racoons are more afraid of humans than we are of them."

"A lot you know," sulked Megan.

Camp smiled at Emily to bolster her spirits. She'd come through this rough stage of the trip without one complaint. "Listen to Emily," Camp urged the girls. "And while you're at it, take some lessons. She has her fire started and black-bean soup cooking. Smoke drives off mosquitoes, too." He glanced pointedly at Megan.

"Yippy skippy." She twirled a finger in the air, stuck out her tongue at Camp, then ran off toward a steamy field of flowering weeds.

Emily exchanged a worried glance with Camp. It was the first time she'd looked directly at him in two days. He took advantage of the crack in her resistance. "Give her time, Em. When she starts to sweat, she'll see the wisdom of bedding down under the wagon. Mmm. That bean soup smells tasty. I swear I don't know how mountain men survived on beef jerky."

"Are you angling for dinner?" she asked, tilting her head like the Emily of old.

"I sure wouldn't turn it down," he drawled.

"Stop by with your bowl in about an hour. I'm offering to feed everyone tonight."

His smile froze. Well, if that didn't put him in his place, Camp didn't know what did. Maybe she'd be more amenable if he won Megan over first. He angled toward the field, hoping for a chance to discuss how he felt about Emily.

A few yards into the meadow, Megan ran screaming toward him. Swooping behind her was a black swarm of bees.

Camp grabbed her, zigzagging past the swarm and going in the opposite direction. He set her on her feet a safe distance away. She didn't even thank him.

"Megan, I wish..." He grappled for words to alleviate the strain between them. But she sailed off, refusing to listen.

At wit's end, during dinner Camp asked Emily to collect the data sheets. He figured she'd bring them by his wagon and he could convince her to stay for tea or something. No such luck. Emily collected the sheets and sent Mark to deliver them.

"You and my mom have a fight?" Mark asked Camp bluntly.

"No. Mark, I like your mother a lot. A whole lot, for that matter. And you kids, too. When this is over, I'd like for us all to get together more."

"Ru-le." Mark's teeth glistened white in the firelight.

"Tell me, Mark. Is Megan afraid I'm trying to take your dad's place?"

Mark's freckles stood out in stark relief. "Mona and Toby have her brainwashed. My dad..."

"Yes?" Camp prompted after a moment of silence.

"He...he was my dad and all—but he wasn't very nice to Mom."

Camp put out a hand, then pulled it back and rubbed his forehead. "Son, it's okay to love someone and not like the way he acts or some of the things he does. I know it sounds weird, but give it time. You'll understand."

"O-kay," Mark said shakily. His head came up as his name was called. "Gina," he said. "I promised to fix her bed under the wagon. Say, Camp, I heard what Brittany said. Are there varmints around?"

"Would Maizie suggest sleeping out if she thought there were?"

"No. Hey, thanks, Camp. You never treat me like a kid. I hope you and Mom...well, you know." Blushing, he left.

It was some time before Camp managed to wipe the smile off his face and settle down to read the papers Mark had dropped off. He finished adding his observations, then crawled under his wagon. Only when he lay back on a crackling bed of branches to stare at the black underbelly of the wagon did he try to analyze his feelings for Emily and her kids. Megan as well as Mark. If anything, Megan needed unconditional love more than her brother. She needed someone to care, yet be firm in guiding her. As sleep stole over him, Camp vowed to set things right with Emily before many more days had passed.

Except that bad weather continued to dog them. At Lower Springs they almost didn't get across Sand Creek. Ugly yellow mud sucked at their boots and stuck to their tires like glue. Maizie ordered teams rotated twice. Camp understood why they'd rented so many extra horses.

Four days later, they faced the swiftest section of the Cimarron, and Maizie expected them to be ecstatic over two giant boulders barely visible to the naked eye. They poked out from the waterlogged grassland still ahead.

"Point of Rocks," she said proudly. "Pioneers cried over those boulders. Meant they were looking at Colorado and within spitting distance of Oklahoma. Also means we're still on the Santa Fe Trail." She chuckled.

"Was there any doubt?" Camp asked, almost too tired to appreciate a joke.

"Navigating by the sun and the stars is tricky, boy. By tomorrow afternoon we'll cross the Cimarron one final time. If this rain doesn't slack, she's gonna be boiling. The ground twixt here and there is like a sponge. I want y'all looking out for one another."

Camp took her at her word. And the person he planned to look out for was Emily. So instead of bringing up the rear as he'd been doing, he forced his team past Sherry's wagon. Pulling even with Emily, Camp smiled across the space between them, which dragged a reluctant smile from her. He regaled her with funny stories and soon had her in stitches. For over an hour they were so engrossed in conversation, neither noticed that Sherry's wagon had fallen behind.

In fact, Camp didn't discover it until they stopped for the night. "Where're Sherry and Brittany?" he asked Emily, peering behind them down a stubbornly empty trail.

"I don't know. Oh, Camp, wouldn't we have noticed if Sherry'd had trouble?"

"Maybe she's admiring the sunset. If she doesn't show by the time we finish unhitching, I'll saddle Mincemeat and ride back."

"I'll go, too. Now, don't say no," she admonished, well aware before he said anything that he was going to object. "Four hands are better than two if Sherry needs help. I'm going with you, and that's final."

His shoulders fell as if in resignation. "Yes, ma'am," he grinned. He'd take time alone with Emily any way he could get it.

CHAPTER ELEVEN

"By 1867 women traveled across the plains in comfort. It was so safe they could serve their men off china plates."
    —Sherry cut this out of a book, taped it to her data
        sheet, noting that it was a big, fat lie.

SHERRY'S TEAM, a mix of Percherons and Belgians today, was much harder to handle than her teddy-bear Clydesdales. After the trial at the river, her arms felt like lead weights, and she knew she and Brittany were falling behind.

"Brittany, I can't see the main body of the train anymore. Won't you please drive for a while? These brutes are yanking my arms from their sockets."

"I told you I don't feel good."

"Well, I'm not surprised. You haven't eaten anything to speak of in three days."

"I hate fruit. And that awful jerky about pulls the caps off my teeth. My folks put a lot of money into them. A fortune, according to my dad."

"If they put that much into them, the caps should hold if you ate shoe leather. You're not anorexic, are you?" Sherry asked all of a sudden.

"No! Who can eat food covered in flies and mosquitoes as big as a barn? Who *wants* to eat? Everything smells like horse shi—"

"I get the picture, Brittany. Oh...damn!"

"What's the matter?" Brittany peered through the opening with frightened eyes.

"Conquistador is limping. I think he picked up a stone." Sherry yanked the animals to a stop. "Will you find me that thingamajig Maizie gave us to dig them out?"

"I don't know where it is. Have you done this before?"

"No. But I've watched Robert. How hard can it be? If you can't find the pick, give me your nail file."

"It's diamond and it's new!"

"It can be platinum-covered gold for all I care. We aren't going another step until that stone comes out."

Brittany threw the file onto the seat. "You owe me a new one."

Sherry soon discovered the task was nowhere near as simple as it had appeared. The horse wouldn't stand still, and the rock was embedded in gunk. Every time she cleared the area around the stone, Conquistador jerked loose or set his foot down. Patience thinning, Sherry hiked the foot onto her knee and started over.

A ghostly fog had moved in by the time she finally removed the rock. Sherry's jeans were caked with mud, her fingers scraped and frozen.

Throughout the entire ordeal, Brittany griped incessantly.

"If you're not going to help, be quiet," Sherry finally snapped.

"It's eerie here," Brittany whined. "How soon before we catch up to the others?"

"Do I look like a psychic? Frankly, I thought Nolan would have come by now."

"Ha! He can't see beyond Emily."

Sherry tossed the file on the seat and unwound the reins. "You keep saying that. Em's had one bad marriage. She's not about to get tangled up with another man."

"Are you blind? The only reason they're not sleeping together is that Megan pitched a royal fit. But kids only count for so long."

"Enough. I know Emily. Wow, it's turning to pea soup out there. We must be closer to the river than I thought. What time is it? I took my watch off to work on that stone and now my hands are too icky to dig it out of my pocket."

"Six o'clock."

"It can't be! We were supposed to cross the Cimarron by four!"

Brittany shoved her watch under Sherry's nose. "Six, see! And in case you haven't noticed, it's getting dark."

"You're right. Hear that?" Sherry led the team a few wagon lengths and cocked an ear. "I can't see it, but I think the river's just ahead."

"All I hear are dogs. Or coyotes! Do you hear that yipping?"

Sherry did, and tried to forget accounts she'd read in that book she'd bought. "We have wood in the wagon. Let's build a fire. I know someone'll be back for us soon."

"They won't. We're lost forever. We're going to die—I know it."

Gritting her teeth, Sherry looped the reins over a cottonwood branch, electing to keep the team hitched. Brittany's theatrics grated on her nerves. Sherry grew even more agitated when the wood she'd dumped in her big metal pot refused to catch fire because the heavy mist that blew around had drenched it.

Suddenly, a figure parted the fog. Sherry glanced up eagerly, expecting to see Nolan. A gasp tore from her lungs as she scrambled away from a tall stranger. A giant of a man, bearded and dark. Unkempt, dishwater-blond hair straggled over the collar of a scruffy jacket. His ripped pants were dirtier than his rundown cowboy boots. In the swirling mist, he looked positively frightening.

The stranger ripped off a muddy glove and reached for something in his belt.

Oh, God—a gun. Sherry fought the fear welling in her throat as Brittany screamed bloody murder, leaped from the wagon seat and slumped against Sherry in a dead faint. "Oh, good grief." Sherry staggered under Brittany's full weight.

"I'll be doggoned. A couple of women out here alone on a night not fit for man or beast." He stopped, discovering the Conestoga. "Is one of us caught in a time warp?"

He had a deep, slow drawl and teeth that flashed wickedly white from the depths of the beard.

Shaking in her boots, Sherry shoved a piece of kindling she still clutched into her jacket pocket. "Don't come any closer," she warned. "I swear I'll shoot."

"Now, hold on." He backed into the thick fog until all that showed were laser-blue eyes and the ragged outline of his bearded jaw.

Brittany roused enough to stand on her own. Babbling hysterically, she threw up her hands and ran behind the wagon.

"Come back here, you coward," Sherry muttered out of the side of her mouth, afraid to take her eyes off the man, who'd begun to speak in that lazy voice again.

"You ladies are a long way from civilization.

Suppose you tell me what y'all are doing out here alone in that confounded contraption."

In a flash of genius, Sherry made up a lie. "We're part of a huge wagon train. The others crossed the river. Our husbands will be back for us any second." She waved her free hand to indicate herself and the now-absent Brittany.

"A wagon train, you say?" He crouched next to the black pot in which Sherry had sheltered a pile of twigs. Snapping open a cigarette lighter, he started the fire that'd only sizzled damply for Sherry. "I'll just keep you company until your menfolk show up." He rose, cool gaze affixed to Sherry's ringless left hand.

Behind the wagon, Brittany began to wail and carry on. "We'll all be killed—I told you so. He'll leave our bodies out here to be picked clean by buzzards. I'm too young to die!"

Edging carefully backward, Sherry reached out and yanked Brittany up on the balls of her feet. "Hush," she hissed. "Don't give him any ideas."

Brittany only blubbered harder.

Sherry wrapped a hand in the front of the girl's jacket and shook her hard. "Listen. I told him the men have already crossed the river and they'll be right back for us. Quit bawling and act like it's true."

The stranger poked his head around the wagon, straight brows pulled together in a fierce frown. Both women screamed and clung together.

"Whoa." He held up grimy hands. "I'm just an ordinary guy from down in Huntsville, Texas. Been up river-panning for gold."

His lopsided grin was far from reassuring to Sherry. The one and only thing she knew about Huntsville, Texas, was that it housed the state's maximum security prison. What if this man was an escapee? He wouldn't let people who could identify him just wander off! In a blind panic, she snatched a bigger chunk of wood from her supply and whacked him upside the head. He toppled like a rock. She heard a splash and knew how close they were to the Cimarron.

"Hurry, Brittany. Climb aboard! Let's make tracks. Duck if you hear shots." Boosting the younger woman into the seat, Sherry felt her legs almost give out. Nevertheless, she untied the reins, scrambled up herself and forced the horses into the murky water. She wasn't sure, but she thought the man had begun to move. Whipping the team into a frenzy, she never looked back, only hunched against expected gunfire.

As they bounced and jolted through the river, spraying water every which way, Sherry gasped out her fears to Brittany.

"You mean he's an outlaw?" shivered Brittany.

"Or a low-down murderer." Sherry gripped the leather straps more tightly and shuddered. "Let's hope he's on foot and doesn't have a horse to follow us."

As if on cue, above the thud of the team's big hooves, they heard a sharper, lighter clippity-clop through the fog. Sherry urged the already blowing horses faster. Brittany mewled louder.

The dark shape of a saddle horse appeared so quickly in front of them that it took all of Sherry's limited power to swing the team to the right and avoid a disaster.

"Oh, God, it's him," Brittany shrieked as the phantom horse swerved and gave chase. When the darkly silhouetted rider leaned out of his saddle, grabbed the harness of the lead horse and fought to bring the team to a halt,

Brittany's wild screech drowned out their captor's voice. "We're dead meat! Dead!"

"Whoa. Sherry, pull up. Dammit, stop! Are you two hurt?" Camp threw his weight against the bit. "What in thunderation is wrong with her?" He squinted at the cowering Brittany.

Sherry couldn't say how or when she recognized her brother's voice. By then she was shaking so hard she had almost no muscle left to do as he asked. But in that last mad race, they'd driven out of the mist. The moon and stars winked in an inky sky as finally Camp and Sherry brought the huge beasts to a standstill.

Emily cantered up on the opposite side of the wagon. "Runaway team?" she asked Sherry.

Camp vaulted from the saddle, uncaring that he landed in a mud hole as he swung up to see why Sherry wasn't talking. He barely caught her when, with a strangled cry, she launched herself at him from the high seat.

"It's okay," he breathed, hugging her and patting her awkwardly. "You're safe. What in blazes happened? I didn't realize you'd fallen so far behind until Maizie signaled to stop for the night."

"We met an escaped convict with a gun," Brittany cried. "A murderer."

Camp pried Sherry away from his chest. "Murder…" Seeing his sister's white face, he stared at the mist boiling behind them. "Escaped convict? How do you know? You wouldn't be putting me on?" Camp frowned, meeting Emily's eyes over Sherry's head.

Sherry pressed a hand to her throat. "He didn't have on black and white stripes, or the orange coveralls you see on TV. But he said he was from Huntsville—and he had the...the *look* of an escapee. Oh, Nolan, let's leave, please."

"Sherry smacked the guy with a piece of firewood. He fell in the river. I hope he drowned," Brittany announced without a shred of compassion.

"You what?" Camp again glanced at Emily as if for verification.

"He...he looked disreputable. All right?" Sherry tossed an uneasy gaze over one shoulder. "In the fog, everything was creepy. I...he said he was panning for gold. I mean...really, in this weather? Can we just go?"

Camp returned Sherry to the seat. "Emily, lead them to Cold Springs. I'll take Mincemeat and have a look around."

"No," all three women exclaimed at once.

"Camp..." Emily rode around and blocked his leaving. "Why would anyone be in this desolate area all alone?"

He caught her restraining hand and kissed her fingers. "Probably some innocent old prospector. If Sherry injured him or worse," he said, "somebody'll have to ride into Ulysses and report it to the police."

Sherry blanched. "God, I never thought. Nolan, I didn't mean to hit him so hard. And he wasn't, you know, old, the way I picture a prospector. That was p-part of the problem. I'm sure he was armed. Oh, I wish you wouldn't go."

"Careful, sis, or I'll get the idea you care." Turning to Emily one last time, Camp murmured, "I'll be fine. You take it easy, too."

"I will, Camp. You can count on me."

He waited long enough to see them move out, before breaching the wall of fog. The idea of an armed prospector sounded ludicrous. But again, they were forty miles from civilization. Something *had* happened. He'd never seen Sherry so rattled. *She hit him,* he mused. Exactly how a pioneer woman would have handled things. That was certainly going into his paper. Too bad he wasn't writing a book.

Grinning, he flipped on the powerful construction flashlight he'd borrowed from Robert before he and Emily left. Sherry's wagon tracks stood out clearly on the muddy ground. The river tumbled and eddied in front of him, shrouded in fog.

He found where the wagon had left the water, but the beam refused to penetrate the cottony mist. Step by wary step his horse moved into the river. Camp thought about what awaited him on the other side. A dead man, or a furious one.

Camp touched his heels to Mincemeat's sides to speed their progress. On the far bank he discovered Sherry's large cast-iron pot lying on its side. He smelled recent smoke, but saw no fire. Another whorl of mist obliterated the scene. Dismounting, he combed the river's edge on foot. Thank goodness he didn't stumble across any dead body. To the right of Sherry's tire tracks he saw signs that something heavy had crawled a short distance through the mud. A tracker he wasn't, but Camp bent and followed the snaky trail.

Finally, footprints.

The ice melted from the solid wad in Camp's chest, and he stopped expecting to find a dead man slumped behind every pile of rocks.

Pushed on by the horse's hot breath on his neck, Camp literally tripped over a heap of wet clothing that in all probability belonged to the person he sought. His light beam swept up and over a shivering naked man. A

guy about his own age who hopped on one foot, trying
to stuff his wet legs into a dry pair of jeans. Beads of
water caught in the man's too-long blond hair. Blue
eyes blinked rapidly in the bright light a moment before
the figure lunged for an army knife Camp saw lying
open on the hood of a bright-red Jeep.

"Hold on there, buddy," Camp growled. "You've got
no call to fear me."

Relaxing, the man dropped the blade, leaned against
the vehicle and finished pulling up his trousers. "For a
minute I was afraid you were that crazy lady who tried
to brain me." The man's last words were muffled as he
shrugged into an out-of-shape sweatshirt with a college
logo on the front. "If you're her man," he muttered,
yanking on socks and a battered pair of sneakers, "you
have my condolences. Last I saw of those two wild
women, they were driving a team across the river like two
bats out of hell. I would have followed to see they didn't
break their fool necks, but the dark-haired one decked
me." He touched a spot above his left ear and grimaced.

"Uh-huh." Camp found himself uttering Maizie's
stock reply. Whoever the blond stranger was, Camp
judged, he wasn't an escaped convict.

"Don't blame you for not being in a hurry to catch
her," the man said with a smile. "If you give me a
minute to stoke the fire, I can offer you coffee. Or
there's beer if you'd rather. The name is Lock. Dr.
Garrett Lock." He leaned forward and extended a broad
hand, which Camp accepted.

"Doctor? Medical, dental or academic?" Camp
released the cold, damp fingers, looped his reins over
the Jeep's bumper and began to loosen the saddle girth.

Hunkering down to fan a low, smoldering flame, the

man in the sweatshirt pointed to the logo on his shirt. "Assistant dean of collaborative programs in Huntsville, Texas. At the college," he added in afterthought.

"Really?" Camp glanced at the overlong, dirt-caked hair, the Jeep and the worn tent. "Quite a ways from home, aren't you, Lock?"

"Yeah. My son and I pan for gold every summer. He's eight. This year, my ex-wife decided to get married. Carla—that's her—hasn't seen Keith since she walked out. Because she's marrying again, she's exerting her rights under our shared custody agreement. Insisted I send Keith to Saint Louis for the summer, so he could meet the jerk she's marrying. I should have canceled this trip, but after two weeks of rattling around the house alone... You have any kids?" He looked at Camp. "Sorry, here I am rambling, and I didn't even catch your name."

"Nolan Campbell. And no, I don't have children. I'm also a Ph.D. History." Leaning on the Jeep's fender, he crossed his ankles and supplied the name of his college in Columbia.

"No kidding?" Lock peppered him with questions as he tossed out old grounds and deftly assembled a new pot of coffee.

Camp answered the rapid-fire queries about his campus, a slight frown creasing his brow, furrowing deeper with each successive question.

"It really is a small world, Campbell. The night before I left Huntsville, I sent in my application for the dean of human services vacancy at your college." He sighed. "Don't get me wrong—I like what I'm doing. But with Carla making noises about seeing more of Keith, it'd behoove me to move closer to her. Not that

I'd want to be in the same town. Columbia's a good compromise. So I called the college job line and learned the dean's position had just been posted."

"Um." Camp stared at his boots. "I didn't realize our dean was leaving." The position Lock had mentioned was the one currently held by Sherry's boss. Camp wondered if she knew. Wouldn't that be something, if her so-called outlaw ended up her boss? A bizarre co-incidence, to say the least.

Lordy, Camp could visualize how the fur would fly. But he was jumping ahead of himself. A dean's opening meant hundreds of applicants. Maybe Lock was qualified, but it was a long shot to assume he'd get the job. "Maybe I will have that beer," Camp decided aloud.

"Sure." Lock's teeth gleamed evenly white as his lips parted in an apologetic smile. "Hope you don't mind drinking alone. After that dunking, I need some-thing hot."

"I understand. I've frozen my buns more than once on this trek." Briefly Camp outlined the paper he was writing and how he'd come to be out here in the wilds himself. In the interest of self-preservation he refrained from mentioning that one of his subjects—the wild woman with the dark hair—was his sister.

Garrett Lock disappeared into his battered tent. He came out with a beer and two folding stools. He also handed Camp a business card. "Whether or not I'm chosen for the position, I'd like to read your published piece. I'm kicking around doing one on displaced home-makers—women reentering the workforce after years spent at home. We're quick to hand them grants to continue their education, but we ignore their low self-esteem and in some cases, their lack of assertiveness. Obviously not a problem in your group." He ruefully touched his head again.

Camp waited while Garrett poured a mug of steaming coffee, then he lifted his can in a toast. "To the women of the Santa Fe Trail—then and now. You know, Lock, my colleagues expect the women on my expedition to fail. I admit I had my doubts at first, too. I've since changed my opinion."

Lock didn't smile. "As a sociologist, I try to keep an open mind. Although in my own situation, I'm afraid I'm only human. To tell you the truth, I'm furious with my ex. Carla's been so wrapped up in becoming a big-shot bank officer, she neglected our son. Till now."

Camp took a swig from his beer and thought about Emily's bad experience with her husband, and now with her in-laws. "Speaking as someone who has feelings for a lady with two kids—one of whom would rather her mom got involved with a space alien than me—I'd guess your ex is going through some rocky times, too."

"Maybe. Hey, how did we hit on this depressing subject? Tell me more about your college and Columbia."

Camp did just that. Then they touched a bit on academic philosophy. Camp enjoyed their conversation immensely. He almost hated to leave. But his beer was finished and he knew the others would worry if he didn't get back soon.

Standing, he tightened Mincemeat's cinch. "I don't have one of my cards with me, Lock. If you decide to take an unofficial look at the campus, I'm in the phone book."

"It helps just knowing there's a friendly face among the faculty if I reach the interview stage. Y'all take care on your trip. I have a shortwave radio, a ham operator out of Houston passed along information of hurricane activity. I was debating whether to head home about the time I met your...friends."

Camp's ears perked. "Hurricane? We still have to cross the North Canadian River twice and the Carizozo."

Lock whistled softly. "'Course, that doesn't mean the rains will blow inland."

"No, but thanks for the warning. We're trying to simulate what the pioneers would have gone through as closely as possible, but that doesn't mean we want to risk anyone's life." Reaching out, he clasped Lock's hand. "Good luck on the job hunt."

"Tell the wildcat she may get another crack at me." As Camp swung into the saddle, Garrett added, "I never asked if she lived in Columbia. Am I liable to run into her in a dark alley?" His face split in a purely male grin.

Camp thought briefly about his direct omission—in not mentioning Sherry's position at the college or her relationship to him. But chances were slight that a man who looked like Grizzly Adams would be offered a job by the staid board of directors at his institution. Smiling, Camp shook his head.

"That's good," Lock said, lifting two fingers in salute. "If she crossed gloves with Evander Holyfield, my money would be on the brunette's knockout punch."

As Camp kneed his mount into the dark river, Garrett Lock faded into an opaque haze. Looking back, he thought it was as if the scene had never happened. Maybe it hadn't. Maybe he'd dreamed the entire thing. Sherry certainly wouldn't believe him if he told her the man she thought was an escaped convict actually had visions of replacing her boss—a guy who wore Italian silk ties and custom-made suits.

Once Camp left the river, the stars popped out overhead and the moon sent silvery shafts of light dancing in and out of the rain-drenched prairie grasses. Gazing at the panorama of stars, he found it difficult to imagine a storm headed this way.

At the outskirts of the row of wagons, Sherry ran to meet him. Her face was pale in the moonlight and dark circles ringed her eyes. "Where have you been? I imagined you lying out there somewhere, shot dead."

Camp climbed off the pinto. "Then you ought to be ecstatic when I tell you I saw nary a dead body nor a man with a gun."

Her hands fluttered to his sleeve. "Thank God. So I didn't kill him. Oh, Nolan, I've been so worried."

"About me or him?" he teased.

"You first…and him. Both." She swallowed several times before throwing her arms around him and planting a kiss on his cheek. "I'm sick from worry. I'm going to bed. Everyone else has. Oh, Emily saved you some hash and asked if you'd please bank her fire."

His eyes automatically swerved to the one remaining campfire. His heart had kicked over like a newly wound watch when he'd thought of Emily waiting up. Now his pulse dropped back to normal. He looped an arm around Sherry's neck and aimed a kiss at her forehead. "I have to see to my horse. Then I'll tend Emily's fire. Honestly, I'm too bushed to eat."

"I'm sorry to have sent you on a wild-goose chase, Nolan. You can bet I'll keep up from now on."

"Good. And I'll keep better watch. Sherry…"

"Yes?" She turned at his serious tone.

"I know we have a tendency to argue. In case I haven't said it in a while...I do love you."

"Are...you...all right, Nolan?"

He caught up, snagged her neck with one hand and pretended to shake her. "I'm fine. Can't a guy tell his sister he loves her once in a blue moon?"

She fidgeted. "Yeah. And same to you, Campbell. Don't let it get out, but I like knowing you'll always be there for me." She gave him a crooked grin. "Enough of this sentimentality. I gotta run."

Camp's bemused expression gave way to one of exasperation as she dashed away. She'd been a difficult baby, too. And an independent teen.

"That was sweet of you," said a soft voice from the shadows of his wagon.

"Emily?" His tone showed his delight at having her appear after all.

"Sherry likes everyone to see her as strong and tough. Underneath she's a marshmallow. A lot lonelier than she lets on."

His head came up as he lifted the saddle from the gelding. "Pretty deep assessment of somebody you've known less than six weeks."

"Camp...I..." Emily almost told him she'd known Sherry a lot longer. That they were friends and had served on intercollegiate committees together. But Sherry didn't want him to know.

"Hey, I didn't mean to take your head off. I forgot you psychologists love to probe a man's soul." Grabbing a brush, he groomed the horse before leading him to a deep patch of grass and affixing his hobble.

Emily remained where he'd left her, hands linked

loosely in front of her, a faint crease between her brows. "We were talking about women. I'd never presume to second-guess men. God knows I made a royal mess of that once."

"Don't be so hard on yourself. I really didn't mean to snap. I'm tired. It's been a long day."

"I know." She sighed. "When we got back home, Brittany carried on for an hour. I'm glad you didn't find anything."

"Nothing of consequence." He suppressed a shiver of guilt at the lie, but decided he really couldn't tell her about Garrett Lock—and risk Sherry finding out. He glanced up at the sky. "Did Maizie mention the possibility of another storm?"

Emily followed his gaze. She grabbed the lapels of her jacket and pulled it a little tighter. "The wind's picked up, and it's gotten colder. But no, she didn't say anything. At least not to me. Come sit by the fire. You must be hungry as well as tired. I saved a plate of hash."

He stopped her with a hand at her elbow. When she turned, he curved a palm around her cheek. "Thanks for looking out for me, Emily. I've wanted a chance to talk. About us."

Her lips turned down and sadness darkened her eyes. "There can't be any us, Camp. Megan may seem all mouth and bluster to you, but this thing with Mona and Toby really shook her. I can't do anything that'll threaten the little security she has."

"You're entitled to a life, Emily."

"I have a life. I have my home, my children, my work."

He felt her tremble at his touch. "Is that enough, Em? What about five years down the road when your nest is empty and your job becomes routine?"

"In five years Mark will still be in high school. I'll grow with my job," she said desperately.

"I'm sure you will. I won't argue with you, Emily. It's not my aim to make your life more difficult. Say, where's that food you promised a starving man?"

She took a deep breath and let it struggle out in a thin laugh. "Don't be so damned accommodating, Campbell. A woman likes to have the illusion that she's worth fighting for. And you know perfectly well where I cook the food."

She would have whirled and marched off toward the flickering fire, but he snatched her hand. "Who do you want me to fight? Megan? Your in-laws? I intend to talk with Megan. And I won't say it hasn't entered my mind to steal you away. All of you."

Another sigh trickled through her lips. "I said it before and I'll say it again—you're a dear, sweet man, Nolan Campbell. But talking to Meggie is like batting your head against a stone wall. Stealing me away is a nice fantasy, but I learned a long time ago that you can't run from your obligations. You're good for my ego, though. I was feeling quite sorry for myself."

"That's the last thing you should do, Emily. Will you stay while I eat? I hate to ask—I'm sure you're beat, too. You did more than your share today, helping dig Gina's wagon out of the mud, and then, riding out with me to find Sherry and Brittany."

"I'm a night owl. It doesn't seem to matter how early I get up, sleep doesn't come easily."

"Something else we have in common, insomnia. Except, when I do drop off, I could sleep till noon. You're up with the roosters. Before the roosters," he corrected.

"Holdover from growing up on a farm. We had to *feed* the roosters."

"And milk the cows and walk nine miles to school in the snow." Mouth quirked in a teasing smile, Camp leaned close to the pot, sniffing the hash as he dished it up. He was grateful that because of Terrill's strategic visits they had more plentiful and more varied meals than had been available to the pioneers. "This smells great. I didn't realize I was so hungry." Taking the fork Emily handed him, he sat back and dug in.

"You know, Camp, I didn't mind life on the farm, although we worked constantly. Oh, I grumbled at the time, I'm sure. All kids faced with chores do. But this trip reinforces the basic values I learned."

Fork halfway to his mouth, Camp stopped to stare at the woman curled comfortably in the lawn chair. Her eyes sparkled like the stars; her cheeks glowed with good health. Suddenly he imagined her puttering around his big old country kitchen. Imagined her capable hands planting flowers, and maybe a garden. He saw Mark chasing down to the stream, fishing pole in hand, followed by Pilgrim, his golden lab. Megan…didn't quite fit. Her image was fuzzy, not clear like the others. He shook his head and quickly took another bite.

"Is something wrong?" Emily shifted in her chair and placed a hand on his arm. "Did the hash dry out? I can scramble some eggs."

"It's not the food. Would you like to live in the country again, Emily?"

She stiffened, then lifted one shoulder slightly. "I haven't thought about it. I've thought of running away to a desert island, or to a remote cabin in the mountains. But I learned from my dad, who farmed and dealt with the fickleness of the elements all his life, that you have to face trouble head-on. He always said you could leave your problems behind but not your conscience. In my case, they amount to the same thing."

"I assume you mean you've dreamed of escaping, of leaving behind your husband's debts—and your in-laws."

"That's all it is—a dream. In today's world it's impossible for an honest person to simply disappear."

"But what if someone paid your in-laws every last cent you owe?"

Face wreathed in smiles, eyes dancing, she said, "That mythical white knight on a fire-breathing steed? I know he doesn't exist."

Camp brooded a moment, trying to fit himself into that armor she teased about. He hadn't tapped the trust fund his grandparents had set up. His folks and Sherry thought he should use some of it to hire a construction crew to finish his house. He'd much preferred doing the work himself. Now...

Emily rose, stretched like a contented cat and took the empty plate from Camp's nerveless hands. "Talk about a tough day. You look positively catatonic. Nice as it is to sit and solve the problems of the world, I suggest we call it a night."

Studying her bright hair and slender back as she efficiently set the pots and bowls to soak, Camp realized she didn't have a clue as to the thoughts running through his head. And because she didn't, he decided to bide his time. No sense jumping the gun, scaring her off. He had several weeks left on this trip. Time to talk Megan around. Time to let all the pieces click in his own mind. Although his arms ached to hold Emily close through the chilly night, he settled for an unsatisfying hug and a friendly good-night kiss.

Emily watched him put out the fire, wondering how

even the simplest kiss from him ignited such a blaze inside her. She wrapped those feelings close as he escorted her to the back of her wagon. And thanked him politely when he offered her a hand up. But she sat in the darkness for a long while, listening to her daughter's even breathing, fancying she'd just left that knight on the fire-breathing steed.

Ah, but she was a fool. If Nolan Campbell hadn't found a damsel in distress to rescue in his thirty-eight years, he wasn't likely to start with a widow who had two kids and more than her share of troubles.

CHAPTER TWELVE

"Not even the toughest men who sought to tame the West messed with Mother Nature."
—Awakened by a storm, Camp recalled this relevant tidbit from one of his lectures.

WIND, blowing things around outside, jolted Camp into wakefulness. He'd sat up long after parting from Emily, integrating Sherry's account of her meeting with Professor Lock into his notes. Sherry skirted certain facts on her data sheet. Brittany's diatribe would make a movie. And then there was his own encounter with the man....

Yawning, he climbed from his sleeping bag, immediately registering a severe drop in temperature. Now he knew why Maizie had insisted they stock up on long underwear. His were still in plastic bags. "Brr!" He rubbed his pebbled flesh. Once he had the long johns out and on his body, he applauded Maizie's foresight.

Outside in the biting wind, Camp grabbed for things such as coffeepots and aluminum lawn chairs that whizzed along the ground. When the wake-up call sounded, he'd collected quite a few, including two webbed chairs belonging to Maizie, whose wagon sat the length of a football field away.

"Thanks, sonny," she panted, running up. "Glad you're

up and around early. Don't know if we're in for a major blow, or if this is a lagging tail from yesterday's storm."

"I heard rumors of a gulf hurricane," he said.

"Don't like the sounds of that. Nosirree!"

"Should we batten down the hatches and stay put?"

Maizie's faded eyes probed the blustery sky that had begun to lighten. "We're sittin' geese here. If we leave soon, with any luck we can make Round Mound or Rabbit Ears before she really cuts loose."

No sooner had she spoken than Robert hurried toward them, resembling a bear in his leather hat with ear flaps and his heavy, plaid mackinaw. "Putrid-looking clouds to the southeast. What's your take on them? Are we headed into trouble?"

Maizie unwrapped a square of bubble gum. "Campbell heard there's a hurricane in the Texas gulf. I figure we got seven, eight hours of drivin' before we know whether she dies on the vine or not. You two tell everybody we're rollin'."

Roll out they did after sorting through the tangle of property. They made short work of necessary chores, and no one mentioned breakfast. Even the horses sniffed the wind and laid back their ears. As usual, the Clydesdales took things in stride. The Belgians and Percherons frisked around, edgy as spring colts.

Camp stopped Mark before he pulled out. "Seems we'll be bucking a stiff head wind, son. Fall in behind Robert. Let his wagon block the wind."

"What about Sherry and the teachers? And Mom's driving four Belgians."

"I know." Camp rested a hand on Mark's arm. "They're all good drivers. Jared's a backup if anyone needs a break. Our first scheduled stop is McNees Crossing. We'll touch base then."

"Okay. And Camp, thanks for not making me turn this wagon over to Jared now. I know he's older and has more experience."

"You're doing fine, Mark. Just remember, a real man recognizes his limitations. He's not afraid to ask for help."

The boy bobbed his head. "I understand. You never preach like Toby. When you say stuff, I understand what you mean. I wish you were my dad, Camp."

Hunched inside his jacket, Camp massaged the back of his neck. "I'll keep that in mind." As he stood dumbly watching Mark guide his team into line, Gina Ames poked her head through the back canvas.

"If it matters, Campbell, you get my vote, too. The way Sherry talked before the trip, I figured you for a real chauvinist. Always nice to be pleasantly surprised." Disappearing again, she tied the canvas closed.

Stunned, Camp moved toward his wagon. What did Gina mean? It sounded as if she and Sherry had been in contact prior to the trip.

"Camp? Is something wrong?" Emily slowed her wagon.

"Nothing." He strode to her side and covered one of her gloved hands with his own. "Are you wearing long underwear?" All the trekkers but Emily looked as if they'd gained five pounds overnight. Camp didn't want her suffering if she'd forgotten.

"What a thing to ask." Her husky laugh volleyed on the wind. "Mine are silk," she said, smoothing a hand along her thigh. "Not as bulky as cotton, and warmer."

"Pu-leeze, Mother!" Megan stuck a tousled head out into the blustery wind. Just as fast, she withdrew it. "If I told a guy what underwear I had on, you'd have a cow."

Emily blushed furiously and slipped a neck scarf she had hidden beneath her jacket up over her ears. She slapped her reins repeatedly and the wagon lumbered off.

Several heartbeats skittered by before Camp blocked out the vision of *his* hand sliding over Emily's slender thigh. Giving himself a firm shake, he followed her lead. As if his team sensed something in the air, they lunged against their traces.

Mile after brutal mile, the wind clawed at the drivers' clothing. Less than two hours on the road, the canvas ripped loose from one side of the teachers' wagon. Sacks, papers and clothing blew out and fell with a thud or danced across the prairie. The entire train stopped. Mark and Jared ran to corral the flapping, ghostly apparitions before they spooked more horses. The heavy canvas bucked and leaped constantly as Camp and Robert fought to tie it down.

Emily and Sherry parked, joining the chase for free-floating debris. They returned with the booty, breathless, faces red and chapped.

"Whew!" Emily rewrapped her neck scarf. "Now I know why pioneer women looked old before their time. This wind is murder!"

Sherry pulled out a tube of lip balm. "I'm sure this is cheating," she said, aiming a grimace at her brother. "But I never agreed to end this trip looking like a crocodile."

He turned up his sheepskin-lined collar. "I don't recall asking you to."

"You said women couldn't give up creature comforts for the time it'd take to go from Missouri to Santa Fe."

"Lyle said that." Camp stripped off one glove. "If you

share that stuff, I promise this weak moment will never find its way into my sordid tale."

"Go ahead, tell the world I'm a wuss." Sherry slugged him on the arm before she handed over the tube.

"Ouch." He rubbed the spot. "Hit some poor devil in the head with a slab of cordwood, and now you beat up on me. Maybe I should warn the world about this streak of violence in Sherilyn Campbell."

She two-stepped around him, thumbing her nose as if ready to box. "Yesterday was self-defense." Pausing, she eyed Camp and Emily, who laughed openly at her antics. "You two look so...so outdoorsy. Like you enjoy this misery."

Camp rested his forehead against Emily's. They both grinned foolishly.

"See what I mean?" Sherry groaned. "There you go again. What's with you two? Anybody would think you're...involved or something."

Camp hurriedly smeared balm on his lips.

Emily hunched against the wind. 'I don't like storms. But...I feel alive out here. Free. You know how tense I've been, Sherry."

Capping the balm, Camp flicked a puzzled glance between the women. "That gives the impression that you two go back a ways."

"Oh." Emily covered her lips. Why had she promised Sherry that she'd hide their friendship from her brother?

"Didn't you think Emily seemed tense the first time you met her?" Sherry asked breezily.

Her reply was too cavalier to suit Camp. He'd wondered before if Sherry and Emily had met through work. Perhaps they thought it'd skew his results. Or his perceptions. He'd have to consider whether it would.

Camp was glad that Maizie cupped her hands and gave her famous "Roll 'em" yell just then. He wanted some time to mull over how Emily's comment fitted with Gina's earlier statement. Or even *if* it did. It stood to reason that Sherry and Emily might have met at a conference, but how would either of them have known Gina?

What bothered him most was the fact that they'd— probably—lied. In some sort of conspiracy, yet, orchestrated—probably—by his loving sister. However, he didn't have time to worry about any of this now.

"See you at McNees Crossing," he said, giving each woman a brisk nod. "Can't say I like the color of that sky."

"Maybe it's the sun trying to break through the clouds," Emily murmured.

"Maybe." Camp didn't tell her that the only other time he'd seen a sky like that, a twister had demolished his uncle's new brick house while the entire family huddled next door in the garage. Camp had been twelve, Sherry just a child. They'd gathered for a Campbell reunion and had steaks barbecuing on the outdoor grill, he recalled, when his mother noticed the muddy yellow sky. The group barely had time to seek refuge before a funnel cloud appeared out of nowhere. He'd never forget the wreckage.

Camp wished he'd made time for a word with Maizie about that sky. But he didn't want to pull out of line and leave Emily unprotected.

Everyone was jittery, miserable and starved by the time Maizie called a short break at McNees Crossing. They sat on a wind-buffeted promontory looking down on the North Canadian River, now a mass of boiling whitecaps and deep whirlpools.

"Get these wagons across to the other side and keep

moving," their leader ordered. "If you've got something to nibble on, do. We're not stopping."

"It's inhumane to drive us like donkeys," Philly shouted. "We need rest and food. We ought to rebel."

Maizie blew a giant pink bubble. The wind popped it. "Fine. Go ahead and stay. Prove you're a jackass. If you'd ever had the pleasure of butting heads with a twister, Philadelphia, you'd be shakin' your bootie. I sure don't fancy being caught on this plateau."

"Twister?" Harv spit. "Those clouds are miles away. You're bluffing. Running us to death because we lost time on account of those brats."

"Uh-huh! It's your pee-rogative to believe what you will. Ford this river one wagon at a time. Robert, you first. Stay east of that scrawny patch of rabbitbrush, and try not to drift downstream. Mark, can you make it on your own?"

Mark huddled in his fleecy jacket. His freckles stood out rust-colored against a pasty face. "I'm pretty tired. If Jared doesn't need to help my mom or Sherry, I'll ask him to drive a stretch for me."

In her aviator's cap that buckled firmly under the chin and a down coat pulled on over her fringed leather jacket, Maizie looked like an unhappy troll. "Emily and Sherry, listen up. I want one person per set of reins. Emily, you're the experienced driver so you take the downriver side, giving Megan the up. Sherry and Brit, do the same. Doris, you and Vi decide which of you has the most power. Jared, give Mark a hand."

Camp looked at the grim faces of the people Maizie had singled out. Megan seemed close to hyperventilating. Brittany's face was a frozen mask.

Robert drove in close to his mother. "What if Camp

and I tie the saddle horses to our wagons, cross, then swim them back to drive the women's wagons over?"

Her eyes turned flinty. "Extra time we don't have, Robby."

"You're the boss," Camp grunted, still disturbed by the bruised-looking sky.

"Glad somebody recognizes that fact." Maizie glowered at Harv Shaw. "Here's the plan. Robert leads, followed by Emily and Megan. Then you, Camp. Sherry and Brittany next. Jared and Mark. Doris and Vi, then Harv. I'll ford last, pushing spare stock ahead of me. Hop to it," she yelled.

Robert made it across without incident. Emily's lead horse stumbled and went to his knees.

Behind and upstream too far, Camp felt powerless to render aid. He continued on, teeth clenched, feeling Emily's struggle to help her horse. Camp's facial muscles didn't relax until the front wheels of Em's wagon found purchase in the shallows. He ran to her, shouting, "Good job!" Megan literally fell into his arms. Surprised, Camp offered comfort. The minute she realized what she'd done, she shoved him aside.

Midpoint in the raging river, Sherry battled her own demons. Brittany stared at the water as if entranced. The lead horse on her side reared, ripping the reins from her limp grasp. Snaking leather confused the team. They panicked, then stopped. No amount of coaxing on Sherry's part could set the animals in motion.

Robert grabbed a rope and ran along the crumbling bank. Slick as any cowboy, he twirled a noose and dropped it neatly over the balky Percheron's head. Between Robert and Camp, who threw his weight into the rope, they forced the team ashore.

Sherry wanted to throttle Brittany. But then the younger woman fell apart, and Sherry felt bad. "It's all right, Brit. We made it okay. Don't cry."

Though shaken by Sherry's experience, the others crossed safely.

"I know you're all right proud of yourselves," shouted Maizie, her words torn from her by the wind. "That storm is moving faster than we are. Save your attaboys and girls till we're in the cradle of Rabbit Ears. Twixt here and there is open prairie. Line up four abreast. I'll bring up the rear again. Anyone spots a funnel, yell like crazy. Everybody up on the seats, ready to jump and roll under the wagons if need be."

"What about me?" Gina tapped her splint and her cast.

"I'll help you," Mark said staunchly. "I won't leave you. That's part of what you're paying me for."

Emily's pride in Mark's mature response was replaced by distress as Megan began to weep. She dragged her daughter closer, taking her own comfort from the warm hand Camp pressed to her shoulder.

Harv Shaw hitched his pseudo-western belt buckle higher on his paunch and swaggered over to Maizie. "Your brochure didn't mention tornadoes."

"Sorry, they're hard to order for every trip," she drawled sarcastically.

His bulbous nose flared. "This isn't funny."

"Damn tootin' it's not. My neck's on the line, too. So quit palavering and hit the road. The sooner we find cover, the better."

"Why did you let all these women and kids come? They'll slow us down."

"Shut up." Camp stalked around Emily and grabbed Harv by his jacket front. "These women aren't pitching half the fit you are. They're doing their jobs! And to top it off, they aren't your concern."

Emily applauded, slow and loud. Sherry and Gina joined in.

Philly brushed Camp's hands aside. He stomped off, muttering darkly. "Far as I'm concerned, it's every man for himself. Don't expect me to baby any damn-fool women. Me and the missus are taking off. Catch us if you can."

"Hold on a dang minute." Maizie chased him. He scrambled onto the high seat, cracked his reins and bounced his wagon off across the open plains.

Maizie spit her wad of gum in his wake. For once Camp wished it'd been a stream of tobacco.

"Want me to catch the jerk and shake some manners into him?" Camp asked.

"Nah. Let him go. There's one on every trip. He's been obnoxious a heap o' years. We aren't likely to change him."

Camp noticed how the women, including Brittany and Megan, suddenly sobered, their fear replaced by grit and determination. He was both humbled and proud, and wished Lyle Roberts could see this display of courage. Modern women might enjoy modern comforts, but these ladies had guts with a capital G. As they moved forward, Camp raised a closed fist to the advancing storm and issued a rebel yell.

With Philly far out in front, the others filtered into two lines. All twenty-eight horses strained against their harnesses. Yet they were driving into such heavy, gusty winds, there were times it felt as if they were standing still.

Except for wild cotton and an occasional tuft of primrose, the grasses had been beaten down by the rain.

Before the travelers often saw silos or farms in the distance; now they might have been the only humans on the planet. They had all bent to shield their faces from the harsh wind, so no one realized the Shaws' wagon had hit a scrub manzanita and blown a rear balloon tire. Not until the first row of wagons practically ran the Shaws down.

"The rest of you keep truckin'," Maizie yelled over the wind's howl. "Robert and I will change that tire. I've got a couple spares in my wagon."

"I'll help, too," Camp shouted.

Maizie waved him on. "You stay with the women. I've seen at least two funnel clouds pass behind us. See? Directly south is Rabbit Ears."

Peering through red-rimmed eyes, Camp saw the protruding rocks still some distance away. Nodding, he motioned for the others to keep moving. He didn't like the thought of leaving anyone behind.

Emily's Belgians arched their thick necks and heaved forward. Sherry's team fought their bits, circled and nearly ripped the traces out of her hands.

Camp pulled alongside. "Let's trade wagons, sis. We can't risk getting stuck out here."

"No. I'll show them who's boss." Muscles bunched, Sherry forced the cantankerous animals into line.

"Maizie said there's a cut between that rounded rock and the flat-topped hill that forms the ears. Head there. Unhitch the teams," he bellowed. "The horses will do better unencumbered. We'll take shelter in the rocks."

Each driver flashed him the thumbs-up sign.

The closer they got to the rock formation, the more wicked the lightning. Hail rained down in large white pellets. Thunder hammered. Peal after peal blended with the pounding gallop of the horses' hooves.

Off to his left, Camp saw a twister unfold. It hovered five or so feet above the ground. For a minute it seemed to chase Mark's wagon. Just as quickly, it veered off and whistled across the open prairie. Camp swallowed a lump lodged in his throat. Sweat popped out on his forehead despite a sharp drop in temperature. Still he urged his team faster. His shoulders ached from the pull of the lathered horses. He honestly didn't know how the women managed with their lesser strength. But they did.

At last Mark's lead wagon entered the dark crevasse snaking into the only shelter for miles around. Camp breathed a little easier after Emily reached it, too. Doris's team disappeared next. Sherry's wagon made the turn seconds before Camp's own. There was no time for congratulations. No sooner had they all freed their teams than there arose a fiendish howl accompanied by thick, churning black clouds.

Stunned, the bedraggled group watched small trees being sucked into a gyrating funnel tearing along the pass. Red dirt swirled as angry black clouds swallowed lightning bolts and put on a laser show. Rumbling, tumbling toward them, it ate the earth like some greedy late-show monster.

Camp screamed for everyone to take cover. No one moved. Instead, they all seemed paralyzed, staring in horror. Except for Emily. She shoved those closest to her flat to the ground. Once she'd helped Sherry and Brittany, Emily ran to assist Gina down from the wagon.

Adrenaline pumping, Camp tore up the rocky trail. He flung Doris, then Vi, into a rocky hollow. With seconds to spare, he used his own body to shield Mark,

Jared and Megan. Over the noise, he heard a horse scream in fright, but dared not raise his head as thick, humid air whistled above him like a banshee.

A saddle horse, tied to the back of Camp's wagon, broke his rope and bolted. At least two of the freed teams galloped wildly back the way they'd come. The most Camp could do was pray he hadn't led his party into a death trap. And what about Emily? Had she reached cover? Last he saw, she was attempting to help Gina.

It seemed that he clung to the sharp rocks forever, listening as the cries of his fellow travelers competed with the ear-splitting shriek of the funnel. In reality, the hideous experience lasted less than twenty seconds. Even after silence descended, it took time for them to untangle their limbs and stop shaking enough to assess the damage.

"It tore the water barrel off the side of my wagon," Gina reported, hobbling along the rutted, cratered ground the microburst had left in its wake.

"We lost the front third of our canvas," Vi relayed anxiously. "Our team looks dazed, but intact," Doris added.

Drained of energy and color, Emily clamped a shaky arm around each of her children. "What's important is that we all came through unscathed. Has the danger passed enough for one of us to ride out and see how Robert and Maizie are doing?" she asked Camp.

"I'll go see in a minute," he said, giving in to a desperate need to touch her hair. "We need to round up all the horses before they break a leg in potholes left by the twister."

"I'll help." Mark pulled from Emily's grasp.

Seeing the concern cross her already pinched features, Camp turned the boy down. "You and Jared start a fire so we can dry things out. Seems the sky is clearing to the south, but we're not necessarily out of danger. I'm assuming, after all that's happened, Maizie'll decide to dig in here for the night."

"You can't handle bringing in all the runaways by yourself, Camp," Emily said quietly. "Once the boys get a fire started, Doris and Vi can break out packets of soup. I'll go with you after the horses if you like."

He did like. The thought of the two of them sharing the one remaining saddle horse—no matter how briefly—appealed immensely to Camp. It took only moments to capture the surefooted gelding he'd snubbed to Mark's wagon earlier. He boosted Emily onto the broad, bare back, then swung up behind her, asking Sherry to hobble and feed the horses that had begun to mill about.

"Do you suppose everyone who got caught out in the open is all right?" Emily asked worriedly the minute they cleared the outcrop of rocks.

"Yes. See?" Camp directed her gaze. "They're driving in now. Looks like all are accounted for." He felt a sigh of relief whisper through Emily's frame.

"Thank goodness. I had visions of us having to try to bury someone on the trail the way the early pioneers did. We may be more technically advanced, but when it comes to the elements we're still at their mercy."

"We certainly are." He laced both arms around her slender waist. "I'm ready for this trip to end, Em. What if something bad had happened to you or the kids? Or to anyone I talked into coming?"

"You didn't talk us into anything. We volunteered."

"Why did you? You'd have made a lot more money teaching summer school."

"The truth, Camp," Emily blurted out, "is that Sherry twisted my arm and Gina's. I'd told Sherry I wanted to spirit the kids away from my in-laws. And Sherry met Gina when Gina attended her program after a rough divorce. It was your sister who convinced her to backpack in the Sierras. Sherry's counting on us to prove that women are tough. The joke's on us. Stacked up against Mother Nature, we aren't tough at all."

"I'll be damned. So Sherry did load the scales. I never would've believed she'd be that devious. Or that you'd all go along with a lie."

"I wouldn't call it devious…exactly. And we didn't lie on our applications. You weren't exactly playing fair, either, Camp. To be totally unbiased you should have booked an equal number of men. Randomly selected, of course."

"Of course," he said, sounding irked. "There's one of our runaway teams. Do you want to walk them back to the cut, or should I?"

Emily started to slide off the gelding. Pausing, she turned and gazed into Camp's eyes. "Sherry did me a favor. I'd never have met you otherwise."

Camp felt the tension leave his body. Swinging down, he took Emily in his arms and kissed her tenderly. "I have a distinct feeling Sherry isn't nearly as pleased about that as we are. If you want the whole truth, I can't be too mad at her, either."

Emily leaned an ear against his chest and listened to his reassuring heartbeat. "She probably considers me a traitor. Then there's Megan. If looks could kill we'd both be dead. What are we going to do, Camp?"

He rubbed his hands over Emily's back. "I'll talk to

Megan, Em. She's part grown-up, part child. I'll find a time when she's not hanging out with Brittany. Maybe tonight."

Emily gazed at him somberly. "My kids have been through so much turmoil. How can I put them through more?"

He drew her up on her toes and covered her mouth fiercely. He would find time to talk with Megan, he vowed, releasing Emily's limp form to stride away.

BUT THE TIME didn't present itself. There was too much work to be done to repair the damage. Relations within the group as a whole were strained, even though preparations for a celebratory dinner were under way by the time Camp brought in the last strayed horse. Dinner for all but the couple from Philadelphia, Camp noticed.

Emily baked the last of her cake mixes. Vi contributed the honey-almond topping. Gina broke out a special blend of coffee she'd been hoarding.

Philly and his wife were very pointedly excluded from the festivities.

"Let's not be petty," Camp said, wanting to ease the rift. "We should all be thankful to be alive." When it became clear that his efforts at mediation had failed, he excused himself to go work on his report. But the words he needed to describe the day wouldn't come. He fell asleep staring moodily into his flickering lantern.

Emily stayed up after the others had said good-night. Memory of the twister remained too real for her to sleep.

Camp's light still glowed. She wondered if he, too, worried about another storm. Tiptoeing to the back of his wagon, she parted the wet canvas. "Camp?" she whispered. He didn't stir. Emily realized he'd fallen asleep with his lantern burning. Afraid that might be dangerous, she climbed over the feed trough and crept toward the light.

She'd lowered the flame when Camp suddenly bolted upright, tumbling her headfirst into his supplies. A small scuffle ended as he emerged from his stupor and felt her curves crushed beneath him.

"Emily?" He blinked sleepy eyes, carefully scanning her damp hair and pale face. With a shaking hand, he smoothed his fingers down her cheek. "It's really you. You were just in my dream."

"A nightmare, you mean?" Her eyes crinkled at the corners. "I missed your help with the dishes. Everyone else always disappears after eating."

He kissed her softly. "Why didn't you wake me sooner?" he murmured, nibbling at her neck.

"Camp, it's late. I should go back to my wagon."

"Why?" He nuzzled her ear, drawing in the scent of her perfume. "You smell like raindrops and jasmine. Mmm, my favorite scents."

"What I smell like is horse," she murmured.

Kissing her arched brow, he eased her out of her jacket, tossed it aside and covered her with a portion of his down sleeping bag. He pulled her against his chest. "You scared me today. What if I'd lost you?" He rubbed his chin over her bright hair.

Sighing, she stretched like a cat. "Don't make me too comfortable. I can't stay."

"Really?" He divested her of her plaid shirt, hesitating when he ran into the silk of her long johns. "Darn…getting you out of these is going to take some fancy contortions." While she pulled the top over her head, Camp let his lips skim the flesh she uncovered, bit by bit.

As the offending article dropped away, Emily brushed her fingers through a lock of his dark hair that had fallen rakishly over his forehead. Suddenly she was struck by a blinding need to feel the naked chest that rose and fell beneath his waffled underwear. Hands unsteady, she worked the hem of his shirt out of his jeans and smoothed her palms over the rough thatch of hair beneath. Heat built within her. Places that obviously still had life. Her urgent reasons for leaving his wagon dimmed as her limbs grew both liquid and weighted. She hadn't felt like this in so long. Too long, she thought, moaning with pleasure.

Camp wasn't a man to make love lightly. By the time their combined breathing had grown ragged and begun to steam the lantern's glass, the thundering of their hearts told him exactly where such explorations would end.

Emily's appearance in his wagon was a gift. A gift he wanted to unwrap slowly and savor to the fullest. "Are you sure?" he breathed against her ear as her questing fingers succeeded in opening the top button of his jeans. "Because if you're not, you have two seconds to say no."

Nothing had ever felt more right to Emily. But they hadn't discussed the important things lovers were supposed to discuss in this day and age. The evidence of his arousal, pressed close to where she was wet and ready to receive him, threatened to make Emily ignore all the facts she preached to her students.

In the nick of time, his question stirred her guilt. "I'm...not...on anything, Camp. I'm sorry." She started to roll away, her body shaking with need and regret.

He tugged her back. "Don't apologize," he murmured, his kisses greedy and desperate. "I should be the one. I wanted this…hoped for it. I…I bought something that day in Dodge." Behind her, he fumbled for a sack. He ripped open the box inside and scattered half the packets, and then, in a fever, they managed to shed jeans, as well as the remaining long underwear, and tear apart one slick packet to sheathe him.

They made slow, delicious love. Giving, taking. Murmuring words of love.

Afterward, Emily lay curled contentedly in Camp's sheltering arms. They talked in fits and spurts and made elaborate plans for their future well into the rainy night.

Twice Emily said she needed to dress and go back to her wagon. Both times Camp wrapped her tighter and kissed her until she snuggled against him and agreed to stay a little longer. Together they laughed over how the wind rocked the wagon like a cradle, never guessing it would lull them to sleep.

"MOTH-ER!"

Emily woke abruptly to a drizzly gray dawn and Megan's frantic shout. In a panic, Emily frantically collected the clothes that lay strewn around Camp's wagon bed. Her cold silk underwear refused to slide onto chilled flesh.

Not sharing her sense of urgency, Camp leaned over and kissed the creamy base of her spine. "Come back to bed," he mumbled.

She shook him off. "Are you crazy?" she hissed, yanking on panties and jeans. "What will Megan think? I've never spent the night with a man."

Camp's lips curved as he sat up and filtered his fingers through her sleep-tangled hair. "Kids are probably more accepting of sex than we are, Em."

Because he'd begun to hunt for his own clothes, he didn't realize that she stiffened when he used the word *sex* to describe what they'd shared last night.

Camp dressed hurriedly and vaulted out of the wagon first. He raised both arms to help her down just as Megan, accompanied by Brittany and Sherry, slopped through the puddles between the two wagons. Megan skidded to a stop. The others piled into her.

Color drained from the girl's face. "I didn't know where you were!" Disgust replaced the fear in her eyes. "You slept with him. How could you?" Covering her face, she ran blindly through the rain.

Camp shielded Emily as best he could. He expected Sherry's support and was disturbed to hear her side with Megan.

Clutching Brittany's arm, Sherry stared at her brother and her friend in confusion. "Find Megan," she urged Brittany. "Tell her she can bunk with us for the time being."

"Yeah," Brittany said stoutly. "This is totally gross. And I'm never going to take another of Nolan's stupid classes."

"That's a relief," Camp murmured to Emily. "I guess that means she's over her crush." When Emily didn't respond, he bent for a closer look at her face.

She tried to wrap her jacket tighter and wad up her wrinkled long johns. Her eyes looked dead. "Oh, see the mess I've made of things!" she cried. "I've played right into Mona's and Toby's hands."

Camp attempted to enfold her again. To his surprise, she shook him off. "I'm not blaming you, Camp. Last night was as much my fault as yours. But I have to consider what to do now. Please, just leave me alone."

Numbed, he watched her splash through muddy bogs to her own wagon.

Last night, they'd talked about seeing each other after the trip. They'd made firm promises, or so he'd thought. Now, in just a few words, Emily had reduced the special experience they'd shared to a one-night stand, and Camp didn't like it. He didn't like it at all.

CHAPTER THIRTEEN

"Women would have been quicker to go West if it wasn't for the rat-finky men who led the expeditions."
—Brittany wrote this in block letters across her data sheet, leaving the rest blank.

AS THE MORNING SKY lightened, a brisk southerly wind blew the rain clouds away. A beautiful double rainbow arched high over Rabbit Ears, promising hope for a better day. Few noticed. They were too busy choosing sides in the latest skirmish.

Camp wallowed in a black mood, but at least he'd built a fire and fixed coffee. Emily didn't even do that. She was hiding, as if they'd done something wrong. That was ridiculous, he fumed. They were adults. Unattached, responsible adults.

In the course of sipping coffee and grumping, Camp noticed a lone rider canter in. Not Sherry's gold-panning professor. A stranger. Maizie's problem, not his. Rising, Camp tossed the last dregs from his cup and hauled out his shaving gear.

Emily crawled from her wagon just as he propped his mirror on his feed trough. She immediately ducked back out of sight.

"Wait!" Camp slung the towel over his shoulder and

lunged for her. He grasped her wrist. "Emily, this is crazy. I love you! But it's as if you're willing to throw away everything that's happened between us."

Her throat worked convulsively for several seconds before any words came. "Love? You can't. I...can't. Oh, Camp." Tears glistened in her blue eyes.

His fingers tightened. "*We* can. Together. You're not fighting alone anymore." Releasing her, he cupped her chin.

Her lower lip trembled. "Don't do this, Camp. Don't make me choose between you and Megan. I stayed in a bad marriage for years because I couldn't...wouldn't forsake my kids. I won't do it n—"

"Hush." He brushed his fingers over her lips to silence what he didn't want to hear. "How could you even think I'd ask you to? You and the kids are a package, Emily. We'll work things out. Have faith."

Sherry and Megan rounded the wagon. Megan's mutinous expression forced Camp to drop his hands. The two skirted Emily as if she had some communicable disease. Their actions made Camp furious.

"Megan's gathering some of her things," Sherry said stiffly.

Emily hopped down and walked away.

Camp stood his ground, facing his sister once Megan had climbed into the wagon. "I'm serious about Emily. I want to marry her, Sherry."

"Marry...?" He watched the reactions flitting across Sherry's face. Shock and bewilderment. Camp waited, expecting congratulations to follow. He waited to no avail. Megan handed an overflowing duffel and a cosmetic case out to Sherry. Then, as if he hadn't spoken, the two brushed past him and disappeared.

So…he and Harv Shaw were to be tarred with the same brush. Social outcasts. Camp steamed all the while he shaved. But…hadn't he read in pioneer journals that women united behind one of their own whom they felt was being mistreated? And men were blackballed for being too familiar. But that was then, not now, dammit! He hadn't mistreated Emily, and his intentions were honorable. In fact, if they'd had more time to talk, he'd planned to discuss paying her debts to free her from Toby and Mona.

"You're sure looking sour today, boy. What's got your tail in a crack?" Maizie sauntered up behind him.

Startled, Camp felt his hand slip. The razor nicked his chin. "Ouch!" He dabbed at the blood. "Do you mind honking or something? Scare a guy out of ten years' growth, why don't you?"

"Sorry. You look full-growed to me." She slapped him hard enough on the shoulder to splatter shaving cream down the front of his clean shirt.

He scowled harder. "You're in fine mettle. Is that why we're dinking around here giving the flies and mosquitoes a field day? Shouldn't we hit the road?"

"I figured after the day we put in yesterday, we all deserved to sleep late. I can see an extra hour's shut-eye didn't improve *your* disposition. I thought you'd be walkin' on air after the helluva job you did herdin' people to safety. I hope you gave yourself credit for heroism in that essay you were workin' on last night. Burned the midnight oil, didn't you?"

Memory of how he'd spent the long night slammed through Camp. "Uh, thanks for the praise, but the piece I'm writing isn't about me. It's about the women. And they deserve most of the credit for the way they handled themselves."

"Yeah. Share the glory—that's fine. Hey, I really came for a different reason. From here to Ute Creek we're on private farmland. The owner sent a rider with an invitation to join 'em this afternoon for a barbecue. Palmer Jones declared a holiday in our honor."

"How'd he know we were here?"

"He had a plane up at first light checking crop damage. The pilot relayed how close we'd come to the path of the tornado. I know Palmer. He's probably majorly grateful that he didn't have to deal with our dead bodies strewn over his new-plowed ground." She guffawed heartily.

Camp couldn't resist a grin. "He's not alone in that."

"You got that right, sonny. With Philadelphia ready to call his lawyer as it is, I shudder to think what would've happened if you hadn't gotten the others into the rocks as fast as you did."

"Isn't there some way to muzzle that nincompoop?"

"Last time I checked we still had freedom of speech in this country."

"Too bad." Camp dabbed at the dot of blood again. "Won't attending this barbecue put us farther behind and give Harv more to bellyache about?"

"The ground's a hog-wallow anyway. What's eatin' you, boy? I thought you'd be happy as a possum in a strawberry patch. The farmers on the trail always threw a wingding for passing wagons. Can't get more authentic than Palmer's hospitality."

"Sorry. Guess I'm not in a party mood. I'd be more inclined if my sister and her pals quit acting as if Emily and I had smallpox."

"Don't they appreciate that you saved their sorry hides?"

Camp's hungry eyes devoured Emily as she sat beside Mark's fire, brushing curls into her gleaming, just-washed hair. "The two are unrelated, Maizie."

"Uh-huh," she grunted. "That ol' green-eyed monster, then?"

He eased out a breath. "Are they right to object? Lord knows there's reason enough on both sides to avoid entanglement, I guess."

"Well, if it means anything…when you turn your back that lady looks at you with her heart in her eyes. Now, it ain't my business, mind you, but seems to me two college professors oughta be able to figure a way around most any problem."

Camp's gaze remained locked on Emily as Maizie walked away. Obviously she didn't understand the extent of Megan's dislike for him. It presented a critical hurdle. However…there'd been a time he was a pretty fair hurdler.

He repacked his razor while Maizie spread the word about the barbecue. Plainly, her message perked up everyone else's spirits. Only, his mood remained pensive. Already he missed Emily's quick wit and her bubbling laughter. To say nothing of the sense of well-being that came over him when they were together. But he'd worked with enough teens to know that it'd take more than a smile or a teddy bear to win Megan's favor. He just wished he knew what it *would* take.

Out of habit, he kept tabs on Emily in the line of wagons. Long after he ceased to see her profile, he imagined how her lips had felt last night on his bare skin. His mind relived every moment in her company as the train wound through miles of fields laid waste by the storm.

The smell of barbecue smoke reached the column

before anyone could see the Jones farm—which turned out to be a huge, multipillared estate with wide verandas reminiscent of Southern plantations.

Palmer and Evelyn Jones were nowhere near as ostentatious as their home. "Welcome, welcome," he boomed in a jocular voice. "Climb down and sit a spell. We'll have that side of beef cooked faster'n you can say bar-bee-cue!" Jones sported a snowy beard that contrasted with leathery skin toasted to the color of teak.

"According to my pilot, you're all luckier than a snake in the Garden of Eden. Storm reminded me of the big twister we had in '52."

"Palmer, dear, don't get started. At least let them eat before you bore them."

He turned to his wife, a plump woman with warm brown eyes. "All right, Evie. Bring on those horse-durveys you and Cora've been fussin' with all morning."

At that signal, a row of duded-up farmhands lounging against the fence doffed summer straw hats and rushed to help the women from their wagons.

Camp watched three cowboy-types stumble over their polished boots trying to be the first to reach Emily and Sherry. He wasn't at all pleased with the gallant giant—a younger version of Clint Eastwood—who won the stampede to Emily.

The saving grace was that Megan Benton looked as miffed as Camp felt. Although that was probably because the cowboys had unmistakably relegated her to the status of kid.

Oblivious to any undercurrents, the locals boisterously led the way to a side yard set with long picnic tables, leaving Camp and Robert to unhitch the wagons. Even Mark and Jared went after the tempting canapés

Mrs. Jones and Cora had begun to pass on trays. But when Mark chanced to glance back, he returned to the wagons to pitch in.

They released the horses into a field of deep grass where Jones had told Maizie to let them graze. Several such fenced fields circled the house, making a lush oasis on the endless brown prairie.

Moments after the last horse was turned out, Mark and Robert joined the revelers. Camp, slower to seek the laughter that rang out from the side yard, plucked a piece of sweet grass to nibble. That was when he noticed Megan slumped against Sherry's wagon, tears streaking her cheeks.

In view of her continuing hostility, he could have left the girl to her own devices. But it went against Camp's nature.

"Megan…" He tossed the stalk of grass before he sauntered toward her. "Sometimes it helps to get frustrations off your chest. As a teacher, I've developed an impartial ear. So if you feel like talking…."

"Butt out," she sniffed, gouging a knuckle into very red eyes.

"If I had a dime for every time a student started out saying that, I'd be a millionaire. Come on, Megan, you don't have to like me to talk to me."

"Why are you so cheery? Mom took up with that other dude fast enough. She doesn't know *you're* alive, either."

Camp heard the bitterness in the girl's hoarse voice. "'Took up with' is a strong term for someone she's just met. I imagine the young man was just flirting with her because Mr. Jones asked his staff to make us feel welcome—that's all." He tried not to grit his teeth. "Anyway, Emily called for you. I heard her."

"She didn't mean it. Because...because she hates that I look like my dad. Mona said. She didn't even cry when they told her Daddy died."

Mona again. "I'm afraid I can't comment on that, Megan. I do know that sometimes people are too shocked to cry at first. I'm reasonably sure you were aware that your parents were having a tough time before the accident. Your grandmother can only guess what your mom felt inside."

"But it's true she hated my dad. They didn't even sleep together," Megan cried.

"When a marriage breaks up, it's never one-sided." Camp weighed his next words carefully, eventually deciding to lay his cards on the table. "There's no question that your mother loves you, Megan. This morning she said that if she had to choose between you and me, I could take a hike."

The tears dried on Megan's cheeks. "Is that why you let the dude horn in?"

Over the top of Megan's flyaway mahogany curls, Camp had been following the outline of a man jogging through the field next to the one with the horses. He'd burst from a small stand of cottonwoods. Camp found it curious that the rail fence surrounding that parcel of land was interspersed with barbed wire.

His gaze left the man momentarily to snap down and clash with Megan's accusing eyes. "That's not it at all. Emily is worth fighting for—even if that means fighting with *you*—until the cows come home. I just can't conceive of doing anything to hurt her." *There, let her chew on that!*

A shout for help interrupted Megan's reply. It came from the puffing man Camp now identified as their obnoxious wagon mate from Philly. Charging fifteen feet behind him, with massive horns lowered, was the biggest, ugliest bull Camp had ever seen.

"Quick, call Mr. Jones or one of his men," Camp ordered Megan over the enraged bellow of the bull. Expecting her to obey, he took off at a run.

"Why would you help that jerk?" Megan yelled.

Believing the panic on Harv's face spoke for itself, Camp scrambled over the fence and dropped inside. Shaw, who carried fifty pounds of extra weight, had begun to flag. "Hurry, man, " Camp shouted. "Don't stop now. Here…I'll give you a boost."

Face as red as the shirt he was wearing, Harv had his hands full trying to keep a grip on his unzipped pants. He lost his grip and they floated down around his knees. It didn't take Einstein to figure out why the man had made a trip into the trees.

Damn, Camp didn't see how he could distract the bull and heave himself, plus someone who outweighed him, over a six-foot fence topped with barbed wire. Rivulets of sweat ran into his eyes as he ducked behind Harv and tried to heave him over the fence.

Harv grunted. "I'm caught on the wire."

Out of the corner of his eye, Camp saw the bull change directions. And he saw two other things. First, the seat of Harv's pants was firmly caught in the top strand of barbed wire. Second, Megan still stood outside the fence, doubled over laughing.

Worse—much worse—the snorting, drooling, plunging bull pawed menacingly a few yards away. Camp shoved frantically at Harv again. His flabby butt bounced immediately back. Camp decided this whole thing must resemble The Three Stooges.

Harv's shouts finally penetrated the party noise. Harv's wife, Sherry and Emily dashed pell-mell toward them.

Just as the bull lowered his head to charge, Camp saw Emily vault the fence.

"Don't just stand there, Campbell," she shouted. "Haul ass."

"No way! Get out of here." He made a move toward her.

"My dad raised Charolais," she said. "I used to run circles around guys like that." She inclined her head toward the bull, which had stopped to paw again.

"Yeah. Well, in another life I medaled in the hundred-yard dash. So you help Harv. I'll distract the bull and hightail it over the gate."

"Too far," she muttered. "Uh-oh. Time's run out. Quit trying to act macho. Harv's too heavy for me to budge."

Before Camp had time to think, she darted at the animal, flailing her arms. Left little choice, he climbed up two rungs so he could better reach the impaled man. Above the sound of blood rushing in his ears, Camp heard people shout. He wanted to check on Emily, but he almost had Harv free. Besides, having seen Emily in action during the tornado, he had to believe she could do what she said.

And she would have if the bull hadn't swerved around her and charged the men.

"Ah!" Camp felt Philly disconnect from the barbs and fall into his wife's waiting arms. Camp should have followed. Instead, he glanced over his shoulder to check on Emily—and smelled the hot, putrid breath of the bull. Next, he heard denim rip, and a searing pain tore up his calf. If not for the hands dragging him over the fence, he'd have lost purchase and become a rag doll for three thousand pounds of royally ticked Santa Gertrudis.

Camp clutched a torn, bloody pant leg, noting with relief that Jones and some of his men had arrived and gotten Emily out, too.

It was Megan's white face that Camp noticed, even more than the sticky blood seeping through his jeans. She was literally shaking. Then Emily appeared, blocking his view. She brushed his hands away and began to mop at blood with a handkerchief that smelled of jasmine. Camp gave himself over to her ministrations.

"The brat just stood there and laughed." Harv's eyes bulged. He'd zipped his pants, but still had a large L-shaped flap in the seat, exposing his underwear.

"I'm awful sorry." Her guilty eyes flew to Camp. "I—I didn't think anything bad would hap-happen," Megan stammered.

Camp felt sorry for her. Anyway, why hadn't Harv asked to use the bathroom in the house? At the very least he should've realized the barbed wire wasn't for looks. Camp thought maybe he was more willing to be magnanimous toward Megan because he felt protective of her. Or because Harv Shaw had been a horse's patoot from the get-go. "Come on, Harv. Where's your sense of humor? We must have looked pretty funny. And you can't blame the bull when they're probably barbecuing his brother. I don't know about you, but I've worked up an appetite. What say we put this aside and go eat?"

Had Camp imagined it or was there a modicum of respect along with the regret in Megan's eyes? Before he managed to ferret it out, Mark ran up, asking if he could bring Camp a soda or anything.

"No, but thanks, sport. I'll be fine once I get this leg taped together. Please, everyone—go back to the party."

Surprisingly, Megan came forward. "Mom, I'll go get the first-aid kit."

"Uh, thanks, honey. We'll meet you at the wagon." Emily helped Camp to his feet. She shook off the hand of the cowboy who tried to take Camp's weight—the young Eastwood who'd been following her around. "Go back to the barbecue, Dylan. My kids and I can manage."

The man's gaze bounced from Emily to Mark to the retreating Megan. "They're yours? But they're…you don't look old enough," he burst out.

"Megan is fourteen, and Mark is twelve. Believe me, I've earned my parenting badge for every one of those years, and then some." She would have slipped her shoulder under Camp's arm again, but Sherry nudged her aside this time.

"You go with Dylan, Em. I know how fussy Nolan is about his clothes. I'll see him back to the wagon, tend his leg and find him a clean pair of jeans."

Some of Emily's joy folded in on itself. But she hated to make a scene. And if Camp wanted her help over Sherry's, he didn't say so. She pasted a smile on her face. "Let me stop and tell Megan not to bother with my first-aid kit, Dylan."

"Sure. Sure. You go on. Uh, do the other ladies all have kids, too?"

"Not Sherry or Brittany. Sherry just took off with her brother, and it appears you'll have to pick a number to wait for Brittany." Doing her best to keep a straight face, Emily pointed out the young woman already ringed by admirers.

Leaving Dylan to his fate, Emily hurried to where Megan waited. "Sherry's taking care of Camp's injury. Why don't we go eat?"

"I'm not hungry. Mom…could we maybe grab some time later to talk? I mean, just the two of us?"

Emily sucked in a sharp breath at Megan's earnest tone. "Why, ye-yes. Any time. I'm always available for you and Mark. You know that, don't you? Your welfare comes first with me."

"Really? Then do you mind if we talk now? Otherwise, I—I might lose my nerve."

"This sounds important. Shall we walk?" Emily linked her arm with Megan's and they strolled back the way they'd come. "Avoiding the bull, of course." She smiled.

Megan looked troubled. "Camp asked me to go for help. I didn't."

"Oh." Emily's loose hold on Megan's arm tightened. "I wondered what Harv was yammering about. This time, your decision had serious consequences. You need to realize that, Megan. Is this what's bothering you?"

"Yes and no. Tell me why you and Daddy lived like strangers in the same house," she blurted.

"Sweetheart…" Emily's voice was strangled. "I, ah, I guess you have a right to know." Little by little, as they walked, she unveiled the truth about Dave's decline and how the money his parents had handed him only made his slide into booze easier and faster.

Eyes huge and weepy, Megan asked in a shaky voice, "Why didn't you just take Mark and me and leave?"

Emily attempted to explain the far-reaching influence of Megan's grandfather in terms she hoped made sense to a fourteen-year-old.

"Toby and Mona are awful," Megan burst out angrily. "How could you let me believe them all this time?"

"How could I not? Don't you understand, Megan?

They had...still have the power to take you and Mark away from me."

The girl threw herself into Emily's arms. "Mama, I'm sorry. I'm so sorry that I help...helped them."

"There, there, hon." Emily hugged her tightly. She, too, cried. "That's why I chose this trip. I'd hoped—but what on earth happened today to bring this about? Not that I'm complaining." She sniffled, wiping first Megan's eyes, then her own.

"Camp's the reason."

"Camp?" Emily drew back. Her heart began to hammer. Did that mean he had talked with Megan? That they'd buried the hatchet? She was almost afraid to hope.

Megan wriggled out of her mother's arms. "He, uh, caught me feeling sorry for myself. I don't 'xactly remember what all he said—except that you loved me enough to tell him to flake off. Gosh, Mom, I figure you *must* love me bushels to dump him like that."

Emily's heart wrenched. She felt it tear in two. She had to force her arms around Megan this time. But she should have known better than to wish for too much good luck. Why wasn't it enough to be mending bridges with Meggie?

It was, and yet...

The piece of Emily's heart that Camp had begun to thaw didn't want to go back into cold storage. Unfortunately, Megan hadn't minced words over the reason for her abrupt turnaround. Emily dared not even contemplate risking the loss of her daughter's tenuous trust. She simply had to avoid Camp at any and all cost.

The remainder of the day posed no problem. Megan

never left Emily's side, and Camp spent the bulk of his time in the company of their host.

Prodded by the hot, drying winds that blew in, Maizie announced they'd leave at dawn. At first there were grumbles, but after cleaning up and delivering a profusion of thanks to Mr. and Mrs. Jones, everyone seemed ready to turn in.

Morning brought harsher winds. No one complained. They were just glad the monsoons had passed. Maizie said there'd be three days of hard driving to reach Wagon Mound, at which point, weather permitting, they'd take a side trip to Fort Union.

Camp half expected Emily to fuss over his injury— would have welcomed it. But she seemed preoccupied. So he left Sherry's original bandage in place.

At their few brief breaks and throughout lunch, Camp observed that Emily and Megan appeared to be tighter than ticks on a hound. That was good. He assumed he'd played a small part in bringing about their reunion, so Camp was at a loss to understand why Emily now went out of her way to avoid him.

Dammit, he'd ask her outright at supper. That plan got sidetracked by a sandstorm that drove them all inside their wagons for the next two days.

Early the third morning, Maizie clanged them awake before dawn. "Rise and shine," she roared in a voice loud enough to wake the dead. "We've gotta make fast tracks today unless we want to bog down in the shallows of the North Canadian River. If this sand keeps rolling we'll be in silt up to our armpits."

"You do have a way with words," Camp grumbled, poking his sleep-rumpled head through the canvas. Sand trapped between two wagon bows dumped on him.

Mark and Jared hooted with laughter at Camp's expense. The others were a little more restrained, except for Sherry.

"At last!" She said, laughing. "God finally agrees that you should bathe. I understand not wanting to wet the cut on your leg, but did you break the arm that holds your razor?"

Camp snorted. "I only let shaving go for two days. Besides, I distinctly remember hearing you say how sexy George Clooney looks with stubble."

"George has that helpless I-need-a-keeper look," Sherry said. "Sorry, bro. You look more like a gorilla."

"Well, since we're related..."

Maizie stuck her thumb and finger between her teeth and whistled shrilly. "Save the family squabble till we hit Wagon Mound. Then you two can trade insults all you want. You'll need that excess energy to push these wagons through sand."

That sobered everyone. Camp withdrew to check the covers on his stores. Emily might act aloof; Sherry, however, seemed more her old teasing self. What was up with Emily? Camp gave up trying to figure her out in the face of hordes of giant blackflies that swarmed around horses already edgy from stinging sand. With each successive break they took, Maizie's temper mushroomed.

"Keep that rear in gear," she yelled at Camp after he slowed his team to a walk in order to check on Emily, who had all but stopped her wagon.

Camp's own composure snapped. He was drenched in sweat and his leg throbbed like the very devil. "We've got women driving three wagons, Maizie," he said angrily. "Maybe *you* have the strength of two mules, but they don't."

Sherry swung around and attacked Camp. "Pu-leeze! Speak for yourself. We didn't come this far to wimp out now. Feel free to quote me in your paper."

"Forget my paper, Sherry. Can't you see that Emily's played out? Last time we switched her teams, she got stuck with four ornery Belgians. They'd pull my arms out of their sockets, too, for crying out loud. It has nothing to do with gender."

"Ha! You say that now, but what's to prevent you changing your tune when you actually write about this incident?"

Emily glanced at Sherry's red face and the tired lines fanning from Camp's eyes. "Why would he be dishonest, Sherry?" Emily asked quietly.

"Yeah, sis. I'm not the one who loaded the dice here. You'd better ask yourself how many friends you'll have if you kill off Emily and Gina."

Sherry sucked in a sharp breath, once again feeling betrayed by Emily. And by Nolan. "I thought they *were* friends," she said in a shaky voice. "Apparently I was wrong." Swiftly, she moved up in the line. She wouldn't let them see her tears.

All Camp saw was a flicker of pain that sliced through Emily's blue eyes. As for his sister, he didn't know her anymore. "Emily...I..." He stretched out a hand. It hung in the wind as Emily slapped her reins. And as she'd done on their first day out, she left Camp in a film of red dust.

Who'd have thought that one simple academic paper had the potential for causing so much trouble? Camp sighed. He knew he only had until Santa Fe to set things right with Emily.

Soon, lethargy crowded everything else from Camp's

mind as their grimy column limped toward the rock formation. Early pioneers had named it Wagon Mound because its outline resembled a Conestoga pulled by a brace of oxen.

Oddly enough, someone driving more modern conveyances—off-road vehicles—had beaten them to the long-awaited shelter. Eight to ten men milled aimlessly beneath a gaudy blue cabana. It looked surreal and out of place to Camp. As the wagons lined up and stopped, flashbulbs suddenly winked in rapid-fire succession.

"What in blazes?" Camp worked to calm his high-strung team. Had they stumbled into a movie set? When the spots before his eyes cleared, the first person he saw was his history colleague Lyle Roberts. And Jeff Scott. Their clean clothes left the biggest impression on Camp. He passed a hand over his bloodshot eyes, wondering if they were a mirage. But no, reporters swarmed the wagons. One particularly aggressive journalist badgered Gina to tell him about her injured leg. The few men Camp didn't recognize turned out to represent syndicated newspapers.

Imprinted on Sherry's grim features, Camp saw a firm belief that he'd arranged for this welcoming committee. Groaning, he dropped the reins long enough to massage his aching leg. Whoever engineered this twist of fate had ruined everything. After this, it was unlikely Sherry *or* Emily would ever speak to him again.

Philly was the only one delighted with the invasion. He swooped down, taking his day in court, so to speak. If there was any part of the trip the man *didn't* bitch about, Camp couldn't figure out what it'd be. But for the life of him, he felt too beat to care.

CHAPTER FOURTEEN

"Exploring the Santa Fe Trail is still a huge adventure. Not for the fainthearted."
—Caption beneath a newspaper photograph of Camp.

LYLE ROBERTS STARTED to clap Camp on the shoulder, then encountering his filthy shirtsleeve, drew back and dusted his hands. "Congrats on making national news, buddy. Our boss is rolling in clover. He loved having the department's name splashed all over TV. But why give so much credit to the women? Outrunning a tornado should have scared them into dropping this project faster than last year's wardrobe."

"What the hell are you talking about? We weren't on television."

"Indirectly you were."

Camp wondered why he'd never noticed before that Lyle had an oily smile.

"An Oklahoma news team interviewed a pilot. He and his boss, some farmer, expounded at length about your escapades. They were unduly impressed that women drove some of the wagons. That's why I rounded up this crew—to counter the damage, so to speak. These women won't look quite so impressive when these guys write their articles."

Grabbing Lyle by the front of his spotless jacket, Camp all but yanked the shorter man off his feet. "See here. My paper isn't a hate vehicle against women."

Lyle's Adam's apple bobbed. "No? At least a *them and us* piece, then. I thought that was the whole idea."

Camp tightened his grip. "Your attitude toward women stinks. The group did a damn fine job coping in every instance. Don't you dare knock them until you've trekked this trail yourself!" Releasing Lyle before he lost it totally, Camp rolled his tired shoulders and limped off to tend to his horses.

Jeff Scott, who'd witnessed most of the byplay, approached Camp. "This publicity gig on the heels of your run-in with a twister was probably bad timing. I'll pass the word. We'll leave now—save our brouhaha for your arrival in Santa Fe."

"You do that," Camp snapped.

"Ah, what's your expected ETA?" Jeff jumped back as Camp detached the forward singletrees, freeing the first two of the giant, dust-covered Percherons.

"Next Friday, barring any other unforeseen problems." Camp's irritation cooled. He'd always found Jeff to be reasonable.

"If by unforeseen you mean stormy weather, relax. The five-day outlook for this area is much improved. Sun, sun and more sun."

"It's not just the rain," Camp said wearily. "Wagons break down. Horses go lame. Sun blisters. This wind stirred up a dust bowl. Good water is scarce. Along the Santa Fe Trail, conditions haven't changed much in a hundred years. That's what I'll explain in my paper. And we had advantages the pioneers lacked. More towns. Better supplies. And no worries about attacks by renegades."

Jeff's jaw tensed. "But you ran afoul of an outlaw. Or so Sherry said."

Camp's shoulders stiffened. He'd forgotten Garrett Lock, Ph.D.—the fellow scholar. Since he couldn't think of a way to set the record straight without embarrassing Sherry, Camp let Jeff's remark pass. Still, Camp had second thoughts about letting these guys walk away with that story. Who knew what they'd print?

"Say, Jeff, why don't you and Lyle tag along with us from here to Santa Fe? Tomorrow we're visiting Fort Union. Frankly, I've always thought a discussion of the frontier escort provided early traders would make a publishable paper."

"I don't know..." Jeff raked a dubious eye over Camp's dirt-encrusted face.

"Come on. Before Lyle spouts off about my group's performance on the trail, he ought to observe them in action."

"I suppose. But we didn't bring any camping gear."

"You're welcome to use my wagon. I'll bunk with Robert Boone."

"Ah, we don't have food, either," Jeff added hastily, as if searching for an excuse.

Camp grinned. "No problem. Men are born hunters, right? We're natural providers. Isn't that what you told Sherry at the college Christmas party?"

Jeff's face turned a sickly green. "Did I say that? I've never shot a gun."

Emily appeared in Camp's peripheral vision. The red dust had coated her normally shiny hair. Untidy or not, she still looked beautiful. When she finally reached him, Camp reined in the warm greeting that rose to the tip of his tongue, lest Jeff see the truth of his feelings. No telling what mischief the men could make of that.

"Emily, you met Jeff Scott in Boonville," Camp said. "I've taken the liberty of inviting him and Lyle to join us for the rest of the trip."

Emily's eyebrows shot up. "Maizie's not too keen on Philly blabbing to the press, Camp. Maybe—"

"I'll talk to her," Camp broke in smoothly.

"Okay. So how many are staying for dinner? We're doing potluck tonight. Something simple. Potato-cheese soup and corn bread."

Jeff patted his stomach. "Great! All we've eaten today is snacks. Your train showed up three hours later than we calculated. By the way, it's good to see you again, Mrs. Benton," he said effusively. "I'm not the best in the kitchen," he added. "But I can manage a potato peeler."

Emily looked Jeff over thoroughly, her eyes revealing nothing of her assessment. "Fine. The rule on the trail is, if you want to eat, you help. Camp, Maizie asked if you, Mark and Jared would hunt up something to burn. We're out of firewood."

"Will do. As soon as I picket my team." It was all Camp could do to hide a grin. He'd bet Jeff had no idea how many potatoes it took to feed this crowd.

"Say, Jeff. Send Lyle and your newshounds to Maizie for a list of chores. She assigns nightly duties. Or Lyle could pull the rocks out of the back of my wagon, build a fire ring and start coffee. Coffee beans are in the canvas sack. The pot and grinder should be there someplace. Water's in that barrel." Camp pointed to the dirt-caked oak container lashed to the right side of his wagon.

Jeff's eyes widened as he darted a quick glance to

Lyle and a photographer, swaggering along the row of wagons. "I'll tell him, but I wouldn't recommend drinking the coffee. Lyle can't even boil water." With that, Jeff trotted off.

Emily's eyes crinkled at the corners as her gaze met Camp's. She opened her mouth to speak, but closed it promptly when Sherry stalked up.

"Hobnobbing with the enemy again, Em?" Sherry whirled on her brother. "Having those macho jerks meet us here was a low, sneaky blow even for you," she accused in a hurt voice.

"But I didn't—"

"Like they just happened to drop out of the sky? Yeah, sure." She turned her back. "Come on, Emily. If we whip up a meal fit for a king, we'll present Lyle Roberts with a culinary feat that'll put his great-grandma to shame." Sherry virtually dragged Emily away.

Camp's weariness struck again with a vengeance. He fed and hobbled his team, giving a lick and a promise with a dandy brush to knock the worst of the red dirt off their once-sleek coats. Tired as he was, maybe he'd skip supper and go to bed early. He didn't have the stomach to listen to Sherry and Lyle sniping at each other all evening.

Emily let Sherry pull her back to the fireside because fixing food for their added guests would take all hands. But she hadn't liked the pallor of Camp's skin and decided to keep an eye on him. Was he coming down with something? He and Robert had done the greater share of the physical labor these last few days. If she'd done any shirking it was only because she'd been preoccupied with Megan.

Megan. If only there was a way to make her judge Camp favorably. Ha! Scant chance of that. She had a better chance of being run over out here by a bus.

While Emily blended ingredients for the soup, Camp dropped off braids of tallgrass to burn in the absence of wood. He came by twice; neither time did he linger. Later, she noticed him carting things from his wagon to Robert's. He'd washed, shaved and put on clean clothes. Was his leg bothering him? It looked as if he was limping.

Maizie clanged the bell announcing supper. Emily got busy dishing up soup and corn bread and lost sight of Camp. When all bowls were filled and everyone seated, it dawned on Emily that he hadn't shown up. *Where was he?* Strangely, it was Megan who threw out the question.

"Where's Mr. Campbell?" Her voice carried just enough to interrupt the talk and laughter being exchanged around the campfire.

Vi glanced up in surprise. "He brought us a huge armload of those grass things to burn. I haven't seen him since."

"Nor I," said Gina. "He refilled my feed trough while the boys braided grass."

Robert paused in the act of pouring honey over his corn bread. "Far as I know, he turned in. He's bunking with me tonight. Gave these guys his wagon." A jab of his knife singled out Lyle, Jeff and the young college reporter who'd elected to stay with the train. "Camp told me the others are leaving after they eat."

"Camp's not sick, is he?" Emily broke in, unable to contain her worry.

"Didn't say so if he is." Robert quirked a brow at Mark and Jared. "Did he mention being sick to you guys?"

The boys stopped shoveling soup into their mouths. "Nope," they chorused.

Emily continued to fret. Since Doris and Vi volunteered to do the dishes, Emily went to check on him. Not wanting to call attention to her concern, she skirted the people who sat around the fire talking after the reporters had taken off.

She peeked into Robert's wagon, but it was too dark to see if Camp looked feverish. Was his breathing normal? Emily listened carefully, the way she did if one of her kids was sick. But Camp wasn't a child, nor was he hers to worry about. Wishing wouldn't make it so. Turning to sneak off as quietly as she'd sneaked over, she ran smack into Sherry Campbell.

"What are you doing?" Sherry whispered.

Unconsciously, Emily raised a protective hand to her throat. "I, um, saved your brother some soup."

"Why? Megan said you'd come to your senses. You have, haven't you, Em?"

Emily's lashes dropped over suddenly wet eyes. "I...I..." Clutching the bowl of soup more tightly, she started past Sherry.

"I don't understand any of this, Em. I'd hate for either you or Nolan to get hurt."

Emily's steps dragged. "Where's the hurt, Sherry? I don't see."

"After all the times you've said you don't think you'll ever recover from a rotten marriage? Well, Nolan's suffering the aftereffects of a broken engagement, too."

"He was engaged?" Emily's chin quivered. "Recently?"

Sherry shrugged. "She married someone else last year. Nolan doesn't talk about it. It's a case of them being mismatched. She expected candlelight and wine from somebody who doesn't have a romantic bone in his body."

Emily recalled the tender way Camp made love. She'd

thought him terribly romantic. Although, who was she to judge? Odd that he hadn't mentioned an engagement. But then, men rarely talked about their failures.

"Have you forgotten how upset you were when you thought I asked you on this trip to set you up with Nolan? I'd feel horribly responsible, Em, if either of you got hurt."

Emily felt an old, familiar frustration. The type that occurred whenever she tried to please and appease. "The last thing I want," she mumbled, "is to jeopardize our friendship."

"Me, too." Sherry looped an arm through Emily's and led her away.

A SULTRY MORNING added to the edgy tempers. Camp's colleagues and the college reporter did nothing, but questioned everyone. Tired of it, the members of the wagon train voted to get under way early.

Maizie was bordering on apoplexy. She was furious that the reporter took down every word Philly said and ignored her remarks completely.

The majority blamed Camp for the burgeoning rift, so he kept to himself.

Try as she might to forget him, Emily's eyes involuntarily tracked Camp. The deep lines bracketing his mouth concerned her. His normally warm eyes were dull. However, he cooked breakfast for his pals and hitched his team.

If Emily had known how much effort it took Camp to carry out each of the duties he performed, she'd have been really worried. This morning he'd finally gotten around to changing the bandage on his leg. The lower half of the cut where the bull's horn had gouged deepest looked swollen and badly infected. Camp cleaned it with alcohol, and just about flew through the canvas roof. He smeared the area with antibiotic cream from his kit and covered it. The rest seemed to be healing.

Lyle's litany of complaints kept Camp's mind off his throbbing leg as the column lumbered steadily across the cracked, baked earth.

"My butt's about to break," Lyle groaned. "I wish I'd hitched a ride back to Santa Fe with the reporters."

"Stuff a sock in it," Jeff warned. "Keep bitching, and if Camp doesn't plant you in that cemetery, I will." He pointed off to the right. "See those hand-carved headstones? Let's walk a while. Hey, wouldn't it be nifty if we stumbled across some old bones, Lyle?"

"*Our* bones, if this keeps up," Lyle said. "I hope Camp puts in his paper that weak pioneers were probably shaken to death."

Camp roused enough to get in a jab. "Women pioneers, right, Lyle? You said there were no weak men."

That shut Lyle up. He clambered out with Jeff, muttering that a walk would do him good. Camp wallowed in the silence. During the brief respite he discovered Emily leaning out every so often to look at him. It cheered him to know that if he fell off his wagon, he wouldn't go unnoticed.

His two talkative colleagues rejoined him much too soon to suit Camp. Especially as it ended Emily's checking on him. It was another five miles before he managed to divert their attention to the vastness of the blue sky. The men failed to see any beauty in scenery. They did shut up, though, as the column neared Fort Union.

The lead wagon flushed a herd of antelope that'd been grazing in an uncut field of grain. All drivers slowed, angling for a better look. But the herd took off.

Whooping, Mark dropped back to keep pace with Camp. "Gina wants to set up for pictures. Man, this is neat. Those other forts were kinda swallowed by towns. This musta been what it was like for the real pioneers."

Camp smiled. What a change from the sullen kid who'd fractured everyone's ears with his boom box at the start of the trip. "Once we pass by, Mark, the antelope will come back. Gina can probably set up a telephoto lens from the fort."

"Good plan." Gina poked her head out of the wagon and waggled an arm. "Hey, Camp, notice anything different? I got rid of the splint last night," she said. "Wish I could lose this leg cast, too. I'm tempted to cut it off myself, but the doctor said not until we reach Santa Fe. It's sure a drag."

Camp's leg wasn't in a cast, but he could understand her feelings. He had zero tolerance for infirmities himself. He turned to a sneering Lyle and said, "She's one tough lady. If you believe women today have gone soft, let me tell you about Gina Ames." He described her injuries and her determination to stay with the train. He broke off as two members of the Park Service popped out of the visitor center to greet them.

If Camp's bad leg was a little shaky when he climbed down, he blamed it on the washboard clay they'd crossed.

"Take the tour," Camp told Lyle and Jeff. "Rusty picked up a stone." He patted the huge horse. Really, though, Camp wanted to shake them and follow Emily at his leisure. Boy, he had it bad. In effect, she'd told him to buzz off, yet he couldn't bring himself to stay away. He loved how her eyes lit with an inner fire each time she experienced something new. He'd never met a woman who derived so much pleasure from simple things. A sunrise. A sunset. Wildflowers.

Perhaps some of her ebullience had even begun to rub off on Megan and Brittany. Megan's face was wreathed in smiles as she skipped along the cobblestone path past the crumbling officers' quarters. And Brittany seemed to be listening intently to what the ranger had to say rather than flirting outrageously with the young man.

The adobe fort was mostly in ruins. The sun beat down mercilessly. Camp found his leg buckling far too often. By the time the rest of the group turned the corner near the military guardhouse, they were far enough ahead that he decided no one would miss him if he returned to the visitors' center. According to the guide, the center boasted a bookstore and a gift shop.

Inside, his eyes adjusted slowly to the artificial light. He sat on the floor and leafed through several books. After choosing two, he hobbled into the gift shop, where he bought small magnets of local stone painted with Conestogas for all the women—including Philly's wife. She deserved a solid-gold Cadillac for putting up with Harv. Anyway, he'd planned to give some commemorative trinket to everyone before they parted. Too bad there weren't many items available for men. As he debated between pencils stamped with the Santa Fe Trail Association logo and fake leather coin purses, the clerk called him aside.

"We just got these in, sir."

Camp studied the key chain she held out for his inspection. Around a Conestoga wagon bow were the words *I followed the Santa Fe Trail.* "These are perfect." He told her how many he needed. "And could I ask a big favor? Would you hide the remaining magnets and wait until we're gone to shelve these key chains?"

"No problem." She bagged his purchases and accepted his credit card. They chatted about the secret gifts even as the first wave of the tour group walked in. Emily and Sherry, followed by Megan and Brittany.

Camp and the clerk stopped in midsentence. He realized how guilty they must look. And for such a benign reason, too.

Sherry waltzed up. "Don't be fooled by his pretty face," she told the clerk. "My brother will twist your words to suit his purpose." Winking at Emily, Sherry explained the mission they were on to the startled clerk.

Camp wagged the two history books he'd bought. "With subjects like you, sis, why stop at a paper when I can fill a book? Wait till you see your role."

"You're kidding?" She pulled back. "You're not. Nolan, history texts flat-out lied about women's roles. I'm calling Yvette to have her meet us in Santa Fe with a reporter from the Women's Hub so we'll get some positive press of our own. Do you have a pay phone?" she demanded of the clerk.

Let Sherry think the worst of him, Camp mused. Suddenly, though, it seemed important that Emily know his work would be an honest account of the trip. But apparently Emily and Megan had also skipped out. He did notice Lyle standing at the end of the counter. Camp swore to himself.

"You'd better muzzle these women, Camp. By the time we roll into Santa Fe, that Yvette will have undermined you so much, you'll probably even be blamed for the tornado."

"Lyle—" Camp grabbed for the corner of a card rack

to keep from falling as an unexpected pain knifed down his leg. "Can't you get it through your head that I'm writing a true comparison-and-contrast, not an exposé? I'll admit that at the time I got roped into this deal I had some reservations about the women holding up. Now, the main thing I've learned is that when the going gets tough, so do the women."

Lyle snorted.

"Don't take my word," said Camp. "See for yourself on the long haul over Glorieta Pass. I'd advise you to sleep well tonight if you don't want the ladies showing you up." Sweeping Lyle aside, Camp limped out the front door.

Concealed behind a row of books, Emily heard everything that was said. Her heart tripped and stumbled in her chest. Oh, why was Sherry never around when Camp displayed the fine traits Emily had come to respect? Well, Sherry might not have been, but Megan and Brittany had returned in time to hear the men's exchange. Emily thought they'd been suitably impressed. She wouldn't pressure Megan just now to revise her opinion of Camp—but soon. Before they parted in Santa Fe. Emily intended to tell Camp that she would see him after they returned home.

Camp begged off joining the others for supper. Once again he missed how closely Emily monitored his every move. In Robert's wagon, Camp rebandaged his leg. It annoyed him that there was no noticeable improvement.

"Maizie, how did Camp seem tonight?" Emily asked out of earshot of the others.

"Fine, I guess." She unwrapped a new pack of gum. "Quiet, maybe. We didn't talk. But then, I'm torqued at him for givin' that jackass from Philadelphia an outlet for his complaints. Why do you ask? Is something wrong with the boy?"

Emily shoved leftover biscuits into a plastic bag. "I'm probably making a mountain out of an anthill. We had words a few days ago. He may be avoiding me."

"More'n likely he ate something that didn't agree. A steady diet of camp cookin'll do that. Or maybe he's plain tuckered. Heat'll do *that*."

"Um. Probably that's it." Emily struggled to contain a yawn. "Mercy. Hiking around the fort today wore me out. Believe I'll turn in, too."

"Do that. Next couple days are gonna be monotonous as hell. You'll see why some folks went crazy trekking this trail. No hills, no trees, no water until we make the bend and start the climb over the pass at San Miguel."

Emily wrinkled her nose. "That ought to test our grit."

"Test more'n that. It'll be a miracle if I don't strangle Philly."

"Or if Sherry doesn't throttle Lyle Roberts. I thought she was going to dump bean soup over his pointed head tonight."

"Yeah," Maizie chuckled. "And every woman here'd be cheering her on. Good night, girl. Can't wait to see what develops tomorrow."

NOTHING DEVELOPED. Except the day was long and monotonous. First, Sherry's wagon broke an axle. It took Maizie, Sherry and Emily three hours to fix it; Sherry had refused help from the men. Then Philly's lead horse stepped in a gopher hole and pulled a tendon. Maizie raked him over the coals for his carelessness. He cried foul, claiming she'd led him across that particular piece of ground on purpose.

Camp was awfully glad when Robert insinuated himself between those two. Today, Camp's head felt the size of a barn door, and he was sweating like a bay steer. Not surprising. The sun hung in the sky—a red ball of fire. Emily slathered sunscreen on herself and the kids so many times, they all resembled greased pigs. Watching her fingers slide over her skin alternated joy with pure torture.

Few words passed between the travelers after Maizie stopped for the night. Not even mosquito netting deterred the bugs that descended on them. The flies were horrible. Camp burned his dirty bandage to keep the flies off it. It was such a disgusting process that he decided to leave his wound unbound.

ABOMINABLE WAS A TERM Camp jotted in his journal numerous times over the next two days. No one in the group escaped visible scars—welts dealt them by repeated strafing missions of flying insects. The only good that resulted was that everyone expended so much energy outwitting the bugs, they had no stamina for back-biting. For once Philly's lip was zipped, as was Lyle's.

On the third day out, the ragtag party reached San Miguel. There, at least, was something of interest to break the tedium of the prairie.

"Whoee! Is that a mirage?" shouted Gina, pointing to the silhouette of an old adobe church that broke the flat, continuous skyline.

"I'll give you half an hour to take pictures," Maizie shouted. "By two o'clock I plan to be well into Glorieta Pass."

The women tumbled out of their wagons, laughing and cavorting like kids who'd escaped a school bus after riding three hours to a field trip.

The men, normally more reticent, climbed down and ran through the old plaza and down a slope to where the Pecos River was little more than a muddy ribbon. All except Camp. His leg still oozed in spite of the antibiotic cream. Thank goodness there were no red streaks that would indicate blood poisoning, but neither was it healing.

On her way back from the river, Emily realized he still sat on his wagon seat in the shade of a gutted adobe house. Screening her eyes with a sunburned arm, she assessed his condition. "Camp, are you sick? Have Jared spell you."

Camp blinked at the soft outline of the face he loved. Heat devils glistened and quivered around Emily's slender body, splintering his concentration. "I'm fine."

She put her hands on her hips. "If this show of machismo is for the sake of your book, it's plain asinine. I'm calling Jared now. So you climb into the back of that wagon. Go on." She gave a nervous laugh. "I must sound like your mother."

He didn't laugh with her. Instead, he tossed her the reins with a sigh and climbed into the wagon box.

Sherry ran up, dashing water from her dripping wet hair. "I never thought I'd soak my head in filthy water. Frankly, it felt better than sex." Not receiving the expected response from her friend, Sherry sobered. "What's wrong? Why are you holding Nolan's team?"

"He's not feeling well. Will you go ask Jared if he'll drive?"

Sherry frowned. "I don't remember Nolan ever being sick a day in his life. But...he spent hours in those last two rivers, ferrying everyone safely across. Who knows what awful germs lurked there. Look at me. I'll probably die of some amoebic invasion." She spiked her muddy hair. "Okay, I'll hunt up Jared before I wash. Nolan will be all right?" It came out in the form of a question.

"Yes. And hurry with Jared. I hear Maizie giving her rebel yell to move out." Emily worried her bottom lip. Camp had caved in too easily. Surely he'd say if something serious was wrong, wouldn't he?

Maizie chafed as the drivers dawdled. But at last the column stretched out for miles across a fallow, arid field. She'd instructed them to leave plenty of room between wagons for the tough pull up Glorieta Pass—where, because of drop-offs on both sides, they had to parallel the highway. In many places on the long upgrade, the drivers found it difficult to stay on the extrawide shoulder. Passing cars honked, making the big horses jittery and hard to handle.

At three o'clock, when they were midway up the steepest slope, automobile traffic going both ways ceased to exist. The drivers began to relax.

All at once a boom shook the ground. Even those lucky enough to be driving teddy-bear Clydesdales fought to keep them from bolting. The earsplitting rumble had barely died away when two bigger booms thundered in succession. The last explosion catapulted a bleary-eyed Camp from his bed.

"What in blazes happened?" he bellowed, scrambling to sit beside Jared.

"Dunno." Jared set the wagon brake and took a firmer grip on the reins. "Yonder comes a couple dudes in hard hats. Looks like they're talkin' to Maizie."

Word eventually filtered down to the end of the line. The pass was supposed to be closed for the next twenty-four hours so that workers could blast a train tunnel through one of the canyons. The signal crew wasn't happy that members of the wagon train had somehow missed posted signs. "Absolutely no one's allowed beyond this point," one disagreeable hulk of a man yelled, waving his hairy arms at Maizie.

She promptly went from wagon to wagon with the news. To Camp, she said, "I'm madder'n a mama wasp, but my sting won't do a lick of good. This is a heckuva place to try to stake our horses. Just do the best you can. The hulk promised to check with his crew chief to see if they'll grant us time at daybreak to cross the pass."

Gina climbed down from her wagon, using crutches to traverse the rough incline. "If we're going to stop for any length of time, I'd like Mark to set up my tripod. The least grouchy of those workmen pointed out that the last of the old wagon swales are visible in the valley off to our left. I figure with my strongest telephoto lens and a four-to-one converter, I can manage a fair picture."

"Fine by me," Maizie said gruffly. "Might as well get something out of this damned inconvenience."

Camp leaned against his wagon, silently cursing further delay. In the last ten minutes he'd begun having chills. He realized his body needed more help fighting off the infection in his leg than the antibiotic cream provided. He let Lyle's bellyaching go in one ear and out the other.

Unexpectedly, the entire hillside shook with the loudest blast yet. Horses whinnied and reared. The report that followed rattled Camp's teeth.

Mark Benton's team bolted. Thrown off stride, the boy wasn't able to stop the runaways headed on a collision course with his mother's wagon.

In a frantic effort to remove her wagon from Mark's path, Emily snapped her team of four bullheaded horses into gear. She didn't realize that Megan had stood to see what was happening, until the right wheel of her wagon struck a granite boulder. "Megan, sit," she hissed.

Then Emily felt the balloon tire rupture; she felt the metal rim grate on the rock outlining the precipice. In spite of the fact that she grappled with all her strength to turn the team, Megan bounced up and out of the wagon. She hung in the air a moment, then flew over the embankment.

The girl's high cry of terror mingled with the sounds of panicked horses and Emily's bloodcurdling scream.

Charged with a burst of adrenaline, Camp arrived at the ledge while several others, stunned by the accident, huddled, looking horrified. He threw himself flat to the ground. "Be careful. Stay back," he warned Emily, who had somehow landed beside him.

"I'll take care of Emily's horses and wagon," shouted Robert.

Inching forward so he could look down into the canyon, Camp gave thanks that his hastily muttered prayers were answered. Megan's fall had been broken by a scrubby bush that grew on a narrow lip some fifty yards below. While Camp assessed the situation, she moved and tried to rub her elbow.

Camp cupped his hands around his mouth. "Lie still. Don't move a muscle. Please, sweetheart. We'll come after you real quick, I promise."

Emily, flanked closely by Sherry and now Mark, let her shaking hands drop from her mouth. "She's alive," Emily gasped. "Oh, how will we get her? From here to there is a sheer drop!"

Camp scooted back. Cold fear licked at his veins. Another shot of dynamite would shake Megan off her precarious perch. Aware that time was the enemy, he scrambled to his feet. The first jolt of adrenaline had faded, leaving him hot and icy at the same time. All that prevented him from vomiting was the more immediate fear for Megan's life. Even as he pulled Emily into a comforting embrace, he began to dispense orders like a drill sergeant. "Em, you and Sherry go tell those signalmen to radio ahead and stop blasting. Robert, bring the longest, sturdiest rope we've got. Jared, find a sound tree or a solid rock to lash it to."

White-faced, Emily reached out and clutched Sherry's hand. The two seemed in shock. Camp dredged up an encouraging smile.

"I'm going down," he muttered out of Emily's earshot. "Megan's stuck on a narrow ledge that could give way at any time."

CHAPTER FIFTEEN

"All's well that ends... Happy trails to you... Women can do anything!"
                    —Possible endings for Nolan Campbell's paper,
                                                    uh...book?

CAMP WAITED to talk rescue strategy with Robert Boone until Emily and Sherry had left on their mission. Thankfully, the schoolteachers diverted Brittany's and Mark's attention as Maizie ran up carrying three ropes. Camp, who'd never been in the Boy Scouts or the navy, tied them solidly into one. He wouldn't let anyone else touch them.

"You ever done any rappelling, boy?" Maizie asked.

Camp shook his head. "Have you?"

"Nope. Why don't we wait to see if that blasting crew can helicopter in a team of paramedics? We don't need two casualties."

Camp's gaze never wavered. "You know how wiggly kids are. All that's holding her is one unhealthy-looking creosote bush. If I didn't try and Megan fell, how could I ever face Emily?"

"If you two don't beat all. Maybe after this you'll quit square dancing and admit you're crazy about each other."

He'd already done that. The problem was Emily's. And everything hinged on the girl stuck on a ledge. The feisty, pretty, scared kid who needed his help. In the silence that followed, Camp knotted the rope around his waist. He concentrated on the task ahead, oblivious to the ring of pasty faces watching his every move.

Jeff, Lyle, the college reporter and the pair from Philadelphia, stood apart from those involved in the rescue attempt.

Robert twisted the rope securely around a sturdy boulder. Slipping on a pair of leather gloves, he braced his feet, looped the sisal around his shoulders and prepared to play it out a little at a time for Camp's descent.

Just before Camp stepped over the side into midair, he saw Jeff Scott align himself with Robert. Oddly enough, the big man from Philadelphia did the same. *Well, would wonders never cease?*

As Camp dangled in space, grabbing at a bush here and there to keep from bouncing off the granite wall, his mind raced on fast-forward. What if Megan had broken bones? Or internal injuries? Camp worried that maybe he shouldn't have been so quick to play hero. Moving her might do permanent harm. He wasn't a paramedic. He couldn't even heal a damned cut on his leg!

On the other hand, he'd already heard her happy cry, probably at the sight of any warm body coming to her rescue. Besides, it didn't make sense to let her wait alone until help from another avenue could arrive.

Camp was close enough for Megan to guide his landing. "Swing left. Can you grab that skinny bush?"

"Thanks. Will I have a ledge to stand on?"

"Some. Boy, am I glad to see you! Standing up in the wagon was pretty dumb, huh?"

"You're outta rope, Campbell," Robert yelled from

above. His voice echoed back to Camp three times from a yawning cavern below.

Camp settled his feet securely on the thin shelf before answering. "It's okay, Robert. I'm down. Just give me time to catch my breath and check Megan over."

"You got it."

Again the muffled echo seemed to leapfrog spookily in space. Something in the way the outcrop on which he stood sheared off sharply, and the way blue sky and jagged rock formations tilted crazily every time he looked down, shifted Camp's pulse into high gear. He hung on to the rope, worried that he'd pass out.

"Can I sit up now?" Megan begged. "Oh…" the young voice quavered. "You only got one rope. How're we both gonna get to the top?"

Trying to get over feeling as if he was Spider-Man stuck on a vertical wall, Camp could manage only a lame chuckle. "Good question, Megan." He couldn't believe that with so many creative minds topside, no one had thought of that very important detail. "We were all too shaken by your nosedive to think clearly. Anyway, don't sit until I decide if it's safe to move you. Is there space for me to kneel?"

"I can't see too good. But if you turn a little toward me, maybe there is. Just be careful. The rocks are sharp."

They were more than sharp; they were knife-edged. And slippery. As Camp turned slowly, his boot slid on loose shale. One rock shot over the lip. They heard it ping off the cliff wall—followed by one distant thump, then another. After that, no noise at all but the sigh of the wind. Sweat popped out on Camp's forehead.

"Wow. Must be a long ways down." Megan's shaky voice barely rose above a whisper.

"Don't think of that," Camp ordered. "Your mom'll kill me if I don't get you back in one piece."

"I guess she probably went ballistic, huh?"

Camp read guilt in the girl's tone, but at least her volume was stronger. His own heart had almost stopped the minute she'd flown over that embankment. He'd come within seconds of hurling himself over the precipice, filled with visions of snatching Emily's daughter back with his bare hands. If that was the description of ballistic, then it wasn't just a mom thing. "Your mom, Mark, me, everyone was scared to death. So let's give you a look-see, then figure out how to lift you out."

Camp did a check of Megan's extremities. She had a scrape on her cheek that was already beginning to bruise. Her left arm and hand were scratched. Not deep, and the blood had already dried. There was a ragged tear in her shirt and another in her jeans. But as Camp gently tested each joint, Megan didn't yelp with pain. "Do you hurt inside? Stomach? Chest?"

She shook her head.

"Your back? Your neck? I need the truth, Megan."

"I hurt, but I can wiggle my toes…and my ears." Red-tinted lips curved in a cheeky grin.

Tipping his face toward the row of faces peering over the rim, he shouted, "No serious injuries. When I give three pulls on the rope, it means I'll be sending her up."

"Yo!" was the single word that drifted down.

Megan dragged a grimy wrist across her nose and sniffed loudly. "You mean I've gotta go up alone?"

Camp, who suddenly felt a stab of vertigo, said curtly, "You didn't have company on the trip down, did you?"

"N-n-no." Huge tears spilled from eyes very like

Emily's. "But then I didn't have time to think about falling. I just did."

"I'm sorry, sweetheart. I didn't mean to bite your head off. You've been very brave. Hang tough a little longer."

"O-kay."

His fingers were so slippery with sweat that Camp had a hard time untying the knots he had so carefully fashioned. The minute he freed the rope from around his waist, he underwent an odd sense of impotence. Standing there defenseless, Camp had a flash of insight. He knew exactly what he'd write. It would have nothing to do with who was stronger, man or woman. But rather how it took everyone working together for people to build on what they'd learned, to survive. That was what the pioneers' quest had been about.

"It's time," Camp muttered. "Let's hoist you back to your mom so she'll breathe easy." Using the utmost care, he twined the crudely fashioned harness around Megan's narrow chest. Repeatedly, he checked the strength of the knots he'd tied.

"I know you didn't have to come after me," she said, clutching his hand.

He gave the second of the two sharp tugs on the rope. "Of course I did. I love your mother, Megan. Everything about her. And that includes you kids." He felt compelled to hug the girl awkwardly and to say, "Tell her for me again, will you?"

"I'm scared. Please, come with me and we'll both tell her."

"Too much weight for those guys to handle." Camp gave the last yank. "Once you're up, they'll toss the rope back down for me." He tried to straighten from his crouched position—to help guide her away from the first outcrop of rocks as the rope tightened and slowly began to lift her from the ledge. A sharp pain knifed through his calf. It hurt so badly it threw him off balance. He let go of Megan and grabbed at his leg. Releasing her allowed the rope to arc. Her feet struck his shoulder, interfering with his already weak hold on the bush. A brittle twig broke off in his hand. Camp felt both his boots slipping.

"Oof." He flailed for a handhold but grasped only air. Megan's scream floated above and below him. His death knell, he thought as wind rushed past his ears. But, dammit, he wasn't ready to go until he heard Emily admit that she loved him. His feet connected with rock. Then his knees did. Then his head. Sky, sun and visions of Emily's smile converged in darkness.

"MAMA, MAMA," Megan shrieked as several sets of hands hauled her out of thin air onto solid ground. "Oh, Mama," she sobbed as Emily's strong arms enveloped her, "He...Camp fell off the ledge. We've got to help him. We've just got to."

The group that pressed in on the rescued girl splintered. Robert, Sherry and Maizie ran to the precipice, flopped prone and draped their heads over the edge.

"Nolan," Sherry called frantically. They heard nothing but the squawk of a bird and the rattle of wind rustling through scrub cedar dotting the hillside. Sherry's voice, uneven with panic, wafted right and left as her brother's name danced around the canyon.

Then...nothing.

Robert cupped his mouth with his hands and yodeled Camp's name three times. The results were the same. Mocking echoes.

Tears coursed down Megan's cheeks. "Mama, he said he loved you. And Mark and me...hateful as I've been. It's my fault. He didn't have to help me—but he did."

Mark clung to his sister's arm and to his mother's hand. Emily noticed that he stoically refused to cry, while she had no defense against the tears that filled her heart and clouded her vision.

"Well," she said, forcing her focus on the next logical step. "Hunt up more rope and a first-aid kit. Camp needs us. I'm going down."

Maizie placed a gnarled hand on Emily's arm. "We'll tell those men to order up a medivac chopper out of Santa Fe pronto. It oughta reach us before dark."

Emily retreated behind a determined smile. "We're wasting time."

"Em, for crying out loud." Sherry waded through the thicket of people clustered around her friend. "He's my brother, but I agree with Maizie. We already know a chopper is on its way. They ordered it for Megan. Oh, sure, I talked big, bragging that modern women are as capable as the pioneers—but what you're proposing...Em, listen to me. This is a job for professionals."

"Save your breath, Sherry," Lyle Roberts snorted. "Look at her eyes. The woman is crazy."

"Crazy in love with Camp," Robert said. "C'mon, Jared...Mark. Let's scout out extra rope."

The three left at once.

Sherry stared at Emily, and feelings of desolation stirred alarmingly in her breast. Her brother and her best friend. Suddenly she felt like an outsider. As if she'd stumbled into emotions she knew nothing about. Perhaps there was time. Most of the women she met through her job suffered from the negative fallout of having loved unwisely. Emily had been one of those women—and she was a counselor, too.

The thought of Nolan with Emily meant she'd have to reexamine all her ideas and beliefs. But that shouldn't matter, she told herself. Not as long as her brother survived this.

Racked with uncertainty, bereft, sick with worry, Sherry crept off to wait alone.

Robert and the boys returned with seven sturdy lengths of rope. Maizie's son knotted them, testing each one. After he'd finished and the rope lay coiled neatly at the foot of a strong cedar, Emily stepped into the harness that'd served both Camp and Megan. Donning gloves, she shrugged off the anxiety she felt emanating from the silent watchers.

Maizie draped a small pair of binoculars around Emily's neck. "Time to call a spade a spade, girl. We don't have any idea how far he fell. If you haven't found him by the time the rope's played out, use the glasses to try to get a fix on him. Memorize landmarks. Maybe save the rescue team shootin' in the dark."

A chill swept over Emily. The combined weight of the binoculars and the first-aid kit clipped to her belt seemed to press in on her, causing panic. Then her two children stepped up and hugged her.

"It's kinda scary swinging out there. But these guys won't let you fall." Megan gazed with trust at the men handling the rope. "I know Camp will feel lots better having you there. He can't have fallen far, Mom. We heard a rock tumble and bump forever. But there weren't any echoes when Camp fell. Only one bump."

Emily stored that information. "Just promise me you kids will stay back from the edge." She trailed a loving hand down their earnest faces. After they nodded, Brittany Powers, of all people, stepped forward, saying the three of them would go recheck the whereabouts of that medivac helicopter. And Emily knew it was time to go.

She'd watched rappelling on TV. That was how she went over the edge. Feet flat against the granite wall, facing those she left behind.

"Good luck," called Gina. "Tell that lunkhead to hurry back here and collect the best darned data sheets yet. Tell him I won't even charge him for the pictures if he decides to write a book."

A smile found its way to Emily's lips. Bless Gina. Emily no longer suffered the niggle of fear that had been eating at her insides. She would find Camp alive. He had an unfinished mission—to write this story. To tell the truth about men and women—modern and pioneer.

Foot by foot she sank into the canyon. She breathed easier after passing the ledge that'd broken Megan's fall. Below that, a grassy slope about four feet wide curved into a bulwark of rocks. Emily saw now that it was a catacomb of caves. Unexpectedly her rear, descending ahead of her legs, struck bedrock. The blow was sharp enough to bring tears to her eyes. As the rope coiled over her knees, Emily glanced around and saw Camp's crumpled form about three feet below her and off to the right. He lay facedown, half in, half out of a granite cave. He lay as still as death. Except for a splash of red that ran from his forehead to his chin, his face was devoid of color.

Emily's heart banged in her chest. Her pulse sounded like a thundering waterfall in her ears. The red was blood. Some dried. Some fresh. She barely had the wherewithal enough to lift her hands to her mouth and yell in a shaky voice, "Stop the rope. I've found him." She recognized her own fright in the echoing words, the reverberations circling like vultures. By the time Robert's question concerning Camp's condition floated down to her, Emily had steeled herself for the worst and scrambled on her hands and knees to press three bare fingers against Camp's jugular. She paid scant attention to the sharp rocks that ripped through her jeans and her gloves. The joy she experienced on feeling a thready pulse overrode all discomfort.

"He's unconscious," she shouted, ignoring the salty tears wetting her cheeks and lips. "But *he's alive.*" Those two precious words exploded on a heartfelt sob of relief. "I'm going to try to determine how badly he's hurt."

The roar of approval raining down from above spurred her onward.

Working swiftly, Emily covered him with the light Mylar blanket from her first-aid kit. It would help retain his body heat and ward off shock. Even now, the sun was sliding out of sight over the ridge, and a cool breeze had risen up. She checked his arms and legs, not feeling any obvious breaks. The knees of his jeans were ripped, but so were hers. These rocks were jagged.

Carefully, Emily tore open medicated pads to wipe the blood from his face. As she touched the large goose egg on his temple that still oozed blood, Camp mumbled and stirred. He flopped from his stomach to his side.

She dabbed at the spot again with the cool sponge. He moaned, blinked twice, then stared at her with huge dark pupils that all but erased the liquid brown of his irises. "Go away, angel," he ordered in a gravelly voice.

"Camp, it's Emily. You lost your footing after you

saved Megan. You have a huge knot on your head. Do you hurt anywhere else?"

He closed his eyes, and for a moment Emily thought he'd slipped into unconsciousness again. Her heart pounded as she stripped away the blanket and began a thorough inspection of his torso and stomach for internal injuries.

"Emily?" Her name sounded thick on his tongue. "For an angel you're stomping all over my pride."

"Oh, Camp." She leaned forward, trailing her fingers across his lips. "You frightened us. Me!"

They both gave a start as a helicopter dipped into the canyon, and the loud whump-whump of its rotors stirred up dust. Like a giant, noisy bird, it hovered at eye level for several jolting heartbeats. Then, as swiftly as it'd swooped in, it rose and disappeared over the ridge.

Before they had time to comment to each other, Maizie's voice warbled. "The rescue team has a fix on your position, Emily. Can you help Camp into a basket if they drop one? The spur you're on isn't wide enough for them to set down another man."

Emily telegraphed Camp a questioning glance.

He said nothing. As she continued to study him, brows furrowed, he sighed and nodded. "I hate going out of here trussed up like a damned Thanksgiving turkey. But I suppose there's no other way."

She shook her head.

"I'm awake," he hollered. "If they toss out a double harness, they can pluck us both out."

"Oh, Camp. Are you sure?" Emily demanded. "That's a nasty head wound."

"Not nearly as bad as the wound to my dignity. I

intended to save Megan, and in so doing earn your undying love—and hers." He grimaced in disgust.

"You did."

"Did what?" Camp's eyes rose to meet her steady gaze.

"Earned Megan's and my undying love."

The sound of the helicopter starting up drowned out his rebel yell. He squeezed her arm and shouted, determined to settle this before the chopper whisked them away. "Are you saying Megan no longer objects? Emily, will you marry me?"

For some reason, the helicopter shut down its engine just then, and the rotors quieted enough that Camp's plea bounced off the cliff walls.

Emily's face flamed red in the last vestiges of sun, and so did his.

"What did she say?" demanded a chorus from above.

"Mom," came the thin voices of Megan and Mark. "It's okay with us."

"I...well, marriage is a big step," Emily whispered. "There're the problems with Mona and Toby. To say nothing of the huge debt I owe them."

The helicopter roared to life again. This time it lifted off and moved out over the canyon.

Camp feared that if he didn't demand a commitment *now,* while she was weakening, it'd be too easy to lose everything they'd gained once life got back to normal. He drew her lips to his and put all his dreams and promises into a single kiss.

They disregarded the downdraft from the rotors that whipped Emily's curls from his hands. Yet he didn't release her until the first cable and harness plopped into her lap. "Say yes," he shouted in her ear. "After all of this, do you believe there's any problem we can't overcome?"

Hands shaking, Emily buckled his safety harness and reached for the second one tumbling from the copter's belly. All through the process of shedding the original rope and connecting the cable straps to her harness, she made him wait. Then, as they wrapped each other in an embrace, ready for the scary upward jerk, she said, "I will marry you, Camp—as long as you publicly admit there's not one darned thing wrong with modern women. I owe your sister that."

He endeavored to land a happy kiss on her mouth, but they were spinning too fast and her eyes were closed tight. Giving up, he growled, "Tell me you know I would have done that anyway."

He felt the rumbling of her laughter. *She did know.* For the first time in longer than Camp cared to remember, in spite of his injuries, all felt right with his world.

On their landing, the chaos he'd predicted set in. Hands of family, friends and strangers wrenched them apart the instant their feet touched the ground. The paramedics who'd flown in examined Camp in one wagon and Megan and Emily in another.

Emily protested, insisting she was fine. And she was. Megan's minor cuts and bruises were treated, and they were both allowed to go.

In the other wagon, Camp didn't fare as well. The blow he'd taken to the head continued to leak blood. But the paramedics were more concerned with the infected cut on his leg.

"We should transport him to Santa Fe," the medics' leader told Maizie. "The blasted man says he won't desert the wagon train. He needs vigorous antibiotic therapy or that wound on his head may end up infected, too."

Maizie unwrapped a stick of gum and folded it into

her mouth. "I can hear what he thinks of your idea." She grinned. "The whole world can hear." She winced, listening as Camp's vocal objections burst through the wagon canvas.

"I understand what you're saying, sonny," she commiserated with the medic. "But I got a policy in this outfit. The customer is always right. Now, we have clearance to scale the pass at daylight, lookin' at maybe an eight-hour trek into Santa Fe. We started this trip together and we'd sure like to finish the same way. Any chance you can give him a shot to tide him over till we reach a doctor? We've got another casualty who'll be goin' to have a cast removed." For Maizie, that was a long-winded speech. She stuffed two more sticks of gum in her mouth, waiting for the medic's reply.

The others crowded close. First the teachers put in a good word for Camp, then Robert.

"Campbell did me a good turn," Philly added gruffly. "It's beyond me why he'd insist on sticking this out. It's the most uncomfortable vacation I've ever taken. However, he wants to stay, so he ought to be allowed."

Emily almost didn't believe her ears. "We'll take care of him," she vowed. "Isn't that right, Sherry? That's what our pioneer sisters would have done."

Lyle Roberts threw up his hands. "You'd let the man die to prove a point. I give up. You win. You're all as tough as shoe leather. And you're also nuts. I intend to tell our department chairman that you all belong in the loony bin."

Almost before the words left his lips, Lyle struggled against an angry press of bodies. "Who knows this pipsqueak is here?" muttered Gina.

"Yeah. We could sort of nudge him over the ledge," Brittany proposed gleefully. "Students would cheer. From what I hear, his classes are totally boring."

Lyle shrank back. "Jeff. Do something."

"Um." Jeff pretended to ponder. "What if Lyle promises to keep his trap shut?"

"He'd better." Mark puffed up like a rooster. "Camp's gonna be me and Megan's new dad." As if that in itself said everything.

"Then the poor sap's getting what he deserves," Lyle said. "Let him write his paper. Nobody who's studied history will believe him." He shoved past Robert and Jared Boone.

The paramedic shut his case and checked around for his co-workers.

Emily pulled him aside. "Don't listen to Lyle. First of all, he's wrong—women's history is a huge new field. And this trip is a history study. Camp's study. He's gone to considerable trouble and expense. How would it look if he didn't finish?"

"Sure you're not in sales?" The medic laughed. "All right. Fine. I'll give Campbell a whopping-big shot."

"Thanks. I'll watch him tonight, and re-dress both wounds if they need it." Emily sought out Sherry with her eyes, daring her to object.

Sherry nodded. It looked as if, no matter what, she was gaining a sister. So why did it feel more like she'd lost a best friend and a brother?

Maizie whistled between her teeth. "We haven't reached Santa Fe yet, folks. Don't think because of all this excitement you can slough off chores."

While the medic dispensed Camp's shot, the others picketed horses and readied a makeshift resting place for the night. After the strain of the day, people mostly kept to their own wagons.

Emily cooked for herself, Megan and Camp. She didn't know who fed Lyle, Jeff and the reporter. Maybe Sherry had. Emily noticed the young college reporter had been following Brittany with his tongue hanging out.

Camp drifted off to sleep before he finished eating. Emily quietly removed his plate and cup. She blew out the lantern. "I'm going to throw my sleeping bag under his wagon, in case he needs me during the night," she told Megan.

"Me, too. In case *you* need me," Megan said. "I apologized to him for everything, Mom."

Emily hugged her child and kissed her on the forehead. It was the first time in over a year that Megan didn't pull away. Emily stayed awake long after Megan's breathing evened out in sleep. So much had happened in such a short time. But she felt good about it. Better than she'd felt about anything in years. Her first marriage had begun with an elopement to Atlantic City. After a quickie wedding, Dave spent what should have been their honeymoon meeting with casino developers.

Yawning, Emily wondered if Camp would mind having a church wedding with all the trappings. A winter wedding. Sherry'd look wonderful in dark-red velvet—provided she'd be maid of honor. Megan and Mark could give her away. Emily fell asleep dreaming of red roses and white carnations.

IN THE MORNING, Camp claimed he felt as good as new. Well enough to drive his own wagon.

"I thought you'd ride with me," Emily said. "I told Jared he could drive yours. There's some young lady he met in Santa Fe on his last trip. Imagine what it'll do for his image to drive a wagon in." Nervous today, she talked in spurts. "Besides, we only have these last few hours to be together. We have a lot to discuss."

Camp threaded his hands through her curls. "We have the rest of our lives, Emily."

"Yes, I know. Oh, Camp. Do what you want, of course. We can talk about a date for our wedding later."

"You're ready to set a date? In that case, Jared, my man—you're welcome to my wagon."

Emily gave a self-conscious laugh. Nevertheless, they whiled away the remaining miles in chatter. In the end they chose Thanksgiving break for the wedding. Both agreed, along with Megan, that it was important to spend Christmas as a family.

"I want you to move to Columbia right away, Emily. I'll take a room with my folks and let you and the kids have the house. After we furnish it fully, that is."

"Kick you out of your house?" Emily shook her head vigorously. "Why can't we all live there?"

"We're doing everything by the book, Em. So your in-laws haven't a prayer of charging you with misconduct. And the first thing we're going to do is pay them off."

She gasped. "But how?"

"My grandfather left me money in trust. His only stipulation was to use it for something that would make me happy. That's you and the kids, Emily."

Her eyes filled with tears. He was offering her love and freedom. No one had ever given her so much. For the remainder of the drive, they hammered out the intricate details. Emily didn't want to go back to the town where her in-laws wielded so much power. Camp agreed. If an opening came up at his college, she could apply or not. As far as he was concerned, it was Emily's choice.

They were surprised to top a rise and see the first of the wagons pull into the outskirts of Santa Fe. A crowd had gathered to greet them. Bands played. Dogs barked, and children stared at the dusty wagons in awe.

Camp spotted the reporters who'd talked to them after the tornado; they were converging on the front wagons with cameramen in tow. "Come on, Em. Let Megan watch the team for a minute. We need to be sure those fools get things straight. It took all of us working as a team to reach Santa Fe. Even Philly came around. That's the story I want told."

"Good luck. You'll have to muzzle Lyle. And isn't that Sherry's friend Yvette? Sherry asked her to bring a staff reporter from the Women's Hub."

They watched Yvette greet Sherry. Camp and Emily were still too far away to hear what the two friends said.

"You actually completed this whole smelly trip," Yvette exclaimed. "You've never looked better, Sherry—outside of those abominably dirty jeans. You've lost weight."

"Maybe five pounds." Sherry wrinkled her nose. "I *feel* good, but you won't *believe* everything that's happened."

Yvette grasped her arm. "Neither will you. Your boss announced his retirement, just as you suspected. I'm glad you filled out that application and left it for me to drop off. You'd have missed the filing deadline by hours."

Sherry clapped her hands. She'd thought her dean might retire. Now that he had and her hat was in the ring, it changed things. Her heart skittered. So Nolan wasn't the only one with good news. Only...what if she didn't reach the interview stage? Guys like Lyle would rub it in forever.

"Yvette, you haven't told anyone I'm applying for the dean's slot, have you?"

"No. But why wouldn't you broadcast such great news?"

"Because." She half turned and saw her brother and Emily coming toward them. "I can't explain now. Please, Yvette, don't spill the beans. Listen to what Nolan has to say. Then you'll understand."

"Married?" Yvette gaped from Camp to the woman who stood at his side. She clucked sympathetically. "Another good woman bites the dust. Well, congratulations…I guess." She slid a glance at Sherry, who'd turned back to her wagon. Camp and Emily left to talk with the reporters.

For the next hour, everyone jabbered at once. Until the outfitter collecting the wagons to make the return trip to Missouri arrived, and the pain of parting struck them all.

"I won't really turn you into the Better Business Bureau," a very subdued Philly promised Maizie. "This trip proved what a man's made of. Uh, and a woman," he added, gazing sheepishly at Sherry. "If any of you are ever in Philadelphia, look me up." He passed everyone a business card.

Camp stuffed the card in his pocket. "I hate goodbyes. Anyway, you're all invited to Emily's and my wedding." He named the date in November. "It'll be a great reunion. I'll send everyone a copy of my paper, too. Is that fair?"

"Suits me," said Maizie. "I want you to know that this trip is one for the books. I owe you my thanks, Campbell. The last few days I haven't even missed my tobacco. Robert's gonna buy me a year's supply of gum before we head home."

"Hip hip hurray!" Vi and Doris led a cheer.

Brittany and Megan squeezed into the circle. "We want to confess to the firecracker caper. We're sorry." They grinned at each other. "Even with all the stuff that happened, we agree this summer's been boss. Rule! The best," Megan interpreted.

Gina limped forward, aided by a cane. "Camp and I, we have a date with the doctor. Oh, and my gift to each of you is going to be a framed picture. I'll mail them."

"Gifts. That reminds me." Camp snapped his fingers. "Hey, Mark. Toss me that blue duffel, will you?"

Gazing adoringly at the man he'd soon call "Dad," Mark brought the bag.

Camp found the sack with the gifts he'd bought at Fort Union. He even gave key chains to the three men who'd joined the excursion late. The reporter, Jeff Scott and Lyle Roberts didn't know what to say. Each looked floored by Camp's generosity as they pumped his hand.

To break the silence, Emily rose on her tiptoes and kissed Camp. Out of breath as she pulled away, she whispered, "That's thanks from everyone for sponsoring the trip. I'll save mine for later. In private." Blushing, she added more loudly, "*After* I edit his academic paper, of course. While he's with the doctor, I'll collect the last data sheets. So make them count, ladies. Make them count. We don't want history repeating itself."

Camp kissed her then. The kiss went on for so long the others drifted away. The couple surfaced and found themselves alone. Laughing, they linked arms and strolled toward the doctor's office.

"The past defines the present, Emily. And the present determines how we look at the past. Lyle is dead wrong about people not paying attention. Our paper will shake a few trees."

"*Our* paper?" Emily's steps faltered. "You actually will let me edit it?"

Camp flattened his hand comfortably at the small of her back. "Oh, did I forget to mention that you and I are going to coauthor this piece? Plus, I really do have an idea for a book that I'll need your help with."

Grinning, she leaned into the hollow of his shoulder. "That book will dislodge a few opinions and revise a few so-called facts. And when the dust settles, Camp, maybe we'll influence the future."

"I think we influenced some people on this trip. Regardless, we'll influence the future of our kids."

"Mark and Megan, you mean?"

"Um…and others." This kiss made him late to see the doctor. Very late, but he didn't care. Professor Campbell felt he had the world by the tail.

HAVING IT ALL

CHAPTER ONE

SHERRY CAMPBELL pirouetted in front of her sleepy roommate, seeking an opinion on her new appearance. She'd undergone a total makeover since returning home from a summer spent trekking on the historic Santa Fe Trail. The pioneer-wagon-train reenactment had left her tanned and trim—a plus, but not her main objective. She'd battled heat, flood and tornadoes to prove a point to male colleagues at her Columbia, Missouri, college. Namely, that modern women were as tough and capable as their pioneer sisters. With help from a few well-chosen friends, she'd fulfilled that mission.

For all the good it had done. Women still had to validate their worth on her campus. Which was why she'd metamorphosed into this stranger—to convince a board of stuffy regents and an administrative interview team that she was capable of replacing the current dean of Human Services. The dean was in charge of Women's Studies, student counseling and the Hub, the women's crisis center that was Sherry's pet project. All the deans at Wellmont College were men. Always had been and, according to some, always would be.

She had a chance to change that.

Allowing herself a small determined smile, Sherry smoothed the navy pin-striped power suit over her flat stomach. "I look so…so buttoned down, Yvette, they'll *have* to sit up and take notice. This is the image they court. I'm not giving them one reason to pass me over for some Ivy Leaguer."

Yvette Miller, the person who'd engineered Sherry's recent transformation, yawned. "I don't pretend to understand what's going on inside your head. You look nothing like your old self."

She and Yvette rarely saw eye to eye anymore, Sherry realized. "I thought I explained that my goal is to blend in with the good old boys," she said, tugging at her short, short hair. Gone were her shoulder-length brunette locks, replaced by a sleek, gold-tipped cap barely two inches long, except for a slight dip over her forehead, where Yvette's beautician friend had left a bit of a wave.

Sherry fingered the discreet gold stud embedded in one earlobe. Already she missed the art-deco earrings that were practically her trademark around campus. Those, and her favorite Mickey Mouse watch. "These suit sleeves would have hidden Mickey. I feel positively naked without him."

"Mickey is funky. That Ironman Timex is what a man would wear."

"You're right." Sherry sighed. "I really hope I'm not a token woman being trotted out to show the community that our administration's open-minded. Rumor has it that of the three final candidates, only one's a woman. *Moi!* And there's a man of color. All very politically correct," she said, wrinkling her nose.

"Still no poop on number three?"

"Nothing, other than that candidate three is also a man. Surprise, surprise."

"Have you asked Nolan? Maybe your business is like mine. In the clothing industry men always have a better pipeline to the top than women do."

"My brother is so mired in his and Emily's wedding plans his pipeline isn't even attached."

"How can you not applaud his wholehearted commitment to Emily and her two kids?" Yvette asked dreamily. "I'd like for some good-looking guy to pay off my debts and whisk me away on a white charger."

"Nolan doesn't have a white charger. He drives a compact. When did you hop on the marital bandwagon? I distinctly remember you saying, 'Another good woman bites the dust,' when you heard their joyous news."

"Well, it's just so romantic. He asked me to find Emily a designer wedding gown regardless of price, because she got shortchanged in her first marriage to that shyster land developer. Nolan wants Emily's wedding at Thanksgiving to be perfect. All women dream of having a perfect wedding. A perfect marriage."

"Mmm." Sherry didn't say the obvious—that a perfect wedding wasn't any guarantee of a perfect marriage. Not only that, she didn't want to admit that she still wasn't sure how she felt about her only sibling marrying her best friend. She wanted to be happy for them, she really did. But what would happen when their bubble popped? And it would. Didn't she work every day with the grim statistics? One in three marriages broke up.

"In college, Sherry, who wore out the bride magazines every month planning our storybook weddings?"

"Back then we were naive enough to think marriage was the be-all and end-all in a woman's life, Yvette. The reality is that few marriages have storybook endings."

"Wait and see. I'll find Mr. Right. You don't even ogle nice buns anymore. It'd do you good to go to a bar with us girls and drool over all that lovely testosterone."

"I see what happens to cast-off wives who are totally dependent on your barroom hunks. Marriage isn't the answer, Yvette. Women are still led down a primrose path. You ought to see how many needy women we turn away from our displaced-housewives program for lack of funding. As dean, I'd have more control over the budget. So, yes, men, or should I say a man in my life, are at the bottom of my priority list."

"Maybe you need to find a new job. Our friends think you've dealt with battered women too long. You've gotten cynical. Rumors are, you hate men. Since your summer trip, even people I know who work with you at the college joke about you being the female Davy Crockett." Yvette moved to inspect her long curly hair in Sherry's mirror. "Trying to prove you're better than a man is not healthy."

"Equal, not better. Terms like 'female Davy Crockett' are meant to put women down. That stuff goes on all the time on campus. Speaking of which, I should leave now. I'd like to get to the boardroom early so I can assess the other two candidates."

She stepped into navy pumps. "So far, Yvette, you and my department secretary are the only ones who know I've tossed my hat in the ring. By tonight candidates' names and faces will be splashed all over the local news."

"If *I* wanted the job, I'd shout it from the rooftops."

"I never thought I'd make final cut. When I learned I had, the family was caught up hiding Emily and her kids from her rotten in-laws. Now they're deep in wedding plans." She shrugged to show it didn't matter. Yet on a purely emotional level it did.

Yvette followed Sherry to the door. "Well, I'm on the road for the next week."

"By the time you get back, maybe they'll be calling me Dean Campbell." Sherry's high spirits lasted until she hit campus and couldn't find a parking place. She'd forgotten this was the last day of registration and the day the faculty returned full force. According to the reader board, it was also new-student orientation. "Rats." Rather than showing up early as planned, she was lucky to dash through the double doors that led to the boardroom on the dot of nine. Almost the last to arrive for the coffee hour.

Talk stopped while all eyes skimmed the latecomer. Sherry's stomach balled as she weathered microscopic inspection by administrators, board members and their perfectly groomed wives. All appeared baffled.

Dr. Harlan Westerbrook, the courtly white-haired college president, left a huddle of men and moseyed toward Sherry. Moseying was his way. A common joke around campus was that he'd be late for his own funeral. Sherry waited to be properly greeted in accordance with the pecking order.

"Sherilyn?" One bushy eyebrow met the president's cottony shock of hair. "I'm so used to seeing you dashing about campus, hair flying like a Gypsy, that I must confess I didn't recognize you."

Smugly satisfied, Sherry wanted to laugh, but said, instead, "Isn't adaptability one of the criteria for this job? As a teacher and counselor at the Hub, I have to blend in with the women we serve. Trust plays a major role in keeping disadvantaged students attending classes. Don't you agree, Doctor?"

"Um, yes… Well, come and meet the other finalists."
Taking Sherry's elbow, the president steered her toward
a short man with olive skin and thinning black hair.
"This is Dr. Eli Aguilar. He's currently department
chairman for minority programs at a prestigious California college." Westerbrook named the institution and
let it impress before he introduced Sherry. "Dr. Sherilyn
Campbell, Eli. Department chairperson of Women's
Studies. This little lady has kept our departing dean on
his toes." Westerbrook patted Sherry's hand. "Reginald
insists she's not responsible for his seeking early retirement, though."

The two men laughed heartily. Sherry didn't smile.
This was typical behavior, intended to keep women
outside the select circles. She offered her hand first. "I
won't apologize for going to the mat with the dean to
retain services vital to troubled women. I'd be interested
in hearing your views on whole-life training for displaced housewives, Dr. Aguilar. It ranks high with me.
Counseling in areas like nutrition and grooming may be
costly, but academic studies alone don't provide an automatic key to success in today's workplace."

Aguilar adjusted his tie a few times before Westerbrook rescued him. "Now Sherilyn," the president
chided, "it's our job to put you three candidates on the
spot—not for you to interrogate one another. Speaking
of candidates, here comes Dr. Lock."

As their chief gazed over her shoulder, Sherry turned
expectantly, one hand extended, a cool smile on her lips.
Her outstretched fingers went limp and her smile died
as she cannoned headlong into the startling punch of
candidate number three's azure blue eyes.

Westerbrook's voice continued to drone in the background, but for the life of her, Sherry couldn't grasp a word he said. Oh, but she *had* to pay attention. *Lock. Dr. Garrett Lock, Assistant Dean of Collaborative programs...somewhere. His background, sociology.* Tongue frozen to the roof of her mouth, Sherry latched on to the newcomer's name and imprinted it in her mind. *Texas.* Westerbrook said Lock had driven to Columbia from Texas. Of course. As he collected her slack hand, he acknowledged her with a honeyed drawl that glued Sherry's toes to the soles of her sensible new pumps.

"Dr. Campbell." Bending slightly, he clasped her hand warmly and kicked up the wattage of his smile. "Any relation to Nolan Campbell? If I recall, his field is history."

Sherry registered the heat sliding up her arm...and little else. Except that Lock's rakish grin exploded like a sunbeam in this dreary walnut-paneled room. He had the most gorgeous sun-streaked blond hair, a good inch longer than her new do. Evenly tanned skin. And teeth so white Sherry thought they must surely be capped.

She tried to respond to his question about Nolan, but the most awful noise wheezed from her throat as if nothing could get past the balloon expanding in her chest. *Hypoglycemia. It sometimes hit when she skipped breakfast. She needed food, fast.*

"Sherilyn is Nolan's sister," Westerbrook answered for her. "Fine man, Nolan. Dedicated professor. I didn't realize you knew a member of our staff."

Garrett extracted his hand from the woman's clammy palm. Something looked familiar about those great cat eyes of hers. Definitely not your normal shade of brown. More like aged amber. He stepped back for a second assessment. Garrett was gifted with a keen memory. He'd hardly forget a woman with such classic bone structure—especially one with hair shorter than his son Keith's latest hatchet job, which came courtesy of Carla's new husband. *The banker* was how Garrett thought of Keith's stepfather. That or *the jerk.* Although he shouldn't place total blame for being uprooted from a job he loved on the man his ex-wife had married. Carla was the one who'd suddenly demanded maternal rights, and as a result Garrett's life had been turned inside out. He might not want this job, but if he didn't get it…well, with him in Huntsville and Carla in St. Louis, Keith would spend half his growing-up years on a plane. An eight-year-old didn't deserve to be zapped around like a yo-yo.

It took Garrett a moment to realize that his sudden fierce frown must be the reason everyone was staring at him so oddly. "Forgive me." He flashed a wide smile. "I was trying to decide if Dr. Campbell resembles her brother. Don't tell him I said so, but when they handed out looks he must've thought they said *books,* and passed because his shelves were full." His joke sparked rollicking laughter from the men. Women gazed at him adoringly.

Sherry did neither. In fact, she'd begun to see that being this close to candidate number three played havoc with her equilibrium and made absolute mush of her brain. "Excuse me," she said abruptly. "The coffee calls. I believe I'll get a cup and then mingle. Dr. Lock…Dr. Aguilar, we'll meet again, I'm sure."

Phew! A flood of relief eased the spasm in her chest as Sherry escaped Lock's presence. What was there about him that so unnerved her? Even now she felt his laser gaze tracking her progress across the room, and her feet tangled. *Stop it!* She consciously erased the frown from between her brows. Filling a cup to the brim with coffee, she gravitated toward the cluster of women Lock had just left. Regents' wives chorused hello, then returned to the topic they'd been discussing.

"Doesn't that handsome Dr. Lock just shiver your timbers?" The speaker was a plump impeccably dressed matron—a power on campus in her own right. Sherry knew of several instances in which this lady had influenced staff hiring.

The matron's bony companion fit the expression that a woman could never be too thin or too rich. She cast her voice in a regal whisper to entice listeners. "Sheldon told me—in confidence, mind you," she murmured, referring to her husband, the current board president, "that Dr. Lock is divorced." She said the word one breathless syllable at a time. "Can you imagine *any* woman foolish enough to let him leave her bed?"

Sherry sympathized with Lock as every last woman undressed him with her eyes. In spite of her own efforts not to turn, her gaze automatically strayed toward him. She recalled her earlier chat with Yvette on the subject of ogling men. Her response now seemed hypocritical in view of the way she all but drooled over Lock.

Sherry spun back. Normally she wasn't the least bit impressed by broad shoulders and tight butts. In Lock's case, though, she was forced to admit that he wore his dark green suit to perfection. Not a single crease where other men's suits were wrinkled. Obviously tailored to fit. His usual attire? Or an indication of how badly he wanted the job. Without appearing obvious, Sherry gave closer scrutiny to the loose way Lock stood, hands on hips, every so often pausing to gesture with a well-manicured hand. Well-manicured but not soft, she noted, remembering how it had felt during the brief meeting of their palms.

He broke off in midsentence, glanced around and caught Sherry giving him the once-over.

Annoyed at the heat suffusing her neck, Sherry deliberately steadied her coffee cup, took a sip, and transferred her inspection to Aguilar. His suit fit well enough. But of her two opponents, she judged Lock the man to beat in this race.

"Sherilyn, dear." A thin voice broke into Sherry's assessment of her competitors. "I understand you piloted a Conestoga across the prairie this summer. Frankly, I never understood why anyone would wish to reenact the old days. Notice I didn't call them the *good* old days. I belong to the historical society for philanthropic reasons. You must come and address our group, dear heart. Lyle Roberts, from the History Department is our professional adviser. He said you even had a run-in with an escaped convict and that you beaned the man. If it'd been me, I would have fainted dead away. You must have nerves of steel. Weren't you frightened at all?"

Sherry, who'd practically forgotten the incident as she prepared for these interviews, drew a fleeting mental image of those blue, blue eyes. No wonder her heart had flip-flopped a moment ago. Lock's eyes were similar in intensity and color to the eyes of…that man. The man who'd loomed out of the fog the night she'd fallen behind the other wagons. But eye color was where the similarity ended. Although… She shivered. Both men hailed from Texas.

Lock exuded city polish. Dallas or Austin would be

Sherry's guess. The bearded ragged stranger claimed to be from Huntsville—home of a maximum security prison. Sherry still suspected he'd been an escapee. Gooseflesh peppered her skin.

"Sometimes," she said, wetting a dry bottom lip, "adrenaline drives us to acts of courage. As a rule, I'm not given to violence. Thank goodness I didn't accidentally kill the man. I wish Lyle would stop talking about it. He's miffed because a handful of women made mockery of his archaic beliefs. Professor Roberts thinks women belong in the kitchen, not in the workforce."

The wife of the board president raised a silver brow. "I've been more than happy to let my husband be the breadwinner during our married life."

Sherry took a big gulp of coffee. She wouldn't touch that statement for love or money. Scratch a vote. But then, she'd already decided these women were biased in Lock's favor. Question—how much influence did they have on their husbands?

She noticed the chill in the air. Now she was almost sorry she'd left the men.

"Sherilyn, do you have immediate plans for starting a family?" the wife of the board president asked next.

"By immaculate conception, you mean?" Sherry murmured, hating herself for giving in to the little green demon perched on her shoulder. Relenting somewhat, she offered a thin smile. "You obviously have me confused with my brother. He's the Professor Campbell who's getting married in November."

Sherry was spared more grilling when Dr. Westerbrook rapped on one of the tables.

"Delightful as this coffee hour has been," he boomed, "we're here for business. If the candidates would step

forward and the guests would be seated, we'll have time
for a few informal questions before we take a tour of the
campus. I trust the selection team has had a chance to
peruse all applications, supplements and curriculum
vitae," he said, employing the academic term for
résumé.

Heads bobbed. Sherry took a deep calming breath
and detached herself from the group of women.

A hush fell over the room as the three finalists set
coffee cups aside and made their way to the teak podium
that bore the college seal. Or rather, two of the candidates
left their cups behind. Sherry realized that Garrett Lock
had ditched his saucer and kept his cup. Smart man. It not
only made him appear more relaxed than the other two,
but he had no worries about what to do with his hands.

Sherry tried thrusting hers into the pockets of her suit
jacket, only to discover that she hadn't removed the
stitching put in at the factory to keep the pockets from
sagging. *Darn.* Why was she so tense? She had the
home-court advantage, so to speak. After all, she knew
the foibles of the people asking the questions. *And their
strengths,* mocked that little voice. Indeed, they wielded
all the power. No wonder her palms were sweating.
And poor Dr. Aguilar. If he smoothed his hand through
his thinning hair many more times, he'd leave these interviews bald.

Garrett, who fell in beside Sherry, raised his cup in
salute. "Let the roasting begin," he muttered near her
ear.

She was surprised—and impressed—that he dared to
joke. But when his clean citrusy scent engulfed her and
his solid shoulder brushed her arm, sending shafts of heat
to her icy fingertips, Sherry wished she'd stood else-

where. She edged a step closer to Dr. Aguilar, determined to ignore Lock's presence and make a good showing.

"I have a question." The board president leaned back in his chair, hooking his thumbs in his vest. "This is for all three candidates, starting with you, Dr. Aguilar. Suppose we asked you to cut twenty percent from the Human Services budget?"

Aguilar thought a moment. "I, ah, would have to see the budget and study it very carefully before making any determination. I'm a very thorough man."

The president rocked back on two chair legs. "Dr. Campbell?"

Sherry's heart plummeted. Naturally he'd smirk. They'd gone through this exercise last year. As department chair she'd been very vocal in her opposition to cuts. She was still opposed. Looking him in the eye, she said, "Enrollment is up. Operating costs, too. We have a staff member on sabbatical and one on paid leave. Cutting anywhere would be disastrous." *There, let Lock try to top her knowledge of the operation.*

All eyes in the room shifted to him. He gestured with his cup and said in a maddeningly slow drawl, "Well, y'all, I've never seen a budget that didn't hide some pork. If you say cut, I'd trim the fat. It's as simple as that."

Sherry's response to the undercurrent of approval manifested itself in the form of a keen desire to kick Garrett Lock right in his skinny butt. *Trim the fat, indeed!* She was so royally ticked off she almost missed the next question. For fifteen minutes thereafter, the candidates fielded rapid-fire questions. Just when she thought they were winding down, she was blindsided by a challenge aimed strictly at her.

"Professor Campbell," demanded the dean of

Science, "as current department chair, do you feel you'd be able to work effectively with either of the other two candidates should they be awarded the position?"

"I—I—I..." she stammered. Clearly it was a question intended to undermine her candidacy. One that took a potshot at women by intimating they were too "emotional" to accept defeat. Anger bubbled, yet Sherry sensed it was crucial that she give calm rational answers.

Surprisingly, help came from Garrett Lock.

"Excuse me, but isn't that question somewhat premature? I don't know about Dr. Aguilar, but I'm not sure I'm ready to hear Dr. Campbell's perception of my shortcomings. What if her opinions adversely influence the team's decision?"

Dr. Westerbrook stood and faced the man who'd posed the question. "Dr. Lock is absolutely right, Byron. At this stage in the process, interrogation must remain equally applicable to all candidates. Now, I think we've kept them on the hot seat long enough for one session. Shall we begin our campus tour?"

Everyone rose dutifully and shuffled toward the doors. Glancing at Byron Imes, Sherry could tell he hadn't liked being publicly chastised. From his scowl, she'd say his vote would, out of spite, go to Eli Aguilar. So far, it appeared she trailed miserably in the overall tally.

Still, it was decent of Lock to stick his neck out—unless he'd done it because he wanted to come off looking the hero. Sherry didn't want to be beholden to him for any reason. Needing to make that clear, she pulled him aside. "If that show was intended to prove your Southern chivalry, then you've made your point.

Don't mistake me for Little Red Riding Hood. I can take care of myself with the worst of the big bad wolves. So back off."

Garrett's eyes narrowed as he watched her stalk away. That walk… He suddenly saw the swing of squared shoulders and a compact shapely rear disappearing through wisps of fog. He squinted, trying desperately to hang on to the vision as Professor Campbell melted into the crowd. It wasn't just her walk that reminded him of the spitfire who'd bopped him over the head this past summer. The memory floated in and out.

While panning for gold alone in a remote corner of Kansas, he'd stumbled across an apparition right out of a history book—a covered wagon. It was apparently being driven by two women. The night hadn't been fit for man nor beast, and he'd offered to help the women, who'd seemed lost and rather desperate. One, without provocation, attacked him with a stick of firewood. Then Nolan Campbell showed up—an affable guy, a historian writing a paper on how modern women handled trekking the Santa Fe Trail. The whole incident was so bizarre that after returning home, he almost believed he'd dreamed it. Except for the lump above his left ear that served to remind him.

The woman who'd hit him had had a mane of lush dark hair spilling over her shoulders. That was fact. Shaking his head to clear it, Garrett was jolted back to the present as two of the regents' wives flanked him, smothering him in a cloud of opposing perfumes.

"Mustn't dawdle, Doctor. If you're going to win, you'll need to strip off those kid gloves and climb into the ring."

Garrett recognized Maxine March, wife of the board president. She clucked over him as if he were a prize at

a silent auction. As if she saw in him an eligible
bachelor to hook up with a friend's single daughter. He
knew that look from Huntsville. Campus communities
were alike in many respects. He needed to let the match-
makers know that he and Keith did okay as bachelors.
His son went to school clean and well fed. As for a
divorced dad's other needs, Garrett had learned to live
with celibacy. Long periods of celibacy. He told himself
it built character.

He wasn't looking for wife number two, and he had
no intention of owing these women favors of any kind.
Yet as he opened his mouth to set them straight, Garrett
remembered why he'd tossed his hat into the ring.

Carla. Keith.

There wasn't another suitable opening on a campus
within a hundred-mile radius. Tempted as he was to chuck
it all, he knew he couldn't. He was stuck with this side-
show—because he intended to walk away with this job.

CHAPTER TWO

THE TOUR SEEMED to lift everyone's spirits. Brick buildings warmed by afternoon sun dotted a campus scattered with trees dressed in crimson fall foliage. Flowering shrubs lined interwoven walkways, scenting the air with a pleasant fragrance.

Sherry never tired of the ever-changing seasons here. She counted herself lucky to teach in such a stimulating atmosphere. In springtime the grass greened and the trees budded with new leaves. Rain washed everything clean. Summer heat brought a quiet period, lazy and relaxed, while autumn reinvigorated everyone with its briskness and beauty. Then winter winds blew in from the north, dropping a soft blanket of snow that students loved, and faculty and staff grumbled about good-naturedly.

Three generations of Campbells had received their higher education at Wellmont College, now in its seventieth year. All had proudly worn the burgundy caps and gowns on graduation day. At times Sherry stood at her office window and dreamed of seeing her own children among the students scurrying between classes. She'd never breathed that fantasy to a soul. Her yearning for babies contradicted how she felt about love, about marriage. Yvette, now, fell in and out of love on a regular basis. She attracted drop-dead gorgeous guys the way flowers attracted bees. And discarded them as ruthlessly as a bee sucked a flower dry. That never used to bother Sherry. Lately it did. She and Yvette were growing in different directions and that saddened Sherry. She supposed they should terminate their present arrangement as housemates before their friendship, which had spanned three decades, deteriorated beyond repair.

Ahead, administrators and board members trudged up the steps and into the counseling center where the departments of Women's Studies and Collaborative Programs shared space. Sherry had an office there, as did the dean of Human Services.

Sherry wondered what her opponents thought of the campus thus far. Maybe they wouldn't like it. It certainly didn't compare in size to the sprawling California institution where Aguilar worked. She hadn't caught the name of Lock's school, but she'd heard Texans were possessive about their particular portion of the vast state. So why was he hoping to move? Advancement, she thought glumly. He was already an assistant dean, and on paper at least, seemed the most experienced of the three.

She looked for the two men to see if their faces gave away their feelings. A casual glance over her shoulder had her sucking in her breath. Lock stood so close that when he exhaled, her skin absorbed his breath. His eyes, fathomless blue, reflected the ivy-covered brickwork. He'd stopped to read the words carved into the ledge circling the six-floor building. "'You must do the thing you think you cannot do,'" he read aloud. "Good advice," he said as if in response to Sherry's scrutiny. "A quote from Eleanor Roosevelt, isn't it?"

"Why, yes." The fact that he knew surprised Sherry. The quote was repeated on all four sides of the building, but Mrs. Roosevelt's name had only been carved on the south side when this building was added in the early 1940s. He couldn't have seen it from where they stood.

By now most of the entourage had disappeared, leaving them alone. Garrett laughed in the face of her amazement. "What can't you believe, Dr. Campbell? That I recognize the quote or that I deem it good advice?"

"Both, I guess," Sherry said honestly.

Bracketing his hips in a very male stance, Garrett shook his head. "Is that an opinion you formed because I'm a man or because I'm from Texas?"

Set to give a terse comeback, Sherry found herself responding favorably to the deep grooves creasing his tanned cheeks. Annoyed by that, she linked her hands loosely over her stomach and pretended to study a crack in the cement. "My remark did sound sexist. I'm really not—no matter what you may hear." Her head came up and Sherry stared straight into his eyes. Why it was important to make herself clear, she couldn't say. Maybe because of what Yvette had said concerning remarks floating from campus into the community.

A small frown gathered between Garrett's straight brows.

Sherry was very glad when someone hollered for them to hurry. Lock was puzzling over her statement far too long. She didn't want to be forced to explain. He probably hadn't heard the rumors. Lies. Sherry didn't hate men. She got darned tired of playing second fiddle to them on this campus. Perhaps it wasn't true of all colleges, but here men got the best jobs. They were promoted faster and held most of the top positions.

Sherry was quick to respond to the summons, leaving Garrett behind. Or so she thought. She hadn't heard his tread and she gave a start when a masculine hand reached around her toward the door. For a second she gaped at the strong wrist and the long fingers gripping the knob. A thin gold watch lay in a dusting of light bronzed hair, gleaming below his starched French cuff. *Nice hands.* But then, she'd thought that earlier. With a jolt, Sherry discovered that he was staring at her quizzically. *Of course.* She needed to step aside and give him room to open the door.

"Excuse me," she mumbled, backing up and right into him. Her heel landed squarely on his foot and she felt him wince.

"Well, that's one way to eliminate the competition," he said pleasantly, a deep dimple winking briefly in his left cheek.

"Sorry. I didn't realize you were so close."

Dr. Westerbrook threw open the door, startling them both. "There you two are. We're waiting for Sherry. As department chair, she'd ordinarily give the grand tour. To avoid any perception of bias, I thought we'd ask the department secretary to fill in. What's her name?" he muttered behind his hand. "I should know."

"Angel," Sherry said. "Angel Baby Webster is her legal name. But I wouldn't advise using it," she said with a teasing grin.

Westerbrook grimaced. "Now I remember. She's rather, uh, flamboyant. Maybe you'd better do the honors, after all. You know how conservative the board is."

"Angel should talk to them. We hired her after she completed our program," she said for Garrett's benefit as they walked toward the waiting group. "Angel is the epitome of what we're about. The first time I saw her as a referral from the battered-women's shelter, she had a black eye, swollen lip and two broken ribs. The father of her six-month-old boy had thrown her down the stairs because the baby was sick and she couldn't keep him from crying. She has two older kids from a previous bad marriage. Our program offered her an alternative to living on the streets—or in prison. When the police arrived at her door, she was one step from carving up the boyfriend because he'd started to slap her kids around." There was more to tell, but Sherry felt a collective uncomfortable shifting of the VIPs.

Wishing she'd kept Angel's story to herself, Sherry elbowed her way to where the secretary sat. She quickly introduced the petite young woman, then said "Angel, please explain how we operate. I've told them you're an expert on our work-study program." Sherry gave her arm a supportive squeeze, then stepped back.

Westerbrook sidled up to Sherry and whispered, "You've accomplished miracles. The dean brought me through the department right after you hired her. She looked like a…a vagrant."

"Many of our students arrive at the shelters with nothing. Did the dean tell you he opposed hiring her? Job placement is the final phase in whole-life training. Education isn't much good unless it puts food on the table and a roof over one's head. I hope no one considers it *fat* that needs trimming from our already meager budget," she said, looking pointedly at Garrett Lock.

The president coughed by way of response. Sherry was disappointed but not surprised. The old guard believed that degree in hand was the primary if not the only duty of this institution. They opposed funding anything that might be misconstrued as vocational training. Westerbrook and his henchmen would graduate ten thousand poli-sci majors, never mind that only one in a thousand would find work in that field.

Sherry decided to abandon the front row. Hassling the president wouldn't advance her cause. Again, unexpectedly, she turned and plowed into Garrett Lock.

This time, as his eyes cruised slowly over the stubborn set of her jaw, he wore a sympathetic expression.

Sherry pushed past him and ended up next to Eli Aguilar. The look on his face remained guarded. Great! She probably ran last in the field of candidates. And if either Lock or Aguilar won, she'd have the same walls to scale as she'd had with Kruger. Or worse, she groaned inwardly. Eli would study every issue to death, and Garrett would hack the life out of the program.

Sherry wasn't sorry when Westerbrook announced that interviews were over for the day. His secretary, Fern Mitchell, opened her briefcase and handed each candidate a revised schedule for the next day.

"As you'll note," Westerbrook said, "we meet at nine tomorrow in the lobby of the theater for coffee with the faculty. Immediately following, delegates from the Faculty Association will present a composite of their questions. So be prepared," he warned. "Lunch in the boardroom will give you a chance to relax and regroup. At two, you'll talk with students. Next day are the individual interviews, and after that friends of the college and other interested parties from the community will host a tea. At seven, there'll be a dinner, where we hope to finalize a decision. I think that's all until tomorrow."

"Wait." Garrett Lock stepped forward. "I don't

know about Eli, but I'd like to see some of the city. Is that possible?"

"We'd be glad to chauffeur you around, Dr. Lock, wouldn't we, Sheldon?" Maxine March nudged her husband.

"I appreciate the offer, Mrs. March, but in the interests of fairness, I thought perhaps Dr. Campbell..." He let the suggestion hang a moment. "Then neither Eli nor I would have greater access to anyone on the selection committee."

"Good thinking, my boy." Westerbrook clapped Garrett on the back.

Sherry started to refuse until she realized Lock was absolutely right.

"I'd like to see the city," Dr. Aguilar agreed. "But my wife is at the hotel. I hate to leave her behind."

Sherry imagined squeezing them all into the Ford Escort she hadn't cleaned properly since school let out. The backseat was littered with folders and the floor with empty diet-soda cans. A brilliant idea struck. "I'm sure that, under the circumstances, Dr. Westerbrook will authorize us to use a vehicle from the motor pool. The white van," she hinted, referring to their newest acquisition, knowing full well he didn't like women to drive the state vehicles, period. She bit her lip to hide a smile as both Lock and Aguilar turned expectantly to the president.

"Ahem." He glanced at his secretary. "The white van? I...I suppose. But I want it returned before dark."

Sherry covered her surprise at his easy capitulation. "I'll go back to the office with Fern to collect the key," she said. "That'll give Dr. Aguilar time to call his wife. Gentlemen, the motor pool is building twelve on your map. We'll meet there in, say, fifteen minutes." She checked her watch. Expecting to see Mickey's gloved hands, she stared blankly at her arm for a moment.

"I'll take a cab to the hotel and wait with my wife. Do you mind? I have a phone call I need to make," Eli told Sherry.

"F-fine." She didn't like being left with Lock. "Maybe Dr. Lock would like to freshen up, too," she said with sudden inspiration.

"I'll just come with you," Garrett put in smoothly.

Sherry didn't want him tagging after her, although she couldn't put her finger on exactly why. Curving her lips into a false smile, she inclined her head graciously. It unnerved her further when he hurried to open the door, then placed a hand lightly on her back to guide her through. At the top of the steps his hand slid to cup her elbow. Did the man not think she was capable of navigating stairs, for pity's sake?

Once they'd reached the bottom, however, and he withdrew his support, for some strange reason Sherry felt like a barge cut loose from its tug. She quickened her steps to catch up with the president's secretary, who walked briskly along the path.

Garrett lengthened his stride, too. He shot her a sidelong glance, trying to recall the last time he'd encountered such a prickly female. Normally he was the one backing away from women who came on too strong. Garrett didn't know why he was annoyed, but he was.

"Nice campus," he said, taking his eyes off her to scan the brick courtyard where students gathered to study and talk.

"Yes, it's a wonderful place to work," she admitted grudgingly. Lock tucked his hands in his pants pockets, and Sherry heard the rattle of change.

"What can you tell me about the town's elementary schools?"

"In what regard?"

A light shrug rustled his crisp shirt collar. "Gangs. Drugs. Anything of that nature."

"Thinking of changing fields?" she asked, sounding hopeful.

"Nothing so drastic. I have a son going into third grade."

"A son. Oh. But I…I'd heard you were divorced," she stammered.

One sun-tipped brow feathered upward. "That's correct."

Flustered, Sherry scrambled to form an answer to his first question. All her dealings had been with single mothers. She didn't personally know any single dads. "I, ah, there're very few problems in our school system. My mom retired last year after teaching in the district for thirty-five years." Sherry waved her hands expansively. "I'm telling you this in case you think I'm whitewashing the situation."

"Frankly, I worried about the opposite." Garrett struggled to hide a sheepish grin. "We are after the same job, remember. You might have said the schools were infested to the max on the off chance I'd drop out of the race."

She stopped and blinked at him. "I do want this job, Dr. Lock. But I wouldn't lie to get it. I've worked hard to improve assistance offered by the crisis center and the rape-relief-counseling program at the Hub. I believe I'm the most qualified to direct Human Services."

"Fair enough." He hesitated. "Call me Garrett, please."

Sherry abruptly picked up her pace. "This afternoon I'm your tour guide. Tomorrow and the next day we go back to being rivals. If I'm chosen, we'll never see each other again. If you are, I'll call you Dean Lock."

"Ouch. You don't pull any punches. Most women—"

"I'm not most women, Doctor. We're here. Excuse me, please. I'll go sign for the car keys." Damn and blast, but the man unnerved her.

Garrett rocked back on his heels as she strode through the door with the frosted glass. He watched her shadow, and for just a moment, a sense of familiarity knotted his stomach. Then it disappeared, leaving him with nothing but the sting of her rebuff. He studied the two women's silhouettes on the glass and noticed that his opponent talked with her hands. Both outlines were tall and slender, but Dr. Campbell was more...voluptuous.

Garrett seesawed from one foot to the other, briefly wondering what lay below that severe blue suit. He clamped down hard on the unexpected arousal he felt. He didn't have those kinds of feelings about women colleagues. And if he ever did, he'd pick one a damned sight less abrasive than Sherilyn Campbell. She wasn't his type. In fact, she was the complete opposite of his type, in personality and appearance.

Her ultrashort hair was a turnoff, Garrett argued silently. He frowned as her silvery laughter wafted through the narrow opening in the door, making mockery of the fact that he'd tried to convince himself he only found women with long hair attractive.

Discovering that he wasn't nearly as impervious to the professor as he wanted to be cooled Garrett's eagerness for the tour he'd instigated. Now he wished he'd let well enough alone.

They walked in complete silence to collect the van. Few words passed between them as Sherry drove to the hotel to pick up Eli Aguilar and his wife. She did slow once to point out the George Caleb Bingham Gallery of Fine Art, adding, "Over there—the building with the black reflective windows—that's the insurance company where my dad's worked for nearly forty years." Thawing a bit, she smiled. "Mom bugs him to retire. They have a house on five acres east of town. Both are horticulture hobbyists. Ever since I was little, they've talked about building a greenhouse. But Dad's a conscientious agent. He can't say no to people who refer clients. I wish he'd slow down."

Garrett noted her wistful expression when she spoke of family. It softened her features. "Quite a feat to live in the same town for forty years. I had hoped— Well, never mind. Things happen," he said, turning to gaze out the side window.

It was on the tip of Sherry's tongue to ask what had made him apply for this job and leave a place he obviously disliked leaving—although she still didn't know what Texas college town that was. Nor was there time to probe. They'd reached the hotel. Sherry spotted Aguilar and a petite pretty woman standing at the entrance.

Garrett got out when Sherry stopped. He opened the van's side door, closing it again once Eli and his wife were buckled into the center seat.

"This is my wife, Marguerite," Eli announced proudly. "I apologize for asking you to go out of your way. I know it was an inconvenience, but we left our three children with their grandparents. I wanted to call and see how they're getting along."

"Three." Garrett whistled through his teeth. "I have one son. He keeps me hopping. 'Course, I'm a single dad," he said, in case Aguilar didn't know.

Sherry couldn't begin to explain the sudden yearning that struck her. Yet it'd struck with greater frequency this past year. When she found herself sitting with groups who discussed their children, she felt a gap in her life. To cover her discomfort, she smiled at Eli's wife in the rearview mirror.

The woman smiled back. "It's kind of you to show us around."

"I thought I'd drive past libraries, museums and hospitals," Sherry said. "The insurance industry, medical services, colleges and a university make up the backbone of our city's economy. I'll circle our biggest shopping mall and go through a new housing development, as well as a more established neighborhood. Barring traffic problems, I'll have you back at your hotel in time for dinner."

The Aguilars nodded in agreement.

Garrett settled comfortably into the seat. "Fine as a frog hair split four ways," he said in a husky drawl.

His remark made no sense to Sherry. But the timbre of his voice had the same effect as someone using her spine as a piccolo. After that, she did most of the talking. Sherry's pride in Columbia was unmistakable. Her passengers were kept so busy craning their necks this way and that no one had time for questions.

Garrett asked the first after they'd completed the circuit and she'd again pulled under the awning at their hotel. "There were no For Sale signs in the residential areas. Not even in that new development. Do they not allow signs or what?"

"They do. Right now our growth exceeds available housing."

"But there are rentals?" Garrett had climbed out,

shut his door and leaned in the side door where the Aguilars got out.

Sherry's hands tightened on the wheel. Did Lock sense he was the leading candidate? Was that why he pressed for details that wouldn't matter if he didn't get the nod? "I'm afraid you'll have to ask someone in real estate," she said stiffly. Purposely glancing at her no-nonsense watch, she added, "You might still catch an agent if you hurry."

"Here's your hat and don't trip on the way out?" Garrett deadpanned. "Seriously, Sherilyn," he said softly, ignoring her earlier insistence that they stick to titles. "Speaking for the Aguilars and myself, we appreciate your time and trouble."

Sherry bit her lip. "It wasn't any trouble…Professor."

"No? Then maybe you'll let me buy you dinner by way of saying thanks." *Dang. Where had that come from?* Garrett could count on one hand the number of women he'd asked out since Carla left. Most of those dinners had been job-related functions that required a partner.

For a few seconds Sherry actually considered accepting his offer. Why was a mystery. News of their hobnobbing would get out and reach the interview team. Shaking her head, she refused. "I can't. My roommate expects me home to cook dinner," she said. "I left meat marinating. But thanks for the offer. See you tomorrow." She pointedly shifted the van into drive so he'd take the hint and withdraw.

Garrett did, all the while picturing some dude in a suit and tie pacing from window to window waiting for her to get home to cook his meal. He had a hard time bringing that frame into focus. Once he did, he felt like a fool for assuming that just because Sherilyn Campbell wore no wedding ring she was free.

Sherry saw him glower at her taillights even after she'd waved to the Aguilars and headed off. Why that look? He had to know that college towns were notorious for gossip. Unless he *hoped* it would compromise her if she'd accepted his invitation. It was her town, after all.

She turned at the corner, effectively cutting off her view of the disturbing Dr. Lock. Sherry didn't want to think he'd play dirty politics, but the truth was she didn't know him at all.

And speaking of truth, she'd made a big deal earlier of her honesty, saying she wouldn't lie. But she'd known very well that Yvette wasn't waiting at home.

Sherry returned the van, then did what she did most nights. She went home to an empty town house and a solitary dinner in front of the TV.

Tonight was marginally different. Pictures of finalists for the dean's position had made the local news. Her phone rang off the hook. Friends called to congratulate or commiserate depending on their point of view. Not her parents or Nolan. They and Emily were probably grouped around the dinner table poring over wedding plans.

Getting up, Sherry put her plate in the dishwasher. Why couldn't she just be pleased for Nolan and Emily? No two people deserved happiness more. A man didn't buy a big house like Nolan had and toil to restore it unless he intended to fill it with a family. And Emily had been stuck too long in a loveless first marriage.

Depressed, yet not fathoming why, Sherry switched the phone to her answering machine and went to bed.

In the morning she slept through her alarm. As a result, she was late for the second day in a row. Today there were more people to stare as she burst into the room. Half the faculty juggled plates and coffee cups while pitching pet projects to the regents. The other half didn't care. Sherry had done her share of politicking at these functions in the past. She'd forgotten how loud it could get until she walked in and a hush fell over the room.

"I overslept," she mumbled, making a beeline for the coffee urn. She felt a pair of eyes drilling her back as she fixed her coffee with two packets of sugar and a generous measure of cream. Normally she drank her coffee black. Somehow the thought of being grilled by peers this morning made her stomach churn. There was a lot of jealousy in academia. When she angled sideways to get a fix on where today's animosity came from, she encountered Garrett Lock's penetrating blue gaze.

Her hand shook and she dumped sugar all over the pristine tablecloth. What had happened between yesterday and today to make him look so fierce? Thank goodness she saw Nolan detach himself from a group and head toward her with arms outstretched. Sherry turned from Lock to meet her brother's bear hug.

Across the room, Garrett registered Sherry Campbell's lateness and her slightly rumpled appearance. He put them together with her remark about oversleeping and pictured her snuggled in bed with the man she had offhandly referred to as her roommate. Was that him now—the long-legged galoot making a spectacle of them center stage?

But no, when Garrett got a good look at the two side by side, it was easy to see their resemblance. That made the man Nolan Campbell. Garrett's jaw sagged. He wouldn't have recognized the historian if they'd bumped into each other on the street. That night on the prairie, the man who'd ridden into his camp—after the crazy woman and her companion had taken off—had badly needed a shave. Rough outdoor clothing had made him appear huskier, too.

What came as an even bigger shock to Garrett—viewing brother and sister together like this—was knowing exactly why Sherilyn Campbell had niggled at his memory. Damned if she wasn't the wild woman who'd done her best to brain him. A fire caught slowly in Garrett's belly.

Nolan Campbell had known it all along. He'd accepted Garrett's hospitality, drunk his beer and shot the breeze amiably, the way men out camping did. All the while lying through his teeth. How could Campbell not have known that his sister had applied for this job? The job he'd been well aware Garrett was applying for! And he must have known she was the one who'd bloodied Garrett's head, too. Well, hell! The distinguished history prof had some explaining to do.

Garrett excused himself from the pocket of faculty members. "I see an old friend." Grinding his teeth, he set a straight course for the Campbells, and as he drew near, heard their raised voices. He wasn't close enough to sort out what the argument was about.

Listening to Nolan, Sherry felt guilty and annoyed in equal parts.

"I can't believe you kept news like this from the family, Sherilyn." He sounded more than a little hurt.

"You were all submerged in wedding plans. And I know you spent every spare minute on the house so that Emily and the kids'll be able to leave Mom and Dad's by the wedding and move out to your place. How's the remodeling going?"

"Fine. Emily's nose is out of joint because you've dropped out of sight. At least now she'll understand. She's counting on you to be her maid of honor, sis."

"I don't know, Nolan. If I get the dean's job, I'll have to really burn the midnight oil." She hoped he didn't pick up on her ambivalence.

But Nolan wasn't listening. His attention had flown to the man approaching from behind her. Sherry knew it was a man from the heavy tread. Nolan's wide smile branded the person a friend. Lord, she hoped it wasn't that obnoxious Lyle Roberts.

Her brother stretched out his hand and stepped around Sherry. "Well, well, after hearing your name on the news, I wondered when we'd meet. You clean up pretty good, Lock."

Garrett didn't take the offered hand. "I'm wracking my brain to remember what we discussed this summer. I trust you got a kick out of sharing bits of my personal history with another candidate. When can I expect it to rise up and haunt me?"

Nolan curled his fingers back into his chest. "There's no call to be rude, Lock. When we met, I didn't have a clue that Sherry had aspirations of becoming a dean."

"That's surprising," Sherry blurted. "Since you fell head over bootstraps for Emily, you haven't been able to see the nose on your face, Nolan Campbell."

Ignoring his sister, Nolan turned back to Garrett. "No offense, pal, but I judged you a hundred-to-one long shot to even get an interview. What with having hair down to your shoulders and being none too clean in spite of an unplanned dip in the river."

Campbell might have missed the subtle message in his sister's words that she was jealous of his impending marriage; Garrett did not. "I suppose it's possible you didn't know about Sherry's plans, Campbell. Difficult to argue with a guy too blinded by love to see that his own sister's pea-green jealous over his getting hitched."

"I'm no such thing," Sherry snapped. "Who asked you to butt in, anyway?"

"Whoa!" Laughing, Nolan held up a hand to stave off the angry pair. "I am deliriously happy, Lock." Nolan provided Garrett with a sketch of what had happened in his life since their chance meeting on the prairie. "I'm afraid I'll have to renege on the good luck I wished you. But if you should get the job, you're invited to Emily's and my wedding. Thanksgiving weekend. Hey, come even if you don't get it." Nolan's grin spread from ear to ear.

Sherry looked in amazement from one man to the other, finally adding things up as she flipped back to that foggy night in August. She didn't much like how the score tallied. With an artist's eye she layered Garrett Lock in the ragged trappings worn by the lunatic who'd materialized out of the fog. Run-down scruffy boots. Longer scraggly hair, as Nolan had said. A beard and…and a *gun!* They were one and the same man. Sherry took a step closer to Nolan, exhaling on a partially restrained gasp. For all she knew, the man was unbalanced.

Her own brother had unwittingly led Lock straight to her.

And who would believe her tale? Not the administrators who looked at him as if he'd hung the moon. Blindly she groped behind her for the cup of coffee she'd filled.

Garrett saw her grab something from the table. He automatically feinted left. She'd cut her hair and dressed like a corporate executive—but this was the same madwoman who a short month ago had tried to brain him with a stick of firewood. What in rambling red blazes should he do now? He wanted this job. Needed it for Keith's sake. But if he got it, he'd have to work with *her*.

"Nolan Campbell, you're a rat!" Sherry rounded on him. "Not one word did you breathe about meeting my victim. The guy I...fended off. Not one! You knew I was sick with worry."

"Well, why didn't *you* mention Kruger's retirement? I would have supported you for the deanship. Do support you. I think we should discuss this later. After we all calm down."

"Calm down?" She stared at one man, then the other, furious with both.

To Garrett's relief, Dr. Westerbrook stepped up to the podium. "Break is over," he announced. "This is faculty members' chance to measure each candidate against the others. You know the time allotted for questions. Candidates, on stage, please."

Working hard to compose his features, Garrett carefully placed Eli Aguilar between himself and the woman he'd once jokingly told Nolan Campbell he hoped never to meet in a dark alley. They'd both laughed as they parted that night. Neither so much as cracked a smile now.

CHAPTER THREE

IT INFURIATED GARRETT that Sherry Campbell acted as if *she* was the injured party and *he* was Jack the Ripper. He leaned around Eli to scowl at her. "I think the least you could do is apologize for hitting me."

"Stay away from me," she warned, putting up a hand to ward him off.

"Same goes," he snapped.

Dr. Aguilar's head whipped first one way, then the other. "Uh…shall I move?"

"Stay," they both hissed.

"All right, all right," Eli said. "Calm down."

The bombardment of questions began the minute they each received a microphone. The delegate from Business stepped to the podium first.

"Relative to your position on the joint deans' committee, if faced with cutbacks, would you—*a* support buying more computers for classroom use, or *b* argue to spend the limited funds for women's special interests? Sherry, you go first."

A setup. The School of Business Management recruited widely, attracting a large number of students, which qualified them for bushels of grants. No program on campus received more support from local business. They needed more computers like a shark needed a snowmobile, but Sherry was determined to be tactful. "Our current computer-student ratio is reportedly the highest in the state. My vote for distribution of funds would depend entirely on what other issues were on the table."

The delegate smirked. "I see. Dr. Aguilar, same question."

"I assume each request would be accompanied by adequate documentation. I'd have to carefully study all petitions before voting." When it was apparent that Eli had said all he was going to, the delegate turned to candidate three. "What would you do, Dr. Lock?"

"I'm pro-student, male *and* female. And pro-technology. I fail to see a conflict of interest."

Sherry glared around Eli at Lock's Cheshire-cat grin. That answer landed the sneaky son of a gun right in the pocket of a big contingent. Throughout the audience, men visibly relaxed. Women leaned forward to give Lock a closer look.

It might seem a small matter, but Sherry, with her background in psychology, read the body language as favorable toward the Texan. If they were playing tennis, it would be fifteen-love for Garrett.

Business had set the tone. Sherry likened the barrage that followed to enemy fire. Lock, however, breezed through unscathed.

Eli came out ahead during questions from Integrated Programs, and again through a grilling by Minority Affairs. It was, after all, his bailiwick.

Overall, hands down, Lock walked away with the match. Feeling sort of shell-shocked, Sherry was glad to have the session behind her. As President Westerbrook called a halt, her main objective was to escape the

crush of faculty descending on the other two candidates. Faculty knew her. Knew where she stood.

But that was supposing the crowd aiming for Lock
had any interest in discussing campus issues, she
thought, running a jaundiced eye over the mob of
females rushing him like a pack of hounds. Disgusted
at her peers' shameless flirting, Sherry slipped behind
the blue velvet stage curtains to regroup. Even then, the
curtain gaped, providing a panoramic view of those
jockeying for Lock's attention.

Sherry sucked in her breath. *Lord, the man did ooze
charisma.* Lock threw back his head and laughed at
something a female faculty member said. Lights from
the stage emphasized his lean jaw and glistened along
the strong tanned column of his throat. Nolan's earlier
words skated around inside Sherry's head. *You clean up
pretty good,* he'd told Lock. An understatement if ever
there was one.

Chills marched up Sherry's spine. So why had Professor Lock appeared that night looking like a derelict?
She didn't know, but in all probability she did owe him
an apology. She might have killed him. Would he
believe she'd paced the campsite, fearful she'd done just
that? Not even Nolan knew how utterly relieved she'd
been when he came back with the news that his search
hadn't turned up a dead body. But that was *all* he'd said,
damn it. If only he'd told her of his meeting with Lock,
she'd have been better prepared.

An irritating pain began to pulse behind her eyes.

She absolutely wouldn't permit any man to cause her
a headache. Sherry charged out from behind the curtain
and into the fray.

The more Garrett charmed the faculty, the greater the

pounding in Sherry's head. She could have kissed Westerbrook's secretary when Fern announced that it was
time for the candidates to convene for lunch.

Only fate would be so cruel as to seat Sherry directly
across from Lock. Worse, he noticed her distress.
Seconds after they sat, he caught her eye and murmured,
"Headache? I'm not surprised. Faculty really raked us
over the coals." Unfurling his napkin, Garrett shifted his
attention from Sherry to the somber interviewers filing
into the room. "Here comes the SWAT team." Lock
pretended to shiver. "Or more like a convention of un-
dertakers. Almost enough to cause second thoughts,
right?"

Sherry dropped her hands from massaging her
temples. The twinkle in his blue eyes sent blood gallop-
ing through her veins. She concentrated on his shirt
collar. "If you're having second thoughts, Lock, why
don't you drop out of the race now and go back
to…Huntsville?"

A muscle at the base of his jaw tightened. She
couldn't know how close he came to saying he'd gladly
leave the field to her if he could. Already he felt
homesick for Texas.

Damn Carla. If it were up to him, Garrett would tell
her what she could do with her belated motherly instincts.
But his lawyer had blown that notion out of his head. He
said judges believed shared custody was best for a child.
Something else he said was even scarier—now that Carla
was married, she might actually appear to be the better
parent should Garrett press for full custody.

His stony silence started wheels grinding inside
Sherry's head. "Maybe the team should delve into your
reasons for leaving Huntsville."

"They're personal," he said, then wished he hadn't played into her hands.

"Ah, the term 'personal' covers a multitude of sins. We farmed a professor out on leave last year when he couldn't keep his hands off female students. Officially he's on sabbatical for *personal* reasons."

Garrett heard both accusation and challenge in her statement. He wadded his napkin and half rose from his chair. To hell with the place cards, he'd find a new seat. But he sank back down as interviewers pulled out chairs on either side of him. They filled the empty space between Sherry Campbell and Eli, too. He appeared oblivious to their squabbles.

The college vice president claimed the seat to Garrett's right. The instant the waiter left after delivering salads, Phipps turned to Garrett. "What was the dispute you had this morning with Nolan Campbell all about?"

Fork poised over his shrimp salad, Garrett's gaze flicked over Sherry's tense face. He tried ducking the query with a minimal shrug. If she wanted to explain the bizarre facts, let her try. Frankly, he wouldn't know where to start.

The ploy didn't work. Barnard—or "Barney"—Phipps repeated his question. People on both sides of the table put their conversations on hold to listen.

Garrett broke a roll and calmly buttered half. "It was nothing really. We had a chance meeting this summer during the study Campbell conducted—the wagon train reenactment. We talked about this and that. I don't know how it came up, but I mentioned that I'd applied for the dean's position here. Campbell claimed he didn't know Dean Kruger was leaving. Today that struck me as odd, given his sister's candidacy."

"Can you answer that, Sherilyn?" The vice president switched to grilling her. "By the way, how did you manage to meet the application deadline? According to a news report, Nolan's group returned from Santa Fe a week after the final date."

Sherry stiffened. "Dean Kruger dropped hints around the department about retiring. I filled out an application in advance. Is there a rule against doing that?"

"None," boomed Dr. Westerbrook from the head of the table. "I'd say it shows initiative. Where is this line of questioning leading, Barney? It's clear Sherilyn was home to receive the supplement we mailed out to semi-finalists."

Phipps twisted the stem of his water glass. "I made no secret of the fact that I thought her answers read like those of a man. And we know her original application was mailed locally."

What was he implying here? That she'd had some *man* complete her application? "That's right," Sherry said, trying not to sound defensive. "I asked Angel, the department secretary, to mail it when the position was announced. Out of curiosity—" Sherry's grip tightened on her fork "—how do women's answers differ from men's? Do we get a different form?"

"Certainly not." Barney touched his napkin to his lips. "Everyone knows men approach problems more analytically than women."

"Indeed?" Sherry's voice quivered with indignation, although she shouldn't have been shocked by his answer. She knew Barney Phipps didn't believe that women belonged in administration. And maybe not on the planet.

"Books have been written on the subject, for goodness' sake." The floundering VP looked to the row of administrators for help. None came to his aid.

When the silence had stretched long enough for Sherry to hear the ice in her tea melt, she decided she didn't want a job she had to cry foul to get. "I kept all my rough drafts," she said lightly. "Anyone know a reputable handwriting analyst?"

"More like a good lawyer." Lock glared first at Phipps, then at Westerbrook, who appeared unhappy with his second-in-command.

Phipps stood. "Excuse me, I just remembered a prior engagement." A collective sigh rose from administrators as the door closed.

"May I remind you," cautioned Westerbrook, "that this institution prides itself on its commitment to equal opportunity."

It seemed a pointless statement in light of the previous exchange. Garrett reached across the table and shackled Sherry's wrist with a warm hand. "You know, you have grounds to force them to give you the job."

She shook him off and picked up her fork. "How would *you* handle it?"

His lips twitched. "Call for sabers under the dueling oaks."

"I thought Texans used six-guns at high noon."

"Sorry, I was born and raised in Louisiana." He pronounced it *Loosyanna* in the slowest sexiest way.

Sherry stabbed more salad with her fork than she could eat in one bite. Then she set the fork down, feeling a need to explain. "My method may appear passive to you. But when I started teaching here, there were no female department chairs. Now we have two. If I play by the old guard's rules, maybe I'll be the first woman dean."

Garrett leaned back. She had guts. Not a response he'd have expected from the hysterical woman he'd met on the prairie. Which one was the real Sherry Campbell?

"Look," Sherry said in an undertone when she caught him staring at her over the dessert sorbet. "I'm no wimp. I can fight in the trenches when I have to."

He gingerly touched two fingers to a spot above his left ear. "I can certainly attest to that."

"Yes, well, I do apologize," she said stiffly. "You burst out of the fog, and…and…looked so scruffy. Then when you mentioned Huntsville, I panicked. I thought…prison." She cleared her throat and spooned up a bite of raspberry ice. "Perhaps if I'd seen you at your campsite the way Nolan did, things might have been different."

He laughed, a deep rumble from his belly. "Yeah. You'd have finished the job you started. When Nolan stumbled in, I'd shucked my wet clothes. He caught me buck naked, my skin blue as Babe, Paul Bunyan's ox."

Sherry tried to imagine it. Or rather, she tried *not* to as she felt heat stealing up her neck into her cheeks. Unfortunately her high color left little doubt that she'd pictured the scene he described. Still, it was hard not to laugh with a man capable of joking about himself. Sherry had met so few men who could do that. Except for Nolan, most of the men on campus took themselves far too seriously.

Garrett frowned; he hadn't meant to sound provocative. Entendres of a sexual nature weren't his style. He wasn't looking to start anything, especially not with a woman who might end up his subordinate. More like *in*-subordinate based on his experience so far with Professor Sherilyn Campbell. He slid her a glance and was surprised to discover her fighting a smile. So she did have a sense of humor. Garrett wouldn't have thought it. Up till now, he'd labeled her tempestuous, if not shrewish.

As if reading his mind, Sherry shrugged. "I'm afraid we started off on the wrong foot. Blame it on knee-jerk reactions linked to our first disastrous meeting. Truth is, you're no chain-gang escapee and I'm not a menace to society." Genuine contrition tinged her words. "The thought of physical abuse sickens me. I can't explain what made me hit you after all I've seen and heard...." Her voice faded to a halt.

"I believe you," Garrett said. And he did. He'd heard the passion in her voice when she discussed the services she struggled to provide for abused women. A far greater range than those available on his campus in Huntsville. Yet if he believed the rumblings he'd heard from some faculty, several claimed that Sherilyn Campbell had a tendency to be too passionate on behalf of the Hub. That maybe she bought too readily into the women's stories. Or had quit looking to see if there were two sides. Even her advocates feared loss of objectivity with regard to men if she became dean. Her enemies, and Garrett knew it was impossible not to make them in the academic community, said she already wore blinders. Case in point, they said: check out how negative she was on the subject of her brother's marriage.

As lunch wound down, Garrett decided to test the waters. "I hope Nolan rented the convention center for his wedding."

"Why?" Sherry pushed her dessert cup away. "Are you in favor of elaborate weddings?"

"No, but from the sound of it, everyone on campus plans to attend."

"Probably."

That didn't leave much of an opening for further discussion. Garrett backed off. What was he after, anyway? He'd never met the prospective bride. And Lord knew he wasn't a walking advertisement for a long and happy marriage.

Sherry stood up. "I'd advise a run to the men's room. If you think faculty hit hard, wait till the students strike. They have so little control over what happens on campus, these forums afford them the illusion of power."

"Are you always such a cynic?"

"A cynic?" Sherry raised a brow. "More like a realist. Student concerns rank low on the academic totem pole. That's fact."

Garrett eyed the swivel of her hips as she set her course for the door. Her suit today was gunmetal gray. Silk, he thought, and soft enough to allow fluid movement. Damn but she had nice legs. Mouth suddenly dry, Garrett darted a guilty glance around the table and discovered his weren't the only appreciative eyes glued to Professor Campbell's backside. Why not? Looking didn't hurt, did it? Touching was where guys got into trouble. Garrett had no intention of touching. Crumpling his napkin, he adjusted his new Brooks Brothers tie. Garrett sure hoped the dang thing impressed the team members, because it had cost what he considered an outrageous amount of money. Not only that, it was choking him.

Man, he hated ties. He could almost believe what a friend said, that they'd been designed by a woman bent on torturing men. He had to smile. That was the reverse of Carla's complaint about panty hose—muttered as she hung them wet on every surface in their minuscule bathroom. He recalled weaving his way through a sea of nylon to reach his shaving gear. Thinking back, Garrett guessed he hadn't minded so much.

Guiltily he caught himself up short. It'd been ages since he reminisced fondly about any aspect of his life with Carla. That cracker-box-size apartment was all they could afford on a first-year instructor's salary. More materialistic than he, Carla had wanted to drop out of school and work so they could get a bigger place. He'd insisted she finish her degree and encouraged her to go for an MBA. Then their method of birth control failed, and Keith was born before Carla graduated from the master's program.

Catering staff cleaned the table around him. Lost in memories, Garrett recalled begging Carla to take a year off. She'd refused. As a result, he'd spent more and more time juggling his job with domestic chores. Which delayed his receiving tenure. Then Carla became obsessed with banking, and that was the beginning of the end of their marriage.

"Dr. Lock."

Garrett roused himself as President Westerbrook called his name. He glanced around, surprised to find he was the only one still seated.

"Did Dr. Campbell leave that sour look on your face?"

Garrett smiled. "She said I'd be smart to hit the men's room before our meeting with the students. I'm weighing the pros and cons."

"Hmpf. Nothing students love more than extracting their pound of flesh from faculty and administrators."

"Will you be there?"

"Are you kidding? Avoiding confrontations with students is ritual with me. Each crop is more inventive than the last. Brr!" He clapped Garrett on the back, pointed him toward the men's room, then took off in the opposite direction.

Garrett arrived last of the three candidates. He noticed students who wore buttons that read Minority Affairs had Eli boxed into a corner. Professor Campbell gestured with a diet soda while chatting with some tough-looking babes. Two were tattooed. At least two more were pregnant and in dire need of maternity clothes. Garrett felt a stab of sympathy. They looked so young. One of his first published papers had been titled *Babies Having Babies*. Something he liked about Well-mont's disadvantaged women's work-study program was that it provided parenting classes and a semester on nutrition. Also one on money management. Whole-life training was a concept few campuses embraced. Garrett wondered if Sherilyn had done any follow-up studies. If they made him dean, he'd suggest it.

A beanpole of a girl with wire-rimmed glasses blew a whistle to gain everyone's attention. Laughter and talk subsided. After introducing herself as student body president, she read off several names. Those students went to stand beside her.

"We have some concerns that aren't being addressed now," the student president said. "Naturally we're interested in learning how each of you feel before we give our input to the interview team. Dr. Aguilar, if you'll respond first, followed by Dr. Lock and Dr. Campbell."

An angelic young woman with blond hair that

brushed the waistband of her jeans took the mike. "Two years ago condom dispensers were installed in the men's rest rooms on campus. Administration won't even discuss placing them in ours. We want them. Where do you stand on this issue?"

Eli's skin turned splotchy red all the way to his bald spot. "I, ah, I'd have to see the statements already submitted. And there's cost to be considered."

All eyes shifted to Garrett. "It should be a line item in the dean of students' budget package. For men and women," he said without hesitation.

The dean of students vaulted from his chair, clearly agitated. "Last year, to kick off National Condom Week, our health department provided packets of condoms to put in campus newspapers. The students *stapled* the packets inside. Not only did I have to deal with their blunder, but parents who saw the paper were outraged to think we'd condone promiscuity on this campus."

Sherry faced him. "Harold, our mission is to teach. Shouldn't we teach responsibility?"

"A student's sexual activity is not our business, Professor Campbell. If anything, we should promote abstinence."

"So," Sherry said softly, "are we removing the dispensers from the men's lavatories? Or is it just women you're saying should abstain?"

Garrett hid a smile behind his hand as Harold's eyes bugged out. Then the dean abruptly got up and stalked from the room.

After that, the questions switched to academics. Students complained that faculty refused to give make-up exams. They claimed to need more night classes.

Lively discussion ensued over the cancellation of a popular yearly conference called Women's Vision, Power and Potential.

All three candidates agreed those were requests worthy of a second look. By four o'clock they were ready to call it a day.

The minute they cleared the building, Garrett stripped off his suit jacket and loosened his tie. "Want a lift to the hotel, Eli? I drove my own vehicle today."

"Sure. I hope my wife's amenable to room service, this evening. I only want to hibernate."

"How about you, Doc?" Garrett turned to Sherry and said unexpectedly, "I'll spring for dinner at your favorite bar and grill, and even throw in a tall cool one."

"Sorry, I already have plans." Sherry didn't, but the thought of accompanying him to some dim smoky pub caused her to break out in a cold sweat.

Garrett slung his coat carelessly over one shoulder. The offer had again sneaked out. For a minute there, he'd forgotten she lived with some fancy dude.

Sherry watched his shoulders slump in spite of the casual wave he tossed when they reached the fork in the path separating staff and visitor parking. She almost said she'd reconsidered his offer. Then because Garrett and Eli struck up a conversation, she kept going, pretending to search her purse for her car keys.

IF THE CANDIDATES believed they'd been raked over coals by the students, the individual interviews with the team were even tougher.

"Whew!" Garrett exclaimed as the three met again after their sessions. "Anybody who thinks deans are just figureheads ought to go through the interview process. From the questions, you'd think these guys were building a dynasty."

"Keep the sense of humor, Lock," Sherry said around a chuckle. "Wait'll the barracudas from the business community chew you up and spit you out."

And she was right. Townspeople vetting the candidates appeared innocent enough with their flashy rings and flashier smiles. Turned out each had a private agenda. All operated on the premise of "Scratch my back if you want endowments." At the end of the coffee hour, the candidates felt worked over by a battering ram.

Later, on their way out the door, Eli shook his head. "Am I such a babe in the woods? Deans here spend half their time politicking and the other half fund-raising."

Garrett, looking the least frazzled, shrugged. "Where I work now, fund-raising falls to the assistant dean. Yours truly." He gave a mock bow. "I try to take it in stride. Hey, it keeps the job from getting boring."

Sherry shouldered her purse. "Thank heaven the wait's almost over. May the best man win. Or woman," she added cheekily, swinging down the path toward her car.

"My kids will be happy if I lose," Aguilar announced unexpectedly to Garrett as they watched her angle between the rows. "The oldest one says he won't leave California. What about your son?"

"He's bummed about leaving his friends. But this job puts us closer to his mother."

"I see. Well, if you get the nod, watch your back. I hear the current Women's Studies chairperson tends to blame men for *all* domestic discord."

"How so?" A little surprised by Eli's uncharacteristic remark, Garrett watched Sherry disappear from sight.

"Haven't you heard that Campbell's a man-eater? I'm not sure I could work with her," Eli said.

"Mmm," was Garrett's only response. "Shall we go? I need to call my son before I dress for tonight's slaughter. He's staying with one of his friends in Huntsville. He doesn't like my being gone this long. I'd hate to miss touching base."

Eli thrust his hands in his pockets and fell in beside Garrett.

SHERRY MADE SURE she arrived early for the banquet. She'd dressed carefully for this event in basic black linen. Her only adornments were her grandmother's pearls and the discreet pearl studs at her ears. Strappy heels and a patent-leather evening bag completed her ensemble. As she entered the banquet room and stepped into a sea of chiffon and glittering sequins worn by the regents' wives, she felt drab. Blast, she should have known they'd put on the dog. Oh, well. She didn't have sequins and chiffon in her wardrobe.

Taking care to skirt the knots of people already deep in conversation, she turned down an offer of champagne and requested ginger ale. Tonight's interrogation would be subtle. If she hoped to win, her answers needed to sparkle. Wandering around the table, Sherry noticed that her place card sat between the other two candidates'. She didn't want to sit next to Garrett Lock. He muddied her thinking.

The minute no one was looking, she switched her card with that of Eli's wife. Twice. Each time someone put it back. Afraid of discovery, she gave up and decided to bite the bullet.

The three candidates didn't meet until they were seated

for dinner. Eli wore tweed over a sweater vest. His wife was elegant in green satin. Lock had on a notch-collared tuxedo with a houndstooth checked tie and matching cummerbund. His stomach was so flat not even one pleat on his cummerbund bunched when he sat. As soon as he took his seat beside her, a light clean tantalizing scent that Sherry couldn't quite place tickled her nose.

Garrett ordered Glenfiddich on the rocks. Eli asked for a Bloody Mary.

"I'll stick with water," Sherry told the waiter as she let the talk flow around her. To her surprise the topic under discussion was gold-panning.

"You don't do it to get rich," Garrett said, bumping Sherry's arm as he swirled the ice in his glass. "'Scuse me," he murmured before returning to the conversation. "I look at gold-panning as a chance to spend time with my son while teaching him to appreciate the environment."

"Three cheers for that old male fire-in-the-belly, let's-commune-with-nature routine," Sherry quipped. "Definitely not the polished academician you see here. Give Lock a tent in the wilds and he becomes the outlaw Josie Wales. I know."

"So you met Garrett this summer, too?" President Westerbrook smiled at Sherry, then turned to Garrett. "Did Sherilyn look like herself, I wonder?"

Garrett's gaze shifted, inching slowly over her slender frame. He said nothing.

Sherry feigned interest in the soup the waiter had just brought. She'd said enough already. Maybe too much. Clearly the men at the table envied Garrett's footloose lifestyle. And the women—the women, hooked on his slow Southern drawl—imagined what it'd be like to spend time alone with him in the wilds. Sherry dipped her spoon in her soup, only to have her arm jostled again by Garrett.

"Sorry," he said. "Banquet seating is a curse when you're left-handed."

Sitting next to him was a curse. Throughout the main course their arms constantly brushed, making Sherry all too aware of his broad shoulders. Worse, a member of the interview team asked Sherry's opinion on the proposed raise in tuition. Right in the middle of her answer, Garrett's leg accidentally bumped hers, and her mind blanked. She completely lost her train of thought, and as a result, she broke off lamely, prompting a row of elevated eyebrows.

With delivery of the main course, questions to the candidates turned personal. From living all her life in a city with more than one institution of higher learning, Sherry knew that during these interviews no area of a candidate's life was sacred.

Garrett appeared dumbfounded when a team member inquired about the details of his divorce. "We split over six years ago," he muttered. "I see no relevance. My ex-wife is remarried."

"You told Sheldon's wife that your boy lives with you, Lock. Our deans often meet early in the morning or late into the evening. Will child care be a problem?"

Garrett stared at the speaker, his right hand squashing his napkin.

Sherry didn't know why she should resent the invasion of his privacy, but she did. "Our women's crises center, the Hub, is something of an authority on local child care," she put in smoothly. "We have a whole rack of brochures." Her response seemed to satisfy team members. They tossed the next barbed question at Eli.

"Thanks," whispered Garrett, scooting his chair closer to Sherry. "I guess I haven't thought ahead to child care. I had no idea they'd ask anything like that."

"Why would you? It's a question working mothers get asked. A woman thinks of her family first. A man thinks of his job."

"Now wait just a darned minute. You don't know me well enough to make snap judgments."

Sherry snatched her dessert spoon and made craters in the chocolate mousse a waiter set in front of her. She glanced around to see who'd heard, already regretting the childish display of temper.

Several sets of eyes were trained on her and Lock. Sherry squirmed in her chair. Her elbow and Garrett's made contact. She jerked aside, knocking over a newly topped-up water glass. The contents, ice included, were dumped in Garrett's lap.

"Oh, heavens!" She lunged for the glass and in so doing, upset his water goblet, too. She fluttered about, sopping up water with her napkin until Garrett grabbed her hand and said tersely, "That's enough!"

Sherry dragged the dripping square of linen to her breast. Gulping, she realized everyone but the three candidates—and President Westerbrook—had fled the table.

Eyes flinty, Garrett rose and shook ice onto the floor. "It seems Dr. Campbell has found a way to clear the field. Excuse me," he said. "Dinner was delightful. I trust someone will call my hotel with the results."

Before Sherry could deny knocking over the glasses on purpose, he vanished.

Folding her napkin with shaking fingers, she reached under her chair for her purse. "It was an accident," she stated firmly. "And it isn't fair to go on without him."

College administrators and team members huddled for a moment. "We probably have sufficient information to make a decision," Sheldon March announced. "Sherilyn, you and Eli may leave. We'll poll the team and I'll call everyone later."

Summarily dismissed, Sherry wrestled with a sick feeling as she slunk out a back door. It was probably petty, but she hated the thought of receiving that call tonight. By tomorrow the results would be on local TV. She could wait for the bad news.

Yvette was still out of town, so once Sherry reached the safety of her home, she turned off the phone and went straight to bed.

CHAPTER FOUR

REPEATED POUNDING on Sherry's front door dragged her from a sound sleep. "All right, all right. I'm coming," she shouted, stumbling around the dark room searching for her robe and slippers. Her heart skittered wildly. People just didn't knock on her door in the middle of the night. Giving up on the slippers, still struggling to get one arm in the robe's sleeve, she hopped barefoot across the cold slab of entryway granite and tried to see through the peephole who was making such a racket.

Her parents. Panic made Sherry forget the sleeve as she worked to release the chain with fingers that shook. "What's wrong?" she cried, at last throwing open the door. "Did something happen to Nolan? Oh, no. Not Emily or the kids?"

"Nothing like that, dear." Her mother stepped inside and gently thrust Sherry's arm through the empty sleeve. "We were worried about you. Sheldon March phoned. He said he'd been trying to reach you since ten. He thought you might be at our house. We tried you, too. When it was after midnight and still no answer, well, your father and I thought we'd better check."

"We know you're an adult," said her father gruffly. "But it's not like you to stay out all night. So we got worried. Not even our community is exempt from nut cases."

Sherry smiled to assure them she wasn't angry. However, she only listened with half an ear. Would March bother her folks to deliver bad news? She shivered against a cool night breeze.

Mr. Campbell noticed. He herded them all inside and shut the door. "You're not sick, are you, Sherilyn?"

She shook her head. "I unplugged my answering machine and turned the ringer down on the phone. Did Sheldon give you a message?"

Her mother's eyes clouded in sympathy, and Sherry's hopes plummeted.

"He did, dear. What with Emily and the children staying with us, and Nolan dashing in and out to complete the remodeling of his home, I feel terrible that your father and I didn't even know you were being considered for a promotion. Why didn't you tell us?"

Sherry thought she'd steeled herself to lose, but from the way her stomach constricted, evidently she wasn't ready to face it. "All of our lives have been so hectic. I would have told you if I'd been selected."

Her parents exchanged guilty glances. "We've been running hither and yon helping Emily square away the wedding. You still should have called. But it does explain why you haven't dropped by. Emily's relieved it was business that kept you away. She's afraid that you're…unhappy about her marrying Nolan. Emily so wants you as her maid of honor, Sherilyn."

Sherry recoiled from the slight censure in her mother's tone. Darn it all, she'd hoped Emily would ask someone else to stand up with her. But she supposed her future sister-in-law felt it was appropriate, not only because they were friends, but because Sherry had been the one who'd invited Emily to take part in Nolan's study. But only to prove that today's women could function fine without men. Not Emily, apparently. It hadn't taken her three months to fall head-over-heels in love.

So okay, Sherry admitted it. Her nose was out of joint.

"Sherry? You look upset. I'm so sorry you lost out on the job, honey." Sherry's mother gave her a bracing hug.

"Who did get it?" Sherry asked dully. "Did Sheldon say?"

"Oh, yes." Mrs. Campbell turned to her husband. "I told you the man's name, Ben. Do you remember?"

Sherry's dad rustled his keys. "Not anyone we knew. Jared, or maybe Garth. Sounded like a cowboy singer."

"Garrett Lock," Sherry supplied. It was no big revelation, but having it spelled out cracked the dam on feelings she'd held at bay thus far. Now she faced real concern for the future of a program to which she'd dedicated so much energy. Coupled with that, a sense of failure seeped in. Personal, yes, but more than that. Her loss set back the upward mobility of women on campus.

"I'm sure it's a crushing disappointment at the moment, Sherry," her mother said gently. "But I've found things usually work out for the best. I'm sure something good will come of this. Give it time, dear."

"Yes," agreed her father. "Maybe it's a blessing in disguise. Your mom and I have been trying to find a way to broach one of our worries—we think you've given up all semblance of a private life for your job. We see more of Yvette than of you. She's always going to parties or out on a date. All you do is work, work, work."

A tic fluttered in Sherry's left eyelid. "Dad. It's after one, and I have to be at the office by eight."

"She's right, Ben." Sherry's mom slipped her arm through that of her spouse and hauled him toward the door. "It's enough that we had to be the bearers of bad tidings. We should have the decency to let her lick her wounds in private."

"Won't work, Mom," Sherry said, all the while wondering if she'd have half of Nan Campbell's verve when she reached sixty. "Your 'good cop, bad cop' routine doesn't work anymore. I've wised up."

"Pity," Nan murmured. "But then, I guess it's time you started working our old flimflam on your own offspring."

"Guilt isn't effective, either." Sherry crossed her arms and leaned a shoulder against the door frame. "I have a Ph.D. in psychology, remember?"

"Then I know you'll march right in there tomorrow and congratulate the winner," her mother whispered, tiptoeing into the dark courtyard that fronted the U-shaped complex of townhomes.

Sherry shut the door with enough force to rattle the stained-glass panels on either side. *Congratulate Garrett Lock?* "It'll be a cold day in...in Texas," she mumbled. Darn. Her mother could still lay on a guilt trip to beat all guilt trips.

As sleep was now out of the question, Sherry went into the kitchen and brewed a pot of Red Zinger tea. Forty minutes later, she dug out the telephone book and looked up the number of the hotel where her rivals were staying. Lifting the receiver, she quickly punched out the main number. A cheery voice answered.

"I'd like to leave messages for two of your guests," she said. "One will be checking out in the morning, so please tuck it under his door. Tell Dr. Eli Aguilar that I enjoyed meeting him and Marguerite. Say it's too bad

there was only one job. Sign it Dr. Sherilyn Campbell."
She spelled her first name. Even after the staff person
read it back, Sherry wasn't sure what she wanted to say
to Lock.

"You said two messages?" the clerk prompted.

"Yes. The second goes to Dr. Garrett Lock. Just say,
congratulations on your appointment. And sign it the
same way as the first."

After she hung up, Sherry worried that her message
sounded too terse. She did have to work with the man.
Somehow she couldn't bring herself to say work *for*
him. Technically they were a team. That had been a big
problem with Kruger. He hid in his office, preferring to
issue edicts in rambling memos. God, she hated those
memos—and the fact that she could never get an appointment with him to discuss any of his preposterous
decrees. He required memos in return, too. Some of hers
were so hot Angel joked that she needed to fan the keys
on her computer as she typed them.

If Lock wanted to get off on the right foot, he'd make
himself more accessible to staff. Come to think of it,
Sherry didn't envy him having to listen to all the initial
gripes that got tossed at a new dean. Faculty members
all had their petty complaints and pet projects. The clas-
sified staff lobbied for less pressure and more help. As
a department chair, she bullied for growth and expansion. And if the board's questions these past three days
were any indication, they planned to tighten the old
purse strings even more.

Sherry sighed. Maybe she was a teensy bit relieved
to know that Garrett Lock would be the one tearing his hair
out attending all those ulcer-inducing meetings and
not her.

The clock in the living room struck three. Why go back to bed for a few short hours? Stifling a yawn, she got out her cookbook and decided to make something gooey and chocolate to take into the department tomorrow. One thing staff agreed on was that chocolate solved a lot of woes. If she appeared bearing chocolate fudge squares, no one would comment on her loss or the road maps in her eyes.

Would Lock be surprised? She'd bet he had her pegged as a sore loser. A sore loser without domestic talents, if he was anything like Nolan's pals in the history department.

By seven, Sherry had showered and dressed in her favorite baggy, hot pink pants, bright orange poet's blouse and comfy Birkenstocks. Mickey was once again ensconced on her wrist. Back to her old self. Almost, she lamented, running gel through her shorn locks. But her heavy hair had always been so difficult to tame. She might just stay with this cut for a while.

Feeling refreshed, she hummed along with a LeAnn Rimes CD she'd popped in the player before smoothing chocolate glaze on the cooled cake. In the middle of slicing finished squares, her doorbell pealed. "What now?" She licked chocolate off her fingers. She might be resigned, but that didn't mean she wanted well-meaning friends stopping by to commiserate. As her mom said, she preferred to lick her wounds in private.

"Yes?" She yanked open the door. The knife she'd been using to cut the cake slipped from her fingers, bounced off the floor and splattered chocolate across the light khaki pants of the man standing there.

Garrett Lock danced back too late to save himself. In doing so, he spilled water down the front of his shirt from the bud vase he held.

"Jeez, I'm sorry." Sherry leaned down and brushed at the spots on his pant leg only to watch in horror as the chocolate smeared and spread. "Oh, no!" she gasped. "I've made it worse."

In trying to see what she'd done, Garrett tilted the vase the other way and poured a stream of water over Sherry's head.

"Stop! I just washed my hair." She leaped up, accidentally knocking the vase out of Garrett's hand. It flew through the air, crashed on the entry floor and exploded. For a heartbeat they both stared at the pale pink rosebud swimming in chocolate-muddied water. Sunlight streaming over Garrett's shoulders glittered off particles of glass embedded in the bruised petals of the delicate flower.

"Oh. Oh," Sherry said softly as she sank onto one knee to rescue the poor bedraggled rose.

"Wait." Garrett quickly jerked her to her feet. Too late. He saw a dark splotch of blood seeping through Sherry's pink pant leg. Hauling her into his arms, he strode into her living room where he dropped her unceremoniously into a rocking chair, still clutching the soggy flower.

Sherry's squeak of protest was cut off by the sound of rending fabric. In one fluid motion he'd ripped her pant leg from the bottom hem to three inches above her knee.

"What…what in *hell* are you doing?" A tic hopscotched beneath her eyelid. "Look what you did to my best linen pants!" she gasped.

"Best…?" He blinked. "I thought they were pajamas. I also thought you'd bloodied your knee. I see now that you hit a blob of chocolate." Closing his eyes, he massaged the lean contours of his cheeks. "I have a cab waiting. I intended to cart you off to the emergency room."

"I can't believe you mutilated my pants." Sherry smacked him with the rose she'd rescued from the muck, much as she would have done to Nolan. Hopping up, she literally shoved him out the door.

"Ouch! Are you nuts? That thing has thorns." Garrett put his arms up to ward off her swats. "I swear, for someone who claims to abhor violence, you get plenty physical," he grumbled.

Sherry slid on the wet flagstone and almost fell. He caught her and held her upright until she shucked off his hands and toppled into the decorative railing that edged her small porch. "You bring out the worst in me, Lock. Shouldn't you be meeting with Westerbrook and the rest of the deans?"

The blue eyes assessing her narrowed marginally. "I got your note of congratulations and decided I'd been rude last night. The hotel gift shop was open and…well, I bought the flower. I was out the door before I happened to think what people would say if I gave it to you on campus. I found you in the phone book. I don't know the area, so I called a cab. You look different, by the way. What have you done to yourself?"

"I've gone back to my old job, as if you didn't know. And let me say again—dumping that water on you last night *was* an accident." Her gaze strayed to the pathetic flower now bent and mangled. Softness crept into her voice. "The rose was a nice gesture, Lock."

"Then do you mind telling me what happened here? Do you throw knives at every man who knocks at your door?"

"I didn't throw it. You were the last person I expected

to see. The knife sort of…fell out of my hand. Um, I really feel bad about the chocolate on your pants. I'll give you the name of my dry cleaner. Tell him to put it on my bill. If you hurry, you should be able to change and still make it to campus to meet the brass." Darn. He'd be on time, but she'd have to rewash her hair. Rumors would fly, after all, about her being a sore loser.

"Are you sure you didn't cut your knee?" He leaned down to check again.

His breath tickled her skin. It was all Sherry could do to stand still for his examination until he muttered, "Yup. You're fit as a fiddle." He stood abruptly and she flinched and flattened her rump against the railing.

"You're sure one jumpy female. Hey, I feel awful, tearing your pants like that."

"We could call it even. I take care of my ruined pants. You take care of yours. And don't feel obliged to replace the rose. Is that your cabby honking?" She leaned over, trying to see out to the parking strip.

Like a shot, Garrett pulled her back. His fingers flexed around her upper arms. "Stop. You make me nervous. That top rail wobbles." He set her nearer the door.

She looked amused. "The railing has always wobbled, and I've lived here five years. That *is* your cab's horn," she said pointedly.

He still seemed unsure whether to go or not. "I hate leaving you with this mess. If you have a broom, I'll sweep up the glass. I'm paying the driver. He can wait."

Somehow picturing this man, who as of today was her boss, inside her home with a broom in his hands, drove Sherry's nerves to red alert. "I'm not the one with an early meeting," she said firmly. "Go."

He did, but only because the cabdriver lay on the

horn and Garrett didn't want any of Sherry's neighbors calling the cops. "I feel like we're still off on the wrong foot," he called as he walked backward along the center walkway.

Sherry's stomach stayed in knots until he totally disappeared. Darn, she'd never met a man who made a habit of throwing her into a tailspin.

Once she'd cleaned up the glass and the watery mess and washed her hair, Sherry peeled off her pants and tossed them in the trash.

"Blast and damn!" Lock attracted accidents. Or else she did.

His concern for her welfare had been commendable, however. That a warm pleasant thought kept him on her mind as Sherry yanked a wild print skirt from the closet. Its riot of colors further lightened her mood.

LATE AGAIN, Sherry detoured past her office to the staff break room. Angel intercepted her, the secretary's cool gray eyes assessing. "Those goodies don't fool me, boss lady. You stayed up half the night crying, didn't you?"

"Nary a tear. I wouldn't give them the satisfaction." Sherry lifted her chin.

"The prez sashayed his drugstore cowboy by here to see his new digs half an hour ago. Think you oughta know I'm probably the only woman on campus who isn't tripping over her feet to kiss up to macho man."

Sherry placed her chocolate squares on the break-room table, along with paper plates and plastic forks, as she listened to Angel. "I expected as much."

"What are we going to do?" Angel asked when Sherry headed into her office.

"Do?"

"Yeah. Are we gonna roll over and play dead or give him hell like we did old man Kruger?"

Sherry stuffed her purse into the locking file where she kept it during working hours. For some reason she recalled how he'd looked, standing in her doorway, holding a rose. "The man deserves a chance, Angel."

"Don't tell me you've fallen for his pretty face, too?"

"Certainly not. It's just…well, I believe a person is innocent until proven guilty. If Lock rides the fence like Kruger, then we'll give him hell." Sherry's lips twitched in the barest hint of a grin.

"He's a man, isn't he? Already has three strikes against him."

Sherry watched Angel turn and dash out to answer the department phone. She remembered the accusation Yvette threw at her the other day—how friends thought she'd become a man hater. It wasn't true, even if her attitude toward men had become a little…jaundiced. Angel, now, had good reason to be bitter, hooking up with two losers before the age of twenty-five. Still, there *were* good men out there.

Sherry made a mental note to watch what she said from now on. She was the teacher—the one charged with straightening out her students sometimes warped views. Taking a moment to give the situation serious thought, Sherry realized her disenchantment with the opposite sex had come about gradually.

The people she dealt with day in and day out were mostly women whose spouses had left them for someone younger. Wives whose husbands abused them physically and mentally. Mothers fighting for custody of their kids. Women unable to get minimal maintenance from the men who'd fathered their children. Who *wouldn't* be jaundiced?

Rearranging a stack of files, Sherry's thoughts turned to her new boss. What was the reason for *his* divorce? He'd certainly evaded the team's questions on that subject. Was it because the truth would hurt him?

Sherry slammed the files into a box. There she was, doing it again. Condemning a man on the basis of his sex. She'd told Angel she was going to give Garrett Lock a fair shake, and she would.

It didn't bode well for him, however, that he didn't bother showing up in the department again all day.

At five minutes to five, Dr. Westerbrook paid Sherry a visit.

"I want you to know, Sherilyn, the decision to hire Garrett was unanimous. Dr. Lock had more administrative experience. Our decision would have been harder if you'd been an assistant dean. There are larger institutions elsewhere in the state that may have openings for assistant deans."

Sherry rocked back in her chair. "Am I to gather that Lock objects to working with me?" Anger clenched her stomach. It took every ounce of professional acumen to keep her tone level.

"Not at all." Westerbrook appeared ruffled. "Sheldon wants assurance that you'll play ball with the new dean. Will you cooperate, Sherilyn?"

"It's not hard to cooperative with an invisible man. Where is the boy wonder?"

"That's the attitude that worries us," Westerbrook exclaimed. "According to the contract, Garrett has two weeks to relocate his household before he starts the job. It's not his fault that Kruger waited until so late to declare his intent to retire. We'll have to begin classes next week without Lock."

"A lot goes on in the first two weeks that needs the dean's attention. Who'll sign overloads and make decisions about adding and dropping classes based on enrollment?"

Westerbrook puffed out his cheeks. "Routine matters. Kruger said he relied heavily on your recommendations." He grasped the doorknob as if wanting to escape. "What if I authorize giving you the title of interim dean? It'll look impressive on your résumé."

Sherry trailed him to the door. "Do I need a résumé?"

"No, of course not," he blustered. "But I assumed that since you'd put in for one administrative post, you'd naturally try for another."

Sherry crossed her arms. "Tell Sheldon March not to get his hopes up. Every college needs a watchdog. I think I'm rather good at it."

"Um…yes. So you'll oversee the department's opening weeks?"

"Lock will owe me big time, but yes, I'll do it." She sounded reluctant but inside she jumped for joy. She and Kruger had always fought bitterly over his dropping classes from the schedule too early. This was one semester they'd be safe.

Still humming happily on the drive home, Sherry had barely cleared the door to her town house and kicked off her shoes when her phone rang. It was Garrett Lock.

"I'm looking at a registration printout," he said without identifying himself. Not that he had to. Sherry would have known that sexy drawl anywhere. "I see two classes with low enrollment. If there's no change by tomorrow, cancel them."

"Where are you? How did you get a printout?"

He chuckled. "I'm in Huntsville. I had the college computer guru link my laptop to the mainframe before I left today. You didn't think I'd shirk my duties, did you?"

That was exactly what she'd thought. So the title of interim dean didn't mean diddly. A figurehead. That was all they wanted. A warm body to take the flak from disgruntled students. She felt her temper sizzle on a short fuse.

"Hello! Are you there?" he asked loudly.

"Cancel them yourself. You don't need me if you have access to enrollment."

There were shouts in the background, then muffled mumbling. "Sorry." He came back on the line. "What was that you said? Things are squirrelly here. Movers are trying to give me an estimate and my son locked them out of his room."

Sherry thought he did sound harried. *The busier, the better.* "You must have a million and one things to do," she soothed. "Leave this kind of stuff in my hands, okay."

There was silence except for the hum of the wire, as if he was weighing her suggestion.

"You can trust me." Sherry injected enough indignation in her tone to push his guilt buttons.

"All right, but keep me posted." He reeled off his e-mail address.

She scribbled it down, never intending to use it.

They rang off. She'd no more than hung up when the phone jingled again. This time it was her mother, inviting her to a family barbecue. "Saturday night. To celebrate your birthday, dear."

"Don't, Mom. I'm acting dean until Dr. Lock com-

pletes his move. I'll probably have to work Saturday."
Her family meant well, but on each successive birthday,
more was made of her single status. She didn't need that
this year, what with losing out on the promotion and
with Nolan so sappy in love. Talk was bound to turn
toward weddings. In fact, she'd be willing to guarantee
it.

"Nonsense," Nan Campbell chided. "You shouldn't
work as late as seven, and you have to eat. Dad's
lighting the barbecue at six-forty-five. Be here." Sherry
found herself staring at a buzzing receiver.

The jarring reminder that she faced turning thirty-
two in a few days left her feeling melancholy. It didn't
help that in the day's mail were two invitations to
wedding showers for Emily and Nolan. Sherry went into
the kitchen and threw herself into a cooking frenzy. After
dirtying half the pans in the cupboard making chicken
cordon bleu for one, she set the table with her grandmother's fine china, lit a taper and poured a glass of
wine.

She was perfectly happy being single. A woman
didn't need a man to enjoy a romantic dinner. It was just
random bad luck that the songs she'd slipped into the
CD player were all about everlasting love.

Sherry picked at her food. In a fit of feeling sorry
for herself, she wished she'd gone out more with
friends. If she had, on evenings such as this she'd feel
free to drop by the pub where the old crowd tended to
hang out.

What was wrong with her? For crying out loud, she
was a psychologist. She was a woman in her prime.
There wasn't a reason in the world for her to feel as if
life had passed her by. No reason at all.

AT WORK THE NEXT DAY, Garrett Lock phoned her four times.

Five times the day after. More on Friday.

By Saturday Sherry viewed the prospective party at her parents' home as an escape from his infuriating meddling in every decision she made.

Emily met Sherry at the door and engulfed her in a hug. Megan and Mark, age fourteen and twelve respectively, Emily's two kids from her previous marriage, blindfolded Sherry the minute their mom returned to the kitchen.

Calling her, Auntie Sherry, the kids led her to a stack of presents. Amid boisterous shouts, they instructed her to guess what was in each package. Sherry had developed a soft spot for these two. Although Megan had started the wagon-train journey as a trial, she'd turned out to be quite a plucky young woman by the end of summer.

"Hey, you guys, I've never been an aunt. I think I'm going to like it." Sherry poked and prodded the many gifts. "It means more packages to open," she teased.

"You rascals," Emily scolded her two. "Untie that scarf and let Sherry see. I think Megan hid a box under the couch that she hoped you'd miss."

As the blindfold came off, Sherry noticed Megan's blush. "Isn't that always the way?" Sherry said gently. "We buy other people what we're dying to have ourselves."

"It's not so much that I want what we bought you as I want *something* new. Everyone here is so busy with wedding stuff Mark and I haven't shopped for school clothes. We start our new schools next week."

Nolan, who'd come in from the patio, shot a worried glance at his bride-to-be. "Emily, maybe you and Mom

should take a day off. Clothes are important to kids
starting a new school. If it's a matter of money—"

"It's not," Emily rushed in. She gazed helplessly at
her future mother-in-law.

Nan turned to her son. "Nolan, you're the one insisting on a big church wedding. These things take time.
I'm afraid we don't have a free minute next week."

Sherry was moved by the kids' long faces. And if she
spent another interminable week at the beck and call of
Garrett Lock, she'd probably go berserk. "Tell you
what, guys, any aunt worth her salt would rescue you.
How about if I take you both to the mall next Saturday?
All day. We'll grab hamburgers or a pizza and do the
concert in the park that evening." She named a well-
known rock group scheduled to perform.

Megan and Mark shouted with glee.

Emily bit her lip. "Sherry, are you sure? Nan said
your job—"

"Positive," Sherry broke in. "Mom and Dad think
I'm working too hard. Besides, the new dean needs to
get rid of the notion that I'm his flunky."

"How are you and Garrett getting on?" Nolan
asked casually.

"Swell." She made a face and picked up one of the
gifts. "He hasn't even been in the office and already I
feel like his personal go-fer. Do this, do that. He's good
at barking orders."

"Give the guy a break. Among other things, he's
having trouble finding a place to live."

"Really? On his salary I shouldn't think it'd be a problem." Sherry did the fake violin thing, and the kids
laughed.

Nolan silenced their antics. "Garrett called in a panic

yesterday and asked me to keep an eye out for houses for sale or rent. He'd like three bedrooms and a yard."

"Tell him to call a realtor." Sherry's conscience niggled as she recalled the corner town house in her complex; just today the owner had posted a sign for sale or lease. It had three bedrooms and a nice backyard. Also a loft bedroom with a city view. But it was much too close to where she lived. From porch to porch, less than a hundred yards.

Sherry pretended interest in folding the paper she'd removed from the gift, which turned out to be a CD carrying case from Mark. Thankfully her terse response motivated a change of subject. Garrett Lock's name didn't come up again all evening. Sherry actually relaxed and enjoyed herself. She even let them ensnare her in the wedding plans. Before she left, she caved in and agreed to be Emily's maid of honor. Something about weddings was infectious.

By the end of the week following her birthday bash, Sherry was ready to wring Lock's neck. If she talked to him once a day, she talked to him fifty times.

Five o'clock, Friday night, she fumed into the telephone, "You're being unreasonable. I have ten students on a degree track who need that class. If they don't get it this semester, they'll have to delay graduation until summer. Six of them won't qualify for grant money if they extend."

"The rules are clear," Garrett said, equally exasperated. "It takes twelve students for the class to run. Find two more students."

"I can't," she wailed. "Cut me some slack here, Lock. The money isn't coming out of your pocket."

"Technically it is. Or it soon will be when I become

a home owner/taxpayer. The best I can do is hold off
another day. Phone me names and social security
numbers of two students by six tomorrow night, and I'll
punch them into the system myself."

She thought of her proposed shopping trip with
Emily's kids. "I can't tomorrow. My…my mom is sick
and I'm needed at home," she said on impulse. "I'll do
it Sunday. Will you give me two days?" Sherry felt
guilty for lying. But darn it, he'd already run her ragged
today. Her back ached. Her eyes burned. She was dead
on her feet. She couldn't stay late. To find students to
fill a class meant tedious hours at the computer going
through individual class schedules of everyone in her
program.

"I'm sorry to hear about your mom. Nothing
serious, I hope."

"Flu," she mumbled, feeling the flush of guilt warm
her neck and cheeks.

He waited a heartbeat. "All right. Two days. Give me
your folks' phone number. Since I'm not sure if I'll be
at the hotel or if the realtor's going to find me something, I'll call you."

"Use my number. I'll access my machine. Their
phone's unlisted," she said lamely, wishing she could
take everything back. One fabrication only seemed to
beget another.

"All right. Good luck, Sherilyn. For the record, I
dislike putting a hardship on students as much as you
do." He clicked off, leaving her with mushy insides
because of the soft way he drawled her name. And
leaving her feeling embarrassed and ashamed because
of the ease with which he'd accepted her lie.

"'Oh, what a tangled web we weave, / when first we practice to deceive,'" she muttered, vowing this was the last time she'd go out on a limb like this.

CHAPTER FIVE

THE FAMILY MINISTER often warned of dire punishment for anyone who broke the ten commandments, Sherry recalled frantically when at ten sharp on Saturday, she and the kids elbowed their way up to a jeans sale table at the mall and she found herself facing none other than Garrett Lock.

Nobody deserves such rotten luck. Nobody.

Garrett recovered first from the shock of seeing her. "Either this sale is a sleeper and worth more than it looks or your mom underwent a miraculous recovery."

"I, ah, she…is better, thank you. Come on, kids, let's check other stores to compare prices." If ever Sherry wanted to sink through the floor and disappear, it was now.

Megan glanced with interest at the man talking with her soon-to-be aunt. Then in the blunt way of teens, she said, "I didn't know Gram was sick. She looked okay to me when she and Mom left to see the florist this morning."

Sherry dropped the jeans she'd been inspecting. She stared in horror at Megan. Now she was truly nailed.

The girl flung the pair of jeans she held onto the table. Eyes defiant, she pushed her brother toward the door. "Your mom said for us to call her Gram, didn't she, Mark?" The statement was carelessly thrown at Sherry.

"Oh, Megan, I'm upset with myself, not you. Never tell even a tiny white lie," she groaned. "They have a way of backfiring. Kids, I'd like you to meet Dr. Lock, my boss at the college. I told him Mom had the flu so I could skip work today and bring you shopping." Her story emerged in nervous spurts.

Garrett smiled at the kids. "I'd have known you anywhere from Nolan's description. He brags on you shamelessly. So? Are you all shopping for school? My son and I are, too. Keith? Where'd he go?" Garrett searched the aisles, then stepped back, practically trampling a small blond boy.

Sherry's heart went out to the child, whose huge blue eyes were framed by thick dark lashes most girls would kill to have. He seemed awkward, as if he hadn't grown into his feet. Or frightened, the way he stared at his sneakers, barely mumbling hello in response to Mark and Megan's greeting. Garrett Lock was so outgoing his son's shyness struck a sympathetic chord in Sherry.

Her imagination kicked into overdrive as Garrett tried unsuccessfully to draw the boy out. Sherry judged that Keith felt intimidated by his dad. Who knew what Garrett was like as a parent? As a husband? She'd heard somewhere that Texas law had a tendency to favor men in cases of divorce. Did the poor tyke miss his mom? Was that it? Had Garrett taken this job to spite his ex-wife? To keep the boy from her?

"What?" With a start Sherry realized Lock had spoken to her.

"I said, I don't expect you to work weekends. I realize now that we set a Sunday deadline. It didn't register at the time. My mind's been jumpy as a frog in a hot skillet. Keith's school starts Monday. If we don't find a house, I may be forced to transfer him a second time when we do."

"Your realtor…?"

"Isn't worth ten cents in Confederate money. He claims the market's bad because of heavier than normal enrollment in all the area colleges." His eyes clouded. "Everything we own is stored, which is why we're shopping. Most of Keith's clothes ended up in boxes at the back of the storage unit."

Megan shifted from one foot to another, a frown of concentration wrinkling her forehead. "I saw a For Sale sign this morning."

Sherry sucked in a breath. Megan must mean the sign outside the corner town house. Sherry purposely closed her ears. Who in their right mind would want their boss next door? She picked up the jeans Mark had said he liked. "I'll go pay for these. Megan, if you want those—" she pointed to the pair Megan had tossed aside "—bring them." Sherry headed for the cash register.

Garrett detained Megan. "Where did you see a For Sale sign?"

Her frown deepened. "On our way here, I think…but I can't exactly remember."

"Oh. Too bad."

"Look," Sherry called back, "I hate to be unsociable, but the kids have long shopping lists. This is the last weekend before school opens, so the stores will get crazy by afternoon." She aimed a smile at Garrett's son, who peeked at her from behind a rack of shirts. "Opening day of school is pretty exciting, Keith."

He continued to watch her with solemn eyes.

Garrett joined his son. "Guess we'll go." He tossed

Sherry a wave, and she fluttered her fingers, wishing he'd hurry up and leave.

Megan bounced over to where Sherry had moved up in the line. "He seems nice. A fox. Don't you just love how he talks? Southern drawls are sooo sexy."

Sherry mumbled something unintelligible. The very last thing she needed was to agree and have it somehow get back to Lock. Chatterbox that Megan was, she might blab anything at the dinner table. Not that Nolan gossiped. But if he somehow let news of that nature slip in his department, those guys would have a field day spreading rumors.

Sherry craned her neck to watch Lock's broad back disappear out the door. Only then did her breakfast settle. In a mall this big she naturally assumed they'd seen the last of the Locks. After paying, she guided the kids to the next store. And the next.

"So we meet again." Garrett's lazy greeting an hour later grated on Sherry's frazzled nerves. She spun toward his voice and landed squarely on the toe of his shiny black boot. "What are you doin—" Thrown off balance, Sherry fell against him.

Garrett caught her. Hopping on one foot, he polished the toe of his damaged boot against the opposite denim-clad leg. "Danged if I don't believe you're trying to maim me for life, Doc."

All ten of Sherry's fingers dug into the soft fabric of his shirt for a moment—until she felt singed by the heat of the hard flesh underneath. It was she who scrambled out of his grasp. "Why are you shopping at Victoria's Secret?" she whispered loudly.

"I…uh…" He glanced around, noting for the first time racks of satin-and-lace undergarments. Taking her arm, he dragged her and her many packages toward the door. "We ran into Mark. He said as soon as you're finished here, y'all plan to eat lunch. I thought we might go together."

She dug in her heels and ground to a stop. "Why?"

"Why what?" He flashed another nervous glance around. No one appeared to be paying attention, but Garrett felt more at ease after stepping out of the store and into the mall.

Sherry signaled to Megan that she'd be right back. Garrett's obvious discomfort stirred amusement and a modicum of sympathy in her. She realized, too, that inviting himself to lunch hadn't been a come-on. So what *was* his purpose? "I repeat, why should we eat together?"

His gaze swerved to his son, who was seated on a bench beside Mark. Garrett's expression changed. Softened. "Keith's having a hard time adjusting to the move. Huntsville is the only home he's known. Mark's older, but the two seem to be getting along. I thought—"

"If Keith's feelings were such a big priority, why did you go after this job in the first place?"

"My reasons are personal." Shutters clicked firmly into place.

What reasons? Too bad she was an advocate of a person's right to privacy. Anyway, secrets didn't stay secret for long on campus. She felt herself giving in. Lunch for the sake of a little boy wasn't a major sacrifice. "Mark knows the way to the pizza parlor. You guys go stake out a table. Megan and I'll join you when we finish here."

"Thanks. I owe you, Doc." He said it as if he meant it.

"No biggie," she mumbled. "And stop calling me Doc. You're one, too."

"I know, but referring to women by their last name goes against my Southern upbringing. I was taught to call ladies ma'am. A courtesy I had to unlearn when I began teaching feminists. Genderless titles are safest. Especially with you. You did object to our being on a first-name basis, remember."

She had. She'd been pretty annoyed, and darn him, it'd be a cold day in Panama before she'd apologize for being a feminist. "At work I insist on formality. Off campus, I guess there's no harm in our using first names," she grudgingly agreed.

Danged if the good Professor Campbell wasn't as bristly as a hedgehog. *Oh.* Did she think he wanted them to be more than colleagues? Garrett tensed briefly until he recalled the ear-dusting campus gossip and relaxed. She wasn't a big fan of men. "Okay, since it's settled, the boys and I will take off. Shall we order or wait?"

"Order yours. Megan and I'll decide after we get there. I'd better go keep her from buying out the store. I'm not sure how much of this stuff her mom'll approve." She waved toward the window.

Garrett made a sweeping assessment of the display. "How old is Megan?"

"Fourteen."

"Don't fourteen-year-old girls still play with dolls?"

"Go—before the manure you're shoveling gets too deep for your boots."

He placed a hand over his heart. "You wound me. At fourteen I was pure as new-driven snow. So were the girls I remember."

She gave a snort. "Like I fell off a turnip truck? I've been reliably informed that sex education in Texas happens out behind the barn—and I heard that from a Texan."

"I believe I hear my pizza calling." He walked off, leaving her looking bemused.

Garrett had sprung from Confederate stock, so he knew better than to provoke a battle he had no hope of winning. Considering who he'd taken on, it was better to sound a retreat.

Sherry watched him collect the boys. In those square-toed boots, Garrett Lock walked with an intriguing roll of his hips. A walk that defied definition. But walk or no walk, he was her boss. She fanned suddenly hot cheeks and ducked back into the store.

Bitten by the shopping bug, Megan didn't want to stop for lunch.

"Mark's already gone to save us a place," Sherry said.

Megan flounced along beside her. "Pizza is so fattening."

"Serious shopping burns a lot of calories," Sherry returned dryly. "Not that you have to worry. What are you? A size three?"

"Five." Megan said it as though five was one step from requiring the services of Omar the tentmaker.

Sherry rolled her eyes. "This place has a salad bar. Heaven forbid that you should put any meat on those nonexistent hips." They were still heatedly discussing what constituted fat when they arrived at the table occupied by Garrett and the boys.

"Fat? Who's fat?" Garrett demanded. "Present company excepted, of course." His assessing blue gaze skipped over Megan's skinny frame to loiter on Sherry's more womanly curves. Obviously liking what he saw, he looked his fill.

She felt like a rabbit caught in the crosshairs of his sight. That smoldering look was precisely why she'd had second thoughts about this impromptu lunch date. *No, not a date. Not by any means.* She dropped her purse on the empty seat between them, then relieved Megan of her shopping bags to build the buffer higher.

"Girls always think they're fat," Mark informed Keith Lock with the superiority of his advanced age. "If you hadda a sister, you'd hafta listen to girls gripe about stuff like that all the time. Girls always think they're fat."

"'Least you've got company," Keith said wistfully.

Megan leaned across the table and slugged her brother in the shoulders.

Rubbing the spot, Mark said to Keith, "You're the lucky one being an only kid. Look at the abuse I gotta take. 'Cause guys can't hit a girl back and they know it."

"Girls shouldn't hit boys, either," Sherry put in after noting a faint frown between Garrett's brows. Although he appeared to be staring at Keith, Sherry thought his disapproval must be aimed at her for not having better control of her charges. "Mark, if you've ordered, would you go tell them Megan and I want the salad bar?" She dug in her purse and handed him some bills. "Take out enough for your pizza, too."

The boy pocketed the money. "Can I keep the change? When Keith and me finish eating, we wanna drop some coin in the techno peeps."

Sherry gaped. "Say what?"

Megan interpreted. "He means they want to play the video games. They have cool ones here. Can I play, too?"

"You may," Sherry said. "All of you may, if we have time."

Keith slouched. "My dad probably won't let me."

"It's just in the back room," Sherry informed Garrett, again wondering if he was a real tyrant. Or did he resent not having a macho son? How many times had she heard that complaint from the moms she counseled? Her heart pinched. Where was Keith's mother that she'd allow him to suffer through this machismo routine?

Garrett was genuinely puzzled by Sherry's harsh expression. *Now what?* What had she read into his thoughts this time? Well, hell. He'd put up with her attitude for Keith's sake. His son had been so down since their move it worried Garrett.

"If you clean your plate," he murmured, "you may do the videos." Garrett hated resorting to bribes, but lately Keith only picked at his food. He'd always been wiry, and it wasn't so much the boy's ribs sticking out that Garrett found troubling as his inertia. Keith didn't seem to care about anything. Not where they were going to live or the prospect of starting school, though he'd always loved his classes. More baffling, he seemed angry at Carla. And wouldn't you know she'd told her lawyer Garrett was turning their son against her. He'd been so careful to hide his feelings from Keith.

Mark's getting up to go and place Sherry and Megan's order jostled Garrett from his private thoughts. "I'll buy drinks," he said, rising, too. "What would you like?"

"Water for me," Megan said.

"Me, too, but I'll fetch mine after we get our salads," Sherry said.

"You'll *fetch* it?" Garrett laughed, his good humor restored for the moment. "Don't razz me anymore about coming from Cowpatty college."

"I never did. I love listening to you talk." The instant the admission left her lips, her face flamed, and so did his.

He muttered something about buying sodas while the line was short.

Megan pushed her chair back. "Hey, there's a girl I met at church. I'll be right back. I want to ask her what kids are gonna wear the first day of school. Go on through the salad line, Aunt Sherry." She left Sherry alone at the table with Garrett's son.

"Um, Keith, around here kids your age wear a lot of denim shorts and T-shirts at the start of school. It's still hot and humid in the classrooms."

He sat straighter. "Really? That's what we wore in Texas. Will you tell my dad? He's been lookin' at dweeby plaid shirts."

Sherry tried not to smile. "Our schools do have strict rules about the kinds of logos on the T-shirts," she cautioned.

"What's a logo?"

"Pictures and advertisements." Then she reduced it to his level. "No shirts with bad words and stuff."

"Oh." He wriggled forward in the seat, swinging his knobby knees. "My dad'd never buy me those."

"What won't Dad buy you, buddy?" Neither Keith nor Sherry had heard Garrett return. Smiling, he pulled out a chair, sat and placed a pitcher of soft drinks and several empty glasses on the table. "My line went faster than Mark's," he said, tilting back in his chair. "Now, what is it you want that I won't buy you, Keith?"

"Nothin'." Keith shut down.

Sherry recognized the sullenness. Exactly how Megan had acted toward Emily at the start of the wag-on-train expedition. Taking pity on Garrett, Sherry

apprised him of what he'd missed. Except for the
remark about dweeby plaid shirts. That was for Keith
to relay.

"See, son? Your new school won't be much different from your old one. That should make you happy."

"I still won't know nobody," he said defiantly.

Garrett sighed. Unconsciously he turned to Sherry
for support.

She didn't know what he wanted from her. Clearly
his son was no happier than she that Garrett had come
to Columbia. What could she say? That it wasn't too late
for him to bow out? It was. Who'd step in knowing he—
or she—was second-best? The person would never get
respect.

The silence dragged out between them.

Mark clomped up in his size-eleven unlaced
sneakers and threw himself into the chair next to Keith.
"Sheesh! What a dork taking orders. Like, how hard is
it to punch in two salads? Here's your plate, Aunt
Sherry. Where's Megan?" He waved a second platter
in the air.

"Talking to someone she met at church."

Nudging Keith, Mark said, "I really like livin' here.
Things are…comfortable, you know?"

Keith's shrug said he didn't agree.

Sherry felt Garrett had been left in the dark. "Emily's
in-laws were pretty controlling. They ran the town and
everyone in it. Columbia's much bigger city, so life
here is a very different experience for these guys."

"A better one!" Mark threw in.

"Uh, thanks," Garrett mumbled. "As new kid on the
block I still have a lot to learn about this place."

She rested an elbow on the table. "I've never lived

anywhere else. I can't imagine moving, although I like to travel."

Keith Lock's lower lip trembled. "I don't see why we hafta move closer to Mom." Leaping up, he knocked his chair over as he ran toward the rest room.

Sherry gasped. "I'm sorry if I caused that."

Garrett fumbled to right the chair. "This isn't like him. Excuse me—I need to go straighten things out."

Megan, who'd wandered back to the table in time to hear Keith's outburst, winced, remembering, no doubt, her recent shouting matches with her mother.

Still shaken by Keith's blowup, Sherry wished she'd declined Garrett's invitation.

"You'd better hurry and get him," Mark hollered after Garrett. "Here comes our pizza."

Needing space, Sherry announced that she was going to the salad bar.

"Me, too." Megan trotted after her. "Keith Lock is one unhappy puppy," she said, heaping lettuce on her plate. "I feel bad for him, don't you?"

"You and Mark are starting new schools," Sherry said, bypassing the croutons and other toppings. "Is transferring really so hard?"

"No. But we're getting a new dad, a big house and a dog. What do you suppose happened that Keith's so bummed at his mother?"

"I don't know, Megan. Those aren't questions one asks a new boss." Although Sherry was more curious than ever. She'd assumed Garrett's move had to do with trying to avoid his ex. Now it sounded as if the opposite was true. Maybe he still loved her.

Sherry's hands tightened involuntarily on her plate. Maybe he was one of those men who obsessed over a wife who'd rejected him. Last year they'd accepted a young woman into the program whose ex-husband wouldn't let go. First he stalked her. In the end he killed her, then turned the gun on himself.

Heart pounding, Sherry watched Garrett and Keith navigate the rows of tables as they returned. The man's face was positively grim. He kept a firm grip on his son's shoulder. Sherry felt so sorry for Keith that she lost her appetite.

"Is that all you're eating?" Megan asked, eyeing the small lump of salad on Sherry's plate.

She thrust her Mickey Mouse watch under Megan's nose. "Look at the time. We still have a lot of shopping to do."

"Gotcha. So let's eat fast and split. Amy—she's the girl I went to see—she bought this really great dress at a boutique on the lower mall. She said they had one left in my size. It's lime green and *so* cool."

"By all means." Sherry sighed with relief. "Eat and we'll split."

Keith ate in silence. Garrett tossed out various topics that nobody took up. Sherry responded with a sentence or less, spread her salad around and kept staring at Garrett in a strange way.

"Have I done something to offend you?" he finally asked, a little exasperated.

"No." She pushed her plate away. "Are you kids finished?" She gathered her purse and packages and stood.

"What's the rush?" Mark asked around a mouthful of pizza. "Me'n Keith were gonna do videos, 'member?"

Sherry started to say no but caught sight of Keith Lock's blue eyes resigned to yet another disappointment. "One game," she said, slipping back to balance on the edge of her chair. "Two, max. And make them short ones, Mark."

"You got it!" He stuffed the last bite into his mouth, latched on to Keith's hand and dragged him toward the dark cavern that housed the noisy games.

Megan rose with more grace, then—forgetting her age—chased after the boys.

Garrett set his slice of pizza aside to pour another soda. "I appreciate what you just did," he said. "I know it's biting into your day." With a quick glance toward the room that'd swallowed the kids, he said, almost too softly for Sherry to hear, "Carla is forever making him promises she doesn't keep."

A million questions whirled through Sherry's mind. She didn't ask a single one. Always conscious that counseling was her job, she tried hard not to grill her friends. She stayed out of people's problems unless they specifically asked for her advice.

The longer she sipped at her water, the more apparent it was that Garrett Lock hadn't been seeking advice. In fact, if anything, he regretted letting slip what he had. On the heels of his unexpected statement, he'd plunged right into shop talk. He quizzed Sherry about the department she chaired—asking how she managed enrollment, determine outcome assessments and handled student quotas. He kept the questions rolling, never giving her an opening to mention Keith's mother.

"Whoa!" She finally held up a hand. "These are things you should bring up at a staff meeting. You *do* plan to meet with us on a regular basis, I hope."

Eyes hooded, he tipped back in his chair and laced his hands over his flat belly.

"You're not," she accused, setting her glass down with a crack. "Dean Kruger kept his department staff in limbo. It was a big mistake."

Garrett walked his fingers together one at a time, starting with his thumbs. "Do you intend to undermine my efforts to administrate unless I agree to play the game your way?"

"You call dissemination of information a game?" Sherry hadn't intended to let her voice rise, but it did. The boys came barreling back, interrupting her glaring match with Garrett. "Don't sit down," Sherry ordered Mark, scrambling up herself. "I'll phone you tomorrow regarding enrollment in that class," she snapped at Lock. "At least information will flow *one* way."

Garrett balled his napkin. "If our work relationship starts off rocky, I don't have a prayer of striking a positive chord with the faculty who report to you. How long are you going to hold it against me that I got the job?"

"What?" she bristled. "To couch this in Texas terms, Lock, except for that teensy lie I told yesterday, I'm about the squarest shooter of all the Human Services chairs you'll deal with. Yes, I'll fight for program expansion, but you'll see me coming. I don't strike from ambush. If there's an uprising in the ranks, I won't be involved." Chin held high, she wove through the tables like a blue-ribbon slalom skier. Megan and Mark caught up with her halfway down the mall.

"He called you a hard-boiled egg," Mark said, puffing in his effort to match his steps to Sherry's. "I said you fly off the handle quick, but cool off fast, too. I didn't want you to get in trouble, Aunt Sherry. I mean, you said he's your boss."

Her steps lagged. Already she felt bad for having

lost her temper in front of the kids. She reached over and ruffled Mark's hair. "So, which of us is the psychologist, huh, kid? Okay, I'm calm now. I doubt we'll see the Locks again today, but how about if I promise to apologize tomorrow when I phone him about enrollment?"

Grinning, Mark strode ahead, whistling.

"He'll have a big head for a week," Megan complained. "How can you be so nice to my dorky brother and rag on a hunk like Dr. Lock?"

Sherry stepped on the escalator, pretending she hadn't heard Megan. Why worry about it right now? As she'd told Mark, she didn't expect to see Garrett again today.

Wrong. The father-son duo lurked outside the boutique where Megan's friend said they'd find the lime green dress.

Deciding there was no time like the present to clear the air, Sherry immediately said, "I apologize for mouthing off."

Garrett pushed away from the wall, caught her wrist and at the same moment she spoke said, "I was out of line at lunch."

Pinpricks of heat spread from his fingers to the underside of Sherry's arm. When it seemed as if the silence was stretched so tight it was about to crack, they both laughed and Sherry pulled free.

Garrett sobered first. "I had no call to go on the attack. If I have an excuse, I guess it's because the dean at my old college called meetings for the purpose of putting faculty on the hot seat. He pitted faculty against department chairs and vice versa."

"Kruger did everything by memo. After ten or so memos filled with backpedaling and double talk, ideas always ended up being shelved. The previous dean was never in his office. Under his leadership all the departments stagnated. The chairman before me got so frustrated he quit. Faculty elected me, and I've spent two years smoothing ruffled feathers. The apathy is terrible. No one likes to lose out on a promotion, but when it comes right down to it, I'm relieved you inherited the whole mess."

He crossed his arms and chewed on his bottom lip as he listened. "I don't claim to be a miracle worker," he said after she'd finished. "We've both taught and you still do, so we know what happens in a house divided. If the dean and department chairs disagree, faculty is always split. I need your support in front of staff, Sherilyn."

The soft pleading way he said her name tracked tiny shivers up Sherry's spine. Coupled with those blue eyes and crooked smile, his voice launched an assault on her senses impossible to thwart. "Ho-kay." She sucked in a deep breath, trying to get out from under his spell. "We'll keep our battles private."

Garrett dropped his chin to his chest and massaged the bridge of his nose. "I prefer not to battle at all, but I'll do my dangedest to see our skirmishes don't turn into war. Now that's settled, I'd better take off. Once I outfit Keith, I have to go sign a contract for his after-school day care. Then…another visit to the realtor."

As Megan beckoned Sherry to come and look at the dress, she said she had to go, too. Later, when she and Megan emerged from the shop with the dress, Mark was waiting there alone. Sherry actually found herself looking around for Lock—and couldn't believe she was doing it.

The three shopped so long they were almost late to the concert. Garrett didn't enter her mind again until nearly midnight when Sherry pulled into her complex and her headlights illuminated the For Sale or Lease sign on the corner unit. She leased her place. Some people in the complex owned their houses. Either way, she didn't want Garrett Lock that close to her.

Would Megan notice the sign and remark on it? she wondered. But no. Both kids bubbled over with news of their purchases and tales of the cool rock band.

Nolan, who awaited their arrival, stuffed the kids and their bags into the car. "Whew," he said to Sherry once the noise subsided. "Have they been like that all day?"

"Not really. We had a good time. They're great kids, Nolan."

"Emily and Mom sent their profound thanks. They accomplished a lot today. I finished sanding floors. Things went so well I finally believe there'll actually be a wedding at Thanksgiving and that my house will be ready to move into."

His joy was contagious. Watching him, Emily and the kids all brim with happiness made Sherry's earlier notion that somehow they'd all end up hurt seem silly. She rose on tiptoe to kiss his bristly cheek. "Tell Emily I'll drop by Monday after work, and we'll go pick out material for my maid-of-honor dress."

"Hey, sis, that's great. I know you're as skittish as I was when it comes to weddings. But I guarantee, when love strikes, you'll fall like a ton of bricks."

"Me? No way. Get these sleepy kids home before Emily thinks you've all been kidnapped."

She waved as Nolan backed out, realizing that Lock had probably been right—she'd been jealous of Nolan and Emily's close bond. Sighing, she let herself into her dark empty house. What was this? An admission that she might need someone else? No way. Once all the lights were on, she felt fine again.

THE EARLY PART of the week flew by. Garrett reclaimed his job on Monday. From then on, Sherry didn't have a moment's peace. A flood of paperwork flowed from his desk to hers as it did to all department chairs who reported to him. For three days a steady stream of people marched in and out of his office. Whenever the traffic stopped, it meant he was in meetings and would come back with double the workload.

Sherry grew adept at sidestepping personal questions concerning her new boss—mostly from unattached female faculty wearing a certain gleam in their eyes. They refused to believe Sherry didn't know anything personal about the handsome Texan.

They'd better believe it. She and Lock had barely exchanged two words since their encounter at the mall. Which was why Sherry was stunned when he stuck his head in her office Wednesday afternoon and announced he was leaving early to meet his movers.

She peered up from one of many student folders piled on her desk, her eyes requiring a moment to focus on the rangy figure lounging against her door frame. He wore close-fitting blue jeans, black boots and a blue shirt that matched his eyes. He carried a soft gray Western-cut jacket slung over one shoulder. "Movers?" she managed to blurt, after running her tongue over dry lips. "I thought your stuff was here in storage."

"I bought a place. Well, actually I've filled out the paperwork. Luckily it's vacant. The owner agreed to rent it to me until the deal closes."

"Where—" The phone rang, cutting her off. "A student," she mouthed, covering the receiver. "Troubled." Listening a moment, she glanced at Garrett again and sliced a finger across her neck.

He studied the credentials on her wall and the plaques he thought said a lot about her. One read: We will find a way—or make one. Another said: Success is an inevitable destination. When it became apparent that she'd be on the phone indefinitely, he tapped his watch, gave her a two-fingered salute and pulled the door closed on his way out.

Sherry raced to her four-o'clock intermediate psych class with only seconds to spare. It was six-thirty by the time she trudged to her car. Tired and hungry—she'd skipped lunch—she was ready to spit nails when she pulled into her complex and found the entry blocked by an enormous moving van.

Her stomach growled as she parked on the street, gathered her briefcase and hiked back to the inner courtyard. A cluster of neighbors lined the walkway, shouting suggestions to movers struggling to push a leather couch through the front door of the town house that'd been vacant when Sherry left for work.

Even in the dusk, she recognized the waitress who lived next door, Alicia Jones—the beautician from three places down—and Yvette. Sherry wondered vaguely when she'd gotten home from her road trip.

Her roommate's back was to Sherry, but she recognized Yvette's seductive pose and her habit of twisting her long blond hair around one finger while she flirted shamelessly.

This time, however, she happened to be flirting with Garrett Lock.

Sherry's stomach pitched and rolled. Feebly she pushed forward.

Garrett glanced up and saw Sherry at the same time she saw him. He knew because of the way her amber eyes opened wide. His own eyes narrowed warily as they exclaimed in unison, "What are *you* doing here?"

In the next breath both chorused, "I live here."

"I signed papers last night." Garrett waved a hand at the corner unit, while Sherry pointed to the lighted house catercorner across the courtyard. "Mine," she whispered.

Yvette, always a toucher and always possessive when it came to men, slid her arm through Garrett's. Sherry understood the warning in her friend's cool green eyes, a warning that said, *back off.*

A noise, not quite recognizable, strangled its way past Sherry's lips. "How…how did you find this particular town house?" she demanded of Garrett.

"Nolan told me about it Sunday. He said it was a nice place—but neglected to say you lived next door." Garrett appeared every bit as disconcerted as she. "Honestly, the morning the cabbie brought me here, I was too turned around to notice."

About to mutter that she'd kill Nolan, Sherry happened to glance up over Lock's head and into the lighted loft bedroom. Keith Lock was outlined there, hugging some sort of stuffed toy. A bear, she thought. His nose was pressed to the glass, his small face pale in the lamplight.

If ever anyone needed a home, that child did. And the truth was, Sherry didn't see much sense in wasting energy railing at situations over which she had no control.

"Tell Keith I said welcome to the neighborhood," she
said to Garrett, shoving her way past the milling throng.
Without a backward glance, she stalked into her one-
time haven of rest.

CHAPTER SIX

SHERRY STRIPPED off her work clothes and stared at the shower, but then decided she needed something physical to work off the head of steam that'd built. Not even the hottest shower would dissolve the irritation knotting her muscles. She pulled on her bike shorts and a crop top, shouldered her in-line skates and collected her helmet, then left the house again.

A big golden harvest moon hung low in the sky, and though night shadows were falling, the evening remained pleasantly warm. The park directly across the street from the town-house complex boasted a wonderful set of lighted trails. From the start of fall classes until Halloween, one of the fraternities patrolled the pathways. At a point where the trails crossed to form a figure eight, their sister sorority operated a hot-dog stand to help pay for a yearly Christmas dance. Sherry was such a steady customer the girls who worked the booth knew her by name.

She was far from ready for a heart-to-heart chat with Yvette, so this spur-of-the-moment outing provided an opportunity to slay three dragons at one time. Sherry's dragons tonight were irritation, hunger and the need to keep peace in the household. She'd seen the same scenario time and again. Yvette threw herself into relationships with abandon. She blundered through the steps like a ritual and to the exclusion of everything else in her life. In Sherry's opinion Yvette always smothered the object of her affections. Love burned bright only so long, then it flamed out.

Sherry's steps slowed as she passed Garrett's house. The crowd had scattered. Through the curtainless window she saw Yvette pointing and waving her hands, obviously helping arrange his furniture. Maybe by this time next week she'd be moving in with him.

As she rounded the moving van, Sherry asked herself why that mattered to her. It couldn't be because she cared for Lock—or cared if he suffered when Yvette found someone new. And she would. Yvette had left a string of casualties. But for all Sherry knew, so had Lock. That might be why Keith looked so sad. Had Garrett moved closer to his ex because mother-son visits would give him greater freedom to sow wild oats?

Now who had an overactive imagination? She'd gone from suspecting Lock was obsessed by his ex-wife to branding him a world-class Casanova.

Sherry peered inside the van as she passed and noticed it was nearly empty. That made Garrett's moving into her neighborhood suddenly very real. She actually hoped she'd somehow dreamed the whole incident. But of course she hadn't.

She dropped onto the first bench at the park entrance to change from her sneakers into her skates. Tying her shoelaces together, she draped the shoes around her neck and immediately glided off.

"Dr. Campbell. Hey, I thought maybe you'd given up skating. I've been here every night since we opened and I haven't seen you around."

Sherry circled and stopped beside a sun-freckled student who flashed her a huge grin. Robert Dickson was the catalyst behind this park project. "Robby, after three years, you must know that opening week is a killer for faculty. And since I'm also a department chair, I work double the time."

"Boy, you must really be under siege. This is the *second* week, not the first."

Sherry wrinkled her nose. "See how time flies when you're having fun?"

"I hear you got a new boss. The sorority women think you should've gotten the job."

"Really? I'll thank them when I stop at the hot-dog stand." Sherry enjoyed a close rapport with the sororities. Most of the girls she'd advised when she'd served as a full-time counselor had graduated. But word filtered down and the current sorority members dropped by if they needed to talk. The older she got the more she felt like a Mother Confessor.

"So, is the new dean a pretty good guy? Letty has an appointment to see him next week. She got two *D*s last semester, and she received a letter saying she can't work in the cafeteria and carry a full class load. But without a job she can't pay tuition."

Sherry gazed at him sympathetically. "That is the rule. I don't know what Dr. Lock will do, but Letty needs to tell him she had a bad time when your dad died. I wondered if either of you'd even be back this year. Who's running the farm?"

"I am. Well, sort of. Dr. Temple adopted the farm as our Ag project this year. His summer class helped with tilling and planting. My class will harvest and ship."

"That's wonderful, Robby. When exactly is Letty's

appointment? I'll put in a good word for her with Dr. Lock. I can't promise anything, but I believe he'll be fair."

"Thanks. She won't fall behind. Guys in my fraternity offered to tutor her in chemistry and physics. You know Letty and I have two brothers and a sister still to put through college. We have to stay on schedule. If Letty misses the nursing boards this spring, she won't get the job she's been promised at the valley hospital."

Sherry nodded and waved goodbye as someone else claimed Robert's attention. She skated off, worrying that she'd stuck her neck out. Frankly, she wasn't at all sure Garrett would make allowances for Letty. He hadn't been willing to bend the rules on the class some of her students needed. Because she'd found only one extra student, instead of the minimum two, he'd canceled the class. Sherry hoped he wasn't by-the-book about everything. Sometimes you had to take a chance on a kid.

She concentrated on the uphill leg of the cinder path, working out in her head what she'd say to Garrett on Monday—provided, of course, that he could give her five minutes.

Her opportunity to speak on Letty's behalf came a lot sooner than that. On her way home after completing the circuit, she took the opportunity to move her car from the street to her covered space, since the van was now gone. Just as she climbed out with her skates and turned to lock the car, Garrett showed up to unload something from the back of his pickup, which was parked beside hers.

"You skate in the dark?" He rested a heavy crate on the tailgate, and in the soft pool of light cast by the carriage lamps hung at intervals along the car park, he took in her windblown hair, sweat-damp neck and arms and the bulky knee pads. "Isn't it dangerous this late?" Frown lines formed between his brows.

She downed the last swig of her bottled water and blotted her face before she told him about the park. It had crossed her mind to ignore him. She certainly didn't want him horning in if he also skated. Although on second thought she figured it was a foolish worry with Yvette occupying his spare time. There were only two recreational events that worked up a sweat in which her roommate participated. One was dancing. Sherry preferred not to think about the other.

"Are the park trails only for adults or can kids use them, too?"

"Whole families," she said. "Why? Do you and Keith skate?" Her heart sank.

"Keith has in-line skates packed somewhere. And a skateboard. He and his friends taught themselves in our previous neighborhood. I hate to think I may have to learn at this age." His smile faded as he cast a worried glance toward the brightly lit town house.

"Keith will soon make friends." Sherry felt compelled to ease the man's obvious anxiety if she could. "The only children in our complex are babies. But on the days I go to work at nine, I see a group of boys walking to the elementary school."

"That's another problem. With my hours, I'll have to drive him. He'll take a bus to the day care facility when school's out."

"Bummer. Well," she said brightly, "after you meet some of the other kids and their folks, maybe you'll turn up a mom who baby-sits in her home before and after school."

"You think?" He scanned her with apprehension. "Where kids get their notions I'll never know, but Keith has it in his head that only babies go to day care."

"Yeah, kids talk. The ones who've been in managed care since birth get pretty jaded, so I hear. The most ideal setup is when one parent is able to stay home, but very few people can manage that these days."

"Boy howdy, don't you know it. And since we're discussing parental responsibility, I'd better be getting back so I can deal with Keith's bed."

"Do you mean you still have to assemble the beds?"

He shook his head as he hoisted the box to his shoulder. "Not assemble. The movers set them up. I just need to find the sheets and put them on."

"Well, I'm sure Yvette will lend a hand."

He caught the sharpness of her tone and delivered a frown that Sherry missed because she stepped aside and let him pass. "I sent Yvette home. I appreciate her offer to help, but if I don't put things away myself, I'll never find them later."

"Really?" Sherry examined him with new eyes, although her mind darted to other things. Absently she asked, "Will you be in the office tomorrow?"

"I hadn't planned to be. I didn't use all the time allotted for my move. I told Westerbrook I'd be out both tomorrow and the next day. Any special reason you ask?"

"You have an appointment on Monday with a student by the name of Letty Dickson. Or she may be listed as Letitia. I'd like a few minutes to talk about her."

"What am I seeing her for?"

"Low grade point average. She got two *D*s last semester. She's scheduled to work twenty hours a week in the cafeteria, so the computer kicked out a letter saying she couldn't. It's mandated that she meet with you to discuss her poor grades."

"That sounds logical." They'd arrived at his gate. He shifted the box to see Sherry more clearly. "Someone who got two *D*s should concentrate on her studies. I agree, she shouldn't work."

"She had a family crisis last semester."

"Okay. Let her drop out of work this year, retake those two classes and better her grades. If she brings her GPA up, she can work again next year. Say ten hours."

"Right, Mr. Hardnose," Sherry flared. "Only next year she won't be back because the family lost its bread-winner, and Letty needs to be working full-time to help send three younger sibs to college." Reaching around him, she opened the gate for Garrett. Then without another word, she walked away.

"Sherilyn, wait," he called, softly drawling her name. "Damn it," he swore when she didn't turn back. "Can't we ever have a discussion without you getting hostile? Run her scores for me and drop them by on your way home tomorrow. Please," he added.

A backward wave was all she gave to let him know she'd heard.

Garrett stood at the gate, slow to shake off the frost of yet another encounter with Dr. Campbell. As he wandered toward his front door, he mulled over the difference in the two roommates. Yvette, attractive as she was, showed the potential of draining a guy with her clingy ways. Sherilyn was the type to leave skid marks on a man's soul. How did those two ever end up living under the same roof? They were as different as sugar and vinegar.

Sherry had no sooner stepped through the front door than Yvette pounced.

"What were you and Garrett talking so chummily about?"

"A student," Sherry said, dumping her helmet and skates in the hall closet.

Yvette flipped her long hair out of her face. "I suppose you think having a job in common with him gives you the inside track."

Bending, Sherry unbuckled her bulky knee pads, tossed them into her helmet and closed the closet door with a loud bang. "Inside track to what?"

"To dating Garrett of course. Don't play coy with me, Sherry."

Sherry rolled her shoulders tiredly. "When, in all the years you've known me, have you seen me act coy? You'll have plenty of competition without me if the parade of women staffers beating a path to his office door is any indication of his popularity."

"He's not the type to get involved in an office romance. Living in his hip pocket is much better. When he comes home, he'll want to relax. And I'll make sure relaxation is synonymous with little ol' me."

"You do that, Yvette. Excuse me, I'm going to take a shower."

"Okay. What and when is dinner?"

Sherry stopped and turned. "It's your night to cook, according to the calendar."

"You must have planned something. You didn't know I'd be home."

"No, I didn't. Whatever happened to us letting each other know about our schedules?" When Yvette didn't answer, Sherry said, "I bought a hot dog at Gamma Sigma's stand."

"Oh. Then I'll go to the pub and grab a burger. Your turn tomorrow. Make something yummy, all right?"

Sherry sighed. She had papers to grade tonight, but Yvette had been on the road two weeks. She was probably sick of eating out. Maybe a little compassion was in order. "How about lasagna? I bought all the stuff the other day. Lasagna and Caesar salad?"

"Great. And peanut-butter-brownie cups for dessert?"

"Yvette, are you all right? I can count on one hand the number of times you've eaten dessert with a meal."

"So? You baked chocolate squares and took them to work last week. You always do that. I might eat sweets if you'd ever leave any here."

"How do you know what I took to work last week?" Sherry asked suspiciously.

"Garrett mentioned it."

Sherry was even more astounded. She hadn't thought he'd come back to the office that day. Obviously he had. "I'm not making brownies. As it is, I'll be up late making the lasagna for tomorrow. If you get home at a decent hour from the pub, you can fix dessert. The recipe's in my box, and it's simple."

"Like anyone would eat anything I cooked. Cooking isn't my thing, as you well know. Even your mom gave up trying to teach me. Anyway, don't count on me being home early tonight. All I've seen for two weeks are bitchy clothing-department managers. After I eat I'll probably play some pool." She paused. "Garrett plays. But he doesn't have a baby-sitter for his kid. Hey, does Emily's daughter baby-sit?"

"Megan? She'd be more apt to play pool," Sherry said dryly. "Just don't put any money on the game. Nolan says she's a real shark."

"Well, I'll call Emily and ask. Garrett needs to be able to come and go as he pleases. He'll need a regular sitter."

Sherry thought about the unhappy little boy she'd met. Keith Lock needed more of his dad's attention, not less. She'd thought Garrett seemed worried about his son. But if he'd indicated otherwise to Yvette, then she must have been mistaken. "I'll likely be in bed when you get home, Yvette. Shall we have dinner at seven tomorrow?"

"Seven-thirty? I have a trunk show for a boutique in Kansas City at noon. They're hosting a champagne brunch to promote one of our new lingerie lines. So please walk softly in the morning. I'm sleeping until ten."

Nodding, Sherry stripped off her sweaty top as she walked down the hall. For a minute there she'd given a fleeting thought to going to the pub with Yvette, just to see what she was missing. But apparently pub crawlers didn't have eight-to-five jobs. No way could she drink beer and play pool until closing time and still hit the ground running first thing the next morning. It was just as well she preferred puttering around the house and left being a party animal to Yvette.

The shower refreshed her. She hummed along with Mariah Carey while assembling ingredients for two pans of lasagna. One to cook and one to freeze for later. Taking pity on Yvette, as she'd eaten in restaurants all week, Sherry relented and fixed a double batch of pea-nut-butter brownies. While they baked, she corrected papers from her first-year psych class. If the placement test was any indication, things did not bode well for this particular class. On the whole, their handwriting was bad and their spelling atrocious. Comprehension wasn't great, either. One said Jung was a game where you

stacked blocks. No one believed B. F. Skinner had
raised his daughter in a box. Three said Freud was a sex
fiend. If they hadn't copied each other, they'd probably
all flunk. Monday she'd crack down on their copying.

Snapping off the kitchen light, Sherry checked to be
sure the outside light was on for Yvette. She expected
Lock's place still to be aglow as he unpacked, but the
windows were dark. Another huge difference between
men and women, she mused. Most women wouldn't go
to bed until every last thing in the kitchen was in order.

SHERRY REFUSED to tiptoe around in the morning for
Yvette's sake. Thursdays were long full days for her,
since they included counseling in the Hub. For comfort
she teamed baggy linen trousers with an oversize poet's
blouse and clogs. Never one to wear much makeup,
Sherry decided on none. She quickly brushed her short
hair, thinking it made her look younger—or was it the
mismatched earrings? Tweety on one ear, Sylvester on
the other. She deliberately mismatched earrings to make
students laugh. Most of the women who timidly drifted
into the Hub didn't have a whole lot of laughs in their
lives. Administration preferred staff to dress more con-
servatively, but too bad.

It was such a nice sunny morning that Sherry thought
it'd be quieter if she took her coffee and newspaper out
on the front porch. Halfway through both, a noise made
her glance up. Garrett Lock stood before her looking
vaguely rumpled. Hair that was usually tamed flopped
over his brow. A slight stubble fuzzed his chin.
Barefoot, he had on gray sweats that looked as if they'd
once been washed with something red.

"Uh…I don't suppose you'd lend me some coffee

and a filter? I found the pot, but I've unpacked three boxes and still no coffee. There's no room on my counter to put anything else."

Sherry grinned. It did her heart good to discover his small imperfections. At the office he was a man of precision. "It's pathetic, Lock, to hear a grown man whine. I thought you'd have every box numbered and labeled as to content." She stood and wafted her cup in the vicinity of his nose. "Who had a fit on Monday when I couldn't lay my hands on J. J. Perry's incoming student record?"

"Have a heart, Campbell. We're talking major caffeine attack here."

"In that case I'd like to see some major groveling."

He dropped to his knees, clasped his hands and beseeched her plaintively—an action that took the wind right out of her sails. Going a step further, he leaned down and kissed her feet. Sherry jumped back and slopped coffee everywhere.

"Stop it, you nut!" she gasped. "What if one of the neighbors sees you?"

Grinning, he sat back on his heels. "If anyone else was up this early, hard-hearted Hannah, I'd already have a cup of java."

"I'll get it. Now. Just please sit in a chair like a normal human being. I'll be right back. Do you have a grinder or do *I* need to grind a batch?"

"Juan Valdez and I have this deal. He grows coffee and then he grinds it. I buy what he exports in industrial-size cans."

"A real connoisseur, huh?"

A crease dented one cheek. "Hot as Texas. Muddy as the Mississippi. A bottomless cup. My only criteria. What can I say? I have no taste."

"I'll grind three batches. Should tide you over till afternoon. Just beware, after three pots of high octane, you might be hooked on the gourmet stuff."

"I'll chance it."

Sherry was still chuckling softly as she burst into the kitchen. Seeing Yvette, hair combed, makeup on, grinding coffee beans, wiped the smile right off her face. Wasn't she going to sleep late?

"Run along to work, Sher. I'll take care of Garrett's...needs."

Taking in the loaded implication, Sherry let her mind hopscotch over a gamut of possibilities. Especially as Yvette wore a minuscule pair of hot-orange shorts and a top that left a great deal of midriff bare.

Crossing her arms, Sherry propped a shoulder against the refrigerator. "That outfit's a little obvious, don't you think? But be my guest. He wants his coffee black."

"*I'm* obvious?" Yvette arched a carefully penciled brow. "You were giggling like a teenager and falling all over him out there."

Sherry straightened, extending her palms. "I offered the man three batches of ground coffee. That's *all*." She spun on her heel and marched out of the kitchen, down the hall and into her bedroom, where she just managed not to slam the door. Closing it quietly, she began shoving books and case studies into her briefcase. Then, ear to the door, she listened for Yvette to leave. After a decent interval, one long enough to ensure they'd gone to Lock's to make coffee—and Sherry tried not to imagine what else—she hefted her briefcase and strode to her car.

THE DAY FLEW BY. Sherry loved counseling, even though in some cases what she provided was a Band-

Aid at best. It saddened her that so many women lacked the funds to get the psychological support they needed. All who came through the Hub had one thing in common, regardless of age. They were women who'd fallen through the funding cracks. Middle-aged, divorced and suddenly dropped from hubby's insurance. Young yet no longer eligible for care under dad's policy. During her first years on the job, Sherry took all their problems home. But the burden was too great. After much soul-searching, she'd come to the realization that she couldn't provide miracles. So she'd put together a strong referral system for women teetering on the edge and gave the others her undivided attention in the fifteen-minute slots allotted her. Today that meant she had to flush her mind of her roommate and her boss.

Well after five, Sherry walked to the door with her last appointment. She'd talked so much that her throat felt raspy. Now she was glad she'd stayed up last night to prepare lasagna. As she locked up, she looked forward to unwinding; she also needed time to set up the best way to proceed with her new cases. If fate was really kind, she'd have an hour to herself before Yvette rolled in.

Concentrating on her plans for the evening, Sherry almost didn't see Keith Lock sitting dejectedly on his porch as she entered the courtyard. The flash of his red T-shirt caught her eye. "Keith," she called, a smile automatic. "Are you taking a breather from unpacking boxes?"

He raised his head from his hands and clambered slowly to his feet. "Hi," he said, moving to the gate. "Where's Mark and Megan? Dad said maybe they'd visit you sometime."

"And so they may. Probably not tonight," she told him honestly.

"Oh." His shoulders bowed as he buried his hands deep in his front pockets. "Are you going skating now?" His eyes brightened momentarily.

Sherry's muscles still protested after last night's rigorous workout. "Sounds like you found the box with your skates. Maybe your dad will take you to the park later."

"He's too busy. He said for me not to bug you, either. But I thought if you were going, I could maybe tag along. I skate pretty good," he added.

Sherry gazed into the hopeful blue eyes and saw her plans for a relaxing evening disappear. "As a matter of fact, I did plan a short turn around the trails. Give me fifteen minutes to change, throw together a salad and stick a casserole in the oven. Meanwhile, you make sure it's okay with your dad."

"It is," Keith said confidently, bestowing her with a gap-toothed grin that altered his appearance to that of a normal happy-go-lucky kid.

Striding off after an involuntary smile in return and a quick glance at her watch, Sherry rushed by Alicia Jones, her beautician neighbor, with barely a nod.

"Did you just come from Garrett's?" The statuesque woman caught Sherry's sleeve with her long curving purple fingernails.

Puzzled, Sherry shook loose. "No. His son, Keith, was outside. Why?"

The woman waved a bakery bag. "I bought extra corn muffins and thought I'd be a good-doobie neighbor. Lorraine," she said, referring to the flight attendant from another unit, "already dropped off a gelatin salad. I mean, really—gelatin'll hardly appeal to a Texan. Everyone knows they have big appetites." She patted her hair.

"Mmm." Sherry narrowly managed to suppress a chuckle. "Gotta run. I have my own dinner to pop in the oven."

"What are you taking Garrett? Sweet potato pie, I'll bet. You're such a good cook it's not fair to the rest of us." The woman pouted.

Sherry lost the battle and did laugh. "I'm not taking him anything. I figure he can do like everyone else who moves—order in Chinese." Leaving her neighbor looking perplexed, Sherry went inside.

Keith was sitting on her porch when she came out fifteen minutes later.

"Hey, those are classy red skates," she said. "You have a helmet and pads for knees and elbows?"

He held them up one at a time for her inspection.

"Okay, sport. And you told your dad we'll be back after one turn around the park?"

"Yep. He's busy tryin' to get rid of another dippy woman. They've been comin' round all afternoon with food."

"They're called housewarming gifts, Keith. A welcome from the neighbors."

He slanted her a sidelong glance through indecently thick sooty lashes. "When my gramma phoned, she said they're women who think Dad'll marry them."

"How old are you, Keith?" Sherry asked, placing a hand on his shoulder to guide him across the street.

"Almost nine. Well, I'll be nine in January."

They stopped at the park bench to change into their skates. Sherry showed Keith how to knot his sneaker shoelaces to carry them around his neck. Then she asked a question that was really none of her concern—and blamed the fact that it'd slipped out on her having been in counselor mode all day. "Are you hoping your mom and dad will get back together, Keith?"

He stumbled a little and she put out a hand to steady him. "Nah. Mom just married Crawford. He don't know nothin' 'bout kids. And he smells prissy. Dad says it's 'cause he's president of a bank. I don't like going there, but Dad says I gotta."

"Oh." Sherry's heart beat faster. She had judged Garrett wrong; apparently he was neither obsessed with his former wife nor trying to get her back.

The path that wound through the trees grew steeper, and they were both panting. Talk died down until they reached the hot dog stand. Sherry dug out money for bottled water for herself and fruit juice for Keith. He wanted a hot dog. "Too close to dinner," she said.

"Jeez. You sound just like dad."

Sherry laughed. The girls running the stand asked veiled questions about Sherry's new buddy. She introduced him as the new dean's son, then wished she hadn't because she saw speculation in the students' eyes.

"I wish you had kids," Keith mumbled after they'd deposited their containers in the trash and started along the trail again. "There aren't any kids here to play with."

"I know. It's too bad," she said sympathetically. "The people who moved out of the house you're in had two girls about your age."

"Dad won't even let me get a puppy. He said the Homeowners' Association rules say no pets."

"That's right. But my brother has a dog and so do my folks. If your dad doesn't object, one of these days I'll take you to play with them."

"That'd be cool…but you'll prob'ly forget."

"I won't," Sherry said fiercely, her heart squeezing with pity for the child who'd so obviously been disappointed a lot in his young life.

"Mom was s'pose to take me to see a paddle-wheel boat on the Mississippi this weekend," he said listlessly. "She phoned this morning and said she can't 'cause of a party she and Crawford got invited to. Dad was ticked off. I told him it didn't matter, but he yelled at her, anyway."

Sherry skated on in silence. She recalled the remark Garrett made at the mall when they met for lunch, about how Carla made promises she didn't keep. Still she felt honorbound to stand up for the woman she'd never met. "I'm sure your mother feels bad, too," Sherry ventured, not sure at all but guessing, based on the women she counseled. Jobs too often dictated a single mom's schedule. Keith's mother had remarried, but that was recent. And maybe her new husband was to blame for this current situation.

"Yeah." Keith shrugged as he plopped down on the bench where they'd sat to don their skates. "I had fun tonight," he said shyly. "Can we do this again?"

"You bet. I don't go every night, but between now and Halloween the trails are pretty safe. Once you're unpacked, though, your dad will probably take you."

"He's got a lot of meetings. I hafta stay at that dorky play school. I don't see why I can't come home by myself. I'm not a baby."

"Your dad would worry, Keith. Anyway, you'll make friends at school. Maybe you can join one of the soccer or Little League teams. I'm sure there are parents who transport kids whose folks both work. Give it time."

He kicked a rock as they crossed the street. "You're

nice, Sherry. Can you come in and play with me while Dad's busy? I have Mr. Potato Head."

"I can't tonight, sprout. I have dinner in the oven and notes to look over before tomorrow."

The boy appeared so crestfallen Sherry wished she was free—though she wouldn't want to join the parade of women throwing themselves at Lock. Speaking of parade, there was Yvette sashaying through Garrett's gate. As Sherry and Keith drew even with her roommate, Sherry saw that Yvette juggled a square casserole dish and the covered container in which Sherry had stored the peanut-butter brownies.

"Hey!" Sherry quickened her steps. "Where are you going with our dinner?"

Surprised, Yvette turned and tossed her silky blond hair over one bare shoulder. "Sher. You're back so soon. I thought you and the kid would skate a lot longer."

Sherry glanced at her watch. "No, I set the oven timer. You should've known I'd be back in time to get the lasagna out."

"It's out. I'm afraid I must confess—I've stolen it to feed Garrett. The poor man is famished after unpacking boxes all day. If you were a real pal, you'd take you know who out for burgers." Yvette gave an exaggerated wink. "I guess not," she murmured, eyes locked on Sherry's stony face. Then she turned to Keith. "Well, c'mon kidlet. Late as it is, you can eat, then hop off to bed."

Keith tossed Sherry a long-suffering I-told-you-so look before he put his head down and trudged up the sidewalk after Yvette's swishing short skirt.

The nitro in Sherry's stomach had burned high enough to explode as Garrett's front door slammed on Keith's heels. If she wasn't so dog-tired and if she didn't have case reports to dictate, she'd march right up there and barge in on them. Of all the gall. After she'd slaved over that lasagna.

She'd make darned sure Yvette got an earful tonight, even if it meant staying up till midnight. Unless… Yvette spent the night at Garrett's. The very thought made Sherry's stomach queasy. But that was probably just hunger, she told herself.

In the end, she ate the Caesar salad Yvette had left behind—left because Sherry hadn't yet mixed the dressing. In the end, she laid a blistering note on Yvette's pillow and went to bed without dictating her reports. Frankly, if Yvette didn't come home, Sherry would rather not know.

But by the time she fell asleep she'd managed to convince herself the only reason she gave a rip-roaring gosh darn was because it might color her work association with the dean.

That was the *only* reason, too.

CHAPTER SEVEN

AT THE END of another hectic day on campus, Sherry marched up to Garrett's front door with Letty Dickson's folder and punched the bell twice. She shouldn't have been surprised when Yvette opened the door, but she was—or disappointed.

"Garrett's busy breaking down moving boxes." Yvette stepped outside and pulled the door almost closed behind her. "Sher, I need a favor. Will you take the kid skating or rent a movie tonight? So I can show Garrett off at the pub. It's Friday night," she wheedled. "I called Emily to see if Megan could baby-sit, but her school has a ball game tonight."

"Why should I do you favors after the stunt you pulled last night?"

"Oh, don't be a spoilsport. The lasagna was a big hit. C'mon, Sher. It's not as if you have a date or anything. You never do."

For some reason that statement rubbed Sherry the wrong way. Was her life so predictable? She chewed the inside of her mouth, thinking back to when she'd had her last date. Valentine's Day a year ago—the new psychologist in town who'd spoken to her class that week. Or was that two years ago? The door, suddenly jerked out of Yvette's hand, ended Sherry's trip down memory lane.

Garrett, who stood a head or more taller than Yvette, stared over her shoulder. "Hi! Keith said he'd heard the doorbell."

Sherry struggled with hello. Garrett wore snug-fitting blue jeans, a navy short-sleeved pullover and sneakers that had seen better days. His sun-streaked hair, boyishly tousled, reminded her of Keith.

"Is that the student's records I asked for? Come on in and we'll go over the case. Yvette was just leaving, isn't that right?"

From Sherry's perspective, he'd issued her roommate a plain "here's your hat" type of goodbye. Yvette was either obtuse or chose not to understand.

"I have plenty of time. The pub doesn't liven up until nine. Sherry was just saying she plans to rent *Raiders of the Lost Ark* and fix popcorn. That'd give Keith something fun to do while we run down to the pub for a couple of hours." Yvette straightened the points of Garrett's collar and trailed her palms down his chest.

His gaze moved to Sherry. She read a combination of reserve and frustration. "I, ah… That's nice of you, Sherilyn, but Nolan called. He's taking Megan and Mark to her high-school football game and invited Keith and me to tag along."

Sherry didn't know how to respond. Yvette took answering out of her hands. "Fine." She curled against Garrett's shoulder. "Tonight we'll do your macho football thing. I'm sure Sherry won't mind saving *Raiders* for another time. The pub's more fun on Saturday night, anyway."

Garrett gently disconnected their limbs. "Sorry, this is dads' night with the kids. And tomorrow I'm helping Nolan put up paneling in his family room. Keith and I are eating with them." He reached out and pulled Sherry across the threshold. "Excuse us, Yvette. Our discussion concerning this student is confidential."

Yvette hovered a moment, as if she considered staying despite his dismissal. Then, with a shrug and a coy smile, she rose on tiptoe and pressed a kiss on Garrett's mouth. By the time he stumbled backward out of her reach, she aimed a not-so-coy smile at Sherry and left.

The reserved Dean Lock looked so alarmed that Sherry almost laughed. However, Keith, who'd been skipping down the stairs and was treated to a bird's eye view of the kiss, didn't find it funny. "Yuck, Dad." He navigated the remaining stairs in two jumps. "Why were you kissin' her? I thought you said—"

"I didn't kiss her, son," Garrett broke in. "She kissed me. There's a difference."

Keith's lashes drifted down over skeptical blue eyes. At some point he realized he and his dad weren't alone. "Sherry, hi!" The boy loped to where she still hovered in the entryway. "Are you here to take me skating? I can't tonight. Me'n Dad are goin' to a football game. Wanna come with us?"

Sherry savored the shock that crossed Garrett's face before she let him off the hook. "A little bird told me the game is a father-kid night out. I wasn't going skating, anyhow, Keith. I'm here to talk to your dad about a student."

"Oh. Okay." He turned to Garrett. "Can I have a bowl of cereal? I'm starved."

Garrett ruffled the boy's unruly curls. "Are you getting ready to shoot up another foot? Isn't this the third bowl of cereal you've eaten since you got home from school?"

"Yeah…but if I had a dog, I wouldn't sit around eatin' and watchin' TV."

"Don't start on the dog bit again," Garrett warned. "Keeping you in cereal is infinitely easier. Besides, I told you, the Association rules don't allow pets."

"I know." Keith hunched his shoulders and shuffled toward the kitchen.

"Now, where were we?" Garrett swiped a hand over his mouth and chin. Then he gestured Sherry toward the living room. "Can I offer you beer or a soda?"

"Neither, thanks. I'm really anxious to get home. Hey, before I forget, thanks for calling a staff meeting for next week. We got your memo today."

Garrett seated her on the couch and took the opposite chair. "I've heard the gripes. I don't want any confusion over the changes coming down the pike."

"Changes? What changes?"

"Ones I want the entire staff to hear at the same time," he said dryly. "Since you're in a hurry to get home, shall we skip to the Dickson girl's problem?"

"As you wish," Sherry said stiffly. She relayed Robby's concerns for his sister and added her own recommendations. "They're a hardworking family. Letty has had her sights set on being a nurse for as long as I can remember. She's a credit to our nursing program."

He flipped through the folder. "An honor student except for last semester." Closing the folder, Garrett tapped it against his lips. "The rules—"

"Screw the rules. Letty isn't just some statistic. She's a person."

His eyes widened marginally at Sherry's outburst. Was Ms. Success-is-a-destination suggesting he flout the rules? "I've never even spoken to this girl. Yet you expect me to step out on a limb. How do I know you aren't waiting to saw it off behind me?"

Sherry looked offended. "I guess I can see where you might worry. After all, we were on opposite sides of the fence during the interviews. Ask someone else. Ask Temple in the Ag department." Sighing, she got to her feet. "Ultimately it's your call. Will you return the folder or shall I? It came from a stack on your desk."

He jumped up, too, and tossed the file on a glass-topped coffee table. "I'll authorize her to work this semester. Second semester I'll reevaluate. If her grades don't dip, I'll lift the restriction altogether."

She mockingly bowed. "Letty won't let you down."

"Hey, we're on the same team. Shall we start the clock over?"

She turned from the door. "Being on the same team doesn't make me a yes man."

His gaze, which rested on her wine red toenails, traveled up her bare legs to hips encased in a paisley print sarong skirt. Somber blue eyes paused momentarily on buttoned-down pocket flaps strategically placed on her sleeveless teal blouse. Garrett's eyes ignited briefly before moving on to stop at lips that might have started out the same color as her toenails but had long since been licked bare.

Sucking in a nervous breath, Sherry yanked open the door just as Garrett exhaled.

"You're absolutely right," he said. "You'll never be a yes man. Or any other kind of man," he muttered.

"Darned tootin'," she shot back, his next statement cut off in the squeak of the hinges. She caught sight of Keith, idly bouncing a ball down the steps. Either he hadn't eaten the cereal or he had and slipped out the back door. "Yo, Keith. Enjoy the ball game. And tomorrow, maybe you and Mark could go fishing in the creek that runs through Nolan's property. If you do, guard your pole against Pilgrim."

"Who's Pilgrim?" He caught the ball one-handed and cocked his head in a gesture reminiscent of Garrett.

"Pilgrim is my brother's golden retriever," she said. "A lovable mutt. But if you don't keep an eye on him, he'll steal your fishing pole just to get attention."

The boy giggled. Sherry thought it was perhaps the first time she'd heard him laugh out loud. Glancing over Keith's head to his dad, who'd followed her to the door, Sherry saw from the soft quirk of his lips that Garrett had also been affected by the joyous sound. Her heart tripped awkwardly. She quickened her pace and hurried past the gate.

It bothered Sherry that she didn't know quite how to pigeonhole Lock. She had a place for men like her dad and granddad. Devoted husbands and fathers who stayed married to the same woman for fifty years. Next came the consummate bachelors. Until recently, Nolan had fit that mold. A separate category held men embittered toward women in general. Last came the dregs. Ex-husbands of the women she worked with every day. Rotten men.

Garrett Lock didn't seem to fit anywhere.

As Sherry inserted her key in the door, it opened and Yvette pounced. "I saw you flirting. What are you trying to do? He's *the* man for me, Sher. Mr. Right. I feel it in my bones."

Sherry's eyebrow vaulted skyward. "Is your new motto get 'em young and raise 'em yourself? I was joking with Keith."

"Don't try to buffalo me, pal. I saw the look on Garrett's face."

Sherry could have said that look was for his son. But Yvette's jealousy got pretty tiresome. "If I had a dollar for every time you claimed a new man was *the one,* I'd be a millionaire. I know you and Vonda had it rough after your mom died and your dad went through all those twenty-year-old babes. But you should take a page from Vonda's book. Ask for the name of her therapist. She's been happily married for eight years now."

"I don't need a shrink. If you were such an almighty expert, you wouldn't sit at home seven nights a week. So stay out of my head. And hands off Garrett." Yvette slung her purse over her shoulder and stormed out.

Sherry flinched as the door slammed. She was buffeted by puffs of the sultry fragrance that permeated the hallway. The scent made it difficult for Sherry to breathe. Or was that because of the situation? Maybe she should move, get out of here. Except the lease was in her name and had eight months to run. Given the trouble Garrett had experienced finding a place, she knew it'd be next to impossible to get anything as nice as this. And why *should* she leave?

Taking refuge in her bedroom, Sherry kicked off her shoes. When they were kids, Sherry and her family had acted as Yvette's anchor. Yvette's dad, a wealthy cardiologist, had overindulged his motherless children with material things. During fling number five or six, he'd forced Yvette off to college. Being neighbors, she and Sherry had drifted into rooming together. Yvette's ability to have fun was a trait Sherry had liked back then. Because she herself was too serious. The bald truth was that neither woman had changed, and what worked at eighteen didn't work now.

Sherry hated these lengthy self-assessments that she'd been subjecting herself to lately. Counselors rarely healed themselves. Those who tried had fools for clients, as the saying went. At least that made her laugh. Frankly, she still found her best therapy in cooking. So that was what she did. Shoving an entire carousel of Elton John into the CD player, she gyrated into the kitchen and rattled pots and pans to her heart's content.

The house was silent the next morning when she slipped out. She didn't know or care if Yvette had come home. She ate breakfast at a nearby café, and when she was sure Nolan, Emily and the kids must have left Sherry's parents to go work on Nolan's house, she drove out to visit the elder Campbells.

"Behold a stranger," Nan quipped when Sherry appeared at the back door.

"Oh, Mom. Hardly a stranger. Just last week Emily and I went out to buy the material and pattern for my dress."

"Almost two weeks ago, Sherry. And you popped in and popped out. I hope you stand still long enough today for me to measure you."

"Emily said you wouldn't start sewing it until mid-October. She also told me Nolan inundated her with handwritten pages of notes from our trip. They're serious about writing a book about the wagon train re-enactment, aren't they?"

"Absolutely. I have to admit they have a knack for humor. I know all those things really happened, but it reads like a farce. I laughed so hard I cried at the account of your meeting with that nice dean Nolan invited for breakfast today."

Sherry whirled from the coffeepot, where she was

helping herself to a cup. "Does Lock know they're putting that horrible tale in their book? Mom, everyone'll know it's us! I'll sue Nolan, I swear."

"You signed a release, dear. That was your idea, I believe."

"Ha!" she fumed. "*Lock* didn't sign anything." She gestured with her cup, paying no attention to the liquid sloshing over the sides.

Her mother patiently wiped up the spill. "He did this morning."

"Why? Doesn't he realize we'll be the butt of jokes around campus?"

"Who on campus will admit they read lighthearted travel-adventure stories?"

Sherry met her mother's laughing eyes. "You're right," she said, at last allowing a smile. "They'll dissect Nolan's academic paper and blow off the book. So, what are you doing today? I really came to see if you wanted to run to St. Louis to shop. Emily said you hadn't found a mother-of-the-groom dress yet."

"I'd love to go with you. Is something wrong? I can't remember ever seeing you not work weekends at the start of a new semester."

Sherry hesitated. "Mom, I need your advice."

"Ah." Nan gave her daughter a big hug. "Advice I'm delighted to give. I didn't think you'd ever meet your match. I say grab the brass ring with both hands."

"Mother, what are you talking about?"

Cloaking a conspiratorial grin, Nan patted her arm. "I mean, go for it, girl. If I was twenty years younger, I'd be in a hurry to snap up that handsome Dr. Lock myself."

"What?" Sherry yelped, and drenched the floor in coffee again. "Oh…but I suppose he is the problem in

a roundabout way," she muttered, doing the mop-up this time. "Get your purse and tell Dad we'll be back before dark. I'll explain on the drive to St. Louis."

She did. And for probably the first time in Sherry's life, her mother didn't have answers. Or, rather, she gave bad advice. Nan said Sherry should either make a play for Garrett and tell Yvette to buzz off, or Sherry ought to find another man she could be serious about and show Yvette she wasn't a threat. Both were stupid ideas. Furthermore, they couldn't even find an appropriate dress for Nan in all those hours.

Sunday, it was mighty chilly around the town house. Yvette flounced around and for once, Sherry didn't try to make peace. By Monday, she was actually reconsidering her mother's suggestions. On a scale of one to ten, dating Garrett earned a four. She assigned a lowly one to going out with other men she'd met through intercampus committee work. And the farmers in the community tended to want wives willing to stay on the farm, which she wasn't.

That afternoon at the staff meeting Garrett blew the first proposition right out of the water—not that it had ever really been viable.

The sneaky bastard met each staff member at the door with a handshake and his killer smile. He'd even bought doughnuts to go with a fresh pot of coffee he'd heisted from Sherry's department, which earned him extra points with the staff.

Sherry took a seat in the back of the room. Thinking of Lock in other than a strictly professional way caused her to feel giddy. Sort of unbalanced.

Everyone else acted relaxed. They munched doughnuts and listened to Garrett toss out solutions to their concerns.

Sherry's mouth was full when he moved to item two on his agenda—and drove a knife through her heart.

"I have here a request from the board of regents. Mandate, I guess you might say," he offered with a shrug. "They want us to spend more time on academic counseling and phase out time spent on students' personal and social deficiencies."

Sherry jumped up, gagging on the doughnut she couldn't swallow. She whirled on colleagues who suddenly acted as if she didn't exist. "Where's your backbone?" she demanded. "We spent two years getting Kruger to at least ride the fence with regards to whole-life counseling for students who have precious little impetus to attend class. Maybe you're all willing to let this metropolitan cowboy waltz in and set our program back fifty years. I'm not." She thumbed herself in the chest so hard, tears sprang to her eyes. "I'm not," she repeated, a quaver creeping into her voice. Before she lost her composure altogether and embarrassed herself with tears, Sherry scooped up her things and fled the room.

In the hall, with the door safely closed between her and the dean, she gulped in air, hating to admit that she more than half expected Garrett to stop her mad flight.

He didn't. Sherry squared her shoulders and strode purposefully past the cubicles where secretaries typed furiously with their heads bent. It occurred to her then that she might have committed a grave error in judgment. Back a new broom into a corner and he had no choice but to sweep his way out. So what if one insignificant department chairperson got caught in the debris?

She sighed as she let herself into her office. From the interviews she should've seen that Lock, unlike Kruger, wasn't a fence rider. He acted. He'd also had called the entire division together. Something his predecessor had avoided like the plague. Damn it. She'd let her temper override good sense again.

She glanced up eagerly as a tap sounded on her door. Through the frosted glass she saw Angel's outline, not Garrett's.

"Come in."

Angel crossed the room and shoved a cup of steaming coffee into Sherry's hands. "Not like you to hide under a rock, boss. Scuttlebutt says the new dean clipped your wings."

Sherry accepted the cup, mouth turned down. "Who said? How?" She waved a hand as if to say, *Don't bother explaining.*

"You asking how I know what happened behind closed doors?" Angel winked. "I have my sources, boss."

"I should have guessed." Sherry lifted her cup in salute. "It pains me to ask, but what went on after I left? Did the dean blast me with both barrels?"

"That's the part I don't get." Angel rolled innocent-looking eyes. "He just went on to the next agenda item. They're up to number six."

Sherry took a seat behind her desk, a faint frown forming between her brows. "Can you lay your hands on a copy of his agenda?"

"Ta-da!" Angel pulled a scrunched paper from her jacket pocket. After smoothing the page, she offered it to Sherry.

Sherry's lips twitched. "You are amazing. Devious but amazing."

"I give you permission to put the amazing part on

my next evaluation. Leave off the devious bit, if you don't mind."

"Evals? Didn't we just do them?" Sherry's muscles tensed at the dark thought of who'd be doing *her* performance evaluation. Garrett Lock.

Angel hesitated. "Lock's secretary is typing names on the forms even as we speak. They'll be on his desk by noon waiting for his memo."

Sherry groaned.

"Aren't you glad you have tenure?" Angel said cheekily, speeding out and closing the door on her ear-to-ear grin.

It forced a smile from Sherry in spite of herself. Angel was right, though, when she'd said Sherry usually didn't run from a battle. Before she'd finished her coffee, Sherry opened her door wide and dug into the million and one tasks that befell her as teacher, counselor and department chair. She dictated the case notes she hadn't gotten to the previous night and handed Angel the tape on her way to her ten o'clock intermediate psychology class. Her route took her down the corridor, past the room where the meeting had been held. It had just broken up. No one spoke, and the brief glimpse Sherry had of Garrett showed him surrounded by staff. *Female* staff. Be that as it may, she owed him another apology. She could do that—even if there were several issues on his agenda she took exception to. During the break between classes, she practiced sounding properly repentant.

Her fifty-minute class stretched to an hour. Then she got tied up helping a new student straighten out a computer glitch in her schedule. Sherry didn't get back to her office until two. Garrett's office was dark, so she approached his secretary.

"He left campus after receiving a call from his son's school."

"Is Keith sick?"

"I really can't say." The woman's icy tone said she wouldn't pass on the information even if she did know.

"If he gets back before three, will you tell him I'd like a word with him?"

The woman nodded, although she plugged her earphones in without writing anything down.

Sherry tried to connect with him again at three-thirty. This time his secretary was away from her desk. When Sherry let herself into her own office, she discovered why. A memo requesting that she make an appointment for her evaluation had been shoved under her door. Kruger had always put off doing evals until the president's secretary rapped his knuckles. Lock obviously had no compunction about rating a staff he barely knew.

She never caught up with Garrett. The next day, she counseled in the Hub. Efforts to reach him by phone during her few breaks didn't pan out. She didn't leave messages because she was hardly in her office and wasn't in the mood for hours of telephone tag. She would never have approached Kruger at home, but she would've talked to Lock if either he or Keith had been around the two evenings she went off to skate.

Yvette, too, was conspicuously absent. A logical assumption might be that the three were together. A possibility that depressed Sherry. These days, even colleagues avoided her on campus. If staff sided with Lock, she'd never win the battle to expand whole-life training services.

By Friday Sherry had given up hope of seeing Garrett. Midafternoon, with Angel gone to a secretaries' meeting, Sherry answered the department phone on the third ring and was shocked to hear Garrett asking to speak with her.

"This is me," she squeaked. "Angel is out and I don't know what happened to our student helpers," she said in a long breathless blur.

"You and I have passed like the hare and the turtle in a footrace all week," he drawled in the slow molasses way that always melted every last shred of Sherry's resistance. "I think we need to set up an appointment to talk."

"Sure." Sherry tripped over her tongue agreeing. "Anytime. You name it."

She heard him flipping his calendar. "How about now?"

"On my way."

Garrett stepped to the door of his office to greet her.

As Sherry didn't hear the click of any computer keys, she assumed his support staff had gone to the same meeting as Angel. Digging a notebook out of her briefcase, she perched on the edge of the leather chair Garrett indicated—one of three grouped at the other end of his office. She'd a whole lot rather have had his desk between them. But she could hardly refute his choice of the more informal conversation area.

After taking a deep breath, she plunged right into the apology she'd spent the week polishing. "I'm sorry I walked out of the staff meeting, Dean Lock. A department chair should set a better example."

He waited and she fidgeted—darned if she'd apologize for defending her position in favor of whole-life training. He studied her so long and with such intensity that she eventually scraped a nervous hand through her short hair, making it stand in spikes.

"Why do I get the feeling you're not really sorry about anything?" he asked.

She hadn't expected such a frank statement and so had nothing to say.

"We both know that BS stands for bullshit," he said. "MS is more of the same. And Ph.D. is piled higher and deeper. Truth is, you make a pressure cooker look calm, Sherilyn. Don't ever wade out on me again after slinging manure. I need ammo to take back to the board. Testimony from law enforcement, women's shelters or from your students' employers. The regents don't want to reduce services at the Hub. They want to scrap the program altogether."

She looked stricken. "Since we're being honest, I'll tell you why I left. Sometimes when I get mad I cry. Men expect that of a woman. I was afraid it would hang me and negate anything I said."

"Fair enough." He pondered, then discarded the notion of telling her he considered tears a human trait. He'd shed some at Keith's birth and after Carla's exit from their lives. But Sherry rushed on before he could. Anyway, it wouldn't have been wise.

"I have another bone to pick," she said. "Agenda item four regarding standardized competency-based assessment. The women who enter our work-study program through the Hub aren't standard. It's unfair to expect them to make any kind of showing compared to the skill levels of normal college students."

"Eloquently put, Dr. Campbell. Did your spies tell you Jess Fowler made essentially the same point at the meeting?"

"Spies?" Sherry tongued a dry bottom lip.

Garrett glanced away, squeezing the bridge of his nose

with his thumb and forefinger. "Yes, spies," he growled. "That's a copy of my agenda you're holding. I typed it on my computer and I thought there was only one copy."

"You typed it? Then how did Angel— I mean, I assumed the secretary who typed it…well, I, ah, I do have my sources." She resorted to Angel's pat response.

"Never mind. It's my fault for keeping Kruger's computer password. I can see I need to change it before I start typing evaluations."

"You type evals, too? Isn't that a waste of *expensive* time?"

"You think I can't type as fast as I can dictate?" He laughed. "Thank goodness your sources aren't omnipotent. Guess they didn't inform you I have two undergraduate degrees. One in sociology, the other in computer science."

"I'm impressed. I keep meaning to take computer classes. I picked up enough rudiments to track enrollment. I can find student files and case notes. That's about it."

"Well, I believe in staff development. I realize computer classes fill up fast, but if you find one you'd like to take and can get in, I'll authorize the department to pay for it."

"That's very generous, considering the board ordered you to trim the budget."

"Ouch. I said I'd cut fat. I didn't promise to cut from the areas *they* pick." He leaned back and tented his fingers. "Enough said. I have a fair idea of the general workings of the program for disadvantaged women. Fill me in on the exact steps. I'll save questions for when you finish." He rummaged for a yellow legal pad.

Sherry explained the lack of services for displaced

homemakers in the original design. She listed classes she'd badgered them to add. Extra counseling. Child care on campus and whole-life training. "That's what sets our program apart. Our success rate is more than double other similar programs."

"Successful, but terribly expensive."

"Compared to what? For the women referred to us from the penal system the alternative would be jail—and you know how much that costs the taxpayers. These women come with a load of baggage. Nine out of ten resent any form of authority. Three counselors brainstormed and designed a series of preliminary requirements that include courses on nutrition, self-esteem, grooming and interactive people skills. These are taken before we discuss academics. The board of regents thinks the extra classes are frivolous."

"Have you had students from the program attend board meetings and explain how much the introductory classes mean?"

"Several times. And not just students from the penal system. We have physically challenged students whose self-esteem needs shoring up. We serve single mothers and divorcees of all ages. Most of them married before they graduated from high school and suddenly found themselves out on their ears with virtually no marketable skills."

Garrett opened his mouth to interrupt when the phone shrilled.

Sherry let it go to the third ring, then just about knocked a funny clay pig paperweight off his desk in her attempt to snag it. The pig's owner motioned her sharply back to her seat.

"There's a student clerk filling in," he said. "She'll

answer it. Now where were we?" The phone rang again, more insistently, as he shuffled notes.

Unable to let the call go unanswered, Sherry dove over Garrett's desk. "Dean Lock's office," she said crisply and efficiently. She listened, then asked the party to hold. Covering the mouthpiece, she whispered, "It's Keith's day care. Do you want to take it or phone them back?"

Garrett looked startled, then grim. "I'll take it." He all but ripped the receiver from her hand. "This is Garrett Lock. My son did what? No, we do not have a dog!" Resting the phone on his shoulder, Garrett shut his eyes. "Why would the driver let him take some scruffy pup on the bus?"

Sherry wondered if she should slip out and give him privacy. She did her best to tune out his end of the conversation. Not easy, as his face grew red and the veins bulged above the collar of his white shirt. Before Sherry could decide whether to leave, he said goodbye and slammed the phone back in its cradle.

It appeared he'd forgotten her presence. Then his eyes lit on her, and he cleared his throat. "I have to go and take care of a matter that's come up. I'd like to talk more about this. If it's not an imposition, could you drop by the house tonight? Ordinarily I wouldn't ask," he said, noting her wary expression. "But we are neighbors. It seems absurd for both of us to drive back here."

Still she hesitated. What if news of their cozy meeting got out? He was an eligible bachelor and she a single teacher. Exactly the juicy stuff rumormongers loved.

"Just say if you have plans. Really, I have to run. Keith found a stray dog. He told the bus driver it was his—that it followed him to school."

"I don't have plans," Sherry said. Her need to convince him to save the Hub won out over what campus gossips might say. "What time is convenient?"

"Is eight or eight-thirty too late? This isn't the first time Keith's been in trouble at school and day care this week." He sighed. "I think he needs more of my time right now. Even so, he'll be in bed by eight-thirty."

"Eight-thirty it is," she said. "Go easy on him, huh? He talks a lot about wanting a dog. Spending last Saturday with Mark and Pilgrim probably made matters worse."

"If I've explained the rules of the Home Association once, I've explained them twenty times. I hate to run out on you like this. Would you ask the student to log messages?"

"Take off," she said, shooing him with her hands. "I'll turn out your lights, set the alarm and tell the staff."

Grateful for her understanding, he thanked her again and dashed out.

She watched the swing of his broad shoulders and felt an uncommon tug on her heart. For Keith, she insisted, unconsciously running her fingers over Lock's silly pig.

CHAPTER EIGHT

AN UNSCHEDULED COUNSELING appointment detained Sherry at work. Unusually heavy traffic further delayed her. It was nearly eight when she walked into the house and met her housemate who was already showered and dressed to go out.

"Where have you been?" Yvette railed without warning.

"At work. Why? Is there some emergency?"

Yvette snatched a video lying on the couch. "I rented this so you could entertain Garrett's kid while we go out."

"Tonight?" Sherry didn't take the plastic case. "Yvette, if you and Garrett had a date, he didn't remember." She glanced at her watch. "I'm due at his place in half an hour to go over the details of one of our programs."

"You sneak! I told you Garrett Lock is the man I want. How can you stab me in the back like this?"

"I didn't. He set the meeting. And four months ago Tony Meyer was the man of your dreams. Darrell Bauer last fall. Kurt somebody before that. Anyway, if you're serious this time, you should be including Keith in your outings."

"A lot you know. The boy's mother is making a big stink over custody. I didn't get the whole story, but I heard Garrett talking to his lawyer. He moved here to appear more accommodating. You know she'll win in the end. Judges always favor mothers. Garrett's going to need consoling when he loses the fight." She twisted a piece of hair. "I intend to be the one he turns to. So be a pal. Call him and cancel the meeting."

Sherry wondered if the custody battle was why Keith had been acting out at school and day care. "Canceling isn't up to me. He's the boss. Besides, he said Keith would be in bed by eight-thirty. That wouldn't allow time for a movie."

"Oh, you can be very persuasive when you set your mind to it, Sher. The incentive is having a house to yourself. If we get married, it'll be all yours."

"Married? That's a big step when you haven't even gone out with the man yet. Has hunting for Emily's wedding dress scrambled your brain?"

"Unlike you, I want to be a wife."

Sherry had a hard time visualizing Yvette as a dean's wife. But, hey, that wasn't her problem. Maybe Yvette *was* serious this time. "Okay," Sherry sighed, and pulled a file of papers out of her briefcase. "But the decision will have to be Lock's."

Yvette opened the door with a jangle of gold bracelets. "Here's the video. Tell Garrett to drop by here for a drink. If I get lucky, you may have to spend the night with the kid."

"No." Sherry shook her head. "I'm sleeping in my own bed tonight and that's final. You want somebody to stay all night, you'd better call a baby-sitting service."

"Okay, okay. No overnighter. Just go."

As Sherry rang Garrett's bell, she wondered how she'd let herself get talked into this. But if they'd truly had a date and he'd forgotten— She almost jumped out of her skin when he bellowed, "Come in!" She eased open the door.

He had a cell phone tucked against one ear and two mitted hands wrapped around a smoking pot. Behind him, the room was blue with smoke. Even as he waved her inside, the smoke alarm bleated. "Oh, hell," he said, gesturing helplessly with the blackened pan. "No, not you," he said into the phone. I've got a crisis here," he snapped. "All right, I'll continue to hold."

By now Sherry saw that Keith wasn't in bed, but huddled in the leather recliner. He had his arms around the most disreputable excuse for a dog Sherry had ever seen. The boy's nose was red as that of Santa's lead reindeer. Huge tears made muddy furrows down ashen cheeks, and giant sobs shook his skinny chest.

Sherry closed the door quietly. Or maybe it only seemed quiet because the alarm made such a racket. Dropping the printouts and the video on the glass-topped coffee table, she went straight to the alarm box, set a straight-backed chair beneath it, climbed up and pried the top off, dropping the batteries.

"Thank you," Garrett mouthed, and went back to talking on the phone.

Sherry hurried to open the front windows, then the back door to let the smoke out. The kitchen was in chaos, she noted as she waved her way through the smoke and navigated around nearly empty packing crates. Dirty cereal bowls still sat on the table. She even tripped over one on the floor. Gazing at it blankly, she finally decided either Keith or Garrett had fed the dog Lucky Charms. She gingerly picked up the bowl, put it in the sink and ran it full of water as Garrett came in and dumped the charred kettle into the other half of the divided sink.

With a dazed expression, he punched the phone's disconnect button. "That was the Humane Society," he announced. "They claim they can't tell me if anyone called about a missing dog, because I don't know what breed this one is." He closed the phone and tossed it on the counter. "I'm not even sure it *is* a dog, except the damned thing barks. I know it has fleas because the manager of the day care is going to make me pay to have the facility sprayed. She spent ten minutes lecturing me on health regulations. Then she suggested I find a new day care for Keith."

"Oh, no. By now most of the good ones are full and have waiting lists."

"Right now that's the least of my worries. First I have to get rid of the dog. Will you go tell Keith I'm not lying about the rules? We can't keep the dog and that's that."

"Slow down." Sherry placed a hand on his arm to calm him. "You have two bathrooms. I'll bathe the dog in the tub. You stick Keith in the shower. Once the pup's clean, we should be able to tell the breed."

"You think so?" Garrett scowled. "If it didn't growl every time I got close, I'd say it was a mop someone threw out with the dirty water."

"So you don't like dogs?"

"Me? I love them. I didn't make the rules here. I do obey them. I can't afford to be thrown out before my deal on this places closes."

"Did you feed the dog sweet cereal?"

"Keith did even after I said not to. I put bean soup on to heat for us and went to phone the animal shelter. Keith insisted the dog was hungry."

"He probably is. I have a solution," she said, all

memory of Yvette's mission flying out of her head as she walked over to Keith and knelt to look at the dog. "No collar. Very likely he is a stray."

"Your solution?" Garrett prompted.

"Oh…I was going to say my folks have an old dog who's pretty easygoing. They're well stocked with dog food, flea soap and combs. Let's take the pup there. My mom's home all day. I'm sure she'd keep him while you run an ad."

Keith brightened considerably at that. He scooted forward, his tears abating.

Garrett gazed at Sherry as if she'd lost her mind.

She stood and faced him. "Do you have a better idea?"

"No. But what if no one claims him? Then what?"

She waved a hand airily. "Cross that bridge when you come to it." She offered the boy an encouraging smile.

"All right," Garrett agreed slowly. "We'll take my pickup. It already has muddy paw prints on the seats. Don't say I didn't warn you about fleas."

The dog whined, burying his nose in Keith's neck the minute the truck door closed. Sherry absently scratched behind the pup's matted ears. She was rewarded with a hearty lap and Keith's grateful smile.

"It's hard to tell, but I think the dog is part poodle and maybe terrier."

"Ninety percent ragamuffin," Garrett muttered.

Keith glanced up in surprise. "I'm calling him Rags. I think it's his name. He came the first time I used it."

Sherry sympathized with a lonely boy's desire to own a pet. During her own childhood, with her parents and Nolan spending long hours at work and school, she didn't know what she'd have done without Murphy, their lop-eared beagle. "Exactly where did you find

Rags?" she asked, inspecting a tender pad on the dog's right foot.

"When Dad dropped me off, Rags was lying outside the fence. He was still there at recess. At lunch I gave him half my sandwich. He crawled under the fence and followed me. A big kid kicked him." Keith's lower lip trembled. "It hurt him, Dad."

Garrett glanced over at his son, eyes dark and enigmatic. "Nevertheless, Keith, what you did was dangerous. You should have told the playground teacher or gone to the office. He might have bitten you. Strays can have rabies."

"Turn here," Sherry said when it seemed Garrett was so intent on lecturing Keith he was about to drive past the Campbell's street.

"He didn't bite me," Keith said stubbornly. "He's scared and hungry is all. He needs a home. If you won't let me keep him, me'n Rags will run away."

"Nonsense, Keith. You don't know what you're saying."

"The driveway's coming up on your left." Sherry raised her hand to point and managed a warning squeeze to Garrett's shoulder before she dropped it again. She might not have kids, but she'd worked with enough parents and children to know that too often such threats weren't idle.

"Let's not make plans until we have him bathed and fed," she said. "Rags will be safe, Keith. I know you'd rather not think about the fact that he might already have a home. But what if he belonged to you and accidentally got out and became lost? Wouldn't you want the person who found him to try and locate you?"

The boy's skinny arms tightened around the dog. "I guess."

Garrett felt himself relax at Sherry's touch. Did she think he didn't realize the seriousness of this mess? He did. Before the move he'd thought himself capable of handling anything that came up with Keith. Carla's demands to be let back in her son's life changed all that. And where *was* she, damn her? If she'd taken Keith to see the stern-wheelers as she'd promised, this entire episode with the dog would probably have been avoided.

Secretly though, Garrett didn't mind that Sherry Campbell had come by a bit early. Or rather, he wouldn't mind *if* she figured out a way to extract him from this debacle. *No,* a little voice argued, *that's not entirely true.* It helped having someone around when push came to shove. Someone as calm and unruffled as Sherry. This was a new side of her. A nice side.

Garrett slowed, peering into the darkness. "Did I miss their driveway? Last time we were here it was daylight."

"After the next block."

Keith slid forward and tried to see around Sherry. "I wish we had a house out here or closer to Nolan. They don't have stupid rules that say you can't have dogs."

"Your dad didn't have much choice, Keith. How about your mother? Will her home accommodate Rags? Provided no one claims him when you run the ad?"

Keith hunched. "Her house is big 'nuff. Everything in it's white. Crawford's afraid I'll get stuff dirty. Don't think he'd like a dog. But I'll ask. Can I call her, Dad?"

Garrett glared at Sherry over Keith's head. He took the corner into the driveway pretty fast and was forced to brake harder than he'd intended. "Let's get this smelly mutt washed first, shall we?" He killed the engine and was none too gentle setting the emergency brake.

Sherry got the message that she'd overstepped her bounds. Boy, was Lock a hard man to please. He didn't want the dog. She'd thought the idea of pawning Rags off on his ex might please him. Obviously not. Well, at least Mark and Megan's presence ought to ease the tension some. It might turn out to be a lucky thing that Nolan had insisted Emily and the kids stay here until after the wedding.

Leading the way through the side gate and into the mudroom off her parents' kitchen, Sherry called out a greeting. Nan Campbell appeared at once.

"What have we here?" Nan aimed the question at Sherry, but smiled at Keith.

"Keith found a dog today, Mom. No tags. He's in bad need of TLC."

"Well, we have plenty of that. If I had a nickel for every stray you dragged home, Sherilyn, I could retire in style."

Keith cocked an ear. "What happened to the dogs you brought home?"

Nan tweaked his button nose. "Practically everyone we know is blessed with man's best friend. Sherry found them all good homes."

Sherry backed out of the pantry, dragging a bag of kibble. "Got a bowl, Mom? After a good meal we'll bathe this little guy—and see what we have under the grime."

"Where's Mark?" Keith glanced around. "I wanna show him my dog."

"Not yours, son," Garrett was quick to correct him.

"He's gonna be. Look at him eat, Dad. I bet he hasn't had food in a long time. We can't let him go back to bad people, can we?"

Sherry waited to see how the man with all the answers worked his way around that logic. Turned out he didn't have to. Nan offered him an out.

"Ben's in the family room watching a football game, Garrett. He'd love company. Nolan, Emily and the kids went out to dinner and a movie. I've been making rice bags for the wedding. Ben came in here during the quarter and said it's too quiet."

Garrett's eyes lit. "I forgot about the game. I've waited all week to see the Chiefs play the Cowboys. Nothing like starting the season out with divided loyalties."

Nan made a face. "Better not venture into the family room if you aren't rooting for the Chiefs. Few things turn my mild-mannered husband into a snarling beast. One of them is anyone making even a slightly disparaging remark about his team. I swear you'd think he owned them."

"Thanks for the warning, Mrs. C. Dang, switching allegiance is tough. Keith, do you think we can go in there and not root for Troy?"

"You go, Dad. I'll stay with Rags."

Garrett frowned. "What? But you love watching the Cowboys play."

"It's okay," Sherry urged the boy. "I'll take good care of Rags. However, I make no promises that you'll recognize him after a bath."

"I want to help." Keith thrust out his jaw. "Dad doesn't think I can take care of a pet. Mrs. Curtis in the school office said keeping dogs clean is important. Even Dad said Rags smelled. Can I stay·and watch how you give him a bath?"

Sherry shrugged. "You may. And it's time. Look, Rags licked his bowl clean. Cleaner than clean. Nab him before he licks a hole in Mom's dish."

They all laughed watching the pup lick the bowl across the floor. All except Garrett. Sherry eyed his frown with some misgiving. For his sake, she hoped Rags did have an owner. But not for Keith's.

"Wow, he's almost white," Sherry said half an hour later after she'd changed the water in the tub twice. They'd bathed him first with a flea soap, then with a better-smelling herbal doggie shampoo.

Keith sat back on his heels and shook water from his shirt and hair. "Boy, is your mom gonna be mad. We got water everywhere."

"I'll clean it up—" Sherry laughed "—while you dry him with the blow-dryer set on low. I hope the noise doesn't scare him, but I don't like seeing him shiver."

"He won't catch cold, will he?" Keith draped the towel around the bedraggled-looking dog. "Dad'll never let me keep him if he gets sick."

"We'll dry him, Keith," Sherry said. She stopped her mopping up long enough to be sure she had the boy's attention. "Keeping him isn't definite."

"I know. I know," he said impatiently. "*If* somebody owns him. Bet they don't." As if agreeing with his new master, the dog wriggled out from beneath the towel and licked Keith's nose. The boy hugged the wet pup and laughed gleefully.

Sherry sighed. She wished she hadn't gotten involved. Garrett Lock had an iron will and so, it appeared, did his son. Woe to anyone who got caught in the crossfire, she thought dolefully, plugging in a blow-dryer she recognized as Emily's. Sherry aimed it at the dog, rather than handing it to Keith, in case Rags objected.

He didn't, but settled on Keith's lap. If a dog was capable of smiling, this one did.

Nan stuck her head into the room once Keith had dried and fluffed most of the silky hair. "Oh, isn't he precious?" She stepped inside, closing the door behind her. "Sherry, I think he's a bichon frise. He hasn't been trimmed, but he's got the curled tail and the buff coloring."

"You mean he's not a mutt?" Sherry left the wet towels and tried to see something of pedigree in the animal sitting so contentedly on Keith's lap.

"I'm not saying he's a purebred. He could have mixed bloodlines. One of the secretaries in your dad's office has one." Nan ran her hands over the soft floppy ears.

"It's not a poodle mix?" Sherry couldn't exactly say when she'd started rooting for Keith's ownership of the little dog. But she realized she had. Chances of a dog with a highfalutin name like bichon frise being a stray were slim to none.

"Don't think so. Dorothy belongs to some state-wide club of bichon owners. If you want to know more, give her a call."

Keith shut off the dryer. He hugged the little animal, the sparkle gone from his eyes. "Will the lady know if somebody's dog ran away?"

"She may," Nan said. "I believe her club has a registry."

Sherry tried discreetly signaling her mother to be quiet. Nan was clearly puzzled by Sherry's signals a moment before understanding dawned. "Oh, Keith, honey. I didn't mean to imply this pup was dognapped or anything."

"Dognapped?" Keith's horror was evident in his voice.

"Thank you, Mother dear," Sherry muttered under her breath. "Give him something else to worry about, why don't you?" Sherry helped the boy up and turned him toward the door. "Keith, why don't you go show Rags to my dad?"

"You're gonna call that Dorothy person, aren't you?" Keith asked, eyes watery, lower lip quivering.

"No." Sherry held up her hand in the scout's-honor fashion. "Stay in here if you'd rather. I intended to ask Mom to rent Rags a room at the Campbell hotel for the night."

"For me, too?" Keith telegraphed Nan a hopeful look.

Sherry rushed to nix that proposal. She had a pretty vivid idea of what Garrett's reaction would be.

"I promise I won't be any trouble. I won't even eat breakfast."

Garrett showed up in the doorway in time to hear Keith. "Whoa. What's this about not eating breakfast, champ? Tomorrow's our morning for chocolate-chip pancakes. It's ritual on weekends," he told Sherry.

If Keith was torn, it was only for a moment. "Fix 'em for Sherry, Dad. I hafta stay here with Rags. I don't want him to think I dumped him with strangers."

Judging by the way Garrett's brows drew together over the bridge of his nose, Sherry knew she hadn't underestimated his reaction one iota. Frankly she doubted Keith had only one night's stay in mind. "Is it halftime?" she asked. At Garrett's curt nod, she hustled her mother past him. "Mom and I will go pop a couple of bags of corn. I'll pour sodas all around." Never had two women beat a hastier retreat. They'd disappeared before Garrett could open his mouth.

Shortly afterward, a disgruntled man and his son followed them into the homey kitchen. The popcorn

corn filled the air with an irresistible aroma that Sherry hoped would trigger an opportunity to sit around the table and talk convivially.

No such luck. Nolan, Emily and the kids returned just as the last kernels popped. Greetings weren't even complete when Nolan helped himself to the steaming bag and a stack of bowls. "We suffered through a terrible science-fiction flick and missed the first half of the ball game. C'mon, guys. Last one to the TV gets no popcorn."

Garrett, Mark and Keith watched him lope from the room. Garrett and Mark gathered soft drinks.

"I'm not a guy," Megan said as they followed Nolan. "But I like the Chiefs, too."

Left in the kitchen to await the second bag of popcorn, Sherry endured Emily's grilling. "You rascal. Holding out on us, huh? Do I smell something cooking between our maid of honor and our best man?"

"Popcorn," Sherry said flippantly. Then spun and gaped. "*Best man?* When did Lock go from being handed a casual invitation to being best man?"

Emily took the bag from the microwave and dumped the contents in a bowl. Sliding it to the center of the table, she sat in the nearest chair. "Nolan's held off asking anyone from his department. He didn't want to step on toes. The other day, when Garrett helped on the house and we all had such a good time, Nolan asked him. He seemed genuinely touched, and agreed. Quit changing the subject." Emily idly picked up a piece of popcorn. "It's not too late to make it a double wedding."

"A double—?" Sherry swallowed a kernel whole. Nan reached over and pounded her on the back. "It's nothing like that, Em," Sherry choked out. She explained the meeting that had taken her to Garrett's tonight.

"Mm-hmm." Emily just smiled.

"Stop that, Em." Sherry flopped back in the chair, at once remembering Yvette. She straightened. "In fact, he had a date with Yvette tonight. So *they're* more likely to take the plunge. She's declared him to be the love of her life."

Nan snorted. "Number what? She's in double digits when it comes to being in love, isn't she?"

"Even so, don't look for Lock and me to set off any rockets. He's my boss, for crying out loud."

Emily closed her eyes and cupped her hands around the popcorn bowl as if it were a crystal ball. "I see love in your stars. I feel it in the cosmic vibes."

Sherry laughed. "Get out hip boots, everyone. I hope you don't expect me to cross your palm with silver, Madame X."

"Okay, skeptic. But mark my words," Emily said smugly.

"Enough nonsense," chided Nan. "Sherry, what's going to happen about Keith and the dog? If he has to give Rags up, that boy will be heartbroken."

Sherry sobered immediately. "I wish it'd been a mutt. Then there'd be a better chance Rags hasn't got an owner. But if no one turns up, I can ask our complex owner to make an exception. Ron's a softie. I didn't tell Garrett and Keith, but Ron looked the other way when the kids who used to live in that house found a kitten."

"If Garrett relents and lets Keith spend the night tonight, on the way home you might introduce that idea gently. I can't decide if Garrett doesn't want to deal with a pet or if he's only concerned with breaking the rules."

Sherry gazed at her mother. "I'll attest to the fact that he's a stickler for rules. But if you convince him to let Keith stay here, I'll offer to talk to Ron."

"Deal." Nan stood. "Come help me tie satin ribbon around the rest of the rice packets. We can watch the game as we work. At the end of third quarter, I'll open the floodgates on the question of sleeping over. I think Mark and Megan will run with the ball from there, don't you?"

"Mom, I never realized you were so devious."

"Mothers have to be to survive kids. Just wait, you'll see."

Sherry shook her head. "Not me. Never." Yet even as the words left her lips, her head and her heart objected. She had to admit to suffering a stab of envy when Nolan, Emily, Megan and Mark had piled into the house tonight full of laughter.

Silly! It's just that old biological clock tick-tick-ticking. She bustled about cleaning up the kitchen.

"You're a regular Suzy Homemaker." Emily grinned, not the least deterred by the fact that Sherry was trying to ignore her.

At the pause between the third and fourth quarter, true to her word, Nan introduced the subject of Keith and Rags spending the night. As predicted, Megan and Mark jumped on the bandwagon. Poor Garrett didn't know what ran over him. Even Murphy barked his two cents' worth, waddled over, sniffed the pup thoroughly, then lapped Rags's face.

The group looked so right together that a bone-deep feeling of contentment mocked Sherry's earlier denial. No, she told herself, it was better—safer—to recognize the scene before her as a sham. She was Lock's subordinate; he'd never allow himself to get involved with a staff member.

Yet she continued to daydream and was surprised when everyone jumped up announcing that the game was over and the Chiefs had won.

"The Cowboys had three men out with injuries." Garrett made allowances.

"Traitor." Nolan poked Garrett in the ribs.

Doubling over, Garrett slapped Nolan's hands away. "You try switching horses in midstream. I've been a Cowboys' fan all my life."

"You're lucky we're non-violent types," joked Sherry's dad. "In a lot of circles them's fightin' words."

Garrett's eyes lit on Sherry and he smiled indulgently. "Not all Campbells are nonviolent. Am I in danger of being murdered on the way home?"

"Not because of football ties. Keep heckling me and maybe yes." Sherry hadn't joked around in some time and realized it felt darned good. Being with her family felt good. When had she started spending so much time at work that she'd forsaken lazy evenings like these?

Garrett shook hands with Ben and Nolan, but his gaze remained on Sherry, who deftly tied a slippery ribbon around the last rice packet in the basket.

"Are you doing groom's cake, too?" she asked her mother. At Nan's nod, Sherry said, "Call me when you're planning to do it. I've wrapped enough groom's cakes for friends' weddings I could cut those foil squares in my sleep."

"Always a bridesmaid, never a bride?" Nolan teased. "After the first of the year, guys, we're going to have to do some serious matchmaking for this lady."

"Not!" Sherry stood and punched her brother's arm.

Keith looked up from his seat on the floor between the two dogs. Dark eyes serious, he said into the sudden silence, "If I was older I'd marry her. She does neat things. Skates. Likes cool music, and she's really good at giving dogs baths."

For too long a time no one spoke. Nolan found his voice first. "All-important criteria for choosing a wife. Here, I picked Emily because she could cook." Mugging, he slung an arm around his sputtering fiancée's shoulders and nuzzled her ear.

After the laughter died, Garrett told Sherry they'd better leave. "I'll pick Keith up at ten tomorrow. And no dallying, son. I'm telling you right now, Rags stays here."

"Okay. But can I visit him every day until you know for sure he don't belong to nobody?"

"I won't promise, Keith. Next week the college starts budget meetings. I expect a lot of early mornings and late nights."

The boy seemed so distraught Sherry blurted without thinking, "If your dad doesn't mind, I'll bring you here to visit Rags."

"Really?" He perked right up. "Gosh, thanks!"

Garrett didn't say anything then. He did after they reached the car. "What are you trying to do, Sherilyn? Undermine me? Why give him false hope?"

"You're totally insensitive. He's lonely and he already loves that dog. There's a fifty-fifty chance no one will answer your ad."

"That'll be ten times worse. Who'd give him a home? I know you think I'm hardhearted. Not even I can take that fuzzy mop to the dog pound."

"What if I asked the complex owner to bend the rules? I know him pretty well."

"That's convenient. How well?" Garrett snapped, unable to disguise a thread of jealousy that he could actually hear in his voice.

Sherry heard it, too. "Ron Erickson is my dad's age. I went all through school with his twin sons. Anyway, what's it to you?"

"Nothing," Garrett muttered. "It's a better solution than your first one of asking Carla and the banker to give the dog a home," he said bitterly.

"If you have such negative feelings about your ex, why did you move here?"

Sighing, Garrett gripped the steering wheel tighter. When the silence dragged on, he explained Carla's belated interest in her son. "My lawyer said to play along. He thought she'd back off. I honestly don't know what I'll do if after all this time some judge gives her custody of Keith. Hell, she abandoned him when he was two. Doesn't that count?"

Sherry chewed at her lip. She'd counseled women who sobbed that same question in her office on numerous occasions. Over the years she'd gotten inured to the father's side of divorce issues. Oddly enough, she found herself in sympathy with Garrett. She didn't want to be. Every avenue she'd worked so hard to establish at the Hub assumed the woman—the mother—was virtually always the injured party. If Garrett's case was valid, how many other men shared his plight? Sherry refused to consider that her feelings might be biased. Garrett was probably one man in a million. And if he was such a great husband and dad… That spawned another question.

"Why haven't you remarried? I know it's not for lack of prospects. I've seen women flock to your door."

"I...I..." he stammered. Although nearly six years had passed since his failure with Carla, Garrett still had trouble admitting he feared a repeat. He found it infinitely easier to let women think he preferred to devote his energies to work and to raising his son. Far safer than venturing his heart again.

"I'm sorry," Sherry mumbled. "I had no right to pry." Then tension was so thick she exhaled in relief on seeing they'd arrived back at the complex. Jumping out, she shut the door before he'd circled the bed of the pickup to assist her—something she noticed he did as a matter of course.

They walked in silence to his gate. Sherry would have hurried on to her place, but Garrett caught her hands, stalling her in the muted lamplight. "Don't rush off before I thank you. Maybe I didn't sound it, but I'm grateful you came along when you did. In Texas I had friends who were single parents. We shared war stories and lent each other a hand. Here, I'm on my own. And Keith..." Garrett swallowed hard and tightened his fingers around her hands. "It hurts me to see him unhappy. With budget talks starting next week, I'll have even less time to spend with him."

Sherry saw the shudder in his chest as he closed his eyes and released a pent-up breath. He'd just laid out another problem that she thought was a women's issue. She really had hidden her head in the sand. Impulsively she squeezed his hand. "I love kids, Garrett. And Keith's a fine bright boy. Why don't I collect him from day care? He and I can skate, rent videos or visit Rags. On the rare days I'm tied up with late meetings, I'm sure Mom would fill in. Just add our names to the authorized list."

Garrett, humbled and touched by her sincerity,

searched for but didn't find subterfuge in the depths of her warm dark eyes.

"I…I don't quite know what to say. I've never had a sitter with a doctorate," he teased, freeing one hand to cup her cheek. The next second, without even knowing he was going to, he kissed her. It was a kiss born of gratitude, but his lips had barely connected with hers before it changed. Hands crushing her soft curves to his chest, Garrett gave himself over to a rare indulgence.

In shock, Sherry did nothing to break away. At least not at first. She rose on tiptoe, reveling in the weightless feeling that came with the unexpected kiss.

The squeal of tires out on the street jarred both of them into separating at the same time. Each tried to appear unaffected. Both breathed raggedly.

Sherry saw excuses building in his blue eyes. Preferring not to hear them, she whispered a husky goodbye and literally ran down the walkway to her town house.

Unsettled as she felt, she wasn't at all prepared for Yvette's verbal attack.

Pacing the entryway, an ugly twist to her mouth, Yvette shrieked, "Some friend! Where have you and Garrett been for three hours?"

"I…I…" Sherry got hold of her raw feelings and explained about the dog.

"Don't add lying to back stabbing! Keith wasn't even with you just now. I saw you kiss Garrett, Sherry." She crossed her arms and tapped a foot. "I want you to move out. Tomorrow isn't soon enough."

That sent a wave of anger through Sherry as nothing else had. "Me? I will not move. The lease is in my name. If anyone leaves it'll be you."

"Well, I don't have money for first and last month's

rent. So we're at a stalemate. But don't think you'll get away with this. When I get through telling people what you've done, you won't have a single friend left." Snatching her purse, Yvette slammed out of the house.

Sherry stifled a cry with her fist. She stared at the door for a long time, hating the fact that a one-time friendship had ended so badly. Yet try as she might, she couldn't make herself feel bad about kissing Garrett Lock.

CHAPTER NINE

THE ENTIRE WEEKEND Sherry didn't catch sight of Garrett again. He called Saturday to ask her advice on wording an ad. She had reservations about it for Keith's sake. But in the end, she suggested also placing a notice in the neighborhood newspaper that was distributed free to homes near the school.

Yvette kept a low profile, too. Though Sherry was in and out running errands and doing laundry, their paths never crossed. Sherry doubted they'd salvage any part of the friendship that'd been forged when they were young. And it saddened her.

She also dwelt on the passion that had erupted between her and Garrett. After examining it from all angles, she'd come to the conclusion that the kiss had sprung from the tension of the moment. Nothing more.

Sherry was sure her assessment was correct when Garrett rushed into her office on Monday morning asking for—no, demanding—figures to take to his first budget exercise. She called them exercises because they were repetitive and raised everyone's blood pressure for weeks.

The way he barked at her, she decided any real or perceived passion they'd shared had flown from his mind two seconds after parting—if that passion had ever been more than a figment of her imagination. If anyone had even jokingly said a simple kiss would have such a profound effect on her, Sherry would have laughed outright. Since he'd certainly erased all memories of it from his backup tapes, she'd show him she could be just as blasé.

"I saw your ad in Sunday's paper," she said by way of polite conversation. "I didn't expect it to run so quickly."

He glanced up blankly from a stack of reports Angel had handed him. "Ad?"

She could almost see his mind screech to a halt. "Lost and found. For Rags," she reminded him, leaning a hip casually on the table where he was seated.

His eyes were level with a chunky gold-chain belt Sherry wore loosely looped around her hips. It circled a lime silk blouse that fell over the orangest orange skirt Garrett had ever seen. A floaty minuscule skirt barely reaching midthigh on legs that were long and smooth and tanned. Garrett coughed, doing his best to refocus on the figures covering the pages now strewn over the tabletop.

"Well, did you get any calls on Sunday afternoon or evening?"

"Calls?" Garrett felt like a damned parrot. Some part of his brain functioned enough to know that. The rest was frozen in a purely male response linked to the vision shimmering before him.

"You think that by not talking about Rags the problem will disappear? I'm here to tell you it won't. Not that you'll care, but last night I phoned Ron and laid the groundwork for Keith to keep Rags in the town house. Ron hasn't agreed yet. But he hasn't said no, either. You're to give him a jingle if the pup's owner doesn't show up."

Garrett managed to assimilate every third word.

Enough to get the drift. "No one called," he admitted gruffly. "Keith is flying in the clouds. I tried to tell him it's early to claim victory. He refuses to listen." Discussing his son served to take Garrett's mind off areas he had no business fantasizing about in the first place. Sherry was so cool today she couldn't have been as turned on as he was by that hellacious kiss Friday night. It'd sent him straight to a cold shower.

Even now he'd like to rattle her cage. See how cool she'd be if he got up, locked the door and announced that his thoughts ran toward the two of them having a friendly wrestling match right on top of this polished-oak conference table.

Bad idea. Garrett shrugged out of a suit jacket that suddenly made him sweat and snapped forward in his chair. Hoping to dismiss her with a roll of one shoulder and the appearance of dedication to the task at hand, he got out his pencil and set some purely meaningless figures down on the ever-present legal pad.

Sherry took the hint. "Guess I'd better quit bugging you. Any other information you need, just yell. I'm sorry we didn't finish our talk regarding the services we offer before you have to slice and dice our budget."

"Me, too," he grunted. And that was an understatement. There was much about Friday he'd like to play over. Ten percent he wouldn't trade, he thought reluctantly, swiveling to watch her leave the conference room.

Dang—the lady from Missouri put more swing in her back stroke than Monica Seles did when she aced Wimbledon.

Garrett tapped his pencil idly, wondering if Sherry played tennis. He wondered a lot of things about her.

None pertained to work or, more specifically, to her department budget. After another five minutes or so of nonproductivity, Garrett stacked the papers one last time, picked them up and told Angel he was taking them back to his office. The look that young woman delivered him cut him down to size. She'd seen his interest in Sherry and made no pretense of liking it. That was okay. Garrett didn't care to have it flashing in neon, either. His interest was illogical. Insane. He met Angel's frigid gaze without flinching.

As Sherry worked in her office, Angel burst through the door, interrupting her dictation. Surprised, she faltered over a word and clicked off the handheld mike. She'd decided to provide Garrett with a list of the points she'd intended to make at the meeting they never had.

As Angel slapped the opened mail on the desk in front of Sherry, she said, "A yard or two more of that orange silk would have made a nice skirt." She hovered on the balls of her feet, scowling fiercely.

Sherry ran a hand through her gel-spiked hair. "Did I miss something? When I came in this morning, didn't you say, and I quote, 'Those are some hot threads, boss.'"

Angel widened her huge velvety eyes. "That was before."

"Before what?" Sherry rocked back in her desk chair to peer critically at the offending article.

"Before our top dog licked his lips as you strolled past like…like you were the feast at his last supper." Making a show of inspecting her glossy nails, she added, "And before I went for coffee and heard about your wild weekend. Guess it's not true what they say in country songs—that Texans have slow hands."

Once Sherry got her chin up off her knees, she folded

her hands on her desk and asked Angel to sit. "Now then—exactly what did you hear and from whom?"

Angel plunked down in the chair. "Those blabbermouth clerks in accounting said your roommate caught you in a compromising spot with you know who." She shrugged. "They said some other stuff, too."

"Like what?" Sherry clasped her hands tighter. Yvette certainly hadn't wasted time spreading her dirt. The secretary to the accounting department chair was the best bet as to source. Lena Martin partied with Yvette's crowd and loved to gossip.

"If you deny it all, boss, I'll hand their heads back on platters."

"That's a gruesome thought. No. We will not lower ourselves to their level. Nothing throws a monkey wrench into a rumor mill faster than no response."

"So it's true?" Angel climbed to her feet. "Men are no damn good. Haven't I taught you anything, boss?"

"Some men are good." Sherry's voice rose sharply. "You had two bad experiences, Angel. Now, you can choose to cloister yourself or you can venture into relationships more slowly, benefiting from wisdom gained."

"You've tumbled big time for the dude, huh?"

Sherry hoped her face wasn't as red as it was hot. "To work, Angel. We weren't discussing me."

"Yeah, but—"

Sherry cut in quickly. "What happened is nothing like they're trying to make out. Yvette has her nose out of joint. The rumors are a result of a tiff we had."

"Girlfriends like that you can do without. It'll be hard, but if you insist, I'll bite my tongue."

"I insist."

But as it turned out, quelling the rumors wasn't so simple. It didn't help that at ten minutes to five her phone rang and Garrett, in a dither, asked her to pick up Keith from his new day care.

Sherry glanced at her watch, then at the pile of dictation she'd barely managed to cut in half. Injecting enthusiasm into her voice, she said, "Sure. Did you clear me with the powers that be? I don't want to be accused of kidnapping."

"I did give them your name," he admitted, "at Keith's insistence. Would you believe I swore I wouldn't foist any more of my problems on you? I even called Carla, foolishly thinking she'd jump at the chance for extra time with him. She claims she wants to see more of him—but on her terms, I guess."

"That's too bad. So…will she give Rags a home if no one claims him?"

The line crackled in her ear with each breath he took. "No dice, huh?" she asked lightly.

"Not an option." Garrett didn't elaborate.

Reading between the lines, Sherry figured he and Carla must have had harsh words. She felt sorrier for Keith. After all her years of counseling women involved in broken relationships, she still naively hoped the adults could set differences aside when it came to doing what was best for their children.

"Our break is over," he said into the silence. "Are you positive you're all right with this? They sprang this late session on us without warning. I could skip out, but I get the feeling they're waiting to see if I do. Like this is a test."

"Probably. And the departments of the people who can't stay will suffer. Keith and I will get along fine.

Don't worry. His bedtime is eight-thirty? Are there other rules I should know?"

"The only one I can think of is no dessert if he doesn't at least try everything on his plate. I suppose I should set more rules. Basically I'm pretty laid-back."

"For kids that's better than being uptight. Oh, one other thing—I assume Keith has a house key?"

"Dang. No. There hasn't been any reason for him to carry one. Look, I'm just downstairs in Frank's office. I'll run my key up to you. There's a spare in the kitchen junk drawer. If you two go anywhere, leave one under the front doormat for me in case the meeting breaks up early."

"Now that's original." She laughed. "First place burglars look, I hear."

"I don't have time to be creative. See you in a minute. And Sherilyn, thanks. I never had to call an agency sitter in Huntsville. I may have to consider it here." He hung up, but she held the receiver against her cheek for a moment, hoping to stretch the tingle of warmth that always accompanied the way he said her name.

Stupid. Dropping the receiver like a hot rock, she got busy locking away the student files that still needed counseling reports. She removed the tape from her machine, then carried it and the records she'd completed into the outer office to leave with Angel. She was still in the process of giving the secretary instructions when Garrett dashed through the door.

Sherry's heart flopped around inside her chest. She wished it would stop doing that every time he appeared.

Rushed though he was, Garrett took a minute to thank Angel for giving up her morning break to run copies of the data he'd needed from Sherry's department for today's meeting. Angel shrugged, but Sherry saw she was pleased. Kruger always made last-minute demands and never thanked anyone. Sherry's respect for Garrett climbed. Angel's self-esteem was higher than when she'd entered the program, but there was a long way to go. The verbal abuse she'd suffered at the hands of both husbands and her dad had taken its toll. The young woman didn't expect much from men and was rarely disappointed unfortunately.

Sherry tried to convey her appreciation in the ardent smile she sent him.

Smiling back, Garrett pulled a key ring from his pocket and fiddled with a key until he worked it free. When he'd entered the office, Sherry and Angel had been the only occupants. Three women staffers noticed him as they walked by the department, then hurried in, full of titters.

Sherry knew all three had designs on Garrett. She groaned inwardly, thinking he'd never get back to his meeting if they waylaid him.

Garrett glanced up and saw them bearing down on him just as the key popped free. He shoved it into Sherry's hand and was already in motion to leave by the time the three reached him. He straightened his tie, gave them a lopsided smile and a quick salute as he hastened toward the door. "I'm late for a budget meeting," he said, cutting off their requests. "I only stopped by to give my house key to Sherilyn."

Four pair of stupefied eyes swerved toward Sherry while Garrett blithely slipped out of the department, leaving her with the evidence dangling in her hand.

She'd kill him. Murder him with her bare hands. The censure in the ring of faces surrounding her was almost more than she could bear, and she attempted to exonerate herself with the truth. "I, ah, I'm baby-sitting his son while he's at the budget talks." Her feeble words fell on stiff backs and deaf ears. Her three colleagues took a hike.

"Baby-sitting?" Angel scowled blackly.

"It's the truth." Sherry spread her hands.

A sunny smile rearranged Angel's pretty features. "That's too hokey to be a lie. I believe you, boss."

One of Sherry's dark brows lifted slightly. "Yippee! A fourth of the rumors squelched."

"I see your point." Angel shut off her computer. "What was he thinking?"

"That he was late for his meeting," Sherry said wryly, realizing it was true. He'd be livid when he heard the gossip. And he'd never recall feeding it.

Angel snapped her fingers. "Go get the kid and parade him through campus. Take him to the cafeteria for supper. Introduce him around."

"The cafeteria? Oh, good plan. He'd get ptomaine poisoning, the dean would have me thrown in jail, then the rumors about me shacking up with Garrett wouldn't matter anymore."

"Okay, no cafeteria. How about the Haywire Hamburger?"

"Angel, you're a genius. I've always said they misnamed that place. They should have called it the Rumor Mill. Only…I so seldom go there, people might get the opposite idea. You know, that I was flaunting my *relationship* with Keith's dad." She made quote marks in the air.

"My kids love to eat there. We'd go with you, but it's too close to payday for me."

"I'll treat you. Keith's the same age as your oldest son. Please, Angel."

"You don't have to twist my arm. It'll take me about half an hour to pick them up from the sitter's and drive there."

"Done. It won't save my reputation entirely, but it's bound to help."

"Yeah. And when the man gets home, explain the facts of life on this campus."

Facts of life. The phrase played in Sherry's head over the course of the evening. A man as virile as Garrett Lock probably *wrote* the facts of life. Wrote and tested. Sherry's mind kept drifting toward areas that were off-limits. Not really off-limits, but certainly dangerous. About the third time Angel had to draw her back from imagining exactly what kind of lover Garrett would be, Sherry scrubbed the thoughts away. She concentrated on showing Keith a good time.

"That was a blast," he said as they climbed into Sherry's car after saying goodbye to Angel and her boisterous brood. "I'm glad you picked me up. Me'n Dad never do anything fun anymore."

"It's hard starting a new job, Keith."

"Yeah, I guess. I saved part of my hamburger for Rags. Can we take it to him?"

"Sure, sport. Then it's home to bed with no stops." She reached over and ruffled his hair. "You don't have homework, do you?"

He leaned back, checking her out with a mischievous smile. "I got a book in my backpack that I'm s'pose to read 'fore I go to bed."

"Really? Why am I just hearing about this now, tiger?"

"'Cause I wanted to go eat burgers. And I wanna see Rags."

His honesty blew her lecture out of the water. "Fair enough." She smiled wryly. "I should have asked earlier about homework. Tomorrow I'll be smarter."

"You gonna pick me up tomorrow? Yay!"

"I'm only assuming your father has meetings all week. Before you get too excited, we'd better find out if he's made other plans."

"I guess you got more important stuff to do than hang out with a kid, huh?"

"Oh, no, Keith. But it's your dad's decision. He said he may call a professional sitter."

Keith's shoulders slumped. "Jason at my old day care said those sitters are meaner 'n snakes. I like you 'cause you call me sport and tiger, and you're nice to dogs and you mess up my hair," he said shyly, slanting a glance through thick dark lashes.

Thrown once again by his candor, she didn't know how to respond. They'd already reached her parents' house, so she said nothing, just fell to brooding.

Emily noticed her moodiness and remarked on it after Nan had finished measuring Sherry for her maid-of-honor dress. "Something's bothering you, Sher. I know you feel I double-crossed you, falling for Nolan the way I did on the heels of announcing I'd never marry again. But...people change." She made a fist of her right hand and placed it over her heart. "Hearts change. I love him, Sherry. I'll spend a lifetime making him happy. I didn't ask him to pay the debt I owed my ex-in-laws. He insisted."

Sherry unfurled the cloth tape measure she'd been folding around her fingers and paced the sewing room, letting it whip like a flag in the wind. "I'm not blind, Em. I see how happy both of you are. Megan and Mark are in seventh heaven." She paused, frowning. "Aren't you the teeniest bit afraid? What if things change again and your feelings for each other don't last?"

Emily studied her friend. "Are we still talking about Nolan and me, Sherry?" she asked softly.

Sherry's pacing grew more erratic. "I feel life as I know it slipping away. Keith...Rags... I'm getting too involved."

"Mmm. And with Keith's dad?"

"No." Sherry made a slicing movement with her hand.

Rising from the chair that sat in front of the sewing machine, Emily matched her steps to Sherry's. "I fought the attraction between Nolan and me. I had a hundred excuses why a relationship was a bad idea. Loving someone is risky. But what's the alternative? Spending a lifetime alone and lonely, that's what."

"I'm not lonely." Sherry recognized the falseness of the statement before the last word died away. "And if I am sometimes? I'll join groups and take more classes."

Emily gazed at her sadly. "How many hours a day can you stay on a treadmill?"

Unwilling to accept the truth of Emily's statement, Sherry bolted for the door. Once there, she waggled her left arm, pointing at her watch. "I have to get Keith home, Em. Eight-thirty's his bedtime. I have papers to grade and a test to set up before tomorrow."

"Stepping up the tempo, Sher?" Emily trailed her down the hall. "It's all right to let yourself like a man. Not all of them bite."

Sherry closed her ears and made a lot of unnecessary noise as she rounded Keith up. He didn't want to leave Rags. Getting out the door was a slow process, further impeded by Nan.

"We're barbecuing chicken tomorrow night," she said. "Why don't you bring Keith for dinner? That way he'll have all evening to spend with Rags."

It was on the tip of Sherry's tongue to refuse. But the boy's obvious delight had her mumbling acceptance. "If his dad has another late meeting," she qualified.

"If he doesn't," Emily piped up, "invite him, too. The more, the merrier."

Sherry knew exactly what had inspired Emily's invitation, and she had no intention of passing it on to Garrett.

Keith chattered like a parrot all the way home. "Can I check the answering machine?" he asked the minute Sherry opened the door. "I hafta see if anybody's claiming Rags."

"Shouldn't you let your dad handle that?" Sherry didn't want to be the one dealing with the boy's broken heart if an owner had called.

"Please," he begged.

"All right."

The phone rang as Keith reached for the machine. His face paled. "Maybe that's someone now."

Sherry grabbed for the phone on the third ring. "Or maybe it's your dad," she hissed. "Hello," she said, sounding out of breath. "Hello," she said a second time into the silence. Then she covered the mouthpiece. "It's your mom, Keith. She wants to talk to you. Here—take the phone."

"Hi, Mom," he said without exuberance. "That's Sherry. Dad's at a meeting. I don't know how late he'll be. Here." He extended the receiver to Sherry. "She wants to talk to you."

"Me?" Puzzled, Sherry put the receiver to her ear.

"I'm the sitter, yes." She grimaced at the woman's frosty tone. "I think I can take a message," she said dryly, torn between telling Carla she had her Ph.D. or acting as if she was half a bubble off plumb—the airhead Carla judged her to be. In the end Sherry opted for coolly professional, knowing from experience that even after ex-wives remarried, they often felt proprietorial when it came to their ex-husbands. "You want Dean Lock to bring Keith to St. Louis this weekend? You'll expect him by 10:00 a.m. Saturday because you're planning a trip to the Mercantile Money Museum. I have that. I'll let him know to call you." Sherry turned away from Keith, who was saying "ick" and "yuck," so his mother wouldn't hear him. "The Magic House is more fun for kids Keith's age," Sherry found herself recommending. "Or the Huck Finn and Tom Sawyer cruises. I know Keith's been looking forward to seeing a stern-wheeler."

Sherry winced at the former Mrs. Lock's immediate putdown. "You're right, it isn't my place to make suggestions. Goodbye." Sherry started to slam the phone down, then thinking better of it, set it gently in the cradle.

"I don't wanna go to any stupid money museum," the boy muttered. "I'm gonna tell Dad I'd rather stay home and play with Rags."

"The museum isn't so bad, Keith. The history of money is interesting. And you get to see counterfeit currency."

"What's that?" He wrinkled his nose.

"I'll let your dad explain," Sherry told him. Eight was a little young to have much interest in money other than for spending. "See if there're any messages on the answering machine and then get ready for bed. If you hurry you can read me the book you brought from school."

"Dad bought me a book about Hercules. Will you read it after I finish mine, Sherry?"

Again she didn't know if she was overstepping her bounds. What if Garrett had bought the book specifically to read to his son himself? She mumbled something noncommittal.

They were both relieved to discover no messages except for one from Garrett, saying he thought he'd be home by ten. He sounded weary.

While Keith showered and put on his pajamas, Sherry wrote a lengthy note explaining Carla's call and left it on the counter.

Garrett got home early, it turned out. Keith was curled beside Sherry on his bed in the loft room when Garrett let himself in and called out a greeting. Keith had read all of his storybook from school and now Sherry was reading aloud.

"Upstairs, Dad. Sherry's almost done reading *Hercules*. Can she finish?"

Garrett reached Keith's room in time to see Sherry uncurl her legs and start to close the book. The scene presented such a cozy picture that first joy, then panic slammed through Garrett's stomach. His son, hair clean from a recent shower, looked sleepy and content as a cat, his head bobbing on Sherry's shoulder. And she resembled a vision he'd imagined too many times in years past when Keith was sick in bed and needed tending. That of a fairy godmom. Garrett had imagined having someone—a female someone—to share the parenting. He stopped at the threshold, not wanting to step inside and disrupt the scene.

Sherry couldn't decipher the strange look on Garrett's face. She must have been right about the book, she decided, scrambling up. "Why don't we ask your dad to read the end? Actually we just got to the action part. The guy stuff."

Garrett shrugged out of his suit jacket and stripped off the tie he'd loosened the minute he left the meeting. "Don't let me interrupt. I'm bushed. Think I'll go take a shower. Did anyone call about the dog?"

"Nope." Keith grinned happily.

"Dang." Garrett heaved a sigh. "Well, I told them to run the ad a full week."

"I did take a message from your ex-wife," Sherry informed him. "I left it on the kitchen counter."

"Why didn't you let her talk to Keith?"

"She did. But she left the message with me. She wants you to call."

Keith yawned. "Mom wants me to go to some dorky money museum this weekend. I don't wanna."

Garrett slung his coat over his shoulder. "She canceled her last visitation."

"So?" Keith flopped back on his pillow. "If I go to St. Louis I won't see Rags for two whole days."

Sherry stood up, closing the book. "I'm sure you two need to talk this through." She handed Garrett the book and tried to slide past him out the door. "Oh, I have your key in my purse. I didn't leave it under the mat."

"I hate having to ask, but can you bail me out again tomorrow night? They set a meeting for three o'clock. I'm sure it'll run past five."

"Goody, goody." Keith hopped up and down on the bed. "Sherry's mom asked us to come over for a barbecue. Oh…you're 'vited, too, Dad."

"I am? What time?" He turned to Sherry with interest.

She shrugged. "Usually six-thirty. I doubt your meeting'll end by then."

"Don't sound so sorry."

She flushed. "I just know these deans. They talk every issue to death."

"You've got that right. Will you schedule some time for me in the morning? I need to know the fudge factors in your department supply budget and in the Hub's, before the others start that double-talk on me."

"You mean you'll go to bat for us? For the Hub?"

"Why wouldn't I? I believe in whole-life training."

"You do?" Sherry tripped over her tongue. "Then why are we always arguing?"

He grinned. "You tell me."

She narrowed her gaze. "Do the regents know how you feel?"

"I can't recall that they asked specifically."

"Well, whaddaya know." Sherry couldn't hide her smile as she stepped back into the room and waved to Keith. There was hope of salvaging the Hub, after all. "G'night, sport. See you tomorrow." To Garrett she said, "I'll clear my morning calendar. I don't have a class till one. Oh, and don't forget the message from your wife," she reminded him, all but skipping down the stairs.

Garrett stood on the top step and watched her descent. Feeling the congenial warmth go with her, he called out impulsively, "Ex-wife. If it turns out I'm taking Keith to St. Louis this weekend, would you like to ride along?"

"G-go to St. Louis with you? Me? What for?" Turning, she gazed at him as if he'd lost his mind.

Her outspokenness stopped him momentarily. "This

is your territory, Doc. I sort of hoped you'd play tour guide. Show me the city."

"Oh, well, sure. I can do that, I guess."

"Good. I'll call Carla tonight and pin her down. Let you know tomorrow."

Sherry hummed happily on the way home. As she entered the town house, she was surrounded by the aroma of garlic.

Yvette scowled up from the sofa, where she watched TV. "My, aren't we cheerful. Did Garrett get home from his meeting?"

"How did you know he had a meeting?" Sherry turned her back on her housemate to close and lock the door.

"I have sources. Why didn't you say you were going to baby-sit the kid? It would have saved us fighting. Don't lock the dead bolt. Poor Garrett's probably starved. I'm taking him our second pan of lasagna." Her announcement was muffled as she disappeared into the kitchen and came out with the steaming casserole. She left with the dish before Sherry had recovered from her initial shock.

Sherry more or less expected Garrett to ship Yvette right back. As the night lengthened without any sign of her return, Sherry felt her earlier joy at being asked to go to St. Louis with him vanish. She drifted off to sleep so many times during her vigil that when Yvette finally did come in and Sherry heard the door close and the lock engage, she was too groggy from sleep to note the time. But it was late. Very late.

GARRETT DIDN'T MENTION his late-night visitor the next morning at their meeting. Neither did Sherry. Professionally, doggedly, she laid out the facts he'd requested.

"Thanks," he said, preparing to dash out of her office. "Now I'll be better able to defend our position on the Hub's value at the roundtable discussions."

When he left, to keep from feeling the loss of his presence, Sherry busied herself refiling student folders.

Garrett promptly stuck his head back in the room. "I couldn't reach Carla last night. She'd already gone to work this morning. I'll call her tonight."

Sherry yanked out another file drawer. "I may have other plans." The lie tasted like ashes in her mouth.

Forced to deal with the disappointment he felt, Garrett said nothing for a moment. "I see." His tone said he didn't.

She lifted a shoulder negligently, still facing away from him.

He stared at the rigid set of her spine as empty seconds ticked by. Already late for a meeting in President Westerbrook's office, Garrett reined in his frustration. "I don't have time to discuss your sudden change of plans. It'll have to be later."

"Fine," Sherry snapped. But he didn't hear, as he'd already retreated.

Luckily she managed to avoid him for the rest of the day. He'd gone to his meeting when she closed the office. Actually she was late picking up Keith. As a result, they drove straight to her folks, where they were drawn into the barbecue preparations.

Immersed in her family's normal highspirited activities, Sherry finally succeeded in putting Garrett Lock out of her mind. Until she saw Emily stiffen and a funny expression cross her face. Sherry turned toward the house in time to see Garrett stroll into the backyard with Yvette clutching his arm.

Aware that Emily was watching her every reaction, Sherry injected pleasure she didn't feel into a passable greeting. And if she thought she could've got away with it, she'd have begged off staying to eat—say she was sick or something. Indeed, both Sherry's head and stomach hurt. Maybe she *was* coming down with the flu.

CHAPTER TEN

YVETTE MOLDED HERSELF to Garrett, at the same time ignoring Keith. Sherry wasn't the only one who noticed. Mark mentioned it, as did Emily. How Garrett could be so obtuse was beyond Sherry. While he didn't overtly flirt back, neither did he appear annoyed that Yvette monopolized him.

Visibly unhappy with his dad, Keith slipped off to play with Rags before he'd taken more than a few bites of dinner. Mark started to follow, but Sherry stalled him and requested a word alone with Keith. Mark slumped back in his seat.

When Sherry ran Keith to ground, he was sitting on the floor in the family room, arms wrapped around the stray pup he hoped to keep. "You okay, tiger? You barely tasted your food."

"Why did *she* have to come with Dad? I don't like her. She called Rags flea-bitten."

"Maybe Yvette was just joking around."

"She wasn't."

Sherry hunkered down and scratched the wiggly pup's ears. All three sat in silence. At last Keith spoke.

"Dad and me did okay in Texas. It's different since we moved. *He's* different."

"Different how?"

"I never had to visit mom. Just talk to her on the phone."

"Things happen in divorce that kids can't control, Keith. Fact is, you still have two parents. The separation is between them and had nothing to do with you. Before your mom remarried, maybe she wasn't in a position to have you visit. It doesn't mean your dad loves you less, Keith, because he's willing to share you with her now. Really, you're lucky to have such an understanding father."

Outside in the hall, Garrett, who'd managed to lose Yvette for the time being, heard Sherilyn and his son talking, and hesitated. Keith had been so withdrawn of late he was reluctant to interrupt their heart-to-heart. To hear Sherry Campbell sticking up for him stirred feelings that hadn't surfaced in a while. From the rumblings on campus, he wouldn't have thought she'd do that for him or any man.

Inside the room, Keith sighed and flung his arms around Sherry's neck. "Gosh, I feel better. Do you think maybe your mom cooked extra chicken? I am sorta hungry."

Sherry tickled him until he giggled. "Cut through the guest bedroom and slip out the sliding glass door. It'll get you to the grill faster." She got to her feet with him and pointed the way.

"Are you coming, too?"

She shook her head. "Think I'll toodle on home. I have a test to write up. You'll be going back with your dad."

"Oh. Okay." Looking more resigned than pleased, he shuffled out.

Impulsively Garrett stepped into the room. "I didn't mean to eavesdrop, but I heard what you told Keith.

Thanks for backing me when you don't know my situation with Carla."

"Yeah, well, it's Keith who needs to hear any truths you're passing out."

Garrett flopped on the couch near where Sherry took a seat on the floor again. "God's truth? I don't know what went wrong with my marriage." Moodily he described Carla's return to college at his request and her subsequent obsession with her career. "One day I came home to a note informing me she'd moved to St. Louis. She said she couldn't explain, but banking excited her—and our marriage was strangling her."

What Garrett didn't impart was that he'd gone through a long phase of self-blame, of thinking Carla had found him lacking as a man and that it therefore stood to reason other women would, too. It seemed easier to use Keith as an excuse for not getting involved. At some point, denying himself female companionship became habit.

Leaning forward, he clasped his hands between his knees. "Some of my colleagues claimed I let Keith fill an emotional void in my life. Maybe I did. I know I'm guilty of raking myself over the coals with what-ifs and should-haves. But the truth is…Carla left me to raise our son alone. Now I'm afraid, after all this time, her weaselly lawyer will make her out the heroine and me the bum. It happens to single dads all the time."

Sherry thought about the times her affidavits had helped make that very thing happen. "You're probably the exception," she murmured. "The divorced dads I meet are neglectful, abusive or deadbeats. Some are all three. A judge will look at your record. Maybe Carla won't want Keith full-time. From what he and you have said, she has a hard time following through on simple visitations."

"I have a letter from Carla's attorney that says I've had him to myself for six years and now it's her turn. As if our son's life is some sort of shuffleboard."

"Courts today are more apt to shuffle parents than the kids. They often ask the child what he or she wants. Keith isn't quite old enough to have his choice given full consideration. Twelve is the magic age. Still, his preference will carry weight."

"I hope it doesn't come to that. Would you like to be fought over like a bone?"

Sherry glanced away, then back at Garrett. She felt a tug-of-war inside her chest concerning her feelings for him. In advising him, she went against her number-one cardinal rule—kids belong with biological moms unless a woman's totally unfit. "Have you and Carla sat down and discussed what each of you believe is best for Keith? Without lawyers to muddy the waters?"

"When I got her first request six months ago, I tried to set up a meeting. Carla said no. Of course, she was deep in wedding plans. I called my lawyer. He said to send Keith to her wedding and that'd probably be the end of it."

"Do you like her husband?"

"No." An abashed grin lifted one corner of Garrett's mouth. "I hate the jerk's cologne."

"Now, that's petty."

"Yeah. But it beats calling him an out-and-out bastard."

"Neither description earns you points in court. Strike that from the record," she said in a deep voice. "Witness conjecture."

They were both laughing at Sherry's rendition of a judge when Yvette burst into the room. "There you are." She threw herself down so close to Garrett she was practically sitting in his lap and sent a challenge to Sherry. "What's so funny?"

Sherry climbed nimbly to her feet, smoothing the pleats of the India-print skirt she'd worn to work. "An inside joke," she said, refusing to be cowed by Yvette's possessiveness. "I was on my way out when Garrett came in." She filtered out Yvette's image and focused on him. "I forgot to ask if you need me to pick up Keith up from day care tomorrow."

"I can't impose. I'll call a sitting service. The joint deans have a six-thirty breakfast meeting in the morning."

"I don't mind taking him to school and picking him up," Sherry said. "I have no conflict tomorrow."

"I'll take the kid to school," Yvette butted in. "What time?"

"Eight." Garrett jerked toward her and frowned. "I'd rather Sherry took him, if anyone does. Involving too many people might confuse Keith."

"Okay." Yvette agreed with a smile. "I'll sleep in. You haven't forgotten the Conways' harvest party tomorrow night, have you Garrett? I RSVP'd for us." She curled ring-clad fingers around his biceps.

Sherry failed an attempt to mask her surprise. And hurt. She'd been going to the Conways' harvest parties longer than Yvette. "Did Janice call with an invitation?"

"Yes, but this year's party is couples only. She knew you wouldn't have a date."

"I…" Sherry swallowed the remark she'd been about to make. Garrett would feel bad and definitely get Keith a sitter if she said she could *get* a date. For a minute she

envisioned what they'd all do if she showed up at the
Conways' with Keith in tow. Smiling at her private joke,
she assured Garrett she'd drop Keith off in the morning
and pick him up after school. "If he doesn't have
homework and you don't mind, maybe we'll go play
miniature golf. After that, we'll hit the virtual-reality
arcade. It's really cool."

Yvette sniffed. "Sherry's such a kid. It's not my idea
of fun. Is it yours, Garrett?"

"Yes, as a matter of fact. But, Sherry, don't feel you
have to entertain Keith."

"I'm not. I'll enjoy it as much or more than he will."

Yvette got pouty then, so Sherry decided to leave.
"I've gotta go. Touch base later."

"Wait, I'll walk you to your car." Garrett tried to
peel Yvette off his arm, but she yanked him back down.

"For heaven's sake, Garrett. Sherry's a nineties'
woman. Don't insult her."

Garrett hovered in the half-upright position a moment.
The blue eyes that sought Sherry's appeared unsure.

Those ingrained manners he'd mentioned, she
thought. Why else would he offer to walk her to her car
when he'd come with another woman? Assuring him
she needed no escort, Sherry left. She stopped to tell her
family and Keith goodbye, aching for the boy. If Garrett
was in the market for a stepmom for his son, he could
certainly make a better choice. But apparently men
didn't select mates with any sort of logic. And Yvette
had been searching for love all her life. In a stable relationship, maybe she'd settle down and be faithful to
one man. It could happen.

Sherry could also meet space aliens on the drive home.

Somewhat melancholy and at loose ends when she got there, Sherry began cleaning the kitchen. She also rinsed out a blouse and finished the test for her advanced-psych class. Having exhausted herself mentally and physically, she fell asleep seconds after crawling into bed.

As a result, she missed hearing Yvette come in—wouldn't have known except that in the morning her bedroom door was shut. Last night it stood open.

Not wanting to risk another confrontation, Sherry decided to forgo coffee. Since Garrett said he had to leave early, maybe Keith would like to go out for breakfast. She packed her book bag and slipped out, relocking the door.

Garrett answered on the third ring of his doorbell. His shirt collar was flipped up and his tie was draped around his neck. Seeing Sherry, he snapped up a sleeve to check his watch.

"I'm early," she said. "I didn't think you'd want to leave Keith alone between the time you leave and when he's due at school."

"Not as a rule. Although I trust him not to get into trouble."

"I didn't mean he would on purpose. But accidents can happen. I don't mind if you give him my work and home numbers in case he needs help and can't reach you."

"I'm never far from my cell phone."

"I forgot you have a cell phone. I wasn't implying you're negligent."

His gaze swept lightly over her. Today she looked like a throwback to a flower child. A voluminous gold skirt skimmed the tops of her hiking boots. A rust-colored blouse hung loosely to her hips, gathered close to her waist by a rope with beaded ends. She left a scent of lilac in her wake as she stepped into the foyer, calmly laying out her plan for taking his son to breakfast. Something moved in Garrett's chest as he listened to her smoky morning voice. A hard-to-describe feeling. One that suggested there was a gaping hole in his life.

Garrett realized he must be staring at her as if he intended to lock her in his bedroom and throw away the key. He grabbed hold of his tie with both hands to keep from grabbing her and devouring her kissable lips. Garrett already knew how she tasted. Sweet. Very, very sweet. A tremor went through him. What was wrong with him? He wasn't in the habit of lusting after women friends, colleagues or baby-sitters. Sherilyn Campbell fit the bill for all three.

Wiping suddenly clammy hands on his white shirt-front, Garrett loped to the foot of the stairs and bellowed for Keith. Equilibrium restored now that he was out of range of her provocative perfume, he tossed Sherry an easy smile.

"Keith will like eating breakfast out. The lucky dog. I'm envious."

Sherry fought an overwhelming temptation to tell him to play hooky. She caught herself in the nick of time. *He's your boss, dummy!*

"You said you had a breakfast meeting, or I'd never have presumed to drop by so early."

"Breakfast to that crew is a box of jelly doughnuts and three pots of leaded coffee."

"And you're a steak-and-grits man?"

"More like cold cereal. Or omelets if someone else is cooking."

"I love to cook. But it's no fun cooking for one." Suddenly she thought how that might sound and backpedaled. "Um, that's not an invitation." She ran nervous fingers up the strap of her shoulder purse and shifted from one foot to the other.

"Too bad. You missed seeing me lap up your lasagna like one of Pavlov's dogs." He screwed his face into a wry grin.

Her surprise at his admission turned into pleasure. "I didn't realize Yvette had told you I made the casserole."

"She didn't. The day Keith and I ate at Nolan's, Emily let the truth slip. She served a side dish of spaghetti. When I wolfed down my third helping, she informed me it was your recipe. Then went on to rave about your lasagna. I put two and two together. You can't have cooked for Nolan. Emily's praise of your cooking surprised him."

"Until he met Em, all Nolan did on weekends was work on his house. My mom cooks at our family gatherings. He's positive I never learned, even though I didn't set out to keep it a secret."

Keith appeared at the head of the stairs. His shirt wasn't tucked in, but his face was scrubbed and his hair combed. He carried sneakers and socks.

"Are you really taking me out for breakfast, Sherry? I heard you ask Dad. I hate grits. Mark went someplace that makes chocolate-chip pancakes. Can we go there?"

"Featherstone Café. Nolan and I used to badger my folks to stop there after church. I'd order strawberry waffles and Nolan would have chocolate-chip pancakes. Going there's okay by me, Keith, if your dad'll let you have chocolate for breakfast."

Garrett gazed at Keith's beaming face, love filling his heart. As a result, his answer emerged sounding deep and a little scratchy. "Anything that brings a smile to your face is fine with me, son. If the food's as good as Sherry remembers, maybe the three of us can leave early for St. Louis on Saturday and stop there to eat."

Sherry's head came around fast. "Who three?" Did he mean Yvette? Probably. No, definitely. After seeing the two of them together last night and hearing about their plans to attend the Conways' harvest party, Sherry had to assume Yvette would naturally replace her as Lock's tour guide on the St. Louis trip.

Deftly tying his tie without a mirror, Garrett pinned Sherry with a look. "Do you have a problem with Saturday? I know last time it came up you sounded a bit vague. Listen, Carla wants Keith there by ten o'clock. If we're having breakfast first, we'll need to leave here by seven."

"You think Yvette can get up that early after partying tonight?"

Forehead creased, Garrett reached for his suit jacket, which hung over one of the newel posts. "I didn't ask Yvette. I asked you."

Sherry gnawed on her bottom lip as she contemplated both his exasperated stance and his words. "But you were together last night and the two of you are going to the Conways' tonight."

Retrieving his briefcase from the closet, Garrett checked his watch before rumpling his son's hair. "If I don't take off, I'll be late for the session. You live with Yvette," he said to Sherry. "You must know the woman doesn't take no for an answer. When she told me about the Conway bash, I thought everyone in town, including you, was going."

"That used to be the case. This couples-only qualifier is new. Look, I don't want to make you late for a budget meeting. I'll go to St. Louis unless you change your mind. Enjoy the harvest party. I'll have Keith home and in bed by eight-thirty."

"You're sure you're all right with this arrangement? If you want to get a date and go to this shindig, I'll be glad to bow out. I'm the Johnny-come-lately here. Those folks are your friends." He realized the minute the words were out that he didn't like the idea of her going with some nameless faceless man. Hadn't Yvette said there'd be dancing by starlight?

Garrett wasn't the world's best dancer. Yet he had no difficulty imagining Sherry cutting a colorful swath across a dance floor. He conjured up a vision as she stood talking to his son. Scowling, he closed out the picture of her tripping lightly around a dance floor held tight to some man's chest.

From Garrett's scowl, Sherry could only conclude that he was still worried about imposing on her and keeping her from the party.

"Keith and I will have a ball at the virtual-reality arcade. Randy and Janice Conway have a daughter Keith's age. You need to meet other parents. Curtis Jensen's son is nine. He plays soccer—and I know that Keith played in Huntsville. The whole Jensen family's involved in mountain biking, too. They'll know how you can join these things."

"Soccer? Yeah, Dad! And I heard a kid talking at school. He said mountain biking at Lake of the Ozarks is the coolest. We should do that."

Garrett laughed. "Well, by all means, we need to get involved in something cool."

"Sherry," the boy said enthusiastically, "you can

come, too. Your mom said the mountain bike in their garage belongs to you."

A denial lay trapped in her throat. Sherry wished Keith wouldn't be so quick to include her in his father's plans. Then Garrett felt he had to be polite. "Count the layers of dust covering that bike, tiger," she said. "I'm not only rusty at mountain biking, I'm corroded. Deal me out."

When Keith looked stricken, she felt compelled to add, "Ask Mark and Nolan to go. I'll bet they'd love taking part in some father-son outings."

"That'd be okay. Wouldn't it, Dad?"

"Whoa. Aren't you two putting the cart before the horse? First I have to meet this Mr. Jensen and find out the particulars. It's not a done deal, son."

Sherry eyed Garrett with amusement. "Spoilsport. Don't you ever take risks?"

Garrett didn't respond because Keith asked him a question. "Dad, when will we know if I can keep Rags?"

Dang, he didn't want to deal with the matter of the dog, either. He felt buffeted between the two of them as they ganged up on him. "I have to go, Keith. We'll talk about the dog when I have time to sit down with you."

Sherry followed him to the door. "Coward," she murmured, stepping outside behind him.

"Yeah, yeah. You're loving every minute of me being on the hot seat, aren't you? I haven't had a single call about the dog. Plus, your mom phoned her friend Dorothy. She checked everyone in her bichon frise club and no one's lost a dog." Throwing a helpless glance back to where his son sat tying his shoes, Garrett muttered, "I suppose it wouldn't hurt if you asked Ron how firm he is on the Association rules. Since they allow families to buy and rent here, they should expect kids to want pets."

She tried not to smile at his reluctant concession. Didn't want to appear smug.

He saw in her eyes how much she wanted to. "Go ahead, crow. The mutt was kind of cute after you got him scrubbed. But don't tell Keith I said so, in case negotiations with Ron fall apart and I have to find another home for Rags."

Sherry propped a shoulder against the door frame. "You're pure caramel under that macho coating, Lock."

He made a face. "Leak that to the other deans and you can kiss funding for your pet project goodbye."

"They're blustering, right? They aren't really serious about closing the doors to the Hub, are they?"

"I'd say they are, yes." Garrett didn't see any way to soft-soap the truth.

His quiet answer jolted Sherry, though it shouldn't have come as any great surprise. She'd fought hard every year to save existing services. The women who desperately needed what the Hub provided would be the losers. And ultimately, so would the community.

Garrett strode the three steps back to lift her chin with the tip of one finger. "I haven't struck out yet. Trust me to save as much of the program as I can."

She hadn't expected his support and therefore wasn't able to express her thanks. A nod was all she managed. It didn't help that her lungs felt squeezed by his proximity and her insides melted at his touch. Thank goodness he didn't linger long enough to figure out what held her tongue.

With a brisk, "See you later," he strode quickly through the gate.

As if her boots were glued to the porch, Sherry didn't move until she heard his truck roar to life. Keith, who'd been busy tucking in his shirt, joined her, forcing her to regroup.

Breakfast with Keith was delightful. For a child who was only eight years old, he had a wide variety of interests. On top of that, he had a stash of really dumb jokes that kept her laughing.

Something Sherry had never reckoned on was the number of college staff who ate at the Featherstone. True to their nosy natures, most dropped by her table for a variety of reasons, but really to meet Keith. Sherry could see the wheels turn in their small minds.

One of the flirtatious professors who'd hit on Garrett—in Sherry's presence—stopped at their table and gushed, "Is this charming child Nolan's soon-to-be son?"

Rarely catty, Sherry didn't know what made her introduce Garrett's son and then calmly go back to eating, instead of mentioning that she was kid-sitting. Sherry noted the jealous flare in Lynn Tabor's eyes before she whirled and swept out.

Hindsight being always better, an hour later Sherry wished she hadn't been so perverse. Especially when Angel recounted numerous new rumors flying around campus.

"Taking Keith to dinner with the kids and me explained why the big man gave you his house key," Angel lectured. "Showing up with him for breakfast at the staff hangout is like flaunting that you and Lock are having an affair."

"Get real, Angel. They're the same gossips who labeled me a man-hater before Lock came on board."

"Right. Which is why these juicy tidbits are so easily spread. They see this hot new jock dean thawing a formerly cold babe."

Sherry stowed her purse. She laughed, shaking her head.

"Boss, you are one naive lady. Kill these rumors now or they'll get uglier."

"After tonight I'm sure they'll die a natural death. Garrett is going to the Conways' harvest party with Yvette. Keith and I plan to hit the arcades."

Angel gazed down her pert nose and slapped the mail on Sherry's desk. "Why didn't you say so before I got all wound up?"

"It's therapeutic to let off steam. Now your mind won't be stuck on silly rumors while you transcribe these three tapes and run 150 copies of this test."

Snatching them up, Angel crossed her eyes, stuck out her tongue and flounced out.

Sherry buckled down to a busy day. She only saw Garrett once, after he'd called and given her fifteen minutes to dig out old figures on the cost of the Hub's special tutorials. He ran by at noon to pick up the twelve copies. Angel had gone to lunch. Otherwise, Sherry wouldn't have seen him at all.

"Our meeting is getting pretty vocal," he announced, then dashed off without filling her in on particulars.

Again Sherry realized she was relieved it was Garrett in there close to the flames instead of Kruger. Or her, she admitted ruefully. But, boy, wouldn't she like to be a mouse in the corner when the others discovered Lock wasn't the team player they thought they'd hired to slash away at the Hub.

For a moment her thoughts were consumed with

Garrett. The glint that came into his eyes when he faced a challenge. His rakish half smile when he won a point. His silky hair that her fingers itched to touch. *What prompted that?*

Angel's noisy return brought Sherry to her senses. Although she couldn't recall what she'd been doing before Garrett walked in.

Shaken, she decided to grab a late lunch in the cafeteria. Judging by the way the few remaining occupants stopped talking when she entered the staff lounge carrying her bowl of soup, Sherry surmised she'd been the topic of conversation. Not wanting to be put in a defensive position, she left and found a quiet bench in the courtyard. From there she hurried off to class and after that, didn't have a minute to herself.

Angel's computer was covered and the department silent by the time Sherry got back to her office to pick up her messages. One was from Ron, and she called him immediately. Good news—he'd convinced the Association to let Keith keep the dog.

"Yes!" Sherry waited until after she'd hung up to punch the air in victory. On the off chance she might catch Garrett at home or in his office, she dialed one after the other. As his home answering machine kicked in, she happened to glance at the clock.

"Yikes!" She scrambled to retrieve her purse. If the meeting was over, he and Yvette were probably at the Conway party. Rather than dwell on why that picture left a sour taste in her mouth, Sherry closed the office and rushed off to collect Keith.

NOLAN CAMPBELL touched Emily's arm and bent close to her ear to be heard above the band the Conways had hired. "Will you be okay on your own? I see Garrett and I want a word with him."

"Is there a problem with him serving as your best man?"

Nolan hesitated. "No. Maybe. I hope not." He angled across the patio, leaving his wife-to-be looking perplexed.

Garrett stood in the shadow of a giant oak tree, nursing the beer he'd accepted on arrival. Yvette wanted to dance. When he'd refused, she found another partner. That suited Garrett. He'd accomplished his goal in coming. Or rather, Sherry's goal. He'd met Randy Conway and decided his daughter was way too spoiled to make an appropriate friend for Keith. He and Curtis Jensen had hit it off. Garrett now possessed all of the facts needed to start Keith in soccer. Plus, he had a map to the mountain-biking trails.

Garrett glanced away from the dance floor as a tall form blocked his view. "Nolan." Straightening, Garrett offered his hand and a hearty smile.

"You son of a bitch." Nolan crowded Garrett and avoided his hand. "If I was a fighter, I'd mop up the dance floor with you."

Garrett's fingers curled into his side. He glanced over his shoulder to see if Nolan's steely gaze was meant for someone else, but encountered only tree trunk. "Hold on, buddy." Garrett stepped forward, absorbing the other man's anger. "A blind man could see you're ticked off. But you have me at a disadvantage." Garrett spoke softly and distinctly.

Jostled by couples coming off the small dance floor, Nolan jerked a thumb toward the side yard lit only by moonlight. "A deaf man could hear the stories floating around campus, *buddy*." He dragged out the word, leaving no doubt he considered it false. "Let's take a walk."

Shrugging, Garrett dropped his unfinished beer into the nearest trash can. When they reached the moon-dappled yard, he turned and hooked his thumbs in his belt. "Suppose you enlighten me."

"In a word, Sherilyn," Nolan snapped.

Garrett waited. His shoulders tensed as his eyes traced the crowd. Was she here? Heart tripping faster, he searched for a glimpse of her impossibly short hair, listened for the sound of her throaty laughter.

Nothing. Of course—she'd taken Keith to the virtual-reality arcade. "Look, man." He spoke more sharply than he'd intended. "Sherilyn volunteered to take Keith tonight. I tried to get her to come to the party, instead of me. She and Yvette ganged up."

"I'm not talking about her time with Keith. Hell, at her age, I don't even have the right to question the hours she spends in your bed. But I think you should know that on our conservative campus it's her reputation being shredded, not yours."

"What in hell are you talking about?" Garrett reared back.

"As if you didn't give her the key to your house in front of three of the biggest gossips on staff."

Garrett wiped at sweat that suddenly beaded his brow. "Is that what set you off? Our initial budget meeting ran late. I asked her to pick Keith up from day care. Well, I didn't ask. She offered, should the need arise. It did, suddenly. How *should* I have given her a key to my house? In a plain brown envelope by campus mail?"

"I suppose Sherry just happened by your place bright

and early this morning, too?" Camp said curtly. "Early enough to take Keith to breakfast at the Featherstone."

"I can't say 'happened by' is accurate. She had it in her head before she came over. She said Keith shouldn't stay alone while I went to a breakfast meeting. Listen, I planned to call a baby-sitting service from the get-go. But this arrangement apparently suits her—and Keith. Frankly, I'm not sure it's anyone else's business. Including yours, *buddy.*" Garrett thumped Nolan's chest twice with his forefinger.

"Sherry is family. You may get bored with the job and move on. She'll stay. In this town you don't live down gossip like having an affair with your boss."

"Should I take out a billboard saying we're not sleeping together?"

Nolan backed away from the fire in Garrett's eyes. "So…nothing's going on?"

"Nothing."

"Why?"

"Pardon me?" Garrett took an exaggerated whiff of Nolan's breath.

"I haven't even had a beer. Don't you find my sister attractive?"

"Yes, but—"

"But what? I never figured you'd believe that trash about her. She's no man-hater."

Garrett tipped his head and wiggled a finger in his ear. "Excuse me. First you threaten to tear me limb from limb for sleeping with your sister. Then you call me a jerk because I'm not. Which is it, pal?"

Nolan rammed both hands into his front pockets and gazed sheepishly at Garrett. "Guess I'm off base on both counts, huh?"

"Mmm." Garrett's reply lodged in his throat as he remembered the heated kiss they'd shared. And the lustful thoughts that kept him awake more nights than he cared to admit. Garrett chose not to tell Nolan just how attractive he did find his sister. Mostly because Garrett's feelings were muddled at best. She was beautiful. Passionate about things she believed in. Easy to talk to. And his son thought the world of her. Beyond that, Garrett wasn't willing to venture. Except he knew he'd rather be with her and Keith tonight than at this dance with her roommate.

Nolan clapped Garrett on the back. "Glad we had this talk. Are you ready to go back and party?"

"I'm ready to go home. If you'll excuse me, I need to tell Yvette."

"She won't leave. Yvette parties till the cows come home."

Garrett shrugged. "We came in separate cars. If she chooses to stay, it's okay by me."

Which didn't stop Yvette from pitching a fit, trying to change his mind. Garrett stood firm, although embarrassed by the scene. As he told his host and hostess goodbye, they made him feel persona non grata. Garrett worried he might inadvertently have added to the lies circling campus. On the other hand, he'd convinced Nolan there was nothing going on between him and Sherilyn. As her brother and a respected member of the faculty, he'd probably set about successfully squelching rumors.

CHAPTER ELEVEN

ON THE DRIVE HOME Garrett had time to think more clearly. Was Sherry aware of the talk? he wondered. He'd lashed out at Nolan in a knee-jerk reaction, but Garrett knew how conservative college administrators could be—and how they reacted to news of divorce or hanky-panky involving staff. They got nervous. Very nervous. And that didn't even address his problems if Carla's lawyer got wind of slanderous gossip.

So what? This was the nineties. Both he and Sherry were single and past the age of consent.

Consent to what? Garrett snorted. A body would think something had happened between them. One kiss did not an affair make. But there were kisses…and *kisses.*

The smart thing to do was end all contact between them outside of work. Sherry hadn't seemed enthusiastic about going with him to St. Louis, anyway. It'd be a simple matter to say he'd changed his mind.

Except he hadn't. "Dang." His son would be disappointed. Who was he kidding? *He* would be disappointed. Until this minute he hadn't realized how much he'd looked forward to Sherry's company on the return trip, after leaving Keith with Carla. Well, it couldn't be helped. As Nolan had so brutally pointed out, Sherry's reputation was on the line. Even conservative administrations looked the other way when male professors strayed. It might be the nineties, but the double standard hadn't changed.

Parking in his designated spot, Garrett turned off the lights and yanked on the emergency brake. He ripped off his tie and, as he did, experienced a quiver low in his stomach at the memory of Sherry watching him tie it this morning. Her golden eyes, had flowed hotly over his chest—and lower. Garrett would bet money she didn't have a clue she'd done it or that he'd noticed.

He'd noticed all right. It was all he could do to keep his hands off her.

He shrugged out of his suit jacket, picked up his briefcase and slammed the car door with more force than necessary. At the gate his steps faltered. Warm light spilled from the windows of his home. In Texas, Keith had always stayed at the sitter's. The house had always been dark when he came home late. Who'd have thought a few blessed lightbulbs would turn a man's guts inside out? Garrett pushed through the gate. If he'd suspected that, he'd have put a lamp on a damn timer.

The porch light, too, shone a welcoming beacon. Had Sherry left it on for him? Why were she and Keith home so early? He quickly checked his watch. Eleven. Not early at all. Where had the time gone? Although it had been after nine when he got to the party. The deans had hammered him all day and into the dinner hour, trying to wear him down and get him to pull the plug on the Hub. He'd trimmed so much fat from other beefy areas that he felt like the local butcher. Sherry would be pleased, he thought as he turned his key in the lock. He'd saved every blasted one of her services.

Stepping inside, Garrett sucked in the scent of

cinnamon and coffee. Another wave of nostalgia overtook his senses, one stretching back to the happy days of his youth. His dad, a writer, had worked at home. His mother always had a pot of coffee on, and she filled the house with the aroma of baked bread at least twice a week.

Until his stomach growled, Garrett had forgotten that he'd missed the barbecue portion of the party. All he'd had to eat since lunch was a handful of pretzels and half a beer. Bypassing the living room where the light was low, he headed for the kitchen, assuming that was where he'd find Sherry. The room was empty. He dropped his coat and case on a chair, staring at a coffee cake that sat cooling on the counter. Powdered sugar frosting still dripped onto the plate. He resisted swiping a finger through it for a taste and backtracked to the living room, calling Sherry's name softly as he went.

The minute he crossed under the arched doorway, Garrett saw why the house remained so still. She lay curled in the corner of his couch, feet bare, student papers floating unheeded from her lap to the floor. She'd fallen asleep.

A lump rose in his throat at the homey picture she presented. A half-full cup of coffee rested on a coaster. The lamp, though low, glinted off red and gold highlights in her sable hair. On a whim Garrett leaned down to see if the thick lashes that lay against her cheeks were a mix of colors, too. With her face shadowed by the sofa's winged back he wasn't able to tell. He did know that up close her skin reminded him of vanilla ice cream.

Twice he reached out to touch her cheek. Twice he drew back and watched the faint rise and fall of her breasts. She slept, lips slightly parted. But no sound whispered through them. She looked like a waif, her face without makeup, hair feathered carelessly around it.

Garrett shifted on the balls of his feet. It felt as if unseen fingers clutched his windpipe, forcing his breath out in ragged spurts.

Sherry stirred. Her eyelids fluttered open. Groggy with sleep, she sensed a presence. *An intruder?* Panic welled in her throat. Then she saw a dark shape looming over her. Rearing back, she screamed. She felt a textbook she'd been using earlier topple from her lap. Papers crunched under her feet as she tried to escape the hands reaching out to her—to clamp across her mouth. Her heart hammered wildly, deafeningly, in her ears. A second scream built. Fear tasted metallic on her tongue.

"Easy, easy." Garrett took his hand from her mouth and lifted her free of the books and papers scattered around her. "Don't scream," he said gruffly, tucking her face against his chest and her head beneath his chin. "It's me, Garrett. The last thing I wanted was to scare you. But you'll wake Keith." Smoothing a hand up and down Sherry's shuddering back, he slowly rocked from side to side.

She felt her heart drop from a gallop to a canter as she absorbed the heat pulsing through Garrett's shirt-front. A shirt that tickled her nose and crinkled crisply in her ear. She should say something to let him know he hadn't permanently warped her psyche. But lethargy seeped into her bones. She felt giddy and weightless, and closed her eyes again.

"Sherilyn? Are you all right?"

Nodding dumbly, Sherry wasn't even aware that her

arms were locked in a stranglehold around his neck. Because his worried questions beat rhythmically against her eardrums, she curved away from him with a sigh. "You scared me into next Juvember." Loosening her grip, she slid to her feet. "I'll live. You must wonder what kind of sitter falls asleep on the job. Lord! A burglar could have waltzed in and walked off with the silver."

A shaky laugh rumbled from Garrett's throat. "You're safe there. The silver went with Carla. As did any crystal, china and linens. Not that we had much. We were both struggling college students. Frankly, the pieces we received as wedding gifts looked out of place in our dinky apartment. I was just glad she left Keith's crib and chest of drawers." His thumbs scraped lightly over her jaw, while his gaze meandered lazily over her sleep-flushed features.

More conscious now, Sherry digested what he'd just said. Some of those wedding gifts must have come from *his* friends and family, and Carla took them all? When she'd counseled divorced wives who poured their hearts out in her office at the Hub, not once had she thought of an ex-husband's needs. Her focus had been on securing a workable household for the displaced mom and kids. Feeling guilty, Sherry stepped away from Garrett. She rubbed at goose bumps that rose on her bare arms.

"What's wrong? Did I hurt you when I yanked you off the couch?" He brushed her fingers aside and inspected her upper arms.

His warm breath skittered across her skin. Laughing nervously, she massaged away a shiver. "Garrett? Why did your lawyer let Carla take so much when you were the one left to provide a home for Keith?"

At the time of his divorce, he and Carla had shared a lawyer to cut costs. A lawyer *she'd* found. Too late, Garrett realized the man was her friend, not his. The one-sided disbursement of joint goods had been a sore point for a long time. One he never talked about. He couldn't think why he'd brought it up now. Garrett thought he'd finally evolved beyond the anger.

"We split six years ago. Maybe I don't have silver and maybe the furniture doesn't get dusted regularly. But I'd gladly stack up Keith's home against any you care to show me."

"I never meant… Garrett, I'm sorry." She closed the distance between them. "Your place has what a child needs most—love." Turning from him, she began to collect her papers and pile them neatly. "Keith and I had a blast at the arcade tonight. He's dead-eye Dick with the control stick. No Tiger Woods at golf, I'm afraid," she said, chuckling at the memory. "Did you have fun at the Conways'?" she asked lightly.

He knelt to help her. "I may as well tell you. I suppose you'll hear, anyway. Your brother gave me kind of a hard time. Then Yvette wanted me to stay longer and I left early. She's…not pleased."

"Oh, Yvette blows up and gets over it. But Nolan? He's normally so laid-back. What set him off?"

"I…" Garrett got very precise straightening the edges of a stack of tests. "Rumors concerning you and me," he growled. "On campus. Have you heard them?" Setting the papers aside, he paced to the fireplace and back, massaging his neck.

She turned aside to keep Garrett from seeing the hot flush climbing up her neck. "A little over a year ago Nolan was dumped by his fiancée, who made some cutting remarks in front of staff. The whole thing got blown out of proportion. It was headline news around campus until the next rumor hit the fan. I give the latest gossip a week—two at most—to run its course."

Garrett shifted a picture of Keith that sat on the mantel. "It's my fault. I should have called you into my office to give you my house key." He was on the verge of telling her about his decision to avoid contact with her outside of work when she glanced up from stuffing some of the papers into her book bag.

"Don't be so quick to take all the blame, Garrett. This morning Lynn Tabor stopped by our table at the restaurant. She confused Keith with Mark. I said he was your son. I just neglected to add that I was doing you a favor running Keith to school."

"Lynn Tabor." Garrett groaned. "So she assumes all women are like her? I've never met anyone who comes on so strong—except for Yvette. I've uninvited Lynn to my house twice. I've started keeping a list of excuses so I don't screw up and do something stupid like kill off my grandfather twice."

Sherry's eyes darkened sympathetically. "I know how Lynn is. She says vile things about people. She loves to stir the pot. Yet I deliberately let her think the worst. If I could take it all back, I would."

Garrett found himself growing angry at Lynn and those who listened and believed her lies. Lynn had probably fueled the first rumors he'd heard about Sherilyn. And Sherilyn had never acknowledged that the stories hurt her. But it didn't take a Rhodes scholar to see how vulnerable she was. Now he was glad he hadn't brushed her off. "You're right, Sherilyn. Campus rumors are shortlived. What do you say we don't let on we've heard them? Hey, join me for a cup of coffee and a slice of that cake some good fairy left in my kitchen. And I'll give you the best news you've heard all day."

A sunny smile brought a dimple to her cheek. "You saved the Hub?" Her shaky question vibrated with hope.

Garrett loved to see the eager anticipation flood her face and brighten her jewel eyes. He was tempted to drag out his response. But the breathless way she danced toward him, a bundle of nervous energy, had him reaching for her and blurting out the truth. "The budget committee didn't like leaving the Hub funding in, but I'm well within the parameters they set for total dollars. Outside of finalizing, it's a done deal."

Sherry threw her arms around his neck. Elated, she rained kisses on his face.

Tongue cloven to the roof of his mouth, Garrett could do little but grin like a fool. Encircling her with his arms was automatic. She made his head swim with the smell of lilacs and shampoo and something he'd begun to recognize as her special womanly scent. All his good intentions to keep a distance between them evaporated like smoke.

He kissed her back, at first matching her soft child-like pecks. Next came slower but as yet impersonal kisses between friends. Then, holding her head in both his hands, Garrett touched Sherry's lips with his tongue and dived into her mouth, kissing her the way a man kisses a woman he wants in his bed. It'd been so long since he'd allowed himself to feel the urge, the truth momentarily escaped him.

Sherry didn't realize she'd been waiting for a repeat performance of the last time they kissed until her fingers framed his face and she strained on tiptoe to feel the satisfying friction of her breasts against his chest—didn't realize it until a fire ignited in her belly, creating a need like none she'd ever experienced. It wasn't that she'd had no prior experience with men, as some on campus hinted. More that she'd never allowed herself to let go. With Garrett it was different. He made her feel boneless, made her lose control. She couldn't hang on to a single solitary thought.

It seemed inevitable that they'd stumble toward the couch in an ungainly crablike walk. Sherry's blouse and bra landed in a heap on the papers she'd so neatly stacked.

Garrett's white shirt hung off his shoulders, opened down the front to expose his broad muscled chest. Yet the sleeves remained fastened at his wrists because both he and Sherry were impatient to feel his lips on her breasts. She moaned at the pleasure that raced through her.

Time held no meaning until the grandfather clock standing at the foot of the stairs chimed twelve. Garrett broke away, dragging in ragged breaths as the sound clanged inside his head. Sliding his thumbs over the peaks of Sherry's nipples, he took pleasure in the way she shuddered. His gaze left her swollen lips and smoky eyes to travel over pale skin illuminated in the glow of the lamp. A lamp that also highlighted the wooden banister that led to the loft. A loft where Keith slept. Since the move, his son often fought bad dreams in the middle of the night.

What was he thinking? What if Keith—? Garrett catapulted off the couch and away from Sherry, unable even to even finish the thought.

"Garrett?" Her voice seemed to come from miles

away as he stood in the middle of the room clenching and unclenching his fists.

She sat up slowly. Noticing his harshly set jaw, she grabbed for her blouse. Heat blazed up her neck and stung her cheeks as she shrugged into the sleeves. Unable to look at Garrett, she fumbled with the buttons. Before she had them all fastened, she wadded up her bra and stuffed it deep in her jeans pocket. Why didn't he say something? He was obviously drowning in remorse. What was the protocol in a situation like this? Should she laugh it off and leave? And then tomorrow morning return to business as usual? As she gathered books and papers, her hands shook noticeably.

All at once Garrett landed on a knee at her feet. "Don't look like that. Like we did something horribly wrong." He cleared his throat. "I just… If Keith… What I'm trying to say is…I don't make this a habit." A wave of his hand encompassed the couch.

"If you think it's my normal modus operandi," she said hotly, "you're mistaken."

"I know that." He caught her fluttering hands and drew his thumbs back and forth across her knuckles.

She stared at his hands, remembering how she liked the feel of them on her skin. On her breasts. How, if things had gone further, they would have both been naked. Not something she cared to have Keith see any more than his father did. They were friends, she and Keith. Sherry knew the boy was confused about his mother's sudden appearance in his life. Confused by her marriage to a man he didn't like. Keith was pretty vocal about not liking it when Yvette kissed his dad. What if…?

"Garrett." Her voice caught. "I'd never do anything

to hurt Keith. This is my fault. I was deliriously happy that you'd saved the Hub. Things got out of hand."

Garrett absorbed her precise little statement. He felt like shaking her until she admitted the truth. But reason stole over him. Letting it go for the moment made sense. He acknowledged what they both knew—that Sherry had become Keith's rock. A liaison between himself and her was trouble looking for a place to happen.

"You're right." He cleared his throat. "You have my word this won't occur again. I hope you're not going to let one lapse on my part affect your relationship with Keith."

She shook her head, not trusting herself to speak.

"Good. So, now shall we have coffee and a slice of that cake?"

"I, ah…no. Have some if you'd like. Or save it for breakfast. It's late. I need to get home, Garrett."

Almost relieved—because he didn't know how he'd have managed to keep his hands to himself as they sat knee to knee at his table—he escorted her to the door. "You'll still go to St. Louis on Saturday? Keith's counting on it."

She nodded. "But it'd be better not to spread the news around. There's no sense causing unnecessary talk."

"I agree." He said it easily, knowing he'd deal later with the lead sinker in his stomach. "I'd walk you home, except if Keith woke up to an empty house, he'd panic."

"No need to feel obliged. I am capable of looking after myself."

"When you care about someone's welfare, it's not an obligation."

Sherry had no comeback for that. She knew Garrett

stood in the doorway and watched her walk all the way home. Twice she battled the urge to turn around and wave, but didn't trust herself not to run back and make a mockery of both their trite proper speeches.

Fighting raw emotion, she unlocked her door, stepped inside and tripped over an array of boxes. Then a sudden blaze of light made her blink in surprise.

Yvette crossed Sherry's line of vision and slammed a stack of Tupperware into one of the boxes. "Well, well, well." She circled Sherry, inspecting her disheveled appearance. "So Garrett left the party early for a quick roll in the hay with his so-called baby-sitter. Wait till everybody on campus hears that Ms. Goody Two-shoes has feet of clay, after all." She ended her tirade with a bitter laugh and called into the kitchen, "Lorraine, come here. This you won't want to miss."

Sherry bit back a groan when the flight attendant who lived a few doors down materialized in the archway. Sherry realized she must look a mess. There was nothing she could do to salvage that situation. Her only avenue was to divert attention from herself. "Care to tell me what's going on?"

"I'm moving in with Lorraine."

"Not with my Tupperware," Sherry said. "I sat through all those parties and shelled out my cash. You never went."

Lorraine smiled. "Because there weren't any men. Come on, Yvette. Let Sherry have her bowls. Neither of us cooks, anyway."

"I figure this stuff's community property." Yvette closed the lid to the box.

"For crying out loud," Sherry exploded. "This isn't a divorce." The minute she said it, Sherry felt a wrench.

As if she heard the bonds of a friendship tearing. "Yvette, look at us. Are we going to let a man drive us to catfights?"

"Garrett's not the Judas—you are, Ms. I'll-never-need-a-man. I, at least, don't pretend to be something I'm not. Let's go, Lorrie." Yvette latched on to the doorknob. "I'll pick up my stuff tomorrow after *she* goes to work."

Sherry stood amid the half-packed cartons for a long time after the two women left. Yvette's barb had hit its mark. Sherry took pride in doing for herself, not depending on a man. She'd taken basic courses in carpentry and auto mechanics. One of her strongest beliefs was that women should have the integrity not to change themselves for men or compromise their own principles. Was she guilty of that herself? She'd have to watch herself around Garrett Lock. She'd let a man she barely knew turn her inside out and upside down.

She went to bed vowing to keep him at arm's length from this day forward.

GOOD PLAN. And one that seemed to work, because it was as if Garrett went to work the next day having made the same vow. He took care not to single Sherry out in a department meeting where he discussed the budget.

She didn't know what arrangements he'd made for Keith, but Sherry didn't see Lock for the remainder of the week. Friday morning, Sherry remembered she hadn't told Garrett that Ron had okayed their keeping Rags. Rather than phone him, she dictated a crisp note. So crisp, Angel remarked on it when she brought the memo in to be signed.

"You and Macho Man had a fight, huh?" Angel stacked the incoming mail.

"I don't know what you mean," Sherry said tersely. "He's our boss. Kindly refer to him as Dean Lock. My superior is all he's ever been."

"Yeah, sure."

"Excuse me?" Sherry glowered at her.

"Nothing," Angel said. "Sheesh. I believe you, I believe you."

"Good. Then go out and squelch the gossip about us."

"No need. Everybody's talking about Trudy Morrison now."

"Trudy? That nice Trudy from English?"

"She's pregnant. No dad in sight."

Sherry schooled her features. She hated the way gossip streaked around their campus.

"You already knew," Angel accused her. "And you didn't tell me?"

"I didn't know. But if she is pregnant—which I doubt—it's her business."

"You're such a killjoy lately. Why don't you just screw Macho Man and get it out of your system? Maybe you'd quit being a grouch."

"What?" Sherry dropped the microphone to her Dictaphone. It bounced twice before she regained possession of it.

Angel tossed her blond braid over one shoulder. "Oops. 'Scuse me, boss lady." She snatched up the correspondence Sherry had signed and ran. "I hear the telephone."

Sherry glanced at her call commander. Not a light blinked. Still, feeling more than a little embarrassed, she let Angel go. If it was that obvious she was frustrated, she simply had to hide it better—and that meant keeping her distance from Lock.

She might have stuck to her resolve if he hadn't popped into her office at twelve, when Angel and both clerks were at lunch. Attached to the phone, Sherry watched him stride to her window and stand looking out over campus, his hands buried in the pockets of tight, dry-cleaner-creased jeans.

Swallowing fast to rid herself of the pain that suddenly attacked her throat, Sherry abruptly terminated the call. "Dean Lock," she managed, "is something wrong?"

He turned slightly, light and shadows playing over his deeply scored cheeks, blue eyes almost indigo in the late-autumn sun. "I promised Keith we'd meet Nolan, Emily and the kids at the high-school football game tonight. President Westerbrook has invited all the deans to his house for cocktails. He's hosting an administrative contingent from Norway. They're here to set up a student-exchange program."

Sherry waited, certain he'd eventually get to the point.

He raked long fingers through already skewed hair. "I'd ask Nolan to pick Keith up from school, but he's not authorized. Not only that, I got your memorandum concerning Rags. When I leave Westerbrook's, I should go by an all-night market and buy dog food, a collar and a doggie bed, if they have such a thing."

When he gazed at her expectantly, Sherry cut through his roundabout speech and ventured a guess. "Would you like me to collect Keith from day care?"

"Would you?"

"You have to ask? Shall I take him to the game? Or would you rather we swung by a pet store?"

"Do you mind going to the game? I'd like to surprise him with the dog myself."

Sherry forgot her promise to be reserved. "I love

football. And I hate going alone. So, Keith and I'll meet you back at your place about ten?"

"Good. Great." He grinned. "Keith has missed you, Sherilyn." He stopped short of saying he had, too.

"I've missed him." Her eyes lingered on Garrett, then she hurriedly glanced away.

"Look, this is stupid. You're still going with us to St. Louis tomorrow, aren't you?"

"Won't you need me to go by and check on Rags?"

"He'd better be okay by himself for a day, or I'm in big trouble. Anyway, Keith's spending the weekend with Carla. I'll drive up Sunday afternoon again and pick him up."

Her heart beat a light tattoo. "I did promise you a tour of St. Louis."

"And breakfast at the Featherstone."

"Rain check? That'd be sure to cause talk."

"I'm inclined to say who cares? Logically, I know you're right. Okay, we'll leave half an hour earlier and stop at a café on the outskirts of town."

"You're sure we won't be compromising our work relationship?"

"I am. And Sherilyn…I feel bad about Yvette moving out. Are you able to make the rent?"

"Yes." It was kind of him to ask.

He rocked forward on his boots. "What we do on our own time is nobody else's business." He looked fierce.

Her palms grew damp at the thought of what Garrett's statement suggested. "Agreed," she whispered. "I'd be happy to walk Rags and feed him if I get home from work before you do."

He dealt her a strange look. "Taking care of Rags is going to be Keith's responsibility."

"Definitely. But I'm offering to help if you get tied up here."

"Accepted. Now I'd better scram before the little pitchers with big ears get back."

Grinning, Sherry trailed him to the door. And she gave it her all to make sure Angel didn't see she was on pins and needles for the rest of the day. She left on time, making no mention to Angel about picking up Keith to go to the game.

Keith was thrilled to see her. They had a good time at the game. Or they did until Emily asked Sherry to drop by the next day for a fitting on her bridesmaid's dress.

"How about Sunday after church? I'm busy tomorrow."

"Working again? Sherry, when will you learn to say no?"

Sherry hadn't realized Keith was listening. He stuck his head around Mark. "Sherry's going to St. Louis tomorrow with Dad and me. I hafta stay through Sunday, but Dad's coming back home tomorrow night."

"Really?" Emily and Nolan chorused. Both studied her with exactly the same gleam in their eyes.

"No big deal," Sherry said as calmly as she could. "Keith's visiting his mom. Garrett asked if I'd give him a quick tour of St. Louis." She held her breath, glad when the home team made a touchdown that claimed Em and Nolan's attention. It ended the game and the crowd started to disperse. Cheers for the winners effectively cut off further talk. They'd parked in different lots, so they said goodbye at the gate.

Garrett was home with Rags and all his new paraphernalia when Sherry walked Keith to the door. Although Garrett invited her inside for coffee, she saw Yvette andLorraine sauntering down the walkway, so she declined.

"I'll see you tomorrow," she murmured. "I don't want to intrude on your special night with Keith."

"Okay." Garrett didn't understand her refusal and was disappointed. He named a time to leave in the morning, then wondered as he watched her disappear into the star-studded night if she really wanted to go to St. Louis with him, or if she felt obligated because he was her boss. Like he'd felt obligated to attend Westerbrook's gathering this evening.

Garrett tucked the notion away, planning to ask her pointblank the next morning.

A plan he immediately forgot when he found her waiting beside his truck first thing Saturday.

They enjoyed a leisurely breakfast at a truck stop on the freeway. Keith bubbled over with excitement. He talked constantly about Rags. But once they reached St. Louis, he fell silent. The change was so obviously connected to his visit with Carla that Sherry felt compelled to offer him some encouragement.

"I'll bet your mom has wonderful things planned for the two of you, tiger." Squeezing his shoulder, Sherry bolstered him with a big smile as Garrett drove past the Gateway Arch. "Look. There's a tram to the observation deck. You feel like you're up in the clouds. It's clear today, so you'll be able to see quite far."

Keith slumped lower in the seat. When they turned down a street of stately homes, the boy slid his sweaty hand into Sherry's. "Will you walk me to the door?" he asked her in a stage whisper.

"Oh, Keith." Sherry darted a quick glance at Garrett.

"It's not my place. But I'll tell you what. If this good weather holds, Monday after school I'll take you skating in the park."

"Okay," he said. "Can Rags go, too?"

"Sure. Why not? You have a leash, I hope?"

"I got one," Garrett said, making a wide swing into a circular drive.

Sherry gazed at the manicured lawn and the huge columns supporting a pristine white structure. She couldn't help it—she whistled through her teeth.

Garrett laughed and so did Keith. Sherry kept her next thought to herself—that the place looked like a funeral home.

She waited in the truck, but couldn't help noticing Garrett's tense walk as he led his resistant child up the marble steps to the door. After what seemed to Sherry like a long time, a beautiful woman answered their knock. When Garrett gestured and the woman assumed a rigid stance, Sherry surmised she was viewing Carla. A blade twisted in her heart. Garrett's ex was gorgeous. He must feel a little bad about losing her. Trying to ignore that disconcerting thought, Sherry turned her gaze elsewhere.

She gave a start when she unexpectedly heard a sharp thump in the pickup's bed. A second later Garrett jerked open the driver's door. He landed in the seat with a *whomp,* and after two twists of the key, ground the gears.

"I could murder her," he snarled, backing out too fast. He jammed on the brakes and stopped abruptly at the street. "Something's come up at work again. Carla can't have Keith stay tonight, after all. In fact, she ordered me to pick him up no later than four." Looping his arms over the steering wheel, he sent Sherry an anxious look.

"Do you mind staying in town for the whole day? It'll mean getting home late."

Sherry shook her head. "So that was Keith's suitcase you threw in back?" she asked insipidly.

"Yeah." He shrugged. "I have to admit Keith wasn't exactly heartbroken. So, what do you want to do?"

"You might be sorry you asked. I need a slip and shoes to go with my dress for the wedding. Since we're here for the duration with all these beautiful malls, you can take me shopping. I could use some help picking out a gift for Nolan and Emily, too."

"You're a good sport, Sherry. I had visions of you throwing a fit. That's what Carla would have done if the situation had been reversed."

Suddenly Sherry's outlook got a whole lot brighter. Garrett didn't sound like a man pining for his ex. Not even a little.

CHAPTER TWELVE

AUTUMN LEAVES had begun to drop from the trees and lay strewn about. Sherry loved to crunch them beneath her feet. The sun straggled through the trees, but there was a nip of fall in the air. "Are you ready for Halloween?" Sherry asked Garrett as they wandered along the pathways of Laumeier Sculpture Park, another pastime she enjoyed. It pleased her that he'd asked to see the work of artists on display there before they went on to the mall.

He caught a red-gold leaf that floated into his hand. Smiling, he tucked it behind Sherry's ear. "Keith's school sent a note home saying the room mothers host a small party on Friday. Will our complex get trick-or-treaters? Mark asked Keith to make the rounds with them in your folks' neighborhood. I'm not keen on them going alone. Figured I'd hang out in the background with a flashlight."

"We have very few kids show up in our area," she said, retrieving the brightly colored leaf and twirling it between her fingers.

He watched her kicking through leaves like a kid. Grasping the hand that didn't hold the leaf, Garrett toyed with the pearl ring on her finger. "Come with us. Nolan said your mom's making fresh doughnuts." He made it sound like the biggest incentive.

Sherry savored the feel of their joined hands, liking the sensation. "Dad makes cider every year, too. When we were kids the whole family fixed popcorn balls. I hope Emily and Nolan keep up the tradition in their home. This year Mom'll go all out for Mark and Megan. I predict she'll be in a blue funk after the wedding, when they finally move into Nolan's house."

Sherry stopped to stare at a bronze sculpture, but Garrett knew she was seeing a time gone by. "So, will you go?" he pressed, carrying her fingers to his lips.

She tried unsuccessfully to snatch her hand back. "I don't want to intrude."

"Sherilyn, it's your family. If anyone's intruding, it's Keith and me."

"Not true," she said. "You were invited. Although—" she grinned "—I could crash the party." She let him keep her hand, after all, and they swung their clasped hands jauntily as they found the next statue.

"The close-knit family you have is what I wanted for Keith. But my mom and dad retired to Florida before I got married. Carla was raised in foster homes. And now," he said broodingly, "I've left the few roots I'd put down in Huntsville."

"So is this a permanent move?" Sherry asked, trying not to sound personally interested. "Some of the staff think you have your eye on a vice presidency at a more prestigious college, and Wellmont is just a stepping stone."

"Me, a VP?" A rumbling laugh shook Garrett's chest. "At Westerbrook's last night, someone introduced me as Wellmont's renegade dean."

"Probably Hadley from Accounting, right?" At his nod, she made a rude noise. "If brains were made of leather, he wouldn't have enough to saddle a flea."

Garrett laughed harder. "Amen to that. Are you sure you weren't born in Texas? You're full of country sayings."

"I listen to country music."

"You do? Something else we have in common."

The way he said something *else* in common chased hot and cold prickles up her spine. Here she thought it was nothing more than basic sexual attraction they shared—which, according to her caseload of displaced wives, faded with the speed of light. The more time she spent around Garrett, the more she realized he possessed a sensitivity missing in other male acquaintances. For one thing, he really listened to a person.

Sherry imagined them being friends, as well as lovers. *Lovers. Will you listen to that.* She stumbled to a stop and gazed across the park at nothing, shocked that she, of all people, contemplated such a thing. *Well, why not?*

Garrett leaned in front of her so he could look her in the eye. He traced the back of one finger down her pink cheek. "Before you hop a shooting star and zap another trillion light years away, how about lunch?"

"Sorry." She blushed, thankful he didn't probe her errant thoughts. "I, ah… Shall we eat at the mall? Then we'll be handy to buy the wedding gift and my shoes."

"I had something more clandestine in mind. Lunch on a lazy riverboat, maybe?"

"Cruises that serve food are overnighters. I've never done one, but I'm told visitors book well in advance. Day jaunts are narrated. If you'd rather do that than shop, you can drop me at the mall and pick me up later."

Garrett curbed his disappointment as he steered her toward his pickup with a hand at the small of her back. "I can't believe you've lived here all your life and have never gone on a dinner cruise. If Keith ever spends a weekend with Carla, you and I should go." Before he'd made his suggestion, Garrett hadn't realized how it'd sound. Sherry's sharp intake of breath told him clearly.

Her heart somersaulted in its rush to accelerate. She'd never gone on a dinner cruise because she'd never met anyone she cared to be confined with for a night of moonlight, champagne and intimacy. Not until now. Now her blood sang at the prospect. "I'd like that," was her only admission.

Garrett glanced away, barely trusting himself to nod. As if both shied from what was happening, they broached again the subject of grabbing sandwiches at the mall.

Right after they ate, Sherry led Garrett on a marathon shopping tour. He surprised her again by actively helping choose Emily and Nolan's wedding gift. And he never once griped about trekking from store to store. Eventually they found the perfect thing—a copper pot to sit on the vintage icebox Emily had refinished.

"You deserve a medal," Sherry said as he carried their packages to his truck. "I didn't hear a single complaint. But maybe you're in shock," she teased.

"It's been five years since I shopped with a woman," he mused. "I can't believe I'd forgotten how intense an experience it is. After my divorce, my mom decided to help me refurbish, and by the week's end my boots had holes in their soles. I tend to shop on a need-to-have basis and avoid malls like the plague."

"You mean your girlfriends never dragged you mall-hopping? That's un-American."

He held the passenger door open and gave her a hand up, debating whether or not to tell her that girlfriends had been scarcer than duck's teeth. He wouldn't want

Sherry to get the idea he was weird or anything. On the other hand, if he insinuated he did things other than shop with his women friends, she would definitely get the wrong picture. So he smiled in a way he hoped said, *Don't ask me to kiss and tell,* and closed her car door solidly. They drove to collect Keith in companionable silence.

Sherry expected Keith to be elated after a day with his mom, and chatty. But the boy slid between Sherry and his father, crossed his arms and sat like a lump.

She finally broke the ice. "How was your trip to the Money Museum?"

Keith hiked a shoulder.

"That's no way to answer a lady, son," Garrett rebuked gently.

"Crawford 'splained too much. He thinks I'm dumb 'cause I don't care where money comes from."

Garrett's fingers tightened on the wheel. Crawford was a dolt, but Garrett knew from experience that if he said anything to Carla, she'd defend the banker to the nth degree. She'd twist things to make it all Garrett's fault. *He* didn't discipline Keith, or *he* spoiled the boy and let him run wild. Garrett had heard it before. To make matters worse, now Sherry was tossing him veiled glances, as if she expected him to do something about Crawford. Life had been so much simpler before Carla surfaced again.

Sherry decided Garrett wasn't going to get involved. "So, Keith," she said, "what about the phony money? Weren't the counterfeit bills cool?"

"They were okay. Crawford got super bummed out when I said they all looked alike."

Garrett scowled. "Where was your mother during all this?"

"She hadda go to the bank to make a big loan."

The muscles in Garrett's jaw flexed. Sherry marveled at his control. If it was up to her, she'd go back and have a talk with Carla. The more Sherry chewed on the reality, however, the more she saw that Garrett was caught between a rock and a hard place. He had Carla's attorney going for his jugular. Just now she held all the advantages. Sherry had witnessed the reverse enough times.

She tried her best to cheer Keith up. "Rags will love having you come home a day early, sport."

Keith's spirits perked immediately. "Go faster, Dad. I don't want Rags to think we left him."

"He'll be fine, Keith." Talk shifted to the dog until they were about a block from home. Suddenly Garrett asked Keith, "Did your mom or Crawford give you a date for your next visit?"

"Mom's gonna call you before Halloween. Crawford doesn't approve of Halloween. I wanna go trick-or-treating with Mark. I don't gotta visit Mom, do I?"

"No. Not on Halloween. Crawford is—"

"Entitled to his opinion," Sherry inserted. She knew Garrett would regret badmouthing Keith's stepdad once he stopped to reconsider. "Hey, I thought of a place I think you'd like, Keith. Maybe sometime your mom can take you to see Mark Twain's boyhood home in Hannibal. It's fun climbing to the top of Cardiff Hill. And I love the tour of the Tom Sawyer caves. Are you familiar with Tom Sawyer and Huck Finn, Keith?"

"Yep. Dad read me the stories. Why don't *we* go? Huh, Dad?"

The possibility germinated. "Yeah. How about next weekend?" Garrett sought Sherry's eyes. "Maybe Sherry'll invite Mark." Garrett had a method to his madness. The boys could explore while he got to spend more time with Sherry.

"Are you asking me to go, too?" She wasn't sure if that was what Garrett meant.

"I'm asking."

Sherry's nerves tingled. "I…well, yes, then." They made plans before parting outside Garrett's gate.

THE TRIP TO HANNIBAL ended up being one of the most wonderful dates Sherry'd ever had. Even though she'd suggested the trip to cheer Keith up, it had all the earmarks of a date. Garrett was attentive. He teased, and flattered and bought her souvenirs.

The boys loved the caves where Tom Sawyer and Becky Thatcher had supposedly been lost. They were decidedly less enthusiastic about the museum.

Garrett had hoped the near-vertical hike up Cardiff Hill would wear the boys out so they'd fall asleep on the way home and he could ask Sherry out again. But the adults were the ones who yawned repeatedly. Keith and Mark sat in the backseat of Sherry's car, plotting how much loot they'd collect trick-or-treating the following Saturday.

CLOUDS MOVED IN as Halloween approached. Miraculously the rain held off. At the elder Campbells' home that night, after the trick-or-treaters returned with pillowcases full of candy, Ben Campbell struck a match to the leaves he'd spent the day raking into a big pile. In spite of thick smoke, the revelers scooted close to the fire to toast hot dogs and marshmallows. Megan, who claimed to be too old for trick-or-treating, told ghost stories guaranteed to spook the boys. An occasional adult was also seen glancing over a shoulder into the darkness beyond the fire.

Pilgrim, Nolan's yellow Lab, and the Campbells' old dog, Murphy, frolicked with Rags. All swiped tidbits of hotdog here and there if anyone's guard dropped.

When at last the fire died, the adults reluctantly called it a day.

Keith scrambled over and hugged Sherry around the neck. "This is the bestest Halloween I've ever had. I love you," he said, fighting a sleepy yawn.

Seated next to Sherry, Emily jabbed Nolan in the ribs.

Sherry saw a telling look pass between them. She also saw Garrett stiffen. Surely he didn't think she'd set out to win his son's affections on purpose. After all, he was the one who'd bugged her to come tonight. Frankly, she'd thought Garrett had been angling for more than friendship on their trip to Hannibal. Obviously not. She must be the only one experiencing wild crazy dreams that tiptoed in at night to disrupt her sleep.

Emily snapped her fingers to jar Sherry from her trance. "I said, if you're free tomorrow night, could you meet me at the church? I have an appointment with a singer to choose songs for the wedding. Nolan says it's up to me. I'd like another opinion."

"Okay. Give me the address," Sherry said absently. "Is your church a drive from here?"

Emily gaped. "We're being married in Nolan's church. Y-your church," she stammered. "As a matter of fact, now it's Garrett and Keith's church, too."

Sherry felt sideswiped. She knew, of course, that Emily and the kids had been attending the family church. The church where her parents had exchanged wedding vows. Emily no longer had contact with her former in-laws or their church, so where else would she get married if not here? Still… Sherry didn't know why, but she'd always assumed she'd be the first Campbell of her generation to walk up that aisle. She acknowledged that it was a silly thought, considering her frequently stated assertions about marriage. And there wasn't even a groom in the offing!

Nan Campbell reached out to her suddenly pale daughter. "Sherry, are you ill? The hot dogs. Ben…" she said, helplessly imploring her husband.

"I'm fine." She would be—in a minute.

Nolan, blind to her feelings, teased her. "Not too late to make it a foursome, sis." He clapped Garrett on the back. "Two for the price of one. Ought to rock the hallowed halls of Wellmont, don't you think?"

Garrett surged to his feet. He ignored Nolan and thanked Sherry's folks for including him and Keith in the festivities. Which wasn't to say that Nolan's shot in the dark hadn't set wheels grinding in Garrett's mind.

Keith fell asleep on the drive home, allowing Garrett far too much time to dwell on Nolan's remark. He understood how others might assume a relationship had developed between him and Sherilyn. He'd spent a lot of time with her lately.

Or had Nolan been goading his sister just for the sake of goading? Clearly marriage was the last thing on her mind. At his heavy handed hint, she'd looked like someone forced to eat a pickle.

That started Garrett wondering how Sherilyn saw him. Only as someone to help her thumb her nose at those on campus who whispered that she hated men?

All the signs said no.

Maybe she just wanted a romp between the sheets. If so, he'd been obtuse. He *had* been the one to call a halt both times when the windows started to steam. Thinking back, Garrett realized a lot of repressed sexual interest smoldered inside each of them. He was tempted to let things play out. •

As he put Keith to bed, Garrett couldn't seem to shake the conviction that if he was smart, he'd forget about Sherry Campbell as anything but a colleague. Explicit scenes nagged him all night.

Next morning, Carla unwittingly offered Garrett opportunity to act on his imagination. She called to request or, rather, demand that he bring Keith to St. Louis the second weekend in November. Crawford's daughter was coming to town, Carla said. And Crawford's daughter had a son Keith's age.

Crawford was a grandpa? Garrett hung up, mulling that over. He didn't know why he'd thought Crawford had been eternally single when he met Carla. Maybe because he was so strict with Keith. Shouldn't a grandfather be better attuned to kids?

Garrett climbed into the shower, trying to keep his mind focused on Crawford's relationship with Keith. Unfortunately last night's dream intruded. A dream of Sherry and him on a moonlit Mississippi riverboat cruise. What had followed...well, it'd been incredible.

Would she go if he invited her? She ran hot and cold. But that time he'd suggested it, she actually sounded favorable.

It'd be a simple matter to phone and ask her. But dreaming of enticing Sherry into his bed was far easier than calling her and risking a no. While Keith ate breakfast, Garrett shut himself in his bedroom where he paced in front of the phone. He rehearsed his speech, yanked up the receiver, then dropped it back and sat down for a minute until his heart quit pounding like a jungle drum.

He reminded himself that good old Crawford hadn't let divorce deter him from pursuing another woman. That did it. Gut churning, head prepared for her refusal, Garrett dialed.

On her end, Sherry listened to his smooth proposition. She recognized it as a proposition because she'd received one or two before. But this was Garrett Lock, a man who just last night had turned seven shades of green at the mention of being involved with her.

Correction. That look—as if he'd sucked a lemon—came at the mention of *marriage*. What he proposed was a no-strings-attached overnighter on the *Ozark Queen*. Moonlight, wine and a night in the sack. At least that was how it sounded.

Sherry feigned a fit of coughing and excused herself to get a drink of water. As she slugged it down, she practiced saying no. It wasn't working. *God strike her dead, but she was going to accept.*

She drew a damp palm over her throat. "Sorry. My toast went down wrong. Two weekends from now, you say?" She cleared her throat. "Um, my calendar is clear." Did that sound worldly enough?

"It is?" Garrett felt like a dope for doubting. "Fine. Good," he managed, clamping down on the ambivalent feelings still churning in his stomach.

Sherry twisted the phone cord around and around her finger. Now what? Was this the time to mention clinical tests? Decide which of them would be responsible for birth control? She wound the cord so tightly it cut off her circulation. Then she chastised herself for acting cowardly. The importance of responsible sex was a drill she hammered relentlessly into students she counseled. In her field she discussed sex openly. But not, apparently, when it involved herself. Feeling the heat of embarrassment, she elected to forgo that discussion. Between now and then she'd drive to the next town and buy condoms.

Searching for a way to avoid the topic, she asked in her best counselor's voice, "How does Keith feel about spending two full days with Crawford?"

Garrett suffered a second stab of guilt. He couldn't very well admit that he hadn't informed his son yet. "About how you'd expect," he mumbled. "He hates leaving Rags."

"I'm sure my mom will dog-sit. Ah, um, I'd appreciate you not mentioning that I'm going with…that we're…"

"Hey, what do you take me for?" Garrett was impatient to get off the phone. All he could think was, What if there wasn't space on the boat after all this? "I, uh, hate to run, but I was just on my way out."

"Oh, sure. Bye then."

The minute Sherry disconnected, Garrett dived for the phone book. He didn't breathe again until the travel agent took his credit card numbers to confirm passage.

"So that's that," he said aloud, after completing the transaction. He managed his first deep breath that didn't sound like air escaping a slow-punctured tire. Dang, but he felt as if he'd just done something illicit. Which was stupid. They were both mature unattached adults. He'd even booked two rooms—in case Sherilyn chickened out. *He* certainly wouldn't.

Midweek, Garrett received an administrative memo from the president's office stating that a contingent from campus had to go to Jefferson City on Wednesday, Thursday and Friday of the following week. The purpose: to protest legislative budget cuts. Garrett frowned at a list topped by Sherry's name. Was she drafted or had she volunteered? Jefferson City was a fair drive. The team wouldn't be back until late Friday night. Did it mean she'd had second thoughts about their weekend trip?

"THESE SILLY MARCHES in the capital don't accomplish anything," Sherry complained to Angel as she assembled material to keep her classes occupied for the three days she'd be gone. "All we do is spin our wheels."

"You didn't volunteer to go?"

"I'd sooner eat worms."

Angel tapped a finger on the memo that had come to Sherry in the form of a command. "I guess the big man delegated you, then, huh? I notice *he's* not on the list."

"Garrett?" Sherry flushed, realizing she'd almost said he wouldn't since they had plans for the weekend.

Angel gave her a speculative look as Sherry hefted her briefcase and bag.

Last to board the van, Sherry was surprised to see mostly deans and a vice provost already seated. Who had included her with the bigwigs and why?

Could it be Garrett? Maybe he'd gotten cold feet about the weekend and figured if the committee returned late on Friday she'd opt out.

He didn't know her if he thought that. She always kept her commitments.

FRIDAY, WHEN SHE DRAGGED home at midnight, Garrett's house was dark. She'd accessed her office voice mail before boarding the van home. He'd left a cryptic message offering her a rain check. Oh, he sounded solicitous, but Sherry fancied she also heard a measure of relief in his voice. The jerk. Make her suffer with those pompous fools for three days, would he? All because *he* didn't have the guts to renege. Well, he could just tell her face-to-face. She fell into bed anticipating how floored he'd be to discover her, suitcase in hand, leaning against his pickup tomorrow.

If it killed her, she'd get up in time to do her hair and nails. A woman had her pride, after all. He'd never know she'd sprung for new clothes. Not that she'd actually planned to wear the sexy red nightie she'd bought spur-of-the-moment at an upscale boutique. But she *had* entertained notions of making Dr. Lock's ears smoke with the near backless, sizzling purple dress she'd purchased for the dinner cruise.

Sherry punched her pillow. She should have saved her money.

AT THE BREAK OF DAWN, Keith shuffled to the pickup ahead of Garrett. First to spot Sherry, he ran to her and enveloped her in a hug. "I heard Dad tell your mom you went to Jefferson City. She's keeping Rags 'cause Dad's gonna gamble on a boat this weekend." He hopped around and trampled on Sherry's toes. "I don't wanna visit Mom and Crawford. If you'n Dad are goin' on a boat, can I go, too? Please," he implored.

Garrett tossed two duffels into the back of the truck before laying a restraining hand on his exuberant son's head. His gaze skimmed Sherry's suitcase, then settled warmly on her face. "Welcome home. You look bright-eyed and bushy-tailed for having spent a week hassling our public servants."

Sherry searched for signs of displeasure in his eyes and saw none. The knots in her stomach unfurled. He did want her to go. Which meant he hadn't volunteered her, after all.

"Can I go, too? Can I, Dad? Can I?" Keith twirled under his father's hand, chanting his request like a mantra.

"Not this time, son. Hey, no long face. You're meeting Crawford's grandson. Your mom said Crawford bought tickets for all of you to see the Rams game."

Keith looked so terribly unhappy Sherry rushed to say, "Next week, if the weather's still good, how about if your dad and I take you someplace special?"

Her announcement piqued Keith and Garrett alike.

"Are you familiar with Precious Moments figu-rines?" When they both nodded, she boosted Keith into the pickup cab. Once they'd buckled in, she explained. "The artist has a chapel in Carthage. There's a park, gardens, a kid's castle. It's neat."

"A castle? Way cool! Can we go there, Dad?"

Garrett backed the truck out and pulled into the traffic. He waved to Lorraine, the flight attendant with whom Yvette now roomed. Sherry hadn't seen Yvette in more than a week. Odd…and disconcerting. They'd been friends so long. Lorraine had just climbed out of a cab. If she saw them, she didn't return the wave. Ob-viously the cold war continued.

Garrett didn't give it a second thought. "I've tenta-tively made other plans for next weekend, Keith. Nolan told me about the largest bass-fishing shop in the world. I have a hankering to buy a bass boat so Keith and I can do a little fishing," he told Sherry.

Keith clearly had a dilemma. "Me'n Dad love to fish," he said, appealing to Sherry with sorrowful eyes.

"No problem, sport. I know the shop he means. My dad and Nolan can get lost in it for days. Better take food and water," she teased.

"But the castle would be cool, too." Keith burrowed closer to Sherry's side. "It's fun when the three of us do stuff together. Ain't it, Dad?"

"Isn't," Garrett corrected softly. "And yes, I guess it is."

A gritty lump clogged Sherry's throat. The wistfulness in Keith's boyish voice and Garrett's deeper one forced her to examine some hard truths. She'd thought she had it all with her career and her independent life. She'd always said she didn't need love—and the things that usually went with it. Like marriage. She'd thought love was something you could control. Not long ago, Emily had tried to tell her that wasn't so; love had its own methods. She'd tuned Emily out.

Garrett gave up trying to sort out the series of dark looks on Sherry's face. She grew quieter and quieter the closer they got to St. Louis. After he'd walked Keith to Carla's door, he climbed back into the truck and sat drumming his fingers on the steering wheel. "Much as I'd like to go on the river cruise, it's your choice whether we go or not, Sherilyn."

She tensed. "I'm here, aren't I?" She hadn't meant to snap. It was just that confronting the way she felt— the way her *heart* felt—about Garrett Lock had sent her nerves into a tizzy.

"In body, maybe, but not in spirit."

Her eyebrows shot up. "If you've changed your mind, just say so."

Garrett patted his shirt pocket. "I bought *two* tickets."

"Would you feel less threatened if I paid for mine?"

He stopped drumming his fingers. "Me? I'm not. But you seem nervous as a goat on Astroturf," he said gruffly. More gently he admitted, "I booked two cabins."

That surprised her, since what she assumed he had in mind— Well, never mind what she assumed. She'd die before admitting she'd actually hoped for something more. "I understand the dinner cruise is considered quite romantic. Should be…fun."

He twisted the ignition key and the engine roared to life. "Yeah," he muttered.

Sherry couldn't be sure, but she thought she detected a tic near the corner of his left eye. Well, he needn't worry that she'd jump his bones.

Garrett parked in the lot next to the docked boat. They continued to sit, watching the river eddy out of sight past the huge boat. Several couples and a family of five headed up the gangplank. The normalcy of the scene released them both. As Garrett climbed out and went to check them in, Sherry waited by the river.

"I'll just put our bags in our rooms," he said on rejoining her. "Meet me middeck near the paddle wheel. The captain said it's a must for first-timers."

"Sounds fine. Oh, you'll need my room key." She pulled it from the packet he'd handed her.

"Listen." Garrett cocked an ear as he took the key. "Is that a live band?"

She leafed through a brochure. "A three-piece jazz

combo in the lounge. A dance band performs in the dining room tonight. If you'd rather hit the casinos like you told my mom, I'll be fine on my own."

"You're the one who said not to tell your folks the truth. Bring that brochure. We'll go to the lounge and discuss options after we shove off. I wouldn't mind trying the slots, but if you're opposed to gambling, I'm okay with doing…whatever."

"I'm not a prude, Garrett. Some of us go into Kansas City for the jazz festival every year. We hit at least one river casino then."

"I like the jazz classics. I'm not much on the really experimental stuff."

"The oldies are my favorite, too." She hooked a thumb toward the lounge. "That kind. Hurry. I hate to miss that trumpet," she said, tapping a toe.

He grinned. Then unexpectedly he curved a finger and traced her chin with a knuckle. "Thanks for not begging off. I hoped you'd come."

She tilted her head, trapping his palm in the curve of her neck. "You might have said so. Bad communication causes most of the problems between men and women. I like honesty—things laid on the line."

He nodded, withdrew his hand, picked up the bags.

As he jogged off, Sherry gazed after him, paying scant heed to being jostled. An errant cloud drifted over the sun, blocking the warmth, and a breeze ruffled her short hair, chilling her bare arms. That was how fairies delivered premonitions, according to Grandmother Campbell. And premonitions never meant good news.

Donning a light jacket, Sherry scampered downstairs where she worked her way through a milling throng of people to wait, as Garrett had directed, near the stern.

The engines gave a mighty rumble somewhere deep in the bowels of the boat. The paddle wheel rocked and shivered. Where was Garrett? He wanted to see this. Sherry didn't think he was going to make it in time.

He surprised her, slipping up behind her to encircle her waist with his arms just as the giant paddle slowly began to turn.

Those standing close to the wire cage, like Sherry, were sprayed. "Sorry," she gasped as she jumped back and landed on Garrett's toe. "I wasn't expecting a shower."

Laughing, he swiped at droplets dripping from her chin into the V of her blouse. The heels of his hands accidentally brushed the tips of her breasts. Both noticed how they peaked. Garrett's laughter died. He stepped to one side and rammed his hands into his jeans pockets.

As the boat churned into the middle of the river, most of the bystanders left. Sherry hovered near the rail listening to the fading footsteps.

"Look." Garrett cleared his throat. "We're no strangers to the birds and the bees. A man and woman can't always dictate how their bodies react."

"I'm the counselor here," she observed dryly. "You're the sociology prof."

He stroked his chin with forefinger and thumb in a parody of professorial mannerisms. "Okay. So when's the next lesson, Doc?"

"Lesson's over. Next on the agenda is a drink and checking out the band that's bringing down the rafters in the lounge."

"Do boats have rafters?" Garrett asked, the beginnings of a smile teasing his lips.

"Beams, then," she said, dragging him up the steps. "Whatever. Are you always so technical?"

"No," he shouted, guiding her toward a table near the band. "Only when I know it's going to get a reaction."

"For that, you'd better buy me a beer."

Glad to have her joking and smiling again, Garrett snapped his fingers to attract a waiter and ordered two dark drafts.

They each had another before the band broke. And one apiece in the casino where they lost two rolls of quarters to the slots. Neither cared, because they'd become bonelessly mellow. It was Sherry who pointed out that they should go back to their cabins and dress for dinner. Garrett would have been satisfied to stay and watch the expressions crossing her face when she won, lost or broke even.

Forty minutes later, when he got a load of Sherry's dress, Garrett was mighty glad he hadn't indulged in a fourth beer. The confection she wore was short, slinky and fell nearly to her waist in back. Tiny crystals sprinkled the flirty skirt, winking each time she moved. Sweat trickled down Garrett's wrists and pooled in the palms of his hands. His tongue felt oversize. "Nice dress," he managed to mumble when she tipped her head to one side and gazed at him oddly.

A sigh whispered through her. Shutting her cabin door, Sherry clasped one of his arms. She'd been afraid the dress was too…too blatantly provocative. Now she felt smug about her purchase. She'd wanted to make him drool. And she had.

Tiny lanterns glowed atop snowy tablecloths in the dining room. Each table, privately secluded among old treasure chests, added to the romantic ambiance. The wine was frosty with a slight bite, the fish grilled to perfection. The band played a mellow mix of old and new, and after dinner Garrett led Sherry to the dance floor.

If Garrett had to label the evening, he'd call the whole thing…romantic, he thought as they bumped cozily against each other while wandering slowly back to their rooms after dancing the night away. He took her key to open her door and recalled Sherry's warning that romance was what the cruise had been designed for. Funny, but right now that suited him.

As Sherry backed inside, he followed to bestow a good-night kiss.

Pleasantly serene, Sherry rose on tiptoe and nipped teasingly at his lips. Teasing stopped and serene shot up in flames when Garrett began kissing her the way she'd dreamed. Too conveniently, a soft bed beckoned, dappled by moonlight that streamed into the room through a high narrow window.

Inhibitions? Left at the foot of the great paddle wheel.

As Sherry's daring new dress floated into a misty purple ring around her bare feet, she considered finding the red nightie. Or she did for all of a heartbeat. Then Garrett shrugged out of his jacket, his shirt, his pants. He was as gorgeous naked as she'd imagined.

She reached for him and they fell on the bed in a tangle of limbs. All thought flew out of Sherry's head. She forgot completely about the foil packets she'd purchased and tucked in her purse.

Luckily he remembered and had brought his own. Shortly thereafter, rational thought ended for Garrett, too. Although as they raced toward heights he'd never hit before, he worried that he'd come too soon. He worried that he wouldn't please her.

It'd been so long. So very, very long.

As far as Sherry was concerned he did everything

just right. His hands, his mouth, his body transported her to places she'd never in her wildest dreams imagined visiting. She spiraled up and up and up until she thought she'd touch the clouds. Then as he tumbled her into a skidding, shuddering release, Sherry Campbell quietly fell in love for the first time ever.

Near dawn, wrapped tight in Garrett's strong arms after yet another awesome bout of lovemaking, Sherry felt compelled to confess what was in her heart. "I love you, Garrett. And I love Keith. We'll be a family," she sighed, stroking his chest. "A spring wedding, don't you think? March? Perfect for new beginnings."

Glorying in her slight weight, Garrett's heart spilled over. Tonight he could believe in everlasting happiness. Tonight, with her, for the first time in a long while, he believed in love. Believed that having it all—not just a career but a wife, a home, a family—was possible.

CHAPTER THIRTEEN

A MARKED CHANGE in the drone of the paddle wheel woke Garrett. He lay flat on his back, a weight pressing against his chest. The lethargy in his limbs kept him from bounding up to check on the noise. A sleepy part of his brain, as yet disconnected from his body, seemed content to drift. *Drift.* He remembered boarding a stern-wheeler with Sherry. *Sherry.* Garrett's mind joined his sleekly content body. It was impossible not to recall the most fantastic night of lovemaking a man had ever had, and the partner responsible for the fulfillment of his fantasies. Incredibly willing. Incredibly giving. He liked the warmth of her body curled against his. Garrett didn't want the day to intrude.

Sherry stirred and lifted her head from the warm pillow where she sprawled at an odd angle. Dazed, she decided she'd slept in the same position too long. She had a kink in her neck and other vague aches. In an attempt to turn she hit a solid obstacle, and Garrett's morning voice rumbled under her ear like the fading echo of thunder.

"Easy, easy. Is this what I have to look forward to? You hogging the bed?"

Sherry smiled as she remembered the glorious night she'd spent loving and being loved by the owner of that gravelly voice. Flopping onto her stomach, she propped both elbows on his broad chest. "Are you always such a grouch in the morning?"

"Is it morning?" His hands settled comfortably on the rounded swell of her buttocks. He'd hoped the night was still young. The feel of her smooth naked flesh warming beneath the slow friction of his palms caused an ache he wouldn't be able to alleviate if he had to dress and return to his room.

She stilled and listened to a variety of muffled noises above and below the cabin. "We've turned and are headed back to St. Louis. The weekend is almost over."

Garrett pulled her down to meet a desperate kiss. His way of telling her that he'd delay the inevitable if he could. He wasn't good with the words even though he had no problem lecturing to a hundred students or arguing successfully in a room filled with peers. Emotional attachments were different. Harder. He couldn't seem to put his feelings into words. Carla had said so in her exit letter. Easing up on the kiss, Garrett worked to catch his breath and said with some difficulty, "It's light out. I have to go."

Sherry strained to reconnect. She scrambled to her knees as he swung his legs off the edge of the bed. Then she giggled. She couldn't help it. "Ah. Have I uncovered your deep dark secret? You're really Dr. Werewolf?"

She looked so adorable crouched in the middle of the bed, not a stitch on, that Garrett, who had only one leg of his pants pulled up, hopped back to collect another kiss. She tugged him down. It was full light by the time he rose again and gently shooed her love-flushed body toward the shower.

"You're insatiable, woman," he scolded, doing his level best to dress as she ran back to steal kisses. "Ordinarily I wouldn't complain, but if we leave this boat with me in my tux and you in that purple dress, I guarantee we'll be the talk of the town."

She disappeared briefly, then reappeared wearing a skimpy towel. "Better?" she said huskily.

Garrett had trouble buttoning his shirt. The sight of those long legs that'd held him so tightly nearly unhinged him.

"Party pooper." She bounced back on the bed. "I expected a man who had a laughing pig on his desk to be more daring."

"Laughing pig?" he choked out. "Ah…the paperweight Keith bought me with his allowance. He said I looked too serious at work." Picking up his shoes, he leaned over and nuzzled her neck. "You think I'm too serious?"

Sherry wound her arms around him and kissed him so hard, colored lightning flashed behind his eyes. Smothering a frustrated growl, Garrett bolted.

"Meet you on deck for brunch in one hour." He ripped open the door and barreled out and into a couple who smirked when they saw his wrinkled shirt and the dress shoes he carried.

At the sound of the closing door, Sherry rose, hugged herself and spun around the room in pure jubilation. She never would have believed that love could create such a confusion of feelings. Weakness and strength. Danger and power.

She vacillated between purring like a kitten and roaring like a lioness.

Love. Who'd have thought Sherry Campbell, Ph.D.,

would ever fall so completely head-over-heels in love? Not one person who knew her, that was for sure.

After she showered and donned her oldest, most comfortable pair of jeans and a faded sweatshirt, she actually peeked in the bathroom mirror to see if the difference she felt inside was visible. Only then did it dawn—her lips and only hers had used the L-word. Garrett had been remarkably silent. Sherry touched the cold glass, and a corresponding chill slithered up her arm.

Nonsense. Of course he felt what she felt. Love was probably old hat to Garrett. He'd been in love before and she hadn't. It didn't take the author of the *Kama Sutra* to understand that what they'd shared last night had been cataclysmic and earth-shattering. For him, too. She'd stake her life on it. But…maybe she was too confident.

She hit the light switch to obliterate her doubting image. Garrett would surely say something when they met for brunch.

He didn't. Though attentive, he avoided the topic of *them.* This, in spite of the fact that Sherry deliberately brought the conversation around to weddings. "It doesn't seem possible that Nolan and Emily are getting married in less than two weeks." Sighing, she gazed at Garrett over the rim of the mimosa she'd ordered to further enhance her romantic illusions.

"Yeah. Can you believe I've held the dean's job for almost three months?" Garrett glanced around for their waiter and signaled for a coffee refill.

Sherry blamed the weakness stealing over her limbs on his clean soapy scent, which wafted across the table.

"Nice weddings take a long time to plan," she

murmured. "Timing is important. Isn't it too bad Nolan and Emily's anniversary will always compete with the holidays?"

"It's their choice. Speaking of holidays, Keith gave me his Christmas list. And one almost as long for Rags. Can you believe it?"

Sherry set her glass down hard. "He wants a brother or sister most. He's very lonely, you know."

"Rags?" Garrett wagged his cup again at the tardy waiter who finally stopped to refill it. "If Keith asked you to soften me up so I'll buy him that kitten we saw at the pet store, the answer is unequivocally no. NO, in capital letters."

Sherry gave up. Not for a second did she think Garrett so obtuse that he didn't know she'd meant Keith wanted siblings. Nor was *she* dense. He was dodging the subject of marriage.

Well, she could be outwardly mature about that. If mountains hadn't moved for him as they had for her, why not be honest?

Because men played games. They liked to reel women out and reel them in again on a whim. She drained her drink and stood. Let him play someone else like a big-mouth bass. This fish was bailing out.

"Excuse me," she said right in the middle of his recounting Keith's Christmas list. "I'm sure you'll figure out what to buy Keith without my help. I'll see you when we dock. For some reason I didn't get a lot of sleep last night. I'm going to take a nap." And she walked off. Stalked was more like it.

Garrett puzzled over her little speech for so long his coffee grew cold in the cup. What did she mean, he'd figure out what to buy Keith without her? Had he been dreaming last night? Didn't Sherry say she loved his son? That they'd be a family?

Women. If he lived to be a hundred, he'd never understand them. So what if last night had been the best sex he'd ever had with anyone? Neither he nor Keith needed another female running hot and cold, messing up their lives. It was better he'd found out now before Keith got too attached and ended up with his heart in shreds. As for Garrett, he'd been down that rocky road with Carla and had no wish to travel it again. Yet it hurt. God, did it hurt.

Throwing some bills on the table, Garrett returned to his cabin. He packed his bag and, though his steps slowed as he passed Sherry's room, he continued on topside. Scant moments before the *Ozark Queen* cut her engines and let the current carry her to the dock, Sherry appeared on deck with her suitcase.

Garrett studied her from behind his dark glasses. She looked rested, he thought, a bit resentful about the sorrow that pinched his heart, but not, apparently, hers. He noticed something more, a cool pulling back, like she'd had second thoughts about last night and now couldn't wait to have the entire expedition over and done with.

Sherry deliberately distanced herself from Garrett. She detested tears, considered them a sign of weakness. Yet she had, in the solitude of her room, shed a few for him and for herself—for a loss she felt so keenly.

If Sherry hadn't seemed completely and icily unapproachable, Garrett might have tried to breech the gap yawning between them on the drive back to Carla's. But how?

He said nothing and, as a result, neither did Sherry.

Keith again waited on Carla's porch. As Garrett turned his truck into the circular lane, the boy tore down the walkway, waving madly, face ringed in smiles.

"Where is everyone?" Garrett asked, climbing out as Keith tossed his duffel into the pickup's bed and scrambled to claim his former seat in the middle.

"Crawford's at work. Mom took Georgette and Arnold to the airport."

"And left you all alone?"

"Don't yell at me. Georgette was plenty mad 'cause Crawford went to the bank hours ago and said he'd send Mom home. She just got here."

"I'm not blaming you, Keith. I don't understand what kind of bank demands they work on Sunday."

Keith scooted nearer Sherry. He peered at her somberly when she shifted away.

"Didn't you guys have fun neither?" he asked, his gaze darting between the two adults.

Garrett started the truck with a roar and jerked it into reverse.

Sherry mumbled something ambiguous as Garrett laid rubber all the way to the street.

Keith hunkered unhappily between them. Regardless of the fact that he announced several times during the drive that he wanted to stop and eat, his dad continued on in moody silence.

Sherry rallied once and asked Keith who'd won in the Rams game.

"We didn't get to go. 'Stead, Crawford helped Arnold with his stupid old coin collection."

"What?" Garrett took his eyes off the highway. "What did he and your mom do with you?"

"Nothin'. Crawford told Mom if I was gonna live

there, I hadda learn to occupy myself." He picked nervously at his fingers. "I don't gotta live there, do I?"

"Not if I can help it," Garrett replied grimly. "Tomorrow I'll have a talk with your mother." Garrett glanced at Sherry, wishing she'd say something to quell the anxiety circling like a flock of buzzards in his stomach.

Her eyes were closed—in a pretext of sleep. He could tell she was pretending. Worry gripped him more tightly. Would a judge recognize Carla and Crawford's supervision of Keith as lackadaisical? Or—considering how much overtime Garrett worked—was his care of Keith any less neglectful?

Custody was Sherry's turf. Garrett would give a lot for her advice. She didn't offer any. And once they arrived at the complex, she collected her bag and left, her goodbye and thanks a shade warmer than frosty.

"What'd you do to Sherry?" Keith demanded before he and Garrett reached their home.

"What makes you think I'm responsible for her bad temper?"

"You always argued with Mom. She said so. And she left. Now I'll bet Sherry's gonna go away, too."

"I rarely argued with your mother. And I'm not responsible for what Sherry does or doesn't do," Garrett yelled as Keith slammed inside and tore upstairs. "Hell." He exhaled noisily. "Do you want to go get Rags tonight?" he shouted from the foot of the stairs. "If so, straighten up and fly right."

Minutes ticked by before Keith's sullen pinched face again appeared at the top of the stairs. "I want my dog, but I don't wanna talk to you."

Garrett's stomach bottomed out as he slowly dropped

his suitcase. "I'm sorry your mother left us, son. And it's time I tried to answer questions you have."

Keith wouldn't look directly at his father. .

Garrett sat on a step and patted the carpet beside him. Without waiting for Keith to join him, he said, "The divorce wasn't my idea, son. I gave your mom everything I knew how to give." He clenched a fist over his heart. "Love wasn't enough to make her happy. Sometimes it isn't, and that's nobody's fault. Not mine. Not yours."

Keith crept down the stairs and slid wiry arms around Garrett's neck. "Sherry's not like that, Dad. Her heart is this big. Bigger." He threw his arms as wide as he could. "She loves kids and dogs and other stuff. Love'd make her plenty happy, I bet."

Garrett closed his eyes and dropped his chin to his chest. He couldn't meet the hope shining in his son's eyes.

An hour later they had Rags home. Keith was lying on the floor watching TV, his dog curled at his side. Garrett sorted through Saturday's mail. There was a letter from Carla's attorney. He ripped it open and read it fast. Then stunned, he read it through more slowly. It contained a lot of legalese, but the gist was a warning for Garrett not to try to rush into a marriage with a virtual stranger for appearance's sake.

The letter fell to his lap. Carla's lawyer had obviously learned via Keith that there was something going on between him and Sherry. Or Carla had suggested as much. Wouldn't they love to drag Sherry's name through the mud? Wasn't it fortunate, then, that she'd cooled off when she had? Folding the letter, Garrett returned it to its envelope. He walked over and stuffed it in his desk with the other correspondence belonging to his case.

"Keith," he said, "tomorrow, I'm hiring someone to look after the house and you. What Sherry needs is for us to do our thing and give her space to do hers."

"No, it's not what she needs." Keith jackknifed into a sitting position. He enfolded Rags in his arms as he glared at Garrett.

Garrett steeled himself to ignore his son's misery. He wondered if there was a way to back out of buying this town house. But he couldn't really afford to lose the earnest money. "Is what I said clear, Keith? After tomorrow there won't be any need for you to call and bother Sherry."

Keith snapped off the TV and ran upstairs. "Sherry doesn't think I'm a bother. When I get big, me'n Rags are gonna live alone. Aren't we, Rags?"

Garrett gazed after the pup scrambling to keep up with the boy. He considered finding a parent-child counselor. It would help if Carla went, too. But she'd refused to consider a marriage counselor. And when did he have time? This job kept him so busy he barely saw Keith now. "Remember—you aren't big yet," he called sternly just before Keith's bedroom door slammed.

Next morning Garrett counted on the boy's anger having blown over.

But Keith remained mute. After dropping him off at school, Garrett called Westerbrook's office and explained he'd be late. "I'm stopping by a domestic employment agency. I can't keep imposing on Dr. Campbell."

Westerbrook coughed. "Wise decision, my boy. In fact I'd planned to have a talk with you today. At church yesterday Sheldon March's wife said somebody saw you, Keith and Sherilyn putting suitcases in your truck.

I'm sure it was perfectly innocent, but talk of that nature causes big trouble on campus."

Garrett was so knocked off his pins he couldn't think of anything to say.

"You understand the position, I'm sure. Faculty would never accept it, what with Sherry reporting to you. They'd dump her as department chair."

"But she's tenured."

"Tenure won't protect her in an elected post. Why belabor a dead issue, eh? All I'm saying is that it's good you've come to your senses and are hiring a sitter. I'll be happy to pass on the reason you're late to the budget committee today. Very happy."

Garrett clutched the receiver to his chest after Westerbrook clicked off the line. The tattletale had to be Yvette's new roommate—the flight attendant—what was her name again? Listening to Westerbrook's warning, Garrett was doubly glad now, for Sherry's sake, that she'd abandoned their deepening relationship. Although he already missed her. When they were together he'd foolishly believed marriage was possible.

With his lousy track record, he should have known better.

ANGEL POUNCED on Sherry the instant she set foot in the department. Hustling her into her private office, the secretary shut the door. "Wait'll you hear the scuttlebutt flying around campus this morning. People are saying you spent the weekend with Dean Lock." Angel laughed uproariously.

Sherry plopped her briefcase on the desk and gazed at Angel with dark-ringed eyes. "I did. I'm a fool, Angel." Sherry walked to the window, leaned a shoulder on the frame and gazed at a row of leafless trees. "I let him break my heart. Compared to that, a few nasty rumors are painless."

"That rat! I'll poison his coffee."

Sherry almost smiled. "I said it before and I'll say it again, no man is worth leaving your kids in foster care while you do hard time, Angel. I walked into this with my eyes open. I'll take my licks on campus. Only…will you run interference between Garrett and me for a few days?"

"You got it, boss. I won't poison his coffee. Just make him wish I had."

"No." Sherry shook her head as she pushed away from the window. "Once I get past seeing him at Nolan and Em's wedding, our only contact will be professional. I can handle that. Remember I told you to think of a lost love as you would a death? I need time to grieve, then I'll be good as new again."

It wasn't until after Angel left quietly without comment that Sherry wondered if her secretary bought into any of this—if she and the others Sherry counseled believed time healed all wounds. Sherry had to believe it, or she wouldn't make it through the day.

But get through it she did. She avoided Garrett before, during and after school on Monday and Tuesday. By Wednesday, she'd begun to breathe easier. Then as she left her one-o'clock class, she glimpsed him hurrying toward his car. Her heart squeezed. Had something happened to Keith? Several seconds passed while she debated chasing after him to ask.

Fortunately a student stopped her, seeking her advice about a topic for a paper, and kept her from making a big mistake. She cared a great deal for Keith Lock. More than she had any right to. Sherry knew Garrett had hired a sitter. Everyone on campus and in the complex knew about the plump grandmotherly woman Garrett had retained to take Sherry's place. Admittedly Sherry missed the time she'd spent with Keith. She missed laughing and talking with Garrett, too.

Her admission might have eased some of Garrett's guilt when, for the second day in a row, he was called to school because his son had picked fights on the playground.

"Is something going on in Keith's life we should know about?" the soft-spoken principal asked Garrett in the private meeting she'd requested.

He clasped his hands between his knees and tapped his thumbs together. "Keith is angry with me. I thought he'd get over it in a day or two, but he hasn't."

"Who is Sherry? According to our records, your ex-wife's name is Carla."

Unprepared for the question, Garrett straightened sharply.

The principal removed her glasses. "Keith didn't mention you when I questioned why he'd flown into a rage. He said he missed doing things with Sherry."

Garrett ran a damp palm over his mouth and chin. "Sherry picked Keith up from day care on a temporary basis until I could hire a full-time sitter."

"Ah. A high-school girl." The woman smiled. "Maybe you could arrange for her to ease out of his life gradually. I gather they skated, played miniature golf and watched videos. Rainy as it's been, he'll soon forget the sporting activities. But perhaps she'd continue the movies once a month or so."

"Sherry isn't a high-school girl. She's a colleague of mine. A professor with a busy schedule."

"But if she's as nice as Keith claims, I'm sure she'd make time to help."

Garrett stood. "He'll see Sherry at her brother's wedding next weekend. Thank you for your time and advice, Mrs. McKay. I'll give it serious thought."

"Keith is a sweet boy. Oh, and, Dr. Lock, normally I don't involve myself in situations with noncustodial parents. But yesterday, I had a call from your ex-wife's lawyer. He beat about the bush in lawyerly fashion. The upshot is I gather she wants Keith to live with her permanently. If she's said as much to Keith, this may be another reason he's acting out."

Cold dread wrapped around Garrett's windpipe, choking off his breath. When he wheezed a few times, the principal stepped to her sideboard and poured him a glass of water. "I assumed you knew. I'm sorry this came as a shock."

"I knew. I thought if I cooperated…" Garrett broke off helplessly.

The principal sat again and laced her hands. "You know, don't you, that Keith's change in classroom behavior will give them a tremendous lever?"

Garrett nodded. "I do. Again, my thanks for the advance warning." He left her office this time without being called back. The boy Garrett collected from the time-out room had torn jeans and an eye beginning to turn interesting shades of purple. And he puffed up belligerently, acting contrite only when it became clear his dad wasn't going to rake him over the coals. Still, he didn't apologize for his behavior.

Twice after Keith had gone to sleep that night Garrett lifted the phone and tried to muster the nerve to call Sherry. He'd given his new sitter the night off, but not even that helped. Garrett turned in after midnight, the phone untouched.

THE MIDDLE OF the next week, Carla called him at work. "I talked to Keith last night. He says he can't come to St. Louis Saturday because of a wedding. Anyone I know?"

"A history professor from my campus. Nolan Campbell."

"Campbell? Any relation to your so-called baby-sitter?"

Garrett didn't like the smirk in Carla's voice. "Nolan is Sherry's brother. But I have a full-time sitter now. I assumed Keith would tell you."

"He did. So things didn't work out with you and Ms. Campbell, hmm?"

"Dr. Campbell," he lashed out. "And there was nothing to work out. I'm busy, Carla. Why the sudden inquisition about my love life? What's really on your mind?"

"The only interest I have in your love life is how it affects my son."

"I could point out that your interest comes about eight years late. But I'll let my lawyer do that in court. Isn't that what all this is leading up to? A custody battle?"

"We don't have our case built yet, Garrett. You'll be the first to know when we do. I just don't understand why Keith turned down a chance to visit us to go to the wedding of a man he can't know well at all. Is this your doing?"

"Keith pals around with Nolan's stepson, Mark. Did you ever think Keith might be more excited about visiting if you didn't run off to work every time he shows up?"

"My work. That's always been a thorn in your side, hasn't it Garrett?"

"Not your work, Carla," Garrett said quietly. "Only your obsession with it to the exclusion of everything else in your life, including your son. I'm not turning Keith against you. You're doing a fine job of it yourself."

"Oh, yes. As if you spend every waking minute with him. Keith has a room full of toys and books here. And Crawford spends quality time with him. Don't try to insinuate I'm a bad parent because I work to help provide a better life. Anyway, for your information, Keith said his class has a parent-child outing to the St. Louis Children's Music concert on the Wednesday after Thanksgiving. He asked me to go. Not you, Garrett. Me!"

She couldn't have hurt Garrett more if she'd cut out his heart with a dull knife. Keith hadn't said one word about the outing. But Garrett would be skewered and roasted on a spit before he let Carla know that. "I suggested it," he lied. "Despite what you think, I'm not trying to prevent you from building a relationship with our son." He paused. "Don't let him down on this, Carla."

"I won't. And since you have him for Thanksgiving, I'm including him in our Christmas plans with Crawford's children."

A protest rose to Garrett's lips, but he let it die. Carla would love to have him contest the original custody decree. It said Keith would spend alternate holidays with each parent. If he spent Thanksgiving with Garrett, Carla was supposed to get him for Christmas. That was the agreement in theory; in practice, Garrett had always had him full-time.

"Okay. I'll see that we have our tree early. Spell out the dates you want him and forward them to me by e-mail. I hate to cut you short, Carla, but I'm late for a meeting."

If he'd surprised her with his generosity, Carla didn't

let on. She hung up immediately. Garrett battled the billowing anger that he seemed unable to quell. Just as fast, he plunged into a loneliness the likes of which he'd never felt before. Not even when Carla had walked out. The thought of spending Christmas without Keith—he couldn't even imagine the void. Christmas was a time for families. He didn't know what people who had no one did over the holiday season. He slid into a depression he couldn't seem to shake.

Garrett kept waiting for Keith to tell him about his invitation to Carla. The boy ignored his father and said nothing. Keith played with Rags and remained aloof and distant. Garrett actually looked forward to Nolan and Emily's wedding.

"Where's our present?" Keith spoke to his dad for the first time in weeks after climbing into the pickup to go to the big event.

"Sherry and I went together on a gift. She took it to wrap."

"Oh. I saw her leave, but she didn't have nothin'. She sure looked pretty, though. Did you see her when she went by our house?"

"No. I must've been getting dressed. Maybe she already took the gift to Nolan's house. A lot of people prefer to not mess with gifts at the reception."

"You been to a lot of weddings?"

"Enough. There's a lot of standing around. We'll know people from church, and I'll introduce you to my colleagues and their families so you won't be totally bored."

"That's okay. Me 'n Mark are handing out groom's cake at the reception. We got a special place to stand and everything."

"Oh." Garrett had assumed they'd be together. He hadn't given any thought to being alone. But alone he was from the minute they stepped inside the church. Keith had rushed off with Mark. And Garrett felt the isolation deep in his bones.

He'd no more than glanced over the crowd when he noticed Sherry flitting from huddle to huddle, a vision in rust and gold satin. Garrett couldn't take his eyes off her. He even found the sprig of white flowers nestled in her short, gold-tipped dark hair enchanting.

A punch of jealousy ripped his joy away when Sherry rose on tiptoe and kissed two beefy guys who'd just arrived. His stomach didn't settle until she turned to speak with a leathery-skinned woman walking between the men. The woman chewed a huge wad of gum.

Garrett heard Camp greet the gum-chewer by name. Maizie. She and Sherry seemed to be the focus of a gaggle of strangers—well, strangers to Garrett in that they weren't from the college community. Two elderly women converged on Sherry. The three shrieked and hugged. Doris and Vi, Sherry called them. A man with a booming voice and a swagger plowed into the center of the group. Someone near Garrett whispered that the loudmouth and his wife had flown in from Philadelphia specifically for the wedding. It finally fell into place for Garrett. These were people Nolan, Emily and Sherry had met on their summer trek.

Garrett lost track of Sherry momentarily. The next time he spotted her, she and Megan were laughing with a stocky female who walked with a slight limp.

"There's Gina," exclaimed Mark. "Everybody we met on the wagon train came to see Mom and Nolan get married. Even that witch Brittany." He pointed to a young woman with shoulder-length blond hair. "Hey, Brit brought a boyfriend, and they both look normal. Cool, huh?"

It was nice, but Garrett had no clue why Brittany shouldn't look normal. Then she turned and Garrett realized he had seen her before—with Sherry at their first fateful meeting. The blonde had done nothing but scream even before Sherry hit him. To say he'd made a bad impression with his scruffy appearance was putting it mildly.

Feeling disassociated from the mainstream of the party, Garrett made his way to the vestibule. Once there, Sherry's dad steered him toward a woman handing out boutonnieres. He thought he might snag a word with Sherry when, as attendants, they witnessed the signing of the marriage certificate. But she barely acknowledged him. She, Emily and Megan took off immediately—to dress the bride, they said.

Retreating, Garrett slapped the nervous groom on the back. "Nolan, old son, you look far too relaxed for a man about to meet his doom."

"I'm counting the hours until the honeymoon. All this folderol is for Emily." Nolan waved a hand. "Her first wedding was disaster. I want to wipe the memory of it from her mind. Most women dream of wearing veils and yards of white lace. I couldn't care less about any of those trappings. But I'll jump through all the hoops because I love her."

Garrett thought about his first wedding as he pocketed the ring. He and Carla had stood before a justice of the peace. Her wedding to Crawford had been a huge white-tie affair.

As he trailed Nolan into the main sanctuary, Garrett remembered the dreamy glow on Sherry's face when she talked of having a spring wedding. A perfect time for new beginnings, she'd said. Funny, he hadn't pegged her as the type to get all misty-eyed about marriage. Showed how little he knew about women. How little he knew about Sherilyn Campbell. And now it was just as well, he lamented.

The music signaled the start of the ceremony, and Garrett took his place beside the groom. The organist struck chords to announce the arrival of the maid of honor. Turning, Garrett watched Sherry drop rose petals along a creamy satin runner. He knew the moment the bride appeared, only because the crowd surged to their feet. However, he missed Emily's entire walk. Garrett's mind's eye placed Sherry in that dress of white froth. And imagined her floating toward him—to accept his ring on her finger.

Garrett tried to focus on the unity candle that sat on a table atop the dais. At the rehearsal, kept brief so everyone could celebrate Thanksgiving in their own homes, Garrett had learned that Nolan and Emily would light the unity candle with tapers placed on either side of it. The candle's inner glow signified the undying flame of love. As the minister opened his Bible and began, "Dearly beloved…" Garrett shifted so he could keep his gaze on Sherilyn.

Emily's voice rose clearly and distinctly for all to hear as she promised to love, honor and cherish Nolan until death.

Garrett rallied long enough to press the rings into Nolan's profusely sweating hand. Ah—so the cool professor wasn't so cool, after all. Which was further evidenced as he twice tangled up his promise to Emily. But Nolan redeemed himself. His voice dropped, he took Emily's face between his shaking hands and recited a poem that spoke eloquently of his everlasting love for her.

Sherry had tears streaking silently down her cheeks. And Megan, who'd lit the candelabrum, scrubbed at hers. Garrett blinked rapidly, his eyes still on Sherilyn. Love might have eluded him; however, every word Nolan spoke applied to the feelings that squeezed unmercifully at Garrett's heart.

Anyone could see how the best man and the maid of honor pined for one another, Nolan thought to himself. So did Emily. And Sherry's parents. Mark, Megan and even Keith noticed it. Not Sherry. She didn't once glance toward Garrett. And he was a man in denial.

Yvette Miller missed the looks, or chose to ignore them. At the huge reception where people laughed, ate and toasted the happy couple, she was never far from Garrett's side. Her friends made a big to-do when Yvette caught the bouquet Emily threw straight at Sherry.

Most of the byplay escaped Garrett. He held his breath, waiting to see what Sherilyn would do when she caught the bride's bouquet. He wanted her to have it. He remembered how she'd fondled the fated rose he'd brought her... It seemed so long ago.

Then Yvette picked the posies right out of midair. Garrett blinked. He felt sad and upset for Sherry. It was at that moment he realized how deeply he loved her. Now, when a relationship between them assured her removal from the department that was so important to her. Now, when it could interfere with his retaining custody of Keith.

During the cutting of the cake, Garrett decided it'd be best for everyone concerned to completely sever ties with Sherry. So he smiled at Yvette when she flirted, even though his heart wasn't in it.

"My car's in the shop, Garrett. I rode in with a friend who couldn't stay for the reception." Yvette stepped in front of Garrett, cutting off his view of Sherilyn.

"You need a lift home?" he asked politely.

Yvette tapped his chest with the white bouquet. "You offering to take me for a ride, big guy?"

Garrett regretted his offer at once, but saw no way to extract himself. "Yes," he mumbled, his eyes drawn to Keith and Mark who ran pell-mell toward him.

"Dad." Keith bounced up and down. "Mark and Megan are gonna stay all night with Sherry. Nolan's mom and dad have lotsa company, and Nolan and Emily are going on a honeymoon for the weekend. Sherry's gonna pop popcorn and show videos. I'm invited! Can we go now and get my sleeping bag?"

Garrett sensed Yvette's sudden interest in his proposed childless state. She was really pretty obvious. He might have consciously decided to forget Sherry; that didn't mean he was interested in a night of meaningless sex.

"No, Keith." Garrett didn't try to qualify his refusal. He just knew he wanted Keith as a buffer.

Yvette snuggled close. "What would it hurt, Garrett?"

"A ride home doesn't entitle you to interfere in decisions regarding my son."

Something flickered in Yvette's green eyes, but she kept hold of Garrett's arm.

"I wanna go with Sherry," Keith whined. "Why can't I? She said to bring Rags."

Never once in all of Keith's young life had Garrett ever fallen back on the lame excuse, "Because I said so." He did now, adding, "Lower your voice, Keith. Stop making a scene in front of my friends and colleagues."

Not only didn't Keith lower his voice, he threw a doozy of a fit.

Garrett added to the scene by half dragging the wailing child out of the reception. It was an awkward retreat, particularly as Yvette clung stubbornly to Garrett's left arm and he was left-handed. All eyes in the room registered the struggle he had opening the door. He swore under his breath.

From the sidelines, Sherry listened to Keith's hiccuping sobs. Everyone who remained in the hall heard the boy sob her name and heard Garrett tell him to hush. If any of their colleagues still believed rumors linking her and the new dean, he'd effectively squelched them. Squelched them, and at the same time delivered her a slap in the face. At least, that was how it felt within a heart that still yearned for him. It hurt so badly Sherry actually thought about quitting her job and moving far, far away.

CHAPTER FOURTEEN

THE LONG THANKSGIVING weekend and the disaster at the wedding reception were minor blips in Garrett's mind as he struggled with the monumental task facing the budget committee on their return to campus. The order—cut another hundred thousand dollars from the academic budget before the state legislature convened in January.

For once Garrett didn't mind that Keith was still sulking. It meant the house was quiet at night except for the click of his calculator. He went home exhausted by the battering he took from other committee members during tense meetings. Again they wanted to slice the Hub completely. Its cost didn't justify the narrow population it served, they said. Garrett didn't know why he stayed awake at night trying to devise ways to save the damned program. When he'd asked for legitimate areas to cut, instead, Sherry hadn't turned in one concrete suggestion. Didn't she realize something had to give?

Between his discouragement at the incessant rain pounding the daylights out of Missouri and Sherilyn's stubborn unwillingness to give him data to work with, Garrett was left brooding over his figures for the third day in a row. He was exhausted; no one knew how tempted he was to chuck everything and just give up.

He didn't expect Sherry to beg for her program, but damn it, he needed her expertise. Her fire. She avoided him on all levels. The tic below one eye reminded Garrett that he was partly to blame. He should never have crossed the invisible line from professional to personal. Never with a woman below him in his chain of command. Remembering her passionate face as she worked with those hardened students, he massaged the ache in the back of his neck, shuffled the stack of departmental budgets and began punching in numbers again. He'd already met with three program chairs. They'd hacked unneeded extras. Garrett wanted Sherry to come forward on her own. On day ten, he sent her a memo demanding they meet the following afternoon.

Next morning when he received an e-mail from Carla spelling out the whole of Keith's school vacation for her custodial visit, Garrett was so bleary-eyed he had to check the dates on the calendar twice. He could hardly believe her request. As anger warred with loneliness and anxiety, he stared at the wall behind his computer screen for a full ten minutes and contemplated how far he'd get if he took Keith and ran.

Carla was wrenching Keith away from him, and there wasn't a damn thing he could do about it. She didn't need to go to court again. The old decree, put together when he'd bent over backward to be fair, gave her alternate holidays and all summer vacations.

Thunder shook the corner window in Garrett's office. Lightning separated the sky, and he felt as if it had torn through his heart. The phone rang three times before he picked it up with a shaking hand.

"Dean Lock? This is Angel. Dr. Campbell forgot she'd agreed to accompany one of our students to her appointment at the Center for Families in Transition this afternoon. Maria Black's husband blew into town unexpectedly. He's making waves. Demanding to see Maria's little girl. Dr. Campbell said if you can stall the committee today, she'll dig out anything you need and bring it tomorrow. You understand, I'm sure. Armando Black is a total jerk."

Garrett drummed his fingers on his desktop. "Is that part of Dr. Campbell's job? Involving herself in a student's divorce?"

Angel's voice took on a bitter edge. "Speaking from experience, I say thank goodness someone like her is willing to go beyond her job. Otherwise, unless a person has a lot of money, no one advocates for kids and ex-wives."

She struck a nerve in Garrett that was too raw. He felt like one of the walking wounded just now. "Oh, I'm sure Maria's lawyer cut her a sweet deal. Tell Dr. Campbell that if she wants to save the Hub, she'll make this meeting with me today. I'll wait." He heard the department secretary scoop in a deep breath.

"I'm sorry, Dean. She left already. With the weather and all, I guess she didn't want to chance making Maria late. That'd be points for Armando."

He picked up a ruler and snapped it in half. "When do you expect her back?"

"Tomorrow morning," Angel said in a small voice.

"Fine. Leave a message on her home answering machine. Never mind, I'll do what I have to do with the Hub, and I'm sure Dr. Campbell will figure it out." He slid a finger over the disconnect button rather than ruin Angel's hearing by slamming down the receiver as he was tempted to do.

In a black mood that matched the clouds rolling

across campus, Garrett selected a felt pen and slashed through Sherry's pet counseling program. According to several members on the budget committee, all Dr. Campbell did in those counseling sessions was teach divorced women how to give men the shaft. Even the indigent had court-appointed lawyers. Too many god-damned shysters. Here was a line item—the Hub passed out literature telling women how to get free legal assist-ance. Free shysters. Without a twinge of remorse, Garrett x'd through the entire amount. And so he pro-gressed, service by service. The retyped budget for the Hub that came up on his computer spreadsheet looked markedly different from Sherilyn's original. He printed it, ran a copy and shoved it under her office door right before he dashed out into the rain and splashed through the puddles to his truck. There weren't a lot of cars left in the staff lot. He hadn't been home on time one night in two weeks.

Sitting through traffic light after traffic light, watching his windshield wipers struggle to combat the steady downpour, did nothing to improve Garrett's mood. And because his baby-sitter had needed this week off to be with her daughter who'd had emergency surgery, Garrett still had to drive to Keith's temporary day care in water nearly up to his hubcaps.

Once he finally reached the facility, he realized he wasn't the only late parent. But he *was* the only father. From the lack of wedding rings on the harried-looking women hustling by, Garrett deduced that at this center there were roughly ten times more single moms than dads. Near the door, Garrett saw the umbrella of the mother who'd just passed him with two children turn inside out. He rushed out to lend her a hand.

"Thanks, but I can handle this myself," she said, raking him with bitter eyes. And indeed, she ripped the umbrella he'd taken from her out of his hand and proceeded to bundle her two little ones and their diaper bags into the car, leaving Garrett standing in the rain. "If I waited around for a man's help," she muttered, climbing into the driver's seat, "I'd either drown or grow mold."

Garrett winced as she slammed her door. He turned up his coat collar, hunched his shoulders against the rain and covered the distance to the building again, where he saw Keith peering anxiously outside.

"Where've you been, Dad?" The boy shrugged into his slicker. "I hate it when I have to wait with all the babies. C'mon. I wanna go home." It took Keith two tries to shut the passenger door of the pickup. "Brr," he said. "Can we have stew for supper?"

Surprised by his son's sudden talkativeness, Garrett agreed. "How about if I build a fire in the fireplace and we eat off TV trays for a change?"

"Don't you have to work tonight?"

Garrett shook his head—although he'd begun to have a twinge or two of guilt at how he'd slashed Sherry's budget to ribbons. On the other hand, Keith seemed guardedly happy over the prospect of their eating together. What was done was done. "Do you have homework, son?"

"Nope. We practiced for our holiday program all day. Oh—don't forget to sign my permission slip to take the bus to St. Louis tomorrow, or else I can't go."

Garrett felt the truck's rear wheels hydroplane in a puddle. He slowed to correct his course, saving his frown until they'd stopped at the next intersection. "I forgot—

the St. Louis Children's Music concert. Keith, surely the school officials won't let you go in this weather."

"Uh-huh, my teacher said."

"Did you remind your mother? Is she definitely meeting you?"

"Yep. Just her and not Crawford. It's gonna be so cool. We get to see Frosty the Snowman and everything. He's not real, but that's okay. I wish I didn't hafta visit Mom and Crawford over Christmas break. Crawford's kids and grandkids are gonna be there." The young voice quavered, and he scooted closer to Garrett.

A stab of loneliness interfered with Garrett's ability to breathe. He ruffled his son's rain-damp hair, not trusting himself to speak. He swallowed a painful lump and then another, but discovered they severely limited his end of the conversation for the remainder of the drive home.

Rags met them at the door with hearty barks. Without the sitter at the house, the poor dog had been confined all day. "Take him out, Keith," Garrett said. "But wipe his feet well before you bring him inside again. Cleaning muddy prints from the carpet isn't my favorite chore."

"Okay. Can I check the answering machine first? It's blinking." It was a habit he'd gotten into after they'd advertised for the dog's owner.

"Go ahead." Garrett stripped off his topcoat. Keith liked to listen to the sales pitches and donation requests that came in during the course of a day. Garrett was happy to leave the task to his son. "I'll go make sure we have a couple of cans of stew." He paused in the act of hanging up his coat as he heard his ex-wife's voice filter into the room.

"Keith, it turns out I can't go to that concert tomorrow. Sorry, but the head of our branch called a department meeting. I'm so close to a promotion I don't dare not attend. But you're grown-up enough to understand. We'll have two weeks together at Christmas. There goes my phone, I've got a client. Bye, honey."

Garrett didn't need to see Keith's face to feel his disappointment. It emanated from the slumped shoulders and the dejected way he hung his head. But what could Garrett say that wouldn't reveal the anger he felt toward Carla at this moment? He passed a shaking hand over his own eyes. How many times did this make now that she'd let Keith down? Too damned many!

"Dad?" Keith's voice wobbled and his eyes shone overbright. "Can you go tomorrow? There's room on the bus. My teacher said so right before she told us to bring our permission slips."

Garrett wanted to say yes more than he wanted to breathe, but today's decree from Westerbrook scheduled budget meetings back-to-back tomorrow. "Son, I can't. I'd like to, but it's too short notice. If I'd known, I could have planned ahead and—"

"That's okay." Keith cut him off, sank down on his knees and gathered his moppy dog in his arms. "When I walk Rags, I'll go ask Sherry. I bet she'd like the concert. She loves music."

Garrett thought how furious Sherry was going to be in the morning when she got a load of what he'd done to the Hub. Dammit, he actually looked forward to doing battle with her. Maybe now she'd give him some helpful suggestions. Any response, even a full-scale eruption, would be more satisfying than her recent passive-aggressive reactions.

"I'd rather you didn't call Sherry."

"Why?" There was a stubborn edge to the single word.

"Because." Garrett knew he sounded no less stubborn. "I said don't, and that's final." The frustrated wave of his hand brought Keith's attention to the renewed rattle of raindrops on the living-room windows. "I wouldn't be surprised if they canceled the trip, Keith."

"They won't. And everybody'll have a mom there but me."

Garrett recalled the first time he'd had to attend a couples function alone, after Carla walked out. He knew the desperation Keith must be feeling. Garrett's heart wrenched for his son. He considered asking Emily if she could spare time to go with Keith. Just as quickly he discarded the idea. Only yesterday Camp told him Emily was steeped in the final stages of their book. An editor had requested sample chapters before the wedding.

Garrett closed his eyes and ran down the list of other women he knew. A pathetically short list. "Maybe Yvette's free, Keith." If Garrett sounded hesitant, it was because he *was* hesitant. Yvette Miller didn't need much encouragement to hang around. Garrett hated to give her any. But neither did he like seeing Keith distraught.

"I don't like her." Jumping up, Keith dumped Rags off his lap. "I don't care what you say, I'm gonna ask Sherry."

"No, son, you are not." Garrett caught Keith by the arm as he raced for the door. He held the boy firmly even though he tried to tear free. "If you persist in this nonsense, Keith, I will not sign your permission form. And if you choose not to ask Yvette, I'm afraid you'll have to resign yourself to being on your own."

"That's not fair." Keith stomped his foot. Tears

furrowed his cheeks. Rags, sensing something had upset his favorite human, began to whine.

"Life isn't fair, Keith. Now what's it going to be?"

In their short test of wills, Keith lost. Shrugging, he dug the form out of his jeans pocket. "I really, really wanna go to the concert," he whispered.

"All right. I'm not doing this to be mean." Garrett took the paper, pulled out his pen and scribbled his name. "Now, let's eat. How about biscuits to go with our stew?"

"I'm not hungry," Keith mumbled. "May I be excused?"

Garrett studied his son a lengthy moment. But he was reluctant to heap one humiliation on another. Pride was important. He inclined his head slightly, allowing Keith to save face. "If you work up an appetite walking Rags, there'll be plenty to eat."

Keith nodded. After stuffing the permission slip in his book bag, he carried his reluctant pet into the stormy night.

They didn't stay out long. Garrett heard the door slam again as the smell of stew began to permeate the house. He sighed, listening to Keith's footsteps march upstairs. Then he turned back to the eight-o'clock news. The Mississippi and the Missouri rivers were both rising. Garrett doubted the concert was going to be an issue tomorrow. Even though the bridge that crossed into the city was high above the river, the roads that led there ran through lowlands.

Keith finished wiping Rags's feet, opened his bedroom door and shoved the pup inside. He closed the door softly and tiptoed into his dad's bedroom. Quietly he lifted the phone and dialed Sherry's number, which he'd carefully committed to memory.

She answered on the first ring. The weather had been so ghastly she'd come straight home after dropping Maria Black off at a shelter following their trying session with a counselor who didn't see through Armando's phony charm.

"Keith? What a surprise. Is everything all right? You're not stranded at day care, are you?" Sherry knew that Garrett might well have been tied up in a late budget session. She realized with a guilty pang that she hadn't done anything to make his time at these meetings easier. And she was worried. They'd already cut funding once, yet the newspapers were filled with rumors of massive legislative cutbacks.

"My mom called, Sherry. She can't go to the concert in St. Louis with my class tomorrow. Will you go? As my friend?" His whispery voice held a trace of recent tears.

Pain wrapped spiky fingers around Sherry's heart, stealing her voice for a minute.

"That's okay," he said in a bleak voice. "I didn't figure you could. Dad can't, either, 'cause it's last minute. I thought maybe…" He dissolved in sniffles.

"Wait." It was impossible not to respond to the anguish in his voice. "I only teach one class tomorrow, and my students are pretty caught up. I still have two days of personal leave coming," she muttered, thinking out loud as she paced the length of the phone cord. Frankly, the way Garrett had withdrawn so completely after the boat trip, she was shocked he'd let Keith ask her. Then she had a dark thought. Perhaps Garrett didn't know.

"Is your dad still at work, Keith?" Sherry more than half expected the boy to grudgingly admit that Garrett was.

"He's home. He picked me up at day care." Keith gave a brief explanation of the sitter's dilemma.

Sherry's heart began to thud loudly. Maybe Garrett had had a change of heart. If he approved of her going with Keith tomorrow, how could she refuse? "I'd be honored to go as your friend, tiger. When and where should I meet you? Are the moms carpooling?"

In a happier more hopeful tone, Keith laid out details.

"A school bus? Two buses? Ah." Sherry cringed inwardly thinking of the two-hour trip to St. Louis crammed on a bus of boisterous third-graders. However, by the time he'd described the concert in an unmistakably excited voice, she hung up feeling some enthusiasm herself. She smiled softly, her heart lighter for bringing joy to Keith. Undoubtedly Garrett would be relieved, too. Really, if truth be known, Sherry was glad she didn't have to drive, considering the weather predictions.

She watched the local news as she prepared soup. But her thoughts kept wandering down the street to Garrett and Keith. Hard as it was, Garrett seemed to cope with Carla's on-again, off-again involvement in Keith's life.

Sherry sat down at the kitchen table with her steaming bowl of vegetable soup, realizing she'd come home angered by divorce after the emotional meeting at the Center for Families in Transition. Divorce didn't close the door on a couple's problems. Hearing the terrible things Armando and Maria screamed at each other, Sherry found herself wondering if they'd ever been in love. In contrast, Garrett's dealings with his ex-wife appeared quite reasonable. Perhaps the principles of the Hub were remiss. Only one-half of a separated couple was recognized when, in fact, where children were involved, the two halves of a couple remained emotionally connected for years.

Sherry laid down her spoon. Excitement began to sing in her blood as she turned over the possibilities in her mind. Whole-life counseling should include men, as well as women. Too bad she had to wait until next week to present this brainstorm to Garrett. What would a few extra days matter? Tomorrow belonged to Keith. He saw her as someone he could count on. She would not shortchange him for the sake of her job or anything else.

Sherry snapped off the television and went to phone Angel. Technically personal days were supposed to be requested in advance and required the signature of the immediate supervisor. Since Garrett was Sherry's immediate supervisor and since he knew the trip with Keith necessitated her taking time off work, he obviously planned to approve her paperwork after the fact.

"Angel," she said, speaking to the department secretary's home answering machine, "I won't be in tomorrow. Please cancel my nine-o'clock class. Tell them to read two chapters ahead and prepare for Monday's quiz. Oh, and don't worry about me. It's not an emergency. Have Garrett sign my leave request and send it on to personnel. His ex copped out on Keith again at the eleventh hour. I'm filling in for her on the third-grader trip to a Christmas concert in St. Louis. Call me if you get home soon. Otherwise, see you bright and early Monday."

Garrett invaded Sherry's dreams that night. At first she lay awake listening to the steady drumming of rain on the roof, trying her level best to be practical and not to read anything personal into his allowing her back in Keith's life. But as the rain slackened, images of Garrett—how it would feel to curl up next to him every night—whisked her off on a tangent. His lovemaking had been tender. Giving. He had felt what she'd felt. She'd seen it in his eyes when Nolan recited that poem at the wedding. So why had he backed off? Fear, maybe? Because he'd had one failed marriage?

One clear thought transcended all others. Keith's phone call tonight represented a major capitulation for Garrett. Keith was the most important person in Garrett's life. That call spelled a definite softening in his feelings for her. Otherwise Garrett wouldn't have let Keith ask her to be his pro-tem parent.

Things would work out between them. This was a start.

Snuggling under her comforter, Sherry yawned and gave fleeting thought to getting up and calling him. Wind gusted outside and whistled around the corner of her bedroom window. She burrowed deeper and decided to phone him while she cooked breakfast.

Sherry woke up with a start and registered the fact that even though her bedside clock said 5:00 a.m., it was much later. Too much light filtered into her room. She turned on the lamp and lunged for her watch. "Oh, no! It's after nine!" The power must have been knocked out sometime during the night. And Keith said the buses were to leave his school at ten.

Flying to the window, Sherry was relieved to see that the rain had let up, even though low black clouds shrouded bare-limbed trees and wind buffeted the evergreen bushes. She let the curtain drop and ran to her closet; she chose boots, black tights and a wool skirt that hung to midcalf. And layers on top. A T-shirt topped by a cardigan that had a collar to fold out over the neck of her raincoat. For good measure, she slung a wool scarf around her neck.

Once dressed, she hurried into the kitchen to fix instant oatmeal. As she poured steaming water over the oats, she tried calling Garrett's house. No answer. Well, she could only hope he'd made Keith dress sensibly. On afterthought she dialed his direct line at the office. After the fifth ring she gave up. Obviously he knew her well enough to trust her to be there for Keith.

The buses were loading when Sherry drove through the school gates. She saw Keith pacing the walkway looking anxious. He didn't see her, and it took her several minutes to find an empty parking space.

"Hi, sport. Sorry I'm late," she apologized as she ran up to him all out of breath.

"Sherry, you came. I knew you would. I knew it." The boy propelled himself into her arms, nearly knocking her off the curb.

Regaining her balance, she hugged him, laughed and ruffled his hair.

A serene-faced woman disconnected herself from a group of rowdy students. "Professor Campbell. I'm Keith's principal. I'm so glad you could make this outing. We've had a number of parents cancel. Keith has mentioned you many times. Frankly, I wasn't sure his father would follow my advice to wean Keith from you slowly."

Sherry glanced up and into dark assessing eyes. "You and Garrett discussed me?" The words "wean Keith from you slowly" spattered goose bumps up her spine.

"In a manner of speaking." The principal's gaze slid away to the two yellow buses. "No matter. You're a lifesaver. Our rules say a minimum of one adult per ten students on a field trip. Counting you, we barely made the quota on our second bus."

Sherry's stomach gave a little lurch. Thirty eight- and nine-year-olds were a lot for three adults to oversee.

The principal noticed Sherry's quick glance at the dark sky and reached over to pat her hand. "I've called the weather bureau at least six times already. They assure me that with the velocity of the wind in another hour, the next front will be Indiana's problem, not ours."

The oatmeal lumped in Sherry's stomach flattened a bit. She smiled down into Keith's eyes and slid an arm around his jean-jacketed shoulders. "So what are we waiting for, tiger? Let's get this show on the road."

His ear-to-ear grin was all the validation and reward Sherry needed for braving several hours on a bus with a load of noisy kids. Because they'd boarded late, the two of them worked their way to the back. Sherry's heart swelled every time Keith paused to introduce her to friends, his hand firmly ensconced in hers.

GARRETT HAD STAYED UP half the night suffering guilt over the hatchet job he'd done on Sherry's program. He'd let his anger at Carla spill over into his work—something he hadn't done in years. About midnight, he'd admitted he'd been angry at Sherry, too. Angry, mixed-up—and in love with her. It wasn't her fault things had moved so fast. They needed to talk. Needed to desperately. His heart cracked and crumbled at his feet every time he passed her on campus and she deliberately crossed the street to avoid him.

He would have taken the first step toward communicating this morning. She'd told him that a lack of communication was at the root of most relationship problems. But he had to get to the campus before she did. In the middle of the night, he'd decided to go down fighting for every service Sherry's department offered. Luckily he had a master key that fit all the offices. He'd retrieve the copy he'd shoved under her door and she'd never be the wiser. He figured she hadn't stopped by her office last night; if she'd found the budget, she would've been pounding on his door regardless of the hour.

Garrett felt like a man given a pardon. This evening, he'd start mending fences. It might be good to see if Nan Campbell would watch Keith while he took Sherry to dinner, then plied her with soft music and warm brandy. That was about the best medicine he could think of to begin healing ills. A good way to say *I'm sorry*.

He pulled back a sleeve and glanced at his watch as he parked. Late though he was after dropping Keith at school, he hoped he'd beaten Sherry to the campus. He also hoped they'd cancel the damned trip to the concert. He'd explained to Keith at great length this morning that they were going to get some things straight with Carla. That was another decision he'd made in the middle of the night—if the lawyers couldn't hammer out an agreement that was fair to Keith in the custody issue between him and Carla, he'd go before a judge and plead his case.

Immediately after he'd collected the budget mistake from Sherry's office floor, he planned to call Carla and let her know he wasn't having any more of her jerking Keith around like a puppet on a string. Maybe they'd make progress if he couched it in terms she understood—such as telling her that if Keith was a client, she'd never cancel an appointment at the last minute. He wasn't trying to keep her from seeing their son, but Keith deserved better than she'd given so far.

It started to spit rain before Garrett had reached the

outside steps. He frowned at the low-riding clouds. Keith's principal had been on the phone with the weather bureau when he'd gone into the school this morning. She'd said they predicted the storm would blow over Missouri. So much for predictions, he thought sourly as he took the steps two at a time to avoid the rain that now pelted faster.

He shook droplets off his winter wool jacket, wishing now that he'd insisted Keith at least take his raincoat. Although, when would they be out in the weather? Only to walk from the bus to the concert hall and back to the bus again. Kids didn't melt, he reminded himself.

"Good," he grunted with satisfaction. He was first in. There were no lights on in the department yet. Garrett flipped on the lights as he made his way down the hall. He dropped his briefcase on his desk. It contained a newly revised version of the budget that he'd pored over until four in the morning. His portion of the cut was a mere twelve thousand dollars. He wasn't going to let the seven other deans force him to accept more.

At midnight, he'd recalled the claims he'd made at the time of his interview—a budget always had fat to trim. Sherry's program provided the community with a much-needed service, and he'd be dammed if he'd let committee members run roughshod over him because he happened to be new. They wanted to cut the Hub completely. He wouldn't let them. Sherry trusted him to save it, and save it he would.

After booting up his computer, Garrett hurried down the hall and unlocked Sherry's office door. The report lay where he'd hoped it would. He felt his shoulders relax even as he picked it up, backed out again and closed the door. Then he turned and ran smack into Angel.

"Are you here to sign Dr. Campbell's personal-leave form?" she asked, eyeing the packet of papers in his hand.

"L-leave?" he stammered, creasing the budget sheets in half so Angel wouldn't be able to see what he'd done.

She set her purse on the desk and pulled a blank form out of a cubbyhole. "Just sign the bottom line and I'll type in the rest. Oh…what should I list as the reason for her absence?"

Garrett gaped at her, then at the paper she'd thrust into his hand along with a pen. "Reason? The truth, of course. Why is she taking the day off?" He half expected Angel to say Sherilyn was accompanying Maria Black to court or something.

Angel crossed her arms and gave him a look that said he must be dense. "Really, Dean Lock. With those gossips in Personnel, you can't want to say she's escorting your son on a field trip."

"She's what?" Garrett dropped the pen. He tried to make sense of Angel's announcement as he searched for the pen. "How? Why…?" he finally managed.

Angel narrowed her eyes, studying him down the length of her nose. "In a message she left on my answering machine at home, she said you knew. She said your ex bowed out and she's replacing her."

"Keith," he growled. "That little monster. I told him not to call her. He must've done it, anyway. That explains why he was so cheerful this morning."

"Does this mean you won't sign Dr. Campbell's leave request?" Angel gave Garrett the evil eye. "No offense, Dean, but you're such a dunce. She really loves your kid—and you, although why is beyond me. No, it's not," she corrected with a wave of her hand. "Women are saps when it comes to picking men."

Garrett was about to protest that Sherry wasn't a sap and, anyway, it was none of Angel's business when the telephone rang. As she reached for it, he scribbled his name on the form and left it for her to handle, deciding it was safer to bail out than get into a discussion that threatened to become far too personal.

At his office door he heard his own telephone. Turning to his secretary, Garrett muttered, "If that's Westerbrook or one of the other committee members, say I have to retype my proposal and I'm going to be late for the meeting."

The woman's cry of alarm halted his steps. Glancing over his shoulder, Garrett saw terror and sorrow and pity cross her face. "In Danville," she said, voice erupting in fits and spurts. "The school bus your son is on skidded off the road and into the Loutre River. The principal is calling all the parents to come to the school and wait for further news."

Garrett watched her hang up the phone as if another man resided inside his skin and had received the awful news. "Keith," he said brokenly, remembering the excited child he'd dropped off at school a little more than an hour ago. "And Sherry," he whispered, thankful somewhere deep in his heart that she'd cared enough for Keith to be there on such short notice. God, what if he lost them both?

Ashen-lipped, he instructed, "Tell Westerbrook." Then, fearing his knees wouldn't obey the need to get him to Keith's school in one piece, Garrett tore out of the office like a man possessed.

CHAPTER FIFTEEN

THE BUS DRIVER was a round jolly woman of indeterminate age. The teacher was so young Sherry doubted the ink on her certificate had dried yet. But the kids loved her, and they listened when she told them to sit and be quiet. Even if it was beyond the capacity of eight- and nine-year-olds to stay quiet long. Fifteen minutes into the drive, the bus pulsed noisily again with their laughter and excited squeals. Another mother, who accompanied her delicate-looking daughter, glanced at Sherry, grimaced and pretended to plug her ears.

Attempting to bring order to chaos, the teacher clapped her hands. "Let's practice the songs we're doing in our upcoming holiday show. Soft voices," she said.

Keith scooted closer to Sherry. "Our program's on the Friday before Christmas. Will you come?"

"Didn't you invite your mom?"

He leaned his curly head on her shoulder. "Only Dad. Mom never has time."

It was said with a careless shrug, but Sherry picked up on his pain. "Remind me when we get home, sport. I'll check my calendar."

"You will? Cool." He sat forward, eyes bright as he joined the other singers.

He had a nice voice. Clear. Pure. Sherry sat back and

smiled. Two songs later, she wondered if Garrett knew that his son had a gift for pitch and tone. He must, she decided, losing herself in thoughts of Garrett. Maybe fathers didn't get worked up over things that weren't athletic. She liked to think Garrett would.

The bus slowed to a crawl. Sherry craned her neck to see out the window, which was clouded with condensation. Reaching across Keith, she rubbed a spot clear. It was darker out than when they'd started. She felt a ripple of unease overtake the singers. The bus driver and the teacher appeared deep in conversation. The urgency of their body language communicated itself to Sherry. "Keith," she murmured, leaning close to his ear, "I'm going to the front of the bus for a minute. You stay right here."

He nodded and slid into the chorus of "Rudolph, the Red-nosed Reindeer."

Lurching down the narrow aisle, Sherry determined that their bus had stopped behind the other one. Through the front window, she saw that the highway ahead was underwater.

"Problems?" She dropped into an empty seat behind the teacher. In answer, the radio crackled and a disembodied voice, presumably from the lead bus, queried whether they should go on or turn back. "Turning here won't be easy," a woman said.

"Your call," advised Mary, the apple-cheeked driver. "Must be raining harder upriver than the forecasters thought. Never seen the Loutre River this high. How deep do you think it is?"

The lead driver didn't respond. Instead, the big yellow bus crept forward. Sherry held her breath as inch by inch the tires churned, soon to be swallowed by swirling, muddy water. As if sensing something amiss, the children let their voices trail off thinly, and silence fell over the interior. Someone began to whimper. The other mother on board, Erica Hanover, tried to console the crying youngster.

Sherry hadn't realized she'd been holding her breath until the companion bus emerged on higher ground beyond the point where water covered the road.

"Well, now. That wasn't so bad," boomed the driver's cheery voice. "This old storm will probably blow out before we head home. Hang on to your seats, kiddos, we're gonna give Lucy Belle here a little bath." The kids all giggled as the woman thrust the bus in gear and lovingly patted the dash.

Sherry made her way back to Keith. She felt the bus skid and cried out in surprise as her thigh smacked a metal seat rim. It hurt, and she almost landed in the lap of a sweet-faced girl whose pigtails wrapped her small head like a crown. "Excuse me," Sherry gasped. Suddenly she was tossed in the opposite direction and fell to her knees. As children began to scream, she crawled uphill to reach Keith. The bus pitched and rolled as she sat down hard and rubbed at a rip in her tights.

Cries of panic escalated. The sound bounced off the ceiling as the bus whirled dizzily. Occupants were tossed first one way, then another. Unsure what was happening, Sherry gripped Keith with one hand and with the other, tried to shield two boys on the opposite side of the aisle. A sheet of water splattered the hole she'd rubbed on the glass earlier. Immediately afterward, the window was slapped by a series of tree branches. With a sick sinking weakness that threatened to bring up the small amount of oatmeal she'd consumed for breakfast, Sherry realized they were no longer on the road.

"Find something solid and hang on, kids!" she shouted. "Stay in your seats and don't let go. We'll ride this out." The bus bucked and shuddered and spun for what seemed an endless amount of time. Sherry had difficulty maintaining a positive face.

She fancied that her whole life passed in a blur. Memories, good, bad and in between skittered through her head. Regrets—yes. She was never going to see her children graduate from Wellmont. Never going to get married so she could *have* kids, even.

And Garrett—he'd be left forever alone because she'd failed to protect the boy he'd entrusted into her care. She met Keith's frightened blue eyes and pinched white face, and vowed if there was any possible way to save him and these other children, she'd use her last breath to do so. For the moment, though, she sheltered as many small bodies as she was physically able to collect. The bumps and shrieks from other parts of the bus told of an appalling lack of adult shelters.

A terrible scrape and screech of metal brought renewed terror to the occupants, prompting wild screams. Then, mercifully, the buffeting stopped and the bus rocked gently as though cradled by invisible arms.

Sherry straightened and put aside Keith and the others who'd clustered in her arms. "Miss Briggs," she called to the teacher above the din, "what is it? Shh, children. Don't anyone move. We're caught on something, I think."

"Looks like we've run aground. No, we're hung up on a tree, maybe," yelled the driver. "The river's raging, but I see land off to the left."

"Does the radio work?" Sherry asked, hope overtaking apprehension. She again ordered the kids in her immediate vicinity to remain seated. Slowly, carefully, she moved forward, checking and attending to injuries as best she could, always wiping away tears. Erica Hanover shook like a leaf, but she tried to calm those closest to her.

After trying several radio frequencies, the white-lipped driver got a faint response. She sliced a hand through the air to quiet the crying. "The other bus reported the accident. All we have to do is sit tight and wait for rescue." She unbuckled the first-aid kit and sucked in a breath when the bus rocked precariously. Taking out a medicated swab, she rolled up her pant leg and wiped a trail of blood that ran down her leg. "Leg might be broken," she muttered, passing Sherry the kit.

Sherry glanced out through the miraculously unbroken glass and into the greedy, sucking floodwater doing its level best to dislodge them from their perch. The young teacher appeared to be in shock. Unless she snapped out of it, that left Sherry, a shaky Erica and a crippled driver to see to the transfer of thirty crying kids, some of them injured. All the prayers she knew and a few she manufactured stuck in her throat. As if things weren't already about as bad as they could get, Keith suddenly launched himself against her thighs and dropped an unexpected bombshell.

"This is all my fault! 'Cause I was bad. Dad said I couldn't ask you to come—and I did. I sneaked into his room and used his phone. Now God's mad."

Sherry's heart had just settled a bit. Keith's declaration sent it skittering again. *Garrett didn't know she'd come with Keith. He hadn't had a change of heart. And if by some chance Angel didn't get her message, no one knew where she was.*

None of which mattered now. Nor did it have any direct bearing on how she felt about Garrett and Keith. She loved them. It was simple, really. Love had always seemed so complicated. It wasn't at all. A studied calm invaded her body as she patted Keith's head. "Honey, God doesn't get mad. And I promise, neither will your dad." She smiled into his teary face. "Trust me," she said. "I want everyone to sit as still as mice. Keith, why don't you and Miss Briggs start another Christmas song?"

Keith brushed a lock of hair from a thin cut that bloodied his forehead and, along with his teacher, sang "Silent Night." At first in a high quavery voice, then growing stronger as the other children joined in.

Sherry shucked off her cardigan and wrapped it around a thin girl who'd begun to shake. She used her scarf to make a sling for a boy whose arm she feared was broken. The teacher rallied and worked the other side of the aisle. She, a gray-faced Erica and Sherry took care of the hurt and the frightened. All thirty kids were gut-wrenchingly scared. So was Sherry.

GARRETT WHEELED into the elementary school parking lot behind a van he knew belonged to the family of one of Keith's classmates. The guy stopped in a bus-loading zone and jumped out. So did Garrett. The woman behind him did the same. Garrett raced into the office in time to hear the principal say the accident had happened about thirty-five minutes east of the city.

"A thirty-five minute drive on a good day," she said. "With this unexpected flash flooding, driving conditions are anything but ideal."

"Has anyone been in contact with the bus driver?" Garrett asked.

"Our other driver. She apparently crossed a low spot in the highway, but when Mary's bus reached the middle of the crossing, a wall of water came out of nowhere and broadsided her bus. Both Montgomery and Warren counties have dispatched rescue crews. News is sketchy, but we must be patient."

Garrett glanced around at the worried faces of the other parents. "Why are we waiting here?" He started elbowing his way to the door.

The principal held up a hand. "Don't do anything foolish, Dr. Lock. The police and volunteer rescue teams are gathering. Rushing up there will only overload highways already devastated by this freak storm."

"Those are our kids," Garrett said emotionally. "How can we sit on our duffs when extra hands may help?"

"Let's go, then," chimed in another man. "My wife planned to go on this trip, but she woke up with the flu. My daughter's alone."

"I have four-wheel drive," announced a father who'd just come in. Most of the men who were present charged out and piled into his vehicle. No one spoke much on the drive. The storm that was supposed to pass over lashed them with dark fury. Garrett conjured up happy visions of Keith and Sherry as if doing so would keep them safe from harm. When they slowed at a railroad track, he remembered Carla. He dragged out his cell phone and placed a call to the bank, only to be informed by someone with a bored voice that both Carla and Crawford were in meetings and had left word they couldn't be disturbed.

Garrett felt unwarranted anger crowd out his good sense. "Tell Carla," he snapped, "that the son she'd promised to be with today is in a school bus trapped in the middle of some damned river." The man seated on his left supplied the name, which Garrett added before he signed off.

"When the rescue teams reach them," the man said, "they'll transport any injured kids to St. Louis."

Garrett didn't want to think about injuries. But of course it was a possibility. He paused, admitting how glad he was that Sherry was there to look out for Keith.

When they reached the area, which police had cordoned off, and saw the roughly tumbling debris-filled river that had jumped its banks, Garrett realized injuries were more than a possibility. A shed bobbed past, followed by a car that cartwheeled out of sight around a bend in the out-of-control tributary. His hands shook and his blood froze.

The men jumped from the vehicle and waded toward the rescuers clustered near a boat. Two men dressed in hip waders and yellow raincoats wrestled a small aluminum boat onto a flatbed truck. Two others were unloading motorized rubber rafts from another truck.

"Any updates?" Garrett demanded. "We all have kids on that bus."

One of the men, a grandfatherly type, looked up. "When we got downstream in this boat—" he tapped the aluminum hull "—we saw the bus hung up on a tree growing out of a sandbar. The kids were singing Christmas carols. Beat all I ever seen. The current's dicey. Near impossible to get this baby close. One of the moms, a spunky little gal, busted out a side window and rigged a rope slide from inside. We got maybe twenty kids and a skinny teacher out. Water's icy, though, and some of 'em were cut and bruised. Top of that, a few hit floating debris. Each batch we hauled ashore, rescue vehicles carted 'em off to various hospitals."

"So you got everyone out?" The fear gripping Garrett's stomach uncoiled in a rush.

"Nope. Weren't that lucky. The bus broke loose and shot downriver about a hundred yards. She went under up to the bottom of the windows. Appears to be lodged on a boulder sticking out of a shoal. Still has the spunky mom, a pretty hysterical mom, an injured driver and mebbe ten kids on board. Problem is, the shoal sits smack in the middle of a big eddy. Tossed this puppy around like so much flotsam. They're gonna try rubber rafts. Maybe they'll roll easier with the swells. Don't know what the crew up there'll do if that fails."

The man who'd given Garrett the lift waded close to the two rescuers. "Any way you have names of the kids already taken off the bus?"

The old fellow rubbed his bald pate. "Me'n Joe are headed upriver to get a lady and her cat hanging on a roof. See that gent?" He pointed to a young man working a base radio attached to a Red Cross vehicle. "He can probably give the hospitals a jingle and get names. The kids were already tagged for their field trip, which helped."

Garrett thanked the men. Then the worried dads converged on the man with the radio. After a suspenseful ten minutes, they pored over the list of rescued children. When Garrett read Keith's name, there was no describing the relief he felt. But where was Sherry's? He ran down the scribbled names more slowly. Her name wasn't there.

"Could there be someone who didn't get reported?" he asked the radioman. Garrett held his breath.

"Nope. The hospitals know who they admitted."

"Is it possible someone didn't need admitting? I mean, if she wasn't injured?"

The volunteer on the radio shook his head. "They were all wet and banged up. Even if they were only treated in Emergency, the hospital logged a name."

Garrett's heart plummeted. Did that mean Sherry was still on board? The first man had said a spunky mom, a hysterical one and the bus driver were the only adults left. Of course, he'd have no way of knowing Sherry wasn't some kid's mom. It'd be like her to stay if she thought she could help. Somehow Garrett knew she wasn't the hysterical woman—and that left the "spunky" one. His heart swelled with pride, although he didn't have a right. She was a treasure, and he'd been a fool.

The owner of the four-wheel-drive vehicle touched Garrett's shoulder. "My daughter, Phillip's girl, and Henry's son are on the list. We're driving on up to St. Louis. Since Keith's there, too, I imagine you'll want to ride along."

Garrett was torn. Keith must be frightened and he could be hurt. Garrett had a burning need to go with the men and check his son's fingers and toes as he had done at birth. But if Sherry was still stuck with the other kids, she might need him more. Keith, at least, was safe and in the hands of medical personnel.

"A lady I care about hasn't been accounted for. Would you find Keith there and tell him I'll be along as soon as I can?"

"I will. But what about transportation, Lock?"

"I'll bum a ride on one of the rescue rigs. Either that, or on the other bus. Looks as if they plan to wait out the rescue here."

"Well, good luck. You better believe I won't be so quick to sign one of those permission slips the next time."

"You and me both." Swamped by second thoughts, Garrett nevertheless jogged over to where two men were getting ready to launch one of the motorized rubber boats. "I think my lady is stranded on that bus. You have room for me?" Until he so possessively claimed Sherry, Garrett hadn't realized it was precisely how he felt about her. *His lady.* Now, if he could just be granted the opportunity to tell her, maybe everything would be right with his world again. He *would* get the opportunity. He refused to think otherwise.

The boatmen took one look at Garrett's determined face and made room. "Lose the vest and tie, buddy," said one. "Hope you're not the queasy type. That ol' bus is on mighty shaky ground. She could topple anytime."

"No," said Garrett, as if by force of his will it would stay afloat.

When they docked downstream, he saw that the situation was worse than he'd imagined. The bus, clinging to the shoal by God only knew what, rocked and teetered in the gusty wind.

"We're trying to snag the front end with a grappling hook to hold the damn bus in place," announced a very wet policeman, one of a small force on the riverbank. "The current's too swift. Keeps tossing it back at us. We're worried about sending boats in. Afraid the force of the river will smack them against the bus and push her off that shoal."

"You know who's on board yet?" Garrett could see

outlines through the foggy windows, but not clearly enough to make out anyone in particular.

"Three women and about ten kids. Bus driver probably has a fractured leg. She refuses to bail out until all the kids are safe. One lady has a cool head. Sent the injured kids out with the first teams. The ones who're left are in better shape. Sorta. The other adult is frantic. Her kid refused to jump earlier. She wouldn't leave the little girl."

"Better shape, but scared witless." Garrett heard sobbing even as faraway as they were. "Can I borrow that?" He pointed to a bullhorn another man was holding.

"Sure." The man handed it over.

"Sherry! Sherilyn, it's Garrett. If you're on the bus, signal me, please."

Sherry's breath bunched and her throat closed. The tears she'd held at bay up to now gathered behind her eyelids. *Why was he here? Didn't he know Keith had gotten out?* She wanted to shout but was afraid to in case the noise dislodged the bus. Carefully she edged to the open window and waved at the group of rescue workers. Was it her imagination or had the water risen? Why couldn't she remember if it'd come to the rim of the window before? She felt a jiggle and heard a sickening groan. The bus rocked wildly. Sherry stopped waving. She held her breath and waited for the bus to break loose and be at the mercy of the torrential river again. Luckily it held.

From the minute he saw her wave, a cold purpose replaced Garrett's fear. "Look, if you can't shoot that grapple out to the bus, why not swim it out?"

"Are you nuts?" A fireman shook his head. "The eddy's too fierce. It'd suck a man down. Unless you're a Navy Seal?" His voice filled with hope.

"An experienced hiker is all." Garrett paced the shore, feeling inept and frustrated by the rampaging water. He watched in silence as yet another attempt to launch the grappling hook fell short. It sank like a rock in the massive whirlpool. Retrieving it was no easy task. It kept catching on weeds.

"Look, we can't just stand here and watch them sink, too. How about if I lash a rope around my waist so you can pull me back? Once I reach the eddy, shoot the grapple. I'll find it and hook it to the bus."

"Might work, but it's pretty risky." Two men consulted for a minute. "You'd have to stay clear, yet be close enough to reach the hook. Need to connect it to the front axle. Otherwise, tension from the winch will rip hunks out of the bus."

The rescue-team organizer shook his head. "It's too chancy. That bus could go at any time and the weight'd crush anyone in the vicinity. I can't be responsible for sending you or any other man on such a dangerous task."

"Then I'll be responsible." Garrett stripped off his watch, his jacket and his shirt. He snatched the bullhorn again. "Sherry, honey, I'm swimming out to attach the hook to the bus. If anything happens to me—" his voice faded, then grew stronger "—be there for Keith." Dropping the horn, he looped a rope through his belt and took the plunge. The shock of the cold water almost did him in. He made it to the eddy by sheer force of will and discovered that another rescuer had followed.

Sherry steepled her fingers over her mouth to keep from crying out. Blood thundered in her ears. What Garrett had said sounded like a declaration of love. But maybe she'd read too much into it. People said and did things under duress they wouldn't ordinarily. "Erica…kids," she whispered through her tears. "Let's sing a happy song for those men out there."

And they did. They sang "Santa Claus is Coming to Town." The warbling voices reached Garrett's ears. He focused every ounce of his energy, imagining Christmas with Sherilyn, Keith and Rags. He conjured up a crackling fire in the grate and saw Sherry and Keith smile as they opened gifts. His partner signaled for the grapple. It sailed through the air, landing five feet from Garrett. It took both men to lift it. Three times they tried to connect with the axle. Three times the bus shifted and groaned, and the current drove them away.

"Won't work," shouted the second man.

"One more try," begged Garrett.

A last-ditch effort. Despite their shivering, they hooked the grapple to a front fender. Weakly they signaled for those on shore to reel them in.

That crew didn't waste any time. While Garrett and the second man were hauled back, others launched two motorized rubber rafts. Their attempt to rescue the remaining kids as they had the others failed. The rafts were too unstable to hover long enough for Sherry and Erica to slide kids down a rope. After four tries, they only managed to transfer two girls into the arms of the frantic boatmen.

Blood flow restored to his chilled limbs thanks to thermal blankets, Garrett paced the shore. "If Sherry slid kids down the rope to a man stationed in the water," he said, "they might get wet, but that guy could pass them out to the boats. I'm game," he added.

"Yeah," said his wet pal. "Alternate boats. Work a round-robin deal, bringing kids ashore two at a time before they get hypothermia."

"What about you?" demanded the team leader. "You'll freeze."

"I'm all ears if you've got a better plan," Garrett said, steely-voiced.

A newcomer sloshed up. "I have two wetsuits in my four-by-four. If the swimmers wear them, they could stay in the river longer and with less danger."

"Damn, Nelson, what took you so long getting through the brush?" said the coordinator. "We only have one volunteer for this crazy scheme. Do we have two?"

Several hands shot up. The chief tagged a young fireman.

Garrett donned the clammy wetsuit and boarded the first of the small boats. About eight feet from the bus, he slid into the freezing water and let it carry him over to the bus. Pumped on adrenaline, he ignored the wind and rain. Rescue efforts went smoothly until his partner handed off the last child and they were left with the three adults—none of whom fit through the window they'd been using as an escape hatch. And the driver had a possible broken leg. The only way the adults could possibly get out would be if they opened the bus door. And the minute they did that, the bus would fill with water, upsetting its tenuous balance.

Precious time ticked away while both boats made a trip to shore and back again. Garrett's teeth clattered. He felt what little body heat he'd conserved slipping away. The first of the yellow rafts was a stone's throw away when Garrett heard a giant rending, like the sound of a train squealing into a station. It didn't take a genius to figure out that the hook, which held by a single prong, had bent the fender out of shape.

Garrett's heart slammed in his chest. To get this close and then not rescue the woman he loved was unthinkable.

"You ladies get out the door fast and swim toward us," the other rescuer yelled.

"Garrett." Sherry's white face appeared at the window. A window through which water now sloshed over and into the bus. "Mary Jones, our driver, is hurt, and Erica Hanover can't swim."

Garrett heard fright nibbling away at Sherry's courage. He swore under his breath. "Hang tough a little longer, babe," he said through lips barely able to form the words. "The minute the door opens, shove Mary out. I'll get her into the first boat. My pal will catch Erica. You shoot right behind her. Swim away from the bus as hard as you can and tread water. I'll come back for you." He waited for an answer, not positive he had the strength left to pull any of it off. "Sherry?"

"Y-yes," she answered. "I'm getting rid of my skirt and boots." She didn't tell him she thought she might have broken a rib when she'd heaved the last sturdy boy out the window. Garrett's skin looked blue. He didn't need extra stress.

"Okay. Ladies, prepare for a shock. The river's like the Arctic." Even as he said it, the rain turned to sleet. "When we count to three, open the door."

As if they'd choreographed the scene a hundred times, Sherry followed his instructions. Mary first. Garrett got her in a fireman's hold. His buddy picked up Erica and swam for the second rubber boat. All might have gone like clockwork if Garrett had been able to boost Mary Jones into the craft as planned. The woman, still fully clothed, simply weighed too much for his tired muscles.

The men in the craft worked diligently to lift her. It proved impossible. In the end, they sped away holding her fast to the side. Garrett had heard Sherry hit the water seconds behind Erica but didn't see where she'd gone while he struggled with the injured driver. As he frantically searched the water around a third craft, a flimsy motorboat he hadn't seen before, a louder noise claimed his sluggish attention. A horrendous screech, a huge sucking sound followed by a loud pop. Garrett saw a fender, severed from the body of the bus, sail through the air over his head. He automatically ducked under the water.

As though from a distance, he heard warning cries from the boat. In spite of the fact that his arms had grown heavy, he surfaced and spotted Sherry's head bobbing in the water. He was so overjoyed to see her he ignored the hiss of the grappling hook that, when freed, snaked the length of the rope. He saw it strike Sherilyn's shoulder.

She and the hook sank without a sound.

Garrett bellowed like a bull as the river sucked her down. A red splash of blood arced across Sherry's white T-shirt moments before she slipped from his limited view. Fighting off the hands reaching to haul him into the small motorboat, Garrett lunged over to where he'd last seen Sherry. But the eddy—he hadn't allowed for the widening whirlpool now gobbling up the bus. Each breath he took burned like fire as he dove below the murky brown water.

The men on the boat kept yelling at him to give up. "Come on!" they shouted. "It's too late for the woman. Save yourself!"

They all urged him to stop except for the man who'd helped Garrett rescue the kids. He stripped off a down jacket and dived in again. He forcefully boosted Garrett over the side into the aluminum craft and discovered that Garrett's fingers were twisted into the fabric of the woman's soggy T-shirt. A second rescuer went over the side to assist his teammate.

Several pair of hands worked to pry Garrett's fingers loose. "Let go," growled a ragged voice. "Trust Johnson and Stroud to get your wife into the boat."

Wife! She wasn't, Garrett's fuzzy brain responded. But he loved her and he couldn't let go. He clung even after the other two men rolled her in. They motored to shore as they had done with the bus driver.

The boat struggled to land with its heavy load. Three more men hit the water to help. Finally, one hauled out a knife and cut Garrett loose from the woman he held in a vicelike grip.

Garrett grinned like a fool when at last they tumbled a sodden Sherry into his lap. His joy fled the minute he saw her face—ghostly white and still as death. In spite of first aid rendered on the spot, the jagged cut that ran from Sherry's shoulder to midway down her spine, continued to ooze blood.

Medics loaded them into ambulances. They worked to staunch the flow of Sherry's blood while trying to bring up her temperature. And Garrett's.

The sleet, pelting down now in fine white crystals, slicked the roadways and made the drive to the hospital interminable and treacherous.

Garrett huddled under a thermal blanket, shivering in spite of the hot fluids the medics forced him to drink. He doubted he'd ever be warm again. Sherilyn hadn't moved. It wasn't fair. She'd saved the children. How could fate then turn and steal her away? How would he face Keith? What could he possibly say to a kid who, against his father's expressed edict, had innocently talked her into coming on this death trip?

The medic thrust another steaming cup of hot boullion into Garrett's red hands. "Her vitals are weak. But she's exhibiting a strong will to live. Talk to her. We aren't sure an unconscious person can hear. Some researchers believe they can."

Garrett scooted closer. "I love you," he said softly. "Keith loves you. Help me out here, lady. Don't you dare let go." He bent over and kissed her icy lips.

The female medic who checked the electrodes connected to Sherry's chest smiled at Garrett. "Keep saying what you're saying. Her pulse is getting stronger."

So he kept up a litany of love-talk, at which he'd always been terrible. At long last the medical vehicle pulled beneath the portico of one of St. Louis's finest hospitals. Then trauma teams whisked Sherry in one direction and him in another.

By the time technicians had checked and released Garrett, who had no lingering ill effects, he'd wearied of asking questions about Sherry and getting no answers. He might be a hero, and the nursing staff all claimed he was, but one thing he wasn't—official kin to Sherilyn Campbell. That cold hard fact precluded his getting any information whatsoever. After he'd produced ID, a nurse led him to Keith. She claimed they were inundated with TV cameras and reporters and had to be careful who they let in to see the victims.

Keith hugged his dad and asked tearfully, "Have you seen Sherry?"

"She's here. But they'll only tell her family how she is, son."

"Then call Nolan or Sherry's mom and dad. Are...are you mad 'cause I asked her when you said I shouldn't?"

"I'm not mad, Keith. Still, there'll be consequences for disobeying."

"Okay. But, Dad, if she's hurt bad it's my fault."

"No. She came because she loves you, Keith. We'll find out how she is." Garrett picked up the phone and dialed Sherry's folks. They couldn't believe she'd been in the wreck that headlined local news. "We're coming to St. Louis," Nan said. "We're leaving now."

"No one will tell me a blasted thing," he complained.

"Tell them you're her fiancé," Nan suggested. "That worked for me when we were in college and Ben suffered a football injury."

Garrett coughed and sat down to steady his legs.

"Well, darn it, Garrett, I know you love her. And last night in a dream, I saw her standing at the altar of our church in a wedding gown. It wasn't coincidence that the groom looked a lot like you."

"That'd be a long shot, Nan. Right now I just want her well."

"Long shot? Nolan told Ben you and Sherry were both AWOL from campus today. He and Emily wondered if you two had eloped."

"A grapple struck her. I'm really worried," he confessed in a thin voice.

"Have faith, Garrett. We'll be there in an hour and get you in to see her."

Word on Sherry's condition came sooner and from a surprising source. Carla and Crawford popped into Keith's room unannounced.

"Keith!" they exclaimed. "We were told you were fine. But your leg?"

"Sherry handed me down the rope. I fell and hit something in the water. A big rock, maybe. Sherry's the one hurt bad." Tears trickled down his pale cheeks. "They won't tell Dad nothin'."

Carla and her husband glanced at Garrett. "We just saw her—in Emergency," Carla said. "She asked about you and Keith. They'd just sewn her up apparently. She was fine enough to give me a lecture about parental responsibility."

Carla sat beside Keith and held his hand. Her eyes filled with tears, and Crawford gripped her shoulder. "You've no idea what hearing about this did to me. Learning that neither Garrett nor the hospital could reach me really shook me up. Garrett, Keith—I've decided not to pursue full custody. My lifestyle didn't allow for motherhood eight years ago and if anything, demands on my time are even greater now. You're part of me, Keith. I don't want to lose touch again, but I have to face facts. All I can ever be is a part-time mother." She sobbed quietly. "I want you to visit us whenever possible. And Garrett—" she faced him "—you've done a fabulous job of raising our son."

Keith gave a whoop, then said with more decorum, "You're okay, too, Mom."

Crawford started to speak, but the door opened and a nurse wheeled Sherry in. "Keith," she gasped. "Your leg? They just told me you'd been admitted."

"Yes," the nurse said dryly. "Dr. Campbell should be in her own room, but she refused to go until we brought her by to see this young man and his father. It's against the rules, you know."

Garrett sprang from his chair and rushed to her side.

Keith sat up in spite of his elevated leg. "My broke leg don't hurt, Sherry. You saved me and all the other kids. You were right, too. Dad's not mad that I invited you."

"Keith." Garrett wagged a finger.

"Well—" the boy looked contrite "—he said I have to lose privileges 'cause I went behind his back. But…he didn't sound all *that* mad."

Carla lobbed a gaze between her son and Sherry. "Has anyone told you, Dr. Campbell, that you'd make a good mother? And wife," she said pointedly to her ex.

Sherry gaped at the woman. "I, uh, know people who wouldn't agree." Was she so transparent that Carla saw right through her half-baked attempt to hide her love for Garrett and Keith?

Crawford, the emotionless banker, certainly did. "A client of mine, the doctor who examined Garrett said he drove them nuts asking about you, Ms. Campbell. Perhaps Garrett'll give us some time alone with Keith while he makes sure you're settled in your room."

"Dr. Lock can stop by 302—briefly," said the nurse who was already backing Sherry's wheelchair out the door. "I figure we have fifteen minutes max to get her into bed before that painkiller kicks in and sends her nighty-night."

"She's looking pretty rocky," Garrett said hesitantly. "Maybe I shouldn't go."

"Do…please." Sherry held up a beseeching hand, then let it fall quickly to her lap. "Unless you'd rather not." Her lashes fluttered down to cover her eyes.

Garrett thought she looked terribly pale, although she had more color than she'd had during the drive to the hospital.

Carla nudged Garrett forward. "Quit looking like a lovesick calf caught in a hailstorm and go get her."

His lips curled in a sheepish grin. "That noticeable, huh?"

"Yeah," Crawford, Keith and Carla all said together.

Garrett frowned at his son. "You're eight years old. What do you know about lovesick looks?"

"I'm almost nine. I watch TV. And you've looked that way since you and Sherry had a fight. Me'n Rags love Sherry, too, so don't blow this, huh, Dad?"

"We did not fight," Garrett said huffily, hitching up jeans dried stiff from the silt in the river. Helluva way to look when a man went to propose to the woman he loved. But then, from that first stormy night they'd met in Kansas, nothing about his relationship with Sherilyn Campbell had been exactly normal.

He entered Sherry's room as the nurse slipped out. "Talk fast," Sherry muttered, her speech slightly slurred.

Garrett gazed at her sweet face. Her short spiky hair made a two-toned splash against the pillow. He remembered how silky it'd felt against his palms that night on the *Ozark Queen*. Afraid of hurting her, he touched the back of her hand—not the one sprouting the IV.

Her smile was off-kilter. Garrett wondered if he'd already lost her to the sedative. But she crooked her finger at him, then patted a spot on her bed.

He sat carefully. "We have a lot to talk about, you and I. Earlier I thought I'd lost you." His voice broke. Nipping in a sharp breath, he attempted to laugh. "Takes getting kicked in the head to show some guy what a danged fool he's been."

Sherry covered his hand with her smaller one. "You were kicked in the head? By whom? When?"

"Figuratively speaking," he said gruffly, threading their fingers and bringing hers to his lips. "You've given me no reason to believe you still consider March a perfect time for new beginnings," he murmured, "but…well, I love you. Will you marry me?"

How she responded so quickly for someone in her shape, Sherry would never know. She lunged forward, flung her arms around Garrett's neck and smothered his lips with a kiss aimed at cutting off any objections he might have raised.

"I take it that means yes," he gasped when they were forced apart to breathe.

"It'd better," chorused Nan and Ben Campbell from the open doorway. "The doctor downstairs said he'd ordered strict bed rest for Sherry. I got the feeling," said Ben dryly, "that the old duffer had something far less strenuous in mind."

Sherry slid back into bed, a silly smile flitting along her lips. "What lousy timing. A marriage proposal at last, and I can't stay awake. But I'm holding you to this, Lock." With that, her lashes drifted down and she was fast asleep.

EPILOGUE

THE CITY HOSTED a parade to honor the hero and heroine who'd kept the local school-bus accident from going down in the annals of history as a tragedy. The parade was front-page news.

As a rule, parades made dull stories. So did averted tragedies. What Sherry Campbell and Garrett Lock provided was better, as far as the reporters were concerned. A love story. The whole world, they soon discovered, loved a love story. At least, the people of Columbia did.

Because the couple had decided on a spring wedding, Garrett and Sherry had reporters dogging them for four months. Also wedding consultants, jewelers, caterers, florists and photographers. Merchants weren't trying to *sell* them services; shop owners begged to *give* them every aspect of a fairytale wedding.

"Shall we elope?" Garrett suggested hopefully. He and Sherry had just sneaked out the back door of the plastic surgeon's who'd conducted a final exam on her now-healed shoulder.

"Are you serious?" Sherry asked as they piled into the back of her father's van.

By pre-arrangement, Ben and Nan Campbell had brought Keith, Megan and Mark along. The whole group was headed to a celebration dinner hosted by Nolan and Emily because an editor was interested in their manuscript, *Who Really Settled the West?*

Garrett hooked one arm around his son's shoulders and tucked Sherry into the crook of the other. "Well, eloping's starting to sound good...."

"But if you 'loped," Keith said, his bright smile fading, "my class—all the kids you helped off the bus—they wouldn't get to be ushers or hand out groom's cake like me and Mark did at Camp and Emily's wedding."

"True," Sherry said. "The kids are looking forward to taking part in our wedding."

"Mom promised I could buy my first pair of high heels to wear when I light your candles," Megan wailed.

"If you eloped," Nan gasped, "that beautiful gown Yvette talked her merchandiser into giving Sherry would go to waste."

"True," Sherry agreed. "But Yvette's apology for starting those rumors means more to me than any gown."

"Speaking of rumors..." Ben smiled at them both in the rearview mirror. "I hear all this publicity has set your board of regents on their ears. In the entire history of Wellmont, they've never let spouses work together in the same department—until now."

Sherry batted her eyes at Garrett. "Sheldon March made it very clear that while I may have helped a few kids out of the bus, you, my love, are the real hero. And since you saved my life, Garrett, he strongly implied I should never oppose you on budget matters again."

Garrett started to snort indignantly, then reared back and favored his soon-to-be-bride with a steely blue gaze worthy of a Texan. "Sheldon's right, little lady, and don't you forget it."

Sherry sputtered. "I was kidding!"

"Me, too." Garrett leaned over and kissed her. Once. Twice. The third time she melted against him with a sigh.

"Those kisses, Lock. That's how you got me to make the Hub co-ed." She held out her left hand and studied the engagement ring Garrett had placed there the day after he proposed—when she was still in the hospital. "Remember how much Angel hated the idea? She called me a traitor and threatened to wax the floor with your butt. Um, Angel changed her tune," she said for the benefit of the others. "After Garrett advertised our new counseling services and twenty divorced and single dads signed up the first day."

"Is that why Angel agreed to be one of your bridesmaids?" he asked.

"Probably. So there's another reason we can't elope."

"I'm tasting defeat, but refresh my memory on why else we shouldn't do it," Garrett muttered.

"To show whatever jerk left that article on my desk about failed second marriages that we're going to beat the odds."

"You'll succeed if you two stay away from water. Bad history there," Nan Campbell put in. "Better add something in your vows about keeping your feet on terra firma."

"Can't," Sherry said. "The owner of the *Ozark Queen* saw our picture in the paper and he offered us the boat for a week."

"Does that 'clude me?" Keith piped up.

Garrett vividly recalled the last trip. Silver moonlight

dancing off the water. Sherry's slinky backless dress—
and everything that occurred thereafter.

Her thoughts similar, Sherry straightened Garrett's
tie while she discreetly slid her foot up and down his
shin.

"Uh…cough…cough…uh," he wheezed.

"Yippee! Dad said yes! I can go. Those are the noises
he makes when he wants to say no, but ends up saying
yes."

"Not this time, Keith." Garrett's voice was strangled. "Honeymoons are strictly a party for two. You and
Rags will stay with Mark, Megan and Pilgrim. But I
promise, son. One day soon Sherry and I will take you
on a river boat. It'll be our first trip as a family."

Keith bounced happily up and down. "Then I'll be
like Mark. I'll have it all."

Mark made a face. "Not quite. You still won't have
a dorky sister."

"Oh." Garrett tweaked Sherry's nose. "I think Professor Campbell and I might be willing to try and
correct that oversight."

Her lips curved in a satisfied smile. "If that's a challenge, Dr. Lock…I accept."

Everything you love about romance...
and more!

Please turn the page for Signature Select™
Bonus Features.

Coffee in the Morning

BONUS FEATURES INSIDE

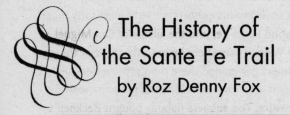

The History of the Sante Fe Trail
by Roz Denny Fox

The Santa Fe Trail was the first of America's great trans-Mississippi pathways to the West. It was opened in 1821 and preceded by two decades the beginnings of the Oregon and California Trails, which were traveled primarily by people seeking new land. The Santa Fe Trail was first and foremost a road for commerce, a trade highway connecting the East with merchants along the way and into Mexico. It was the only East-West trail that extended into a foreign country.

William Becknell and five companions from Missouri's Boonslick County headed west across the plains planning to trade with Indians, exchanging fabric and their goods for horses and mules, and to hunt. There are many historians, however, who insist that Becknell's goal was always to expand a waiting market for textiles and manufactured goods deep into what was then a Spanish province, one that which prohibited trade with foreigners (the American territory.)

4

In spite of the well-known trade barrier, Becknell and his cohorts drove at least forty miles beyond Santa Fe, into the village of San Miguel del Vado. It was sheer luck, some say, that the soldiers garrisoned there didn't throw Becknell's traders into irons, but received his party with pleasure. The soldiers happily bought Becknell's entire stock at a high profit.

It's thought that because Mexico had achieved its independence from Spain mere months before Becknell's party arrived, what had previously been a terrible risk suddenly paid off.

His success excited many others who saw the enormous potential of the Southwest trade options.

Becknell's first few trips would ultimately be followed by thousands of wagons transporting a large assortment of goods. The most popular trade items were cotton cloth, printed calico, woolens and silks. The traders also sold a broad assortment of American-made goods that brought silver pesos, mules, beaver pelts and other desirable things back to the Missouri area. As well, silver coin and gold bullion bolstered the currency-starved Missouri banks.

The significance of the Santa Fe route to commerce stretched far beyond the 865 arduous miles from Franklin, Missouri, to Santa Fe, New Mexico. It doubled and tripled the need for European textiles then being shipped to ports along the Eastern seaboard. Freight was carried in barges along the Mississippi River, which encouraged other travelers, who were guided on their journeys only by rivers, springs, natural landmarks and the scars left in the land by previous wagon trains. By 1840, soldiers patrolling the Western plains began to travel this route, and erected forts along the trail. Following the soldiers were missionaries, gold-seekers, young men hunting for adventure and emigrant families.

After gold was discovered in California in 1848, groups of men called Forty-Niners initially used the trail. Ultimately they forged other routes West.

Those who traveled the Santa Fe Trail encountered many hardships. Robbers, Indian attacks, disease, extreme weather and sometimes a lack of water spelled disaster for many a wagon train. As the U.S. Army forayed out from the forts and claimed land and subsequently made it safe for emigrants, the trail was considered a lifeline between the new territory and "the states." In 1850, a regular mail service started between Independence, Missouri and Santa Fe, New Mexico.

Travel over the Santa Fe Trail declined when the Atchison, Topeka & Santa Fe Railway opened in 1873, although merchants who couldn't afford the train or who didn't trust the Iron Horse, made use of the trail until late in 1878. From then until

1987 the trail was virtually unused. The Daughters of the American Revolution saw its significance and requested that it be designated as a National Historic Trail. They set out to locate and map the entire trail. The Santa Fe Trail Association was formed; today its purpose is to preserve as much of the original trail and save it from encroachment wherever possible.

Modern-day travelers can still see many famous landmarks along the old trail, including natural markers such as Rabbit Ears, Wagon Mound and Starvation Peak. Traces of ruts left by traders' wagons can be seen at various points from the Missouri River to downtown Santa Fe. Many of the forts that were vital to the success of the Santa Fe Trail are also open for public viewing.

The Santa Fe Trail was instrumental in opening the American West, and we are fortunate that so much of it remains visible. What an opportunity to relive history!

The Writing Life:
Following the Sante Fe Trail
by Roz Denny Fox

Probably the question most asked of a writer is:
"Where do you get your ideas?"

Often it's impossible to say where ideas come
from, because writers all work differently. A story
idea can strike fully formed, or begin as a fleeting
thought, as was the case with the stories in
this volume.

Some years ago, I chanced upon an historical
marker in Santa Fe that said it indicated the
end of the original Santa Fe Trail. Where was the
trailhead? I wondered. Having been born and
raised in Oregon, I'd studied the Oregon Trail.
I'm sure I'd also learned about other trails west,
such as the Chisholm and the Santa Fe, although
my memories were vague. I write contemporary
fiction and was prepared to let my question about
the trailhead die a natural death. But it lingered in
my mind.

Not long afterward, I heard that an old school friend, who worked for a new Oregon wine company marketed under the Oregon Trail label, planned to travel the Oregon trail to advertise their wine—in an old-style Conestoga wagon. Interesting. Add that tidbit to the previous one, and the Santa Fe Trail remained stuck in my mind as I got on with my life. Then one day I read a news article about a group in Utah, who'd organized a wagon train to recreate a trek made by their ancestors.

Ah, but I love my creature comforts. In fact, our family jokes about Mom preferring "motel" camping. I pictured what it'd be like for someone like me to walk in the shoes of a pioneer woman.

Thoughts tend to nag me. I wrote away for information on the old Santa Fe Trail and got in touch with the Santa Fe Trail Association. In spite of encroaching growth countrywide, they've preserved many parts of the original route, and have installed historical markers from Franklin, Missouri, across Kansas, to where the trail splits, and then through Colorado into New Mexico, and across the Texas Panhandle into Santa Fe.

By now I'd talked about the trail enough to interest my husband. He liked driving trips. Over morning coffee, which we always have together, he suggested we use our vacation to follow the trail. I was game—as long as we could stay in motels. It was dreadfully hot the day we left. And I'd read about mosquitos and varmints along the route. So I reiterated that there'd be no sleeping in tents for me. And that my days needed to start with a cup of *good* coffee. Which is when I considered what kind of characters would populate my story.

I'd worked at colleges and always found that their bookstores stocked great local lore. Our first stop in Missouri was a college with vine-covered walls. A charming, bustling campus. I saw it—or a version of it—in my book. I also stumbled on the notion that a college history professor would be the ideal person to send on a wagon-train reenactment. Now, this may be where people start thinking writers are weird. This professor I'd dreamed up told me he didn't *want* to go on any dusty wagon train. He had serious stuff to do, like publish a paper.

He and I *both* needed coffee.

We drove to Franklin, Missouri, a lovely town steeped in history. In 1821, William Becknell from Boonslick County and five companions opened a trade trail that started there. 865 miles—can you imagine?—in a Conestoga wagon, no less. It's thought Becknell was successful because New Mexico had achieved its independence from

Spain, and the old trade restrictions that might have gotten his party killed or imprisoned had been lifted.

I loved tramping around Boonville, too, and borrowed a fictional descendant of Daniel Boone's to head up my wagon train. Maizie Boone. I could visualize her. A stalwart woman befitting her name, but soft on family. Reminded me a lot of my mother, who homesteaded in Oregon when women didn't do such things.

I enjoyed staying in a lovely motel that night in Independence. Talk about history! This town is filled with it. The President Truman Museum is a must-see if you get there.

Arrow Rock was our the first stop the next morning. The bluff overlooks the Missouri River. Driving, we got there fast, and I wondered how long it'd take my characters in their wagon train. We toured restored homes and the Old Tavern, made of walnut, oak and brick, plus a courthouse and a jail that dated from the 1800s. Then we took a side trip to Fort Leavenworth, Kansas, before heading to Council Grove. I bought a book called *Following the Santa Fe Trail—A Guide for Modern Travelers*. That was us, and the book was worth every cent. Still, no matter how clear directions are, old roads close, new ones crop up, and of course I'll never forget the very long detour through acres of milo fields in Kansas.

I learned that forts along the way kept the westward travelers alive. Gave them a chance to mingle, discuss routes, hard times and everything they'd left behind. Meeting at the forts, talking with soldiers and fellow pioneers, also gave them news about the fate of wagon trains who'd gone before.

One morning, I considered who the heroine of my emerging wagon train story should be. Emily Benton came to me in a flash. She and Professor Nolan Campbell, fondly called Camp, were a good match. Perfect. I toasted them with fresh-ground coffee.

The days were hot, the nights cool. We experienced an unexpected wind storm, and I knew my characters would weather tough times. We hiked a ways to look at trail depressions. You can see wagon-wheel ruts. It was an eerie feeling gazing down on ghost tracks left by pioneers.

Council Grove in the Flint Hills has replanted the indigenous prairie grass. Blue stem that undulates in the breeze and honestly looks like ocean waves. I loved the town, and it evoked so many ideas. I must've taken ten pictures of the statue called: *Madonna of the Trail,* a work-worn woman in a long patched dress, bonnet and laced-up boots, holding an infant while a toddler clings to her skirt. It was her face that haunted me. The sculptor captured the misery of long months on a relentless trail.

Walking tours of the town reveal how the old blends with the new. A comfortable mix. I gained much information at the Hays House Restaurant, and the Last Chance Store. I'm here to tell you we've got it easy! I appreciated my bed that night and my coffee the next morning.

Fort Riley was a mere blip on our radar. It remains an active Kansas military post, and the men and women stationed there must feel a touch of the past.

We stopped at so many places with interesting names like Lost Spring and Cottonwood Crossing. We had a detailed map and still got lost several times. I gained a new respect for pioneers, especially the women. I think that at every point we visited, my story people gained strength and wisdom. I felt fortunate to be able to soak up all of this history and inspiration.

Walnut Creek Crossing was listed on the marker as one of the most dangerous points on the Santa Fe Trail. It was home to Fort Zarah, a stage line, and a government mail-exchange drop. Hardly anything remains today. The sandstone fort literally crumbled and blew away on the wind.

Feeling that prairie wind, I understood. It actually buffeted our car. We'd packed a picnic lunch and a thermos of coffee, which we enjoyed in the car, away from bugs and stinging wind.

Pawnee Rock was a campground for caravans, but also the site of a terrible Indian ambush. It looked like a small hill with a rock face. But to weary travelers in a bumpy wagon, I'm sure it seemed an oasis.

At Fort Larned, the Pawnee River flows past. Here were a series of green and white historical markers. At the cemetery, we passed through an iron gate that opened out onto wide swales left by the wagons. I swear I heard the squeak of wagon wheels. A storm erupted soon after we got there, and we didn't see as much as I'd hoped to. It was late and we wanted to make Dodge City. A hotel, of course. A dinner of steak, potatoes and coffee—lots of it, hot and fresh. I loved Dodge City. You can sense the passage of cattle, pioneers and gunslingers. It's wonderful in every way.

Among other places, we visited the teachers' hall of fame—a fitting tribute to a noble profession. We went to Fort Dodge and Fort Larned, where self-guided tours take a day. We saw the Long Branch Saloon and the original Boot Hill Cemetery, an old locomotive from the Santa Fe

Rail line and Dodge Jail. Pieces of history that not only inspired my characters' situations but created memories I'll cherish.

On the north side of Highway 50 we visited Point of Rocks, an important landmark for wagoners. West of there, we visited more wagon ruts that have remained visible for over a hundred years. It was a dreary, rainy day, with not many people about. I have to say it was the most moving experience of our trip. I'm at a loss to explain the connection I felt with the many pioneers who'd passed this way. Listen, and you can hear the clop, clop, clop of plodding oxen. The groan of loaded wagons and the clink and creak of heavy yokes. There's so much to see in Dodge City that we wished we'd scheduled an extra day. If you go there, check out the brick streets. All sixteen miles of them. And of course there's Wyatt Earp history galore. I can't move on without mentioning a wonderful cowboy statue that drives home how vital cattle drives were back then. Oh, and plenty of spots to indulge in fresh-ground gourmet coffee. Dodge City added a nice texture to my books.

Next were Bent's Old Fort and Bent's New Fort, situated on the Arkansas River. Easy to see how necessary the Bent Forts were to those who took the high mountain route up and over Raton

Pass. As we continued our trip, fall was winding down. Our mornings were crisp now and the nights cold—a reminder that wagon trains had to plan well to cross the rugged pass before snow started to fall.

We encountered a lot of highway construction and traffic was held up for hours, so we elected to retrace our steps and take the lower Cimarron Route into Santa Fe. I considered that lucky as we were able to visit Rabbit Ears, Round and Wagon Mound, landmark rock formations inside New Mexico, visible for miles. The distinctive hills guided many a wagon train through sandstorms or Indian attacks. At Wagon Mound, you can see evidence of the frequent casualties suffered by pioneers. There are two very old cemeteries, one Catholic, one Protestant. Both have a mix of marble, stone and wood markers worn by the weather. And many sites are marked by nothing more than a heap of rocks gathered from the nearby hill. Those markers show plainly how people from all economic levels ventured west in spite of harsh conditions. It was there that I began to wonder if my fictional wagon travelers had what it would take to complete a summer-long trek. My doubts deepened when we took a side trip to old Fort Union. What remains of its adobe walls is so primitive, so far from modern civilization, that for the first time I was able to really experience what our pioneer sisters probably did. Here, dry native grasses flourish. We were surprised and delighted to see several bands of antelope, even though the wind blew hard and constant. As we walked the trails around the fort, a fine red dust got into our eyes and felt gritty on our teeth. I took a lot of photographs as a reminder of how it felt to step back in time.

Although the fort is under management of the National Parks Service, tours are self-guided. There are signs and markers to show the rough outline of the fort. Visitors are warned to watch for rattlers, and indeed we saw some. We also found rows of wagon tracks, their grooves worn deeper than any others we'd seen. Judging by these ruts, the wagon travelers left the fort driving three or four abreast.

Going by car, it wasn't much farther to Santa Fe. Up to this point, we'd had good weather except for a few showers. No one could've been more shocked than we were when, a few miles after leaving the blowing sand of Fort Union, it began to snow. We hadn't packed for this kind of weather. I suppose lots of pioneers felt the same. Traffic was snarled. No one was prepared for the unseasonable storm, and it took us hours to reach the outskirts of Santa Fe. And then we were told there were no rooms to be had! Our only alternative—drive on to Albuquerque in the treacherous weather. Even there, hordes of fall travelers were stranded. A helpful hotel worker phoned around the city until he located a room for us, otherwise, we would've had to spend the night in the car. I suppose then I would truly have experienced a taste of what I planned to put my characters through. But like Sherry Campbell, the heroine of the second book, I couldn't wait to get out of the weather and wash off the dust of the trail in a thoroughly modern shower. Followed by coffee. Never had I enjoyed a hot cup of coffee more than at the end of this journey.

Not all story ideas take so long to come together, nor do they all result in such exciting vacations. It's nice when they do. I loved writing about Emily, Camp, Sherry and Garrett and their children. I was delighted when I was offered the opportunity to revisit everyone, especially since I'd be able to look into the lives of their children, Megan and Mark Benton and Keith Lock. It's fun to see how well they turned out as grown-ups. I hope you'll be as excited to read about them as I was to follow their careers and give them their own love stories. Real family sagas are about growth and love and continuing a legacy. Except that Megan Benton isn't as fond of coffee as her stepdad, Nolan Campbell, or her aunt Sherry. Megan prefers her mom's special hot chocolate recipe. She needs it where I made her live, in the cold Upper Peninsula of Michigan. Look for her story next month in *Hot Chocolate on a Cold Day*.

Turn the page for a taste!

BONUS FEATURE

Here's a sneak peek...

20

Hot Chocolate on a Cold Day
by
Roz Denny Fox

Despite their high-maintenance families and high-risk jobs, Megan Benton and Sterling Dodge find plenty of ways to stay warm during the blustery months of March.

A brand-new novel...coming in April 2006.

CHAPTER 1

St. Ignace, Michigan

WHERE WERE THE NEW RENTERS? Megan Benton
parted heavy drapes designed to shut out the
cold, and for the umpteenth time in half an hour
scanned the street below her top-floor Victorian
rental. The thermometer she'd set in her window
box said twenty-six degrees. Practically balmy
compared to the minus fifteen that had gripped
Michigan's Upper Peninsula at her arrival on
New Year's Day. Last week, March blew in and
the ice had finally begun to break up in the
channel and harbor.

Steam rising from her cup of hot chocolate
obscured her view of the marina at the bottom
of the hill. She let the drape fall, then made her
way into the bedroom to dress in her Coast
Guard uniform. As she struggled into long johns
and skier-weight overalls, she thought enviously
of her last duty station in Mobile, Alabama.

Having been born and raised in northern Missouri, she never would have guessed that her Midwest blood could have thinned so much in the few weeks she'd spent in Mobile's helicopter training school. After a scant two months in the northland, crew mates who were like a mob of brothers still ribbed her mercilessly about how she bundled up whenever they had to navigate the Mackinac Straits.

A knock sounded at her front door just as she downed a last swig of chocolate. Leaving off her jacket, Megan pasted on a smile to welcome the new folks her landlord had said would be moving in downstairs.

The house owner, crusty old Hank Meade, was off fishing warmer waters. He'd phoned to ask if Megan would mind if his rental agent left a key with her to make it easier for the renters to pick up. A family, Hank had indicated. With kids. Megan loved kids. Nevertheless, she had mixed feelings about acquiring neighbors. For two months she'd had Lady Vic, as she called the place, to herself. Usually she ran five miles every morning for exercise. But because it was so cold, she'd fallen into the habit of an early-morning aerobics program in her bedroom, where she cranked up hip-hop music to get her blood

22

moving. Neighbors meant she'd have to use earphones, she lamented, yanking open the door.

The face staring down at her wasn't one she expected. Stunned, she gaped at Mark, her brother. Two years younger than her twenty-five, Mark had shot up and surpassed her skinny, five-three frame when they were still in high school. She wondered now if she was hallucinating.

This past Christmas, she'd spent a week at home. Mark had remained at his university in western Missouri, determined, according to their mom and stepdad, to graduate in January with his master's in psychology. When Megan had last called home, their mom had said Mark would walk straight from school into a job at the college in Columbia, where their folks lived and worked. Yet here he stood.

"Hey, did you take a wrong turn in St. Louis, or are you just plain lost?"

Grinning, Mark blew on red-chapped, gloveless fingers. "Invite me in and I'll tell you my sad story. It's colder than a coal miner's patootie out here."

Whooping with delight, Megan launched herself into his arms and let him swing her around and around until they both stumbled inside, punching each other happily. "I can offer you a cup of something warm. And shut the door, you goof. You weren't born in a barn. Wait—do the folks know you're here?"

"Yeah, they know." Shrugging out of a Gore-Tex ski jacket, Mark Benton removed his knit cap and tossed both on his sister's flowered couch before following her into a bright yellow kitchen. Using his hands to bring order to his unruly auburn hair, he propped a hip against the counter as Megan darted from cupboard to stove, where she lit the gas burner under a well-used saucepan.

"Something in your tone tells me all isn't well in little ol' Columbia. Okay, brother, out with it. I have to leave for the station in fifteen minutes. When we talked after the holidays, you told me you were flat broke. Mom said if you finished your dissertation on time you were a shoo-in for a counseling job at Wellmont. So what's up?"

Mark wrinkled his lightly freckled nose. "Right! *Mom's* campus. Where she's head of women's studies, and our stepdad teaches history. Where Aunt Sherry's in charge of the Crisis Center, and Uncle Garrett's just been made vice-chancellor. On top of that, there's a whole danged wing at Wellmont named for our great-grandfather."

"Campbell Hall is a dormitory, not a wing."

"So? It's intimidating," he mumbled, watching Megan pour steaming water over mounds of cocoa she mixed with a dash of salt. Once the mixture had heated through, she added sugar and milk, and let it come to a boil, stirring absently. Then she removed the pan from the burner and dumped in a splash of vanilla. She poured a crockery cup full and topped it with two fat marshmallows. Megan thrust the mug into her brother's hands with a frown.

"And…you're here because you don't want to join a place where most of the family works? Where you're guaranteed good pay and benefits? Have you seen the U.S. jobless stats for new grads, Mark?"

He fished out a gooey marshmallow and popped it into his mouth. "Now you sound like Mom and Camp," he said. Both of them had long ago begun calling their stepfather, Nolan Campbell, by his nickname. "I just…well, thought you'd understand since Mom did her level best to steer you into education. Yet here you are, a Coast Guard officer."

"That's different. I made up my mind to go into search and rescue the summer I fell off that cliff and Camp risked his life to save me…." She let her statement trail off. "That fall I joined ROTC. My career choice shouldn't have shocked anyone. But you, Mark, have spent the better part of six years getting a master's in child psychology. You interned for a year. And starting at Wellmont doesn't mean you have to stay there forever."

Mark stepped over to a window, staring out as he sipped his hot chocolate. "I wish I could say that counseling's what I want to do for even part of my life, Meg. If you recall, Gina Ames got me hooked on photography the same summer. Last year, at her urging, I sent one of my photos to a contest. I won! I'll be doing a one-man show in New York City."

"Gosh, a one-man show sounds impressive, but—"

"It is," he hastened to say. "Yet Mom dismisses photography as a silly hobby. What I'd like," Mark said, turning and sounding eager for the first time in their discussion, "is to try my hand at freelancing. Gina has contacts. All I have to do is create a portfolio of worthwhile photos."

"Oh, wow! I see your dilemma. Mom and Camp paid for your schooling, and you're thinking of taking off in a whole different direction."

"If photography works out, I'll pay them back. For now, Gram volunteered to grub-stake me until the show in New York this fall."

"Gram? As in *Mona* Gram? You took Benton money?" The Benton wealth had caused a serious rift between their mother and her former in-laws

"Mona can spare the bucks. Did you get the news article I sent outlining her net worth after Grandpa Toby died? He left Mona a millionaire twice over."

"That's not the point. Mom will have a cat-fit if you take one red cent from her."

Mark's temper flared. "Mona's *our* blood grand-mother, Megan. And she's getting on in years. It hurt her that you were home at Christmas and never drove seventy miles to visit her. Since Toby died, she rattles around in that big house."

"I only had a week at home. I bought and wrap-ped a cashmere sweater, signed both our names like we agreed and sent it for her Christmas." Megan tucked her thumbs under her bright orange suspenders and twisted her lips to one side. "She smothers me, Mark. Plus she makes snide comments about Mom marrying Camp. It's been eleven years. Why can't she let it go?"

"Then she'd have to admit Dad was a jerk. She'll never do that. Dad was their only child. Their pride and joy. But Megan...we're her only relatives now. I'm not like you, I can't flip a switch and erase the fact that I'm a Benton."

Megan didn't want to argue. "So, uh, how long can you stay? A week? Two? Longer?" The last sounded hopeful.

BONUS FEATURE

Mark's eyes grew guarded. "Is a month too long? Maybe two? I'd like to stay for a while to see if I can produce quality photos. I figure the landscapes around here should be pretty interesting."

Megan broke into a wide grin and smacked his arm. "You stay two months, buddy, you're no guest. Starting tomorrow, we split household chores. Cooking, cleaning, laundry. The works."

"Speaking of cooking, I'm starved. You got anything to eat around here?"

"Peanut-butter cookies that I made this morning." She hauled out a fat pink pig-shaped cookie jar. "I probably have cheese and crackers on hand. If the cheese isn't moldy."

From his superior height Mark gazed on her with amused affection. "Some things never change. You always had terrible eating habits. Point me toward the local grocery store. After I unpack, I'll make a list and shop. If you don't object to me using Mona's money, that is."

"I'll pay," Megan said quickly. "I make a good salary. I don't want Mona's handout. If you're willing to split chores, I'll gladly feed you, Mark."

"Okay," he said. "But I wish you wouldn't be so hard on Gram."

"Uh...come with me. I'll show you where you can bunk. Isn't this a great old house? I have more space here than we did in that dinky duplex

Mom rented after Dad died. Oh, say, will you do me another favor? I'm getting downstairs neighbors." She pointed to a key lying on her kitchen table. "They were supposed to be here already, but they're late. I'd planned to leave them a note and take the key across the street to Mrs. Ralston. She's a busybody, so I'd rather leave it with you. Will you hold off going to the store until after the new family puts in an appearance?"

"Sure. They got a name?"

"Don't know what it is." She shook her head, then laughed. "But who else will come asking for a key?"

Sterling Dodge paid the toll and eased his dirt-streaked black four-wheel-drive Land Rover onto the five-mile suspension span of Mackinac Bridge, which connected Michigan's Upper and Lower Peninsulas. Below, the wind whipped angry whitecaps into a froth across a broad expanse of blue so dark that in places the water looked black.

"Je-zus. It's the end of the earth," spat Sterling's fourteen-year-old brother-in-law, Joel Atwater. A comment seconded by his older sister, Lauren, who jammed a pillow behind her head.

"Joel," Sterling snapped. "I'm not telling you again to watch your mouth. Next time it'll affect your allowance." Sterling then called to his son, the youngest of his three passengers. Tyler was kicking rhythmically against the back of his dad's seat. At four, he mimicked the older kids, who'd lived with Sterling and his wife, Blythe, since their wedding. Now with Blythe gone, Sterling was left the sole guardian.

His wife's siblings had gotten out of hand back on Long Island, and he knew primarily that was because of Blythe's inattention. The kids had cultivated bad friendships and worse habits. That was the catalyst for Sterling's seeking this new job. He hoped it wasn't too late to turn their lives around.

The teens were angry about the control he had over them and their trust fund. He couldn't blame them, as thanks to Blythe's resistance, he'd never taken a hand in raising them before. This wasn't a situation he'd ever envisioned. At the time he married Blythe, he would never have believed life would change so much that he'd uproot everyone and move to a state miles away from where they'd all been born.

"Listen, I know you're sick of driving, and you're probably hungry. Me, too. But it's not my fault we hit a spot on the highway where the road washed out and we had to backtrack. I would've stopped at a restaurant if Hank Meade, the guy

30

we're renting from, hadn't made it clear that the woman upstairs who has our key works swing shift. We have twenty minutes before she takes off."

"Big frickin' deal. Who cares?" Joel flung himself so hard against his seat he rocked the big SUV. "If we'd stayed in New York, I'd be hanging with my buds and eatin' burgers about now." He slapped on earphones and turned up his CD.

Sterling raised a black eyebrow. "That's one reason we're here, Joel," he said, raising his voice to no avail. "This is a school day. You had how many unexcused absences in the last six months?"

Lauren tossed her head. "Like you care? If Blythe hadn't been killed during that stakeout, you would've already cut and run. I wish you had. Then the court would've put me in charge of my own life—and Joel's." She crossed her arms, looking mutinous.

"Enough," Sterling said tiredly. He sensed that his son, already traumatized by recent events, had gone stock still in his booster seat. "Lauren…" Sterling said with a sigh, "My separating from Blythe was never a done deal. Yes, I asked a lawyer friend, Jeff Gaines, to check on options. I'm sorry you had to take his return call."

"Like I believe you? Too bad he phoned while you were at the funeral home arranging to bury our sister."

BONUS FEATURE

The implication in the girl's scathing response hit Sterling between his shoulder blades. The pain was so palpable he had to massage his neck to ease the tension. In hindsight, he regretted having called Jeff. Because now he was at a loss when it came to explaining what had led to his inquiry about possible divorce. The welfare of these kids had fallen to Sterling's wife when Joel was in fourth grade. The elder Atwaters were brutally murdered in a house robbery turned violent after they'd surprised the thieves. Joel had been at a sleepover, and he and Blythe were delayed at one of their wedding showers.

32   Mere days away from their wedding, they'd foregone a honeymoon and taken the kids in. From the outset, Blythe had told him to butt out of anything concerning the kids—particularly discipline. So, he had no earthly idea how to tell them that their sister had changed a hundred percent from the woman he'd once loved. First, she'd developed a rabid need for excitement. And without any discussion between them, she'd gone to police college and become a city cop. Granted, he'd never understood that choice. The kids needed her. Plus, she'd accidentally gotten pregnant. Accidentally, because she'd made it plain she didn't want a baby. Yet even with extra mouths to feed, she didn't need to work, or not

for financial reasons, anyway. He did fine as a ferry boat captain. They had a nice house left to him by his grandparents. At the very least, she should've taken a part-time job, he thought, and certainly something far less dangerous. Especially after Tyler was born. No, Sterling would not apologize for not liking his wife's career. And as much as they'd battled over her job, they'd had twice the arguments over her refusal to set limits on her siblings. Still, that wasn't why he'd contemplated divorce. If they only knew... But he couldn't hurt the kids the way he'd been hurt.

Sterling dug deep for patience as he left the bridge, finally entering the seaside hamlet of St. Ignace. "This is it," he exclaimed. "Our town. Temporarily."

"Whoop-de-do," Joel ground out. He ripped off his earphones and pressed his nose to the side window. "Hey, Lauren, what's there to do in this jerk-water hole?"

"Joel," Sterling chided gently. "It's only until a carpenter fixes the dry rot problem in the home I bought on Mackinac Island."

"How long?" Lauren demanded. "Joel's right, this dinky place sucks."

Sterling slowed, rechecking the directions he'd plugged into his GPS system. According to the readout, he had to be practically on top of the house. Ducking, he read gilt-edged numbers painted on a sprawling blue monstrosity. The house, which was at the end of a cul-de-sac, had four upper-story dormers. Twin porches sat on white spindles that didn't look strong enough to hold them up. Unfortunately, the house number matched the one blinking on his screen.

At least he'd skated in with minutes to spare. He made a U-turn and hoped his trailer didn't hang over the sidewalk. A compact car and a pickup took up most of the parking area.

"According to Captain Meade, the woman upstairs has our key. You kids want to run and get it? I see stairs to the right of the car with the Missouri license plates."

"Me wanna go, too!" Tyler strained against the harness holding him fast.

Lauren and Joel both had their doors open. "Is it okay if the kid goes with?" Lauren asked Sterling.

Sterling's shoulders relaxed minutely. At least the kids loved Tyler, and in many ways Lauren was more nurturing than Blythe had been. "Thanks." Sterling released his seat belt and leaned back to rummage in a pile of coats in the seat next to his son. He pulled out Tyler's jacket. "Judging from that wind, you kids had better find your coats."

34

Joel curled a pierced bottom lip that held two rings. He slammed his car door so hard the whole vehicle shook.

Sterling stopped stuffing Tyler's arms into coat sleeves. Meeting Lauren's uncompromising gaze, he said gently, "Look, we're not going back, so it'll be easier if we try to make a go of this."

Lauren banged her door, as well and lifted her young nephew up on her hip.

AFTER SHOWING MARK his room, and pointing out an adjoining half bath that would be his, Megan left her brother to unpack the duffel bags he'd hauled in from his car. Grabbing the jacket that completed her winter uniform, she paused to say goodbye. A banging on her front door interrupted any last-minute instructions she might have had.

"Mark, I'm guessing that'll be our *late* neighbors. Come with me and say hi. We'll get all the introductions out of the way."

She crossed the living room, detouring to get the key. Ahead of her now, Mark opened the door. A gust of wind tore it from his grasp. From her vantage point, Megan was afforded a view of a ragtag trio huddled on her porch. Mark's body blocked their view of her, and gave her time to assess them.

Having grown up a rebel, she instantly recognized the same qualities in the teenage boy who sported loops of chains hanging from baggy black pants. His multipierced ears, lip rings and bleached hair greased into orange spikes gave her a bit of a shock. Megan had long since shed her Goth lipstick, nail polish and flashy rings on every finger. Hiding her dismay, she turned her attention to the woman attempting to balance a suddenly shy four- or five-year-old boy on a nonexistent hip. She was a classic beauty. Megan couldn't readily determine her age. Late teens to mid-twenties? Wind swirled a mane of spun gold around a triangular face. Thick-lashed, chocolate-colored eyes added to the newcomer's exotic appeal. "I came for a key," she said.

Mark was acting like a dunce. It took a moment of silence for Megan to see the problem. Her brother was struck mute by the young woman's beauty. Or maybe he was plotting light angles and lens exposures to photograph her.

Ducking beneath his arm, Megan came up smiling and dangling the key. "I'm Megan Benton. This man of few words is my brother, Mark." She jabbed his ribs, and he finally breathed out the air trapped in his lungs.

"I'm about to take off for the Coast Guard

station where I work, but you all look frozen. Come in and warm up. I made extra hot chocolate. Mark can get you drinks, and you guys can get better acquainted." She gestured toward her kitchen, key still in hand.

The little boy, a darling tyke with huge gray eyes, untucked his curly head from where it was buried in the young woman's shoulder. He offered a shy, willing smile, and immediately wriggled down to tug the girl toward the open door.

Megan smiled at him, and wondered if the woman was the little charmer's mom or older sister. She and the teenage boy bore marked similarities in the shape of their faces. The younger boy had hair like hers, but the resemblance ended there. It was the older boy, however, who reached out a bare arm, tattooed to the shoulder with a snake and a skull with crossbones, and snatched the key from Megan.

"We can't come in," the woman said, bending to lift the little boy. "Sterling's waiting." She hiked a thumb toward the stairs. "We haven't had lunch yet, and he wants us moved in before dark."

Megan strained to peer over the rail. On the sidewalk, a man stood knee-deep in suitcases. Long-legged, and broad-shouldered, he seemed impervious to the wind gusting off the bay, in spite of the fact that it whipped his jet-black hair around his ears. Megan would have called out a greeting and invited him up for a hot drink, too, had he not glanced up and glowered at her.

Mark roused himself. "Megan's off to work, but I'm hanging around doing nothing. I'll give you guys a hand unloading."

The eldest boy swaggered. "We got it covered, dude. We're not gonna be in this dump long enough to get friendly." Whirling on the heel of a heavy black boot, he clattered down the wooden steps. His sister, if that was who she was, tried to follow. But the little guy dug in, crying, "I want hot chocolate!"

38   *Dump?* Megan wanted to smack the smart-assed kid. Instead, she turned to the crying youngster, who'd refused to let the woman pick him up. "Maybe another day," she said, dropping to one knee in front of him. "What's your name?" She mustered a gentle smile.

"Tyler," he said through his tears. The young woman calling the shots descended a couple of steps and scooped him up in spite of his protests. Containing him against his will, she was able to make her way downstairs. His sobs reached up to Megan and Mark, still hovering in the open doorway.

It wasn't until the man, the one the blond girl had called Sterling, threw another intimidating glare at them, that the pair upstairs quickly withdrew.

"Joy, oh joy," Megan murmured. "Aren't *they* going to be lovely neighbors?"

"Mmm-hmm."

As she shoved her arms into her jacket and tucked her mop of sable hair under the requisite blue Coast Guard baseball-style cap, Megan paused to eye her brother. He'd slightly opened the front drape in an attempt to peer over the porch.

Walking toward him, she punched his arm hard. "Listen, Mark, we'd better listen to that punk teen. They're not planning to be here long enough to bother making friends."

Her brother sprang back. "Why'd you hit me?"

"Because you have that *look*. That I'm-*very*-interested look."

"Can you blame me? She's gorgeous! Did you catch her name?"

"Ma-a-rk! None of them gave us names, except for the little boy. That's what I'm saying. Do I have to spell it out? They aren't interested in being neighborly." She slid back her sleeve and glanced at her watch. "Holy smokes, I've gotta go. I'm gonna be late signing in. The crew will go out to check lighthouses without me."

"You check lighthouses?"

She nodded and jerked open the door. "My

BONUS FEATURE

unit's responsible for maintaining the status quo of twenty-one maritime lights, thirteen of which are on buoys located offshore. We make sure they haven't broken loose from anchors, and we change burned out light bulbs. My shift ends at eleven. I'm home by eleven-fifteen. Don't feel you have to wait up, though. I usually fix something easy like bacon and eggs. I'll try to be quiet."

"I'll probably be up. It hasn't been that long since I stayed up nights studying for finals. Takes a while to unwind from that."

"Suit yourself. Oh, that reminds me. Here's money for groceries." She pulled a money clip out of her pants pocket and peeled off a sheaf of twenties as she gave directions to the store. Dispensing a final wave, Megan tripped lightly down the stairs. She held her key tight so the wind couldn't rip it away. The sporty red imported pickup with oversize tires, a roll bar and a full set of fog lights was hers. Mark, she saw, still drove the beater compact their stepdad had helped him refurbish in high school. She recalled envying how the two bonded over that car.

Their stepdad, Nolan Campbell, was a man's man. Even though their mom, Emily, had filed off many of his rougher edges, it seemed to Megan that her stepfather was more comfortable with Mark than with her. Although Camp stood up for her more than once—most memorably when she'd been fleecing a bunch of rowdy cowboys at pool. Her mom threw a fit, but Camp let her finish winning. Megan grinned now as the memory flooded back.

Unlocking her pickup, Megan noticed that the way their neighbor had parked his trailer had blocked her in. Already late, she'd have to waste time hunting him down.

Luckily he emerged from his apartment. "Hey," Megan called. "I need to get out, and you have me boxed in. Would you mind pulling up a foot or so?"

He continued toward her at a languid gait Megan admired. It took a moment for her to realize he wasn't viewing her with similar regard. In fact, he studied her uniform with obvious distaste. Maybe he thought the bulky blue pants and blue-and-orange jacket made her look like a fat ladybug. They did, but they were toasty warm.

"I'm your upstairs neighbor, Megan Benton. Lieutenant Benton," she added, thrusting out a hand. "I would've brought you a thermos of cocoa and some cookies as a better welcome, but I'm late for duty." Her implication was because he'd blocked her in.

He avoided her outstretched hand and lowered

BONUS FEATURE

indecently long eyelashes as he slid two fingers in to a tight front pocket of his worn jeans. Megan held her breath, but he succeeded in retrieving a set of keys. Setting those long legs in motion, he skirted her pickup and had the door of his SUV open before she could move.

"Hey…" she called. "I didn't catch your name."

"Dodge," he growled. "Sterling Dodge." Clearly he didn't want to share even that much.

Megan blinked as his door slammed. It couldn't be plainer. He and his whole tribe had come with bad attitudes. Wasn't that going to be fun?

42   She climbed into her pickup, wondering what the surly man did for a living. What had motivated him to move his family here this time of year? The area was ninety percent dependent on summer tourism. It took a hardy soul to live here year-round.

Taking only seconds to warm her engine, Megan drove off without checking to see if Dodge remained in his vehicle or if he'd gone back to unloading the trailer that bore New York license plates. Since New York was known far and wide for its job opportunities, she found his timing even more curious. But they didn't plan to stay long, or so Dodge's eldest son had said.

If the two older kids were his. The man had jet-black hair shot with silver. The two blond kids had brown eyes. Dodge's gray ones were as chilly as Mackinac Straits after a wintry storm. And he might be from New York, but nothing about his attire or whipcord body looked citified or soft. He wore a lumberjack shirt with the sleeves rolled midway up his tanned, muscular forearms. And well-worn blue jeans, tucked into scuffed boots. Maybe he was a logger from upstate New York. Although logging was about gone from Michigan.

Her mysterious unfriendly neighbor remained on her mind long after Megan signed in at the station. Long after she and the crew boarded their *Reliance* cutter, its twin diesel engines and midship helicopter deck designed to patrol a vital shipping channel emerging from the grip of winter.

Frowning, she scanned melting ice floes. Megan had only just realized that she and Mark hadn't seen any sign of a wife or mother in their new neighbor's entourage. Granted, she could've stayed in the warm SUV until the kids got back with the key. Unless the pretty blonde was a second wife. If so, she was either brave or naive. Megan shivered recalling Dodge's icy stare.

"Lieutenant, are you with us today?" Commander Donovan barked out when Megan failed twice to respond to a question.

"Sorry, sir." She snapped to attention and hastily raised the binoculars swinging from a cord hung around her neck. "Guess my mind wandered for a minute."

"That's not like you, Benton. Everything all right?"

"Yes, sir. Well…my younger brother came to visit unexpectedly. Because of that, combined with new neighbors moving into the apartment below mine, I got to the station late. I'm still playing catch-up."

44 The grizzled old commander studied the choppy sea. "Hell of a time for anyone to visit or move to St. Ignace. Are they nuts? About now is when I'd shell out premium rates for a week's vacation in the Bahamas."

Everyone within hearing range laughed. Megan, too, especially since she knew how much Donovan loved the north country. "I can't speak for my neighbors, but my brother just graduated with a master's degree in psych. Hmm…maybe I'll bring him around to see if he can figure out what makes this crew tick," she teased. They were a small station and tended to operate more like a family than a larger crew might.

"Bring him on, Benton," shouted a fellow

lieutenant. "Maybe he'll spill your secrets—like how you got to be a pool shark."

Megan grinned from ear to ear and hung over the ice-crusted rail to scan the waves for any sign of a boat, barge or container ship that might be in trouble. Her fleet also patrolled a section of the busiest waterway between the U.S. and neighboring Canada. Over the summer, pleasure boaters would appear in droves, tripling their workload. As well as rendering aid in boating accidents, their crew conducted boat-safety education classes in local schools, kept their eyes peeled for all types of smugglers and assisted other agencies involved in Homeland Security. Megan had never enjoyed a dull existence. This career kept her hopping, and she loved it.

As if to punctuate her thoughts, midway through the evening a distress call came in. "What have we got?" she asked, rushing to the foredeck.

"A car drove off the Mackinaw City loading dock at the ferry terminal."

"Accidentally or on purpose?" Like other team members, Megan readied emergency equipment on board as she processed information. She and the crew were trained for amphibious helicopter rescue. But if a car went into the drink, that meant the even more dangerous task of sending down divers.

BONUS FEATURE

"An accident. Stupid kid took his mom's car for a joyride. Cops gave chase, he lost control and shot off the pier. Broke the guard chain. Good thing the ferries don't start running again for another week, or it'd be a bigger mess."

Her companions' faces were grim. They all knew the chances of anyone's surviving the icy water. The Great Lakes were always cold. Even in summer rescue workers had from fifteen to thirty minutes to save someone. The fact that the icebreakers under Donovan's command had only recently stopped running, and darkness had descended, didn't bode well for the crazy kid now sitting in Lake Huron.

The commander stepped out onto the bridge. "A diving team from Sault Ste. Marie should be on site by the time we get there. Our job will be to drop grapples their divers will attach to the kid's car. We'll winch up the auto while the Soo guys attempt to extract the victim."

Knowing their jobs backward and forward thanks to simulations run time and again didn't lessen the crew's heightened flow of adrenaline as the cutter's engines picked up speed. The dock was already a hub of activity, with cops and paramedics preparing for their roles. The Coast Guard vessel from Sault Ste. Marie had anchored fifty yards out. Her powerful lights bounced off the murky water.

Megan's vessel pulled bow to bow with the other ship. Her heart began to hammer as she watched the black, silent sea. But the water wasn't silent for long. Divers suited up in full wet gear went in feetfirst off the neighboring boat.

Megan's duty in this rescue was to lower a midship grapple. The minute the middle diver surfaced and gave his cue, she raised her arm and circled her hand several times. That told her assistant to begin tightening the winch. The cables groaned, went taut and Megan felt sweat slide down her cleavage.

Waiting was the most difficult. It was easier to be the one actively trying to rescue a victim. What seemed like hours later—but was only a few minutes—excited shouts from one of the divers echoed from shore. That happy shout said their collective prayers were at least partially answered. The kid had been sprung from his watery grave. Colored flares shot from the neighboring ship, indicating he was alive.

Megan wiped her brow and coiled in her grapple, relieved by the news.

The thing about search and rescue, she decided three hours later when they were back in the station warming up and filing reports, was

BONUS FEATURE

that nothing felt as good as a happy ending. Tonight, training had paid off. And luck. Megan never discounted luck. Four experienced divers made the rescue look easy, when every Coast Guard member knew there was a thin line between success and death.

Finished with her report, Megan flipped it into the out-basket and unhooked her jacket from a rack on the wall. "I'm out of here. See you all tomorrow."

"Want to hit the tavern for a celebration beer?" Lieutenant Jim Elkhorn called, peering over his cubicle.

48   Megan shook her cap. "Rain check, Jim? My brother just got into town. He may be waiting up for me."

"Is he a pool shark, too?"

She laughed, knowing Jim complained loudest at being beaten regularly by a girl. "Mark's a mountain biker, and a fair bowler. But even you could beat him at pool," she said, tugging her cap over disheveled curls. With a quick wave, she hurried into the frigid night. She got along well with all the guys, but still wished the station would get another woman. The last one had requested a duty station closer to her ailing parents. She'd left shortly after Megan arrived.

On the drive home, Megan found herself

hoping Mark had waited up. After a rescue she found it impossible to sleep. Nerves that had been stretched tight remained jumpy. So she was happy to see that lights burned upstairs and down at Lady Vic. Squeezing between the big Land Rover and Mark's car, Megan noticed her neighbor on his porch. When she got out, she saw steam curling from a mug he held. Her mouth watered, all but tasting hot chocolate, although he was probably drinking coffee.

"Hi," she said, removing her cap as she approached. "You got all moved in?"

Half turning, the man gave a curt nod.

Megan set a foot on his lower porch step. She was near enough to see his gray eyes glitter silvery in light falling from the bridge. "I guess you're out here enjoying our Mighty Mac." She chuckled, and was only faintly aware that he didn't join in. "You probably think the *Mighty Mac* is a super-size hamburger. It's an affectionate name for our bridge—the longest in the country. One of the greatest engineering marvels in the world. Took four years to construct." Megan rattled off a stream of other statistics, expecting a response from the man in the quilted vest. Coast Guard personnel tended to sound like Upper Peninsula old-timers by the time visitor season rolled around. She was delighted she'd remembered so many facts.

Her neighbor let too much time pass for polite conversation, then muttered, "I came out here to enjoy the silence."

Megan's head snapped up. She was slower to remove her foot from his porch, although remove it she did. Holding back a terse word hovering on the tip of her tongue, she executed a perfect about-face and marched across the asphalt to stomp up the thirty-three steps that led to her apartment.

...NOT THE END...

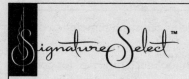

Signature Select™

"Roz Denny Fox is my kind of writer!…
She steals your heart."—*New York Times*
bestselling author Vicki Lewis Thompson

National bestselling author

ROZ *Denny* FOX

Hot Chocolate on a Cold Day

Despite their high-maintenance families and high-risk jobs, Megan Benton and Sterling Dodge find plenty of ways to stay warm during the blustery month of March.

*A brand-new novel…
coming in April 2006.*

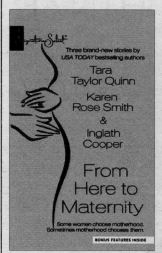

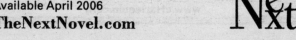

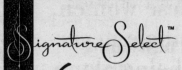
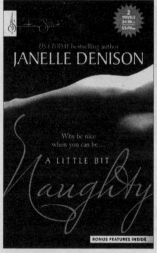

If you enjoyed what you just read,
then we've got an offer you can't resist!

Take 2 bestselling love stories FREE!

Plus get a FREE surprise gift!

COMING NEXT MONTH

Signature Select Collection
FROM HERE TO MATERNITY by Tara Taylor Quinn,
Karen Rose Smith, Inglath Cooper
Some women choose motherhood. Sometimes motherhood
chooses *them*. Enjoy this heartwarming anthology—just in time
for Mother's Day!

Signature Select Saga
HOT CHOCOLATE ON A COLD DAY by Roz Denny Fox
Despite their high-maintenance families and high-risk jobs, Megan
Benton and Sterling Dodge find plenty of ways to stay warm during
the blustery month of March.

Signature Select Miniseries
A LITTLE BIT NAUGHTY by Janelle Denison
Two sisters find blazing chemistry with the two least likely men of
all in TEMPTED and NAUGHTY—two sizzling page-turning novels
that are editorially connected.

Signature Select Spotlight
HER PERFECT LIFE by Vicki Hinze
Katie Slater's life is perfect. She's a wife, mother of two and a pilot
in the United States Air Force. But then she's shot down by the enemy,
left for dead by a man she trusted and taken as a prisoner of war in
Iraq. Now, six years later, she's back home...only home isn't there
anymore...and her perfect life has become a total mystery.

Signature Select Showcase
SWANSEA DYNASTY by Fayrene Preston
Built on the beautiful, windswept shore of Maine, the great house
of SwanSea was built by Edward Deverell as a monument to himself,
his accomplishments and his family dynasty. Now, more than one
hundred years later, the secrets of past and present converge as his
descendants deal with promises, danger and passion.